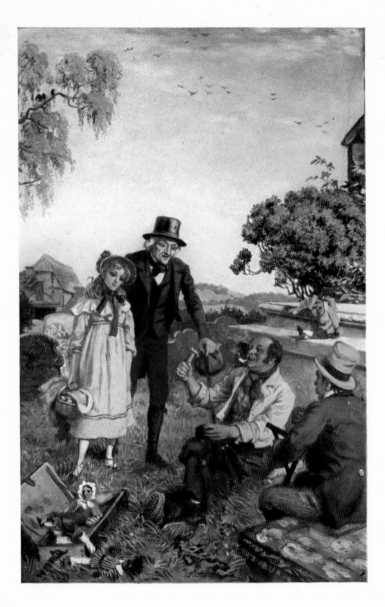

The itinerant showmen.
—*Old Curiosity Shop*, ch. xvi., p. 120.

THE
OLD CURIOSITY
SHOP

BY

CHARLES DICKENS

Made in U. S. A.

M. A. DONOHUE & COMPANY
CHICAGO   ::   NEW YORK

INTRODUCTION

TO

THE OLD CURIOSITY SHOP.

EARLY in the year 1840, during a visit to Walter Savage
Landor, then resident at Bath, the fancy which led to the
creation of Little Nell first dawned upon Charles Dickens.
His original idea was to utilize it only for a short story
of a few chapters, but the discovery, which was made
very early in the career of *Master Humphrey's Clock*,
that the somewhat desultory plan of that work had failed
to hit the public taste as had been hoped and expected,
and that it was absolutely necessary to strengthen it by
the immediate publication of a continuous story, involved
a complete alteration in the original design, and *The Old
Curiosity Shop*, which had been commenced in the fourth
number of the *Clock*, thenceforward took, until its completion, the whole of its author's attention. How *Master
Humphrey's Clock* came in course of time to be abandoned
altogether is told in the introduction to the volume of
this series in which the work is reprinted.

Fortunately the capabilities of the story, when it came
to be worked at seriously, proved themselves to be far
greater than had at first sight appeared to be the case,
and it was not long before Charles Dickens was able to
write, "I feel the story extremely myself, which I take
to be a good sign; and am already warmly interested in
it. I shall run it on now for four whole numbers together to give it a fair chance." Thenceforward the interruptions which the original plan of the *Clock* had
necessitated gradually faded out of the scheme, and the
story was worked at and published as a thing by itself.

There had been some hesitation as to the title, which
had been suggested in the following forms; "PERSONAL

Adventures of Master Humphrey; " "The Old Curiosity Shop; " " Master Humphrey's Tale; " "Master
Humphrey's Narrative; " "A Passage in Master Hum
phrey's Life; " and " The Old Curiosity Dealer and the
Child," but the best of these was ultimately chosen, and
The Old Curiosity Shop became the fitting shrine of by
far the most popular, as well as the most beautiful, of
the pathetic characters of Charles Dickens.

Some considerable trouble was, of course, given by
the necessity of turning out a weekly instalment, while
there was no chance, under the circumstances, of getting
at all ahead of the printer, and the very confined space
available in each number was another sore trial—" I was
obliged to cramp most dreadfully what I thought a pretty
idea in the last chapter. I hadn't room to turn," a letter
at this time says. Furthermore the difficulties of construction were seriously aggravated by the fact that the
conclusion of the story was not determined upon until
half of it, at least, had been written, and it is difficult to
understand how all these troubles were gradually surmounted with the brilliantly successful result that every
one knows.

The story took up the whole of the year—a considerable portion of it was written at Charles Dickens's favorite
little seaside village of Broadstairs—and, indeed, was not
finished until nearly the end of January, 1841. How
deeply it had in its progress impressed itself upon its
author's mind is evidenced by his mournful little lament
to Mr. Forster, "After you left last night "—the letter
is dated the 17th of January, 1841—" I took my desk
up-stairs; and writing until four o'clock this morning,
finished the old story. It makes me very melancholy to
think that all these people are lost to me forever, and I
feel as if I never could become attached to any new set
of characters." It was some such sense of liking for old
friends, no doubt, which led to the not very happy revival of Mr. Pickwick and the Wellers in *Master Humphrey's Clock*.

Still more remarkable and interesting, however, is the
extraordinary suffering which the death of Little Nell
caused her creator. This end to her career had not been
originally intended, but was mainly the outcome of
a wise and acute piece of criticism on the part of Mr.

Forster, who thus describes what Charles Dickens himself called his "valued suggestion" and its result on the book; "I was responsible for its tragic ending. He had not thought of killing her, when, about half way through, I asked him to consider whether it did not necessarily belong, even to his own conception, after taking so mere a child through such a tragedy of sorrow, to lift her also out of the commonplace of ordinary happy endings, so that the gentle pure little figure and form should never change to the fancy. All that I meant he seized at once, and never turned aside from it again."

But the necessity of accepting this tragic ending to the story caused Charles Dickens positive anguish, as a few extracts from his correspondence will abundantly show. To Mr. Forster he wrote at various times: "You can't imagine (gravely I write and speak) how exhausted I am to-day with yesterday's labours. I went to bed last night utterly dispirited and done up. All night I have been possessed by the child; and this morning I am unrefreshed and miserable. I don't know what to do with myself." "I have only this moment put the finishing touch to it. The difficulty has been tremendous, the anguish unspeakable." And, just before the end, "This part of the story is not to be galloped over, I can tell you. I think it will come famously—but I am the wretchedest of the wretched. It casts the most horrible shadow upon me, and it is as much as I can do to keep moving at all. I tremble to approach the place a great deal more than Kit; a great deal more than Mr. Garland; a great deal more than the Single Gentleman. I shan't recover it for a long time. Nobody will miss her like I shall. It is such a very painful thing to me, that I really cannot express my sorrow. Old wounds bleed afresh when I only think of the way of doing it; what the actual doing of it will be, God knows. I can't preach to myself the schoolmaster's consolation though I try." To George Cattermole, who illustrated most of the Little Nell portion of the book, and to whom Charles Dickens wrote very elaborate descriptions of scenes with which he wished particular care taken, he said, "I am breaking my heart over this story, and cannot bear to finish it," and "I am for the time being nearly dead with work and grief for the loss of my child." To the Rev. William Harness, declining a dinner invitation, he wrote, " I must occupy myself in finishing the ' Curiosity Shop,' and it is such a painful task to me that I must concentrate myself upon it tooth and nail, and go out nowhere until it is done." And to Mr. R. Monckton Milnes, afterwards Lord Houghton, " That Nellicide was the act of Heaven, as you may see any of these fine mornings when you look about you. If you knew the pain it gave me—but what am I talking of ? if you don't know, nobody does." It would be well, I think, if a certain class of critics, great and small,[1] who are so fond of using certain conventional cant phrases about Charles Dickens's pathos being exaggerated, and forced, and overstrained, and all the rest of it, would reflect for a moment that in such a case as this, for instance, what he gave to the public was simply what he felt himself.[2]

[1] Such, for instance, as the extremely " cock-sure " writer of an article in the number of the *Contemporary Review* for February, 1869, who laid down the law in this absurdly uncompromising fashion : " Mr. Dickens's pathos we can only regard as a complete and absolute failure. It is unnatural and unlovely. He attempts to make a stilted phraseology and weak and sickly sentimentality do duty for genuine emotion. The result is that, when he would move us most deeply, he is apt to become rather a bore. Hard-hearted as it may sound, we must confess to having found little Paul Dombey, Little Nell, and Tiny Tim exceeding tiresome, and to have been glad to be rid of them on any terms. . . . The pathos is ' stagey '; it lacks simplicity, grace, dignity." I suppose it must be a pleasant thing to be so superior to the weaknesses of vulgar mortals as this gentleman seems to pride himself on being.

[2] It was *The Old Curiosity Shop* and the pathos of Little Nell which so moved the rough miners in Bret Harte's *Dickens in Camp*, it will be remembered. The poem has often been quoted, but it will bear repetition in this place.

> Above the pines the moon was slowly drifting,
>   The river sang below ;
> The dim Sierras, far beyond, uplifting
>   Their minarets of snow :
>
> The roaring camp fire, with rude humor, painted
>   The ruddy tints of health
> On haggard face and form that drooped and fainted
>   In the fierce race for wealth ;
>
> Till one arose, and from his pack's scant treasure
>   A hoarded volume drew,
> And cards were dropped from hands of listless leisure
>   To hear the tale anew ;

The death of Little Nell had also a painful effect on Macready, as the following extracts from his diary will show :—

"*Jan.* 21, 1841.—Called on Dickens. . . . asked Dickens to spare the life of Nell in his story (Master Humphrey's Clock), and observed that he was cruel. He blushed, and men who blush are said to be either proud or cruel; he is not proud, and therefore—or as Dickens added—the axiom is false.

And then, while round them shadows gathered faster,
  And as the firelight fell,
He read aloud the book wherein the Master
  Had writ of " Little Nell " :

Perhaps 'twas boyish fancy—for the reader
  Was youngest of them all,—
But, as he read, from clustering pine and cedar
  A silence seemed to fall;

The fir-trees gathering closer in the shadows,
  Listened in every spray,
While the whole camp, with " Nell " on English meadows,
  Wandered and lost their way:

And so in mountain solitudes—o'ertaken
  As by some spell divine—
Their cares dropped from them like the needles shaken
  From out the gusty pine.

Lost is that camp, and wasted all its fire;
  And he who wrought that spell ?—
Ah, towering pines and stately Kentish spire,
  Ye have one tale to tell !

Lost is that camp! but let its fragrant story
  Blend with the breath that thrills
With hop-vines' incense all the pensive glory
  That fills the Kentish hills.

And on that grave where English oak and holly
  And laurel wreaths entwine,
Deem it not all a too presumptuous folly,—
  This spray of western pine !

Mr. Forster was surely right when he said of Charles Dickens in this connection, " There is hardly any form of posthumous tribute which I can imagine likely to have better satisfied his desire of fame, than one which should thus connect with the special favorite among all his heroines, the restraints and authority exerted by his genius over the rudest and least civilized of competitors in that far fierce race for wealth."

Jan. 22.—Found at home notes from Ransom, and one from Dickens with an onward number of "Master Humphrey's Clock." I saw one print in it of the dear dead child that gave a dead chill through my blood. I dread to read it, but I must get it over.

I have read the two numbers; I never have read printed words that gave me so much pain. I could not weep for some time. Sensation, sufferings have returned to me, that are terrible to awaken : it is real to me; I cannot criticise it.

The allusion in the last paragraph is to the death of Macready's little daughter Harriet Joanna, who died on the 25th of November, 1840, in her fourth year.

A graceful tribute to the admirable illustrations which are so closely associated in the minds of all lovers of Little Nell with her touching story and pathetic end may be quoted here from a letter addressed by Charles Dickens to George Cattermole :—

I cannot close this hasty note, my dear fellow, without saying that I have deeply felt your hearty and most invaluable co-operation in the beautiful illustrations you have made for the last story, that I look at them with a pleasure I cannot describe to you in words, and that it is impossible for me to say how sensible I am of your earnest and friendly aid. Believe me that this is the very first time any designs for what I have written have touched and moved me, and caused me to feel that they expressed the idea I had in my mind. I am most sincerely and affectionately grateful to you, and am full of pleasure and delight.

It may be noted that several of the characters in *The Old Curiosity Shop* had their prototypes in the unlucky days of the Marshalsea and the blacking warehouse in Hungerford Stairs. Thus the Marchioness was first suggested by the maid-of-all-work who waited upon the Dickens family in Bayham Street, and afterwards in the debtors' prison ; the Garlands were drawn from the landlord of Charles Dickens's lodging in those days and his family—" He was a fat, good-natured, kind old gentleman. He was lame and had a quiet old wife ; and he had a very innocent grown-up son, who was lame too "—and the poetical Mr. Slum was derived from one of the ingenious gentlemen who wrote the poetical advertisements of Warren's blacking.

After the discontinuance of *Master Humphrey's Clock*

The Old Curiosity Shop was published in its original imperial octavo form, with the pagination and running head title retained but without its *Clock* setting, and as an independent book, at thirteen shillings. This edition contained the dedication to Samuel Rogers and the preface which had been published with the first volume of *Master Humphrey's Clock*, and which ran as follows:—

When the author commenced this Work, he proposed to himself three objects.

First. To establish a periodical, which should enable him to present, under one general head, and not as separate and distinct publications, certain fictions which he had it in contemplation to write.

Secondly. To produce these Tales in weekly numbers; hoping that to shorten the intervals of communication between himself and his readers, would be to knit more closely, the pleasant relations they had held, for Forty Months.

Thirdly. In the execution of this weekly task, to have as much regard as its exigencies would permit, to each story as a whole, and to the possibility of its publication at some distant day, apart from the machinery in which it had its origin.

The characters of Master Humphrey and his three friends, and the little fancy of the clock, were the results of these considerations. When he sought to interest his readers in those who talked, and read, and listened, he revived Mr. Pickwick and his humble friends; not with any intention of re-opening an exhausted and abandoned mine, but to connect them in the thoughts of those whose favorites they had been, with the tranquil enjoyments of Master Humphrey.

It was never the intention of the author to make the Members of Master Humphrey's Clock, active agents in the stories they are supposed to relate. Having brought himself in the commencement of his undertaking to feel an interest in these quiet creatures, and to imagine them in their old chamber of meeting, eager listeners to all he had to tell, the author hoped—as authors will—to succeed in awakening some of his own emotion in the bosoms of his readers. Imagining Master Humphrey in his chimney corner, resuming night after night, the narrative,—say, of the Old Curiosity Shop—picturing to himself the various sensations of his hearers—thinking how Jack Redburn might incline to poor Kit, and perhaps lean too favorably even towards the lighter vices of Mr. Richard Swiveller—how the deaf gentleman would have his favorite and Mr. Miles his—and how all these gentle spirits would trace some faint reflection of their past lives in the varying currents of the tale—he has insensibly fallen into the belief that they are present to his readers as they are to him, and has forgotten that like one whose vision is disordered he may be conjuring up bright figures when there is nothing but empty space.

The short papers which are to be found at the beginning of the volume were indispensable to the form of publication and the limited extent of each number, as no story of length and interest could be begun until " The Clock," was wound up and fairly going.

The author would fain hope that there are not many who would disturb Master Humphrey and his friends in their seclusion ; who would have them forego their present enjoyments, to exchange those confidences with each other, the absence of which is the foundation of their mutual trust. For when their occupation is gone, when their tales are ended, and but their personal histories remain, the chimney corner will be growing cold, and the clock will be about to stop forever.

One other word in his own person, and he returns to the more grateful task of speaking for those imaginary people whose little world lies within these pages.

It may be some consolation to those well-disposed ladies and gentlemen who, in the interval between the conclusion of his last work and the commencement of this, originated a report that he had gone raving mad, to know that it spread as rapidly as could be desired, and was made the subject of considerable dispute ; not as regarded the fact, for that was as thoroughly established as the duel between Sir Peter Teazle and Charles Surface in The School for Scandal ; but with reference to the unfortunate lunatic's place of confinement : one party insisting positively on Bedlam, another inclining favorably towards St. Luke's, and a third swearing strongly by the asylum at Hanwell ; while each backed its case by circumstantial evidence of the same excellent nature as that brought to bear by Sir Benjamin Backbite on the pistol shot, which struck against the little bronze bust of Shakespeare over the fireplace, grazed out of the window at a right angle, and wounded the postman, who was coming to the door with a double letter from Northamptonshire.

It will be a great affliction to these ladies and gentlemen to learn—and he is so unwilling to give pain, that he would not whisper the circumstance on any account, did he not feel in a manner bound to do so, in gratitude to those amongst his friends who were at the trouble of being angry at the absurdity—that their inventions made the author's home unusually merry, and gave rise to an extraordinary number of jests, of which he will only add, in the words of the good Vicar of Wakefield, " I cannot say whether we had more wit among us than usual; but I am sure we had more laughing."

DEVONSHIRE TERRACE, YORK GATE,
    September, 1840.

In the first double-column crown octave cheap edition of 1848, *The Old Curiosity Shop* was published third in the series in a volume of three hundred and forty-four pages bound in cloth at four shillings, and was embellished with a frontispiece from a painting by George Cattermole. It also contained the following new preface dated London, September, 1848 :—

PREFACE.

In April, 1840, I issued the first number of a new weekly publication, price threepence, called MASTER HUMPHREY'S CLOCK. It was intended to consist, for the most part, of detached papers, but was to include one continuous story, to be resumed from time to time, with such indefinite intervals between each period of resumption as might best accord with the exigencies and capabilities of the proposed Miscellany.

The first chapter of this tale appeared in the fourth number of MASTER HUMPHREY'S CLOCK, when I had already been made uneasy by the desultory character of that work, and when, I believe, my readers had thoroughly participated in the feeling. The commencement of a story was a great satisfaction to me, and I had reason to believe that my readers participated in this feeling too. Hence, being pledged to some interruptions and some pursuit of the original design, I cheerfully set about disentangling myself from those impediments as fast as I could ; and, that done, from that time until its completion THE OLD CURIOSITY SHOP was written and published from week to week, in weekly parts.

When the story was finished, that it might be freed from the incumbrance of associations and interruptions with which it had no kind of concern, I caused the few sheets of MASTER HUMPHREY'S CLOCK, which had been printed in connection with it, to be cancelled ; and, like the unfinished tale of the windy night and the notary in The Sentimental Journey, they became the property of the trunkmaker and the butterman. I was especially unwilling, I confess, to enrich those respectable trades with the opening paper of the abandoned design, in which MASTER HUMPHREY described himself and his manner of life. Though I now affect to make the confession philosophically, as referring to a by-gone emotion, I am conscious that my pen winces a little even while I write these words. But it was done, and wisely done, and MASTER HUMPHREY'S CLOCK, as originally constructed, became one of the lost books of the earth—which we all know, are far more precious than any that can be read for love or money.

In reference to the tale itself, I desire to say very little here. The many friends it has won me, and the many hearts it has turned to me when they were full of private sorrow, invest it with an interest, in my mind, which is not a public one, and the rightful place of which appears to be " a more removed ground."

I will merely observe, therefore, that, in writing the book, I had it always in my fancy to surround the lonely figure of the child with grotesque and wild, but not impossible companions, and to gather about her innocent face and pure intentions, associates as strange and uncongenial as the grim objects that are about her bed when her history is first foreshadowed.

MASTER HUMPHREY (before his devotion to the trunk and butter business) was originally supposed to be the narrator of the story. As it was constructed from the beginning, however, with a view to separate publication when completed, his demise has not involved the necessity of any alteration.

I have a mournful pride in one recollection associated with
"little Nell." While she was yet upon her wanderings, not then
concluded, there appeared in a literary journal, an essay of which
she was the principal theme, so earnestly, so eloquently, and tenderly appreciative of her, and of all her shadowy kith and kin,
that it would have been insensibility in me, if I could have read it
without an unusual glow of pleasure and encouragement. Long
afterwards, and when I had come to know him well, and to see him,
stout of heart, going slowly down into his grave, I knew the writer
of that essay to be THOMAS HOOD.

LONDON, *September*, 1848.

Of later illustrated editions the most noticeable is that
which was comprised in the "Household Edition" of
Messrs. Chapman and Hall—a volume of two hundred and
seventy-four pages, with thirty-nine excellent illustrations by Charles Green, published, in paper covers at
three shillings, and in cloth at four shillings, in 1876. In
the "Library Edition" *The Old Curiosity Shop* was
bound up with "Reprinted Pieces," the whole making
two volumes.

Among outside or extra illustrations to *The Old Curiosity Shop* was a series which was thus advertised on the
wrapper of No. 37 of *Master Humphrey's Clock*: "Early
in November will be published (with the volume) part 1,
price 2s., containing six etchings of "Hands to Humphrey's Clock, or Sketches from the Clock Case" to illus-
trate The Old Curiosity Shop, by Jacob Parallel, London,
C. Berger, Holywell Street, Strand. A Part will be published at the completion of each volume." A list of the
illustrations in Parts 1 and 2 was afterwards given on the
wrappers of No. 52, the 27th of March, 1841. Also known
to Dickens collectors are four lithos by T. C. W. illustrating the first portion of the *Clock*, imperial octavo, undated
and without publisher's name ; and " Sketches of Character from Master Humphrey's Clock by Brush." These
are the three etchings—portraits of Master Humphrey,
Nell, and the Grandfather—which were published in one
part at a shilling by W. T. Davey, 16 Great Sutton Street,
Clerkenwell, and W Britain, 11 Paternoster Row, with
an address in which it is stated that "the following
sketches are the commencement of a series illustrating the
principal characters in Master Humphrey's Clock, to appear at monthly intervals in parts similar to the present."

Whether any further parts were published I have not been able to ascertain.

When the first cheap edition was published a series of plates illustrative of the *Clock* novels, by Hablot Browne, was also issued by Messrs. Chapman and Hall, with the approbation of the author, those for *The Old Curiosity Shop* being Little Nell and her Grandfather, the Marchioness, Barbara, and the Deathbed of Nell. These were published in a green wrapper at a shilling, and are now extremely scarce.

Among the pictures in Charles Dickens's collection—which were, under the provisions of his will, sold at Christie's—were three illustrative of *The Old Curiosity Shop*. These were Little Nell and her Grandfather in the tent making nosegays for the race-course, a drawing by F. W. Topham, presented to Charles Dickens by the artist, which sold for £288 : 16s.; Little Nell in the Churchyard, a painting by Mrs. M'Ian, presented by the artist, sale price £44 : 2s.; Little Nell at home in the Old House, a drawing by George Cattermole, sale price £168; and the Grandfather at Little Nell's grave, the companion drawing, which brought £189.

The original manuscript of *The Old Curiosity Shop* is at South Kensington.

Of plagiarisms or imitations of *The Old Curiosity Shop* of any importance I have not been able to find any record, but Mr. Kitton in his *Dickensiana* says that the first volume of Parley's Penny Library, edited by Mr. Samuel Goodrich under the pseudonym of Peter Parley, contained a number of selections from *The Old Curiosity Shop* in the form of dialogues, and that "Dickens was naturally incensed at this wholesale piracy."

The story has frequently been adapted for stage purposes. The first version was by Mr. Edward Stirling—it was described as a "burletta in two acts, founded on the celebrated, widely circulated, and universally admired papers by Boz"—and was first performed at the Adelphi Theatre, with Mrs. Keeley as Nell and Frederick Yates as Quilp, on the 9th of November, 1840; the best was probably that by Andrew Halliday, which was produced at the Olympic Theatre on the 19th of November, 1870. An adaptation of my own, which was produced at the Opera Comique Theatre on the 12th of January, 1884, was

2

deprived of any merit it may have possessed by the inter-
polation by the American lady for whom I wrote the
piece (she "doubled" Nell and the Marchioness), of a
preposterous act from a ridiculous version by Mr. John
Brougham which she had been accustomed to play in the
United States.

CHARLES DICKENS
THE YOUNGER.

THE OLD CURIOSITY SHOP.

CHAPTER THE FIRST.

NIGHT is generally my time for walking. In the summer I often leave home early in the morning, and roam about fields and lanes all day, or even escape for days or weeks together, but saving in the country I seldom go out until after dark, though, Heaven be thanked, I love its light and feel the cheerfulness it sheds upon the earth, as much as any creature living.

I have fallen insensibly into this habit, both because it favors my infirmity and because it affords me greater opportunity of speculating on the characters and occupations of those who fill the streets. The glare and hurry of broad noon are not adapted to idle pursuits like mine; a glimpse of passing faces caught by the light of a street lamp or a shop window is often better for my purpose than their full revelation in the daylight, and, if I must add the truth, night is kinder in this respect than day, which too often destroys an air-built castle at the moment of its completion, without the smallest ceremony or remorse.

That constant pacing to and fro, that never-ending restlessness, that incessant tread of feet wearing the rough stones smooth and glossy—is it not a wonder how the dwellers in narrow ways can bear to hear it! Think of a sick man in such a place as Saint Martin's Court, listening to the footsteps, and in the midst of pain and weariness obliged, despite himself (as though it were a task he must perform) to detect the child's step from the man's, the slipshod beggar from the booted exquisite, the lounging from the busy, the dull heel of the sauntering outcast from

the quick tread of an expectant pleasure-seeker—think of
the hum and noise being always present to his senses, and
of the stream of life that will not stop, pouring on, on, on,
through all his restless dreams, as if he were condemned
to lie dead but conscious, in a noisy churchyard, and had
no hope of rest for centuries to come.

Then the crowds forever passing and repassing on the
bridges (on those which are free of toll at least) where
many stop on fine evenings looking listlessly down upon
the water with some vague idea that by and by it runs
between green banks which grow wider and wider until
at last it joins the broad vast sea—where some halt
to rest from heavy loads and think as they look over the
parapet that to smoke and lounge away one's life and lie
sleeping in the sun upon a hot tarpaulin, in a dull slow
sluggish barge, must be happiness unalloyed—and where
some, and a very different class, pause with heavier loads
than they, remembering to have heard or read in some
old time that drowning was not a hard death, but of all
means of suicide the easiest and best.

Covent Garden Market at sunrise too, in the spring
or summer, when the fragrance of sweet flowers is in the
air, overpowering even the unwholesome streams of last
night's debauchery, and driving the dusky thrush, whose
cage has hung outside a garret window all night long, half
mad with joy! Poor bird! the only neighboring thing
at all akin to the other little captives, some of whom,
shrinking from the hot hands of drunken purchasers,
lie drooping on the path already, while others, sod-
dened by close contact, await the time when they shall
be watered and freshened up to please more sober company, and make old clerks who pass them on their road to
business, wonder what has filled their breasts with visions
of the country.

But my present purpose is not to expatiate upon my
walks.   An adventure which I am about to relate, and to
which I shall recur at intervals, arose out of one of these
rambles, and thus I have been led to speak of them by
way of preface.

One night I had roamed into the City, and was walking
slowly on in my usual way, musing upon a great many
things, when I was arrested by an inquiry, the purport of
which did not reach me, but which seemed to be addressed

to myself, and was preferred in a soft sweet voice that struck me very pleasantly. I turned hastily round and found at my elbow a pretty little girl, who begged to be directed to a certain street at a considerable distance, and indeed in quite another quarter of the town.

" It is a very long way from here," said I, " my child."

" I know that, Sir," she replied timidly. " I am afraid it is a very long way, for I came from there to-night."

" Alone? " said I, in some surprise.

" Oh yes, I don't mind that, but I am a little frightened now, for I had lost my road."

" And what made you ask it of me? Suppose I should tell you wrong."

" I am sure you will not do that," said the little creature, " you are such a very old gentleman, and walk so slow yourself."

I cannot describe how much I was impressed by this appeal and the energy with which it was made, which brought a tear into the child's clear eye, and made her slight figure tremble as she looked up into my face.

" Come," said I, " I'll take you there."

She put her hand in mine as confidingly as if she had known me from her cradle, and we trudged away together: the little creature accommodating her pace to mine, and rather seeming to lead and take care of me than I to be protecting her. I observed that every now and then she stole a curious look at my face as if to make quite sure that I was not deceiving her, and that these glances (very sharp and keen they were too) seemed to increase her confidence at every repetition.

For my part, my curiosity and interest were at least equal to the child's, for child she certainly was, although I thought it probable from what I could make out, that her very small and delicate frame imparted a peculiar youthfulness to her appearance. Though more scantily attired than she might have been she was dressed with perfect neatness, and betrayed no marks of poverty or neglect.

" Who has sent you so far by yourself? " said I.

" Somebody who is very kind to me, Sir."

" And what have you been doing? "

" That I must not tell," said the child firmly.

There was something in the manner of this reply which

caused me to look at the little creature with an involuntary expression of surprise; for I wondered what kind of errand it might be that occasioned her to be prepared for questioning. Her quick eye seemed to read my thoughts, for as it met mine she added that there was no harm in what she had been doing, but it was a great secret—a secret which she did not even know herself.

This was said with no appearance of cunning or deceit, but with an unsuspicious frankness that bore the impress of truth. She walked on as before, growing more familiar with me as we proceeded and talking cheerfully by the way, but she said no more about her home, beyond remarking that we were going quite a new road and asking if it were a short one.

While we were thus engaged, I revolved in my mind a hundred different explanations of the riddle and rejected them every one. I really felt ashamed to take advantage of the ingenuousness or grateful feeling of the child for the purpose of gratifying my curiosity. I love these little people; and it is not a slight thing when they, who are so fresh from God, love us. As I had felt pleased at first by her confidence I determined to deserve it, and to do credit to the nature which had prompted her to repose it in me.

There was no reason, however, why I should refrain from seeing the person who had inconsiderately sent her to so great a distance by night and alone, and as it was not improbable that if she found herself near home she might take farewell of me and deprive me of the opportunity, I avoided the most frequented ways and took the most intricate, and thus it was not until we arrived in the street itself that she knew where we were. Clapping her hands with pleasure and running on before me for a short distance, my little acquaintance stopped at a door and remaining on the step till I came up knocked at it when I joined her.

A part of this door was of glass unprotected by any shutter, which I did not observe at first, for all was very dark and silent within, and I was anxious (as indeed the child was also) for an answer to our summons. When she had knocked twice or thrice there was a noise as if some person were moving inside, and at length a faint light appeared through the glass which, as it approached very slowly, the bearer having to make his way through a great many scattered articles, enabled me to see both what kind of person it was who advanced and what kind of place it was through which he came.

It was a little old man with long gray hair, whose face and figure as he held the light above his head and looked before him as he approached, I could plainly see. Though much altered by age, I fancied I could recognize in his spare and slender form something of that delicate mould which I had noticed in the child. Their bright blue eyes

were certainly alike, but his face was so deeply furrowed and so very full of care, that here all resemblance ceased.

The place through which he made his way at leisure was one of those receptacles for old and curious things which seem to crouch in odd corners of this town and to hide their musty treasures from the public eye in jealousy and distrust. There were suits of mail standing like ghosts in armor here and there, fantastic carvings brought from monkish cloisters, rusty weapons of various kinds, distorted figures in china and wood and iron and ivory: tapestry and strange furniture that might have been designed in dreams. The haggard aspect of the little old man was wonderfully suited to the place; he might have groped among old churches and tombs and deserted houses and gathered all the spoils with his own hands. There was nothing in the whole collection but was in keeping with himself; nothing that looked older or more worn than he.

As he turned the key in the lock, he surveyed me with some astonishment which was not diminished when he looked from me to my companion. The door being opened, the child addressed him as grandfather, and told him the little story of our companionship.

" Why bless thee, child," said the old man patting her on the head, " how couldst thou miss thy way? What if I had lost thee, Nell! "

" I would have found my way back to *you*, grandfather," said the child boldly; " never fear."

The old man kissed her, then turning to me and begging me to walk in, I did so. The door was closed and locked. Preceding me with the light, he led me through the place I had already seen from without, into a small sitting-room behind, in which was another door opening into a kind of closet, where I saw a little bed that a fairy might have slept in, it looked so very small and was so prettily arranged. The child took a candle and tripped into this little room, leaving the old man and me together.

" You must be tired, Sir," said he as he placed a chair near the fire, " how can I thank you? "

" By taking more care of your grandchild another time, my good friend," I replied.

" More care! " said the old man in a shrill voice, " more care of Nelly! Why, who ever loved a child as I love Nell? "

He said this with such evident surprise that I was perplexed what answer to make, and the more so because coupled with something feeble and wandering in his manner, there were in his face marks of deep and anxious thought which convinced me that he could not be, as I had been at first inclined to suppose, in a state of dotage or imbecility.

" I don't think you consider—" I began.

" I don't consider! " cried the old man interrupting me,

" I don't consider her ! Ah, how little you know of the truth ! Little Nelly, little Nelly ! "

It would be impossible for any man, I care not what his form of speech might be, to express more affection than the dealer in curiosities did, in these four words. I waited for him to speak again, but he rested his chin upon his hand and shaking his head twice or thrice fixed his eyes upon the fire.

While we were sitting thus in silence, the door of the closet opened, and the child returned, her light brown hair hanging loose about her neck, and her face flushed with the haste she had made to rejoin us. She busied herself immediately in preparing supper, and while she was thus engaged I remarked that the old man took an opportunity of observing me more closely than he had done yet. I was surprised to see that all this time everything was done by the child, and that there appeared to be no other persons but ourselves in the house. I took advantage of a moment when she was absent to venture a hint on this point, to which the old man replied that there were few grown persons as trustworthy or as careful as she.

" It always grieves me," I observed, roused by what I took to be his selfishness, " it always grieves me to contemplate the initiation of children into the ways of life, when they are scarcely more than infants. It checks their confidence and simplicity—two of the best qualities that Heaven gives them—and demands that they share our sorrows before they are capable of entering into our enjoyments."

" It will never check hers," said the old man looking steadily at me, " the springs are too deep. Besides, the children of the poor know but few pleasures. Even the cheap delights of childhood must be bought and paid for."

" But—forgive me for saying this—you are surely not so very poor "—said I.

" She is not my child, Sir," returned the old man. " Her mother was, and she was poor. I save nothing—not a penny—though I live as you see, but "—he laid his hand upon my arm and leant forward to whisper—" she shall be rich one of these days, and a fine lady. Don't you think ill of me, because I use her help. She gives it cheerfully as you see, and it would break her heart if she knew that I suffered anybody else to do for me what her little hands could undertake. I don't consider!"— he cried with sudden querulousness, "why, God knows that this one child is the thought and object of my life, and yet he never prospers me—no, never!"

At this juncture, the subject of our conversation again returned, and the old man motioning to me to approach the table, broke off, and said no more.

We had scarcely begun our repast when there was a knock at the door by which I had entered, and Nell bursting into a hearty laugh, which I was rejoiced to hear, for it was childlike and full of hilarity, said it was no doubt dear old Kit come back at last.

"Foolish Nell!" said the old man fondling with her hair. "She always laughs at poor Kit."

The child laughed again more heartily than before, and I could not help smiling from pure sympathy. The little old man took up a candle and went to open the door. When he came back, Kit was at his heels.

Kit was a shock-headed shambling awkward lad with an uncommonly wide mouth, very red cheeks, a turned-up nose, and certainly the most comical expression of face I ever saw. He stopped short at the door on seeing a stranger, twirled in his hand a perfectly round old hat without any vestige of a brim, and resting himself now on one leg and now on the other and changing them constantly, stood in the doorway, looking into the parlor with the most extraordinary leer I ever beheld. I entertained a grateful feeling towards the boy from that minute, for I felt that he was the comedy of the child's life.

"A long way, wasn't it, Kit?" said the little old man.

"Why then, it was a goodish stretch, master," returned Kit.

"Did you find the house easily?"

"Why then, not over and above easy, master," said Kit.

"Of course you have come back hungry?"

"Why then, I do consider myself rather so, master," was the answer.

The lad had a remarkable manner of standing sideways as he spoke, and thrusting his head forward over his shoulder, as if he could not get at his voice without that accompanying action. I think he would have amused one anywhere, but the child's exquisite enjoyment of his oddity, and the relief it was to find that there was something she associated with merriment in a place that appeared so unsuited to her, were quite irresistible. It was a great point too that Kit himself was flattered by the sensation he created, and after several efforts to preserve his gravity, burst into a loud roar, and so stood with his mouth wide open and his eyes nearly shut, laughing violently.

The old man had again relapsed into his former abstraction and took no notice of what passed, but I remarked that when her laugh was over, the child's bright eyes were dimmed with tears, called forth by the fulness of heart with which she welcomed her uncouth favorite after the little anxiety of the night. As for Kit himself (whose laugh had been all the time one of that sort which very little would change into a cry) he carried a large slice of bread and meat and a mug of beer into a corner, and applied himself to disposing of them with great voracity.

"Ah!" said the old man turning to me with a sigh as if I had spoken to him but that moment, "you don't know what you say when you tell me that I don't consider her."

"You must not attach too great weight to a remark founded on first appearances, my friend," said I.

"No," returned the old man thoughtfully, "no. Come hither, Nell."

The little girl hastened from her seat, and put her arm about his neck.

"Do I love thee, Nell?" said he. "Say—do I love thee, Nell, or no?"

The child only answered by her caresses, and laid her head upon his breast.

"Why dost thou sob," said the grandfather pressing her closer to him and glancing towards me. "Is it because thou know'st I love thee, and dost not like that I should seem to doubt it by my question? Well, well—then let us say I love thee dearly."

"Indeed, indeed you do," replied the child with great earnestness, "Kit knows you do."

Kit, who in despatching his bread and meat had been swallowing two-thirds of his knife at every mouthful with

the coolness of a juggler, stopped short in his operations
on being thus appealed to, and bawled "Nobody isn't
such a fool as to say he doesn't," after which he inca-
pacitated himself for further conversation by taking a
most prodigious sandwich at one bite.

"She is poor now "—said the old man patting the child's
cheek, "but I say again that the time is coming when
she shall be rich. It has been a long time coming, but it
must come at last; a very long time, but it surely must
come. It has come to other men who do nothing but
waste and riot. When *will* it come to me!"

"I am very happy as I am, grandfather," said the child.

"Tush, tush!" returned the old man, "thou dost not
know—how should'st thou!" Then he muttered again
between his teeth, "The time must come, I am very sure
it must. It will be all the better for coming late;" and
then he sighed and fell into his former musing state, and
still holding the child between his knees appeared to be
insensible to everything around him. By this time it
wanted but a few minutes of midnight and I rose to go,
which recalled him to himself.

"One moment, Sir," he said. "Now, Kit—near midnight, boy, and you still here! Get home, get home,
and be true to your time in the morning, for there's work
to do. Good night! There, bid him good night, Nell,
and let him be gone!"

"Good night, Kit," said the child, her eyes lighting
up with merriment and kindness.

"Good night, Miss Nell," returned the boy.

"And thank this gentleman," interposed the old man,
"but for whose care I might have lost my little girl to-
night."

"No, no, master," said Kit, "that won't do, that won't."

"What do you mean?" cried the old man.

"I'd have found her, master," said Kit, "I'd have found
her. I'd bet that I'd find her if she was above ground, I
would, as quick as anybody, master. Ha ha ha!"

Once more opening his mouth and shutting his eyes,
and laughing like a stentor, Kit gradually backed to the
door, and roared himself out.

Free of the room, the boy was not slow in taking his
departure; when he had gone, and the child was occupied
in clearing the table, the old man said:

"I haven't seemed to thank you, Sir, enough for what you have done to-night, but I do thank you humbly and heartily, and so does she, and her thanks are better worth than mine. I should be sorry that you went away and thought I was unmindful of your goodness, or careless of her—I am not indeed."

I was sure of that, I said, from what I had seen. "But," I added, "may I ask you a question?"

"Ay, Sir," replied the old man, "what is it?"

"This delicate child," said I, with so much beauty and intelligence—has she nobody to care for her but you? Has she no other companion or adviser?"

"No," he returned looking anxiously in my face, "no, and she wants no other."

"But are you not fearful," said I, "that you may mis-understand a charge so tender? I am sure you mean well, but are you quite certain that you know how to ex-ecute such a trust as this? I am an old man, like you, and I am actuated by an old man's concern in all that is young and promising. Do you not think that what I have seen of you and this little creature to-night must have an interest not wholly free from pain?"

"Sir," rejoined the old man after a moment's silence, "I have no right to feel hurt at what you say. It is true that in many respects I am the child, and she the grown person—that you have seen already. But waking or sleep-ing, by night or day, in sickness or health, she is the one object of my care, and if you knew of how much care, you would look on me with different eyes, you would indeed. Ah! it's a weary life for an old man—a weary, weary life —but there is a great end to gain and that I keep before me."

Seeing that he was in a state of excitement and impa-tience, I turned to put on an outer coat which I had thrown off on entering the room, purposing to say no more. I was surprised to see the child standing patiently by with a cloak upon her arm, and in her hand a hat and stick.

"Those are not mine, my dear," said I.

"No," returned the child quietly, "they are grand-father's."

"But he is not going out to-night."

"Oh yes he is," said the child, with a smile.

"And what becomes of you, my pretty one?"

" Me ! I stay here of course. I always do."

I looked in astonishment towards the old man, but he was, or feigned to be, busied in the arrangement of his dress. From him I looked back to the slight gentle figure of the child. Alone! In that gloomy place all the long, dreary night.

She evinced no consciousness of my surprise, but cheerfully helped the old man with his cloak, and when he was ready took a candle to light us out. Finding that we did not follow as she expected, she looked back with a smile and waited for us. The old man showed by his face that he plainly understood the cause of my hesitation, but he merely signed to me with an inclination of the head to pass out of the room before him, and remained silent. I had no resource but to comply.

When we reached the door, the child setting down the candle, turned to say good night and raised her face to kiss me. Then she ran to the old man, who folded her in his arms and bade God bless her.

" Sleep soundly, Nell," he said in a low voice, " and angels guard thy bed ! Do not forget thy prayers, my sweet."

" No indeed," answered the child fervently, " they make me feel so happy ! "

" That's well ; I know they do ; they should," said the old man. " Bless thee a hundred times ! Early in the morning I shall be home."

" You'll not ring twice," returned the child. " The bell wakes me, even in the middle of a dream."

With this, they separated. The child opened the door (now guarded by a shutter which I had heard the boy put up before he left the house) and with another farewell whose clear and tender note I have recalled a thousand times, held it until we had passed out. The old man paused a moment while it was gently closed and fastened on the inside, and, satisfied that this was done, walked on at a slow pace. At the street-corner he stopped, and regarding me with a troubled countenance said that our ways were widely different and that he must take his leave. I would have spoken, but summoning up more alacrity than might have been expected in one of his appearance, he hurried away. I could see that twice or thrice he looked back as if to ascertain if I were still watching him, or perhaps to assure himself that I was not following at a distance. The obscurity of the night favored his disappearance, and his figure was soon beyond my sight.

I remained standing on the spot where he had left me, unwilling to depart, and yet unknowing why I should loiter there. I looked wistfully into the street we had lately quitted, and after a time directed my steps that way. I passed and repassed the house, and stopped and listened at the door; all was dark, and silent as the grave.

Yet I lingered about, and could not tear myself away, thinking of all possible harm that might happen to the child—of fires and robberies and even murder—and feeling as if some evil must ensue if I turned my back upon the place. The closing of a door or window in the street brought me before the curiosity-dealer's once more; I crossed the road and looked up at the house to assure myself that the noise had not come from there. No, it was black, cold, and lifeless as before.

There were few passengers astir; the street was sad and dismal, and pretty well my own. A few stragglers from the theatres hurried by, and now and then I turned aside to avoid some noisy drunkard as he reeled homewards, but these interruptions were not frequent and soon ceased. The clocks struck one. Still I paced up and down, promising myself that every time should be the last, and breaking faith with myself on some new plea as often as I did so.

The more I thought of what the old man had said, and of his looks and bearing, the less I could account for what I had seen and heard. I had a strong misgiving that his nightly absence was for no good purpose. I had only come to know the fact through the innocence of the child, and though the old man was by at the time, and saw my undisguised surprise, he had preserved a strange mystery upon the subject and offered no word of explanation. These reflections naturally recalled again more strongly than before his haggard face, his wandering manner, his restless anxious look. His affection for the child might not be inconsistent with villainy of the worst kind; even that very affection was in itself an extraordinary contradiction, or how could he leave her thus? Disposed as I was to think badly of him, I never doubted that his love for her was real. I could not admit the thought, remembering what had passed between us, and the tone of voice in which he had called her by her name.

"Stay here of course," the child had said in answer to my question, "I always do!" What could take him from home by night, and every night! I called up all the strange tales I had ever head of dark and secret deeds committed in great towns and escaping detection for a long series of years; wild as many of these stories were, I could not find one adapted to this mystery, which only became the more impenetrable, in proportion as I sought to solve it.

Occupied with such thoughts as these, and a crowd of others all tending to the same point, I continued to pace the street for two long hours; at length the rain began to descend heavily, and then overpowered by fatigue though no less interested than I had been at first, I engaged the nearest coach and so got home. A cheerful fire was blazing on the hearth, the lamp burnt brightly, my clock received me with its old familiar welcome; everything was quiet, warm and cheering, and in happy contrast to the gloom and darkness I had quitted.

But all that night, waking or in my sleep, the same

thoughts recurred and the same images retained possession of my brain. I had ever before me the old dark
murky rooms—the gaunt suits of mail with their ghostly
silent air—the faces all awry, grinning from wood and
stone—the dust and rust and worm that lives in wood—
and alone in the midst of all this lumber and decay and
ugly age, the beautiful child in her gentle slumber, smiling through her light and sunny dreams.

CHAPTER THE SECOND.

AFTER combating, for nearly a week, the feeling which
impelled me to revisit the place I had quitted under the
circumstance already detailed, I yielded to it at length;
and determining that this time I would present myself by
the light of day, bent my steps thither early in the afternoon.

I walked past the house, and took several turns in the
street, with that kind of hesitation which is natural to
a man who is conscious that the visit he is about to pay
is unexpected, and may not be very acceptable. However, as the door of the shop was shut, and it did not appear likely that I should be recognized by those within,
if I continued merely to pass up and down before it, I
soon conquered this irresolution, and found myself in the
Curiosity Dealer's warehouse.

The old man and another person were together in the
back part, and there seemed to have been high words between them, for their voices which were raised to a very
loud pitch suddenly stopped on my entering, and the old
man advancing hastily towards me, said in a tremulous
tone that he was very glad I had come.

"You interrupted us at a critical moment," he said,
pointing to the man whom I had found in company with
him; "this fellow will murder me one of these days. He
would have done so, long ago, if he had dared."

"Bah! You would swear away my life if you could,"
returned the other, after bestowing a stare and a frown on
me; "we all know that!"

"I almost think I could," cried the old man, turning
feebly upon him. "If oaths, or prayers or words, could

3

rid me of you, they should. I would be quit of you, and would be relieved if you were dead."

"I know it," returned the other. "I said so, didn't I? But neither oaths, nor prayers, nor words, *will* kill me, and therefore I live, and mean to live."

"And his mother died!" cried the old man, passionately clasping his hands and looking upward; "and this is Heaven's justice!"

The other stood lounging with his foot upon a chair, and regarded him with a contemptuous sneer. He was a young man of one-and-twenty or thereabouts; well made, and certainly handsome, though the expression of his face was far from prepossessing, having in common with his manner and even his dress, a dissipated insolent air which repelled one.

"Justice or no justice," said the young fellow, "here I am and here I shall stop till such time as I think fit to go, unless you send for assistance to put me out—which you won't do, I know. I tell you again that I want to see my sister."

"*Your* sister!" said the old man bitterly.

"Ah! You can't change the relationship," returned the other. "If you could, you'd have done it long ago. I want to see my sister, that you keep cooped up here, poisoning her mind with your sly secrets and pretending an affection for her that you may work her to death, and add a few scraped shillings every week to the money you can hardly count. I want to see her; and I will."

"Here's a moralist to talk of poisoned minds! Here's a generous spirit to scorn scraped up shillings!" cried the old man, turning from him to me. "A profligate, Sir, who has forfeited every claim not only upon those who have the misfortune to be of his blood, but upon society which knows nothing of him but his misdeeds. A liar too," he added, in a lower voice as he drew closer to me, "who knows how dear she is to me, and seeks to wound me even there, because there is a stranger by."

"Strangers are nothing to me, grandfather," said the young fellow catching at the word, "nor I to them, I hope. The best they can do, is to keep an eye to their business and leave me to mine. There's a friend of mine waiting outside, and as it seems that I may have to wait some time, I'll call him in, with your leave."

Saying this, he stepped to the door, and looking down the street beckoned several times to some unseen person, who, to judge from the air of impatience with which these signals were accompanied, required a great quantity of persuasion to induce him to advance. At length there sauntered up, on the opposite side of the way—with a bad pretence of passing by accident—a figure conspicuous for its dirty smartness, which after a great many frowns and jerks of the head, in resistance of the invitation, ultimately crossed the road and was brought into the shop.

"There. It's Dick Swiveller," said the young fellow, pushing him in. "Sit down, Swiveller."

"But is the old min agreeable?" said Mr. Swiveller in an under tone.

"Sit down," repeated his companion.

Mr. Swiveller complied, and looking about him with a propitiatory smile, observed that last week was a fine week for the ducks, and this week was a fine week for the dust; he also observed that whilst standing by the post at the street corner, he had observed a pig with a straw in his mouth issuing out of the tobacco-shop, from which appearance he augured that another fine week for the ducks was approaching, and that rain would certainly ensue. He furthermore took occasion to apologize for any negligence that might be perceptible in his dress, on the ground that last night he had had "the sun very strong in his eyes;" by which expression he was understood to convey to his hearers in the most delicate manner possible, the information that he had been extremely drunk.

"But what," said Mr. Swiveller with a sigh, "what is the odds so long as the fire of soul is kindled at the taper of conwiviality, and the wing of friendship never moults a feather! What is the odds so long as the spirit is expanded by means of rosy wine, and the present moment is the least happiest of our existence!"

"You needn't act the chairman here," said his friend, half aside.

"Fred!" cried Mr. Swiveller, tapping his nose, "a word to the wise is sufficient for them—we may be good and happy without riches, Fred. Say not another syllable. I know my cue; smart is the word. Only one little whisper, Fred—*is* the old min friendly?"

" Never you mind," replied his friend.

" Right again, quite right," said Mr. Swiveller, " **caution** is the word, and caution is the act." With that, he **winked** as if in preservation of some deep secret, and folding his arms and leaning back in his chair, looked up at the ceiling with profound gravity.

It was perhaps not very unreasonable to suspect from what had already passed, that Mr. Swiveller was not quite recovered from the effects of the powerful sunlight to which he had made allusion ; but if no such suspicion had been awakened by his speech, his wiry hair, dull eyes,

and sallow face, would still have been strong witnesses against him. His attire was not, as he had himself hinted, remarkable for the nicest arrangement, but was in a state of disorder which strongly induced the idea that he had gone to bed in it. It consisted of a brown body-coat with a great many brass buttons up the front and only one behind, a bright check neckerchief, a plaid waistcoat, soiled white trousers, and a very limp hat, worn with the wrong side foremost, to hide a hole in the brim. The breast of his coat was ornamented with an outside pocket from which there peeped forth the cleanest end of a very large and very ill-favored handkerchief; his dirty wristbands were pulled down as far as possible and ostentatiously folded back over his cuffs; he displayed no gloves, and carried a yellow cane having at the top a bone hand with the semblance of a ring on its little finger and a black ball in its grasp. With all these personal advantages (to which may be added a strong savor of tobacco-smoke, and a prevailing greasiness of appearance) Mr. Swiveller leant back in his chair with his eyes fixed on the ceiling, and occasionally pitching his voice to the needful key, obliged the company with a few bars of an intensely dismal air, and then, in the middle of a note, relapsed into his former silence.

The old man sat himself down in a chair, and, with folded hands, looked sometimes at his grandson and sometimes at his strange companion, as if he were utterly powerless and had no resource but to leave them to do as they pleased. The young man reclined against a table at no great distance from his friend, in apparent indifference to everything that had passed; and I—who felt the difficulty of any interference, notwithstanding that the old man had appealed to me, both by words and looks—made the best feint I could of being occupied in examining some of the goods that were disposed for sale, and paying very little attention to the persons before me.

The silence was not of long duration, for Mr. Swiveller, after favoring us with several melodious assurances that his heart was in the Highlands, and that he wanted but his Arab steed as a preliminary to the achievement of great feats of valor and loyalty, removed his eyes from the ceiling and subsided into prose again.

"Fred," said Mr. Swiveller stopping short as if the idea had suddenly occurred to him, and speaking in the same audible whisper as before, "*is* the old min friendly?"

"What does it matter?" returned his friend peevishly.

"No, but *is* he?" said Dick.

"Yes, of course. What do I care whether he is or not."

Emboldened as it seemed by this reply to enter into a more general conversation, Mr. Swiveller plainly laid himself out to captivate our attention.

He began by remarking that soda-water, though a good

thing in the abstract, was apt to lie cold upon the stomach unless qualified with ginger, or a small infusion of brandy, which latter article he held to be preferable in all cases, saving for the one consideration of expense. Nobody venturing to dispute these positions, he proceeded to observe that the human hair was a great retainer of tobacco-smoke, and that the young gentlemen of Westminster and Eton, after eating vast quantities of apples to conceal any scent of cigars from their anxious friends, were usually detected in consequence of their heads possessing this remarkable property; whence he concluded that if the Royal Society would turn their attention to the circumstance, and endeavor to find in the resources of science a means of preventing such untoward revelations, they might indeed be looked upon as benefactors to mankind. These opinions being equally incontrovertible with those he had already pronounced, he went on to inform us that Jamaica rum, though unquestionably an agreeable spirit of great richness and flavor, had the drawback of remaining constantly present to the taste next day; and nobody being venturous enough to argue this point either, he increased in confidence and became yet more companionable and communicative.

"It's a devil of a thing, gentlemen," said Mr. Swiveller, "when relations fall out and disagree. If the wing of friendship should never moult a feather, the wing of relationship should never be clipped, but be always expanded and serene. Why should a grandson and grandfather peg away at each other with mutual wiolence when all might be bliss and concord? Why not jine hands and forgit it?"

"Hold your tongue," said his friend.

"Sir," replied Mr. Swiveller, "don't you interrupt the chair. Gentlemen, how does the case stand, upon the present occasion? Here is a jolly old grandfather—I say it with the utmost respect—and here is a wild young grandson. The jolly old grandfather says to the wild young grandson, 'I have brought you up and educated you, Fred; I have put you in the way of getting on in life; you have bolted a little out of the course, as young fellows often do; and you shall never have another chance, nor the ghost of half a one.' The wild young grandson makes answer to this and says. 'You're as rich as rich can be;

you have been at no uncommon expense on my account,
you're saving up piles of money for my little sister that
lives with you in a secret, stealthy, hugger-muggering
kind of way and with no manner of enjoyment—why
can't you stand a trifle for your grown-up relation?'
The jolly old grandfather unto this, retorts, not only that
he declines to fork out with that cheerful readiness which
is always so agreeable and pleasant in a gentleman of his
time of life, but that he will blow up, and call names, and
make reflections whenever they meet. Then the plain
question is, an't it a pity that this state of things should
continue, and how much better would it be for the old
gentleman to hand over a reasonable amount of tin, and
make it all right and comfortable?"

Having delivered this oration with a great many waves
and flourishes of the hand, Mr. Swiveller abruptly thrust
the head of his cane into his mouth as if to prevent himself from impairing the effect of his speech by adding
one other word.

"Why do you hunt and persecute me, God help me!"
said the old man turning to his grandson. "Why do you
bring your profligate companions here? How often am
I to tell you that my life is one of care and self-denial,
and that I am poor?"

"How often am I to tell you," returned the other, looking coldly at him, "that I know better?"

"You have chosen your own path," said the old man.
"Follow it. Leave Nell and me to toil and work."

"Nell will be a woman soon," returned the other, "and,
bred in your faith, she'll forget her brother unless he
shows himself sometimes."

"Take care," said the old man with sparkling eyes,
"that she does not forget you when you would have her
memory keenest. Take care that the day don't come
when you walk barefoot in the streets, and she rides by
in a gay carriage of her own."

"You mean when she has your money?' retorted the
other. "How like a poor man he talks!"

"And yet," said the old man dropping his voice and
speaking like one who thinks aloud, "how poor we are,
and what a life it is! The cause is a young child's, guilt-
less of all harm or wrong, but nothing goes well with it!
Hope and patience, hope and patience!"

These words were uttered in too low a tone to reach the ears of the young men. Mr. Swiveller appeared to think that they implied some mental struggle consequent upon the powerful effect of his address, for he poked his friend with his cane and whispered his conviction that he had administered "a clincher," and that he expected a commission on the profits. Discovering his mistake after a while, he appeared to grow rather sleepy and discontented, and had more than once suggested the propriety of an immediate departure, when the door opened, and the child herself appeared.

CHAPTER THE THIRD.

THE child was closely followed by an elderly man of remarkably hard features and forbidding aspect, and so low in stature as to be quite a dwarf, though his head and face were large enough for the body of a giant. His black eyes were restless, sly, and cunning; his mouth and chin, bristly with the stubble of a coarse hard beard; and his complexion was one of that kind which never looks clean or wholesome. But what added most to the grotesque expression of his face, was a ghastly smile, which, appearing to be the mere result of habit and to have no connection with any mirthful or complacent feeling, constantly revealed the few discolored fangs that were yet scattered in his mouth, and gave him the aspect of a panting dog. His dress consisted of a large high-crowned hat, a worn dark suit, a pair of capacious shoes, and a dirty white neckerchief sufficiently limp and crumpled to disclose the greater portion of his wiry throat. Such hair as he had, was of a grizzled black, cut short and straight upon his temples, and hanging in a frowgy fringe about his ears. His hands, which were of a rough coarse grain, were very dirty; his finger-nails were crooked, long, and yellow.

There was ample time to note these particulars, for besides that they were sufficiently obvious without very close observation, some moments elapsed before any one broke silence. The child advanced timidly towards her brother and put her hand in his, the dwarf (if we may call him so) glanced keenly at all present, and the curiosity·

dealer, who plainly had not expected his uncouth visitor, seemed disconcerted and embarrassed.

"Ah!" said the dwarf, who with his hand stretched out above his eyes had been surveying the young man attentively, "that should be your grandson, neighbor!"

"Say rather that he should not be," replied the old man. "But he is."

"And that!" said the dwarf, pointing to Dick Swiveller.

"Some friend of his, as welcome here as he," said the old man.

"And that!" inquired the dwarf wheeling round and pointing straight at me.

"A gentleman who was so good as to bring Nell home the other night when she lost her way, coming from your house."

The little man turned to the child as if to chide her or express his wonder, but as she was talking to the young man, held his peace, and bent his head to listen.

"Well, Nelly," said the young fellow aloud. "Do they teach you to hate me, eh?"

"No, no. For shame. Oh, no!" cried the child.

"To love me, perhaps?" pursued her brother with a sneer.

"To do neither," she returned. "They never speak to me about you. Indeed they never do."

"I dare be bound for that," he said, darting a bitter look at the grandfather. "I dare be bound for that, Nell. Oh! I believe you there!"

"But I love you dearly, Fred," said the child.

"No doubt!"

"I do indeed, and always will," the child repeated with great emotion, "but, oh! if you would leave off vexing him and making him unhappy, then I could love you more."

"I see!" said the young man, as he stooped carelessly over the child, and having kissed her, pushed her from him: "There—get you away now you have said your lesson. You needn't whimper. We part good friends enough, if that's the matter."

He remained silent, following her with his eyes, until she had gained her little room and closed the door; and then turning to the dwarf, said abruptly,

"Harkee, Mr.—"

"Meaning me?" returned the dwarf. "Quilp is my name. You might remember. It's not a long one—Daniel Quilp."

"Harkee, Mr. Quilp, then," pursued the other. "You have some influence with my grandfather there."

"Some," said Mr. Quilp emphatically.

"And are in a few of his mysteries and secrets."

"A few," replied Quilp, with equal dryness.

"Then let me tell him once for all, through you, that I will come into and go out of this place as often as I like, so long as he keeps Nell here; and that if he wants to be quit of me, he must first be quit of her. What have I done to be made a bugbear of, and to be shunned and dreaded as if I brought the plague? He'll tell you that I have no natural affection; and that I care no more for Nell, for her own sake, than I do for him. Let him say so. I care for the whim, then, of coming to and fro and reminding her of my existence. I *will* see her when I please. That's my point. I came here to-day to maintain it, and I'll come here again fifty times with the same object and always with the same success. I said I would stop till I had gained it. I have done so, and now my visit's ended. Come, Dick."

"Stop!" cried Mr. Swiveller, as his companion turned towards the door. "Sir!"

"Sir, I am your humble servant," said Mr. Quilp, to whom the monosyllable was addressed.

"Before I leave the gay and festive scene, and halls of dazzling light, Sir," said Mr. Swiveller, "I will, with your permission, attempt a slight remark. I came here, Sir, this day, under the impression that the old min was friendly."

"Proceed, Sir," said Daniel Quilp; for the orator had made a sudden stop.

"Inspired by this idea and the sentiments it awakened, Sir, and feeling as a mutual friend that badgering, baiting, and bullying, was not the sort of thing calculated to expand the souls and promote the social harmony of the contending parties, I took upon myself to suggest a course which is *the* course to be adopted on the present occasion. Will you allow me to whisper half a syllable, Sir?"

Without waiting for the permission he sought, Mr.

Swiveller stepped up to the dwarf, and leaning on his shoulder and stooping down to get at his ear, said in a voice which was perfectly audible to all present,

" The watch-word to the old min is—fork."

" Is what?" demanded Quilp.

" Is fork, Sir, fork," replied Mr. Swiveller, slapping his pocket. " You are awake, Sir?"

The dwarf nodded. Mr. Swiveller drew back and nodded likewise, then drew a little further back and nodded again, and so on. By these means he in time reached the door, where he gave a great cough to attract the dwarf's attention and gain an opportunity of expressing in dumb show, the closest confidence and most inviolable secrecy. Having performed the serious pantomime that was necessary for the due conveyance of these ideas, he cast himself upon his friend's track, and vanished.

" Humph!" said the dwarf with a sour look and a shrug of his shoulders, " so much for dear relations. Thank God I acknowledge none! Nor need you either," he added, turning to the old man, " if you were not as weak as a reed, and nearly as senseless."

" What would you have me do?" he retorted in a kind of helpless desperation. " It is easy to talk and sneer. What would you have me do?"

"What would I do if I was in your case?" said the dwarf.

"Something violent, no doubt."

"You're right there," returned the little man, highly gratified by the compliment, for such he evidently considered it; and grinning like a devil as he rubbed his dirty hands together. " Ask Mrs. Quilp, pretty Mrs. Quilp, obedient, timid, loving Mrs. Quilp. But that reminds me —I have left her all alone, and she will be anxious and know not a moment's peace till I return. I know she's always in that condition when I'm away, though she doesn't dare to say so, unless I lead her on and tell her she may speak freely and I won't be angry with her. Oh! well-trained Mrs. Quilp!"

The creature appeared quite horrible with his montrous head and little body, as he rubbed his hands slowly round, and round, and round again—with something fantastic even in his manner of performing this slight

action—and, dropping his shaggy brows and cocking his
chin in the air, glanced upward with a stealthy look of
exultation that an imp might have copied and appropriated to himself.

"Here," he said, putting his hand into his breast and
sidling up to the old man as he spoke ; " I brought it myself for fear of accidents, as, being in gold, it was something large and heavy for Nell to carry in her bag. She
need be accustomed to such loads betimes though, neighbor, for she will carry weight when you are dead."

"Heaven send she may! I hope so," said the old man
with something like a groan.

"Hope so!" echoed the dwarf, approaching close to his
ear; "neighbor, I would I knew in what good invest-
ment all these supplies are sunk. But you are a deep
man, and keep your secret close."

"My secret!" said the other with a haggard look.
"Yes, you're right—I—I—keep it close—very close."

He said no more, but taking the money turned away
with a slow uncertain step, and pressed his hand upon his
head like a weary and dejected man. The dwarf watched
him sharply, while he passed into the little sitting-room
and locked it in an iron safe above the chimney-piece; and
after musing for a short space, prepared to take his leave,
observing that unless he made good haste, Mrs. Quilp
would certainly be in fits on his return.

"And so, neighbor," he added, "I'll turn my face
homewards, leaving my love for Nelly and hoping she
may never lose her way again, though her doing so *has*
procured me an honor I didn't expect." With that he
bowed and leered at me, and with a keen glance around
which seemed to comprehend every object within his
range of vision, however small or trivial, went his way.

I had several times essayed to go myself, but the old
man had always opposed it and entreated me to remain.
As he renewed his entreaties on our being left alone, and
adverted with many thanks to the former occasion of our
being together, I willingly yielded to his persuasions, and
sat down, pretending to examine some curious miniatures
and a few old medals which he placed before me. It
needed no great pressing to induce me to stay, for if my
curiosity had been excited on the occasion of my first
visit, it certainly was not diminished now.

Nell joined us before long, and bringing some needle-work to the table, sat by the old man's side. It was pleasant to observe the fresh flowers in the room, the pet bird with a green bough shading his little cage, the breath of freshness and youth which seemed to rustle through the old dull house and hover round the child. It was curious, but not so pleasant, to turn from the beauty and grace of the girl, to the stooping figure, care-worn face, and jaded aspect of the old man. As he grew weaker and more feeble, what would become of this lonely little creature; poor protector as he was, say that he died—what would her fate be, then?

The old man almost answered my thoughts, as he laid his hand on hers, and spoke aloud.

" I'll be of better cheer, Nell," he said ; " there must be good fortune in store for thee—I do not ask it for myself, but thee. Such miseries must fall on thy innocent head without it, that I cannot believe but that, being tempted, it will come at last ! "

She looked cheerfully into his face, but made no answer.

" When I think," said he, " of the many years—many in thy short life—that thou hast lived alone with me ; of thy montonous existence, knowing no companions of thy own age nor any childish pleasures ; of the solitude in which thou hast grown to be what thou art, and in which thou hast lived apart from nearly all thy kind but one old man ; I sometimes fear I have dealt hardly by thee, Nell."

" Grandfather ! " cried the child in unfeigned surprise.

" Not in intention—no no," said he. " I have ever looked forward to the time that should enable thee to mix among the gayest and prettiest, and take thy station with the best. But I still look forward, Nell, I still look forward, and if I should be forced to leave thee, mean-while, how have I fitted thee for struggles with the world? The poor bird yonder is as well qualified to encounter it, and be turned adrift upon its mercies—Hark ! I hear Kit outside. Go to him, Nell, go to him."

She rose, and hurrying away, stopped, turned back, and put her arms about the old man's neck, then left him and hurried away again—but faster this time, to hide her fall-ing tears.

" A word in your ear, Sir," said the old man in a hur-ried whisper. " I have been rendered uneasy by what you said the other night, and can only plead that I have done all for the best—that it is too late to retract, if I could (though I cannot)—and that I hope to triumph yet. All is for her sake. I have borne great poverty myself, and would spare her the sufferings that poverty carries with it. I would spare her the miseries that brought her mother, my own dear child, to an early grave. I would leave her—not with with resources which could be easily spent or squandered away, but with what would place her beyond the reach of want for ever. You mark me, Sir? She shall have no pittance, but a fortune—Hush! I can say no more than that, now or at any other time, and she is here again!"

The eagerness with which all this was poured into my ear, the trembling of the hand with which he clasped my arm, the strained and starting eyes he fixed upon me, the wild vehemence and agitation of his manner, filled me with amazement. All that I had heard and seen, and a great part of what he had said himself, led me to suppose that he was a wealthy man. I could form no comprehension of his character, unless he were one of those miserable wretches who, having made gain the sole end and object of their lives and having succeeded in amassing great riches, are constantly tortured by the dread of poverty, and beset by fears of loss and ruin. Many things he had said which I had been at a loss to understand, were quite reconcileable with the idea thus presented to me, and at length I concluded that beyond all doubt he was one of this unhappy race.

The opinion was not the result of hasty consideration, for which indeed there was no opportunity at that time, as the child came back directly, and soon occupied herself in preparations for giving Kit a writing lesson, of which it seemed he had a couple every week, and one regularly on that evening, to the great mirth and enjoyment both of himself and his instructress. To relate how it was a long time before his modesty could be so far prevailed upon as to admit of his sitting down in the parlor, in the presence of an unknown gentleman—how, when he did sit down, he tucked up his sleeves and squared his elbows and put his face close to the copy-book and squinted horribly at the lines—how, from the very first moment of having the pen in his hand, he began to wallow in blots, and to daub himself with ink up to the very roots of his hair—how, if he did by accident form a letter properly, he immediately smeared it out again with his arm in his preparations to make another—how, at every fresh mistake, there was a fresh burst of merriment from the child and a louder and not less hearty laugh from poor Kit himself—and how there was all the way through, notwithstanding, a gentle wish on her part to teach, and an anxious desire on his to learn—to relate all these particulars would no doubt occupy more space and time than they deserve. It will be sufficient to say that the lesson was given—that evening passed and night came on—that the old man again grew restless and impatient —that he quitted the house secretly at the same hour as before—and that the child was once more left alone within its gloomy walls.

And now, that I have carried this history so far in my own character and introduced these personages to the reader, I shall for the convenience of the narrative detach myself from its further course, and leave those who have prominent and necessary parts in it to speak and act for themselves.

CHAPTER THE FOURTH.

MR. and Mrs. Quilp resided on Tower Hill; and in her bower on Tower Hill Mrs. Quilp was left to pine the absence of the lord, when he quitted her on the business which he has been already seen to transact.

Mr. Quilp could scarcely be said to be of any particular trade or calling, though his pursuits were diversified and his occupations numerous. He collected the rents of whole colonies of filthy streets and alleys by the waterside, advanced money to the seamen and petty officers of mer- chant vessels, had a share in the ventures of divers mates of East Indiamen, smoked his smuggled cigars under the very nose of the Custom House, and made appointments on 'Change with men in glazed hats and round jackets pretty well every day. On the Surrey side of the river was a small rat-infested dreary yard called " Quilp's Wharf," in which were a little wooden counting-house burrowing all away in the dust as if it had fallen from

the clouds and ploughed into the ground; a few fragments
of rusty anchors; several large iron rings; some piles of
rotten wood; and two or three heaps of old sheet copper,
crumpled, cracked, and battered. On Quilp's Wharf,
Daniel Quilp was a ship-breaker, yet to judge from these
appearances he must either have been a ship-breaker on
a very small scale, or have broken his ships up very small
indeed. Neither did the place present any extraordinary
aspect of life or activity, as its only human occupant was
an amphibious boy in a canvas suit, whose sole change
of occupation was from sitting on the head of a pile and
throwing stones into the mud when the tide was out, to
standing with his hands in his pockets gazing listlessly
on the motion and on the bustle of the river at high-water.

The dwarf's lodging on Tower Hill comprised, besides
the needful accommodation for himself and Mrs. Quilp, a
small sleeping-closet for that lady's mother, who resided
with the couple and waged perpetual war with Daniel;
of whom, notwithstanding, she stood in no slight dread.
Indeed, the ugly creature contrived by some means or
other—whether by his ugliness or his ferocity or his
natural cunning is no great matter—to impress with a
wholesome fear of his anger, most of those with whom
he was brought into daily contact and communication.
Over nobody had he such complete ascendancy as Mrs.
Quilp herself—a pretty little, mild-spoken, blue-eyed
woman, who having allied herself in wedlock to the dwarf
in one of those strange infatuations of which examples
are by no means scarce, performed a sound practical penance for her folly, every day of her life.

It has been said that Mrs. Quilp was pining in her
bower. In her bower she was, but not alone, for besides
the old lady her mother of whom mention has recently
been made, there were present some half-dozen ladies of
the neighborhood who had happened by a strange accident
(and also by a little understanding among themselves) to
drop in one after another, just about tea-time. This being
a season favorable to conversation, and the room being a
cool, shady, lazy kind of place, with some plants at the
open window shutting out the dust, and interposing
pleasantly enough between the tea table within and the
old Tower without, it is no wonder that the ladies felt an
inclination to talk and linger, especially when there are

taken into account the additional inducements of fresh butter, new bread, shrimps, and water-cresses.

Now, the ladies being together under these circumstances, it was extremely natural that the discourse should turn upon the propensity of mankind to tyrannize over the weaker sex, and the duty that devolved upon the weaker sex to resist that tyranny and assert their rights and dignity. It was natural for four reasons : firstly, because Mrs. Quilp being a young woman and notoriously under the dominion of her husband ought to be excited to rebel ; secondly, because Mrs. Quilp's parent was known to be laudably shrewish in her disposition and inclined to resist male authority ; thirdly, because each visitor wished to show for herself how superior she was in this respect to the generality of her sex; and fourthly, because the company being accustomed to scandalize each other in pairs, were deprived of their usual subject of conversation now that they were all assembled in close friendship, and had consequently no better employment than to attack the common enemy.

Moved by these considerations, a stout lady opened the proceedings by inquiring, with an air of great concern and sympathy, how Mr. Quilp was ; whereunto Mr. Quilp's wife's mother replied sharply, "Oh ! he was well enough—nothing much was ever the matter with him—and ill weeds were sure to thrive." All the ladies then sighed in concert, shook their heads gravely, and looked at Mrs. Quilp as at a martyr.

"Ah ! " said the spokeswoman, " I wish you'd give her a little of your advice, Mrs .Jiniwin "—Mrs. Quilp had been a Miss Jiniwin it should be observed—"nobody knows better than you, ma'am, what us women owe to ourselves."

"Owe indeed, ma'am ! " replied Mrs. Jiniwin. " When my poor husband, her dear father, was alive, if he had ever ventur'd a cross word to *me*, I'd have——" the good old lady did not finish the sentence, but she twisted off the head of a shrimp with a vindictiveness which seemed to imply that the action was in some degree a substitute for words. In this light it was clearly understood by the other party, who immediately replied with great approbation, "You quite enter into my feelings, ma'am, and it's jist what I'd do myself."

"But you have no call to do it," said Mrs. Jiniwin. "Luckily for you, you have no more occasion to do it than I had."

"No woman need have, if she was true to herself," rejoined the stout lady.

"Do you hear that, Betsy?" said Mrs. Jiniwin, in a warning voice. "How often have I said the very same words to you, and almost gone down on my knees when I spoke 'em!"

Poor Mrs. Quilp, who had looked in a state of helplessness from one face of condolence to another, colored, smiled, and shook her head doubtfully. This was the signal for a general clamor, which beginning in a low murmur gradually swelled into a great noise in which everybody spoke at once, and all said that she being a young woman had no right to set up her opinions against the experiences of those who knew so much better; that it was very wrong of her not to take the advice of people who had nothing at heart but her good; that it was next door to being downright ungrateful to conduct herself in that manner; that if she had no respect for herself she ought to have some for other women, all of whom she compromised by her meekness; and that if she had no respect for other women, the time would come when other women would have no respect for her; and she would be very sorry for that, they could tell her. Having dealt out these admonitions, the ladies fell to a more powerful assault than they had yet made upon the mixed tea, new bread, fresh butter, shrimps, and water-cresses, and said that their vexation was so great to see her going on like that, that they could hardly bring themselves to eat a single morsel.

"It's all very fine to talk," said Mrs. Quilp with much simplicity, "but I know that if I was to die to-morrow, Quilp could marry anybody he pleased—now that he could, I know!"

There was quite a scream of indignation at this idea. Marry whom he pleased! They would like to see him dare to think of marrying any of them; they would like to see the faintest approach to such a thing. One lady (a widow) was quite certain she should stab him if he hinted at it.

"Very well," said Mrs. Quilp, nodding her head, "as

I said just now, it's very easy to talk, but I say again that I know—that I'm sure—Quilp has such a way with him when he likes, that the best-looking woman here couldn't refuse him if I was dead, and she was free, and he chose to make love to her. Come!'"

Everybody bridled up at this remark, as much as to say "I know you mean me. Let him try—that's all." And yet for some hidden reason they were all angry with the widow, and each lady whispered in her neighbor's ear that it was very plain the said widow thought herself the person referred to, and what a puss she was!

"Mother knows," said Mrs. Quilp, "that what I say is quite correct, for she often said so before we were married. Didn't you say so, mother?"

This inquiry involved the respected lady in rather a delicate position, for she certainly had been an active party in making her daughter Mrs. Quilp, and, besides, it was not supporting the family credit to encourage the idea that she had married a man whom nobody else would have. On the other hand, to exaggerate the captivating qualities of her son-in-law would be to weaken the cause of revolt, in which all her energies were deeply engaged. Beset by these opposing considerations, Mrs. Jiniwin admitted the powers of insinuation, but denied the right to govern, and with a timely compliment to the stout lady brought back the discussion to the point from which it had strayed.

"Oh! It's a sensible and proper thing indeed, what Mrs. George has said!" exclaimed the old lady. "If women are only true to themselves!—But Betsy isn't, and more's the shame and pity."

"Before I'd let a man order me about as Quilp orders her," said Mrs. George; "before I'd consent to stand in awe of a man as she does of him, I'd—I'd kill myself, and write a letter first to say he did it!"

This remark being loudly commended and approved of, another lady (from the Minories) put in her word:

"Mr. Quilp may be a very nice man," said this lady, "and I suppose there's no doubt he is, because Mrs. Quilp says he is, and Mrs. Jiniwin says he is, and they ought to know, or nobody does. But still he is not quite a—what one calls a handsome man, nor quite a young man neither, which might be a little excuse for him if anything could be; whereas his wife is young, and is good-looking, and is a woman—which is the great thing after all."

"This last clause being delivered with extraordinary pathos, elicited a corresponding murmur from the hearers, stimulated by which the lady went on to remark that if such a husband was cross and unreasonable with such a wife, then—

"If he is!" interposed the mother, putting down her tea-cup and brushing the crumbs out of her lap, preparatory to making a solemn declaration. "If he is! He is the greatest tyrant that ever lived, she daren't call her soul her own, he makes her tremble with a word and even with a look, he frightens her to death, and she hasn't the spirit to give him a word back, no, not a single word."

Notwithstanding that the fact had been notorious beforehand to all the tea-drinkers, and had been discussed and expatiated on at every tea-drinking in the neighborhood for the last twelve months, this official communication was no sooner made than they all began to talk at once and to vie with each other in vehemence and volubility. Mrs. George remarked that people would talk, that people had often said this to her before, that Mrs. Simmons then and there present had told her so twenty times, that she had always said, "No, Henrietta Simmons, unless I see it with my own eyes and hear it with my own ears, I never will believe it." Mrs. Simmons corroborated this testimony and added strong evidence of her own. The lady from the Minories recounted a successful course of treatment under which she had placed her own husband, who, from manifesting one month after marriage unequivocal symptoms of the tiger, had by this means become subdued into a perfect lamb. Another lady recounted her own personal struggle and final triumph, in the course whereof she had found it necessary to call in her mother and two aunts, and to weep incessantly night and day for six weeks. A third, who in the general confusion could secure no other listener, fastened herself upon a young woman still unmarried who happened to be amongst them, and conjured her as she valued her own peace of mind and happiness to profit by this solemn occasion, to take example from the weakness of Mrs.

Quilp, and from that time forth to direct her whole
thoughts to taming and subduing the rebellious spirit of
man. The noise was at its height, and half the company
had elevated their voices into a perfect shriek in order to
drown the voices of the other half, when Mrs. Jiniwin
was seen to change colour and shake her fore-finger
stealthily, as if exhorting them to silence. Then, and
not until then, Daniel Quilp himself, the cause and oc
casion of all this clamor, was observed to be in the room,
looking on and listening with profound attention.

"Go on, ladies, go on," said Daniel. "Mrs. Quilp,
pray ask the ladies to stop to supper, and have a couple
of lobsters and something light and palatable."

"I—I—didn't ask them to tea, Quilp," stammered his
wife. "It's quite an accident."

"So much the better, Mrs. Quilp; these accidental
parties are always the pleasantest," said the dwarf, rubbing his hands so hard that he seemed to be engaged in
manufacturing, of the dirt with which they were encrusted,
little charges for popguns. "What! Not going, ladies,
you are not going, surely!"

His fair enemies tossed their heads slightly as they sought their respective bonnets and shawls, but left all verbal contention to Mrs. Jiniwin, who finding herself in the position of champion, made a faint struggle to sustain the character.

"And why *not* stop to supper, Quilp," said the old lady, "if my daughter had a mind?"

"To be sure," rejoined Daniel. "Why not?"

"There's nothing dishonest or wrong in a supper, I hope?" said Mrs. Jiniwin.

"Surely not," returned the dwarf. "Why should there be? Nor anything unwholesome either, unless there's lobster-salad or prawns, which I'm told are not good for digestion."

"And you wouldn't like *your* wife to be attacked with that, or anything else that would make her uneasy, would you?" said Mrs. Jiniwin.

"Not for a score of worlds," replied the dwarf with a grin. "Not even to have a score of mothers-in-law at the same time—and what a blessing that would be!"

"My daughter's your wife, Mr. Quilp, certainly," said the old lady with a giggle, meant for satirical and to imply that he needed to be reminded of the fact; your wedded wife."

"So she is, certainly. So she is," observed the dwarf.

"And she has a right to do as she likes, I hope, Quilp," said the old lady trembling, partly with anger and partly with a secret fear of her impish son-in-law.

"Hope she has!" he replied. "Oh! Don't you know she has? Don't you know she has, Mrs. Jiniwin?"

"I know she ought to have, Quilp, and would have, if she was of my way of thinking."

"Why ain't you of your mother's way of thinking, my dear?" said the dwarf, turning round and addressing his wife, "why don't you always imitate your mother, my dear? She's the ornament of her sex—your father said so every day of his life. I am sure he did."

"Her father was a blessed creetur, Quilp, and worth twenty thousand of some people," said Mrs. Jiniwin; "twenty hundred million thousand."

"I should like to have known him," remarked the dwarf. "I dare say he was a blessed creature then; but

I'm sure he is now. It was a happy release. I believe he had suffered a long time?"

The old lady gave a gasp, but nothing came of it; Quilp resumed, with the same malice in his eye and the same sarcastic politeness on his tongue.

"You look ill, Mrs. Jiniwin; I know you have been exciting yourself too much—talking perhaps, for it is your weakness. Go to bed. Do go to bed."

"I shall go when I please, Quilp, and not before."

"But please to go now. Do please to go now," said the dwarf.

The old woman looked angrily at him, but retreated as he advanced, and falling back before him, suffered him to shut the door upon her and bolt her out among the guests, who were by this time crowding down stairs. Being left alone with his wife, who sat trembling in a corner, with her eyes fixed upon the ground, the little man planted himself before her, and folding his arms looked steadily at her for a long time without speaking.

"Mrs. Quilp," he said at last.

"Yes, Quilp," she replied meekly.

Instead of pursuing the theme he had in his mind, Quilp folded his arms again, and looked at her more sternly than before, while she averted her eyes, and kept them on the ground.

"Mrs. Quilp."

"Yes, Quilp."

"If ever you listen to these beldames again, I'll bite you."

With this laconic threat, which he accompanied with a snarl that gave him the appearance of being particularly in earnest, Mr. Quilp bade her clear the teaboard away, and bring the rum. The spirit being set before him in a huge case-bottle, which had originally come out of some ship's locker, he ordered cold water and the box of cigars; and these being supplied, he settled himself in an arm-chair with his large head and face squeezed up against the back, and his little legs planted on the table.

"Now, Mrs. Quilp," he said; "I feel in a smoking humor, and shall probably blaze away all night. But sit where you are, if you please, in case I want you."

His wife returned no other reply than the customary "Yes, Quilp," and the small lord of the creation took his

first cigar and mixed his first glass of grog. The sun
went down and the stars peeped out, the Tower turned
from its own proper colors to gray and from gray to
black, the room became perfectly dark and the end of the
cigar a deep fiery red, but still Mr. Quilp went on smoking and drinking in the same position, and staring listlessly out of window with the dog-like smile always on
his face, save when Mrs. Quilp made some involuntary

movement of restlessness or fatigue; and then it expanded
into a grin of delight.

CHAPTER THE FIFTH.

WHETHER Mr. Quilp took any sleep by snatches of a
few winks at a time, or whether he sat with his eyes
wide open all night long, certain it is that he kept his
cigar alight, and kindled every fresh one from the ashes
of that which was nearly consumed, without requiring
the assistance of a candle. Nor did the striking of the
clocks, hour after hour, appear to inspire him with any
sense of drowsiness or any natural desire to go to rest,
but rather to increase his wakefulness, which he showed,
at every such indication of the progress of the night, by

a suppressed cackling in his throat, and a motion of his shoulders, like one who laughs heartily but at the same time slily and by stealth.

At length the day broke, and poor Mrs. Quilp, shivering with the cold of early morning and harassed by fatigue and want of sleep, was discovered sitting patiently on her chair, raising her eyes at intervals in mute appeal to the compassion and clemency of her lord, and gently reminding him by an occasional cough that she was still unpardoned and that her penance had been of long duration. But her dwarfish spouse still smoked his cigar and drank his rum without heeding her; and it was not until the sun had some time risen, and the activity and noise of city day were rife in the street, that he deigned to recognize her presence by any word or sign. He might not have done so even then, but for certain impatient tappings at the door which seemed to denote that some pretty hard knuckles were actively engaged upon the other side.

" Why dear me ! " he said looking round with a malicious grin, " it's day ! Open the door, sweet Mrs. Quilp ! "

His obedient wife withdrew the bolt, and her lady mother entered.

Now, Mrs. Jiniwin bounced into the room with great impetuosity ; for, supposing her son-in-law to be still a-bed, she had come to relieve her feelings by pronouncing a strong opinion upon his general conduct and character. Seeing that he was up and dressed, and that the room appeared to have been occupied ever since she quitted it on the previous evening, she stopped short, in some embarrassment.

Nothing escaped the hawk's eye of the ugly little man, who, perfectly understanding what passed in the old lady's mind, turned uglier still in the fulness of his satisfaction, and bade her good morning, with a leer of triumph.

" Why, Betsy," said the old woman, " you haven't been a—you don't mean to say you've been a—"

" Sitting up all night ? " said Quilp, supplying the conclusion of the sentence. " Yes she has ! "

" All night ! " cried Mrs. Jiniwin.

" Ay, all night. Is the dear old lady deaf ? " said Quilp, with a smile of which a frown was part. " Who says man and wife are bad company? Ha ha! The time has flown."

"You're a brute!" exclaimed Mrs. Jiniwin.

"Come come," said Quilp, wilfully misunderstanding her, of course, "you mustn't call her names. She's married now, you know. And though she *did* beguile the time and keep me from my bed, you must not be so tenderly careful of me as to be out of humor with her. Bless you for a dear old lady. Here's your health!"

"I am *much* obliged to you," returned the old woman, testifying by a certain restlessness in her hands a vehement desire to shake her matronly fist at her son-in-law. "Oh! I'm very much obliged to you!"

"Grateful soul!" cried the dwarf. "Mrs. Quilp."

"Yes, Quilp," said the timid sufferer.

"Help your mother to get breakfast, Mrs. Quilp. I am going to the wharf this morning—the earlier, the better, so be quick."

Mrs. Jiniwin made a faint demonstration of rebellion by sitting down in a chair near the door and folding her arms as if in a resolute determination to do nothing. But a few whispered words from her daughter, and a kind inquiry from her son-in-law whether she felt faint, with a hint that there was abundance of cold water in the next apartment, routed these symptoms effectually, and she applied herself to the prescribed preparations with sullen diligence.

While they were in progress, Mr. Quilp withdrew to the adjoining room, and, turning back his coat-collar, proceeded to smear his countenance with a damp towel of very unwholesome appearance, which made his complexion rather more cloudy than it was before. But, while he was thus engaged, his caution and inquisitiveness did not forsake him, for with a face as sharp and cunning as ever, he often stopped, even in this short process, and stood listening for any conversation in the next room, of which he might be the theme.

"Ah!" he said after a short effort of attention, "it was not the towel over my ears, I thought it wasn't. I'm a little hunchy villain and a monster, am I, Mrs. Jiniwin? Oh!"

The pleasure of this discovery called up the old dog-like smile in full force. When he had quite done with it, he shook himself in a very doglike manner, and rejoined the ladies.

Mr. Quilp now walked up to the front of a looking-glass, and was standing there putting on his neckerchief, when Mrs Jiniwin, happening to be behind him, could not resist the inclination she felt to shake her fist at her tyrant son-in-law. It was the gesture of an instant, but as she did so and accompanied the action with a mena-cing look, she met his eye in the glass, catching her in the very act. The same glance at the mirror conveyed to her the reflection of a horribly grotesque and distorted face with the tongue lolling out; and the next instant the dwarf, turning about with a perfectly bland and placid look, inquired in a tone of great affection.

" How are you now, my dear old darling?"

Slight and ridiculous as the incident was, it made him appear such a little fiend, and withal such a keen and knowing one, that the old woman felt too much afraid of him to utter a single word, and suffered herself to be led with extraordinary politeness to the breakfast-table. Here he by no means diminished the impression he had just produced, for he ate hard eggs, shell and all, de-voured gigantic prawns with the heads and tails on, chewed tobacco and water-cresses at the same time and with extraordinary greediness, drank boiling tea without winking, bit his fork and spoon till they bent again, and in short performed so many horrifying and uncommon acts that the women were nearly frightened out of their wits, and began to doubt if he were really a human creature. At last, having gone through these proceedings and many others which were equally a part of his system, Mr. Quilp left them, reduced to a very obedient and humbled state, and betook himself to the river-side, where he took boat for the wharf on which he had bestowed his name.

It was flood tide when Daniel Quilp sat himself down in the wherry to cross to the opposite shore. A fleet of barges were coming lazily on, some sideways, some head first, some stern first; all in a wrong-headed, dogged, obstinate way, bumping up against the larger craft, run-ning under the bows of steamboats, getting into every kind of nook and corner where they had no business, and being crunched on all sides like so many walnut-shells;

while each with its pair of long sweeps struggling and splashing in the water looked like some lumbering fish in pain. In some of the vessels at anchor all hands were busily engaged in coiling ropes, spreading out sails to dry, taking in or discharging their cargoes; in others no life was visible but two or three tarry boys, and perhaps a barking dog running to and fro upon the deck or scrambling up to look over the side and bark the louder for the view. Coming slowly on through the forests of masts was a great steam-ship, beating the water in short impatient strokes with her heavy paddles as though she

wanted room to breathe, and advancing in her huge bulk like a sea monster among the minnows of the Thames. On either hand were long black tiers of colliers; between them vessels slowly working out of harbor with sails glistening in the sun, and creaking noise on board, re-echoed from a hundred quarters. The water and all upon it was in active motion, dancing and buoyant and bubbling up; while the old gray Tower and piles of building on the shore, with many a church-spire shooting up between, looked coldly on, and seemed to disdain their chafing, restless neighbor.

Daniel Quilp, who was not much affected by a bright morning save in so far as it spared him the trouble of carrying an umbrella, caused himself to be put ashore hard by the wharf, and proceeded thither through a narrow lane which, partaking of the amphibious character of its frequenters, had as much water as mud in its composition, and a very liberal supply of both. Arrived at his destination, the first object that presented itself to his view was a pair of very imperfectly shod feet elevated in the air with the soles upwards, which remarkable appearance was referable to the boy, who being of an eccentric spirit and having a natural taste for tumbling, was now standing on his head and contemplating the aspect of the river under these uncommon circumstances. He was speedily brought on his heels by the sound of his master's voice, and as soon as his head was in its right position, Mr. Quilp, to speak expressively in the absence of a better verb, "punched it" for him.

"Come, you let me alone," said the boy, parrying Quilp's hand with both his elbows alternately. "You'll get something you won't like if you don't, and so I tell you."

"You dog," snarled Quilp, "I'll beat you with an iron rod, I'll scratch you with a rusty nail, I'll pinch your eyes, if you talk to me—I will."

With these threats he clenched his hand again, and dexterously diving in between the elbows and catching the boy's head as it dodged from side to side, gave it three or four good hard knocks. Having now carried his point and insisted on it, he left off.

"You won't do it again," said the boy, nodding his head and drawing back, with the elbows ready in case of the worst; "now—"

"Stand still, you dog," said Quilp. "I won't do it again, because I've done it as often as I want. Here. Take the key."

"Why don't you hit one of your size?" said the boy approaching very slowly.

"Where is there one of my size, you dog?" returned Quilp. "Take the key, or I'll brain you with it"—indeed he gave him a smart tap with the handle as he spoke. "Now, open the counting-house."

The boy sulkily complied, muttering at first, but desisting when he looked round and saw that Quilp was following him with a steady look. And here it may be remarked, that between this boy and the dwarf there existed a strange kind of mutual liking. How born or bred, or how nourished upon blows and threats on one side, and retorts and defiances on the other, is not to the purpose. Quilp would certainly suffer nobody to contradict him but the boy, and the boy would assuredly not have submitted to be so knocked about by anybody but Quilp, when he had the power to run away at any time he chose.

"Now," said Quilp, passing into the wooden counting-house, "you mind the wharf. Stand upon your head again, and I'll cut one of your feet off."

The boy made no answer, but directly Quilp had shut himself in, stood on his head before the door, then walked on his hands to the back and stood on his head there, and then to the opposite side and repeated the performance. There were indeed four sides to the counting-house, but he avoided that one where the window was, deeming it probable that Quilp would be looking out of it. This was prudent, for in point of fact the dwarf, knowing his disposition, was lying in wait at a little distance from the sash armed with a large piece of wood, which, being rough and jagged and studded in many parts with broken nails, might possibly have hurt him.

It was a dirty little box, this counting-house, with nothing in it but an old rickety desk and two stools, a hat-peg, an ancient almanack, an inkstand with no ink and the stump of one pen, and an eight-day clock which hadn't gone for eighteen years at least, and of which the minute-hand had been twisted off for a tooth-pick. Daniel Quilp pulled his hat over his brows, climbed on to the desk (which had a flat top), and stretching his short length upon it went to sleep with the ease of an old practitioner; intending, no doubt, to compensate himself for the deprivation of last night's rest, by a long and sound nap.

Sound it might have been, but long it was not, for he had not been asleep a quarter of an hour when the boy opened the door and thrust in his head, which was like a bundle of badly-picked oakum. Quilp was a light sleeper and started up directly.

"Here's somebody for you," said the boy.

"Who?"

"I don't know."

"Ask!" said Quilp, seizing the trifle of wood before mentioned and throwing it at him with such dexterity that it was well the boy disappeared before it reached the spot on which he had stood. "Ask, you dog."

Not caring to venture within range of such missiles again, the boy discreetly sent in his stead the first cause of the interruption, who now presented herself at the door.

"What, Nelly!" cried Quilp.

"Yes,"—said the child, hesitating whether to enter or retreat, for the dwarf just roused, with his dishevelled hair hanging all about him and a yellow handkerchief over his head, was something fearful to behold; "it's only me, Sir."

"Come in," said Quilp, without getting off the desk. "Come in. Stay. Just look out into the yard, and see whether there's a boy standing on his head."

"No, Sir," replied Nell. "He's on his feet."

"You're sure he is?" said Quilp. "Well. Now, come in and shut the door. What's your message, Nelly?"

The child handed him a letter; Mr. Quilp, without changing his position further than to turn over a little more on his side and rest his chin on his hand, proceeded to make himself acquainted with its contents.

CHAPTER THE SIXTH.

LITTLE NELL stood timidly by, with her eyes raised to the countenance of Mr. Quilp as he read the letter, plainly showing by her looks that while she entertained some fear and distrust of the little man, she was much inclined to laugh at his uncouth appearance and grotesque attitude. And yet there was visible on the part of the child a painful anxiety for his reply, and a consciousness of his power to render it disagreeable or distressing, which was strongly at variance with this impulse and restrained it more effectually than she could possibly have done by any efforts of her own.

That Mr. Quilp was himself perplexed, and that in no
small degree, by the contents of the letter, was sufficiently
obvious.   Before he had got through the first two or
three lines he began to opened his eyes very wide and to
frown most horribly, the next two or three caused him
to scratch his head in an uncommonly vicious manner,
and when he came to the conclusion he gave a long dismal whistle indicative of surprise and dismay.   After
folding and laying it down beside him, he bit the nails of
all his ten fingers with extreme voracity; and taking it
up sharply, read it again.   The second perusal was to all

appearance as unsatisfactory as the first, and plunged
him into a profound reverie from which he awakened to
another assault upon his nails and a long stare at the child,
who with her eyes turned towards the ground awaited
his further pleasure.

"Halloa here!" he said at length, in a voice, and with
a suddenness, which made the child start as though a gun
had been fired off at her ear.   "Nelly!"

"Yes, Sir."

" Do you know what's inside this letter, Nell ? "

" No, Sir ! "

" Are you sure, quite sure, quite certain, upon your soul ? "

" Quite sure, Sir."

" Do you wish you may die if you do know, hey ? " said the dwarf.

" Indeed I don't know," returned the child.

" Well ! " muttered Quilp as he marked her earnest look. " I believe you. Humph ! Gone already ? Gone in four-and-twenty hours ! What the devil has he done with it, that's the mystery ! "

This reflection set him scratching his head and biting his nails once more. While he was thus employed his features gradually relaxed into what was with him a cheerful smile, but which in any other man would have been a ghastly grin of pain, and when the child looked up again she found that he was regarding her with extraordinary favor and complacency.

" You look very pretty to-day, Nelly, charmingly pretty. Are you tired, Nelly ? "

" No, Sir. I'm in a hurry to get back, for he will be anxious while I am away."

" There's no hurry, little Nell, no hurry at all," said Quilp. " How should you like to be my number two, Nelly ? "

" To be what, Sir ? "

" My number two, Nelly, my second, my Mrs. Quilp," said the dwarf.

The child looked frightened, but seemed not to understand him, which Mr. Quilp observing, hastened to explain his meaning more distinctly.

" To be Mrs. Quilp the second, when Mrs. Quilp the first is dead, sweet Nell," said Quilp, wrinkling up his eyes and luring her towards him with his bent forefinger, " to be my wife, my little cherry-cheeked, red-lipped wife. Say that Mrs. Quilp lives five years, or only four, you'll be just the proper age for me. Ha ha ! Be a good girl, Nelly, a very good girl, and see if one of these days you don't come to be Mrs. Quilp of Tower Hill."

So far from being sustained and stimulated by this delightful prospect, the child shrank from him in great agitation, and trembled violently. Mr. Quilp, either because frightening anybody afforded him a constitutional delight, or because it was pleasant to contemplate the death of Mrs. Quilp number one, and the elevation of Mrs. Quilp number two to her post and title, or because he was determined for purposes of his own to be agreeable and good-humored at that particular time, only laughed and feigned to take no heed of her alarm.

"You shall come with me to Tower Hill, and see Mrs. Quilp that is, directly," said the dwarf. "She's very fond of you, Nell, though not so fond as I am. You shall come home with me."

"I must go back indeed," said the child. "He told me to return directly I had the answer."

"But you haven't it, Nelly," retorted the dwarf, "and won't have it, and can't have it, until I have been home, so you see that to do your errand, you must go with me. Reach me yonder hat, my dear, and we'll go directly." With that, Mr. Quilp suffered himself to roll gradually off the desk until his short legs touched the ground, when he got upon them and led the way from the counting-house to the wharf outside, when the first objects that presented themselves were the boy who had stood on his head and another young gentleman of about his own stature, rolling in the mud together, locked in a tight embrace, and cuffing each other with mutual heartiness.

"It's Kit!" cried Nelly, clasping her hands, "poor Kit who came with me! oh pray stop them, Mr. Quilp!"

"I'll stop 'em," cried Quilp, diving into the little counting-house and returning with a thick stick, "I'll stop 'em. Now, my boys, fight away. I'll fight you both. I'll take both of you, both together, both together!"

With which defiances the dwarf flourished his cudgel, and dancing round the combatants and treading upon them and skipping over them, in a kind of frenzy, laid about him, now on one and now on the other, in a most desperate manner, always aiming at their heads and dealing such blows as none but the veriest little savage would have inflicted. This being warmer work than they had calculated upon, speedily cooled the courage of the belligerents, who scrambled to their feet and called for quarter.

"I'll beat you to a pulp, you dogs," said Quilp, vainly endeavoring to get near either of them for a parting blow. "I'll bruise you till you're copper-colored, I'll break your faces till you haven't a profile between you, I will."

"Come, you drop that stick or it'll be worse for you," said his boy, dodging round him and watching an opportunity to rush in; "you drop that stick."

"Come a little nearer, and I'll drop it on your skull, you dog," said Quilp with gleaming eyes; "a little nearer —nearer yet."

But the boy declined the invitation until his master was apparently a little off his guard, when he darted in and seizing the weapon tried to wrest it from his grasp. Quilp, who was as strong as a lion, easily kept his hold until the boy was tugging at it with his utmost power, when he suddenly let it go and sent him reeling backwards, so that he fell violently upon his head. The success of his manœuvre tickled Mr. Quilp beyond description, and he laughed and stamped upon the ground as at a most irresistible jest.

"Never mind," said the boy, nodding his head and rubbing it at the same time; "you see if ever I offer to strike anybody again because they say you're a uglier dwarf than can be seen anywheres for a penny, that's all."

"Do you mean to say, I'm not, you dog?" returned Quilp.

"No!" retorted the boy.

"Then, what do you fight on my wharf for, you villain? ' said Quilp.

"Because he said so," replied the boy, pointing to Kit, "not because you an't."

"Then why did he say," bawled Kit, "that Miss Nelly was ugly, and that she and my master was obliged to do whatever his master liked? Why did he say that?"

"He said what he did because's he's a fool, and you said what you did because you're very wise and clever— almost too clever to live, unless you're very careful of yourself, Kit," said Quilp, with great suavity in his manner, but still more of quiet malice about his eyes and mouth. "Here's sixpence for you, Kit. Always speak the truth. At all times, Kit, speak the truth. Lock the counting-house, you dog, and bring me the key."

The other boy, to whom this order was addressed, did as he was told, and was rewarded for his partizanship in

behalf of his master, by a dexterous rap on the nose with
the key, which brought the water into his eyes. Then
Mr. Quilp departed with the child and Kit in a boat, and
the boy revenged himself by dancing on his head at intervals on the extreme verge of the wharf, during the
whole time they crossed the river.

There was only Mrs. Quilp at home, and she, little expecting the return of her lord, was just composing herself
for a refreshing slumber when the sound of his footsteps
roused her. She had barely time to seem to be occupied
in some needle-work, when he entered, accompanied by
the child; having left Kit downstairs.

"Here's Nelly Trent, dear Mrs. Quilp," said her husband. "A glass of wine, my dear, and a biscuit, for she
has had a long walk. She'll sit with you, my soul, while
I write a letter."

Mrs. Quilp looked tremblingly in her spouse's face to
know what this unusual courtesy might portend, and obedient to the summons she saw in his gesture, followed
him into the next room.

"Mind what I say to you," whispered Quilp. "See if
you can get out of her anything about her grandfather,
or what they do, or how they live, or what he tells her.
I've my reasons for knowing, if I can. You women talk
more freely to one another than you do to us, and you
have a soft, mild way with you that'll win upon her. Do
you hear?"

"Yes, Quilp."

"Go, then. What's the matter now?"

"Dear Quilp," faltered his wife, "I love the child—if
you *could* do without making me deceive her——"

The dwarf muttering a terrible oath looked round as if
for some weapon with which to inflict condign punishment upon his disobedient wife. The submissive little
woman hurriedly entreated him not to be angry, and
promised to do as he bade her.

"Do you hear me," whispered Quilp, nipping and pinching her arm; "worm yourself into her secrets; I know
you can. I'm listening, recollect. If you're not sharp
enough I'll creak the door, and woe betide you if I have
to creak it much. Go!"

Mrs. Quilp departed according to order, and her amiable husband, ensconcing himself behind the partly

opened door, and applying his ear close to it, began to listen with a face of great craftiness and attention.

Poor Mrs. Quilp was thinking, however, in what manner to begin or what kind of inquiries she could make; and it was not until the door, creaking in a very urgent manner, warned her to proceed without further consideration, that the sound of her voice was heard.

"How very often you have come backwards and forwards lately to Mr. Quilp, my dear."

"I have said so to grandfather, a hundred times," returned Nell innocently.

"And what has he said to that?"

"Only sighed, and dropped his head, and seemed so sad and wretched that if you could have seen him I am sure you must have cried; you could not have helped it more than I, I know. How that door creaks!"

"It often does," returned Mrs. Quilp, with an uneasy glance towards it. "But your grandfather—he used not to be so wretched?"

"Oh no!" said the child eagerly, "so different! we were once so happy and he so cheerful and contented! You cannot think what a sad change has fallen on us since."

"I am very, very sorry, to hear you speak like this, my dear!" said Mrs. Quilp. And she spoke the truth.

"Thank you," returned the child, kissing her cheek, "you are always kind to me, and it is a pleasure to talk to you. I can speak to no one else about him, but poor Kit. I am very happy still, I ought to feel happier perhaps than I do, but you cannot think how it grieves me sometimes to see him alter so."

"He'll alter again, Nelly," said Mrs. Quilp, "and be what he was before."

"Oh if God would only let that come about!" said the child with streaming eyes; "but it is a long time now, since he first began to—I thought I saw that door moving!"

"It's the wind," said Mrs. Quilp faintly. "Began to—?"

"To be so thoughtful and dejected, and to forget our old way of spending the time in the long evenings," said the child. "I used to read to him by the fireside, and he sat listening, and when I stopped and we began to talk,

he told me about my mother, and how she once looked
and spoke just like me when she was a little child.   Then
he used to take me on his knee, and try to make me
understand that she was not lying in her grave, but had
flown to a beautiful country beyond the sky, where nothing died or ever grew old—we were very happy once!"

"Nelly, Nelly!"—said the poor woman, "I can't bear
to see one as young as you, so sorrowful. Pray don't
cry."

"I do so very seldom," said Nell, "but I have kept
this to myself a long time, and I am not quite well, I
think, for the tears come into my eyes and I cannot keep
them back. I don't mind telling you my grief, for I know
you will not tell it to any one again."

Mrs. Quilp turned away her head and made no answer.

"Then," said the child, "we often walked in the fields
and among the green trees, and when we came home at
night, we liked it better for being tired, and said what a
happy place it was.   And if it was dark and rather dull,
we used to say, what did it matter to us, for it only made
us remember our last walk with greater pleasure, and
look forward to our next one. But now we never have
these walks, and though it is the same house it is darker
and much more gloomy than it used to be, indeed!"

She paused here, but though the door creaked more
than once, Mrs. Quilp said nothing.

"Mind you don't suppose," said the child earnestly,
"that grandfather is less kind to me than he was. I
think he loves me better every day, and is kinder and
more affectionate than he was the day before. You do
not know how fond he is of me!"

"I am sure he loves you dearly," said Mrs. Quilp.

"Indeed, indeed he does!" cried Nell, "as dearly as I
love him. But I have not told you the greatest change
of all, and this you must never breathe again to any one.
He has no sleep or rest, but that which he takes by day
in his easy chair; for every night and nearly all night
long he is away from home.

"Nelly!"

"Hush!" said the child, laying her finger on her lip
and looking round.   "When he comes home in the morning, which is generally just before day, I let him in.
Last night he was very late, and it was quite light. I

saw that his face was deadly pale, that his eyes were bloodshot, and that his legs trembled as he walked. When I had gone to bed again, I heard him groan. I got up and ran back to him, and heard him say, before he knew that I was there, that he could not bear his life much longer, and if it was not for the child, would wish to die. What shall I do! Oh! what shall I do!"

The fountains of her heart were opened; the child, overpowered by the weight of her sorrows and anxieties, by the first confidence she had ever shown, and the sympathy with which her little tale had been received. hid her face in the arms of her helpless friend, and burst into a passion of tears.

In a few moments Mr. Quilp returned, and expressed the utmost surprise to find her in this condition, which he did very naturally and with admirable effect, for that kind of acting had been rendered familiar to him by long practice, and he was quite at home in it.

"She's tired you see, Mrs. Quilp," said the dwarf, squinting in a hideous manner to imply that his wife was to follow his lead. "It's a long way from her home to the wharf, and then she was alarmed to see a couple of young scoundrels fighting, and was timorous on the water besides. All this together has been too much for her. Poor Nell!"

Mr. Quilp unintentionally adopted the very best means he could have devised for the recovery of his young visitor, by patting her on the head. Such an application from any other hand might not have produced a remarkable effect, but the child shrank so quickly from his touch and felt such an instinctive desire to get out of his reach, that she rose directly and declared herself ready to return.

"But you'd better wait, and dine with Mrs. Qulip and me," said the dwarf.

"I have been away too long, Sir, already," returned Nell, drying her eyes.

"Well," said Mr. Quilp, "if you will go, you will, Nelly. Here's the note. It's only to say that I shall see him to-morrow or maybe next day, and that I couldn't do that little business for him this morning. Good-bye, Nelly. Here, you, Sir; take care of her, d'ye hear?"

Kit, who appeared at the summons, deigned to make no reply to so needless an injunction, and after staring at

Quilp in a threatening manner as if he doubted whether
he might not have been the cause of Nelly shedding tears,
and felt more than half-disposed to revenge the fact upon
him on the mere suspicion, turned about and followed his
young mistress, who had by this time taken her leave of
Mrs. Quilp and departed.

" You're a keen questioner, an't you, Mrs. Quilp?" said
the dwarf, turning upon her as soon as they were left
alone.

"What more could I do?" returned his wife mildly.

" What more could you do!" sneered Quilp, "couldn't
you have done something less? couldn't you have done
what you had to do, without appearing in your favorite
part of the crocodile, you minx?"

"I am very sorry for the child, Quilp," said his wife.
"Surely I've done enough. I've led her on to tell her
secret when she supposed we were alone; and you were
by, God forgive me."

" You led her on! You did a great deal truly!" said
Quilp. " What did I tell you about making me creak the
door? It's lucky for you that from what she let fall, I've
got the clue I want, for if I hadn't, I'd have visited the
failure upon you, I can tell you."

Mrs. Quilp being fully persuaded of this, made no reply.
Her husband added with some exultation,

"But you may thank your fortunate stars—the same
stars that made you Mrs. Quilp—you may thank them
that I'm upon the old gentleman's track, and have got a
new light. So let me hear no more about this matter now
or at any other time, and don't get anything too nice for
dinner, for I shan't be home to it."

So saying, Mr. Quilp put his hat on and took himself
off, and Mrs. Quilp, who was afflicted beyond measure by
the recollection of the part she had just acted, shut herself up in her chamber, and smothering her head in the
bed-clothes bemoaned her fault more bitterly than many
less tender-hearted persons would have mourned a much
greater offence; for, in the majority of cases, conscience
is an elastic and very flexible article, which will bear a
deal of stretching and adapt itself to a great variety of
circumstances. Some people by prudent management
and leaving it off piece by piece like a flannel waistcoat
in warm weather, even contrive, in time, to dispense with

it altogether; but there be others who can assume the garment and throw it off at pleasure; and this, being the greatest and most convenient improvement, is the one most in vogue.

CHAPTER THE SEVENTH.

"Fred," said Mr. Swiveller, "remember the once popular melody of 'Begone dull care;' fan the sinking flame of hilarity with the wing of friendship; and pass the rosy wine."

Mr. Richard Swiveller's apartments were in the neighborhood of Drury Lane, and in addition to this conveniency of situation had the advantage of being over a tobacconist's shop, so that he was enabled to procure a refreshing sneeze at any time by merely stepping out upon the staircase, and was saved the trouble and expense of maintaining a snuff-box. It was in these apartments that Mr. Swiveller made use of the expressions above recorded for the consolation and encouragement of his desponding friend; and it may not be uninteresting or improper to remark that even these brief observations partook in a double sense of the figurative and poetical character of Mr. Swiveller's mind, as the rosy wine was in fact represented by one glass of cold gin-and-water, which was replenished as occasion required from a bottle and jug upon the table, and was passed from one to another, in a scarcity of tumblers which, as Mr. Swiveller's was a bachelor's establishment, may be acknowledged without a blush. By a like pleasant fiction his single chamber was always mentioned in the plural number. In its disengaged times, the tobacconist had announced it in his window as "apartments" for a single gentleman, and Mr. Swiveller, following up the hint, never failed to speak of it as his rooms, his lodgings, or his chambers, conveying to his hearers a notion of indefinite space, and leaving their imaginations to wander through long suites of lofty halls, at pleasure.

In this flight of fancy, Mr. Swiveller was assisted by a deceptive piece of furniture, in reality a bedstead, but in semblance a bookcase, which occupied a prominent situation in his chamber and seemed to defy suspicion and

challenge inquiry. There is no doubt that by day Mr.
Swiveller firmly believed this secret convenience to be a
bookcase and nothing more; that he closed his eyes to
the bed, resolutely denied the existence of the blankets,
and spurned the bolster from his thoughts. No word of
its real use, no hint of its nightly service, no allusion to
its peculiar properties, had ever passed between him and
his most intimate friends. Implicit faith in the deception
was the first article of his creed. To be the friend of
Swiveller you must reject all circumstantial evidence, all
reason, observation, and experience, and repose a blind
belief in the bookcase. It was his pet weakness, and he
cherished it.

"Fred!" said Mr. Swiveller, finding that his former
adjuration had been productive of no effect. "Pass the
rosy."

Young Trent with an impatient gesture pushed the
glass towards him, and fell again into the moody attitude
from which he had been unwillingly roused.

"I'll give you, Fred," said his friend, stirring the mix-
ture, "a little sentiment appropriate to the occasion.
Here's may the——"

"Pshaw!" interposed the other. "You worry me to
death with your chattering. You can be merry under
any circumstances."

"Why, Mr. Trent," returned Dick, "there is a proverb
which talks about being merry and wise. There are
some people who can be merry and can't be wise, and
some who can be wise (or think they can) and can't be
merry. I'm one of the first sort. If the proverb's a good
'un, I suppose it's better to keep to half of it than none;
at all events I'd rather be merry and not wise, than like
you, neither one nor t'other."

"Bah!" muttered his friend, peevishly.

"With all my heart," said Mr. Swiveller. "In the
polite circles I believe this sort of thing isn't usually said
to a gentleman in his own apartments, but never mind
that. Make yourself at home." Adding to this retort
an observation to the effect that his friend appeared to
be rather "cranky" in point of temper, Richard Swiveller
finished the rosy and applied himself to the composition
of another glassful, in which, after tasting it with great
relish, he proposed a toast to an imaginary company.

" Gentlemen, I'll give you, if you please, Success to the ancient family of the Swivellers, and good luck to Mr. Richard in particular—Mr. Richard, gentlemen," said Dick with great emphasis, " who spends all his money on his friends and is *Bah! 'd* for his pains.   Hear, hear! "

" Dick! " said the other, returning to his seat after having paced the room twice or thrice, " will you talk seriously for two minutes, if I show you a way to make your fortune with very little trouble?"

" You've shown me so many," returned Dick; " and nothing has come of any one of 'em but empty pockets—"

" You'll tell a different story of this one, before a very long time is over," said his companion drawing his chair to the table.   " You saw my sister Nell?"

" What about her?" returned Dick.

" She has a pretty face, has she not?"

" Why, certainly," replied Dick, " I must say for her that there's not any very strong family likeness between her and you."

" Has she a pretty face?" repeated his friend impatiently.

" Yes," said Dick, " she has a pretty face, a very pretty face.   What of that?"

" I'll tell you," returned his friend.   " It's very plain that the old man and I will remain at daggers-drawn to the end of our lives, and that I have nothing to expect from him.   You see that, I suppose?"

" A bat might see that, with the sun shining," said Dick.

" It's equally plain that the money which the old flint —rot him—first taught me to expect that I should share with her at his death, will all be hers, is it not?"

" I should say it was," replied Dick; " unless the way in which I put the case to him, made an impression.   It may have done so.   It was powerful, Fred.   'Here is a jolly old grandfather'—that was strong, I thought—very friendly and natural.   Did it strike you in that way?"

" It didn't strike *him*," returned the other, " so we needn't discuss it.   Now look here.   Nell is nearly fourteen."

" Fine girl of her age, but small," observed Richad Swiveller parenthetically.

" If I am to go on, be quiet for one minute," returned

Trent, fretting at the very slight interest the other appeared to take in the conversation. " Now I'm coming to the point."

" That's right," said Dick.

" The girl has strong affections, and brought up as she has been, may, at her age, be easily influenced and persuaded. If I take her in hand, I will be bound by a very little coaxing and threatening to bend her to my will. Not to beat about the bush (for the advantages of the scheme would take a week to tell) what's to prevent your marrying her ? "

Richard Swiveller, who had been looking over the rim of the tumbler while his companion addressed the foregoing remarks to him with great energy and earnestness of manner, no sooner heard these words than he evinced the utmost consternation, and with difficulty ejaculated the monosyllable,

" What ! "

" I say, what's to prevent," repeated the other with a steadiness of manner, of the effect of which upon his companion he was well assured by long experience, " what's to prevent your marrying her ? "

" And she 'nearly fourteen'!" cried Dick.

"I don't mean marrying her now"—returned the brother angrily; "say in two years' time, in three, in four. Does the old man look like a long-liver?"

"He don't look like it," said Dick shaking his head, "but these old people—there's no trusting 'em, Fred. There's an aunt of mine down in Dorsetshire that was going to die when I was eight years old, and hasn't kept her word yet. They're so aggravating, so unprincipled, so spiteful—unless there's apoplexy in the family, Fred, you can't calculate upon 'em, and even then they deceive you just as often as not."

"Look at the worst side of the question then," said Trent as steadily as before, and keeping his eyes upon his friend. "Suppose he lives."

"To be sure," said Dick. "There's the rub."

"I say," resumed his friend, "suppose he lives, and I persuaded, or if the word sounds more feasible, forced, Nell to a secret marriage with you. What do you think would come of that?"

"A family and an annual income of nothing, to keep 'em on," said Richard Swiveller after some reflection.

"I tell you," returned the other with an increased earnestness, which, whether it were real or assumed, had the same effect on his companion, "that he lives for her, that his whole energies and thoughts are bound up in her, that he would no more disinherit her for an act of disobedience than he would take me into his favor again for any act of obedience or virtue that I could possibly be guilty of. He could not do it. You or any other man with eyes in his head may see that, if he chooses."

"It seems improbable certainly," said Dick, musing.

"It seems improbable because it is improbable," his friend returned. "If you would furnish him with an additional inducement to forgive you, let there be an irreconcileable breach, a most deadly quarrel, between you and me—let there be a pretence of such a thing, I mean, of course—and he'll do so fast enough. As to Nell, constant dropping will wear away a stone; you know you may trust to me as far as she is concerned. So, whether he lives or dies, what does it come to? That you become the sole inheritor of the wealth of this rich old hunks, that you and I spend it together, and that you get into the bargain a beautiful young wife."

" I suppose there's no doubt about his being rich "—
said Dick.

" Doubt! Did you hear what he let fall the other day
when we were there? Doubt! What will you doubt
next, Dick?"

It would be tedious to pursue the conversation through
all its artful windings, or to develop the gradual approaches by which the heart of Richard Swiveller was
gained. It is sufficient to know that vanity, interest,
poverty, and every spendthrift consideration urged him
to look upon the proposal with favor, and that where all
other inducements were wanting, the habitual carelessness of his disposition stepped in and still weighed down
the scale on the same side. To these impulses must be
added the complete ascendancy which his friend had
long been accustomed to exercise over him—an ascendancy
exerted in the beginning sorely at the expense of the unfortunate Dick's purse and prospects, but still maintained
without the slightest relaxation, notwithstanding that
Dick suffered for all his friend's vices, and was in nine cases
out of ten looked upon as his designing tempter when he
was indeed nothing but his thoughtless light-headed tool.

The motives on the other side were something deeper
than any which Richard Swiveller entertained or understood, but these being left to their own development, require no present elucidation. The negotiation was concluded very pleasantly, and Mr. Swiveller was in the act
of stating in flowery terms that he had no insurmountable objection to marrying anybody plentifully endowed
with money or movables, who could be induced to take
him, when he was interrupted in his observations by a
knock at the door, and the consequent necessity of crying
" Come in."

The door was opened, but nothing came in except a
soapy arm and a strong gush of tobacco. The gush of
tobacco came from the shop downstairs, and the soapy
arm proceeded from the body of a servant girl, who being
then and there engaged in cleaning the stairs had just
drawn it out of a warm pail to take in a letter, which
letter she now held in her hand, proclaiming aloud with
that quick perception of surnames peculiar to her class
that it was for Mister Snivelling.

Dick looked rather pale and foolish when he glanced at

the direction, and still more so when he came to look at
the inside, observing that this was one of the inconveniences of being a lady's man, and that it was very easy
to talk as they had been talking, but he had quite forgotten her.

" *Her.* Who?" demanded Trent.

"Sophy Wackles," said Dick.

"Who's she?"

"She's all my fancy painted her, Sir, that's what she
is," said Mr. Swiveller, taking a long pull at "the rosy"
and looking gravely at his friend. "She is lovely, she's
divine. You know her."

"I remember," said his companion carelessly. "What
of her?"

"Why, Sir," returned Dick, "between Miss Sophia
Wackles and the humble individual who has now the
honor to address you, warm and tender sentiments have
been engendered, sentiments of the most honorable and
inspiring kind. The Goddess Diana, Sir, that calls aloud
for the chase, is not more particular in her behavior
than Sophia Wackles; I can tell you that."

"Am I to believe there's anything real in what you
say?" demanded his friend; "you don't mean to say that
any love-making has been going on?"

"Love-making, yes. Promising, no," said Dick.
"There can be no action for breach, that's one comfort.
I've never committed myself in writing, Fred."

"And what's in the letter, pray?"

"A reminder, Fred, for to-night—a small party of
twenty, making two hundred light fantastic toes in all,
supposing every lady and gentleman to have the proper
complement. I must go, if it's only to begin breaking
off the affair—I'll do it, don't you be afraid. I should
like to know whether she left this herself. If she did,
unconscious of any bar to her happiness, it's affecting,
Fred."

To solve this question, Mr. Swiveller summoned the
handmaid and ascertained that Miss Sophy Wackles had
indeed left the letter with her own hands; and that she
had come accompanied, for decorum's sake no doubt, by
a younger Miss Wackles; and that on learning that
Mr. Swiveller was at home and being requested to walk upstairs, she was extremely shocked and professed that she

would rather die. Mr. Swiveller heard this account with
a degree of admiration not altogether consistent with the
project in which he had just concurred, but his friend
attached very little importance to his behavior in this
respect, probably because he knew that he had influence
sufficient to control Richard Swiveller's proceedings in
this or any other matter, whenever he deemed it necessary, for the advancement of his own purposes, to exert it.

CHAPTER THE EIGHTH.

BUSINESS disposed of, Mr. Swiveller was inwardly reminded of its being nigh dinner-time, and to the intent
that his health might not be endangered by longer abstinence, despatched a message to the nearest eating-house
requiring an immediate supply of boiled beef and greens
for two. With this demand, however, the eating-house
(having experience of its customer) declined to comply,
churlishly sending back for answer that if Mr. Swiveller
stood in need of beef perhaps he would be so obliging as
to come there and eat it, bringing with him, as grace before meat, the amount of a certain small account which
had been long outstanding. Not at all intimidated by
this rebuff, but rather sharpened in wits and appetite,
Mr. Swiveller forwarded the same message to another
and more distant eating-house, adding to it by way of
rider that the gentleman was induced to send so far, not
only by the great fame and popularity its beef had acquired, but in consequence of the extreme toughness of
the beef retailed at the obdurate cook's shop, which rendered it quite unfit not merely for gentlemanly food but
for any human consumption. The good effect of this
politic course was demonstrated by the speedy arrival of
a small pewter pyramid, curiously constructed of platters
and covers, whereof the boiled-beef-plates formed the
base, and a foaming quart-pot the apex; the structure
being resolved into its component parts afforded all things
requisite and necessary for a hearty meal, to which
Mr. Swiveller and his friend applied themselves with
great keenness and enjoyment.

"May the present moment," said Dick, sticking his fork into a large carbuncular potato, "be the worst of our lives! I like this plan of sending 'em with the peel on; there's a charm in drawing a potato from its native element (if I may so express it) to which the rich and powerful are strangers. Ah! 'Man wants but little here below, nor wants that little long!' How true that is! —after dinner."

"I hope the eating-house keeper will want but little and that *he* may not want that little long," returned his companion; "I suspect you've no means of paying for this!"

"I shall be passing presently, and I'll call," said Dick, winking his eye significantly. "The waiter's quite helpless. The goods are gone, Fred, and there's an end of it."

In point of fact, it would seem that the waiter felt this wholesome truth, for when he returned for the empty plates and dishes and was informed by Mr. Swiveller with dignified carelessness that he would call and settle when he should be passing presently, he displayed some perturbation of spirit, and muttered a few remarks about "payment on delivery," and "no trust," and other unpleasant subjects, but was fain to content himself with inquiring at what hour it was likely the gentleman would call, in order that being personally responsible for the beef, greens, and sundries, he might take care to be in the way at the time. Mr. Swiveller, after mentally calculating his engagements to a nicety, replied that he should look in at from two minutes before six to seven minutes past; and the man disappearing with this feeble consolation, Richard Swiveller took a greasy memorandum-book from his pocket and made an entry therein.

"Is that a reminder, in case you should forget to call?" said Trent with a sneer.

"Not exactly, Fred," replied the imperturbable Richard, continuing to write with a business-like air, "I enter in this little book the names of the streets that I can't go down while the shops are open. This dinner to-day closes Long Acre. I bought a pair of boots in Great Queen Street last week, and made that no thoroughfare too. There's only one avenue to the Strand left open now, and I shall have to stop up that to-night with a pair of gloves. The roads are closing so fast in every direction, that in

6

about a month's time, unless my aunt sends me a remittance, I shall have to go three or four miles out of town to get over the way."

"There's no fear of her failing, in the end?" said Trent.

"Why, I hope not," returned Mr. Swiveller, "but the average number of letters it takes to soften her is six, and this time we have got as far as eight without any effect at all. I'll write another to-morrow morning. I mean to blot it a good deal and shake some water over it out of the pepper-castor, to make it look penitent. 'I'm in such a state of mind that I hardly know what I write'— blot—'if you could see me at this minute shedding tears for my past misconduct'—pepper-castor—'my hand trembles when I think'—blot again—if that don't produce the effect, it's all over."

By this time Mr. Swiveller had finished his entry, and he now replaced his pencil in its little sheath and closed the book, in a perfectly grave and serious frame of mind. His friend discovered that it was time for him to fulfil some other engagement, and Richard Swiveller was accordingly left alone, in company with the rosy wine and his own meditations touching Miss Sophy Wackles.

"It's rather sudden," said Dick shaking his head with a look of infinite wisdom, and running on (as he was accustomed to do) with scraps of verse as if they were only prose in a hurry; "when the heart of a man is depressed with fears, the mist is dispelled when Miss Wackles appears: she's a very nice girl. She's like the red red rose that's newly sprung in June—there's no denying that—she's also like a melody that's sweetly played in tune. It's really very sudden. Not that there's any need, on account of Fred's little sister, to turn cool directly, but it's better not to go too far. If I begin to cool at all I must begin at once, I see that. There's the chance of an action for breach, that's one reason. There's the chance of Sophy's getting another husband, that's another. There's the chance of—no, there's no chance of that, but it's as well to be on the safe side."

This undeveloped consideration was the possibility, which Richard Swiveller sought to conceal even from himself, of his not being proof against the charms of Miss Wackles, and in some unguarded moment, by linking his fortunes to hers forever, of putting it out of his own power to further the notable scheme to which he had so readily become a party. For all these reasons, he decided to pick a quarrel with Miss Wackles without delay, and casting about for a pretext determined in favor of groundless jealousy. Having made up his mind on this important point, he circulated the glass (from his right hand to his left, and back again) pretty freely, to enable him to act his part with the greater discretion, and then, after making some slight improvements in his toilet, bent his steps towards the spot hallowed by the fair object of his meditations.

This spot was at Chelsea, for there Miss Sophia Wackles resided with her widowed mother and two sisters, in conjunction with whom she maintained a very small day-school for young ladies of proportionate dimensions; a circumstance which was made known to the neighborhood by an oval board over the front first-floor window, whereon appeared in circumambient flourishes the words "Ladies Seminary;" and which was further published and proclaimed at intervals between the hours of half-past nine and ten in the morning, by a straggling and solitary young lady of tender years standing on the scraper on the tips of her toes and making futile attempts to reach the knocker with a spelling-book. The several duties of instruction in this establishment were thus discharged. English grammar, composition, geography, and the use of the dumb-bells, by Miss Melissa Wackles; writing, arithmetic, dancing, music, and general fascination, by Miss Sophy Wackles; the art of needle-work, marking, and samplery, by Miss Jane Wackles; corporal punishment, fasting, and other tortures and terrors, by Mrs. Wackles. Miss Melissa Wackles was the eldest daughter, Miss Sophy the next, and Miss Jane the youngest. Miss Melissa might have seen five-and-thirty summers or thereabouts, and verged on the autumnal; Miss Sophy was a fresh, good-humored, buxom girl of twenty; and Miss Jane numbered scarcely sixteen years. Mrs. Wackles was an excellent but rather venomous old lady of three-score.

To this Ladies' Seminary then, Richard Swiveller hied with designs obnoxious to the peace of the fair Sophia, who, arrayed in virgin white, embellished by no ornamen

but one blushing rose, received him on his arrival, in the
midst of very elegant not to say brilliant preparations;
such as the embellishment of the room with the little
flower-pots which always stood on the window-sill outside, save in windy weather when 'they blew into the
area; the choice attire of the day-scholars who were allowed to grace the festival; the unwonted curls of Miss
Jane Wackles who had kept her head during the whole
of the preceding day screwed up tight in a yellow play-
bill; and the solemn gentility and stately bearing of the
old lady and her eldest daughter, which struck Mr. Swiveller as being uncommon but made no further impression upon him.

The truth is—and, as there is no accounting for tastes,
even a taste so strange as this may be recorded without
being looked upon as a wilful and malicious invention—
the truth is that neither Mrs. Wackles nor her eldest
daughter had at any time greatly favored the pretensions of Mr. Swiveller, being accustomed to make slight
mention of him as "a gay young man" and to sigh and
shake their heads ominously whenever his name was
mentioned. Mr. Swiveller's conduct in respect to Miss
Sophy having been of that vague and dilatory kind which
is usually looked upon as betokening no fixed matrimonial
intentions, the young lady herself began in course of time
to deem it highly desirable, that it should be brought to an
issue one way or other. Hence she had at last consented
to play off against Richard Swiveller a stricken market-
gardener known to be ready with his offer on the smallest encouragement, and hence—as this occasion had been
specially assigned for the purpose—that great anxiety on
her part for Richard Swiveller's presence which had
occasioned her to leave the note he has been seen to receive. "If he has any expectations at all or any means
of keeping a wife well," said Mrs. Wackles to her eldest
daughter, "he'll state 'em to us now or never."—"If he
really cares about me," thought Miss Sophy, "he must
tell me so, to-night."

But all these sayings and doings and thinkings being
unknown to Mr. Swiveller, affected him not in the least;
he was debating in his mind how ne could best turn jealous, and wishing that Sophy were for that occasion only
far less pretty than she was, or that she were her own

sister, which would have served his turn as well, when the company came, and among them the market-gardener, whose name was Cheggs. But Mr. Cheggs came not alone or unsupported, for he prudently brought along with him his sister, Miss Cheggs, who making straight to Miss Sophy and taking her by both hands, and kissing her on both cheeks, hoped in an audible whisper that they had not come too early.

"Too early, no!" replied Miss Sophy.

"Oh my dear," rejoined Miss Cheggs in the same whisper as before, "I've been so tormented, so worried, that it's a mercy we were not here at four o'clock in the afternoon. Alick has been in *such* a state of impatience to come! You'd hardly believe that he was dressed before dinner-time and has been looking at the clock and teasing me ever since. It's all your fault, you naughty thing."

Hereupon Miss Sophy blushed, and Mr. Cheggs (who was bashful before ladies) blushed too, and Miss Sophy's mother and sisters, to prevent Mr. Cheggs from blushing more, lavished civilities and attentions upon him, and left Richard Swiveller to take care of himself. Here was the very thing he wanted, here was good cause, reason and foundation for pretending to be angry; but having this cause reason and foundation which he had come expressly to seek, not expecting to find, Richard Swiveller was angry in sound earnest, and wondered what the devil Cheggs meant by his impudence.

However, Mr. Swiveller had Miss Sophy's hand for the first quadrille (country-dances being low, were utterly proscribed) and so gained an advantage over his rival, who sat despondingly in a corner and contemplated the glorious figure of the young lady as she moved through the mazy dance. Nor was this the only start Mr. Swiveller had of the market-gardener, for determining to show the family what quality of man they trifled with, and influenced perhaps by his late libations, he performed such feats of agility and such spins and twirls as filled the company with astonishment, and in particular caused a very long gentleman who was dancing with a very short scholar, to stand quite transfixed by wonder and admiration. Even Mrs. Wackles forgot for the moment to snub three small young ladies who were inclined to be happy,

and could not repress a rising thought that to have
such a dancer as that in the family would be a pride
indeed.

At this momentous crisis, Miss Cheggs proved herself a
vigorous and useful ally, for not confining herself to expressing by scornful smiles a contempt for Mr. Swiveller's
accomplishments, she took every opportunity of whispering into Miss Sophy's ear expressions of condolence and
sympathy on her being worried by such a ridiculous creature, declaring that she was frightened to death lest Alick
should fall upon, and beat him, in the fullness of his wrath,
and entreating Miss Sophy to observe how the eyes of the

said Alick gleamed with love and fury; passions, it may
be observed, which being too much for his eyes rushed
into his nose also, and suffused it with a crimson glow.

"You must dance with Miss Cheggs," said Miss Sophy
to Dick Swiveller, after she had herself danced twice
with Mr. Cheggs and made great show of encouraging his
advances. "She's such a nice girl—and her brother's
quite delightful."

"Quite delightful is he?" muttered Dick. "Quite delighted too, I should say, from the manner in which he's looking this way."

Here Miss Jane (previously instructed for the purpose) interposed her many curls and whispered her sister to observe how jealous Mr. Cheggs was.

" Jealous! Like his impudence! " said Richard Swiveller.

" His impudence, Mr. Swiveller! " said Miss Jane, tossing her head. " Take care he don't hear you, Sir, or you may be sorry for it."

"Oh pray, Jane—" said Miss Sophy.

" Nonsense! " replied her sister. " Why shouldn't Mr. Cheggs be jealous if he likes ? I like that, certainly. Mr. Cheggs has as good a right to be jealous as anybody else has, and perhaps he may have a better right soon if he hasn't already. You know best about that, Sophy! "

Though this was a concerted plot between Miss Sophy and her sister, originating in humane intentions and having for its object the inducing Mr. Swiveller to declare himself in time, it failed in its effect ; for Miss Jane being one of those young ladies who are prematurely shrill and shrewish, gave such undue importance to her part that Mr. Swiveller retired in dudgeon, resigning his mistress to Mr. Cheggs and conveying a defiance into his looks which that gentleman indignantly returned.

"Did you speak to me, Sir ? " said Mr. Cheggs, following him into a corner. " Have the kindness to smile, Sir, in order that we may not be suspected. Did you speak to me, Sir?"

Mr. Swiveller looked with a supercilious smile at Mr. Cheggs's toes, then raised his eyes from them to his ankle, from that to his shin, from that to his knee, and so on very gradually, keeping up his right leg, until he reached his waistcoat, when he raised his eyes from button to button until he reached his chin, and travelling straight up the middle of his nose came at last to his eyes, when he said abruptly,

" No, Sir, I didn't."

" Hem! " said Mr. Cheggs, glancing over his shoulder, "have the goodness to smile again, Sir. Perhaps you wished to speak to me, Sir."

" No, Sir, I didn't do that, either."

"Perhaps you may have nothing to say to me *now*, Sir," said Mr. Cheggs fiercely.

At these words Richard Swiveller withdrew his eyes from Mr. Cheggs's face, and travelling down the middle of his nose and down his waistcoat and down his right leg, reached his toes again, and carefully surveyed them; this done, he crossed over, and coming up the other leg and thence approaching by the waistcoat as before, said when he had got to his eyes "No, Sir, I haven't."

"Oh indeed, Sir!" said Mr. Cheggs. "I'm glad to hear it. You know where I'm to be found, I suppose, Sir, in case you *should* have anything to say to me?"

"I can easily inquire, Sir, when I want to know."

"There's nothing more we need say, I believe, Sir?"

"Nothing more, Sir"—With that they closed the tremendous dialogue by frowning mutually. Mr. Cheggs hastened to tender his hand to Miss Sophy, and Mr. Swiveller sat himself down in a corner in a very moody state.

Hard by this corner, Mrs. Wackles and Miss Wackles were seated, looking on at the dance; and unto Mrs. and Miss Wackles, Miss Cheggs occasionally darted when her partner was occupied with his share of the figure, and made some remark or other which was gall and wormwood to Richard Swiveller's soul. Looking into the eyes of Mrs. and Miss Wackles for encouragement, and sitting very upright and uncomfortable on a couple of hard stools, were two of the day-scholars; and when Miss Wackles smiled, and Mrs. Wackles smiled, the two little girls on the stools sought to curry favor by smiling likewise, in gracious acknowledgment of which attention the old lady frowned them down instantly, and said that if they dared to be guilty of such an impertinence again, they should be sent under convoy to their respective homes. This threat caused one of the young ladies, she being of a weak and trembling temperament, to shed tears, and for this offence they were both filed off immediately, with a dreadful promptitude that struck terror into the souls of all the pupils.

"I've got such news for you," said Miss Cheggs approaching once more, "Alick has been saying such things to Sophy. Upon my word, you know, it's quite serious and in earnest, that's clear."

"What's he been saying, my dear?" demanded Mrs. Wackles.

"All manner of things," replied Miss Cheggs, "you can't think how out he has been speaking!"

Richard Swiveller considered it advisable to hear no more, but taking advantage of a pause in the dancing, and the approach of Mr. Cheggs to pay his court to the old lady, swaggered with an extremely careful assumption of extreme carelessness towards the door, passing on the way Miss Jane Wackles, who in all the glory of her curls was holding a flirtation (as good practice when no better was to be had) with a feeble old gentleman who lodged in the parlor. Near the door sat Miss Sophy, still fluttered and confused by the attentions of Mr. Cheggs, and by her side Richard Swiveller lingered for a moment to exchange a few parting words.

"My boat is on the shore and my bark is on the sea, but before I pass this door I will say farewell to thee," murmured Dick, looking gloomily upon her.

"Are you going?" said Miss Sophy, whose heart sank within her at the result of her stratagem, but who effected a light indifference notwithstanding.

"Am I going!" echoed Dick bitterly. "Yes, I am. What then?"

"Nothing, except that it's very early," said Miss Sophy; "but you are your own master, of course."

"I would that I had been my own mistress too," said Dick, "before I had ever entertained a thought of you. Miss Wackles, I believed you true, and I was blest in so believing, but now I mourn that e'er I knew, a girl so fair yet so deceiving."

Miss Sophy bit her lip and affected to look with great interest after Mr. Cheggs, who was quaffing lemonade in the distance.

"I came here," said Dick, rather oblivious of the purpose with which he had really come, "with my bosom expanded, my heart dilated, and my sentiments of a corresponding description. I go away with feelings that may be conceived but cannot be described, feeling within myself the desolating truth that my best affections have experienced this night a stifler?"

"I am sure I don't know what you mean, Mr. Swiveller," said Miss Sophy with downcast eyes. "I'm very sorry if——"

"Sorry, Ma'am!" said Dick, "sorry in the possession of a Cheggs! But I wish you a very good night, concluding with this slight remark, that there is a young lady growing up at this present moment for me, who has not only great personal attractions but great wealth, and who has requested her next of kin to propose for my hand, which, having a regard for some members of her family, I have consented to promise. It's a gratifying circumstance which you'll be glad to hear, that a young and lovely girl is growing into a woman expressly on my account, and is now saving up for me. I thought I'd mention it. I have now merely to apologize for trespassing so long upon your attention. Good night."

"There's one good thing springs out of all this," said Richard Swiveller to himself when he had reached home and was hanging over the candle with the extinguisher in his hand, "which is, that I now go heart and soul, neck and heels, with Fred in all his scheme about little Nelly, and right glad he'll be to find me so strong upon it. He shall know all about that to-morrow, and in the mean time, as it's rather late, I'll try and get a wink or two of the balmy."

"The balmy" came almost as soon as it was courted. In a very few minutes Mr. Swiveller was fast asleep, dreaming that he had married Nelly Trent and come into the property, and that his first act of power was to lay waste the market-garden of Mr. Cheggs and turn it into a brick-field.

CHAPTER THE NINTH.

THE child, in her confidence with Mrs. Quilp, had but feebly described the sadness and sorrow of her thoughts, or the heaviness of the cloud which overhung her home, and cast dark shadows on its hearth. Besides that it was very difficult to impart to any person not intimately acquainted with the life she led, an adequate sense of its gloom and loneliness, a constant fear of in some way committing or injuring the old man to whom she was so tenderly attached, had restrained her even in the midst of her heart's overflowing, and made her timid of allusion to the main cause of her anxiety and distress.

For, it was not the monotonous days uncheckered by variety and uncheered by pleasant companionship, it was not the dark dreary evenings or the long solitary nights, it was not the absence of every slight and easy pleasure for which young hearts beat high, or the knowing nothing of childhood but its weakness and its easily wounded spirit, that had wrung such tears from Nell. To see the old man struck down beneath the pressure of some hidden grief, to mark his wavering and unsettled state, to be agitated at times with a dreadful fear that his mind was wandering, and to trace in his words and looks the dawning of despondent madness; to watch and wait and listen for confirmation of these things day after day, and to feel and know that, come what might, they were alone in the world with no one to help or advise or care about them—these were causes of depression and anxiety that might have sat heavily on an older breast with many influences at work to cheer and gladden it, but how heavily on the mind of a young child to whom they were ever present, and who was contantly surrounded by all that could keep such thoughts in restless action!

And yet, to the old man's vision, Nell was still the same. When he could for a moment disengage his mind from the phantom that haunted and brooded on it always, there was his young companion with the same smile for him, the same earnest words, the same merry laugh, the same love and care that sinking deep into his soul seemed to have been present to him through his whole life. And so he went on, content to read the book of her heart from the page first presented to him, little dreaming of the story that lay hidden in its other leaves, and murmuring within himself that at least the child was happy.

She had been once. She had gone singing through the dim rooms, and moving with gay and lightsome step among their dusty treasures, making them older by her young life, and sterner and more grim by her gay and cheerful presence. But now the chambers were cold and gloomy, and when she left her own little room to while away the tedious hours, and sat in one of them, she was still and motionless as their inanimate occupants. and had no heart to startle the echoes—hoarse from their long silence—with her voice.

In one of these rooms was a window looking into the

street, where the child sat, many and many a long evening, and often far into the night, alone and thoughtful. None are so anxious as those who watch and wait, and at these times, mournful fancies came flocking on her mind, in crowds.

She would take her station here at dusk, and watch the people as they passed up and down the street, or appeared at the windows of the opposite houses, wondering whether those rooms were as lonesome as that in which she sat, and whether those people felt it company to see her sitting there, as she did only to see them look out and draw in their heads again. There was a crooked stack of chimneys on one of the roofs, in which by often looking at them she had fancied ugly faces that were frowning over at her and trying to peer into the room, and she felt glad when it grew too dark to make them out, though she was sorry too, when the man came to light the lamps in the street, for it made it late, and very dull inside. Then she would draw in her head to look round the room and see that everything was in its place and hadn't moved; and looking out into the street again, would perhaps see a man passing with a coffin on his back, and two or three others silently following him to a house where somebody lay dead, which made her shudder and think of such things until they suggested afresh the old man's altered face and manner, and a new train of fears and speculations. If he were to die—if sudden illness had happened to him, and he were never to come home again, alive—if, one night, he should come home, and kiss and bless her as usual, and after she had gone to bed and had fallen asleep and was perhaps dreaming pleasantly, and smiling in her sleep, he should kill himself and his blood come creeping, creeping, on the ground to her own bedroom door! These thoughts were too terrible to dwell upon, and again she would have recourse to the street, now trodden by fewer feet and darker and more silent than before. The shops were closing fast, and lights began to shine from the upper windows, as the neighbors went to bed. By degrees these dwindled away and disappeared, or were replaced here and there by a feeble rush-candle which was to burn all night. Still there was one late shop at no great distance which sent forth a ruddy glare upon the pavement even yet, and looked bright and companionable. But in a little time this closed, the light was extinguished, and all was gloomy and quiet, except when some stray footsteps sounded on the pavement, or a neighbor, out later than his wont, knocked lustily at his house-door to rouse the sleeping inmates.

When the night had worn away thus far (and seldom now until it had) the child would close the window, and steal softly downstairs, thinking as she went that if one of those hideous faces below, which often mingled with her dreams, were to meet her by the way, rendering itself visible by some strange light of its own, how terrified she would be. But these fears vanished before a well-trimmed lamp and the familiar aspect of her own room. After praying fervently and with many bursting tears for the old man, and the restoration of his peace of mind and the happiness they had once enjoyed, she would lay her head upon the pillow and sob herself to sleep, often starting up again, before the daylight came, to listen for the bell, and respond to the imaginary summons which had roused her from her slumber.

One night, the third after Nelly's interview with Mrs. Quilp, the old man, who had been weak and ill all day, said he should not leave home. The child's eyes sparkled at the intelligence, but her joy subsided when they reverted to his worn and sickly face.

"Two days," he said, "two whole, clear days have passed, and there is no reply. What *did* he tell thee, Nell?"

"Exactly what I told you, dear grandfather, indeed."

"True," said the old man, faintly. "Yes. But tell me again, Nell. My head fails me. What was it that he told thee? Nothing more than that he would see me to-morrow or next day? That was in the note."

"Nothing more," said the child. "Shall I go to him again to-morrow, dear grandfather? Very early? I will be there and back, before breakfast."

The old man shook his head, and sighing mournfully, drew her towards him.

"'Twould be of no use, my dear, no earthly use. But if he deserts me, Nell, at this moment—if he deserts me now, when I should, with his assistance, be recompensed for all the time and money I have lost, and all the agony of mind I have undergone, which makes me what you see, I am ruined, and—worse, far worse than that—have ruined thee, for whom I ventured all. If we are beggars—!"

"What if we are?" said the child boldly. "Let us be beggars, and be happy."

"Beggars—and happy!" said the old man. "Poor child!"

"Dear grandfather," cried the girl with an energy which shone in her flushed face, trembling voice, and impassioned gesture, "I am not a child in that I think, but even if I am, oh hear me pray that we may beg, or work in open roads or fields, to earn a scanty living, rather than live as we do now."

"Nelly!" said the old man.

"Yes, yes, rather than live as we do now," the child repeated, more earnestly than before. "If you are sorrowful, let me know why and be sorrowful too; if you waste away and are paler and weaker every day, let me be your nurse and try to comfort you. If you are poor, let us be poor together, but let me be with you, do let me be with you, do not let me see such change and not know why, or I shall break my heart and die. Dear grandfather, let us leave this sad place to-morrow, and beg our way from door to door."

The old man covered his face with his hands, and hid it in the pillow of the couch on which he lay.

"Let us be beggars," said the child passing an arm round his neck, "I have no fear but we shall have enough, I am sure we shall. Let us walk through country places, and sleep in fields and under trees, and never think of money again, or anything that can make you sad, but rest at nights, and have the sun and wind upon our faces in the day, and thank God together. Let us never set foot in dark rooms or melancholy houses any more, but wander up and down wherever we like to go, and when you are tired, you shall stop to rest in the pleasantest place that we can find, and I will go and beg for both."

The child's voice was lost in sobs as she dropped upon the old man's neck; nor did she weep alone.

These were not words for other ears, nor was it a scene for other eyes. And yet other ears and eyes were there and greedily taking in all that passed, and moreover they were the ears and eyes of no less a person than **Mr. Daniel Quilp**, who, having entered unseen when the child first placed herself at the old man's side, refrained—actuated, no doubt, by motives of the purest delicacy—from interrupting the conversation, and stood looking on with his accustomed grin. Standing, however, being a tiresome attitude to a gentleman already fatigued with walking, and the dwarf being one of that kind of persons who

usually make themselves at home, he soon cast his eyes upon a chair into which he skipped with uncommon agility, and perching himself on the back with his feet upon the seat, was thus enabled to look on and listen with greater comfort to himself, besides gratifying at the same time that taste for doing something fantastic and monkey-like, which on all occasions had strong possession of him. Here, then, he sat, one leg cocked carelessly over the other, his chin resting on the palm of his hand, his head turned a little on one side, and his ugly features twisted into a complacent grimace. And in this position the old man, happening in course of time to look that way, at length chanced to see him, to his unbounded astonishment.

The child uttered a suppressed shriek on beholding this agreeable figure; in their first surprise both she and the old man, not knowing what to say, and half doubting its reality, looked shrinkingly at it. Not at all disconcerted by this reception, Daniel Quilp preserved the same attitude, merely nodding twice or thrice with great condescension. At length the old man pronounced his name, and inquired how he came there.

"Through the door," said Quilp pointing over his shoulder with his thumb. "I'm not quite small enough to get through key-holes. I wish I was. I want to have some talk with you, particularly, and in private—with nobody present, neighbor. Good-bye, little Nelly."

Nell looked at the old man, who nodded to her to retire, and kissed her cheek.

"Ah!" said the dwarf, smacking his lips, "what a nice kiss that was—just upon the rosy part. What a capital kiss!"

Nell was none the slower in going away, for this remark. Quilp looked after her with an admiring leer, and when she had closed the door, fell to complimenting the old man upon her charms.

"Such a fresh, blooming, modest little bud, neighbor," said Quilp, nursing his short leg, and making his eyes twinkle very much; "such a chubby, rosy, cosy, little Nell!"

The old man answered by a forced smile, and was plainly struggling with a feeling of the keenest and most exquisite impatience. It was not lost upon Quilp, who delighted in torturing him, or indeed anybody else when he could.

"She's so," said Quilp, speaking very slowly, and feigning to be quite absorbed in the subject, "so small, so compact, so beautifully modelled, so fair, with such blue veins and such a transparent skin, and such little feet, and such winning ways—but bless me, you're nervous! Why neighbor, what's the matter? I swear to you," continued the dwarf dismounting from the chair and sitting down in it, with a careful slowness of gesture very different from the rapidity with which he had sprung up unheard, "I swear to you that I had no idea old blood ran so fast or kept so warm. I thought it was sluggish in its course, and cool, quite cool. I am pretty sure it ought to be. Yours must be out of order, neighbor."

"I believe it is," groaned the old man, clasping his head with both hands. "There's burning fever here, and something now and then to which I fear to give a name."

The dwarf said never a word, but watched his companion as he paced restlessly up and down the room, and presently returned to his seat. Here he remained, with his head bowed upon his breast for some time, and then suddenly raising it, said,

"Once, and once for all, have you brought me any money?"

"No!" returned Quilp.

"Then," said the old man, clenching his hands desperately, and looking upward, "the child and I are lost!"

"Neighbor," said Quilp glancing sternly at him, and beating his hand twice or thrice upon the table to attract his wandering attention, "let me be plain with you, and play a fairer game than when you held all the cards, and I saw but the backs and nothing more. You have no secret from me now."

The old man looked up, trembling.

"You are surprised," said Quilp. "Well, perhaps that's natural. You have no secret from me now, I say; no, not one. For now I know that all those sums of money, that all those loans, advances, and supplies that you have had from me, have found their way to—shall I say the word?"

"Ay!" replied the old man, "say it, if you will."

"To the gaming-table," rejoined Quilp, "your nightly haunt. This was the precious scheme to make your fortune, was it; this was the secret certain source of wealth in which I was to have sunk my money (if I had been the fool you took me for); this was your inexhaustible mine of gold, your El Dorado, eh?"

"Yes," cried the old man, turning upon him with gleaming eyes, "it was. It is. It will be till I die."

"That I should have been blinded," said Quilp looking contemptuously at him, "by a mere shallow gambler!"

7

"I am no gambler," cried the old man fiercely. "I call Heaven to witness that I never played for gain of mine, or love of play; that at every piece I staked, I whispered to myself that orphan's name and called on Heaven to bless the venture, which it never did. Whom did it prosper? Who were those with whom I played? Men who lived by plunder, profligacy, and riot, squandering their gold in doing ill and propagating vice and evil. My winnings would have been from them, my winnings would have been bestowed to the last farthing on a young sinless child whose life they would have sweetened and made happy. What would they have contracted? The means of corruption, wretchedness, and misery. Who would not have hoped in such a cause—tell me that; now who would not have hoped as I did?"

"When did you first begin this mad career?" asked Quilp, his taunting inclination subdued for a moment by the old man's grief and wildness.

"When did I first begin?" he rejoined, passing his hand across his brow. "When *was* it, that I first began? When should it be, but when I began to think how little I had saved, how long a time it took to save at all, how short a time I might have at my age to live, and how she would be left to the rough mercies of the world, with barely enough to keep her from the sorrows that wait on poverty; then it was that I began to think about it."

"After you first came to me to get your precious grandson packed off to sea?" said Quilp.

"Shortly after that," replied the old man. "I thought of it a long time, and had it in my sleep for months. Then I began. I found no pleasure in it, I expected none. What has it ever brought to me but anxious days and sleepless nights, but loss of health and peace of mind and gain of feebleness and sorrow!"

"You lost what money you had laid by, first, and then came to me. While I thought you were making your fortune (as you said you were) you were making yourself a beggar, eh? Dear me! And so it comes to pass that I hold every security you could scrape together, and a bill of sale upon the—upon the stock and property," said Quilp standing up and looking about him, as if to assure himself that none of it had been taken away. "But did you never win?"

"Never!" groaned the old man. "Never won back my loss!"

"I thought," sneered the dwarf, "that if a man played long enough he was sure to win at last, or at the worst not to come off a loser."

"And so he is," cried the old man, suddenly rousing himself from his state of despondency, and lashed into the most violent excitement, "so he is; I have felt that from the first, I have always known it, I've seen it, I never felt it half so strongly as I feel it now. Quilp, I have dreamed three nights of winning the same large sum, I never could dream that dream before, though I have often tried. Do not desert me now I have this chance. I have no resource but you, give me some help, let me try this one last hope."

The dwarf shrugged his shoulders and shook his head.

"See, Quilp, good tender-hearted Quilp," said the old man, drawing some scraps of paper from his pocket with a trembling hand, and clasping the dwarf's arm, "only see here. Look at these figures, the result of long calculation, and painful and hard experience. I *must* win. I only want a little help once more, a few pounds, but two score pounds, dear Quilp."

"The last advance was seventy," said the dwarf; "and it went in one night."

"I know it did," answered the old man, "but that was the very worst fortune of all, and the time had not come then. Quilp, consider, consider," the old man cried, trembling so much the while that the papers in his hand fluttered as if they were shaken by the wind, "that orphan child. If I were alone, I could die with gladness—perhaps even anticipate that doom which is dealt out so unequally, coming as it does on the proud and happy in their strength, and shunning the needy and afflicted and all who court it in their despair—but what I have done, has been for her. Help me for her sake I implore you—not for mine, for hers!"

"I'm sorry I've got an appointment in the City," said Quilp, looking at his watch with perfect self-possession, "or I should have been very glad to have spent half an hour with you while you composed yourself—very glad."

"Nay, Quilp, good Quilp," gasped the old man, catching at his skirts—"you and I have talked together more

than once of her poor mother's story. The fear of her
coming to poverty has perhaps been bred in me by that.
Do not be hard upon me, but take that into account.
You are a great gainer by me. Oh spare me the money
for this one last hope!"

"I couldn't do it really," said Quilp with unusual
politeness, "though I tell you what—and this is a circumstance worth bearing in mind as showing how the
sharpest among us may be taken in sometimes—I was so
deceived by the penurious way in which you lived, alone
with Nelly—"

"All done to save money for tempting fortune, and
make her triumph greater," cried the old man.

"Yes yes, I understand that now," said Quilp; "but I
was going to say, I was so deceived by that, your miserly
way, the reputation you had among those who knew you
of being rich, and your repeated assurances that you
would make of my advances treble and quadruple the interest you paid me, that I'd have advanced you even now
what you want, on your simple note of hand, though I had
been led to suspect something wrong, if I hadn't unexpectedly become acquainted with your secret way of life."

"Who is it," retorted the old man desperately, "that
notwithstanding all my caution, told you that? Come.
Let me know the name—the person."

The crafty dwarf, bethinking himself that his giving
up the child would lead to the disclosure of the artifice
he had employed, which, as nothing was to be gained by
it, it was as well to conceal, stopped short in his answer
and said, "Now, who do you think?"

"It was Kit, it must have been the boy; he played the
spy and you tampered with him?" said the old man.

"How came you to think of him?" said the dwarf in
a tone of great commiseration. "Yes, it was Kit. Poor
Kit!"

So saying, he nodded in a friendly manner, and took
his leave, stopping when he had passed the outer door a
little distance, and grinning with extraordinary delight.

"Poor Kit!" muttered Quilp. "I think it was Kit
who said I was an uglier dwarf than could be seen anywhere for a penny, wasn't it. Ha ha ha! Poor Kit!"

And with that he went his way, still chuckling as he
went.

CHAPTER THE TENTH.

DANIEL QUILP neither entered nor left the old man's house, unobserved. In the shadow of an archway nearly opposite, leading to one of the many passages which diverged from the main street, there lingered one who having taken up his position when the twilight first came on, still maintained it with undiminished patience, and leaning against the wall with the manner of one who had a long time to wait, and being well used to it was quite resigned, scarcely changed his attitude for the hour together.

This patient lounger attracted little attention from any of those who passed, and bestowed as little upon them. His eyes were constantly directed towards one object, the window at which the child was accustomed to sit. If he withdrew them for a moment, it was only to glance at a clock in some neighboring shop, and then to strain his sight once more in the old quarter with increased earnestness and attention.

It has been remarked that this personage evinced no weariness in his place of concealment, nor did he, long as his waiting was. But as the time went on, he manifested some anxiety and surprise, glancing at the clock more frequently and at the window less hopefully than before. At length the clock was hidden from his sight by some envious shutters, then the church steeples proclaimed eleven at night, then the quarter past, and then the conviction seemed to obtrude itself upon his mind that it was of no use tarrying there any longer.

That the conviction was an unwelcome one, and that he was by no means willing to yield to it, was apparent from his reluctance to quit the spot; from the tardy steps with which he often left it, still looking over his shoulder at the same window; and from the precipitation with which he as often returned, when a fancied noise or the changing and imperfect light induced him to suppose it had been softly raised. At length he gave the matter up as hopeless for that night, and suddenly breaking into a run as though to force himself away, scampered off at his utmost speed, nor once ventured to look behind him lest he should be tempted back again.

Without relaxing his pace or stopping to take breath, this mysterious individual dashed on through a great many alleys and narrow ways until he at length arrived in a square paved court, when he subsided into a walk, and making for a small house from the window of which a light was shining, lifted the latch of the door and passed in.

"Bless us!" cried a woman turning sharply round, "who's that? Oh! It's you, Kit!"

"Yes, mother, it's me."

"Why, how tired you look, my dear!"

"Old master an't gone out to-night," said Kit; "and so she hasn't been at the window at all." With which words, he sat down by the fire and look very mournful and discontented.

The room in which Kit sat himself down in this condition was an extremely poor and homely place, but with that air of comfort about it, nevertheless, which—or the spot must be a wretched one indeed—cleanliness and order can always impart in some degree. Late as the Dutch clock showed it to be, the poor woman was still hard at work at an ironing table; a young child lay sleeping in a cradle near the fire; and another, a sturdy boy of two or three years old, very wide awake, with a very tight night-cap on his head, and a night-gown very much too small for him on his body, was sitting bolt upright in a clothes-basket, staring over the rim with his great round eyes, and looking as if he had thoroughly made up his mind never to go to sleep any more; which, as he had already declined to take his natural rest and had been brought out of bed in consequence, opened a cheerful prospect for his relations and friends. It was rather a queer-looking family; Kit, his mother, and the children, being all strongly alike.

Kit was disposed to be out of temper, as the best of us are too often—but he looked at the youngest child who was sleeping soundly, and from him to his other brother in the clothes-basket, and from him to their mother, who had been at work without complaint since morning, and thought it would be a better and kinder thing to be good-humored. So he rocked the cradle with his foot, made a face at the rebel in the clothes-basket, which put him in high good-humor directly and stoutly determined to be talkative and make himself agreeable.

"Ah mother!" said Kit, taking out his clasp-knife and falling upon a great piece of bread and meat which she had had ready for him, hours before, "what a one you are! There an't many such as you, *I* know."

"I hope there are many a great deal better, Kit," said Mrs. Nubbles; "and that there are, or ought to be, accordin' to what the parson at chapel says."

"Much *he* knows about it," returned Kit contemptuously. "Wait till he's a widder and works like you do, and gets as little, and does as much, and keeps his spirits up the same, and then I'll ask him what's o'clock and trust him for being right to half a second."

"Well," said Mrs. Nubbles, evading the point, "your beer's down there by the fender, Kit."

"I see," replied her son, taking up the porter pot, "my love to you, mother. And the parson's health too if you like. I don't bear him any malice, not I!"

"Did you tell me just now that your master hadn't gone out to-night?" inquired Mrs. Nubbles.

"Yes," said Kit, "worse luck."

"You should say better luck, I think," returned his mother, "because Miss Nelly won't have been left alone."

"Ah!" said Kit, "I forgot that. I said worse luck, because I've been watching ever since eight o'clock, and seen nothing of her."

"I wonder what she'd say," cried his mother, stopping in her work and looking round, "if she knew that every night, when she—poor thing—is sitting alone at that window, you are watching in the open street for fear any harm should come to her, and that you never leave the place or come home to your bed though you're ever so tired, till such time as you think she's safe in hers."

"Never mind what she'd say," replied Kit, with something like a blush on his uncouth face; "she'll never know nothing, and consequently, she'll never say nothing."

Mrs. Nubbles ironed away in silence for a minute or two, and coming to the fireplace for another iron, glanced stealthily at Kit while she rubbed it on a board and dusted it with a duster, but said nothing until she had returned to her table again, when holding the iron at an alarmingly short distance from her cheek, to test its temperature, and looking round with a smile, she observed:

"I know what some people would say, Kit—"

"Nonsense," interposed Kit with a perfect apprehension of what was to follow.

"No, but they would indeed. Some people would say that you'd fallen in love with her, I know they would."

To this, Kit only replied by bashfully bidding his mother "get out," and forming sundry strange figures with his legs and arms, accompanied by sympathetic contortions of his face. Not deriving from these means the relief which he sought, he bit off an immense mouthful from the bread and meat, and took a quick drink of the porter, by which artificial aids he choked himself and effected a diversion of the subject.

"Speaking seriously though, Kit," said his mother taking up the theme afresh, after a time, "for of course I was only in joke just now, it's very good and thoughtful, and like you, to do this, and never let anybody know it, though some day I hope she may come to know it, for

I'm sure she would be very grateful to you, and feel it very much. It's a cruel thing to keep the dear child shut up there. I don't wonder that the old gentleman wants to keep it from you."

"He don't think it's cruel, bless you," said Kit, "and don't mean it to be so, or he wouldn't do it—I do consider, mother, that he wouldn't do it for all the gold and silver in the world. No, no, that he wouldn't. I know him better than that."

"Then what does he do it for, and why does he keep it so close from you?" said Mrs. Nubbles.

"That I don't know," returned her son. "If he hadn't tried to keep it so close though, I should never have found it out, for it was his getting me away at night and sending me off so much earlier than he used to, that first made me curious to know what was going on. Hark! what's that?"

"It's only somebody outside."

"It's somebody crossing over here"—said Kit standing up to listen, "and coming very fast too. He can't have gone out after I left, and the house caught fire, mother!"

The boy stood for a moment, really bereft, by the apprehension he had conjured up, of the power to move. The footsteps drew nearer, the door was opened with a hasty hand, and the child herself, pale and breathless, and hastily wrapped in a few disordered garments, hurried into the room.

"Miss Nelly! What is the matter!" cried mother and son together

"I must not stay a moment," she returned, "grandfather has been taken very ill, I found him in a fit upon the floor—"

"I'll run for a doctor"—said Kit, seizing his brimless hat. I'll be there directly, I'll—"

"No, no," cried Nell, "there is no one there, you're not wanted, you—you—must never come near us any more!"

"What!" roared Kit.

"Never again," said the child. "Don't ask me why, for I don't know. Pray don't ask me why, pray don't be sorry, pray don't be vexed with me, I have nothing to do with it indeed!"

Kit looked at her with his eyes stretched wide, and

opened and shut his mouth a great many times, but couldn't get out one word.

" He complains and raves of you," said the child, " I don't know what you have done, but I hope it's nothing very bad."

" *I* done ! " roared Kit.

" He cries that you're the cause of all his misery," returned the child with tearful eyes; " he screamed and called for you, they say you must not come near him or he will die. You must not return to us any more. I came to tell you. I thought it would be better that I should come than somebody quite strange. Oh, Kit, what *have* you done ? You, in whom I trusted so much, and who were almost the only friend I had ! "

The unfortunate Kit looked at his young mistress harder and harder, and with eyes growing wider and wider, but was perfectly motionless and silent.

" I have brought his money for the week," said the child, looking to the woman and laying it on the table— " and—and—a little more, for he was always good and kind to me. I hope he will be sorry and do well somewhere else and not take this to heart too much. It grieves me very much to part with him like this, but there is no help. It must be done. Good night ! "

With the tears streaming down her face, and her slight figure trembling with the agitation of the scene she had left, the shock she had received, the errand she had just discharged, and a thousand painful and affectionate feelings, the child hastened to the door, and disappeared as rapidly as she had come.

The poor woman, who had no cause to doubt her son, but every reason for relying on his honesty and truth, was staggered, notwithstanding, by his not having advanced one word in his defence. Visions of gallantry, knavery, robbery; and of the nightly absences from home for which he had accounted so strangely, having been occasioned by some unlawful pursuit; flocked into her brain and rendered her afraid to question him. She rocked herself upon a chair, wringing her hands and weeping bitterly, but Kit made no attempt to comfort her and remained quite bewildered. The baby in the cradle woke up and cried, the boy in the clothes-basket fell over on his back with the basket upon him and was seen no more, the mother wept louder yet and rocked faster, but Kit, insensible to all the din and tumult, remained in a state of utter stupefaction.

CHAPTER THE ELEVENTH.

Quiet and solitude were destined to hold uninterrupted rule no longer, beneath the roof that sheltered the child. Next morning the old man was in a raging fever accompanied with delirium, and sinking under the influence of this disorder he lay for many weeks in imminent peril of his life. There was watching enough now, but it was the watching of strangers who made of it a greedy trade, and who, in the intervals of their attendance upon the sick man huddled together with a ghastly good-fellowship, and ate and drank and made merry; for disease and death were their ordinary household gods.

Yet in all the hurry and crowding of such a time, the child was more alone than she had ever been before; alone in spirit, alone in her devotion to him who was wasting away upon his burning bed; alone in her unfeigned sorrow, and her unpurchased sympathy. Day after day, and night after night, found her still by the pillow of the unconscious sufferer, still anticipating his every want, and still listening to those repetitions of her name and those anxieties and cares for her, which were ever uppermost among his feverish wanderings.

The house was no longer theirs. Even the sick chamber seemed to be retained on the uncertain tenure of Mr. Quilp's favor. The old man's illness had not lasted many days when he took formal possession of the premises and all upon them, in virtue of certain legal powers to that effect, which few understood and none presumed to call in question. This important step secured, with the assistance of a man of law whom he brought with him for the purpose, the dwarf proceeded to establish himself and his coadjutor in the house, as an assertion of his claim against all comers; and then set about making his quarters comfortable after his own fashion.

To this end, Mr. Quilp encamped in the back parlor, having first put an effectual stop to any further business

by shutting up the shop. Having looked out from among
the old furniture the handsomest and most commodious
chair he could possibly find, which he reserved for his
own use, and an especially hideous and uncomfortable
one, which he considerately appropriated to the accommodation of his friend, he caused them to be carried into
this room and took up his position in great state. The
apartment was very far removed from the old man's
chamber, but Mr. Quilp deemed it prudent, as a precaution against infection from fever, and a means of wholesome fumigation, not only to smoke himself without
cessation, but to insist upon it that his legal friend did
the like. Moreover, he sent an express to the wharf for
the tumbling boy, who arriving with all despatch was
enjoined to sit himself down in another chair just inside
the door, continually to smoke a great pipe which the
dwarf had provided for the purpose, and to take it from
his lips under any pretence whatever, were it only for
one minute at a time, if he dared. These arrangements
completed, Mr. Quilp looked round him with chuckling
satisfaction, and remarked that he called that comfort.

The legal gentleman, whose melodious name was Brass,
might have called it comfort also but for two drawbacks,
one was that he could by no exertion sit easily in his
chair, the seat of which was very hard, angular, slippery,
and sloping; the other that tobacco-smoke always caused
him great internal discomposure and annoyance. But as
he was quite a creature of Mr. Quilp's and had a thousand reasons for conciliating his good opinion, he tried
to smile, and nodded his acquiescence with the best grace
he could assume.

This Brass was an attorney of no very good repute from
Bevis Marks in the City of London; he was a tall, meagre
man, with a nose like a wen, a protruding forehead,
retreating eyes, and hair of a deep red. He wore a long
black surtout reaching nearly to his ankles, short black
trousers, high shoes, and cotton stockings of a bluish
gray. He had a cringing manner but a very harsh voice,
and his blandest smiles were so extremely forbidding,
that to have had his company under the least repulsive
circumstances, one would have wished him to be out of
temper that he might only scowl.

Quilp looked at his legal adviser, and seeing that he

was winking very much in the anguish of his pipe, that
he sometimes shuddered when he happened to inhale its
full flavor, and that he constantly fanned the smoke
from him, was quite overjoyed and rubbed his hands with
glee.

"Smoke away, you dog," said Quilp turning to the boy;
"fill your pipe again and smoke it fast, down to the last
whiff, or I'll put the sealing-waxed end of it in the fire
and rub it red hot upon your tongue."

Luckily the boy was case-hardened, and would have

smoked a small lime-kiln if anybody had treated him
with it. Wherefore he only muttered a brief defiance of
his master, and did as he was ordered.

"Is it good, Brass, is it nice, is it fragrant, do you feel
like the Grand Turk?" said Quilp.

Mr. Brass thought that if he did, the Grand Turk's
feelings were by no means to be envied, but he said it
was famous, and he had no doubt he felt very like that
Potentate.

"This is the way to keep off fever," said Quilp, "this
is the way to keep off every calamity of life. We'll never

leave off all the time we stop here—smoke away, you dog, or you shall swallow the pipe."

"Shall we stop here long, Mr. Quilp?" inquired his legal friend, when the dwarf had given his boy this last gentle admonition.

"We must stop, I suppose, till the old gentleman up-stairs is dead," returned Quilp.

"He he he!" laughed Mr. Brass, "oh! very good!"

"Smoke away!" cried Quilp. "Never stop! you can talk as you smoke. Don't lose time."

"He he he!" cried Brass faintly, as he again applied himself to the odious pipe. "But if he should get better, Mr. Quilp?"

"Then we shall stop till he does, and no longer," returned the dwarf.

"How kind it is of you, Sir, to wait 'till then!" said Brass. "Some people, Sir, would have sold or removed the goods—oh dear, the very instant the law allowed 'em. Some people, Sir, would have been all flintiness and granite. Some people, Sir, would have—"

"Some people would have spared themselves the jab-bering of such a parrot as you," interposed the dwarf.

"He he he!" cried Brass. "You have *such* spirits!"

The smoking sentinel at the door interposed in this place, and without taking his pipe from his lips, growled,

"Here's the gal a comin' down."

"The what, you dog?" said Quilp.

"The gal," returned the boy. "Are you deaf?"

"Oh!" said Quilp, drawing in his breath with great relish as if he were taking soup, "you and I will have such a settling presently; there's such a scratching and bruising in store for you, my dear young friend. Aha! Nelly! How is he now, my duck of diamonds?"

"He's very bad," replied the weeping child.

"What a pretty little Nell!" cried Quilp.

"Oh beautiful, Sir, beautiful indeed," said Brass. "Quite charming!"

"Has she come to sit upon Quilp's knee," said the dwarf, in what he meant to be a soothing tone, "or is she going to bed in her own little room inside here—which is poor Nelly going to do?"

"What a remarkable pleasant way he has with chil-dren!" muttered Brass, as if in confidence between him-

self and the ceiling; "upon my word it's quite a treat to hear him."

"I'm not going to stay at all," faltered Nell. "I want a few things out of that room, and then I—I—won't come down here any more."

"And a very nice little room it is!" said the dwarf looking into it as the child entered. "Quite a bower. You're sure you're not going to use it, you're sure you're not coming back, Nelly?"

"No," replied the child, hurrying away, with the few articles of dress she had come to move; "never again, never again."

"She's very sensitive," said Quilp, looking after her. "Very sensitive; that's a pity. The bedstead is much about my size. I think I shall make it *my* little room."

Mr. Brass encouraging this idea, as he would have encouraged any other emanating from the same source, the dwarf walked in to try the effect, which he did by throwing himself on his back upon the bed with his pipe in his mouth, and then kicking up his legs and smoking violently. Mr. Brass applauding this picture very much, and the bed being soft and comfortable, Mr. Quilp determined to use it, both as a sleeping place by night and as a kind of divan by day, and in order that it might be converted to the latter purpose at once, remained where he was and smoked his pipe out. The legal gentleman being by this time rather giddy and perplexed in his ideas (for this was one of the operations of the tobacco upon his nervous system), took the opportunity of slinking away into the open air where in course of time he recovered sufficiently to return with a countenance of tolerable composure. He was soon led on by the malicious dwarf to smoke himself into a relapse, and in that state stumbled upon a settee where he slept till morning.

Such were Mr. Quilp's first proceedings on entering upon his new property. He was for some days restrained by business from performing any particular pranks, as his time was pretty well occupied between taking, with the assistance of Mr. Brass, a minute inventory of all the goods in the place, and going abroad upon his other concerns which happily engaged him for several hours at a time. His avarice and caution being now thoroughly awakened, however, he was never absent from the house one night,

and his eagerness for some termination, good or bad, to the old man's disorder, increasing rapidly as the time passed by, soon began to vent itself in open murmurs and exclamations of impatience.

Nell shrank timidly from all the dwarf's advances towards conversation and fled from the very sound of his voice, nor were the lawyer's smiles less terrible to her than Quilp's grimaces. She lived in such continual dread and apprehension of meeting one or other of them upon the stairs or in the passages if she stirred from her grandfather's chamber, that she seldom left it for a moment until late at night, when the silence encouraged her to venture forth and breathe the purer air of some empty room.

One night she had stolen to her usual window and was sitting there very sorrowfully, for the old man had been worse that day, when she thought she heard her name pronounced by a voice in the street, and looking down, recognized Kit, whose endeavors to attract her attention had roused her from her sad reflections.

"Miss Nell!" said the boy in a low voice.

"Yes," replied the child, doubtful whether she ought to hold any communication with the supposed culprit, but inclining to her old favorite still, "what do you want?"

"I have wanted to say a word to you for a long time," the boy replied, "but the people below have driven me away and wouldn't let me see you. You don't believe— I hope you don't really believe—that I deserve to be cast off as I have been; do you, Miss?"

"I must believe it," returned the child. "Or why would grandfather have been so angry with you?"

"I don't know," replied Kit. "I'm sure I've never deserved it from him, no, nor from you. I can say that with a true and honest heart any way. And then to be driven from the door, when I only came to ask how old master was—!"

"They never told me that," said the child. "I didn't know it indeed. I wouldn't have had them do it for the world."

"Thank'ee, Miss," returned Kit, "it's comfortable to hear you say that. I said I never would believe that it was your doing."

"That was right!" said the child eagerly.

" Miss Nell," cried the boy, coming under the window and speaking in a lower tone, "there are new masters down-stairs. It's a change for you."

" It is indeed," replied the child.

" And so it will be for him when he gets better," said the boy, pointing towards the sick room.

"—If he ever does," added the child, unable to restrain her tears.

" Oh, he'll do that, he'll do that," said Kit, " I'm sure he will. You mustn't be cast down, Miss Nell. Now don't be, pray."

These words of encouragement and consolation were few and roughly said, but they affected the child and made her for the moment weep the more.

" He'll be sure to get better now," said the boy anxiously, "if you don't give way to low spirits and turn ill yourself, which would make him worse and throw him back just as he was recovering. When he does, say a good word—say a kind word for me, Miss Nell."

" They tell me I must not even mention your name to him for a long, long time," rejoined the child, " I dare not ; and even if I might, what good would a kind word do you, Kit ? We shall be very poor. We shall scarcely have bread to eat."

" It's not that I may be taken back," said the boy, "that I ask the favor of you. It isn't for the sake of food and wages that I've been waiting about so long in hopes to see you. Don't think that I'd come in a time of trouble to talk of such things as them."

The child looked gratefully and kindly at him, but waited that he might speak again.

" No, it's not that," said Kit hesitating, " it's something very different from that. I haven't got much sense I know, but if he could be brought to believe that I'd been a faithful servant to him, doing the best I could, and never meaning harm, perhaps he mightn't—"

Here Kit faltered so long that the child entreated him to speak out, and quickly, for it was very late, and time to shut the window.

" Perhaps he mightn't think it over venturesome of me to say—well then, to say this,"—cried Kit with sudden boldness. " This home is gone from you and him. Mother and I have got a poor one, but that's better than

8

this with all these people here; and why not come there, till he's had time to look about and find a better!"

The child did not speak. Kit, in the relief of having made his proposition, found his tongue loosened, and spoke out in its favor with his utmost eloquence.

"You think," said the boy, "that it's very small and inconvenient. So it is, but it's very clean. Perhaps you think it would be noisy, but there's not a quieter court than ours in all the town. Don't be afraid of the children; the baby hardly ever cries, and the other one is very good—besides, *I'd* mind 'em. They wouldn't vex you much, I'm sure. Do try, Miss Nell, do try. The little front room upstairs is very pleasant. You can see a piece of the church-clock through the chimneys and almost tell the time; mother says it would be just the thing for you, and so it would, and you'd have her to wait upon you both, and me to run of errands. We don't mean money, bless you; you're not to think of that. Will you try him, Miss Nell? Only say you'll try him. Do try to make old master come, and ask him first what I have done—will you only promise that, Miss Nell?"

Before the child could reply to this earnest solicitation, the street-door opened, and Mr. Brass thrusting out his night-capped head called in a surly voice, "Who's there!" Kit immediately glided away, and Nell, closing the window softly, drew back into the room.

Before Mr. Brass had repeated his inquiry many times, Mr. Quilp, also embellished with a night-cap, emerged from the same door and looked carefully up and down the street, and up at all the windows of the house from the opposite side. Finding that there was nobody in sight he presently returned into the house with his legal friend, protesting (as the child heard from the staircase) that there was a league and plot against him, that he was in danger of being robbed and plundered by a band of conspirators who prowled about the house at all seasons, and that he would delay no longer but take immediate steps for disposing of the property and returning to his own peaceful roof. Having growled forth these and a great many other threats of the same nature, he coiled himself once more in the child's little bed, and Nell crept softly up the stairs.

It was natural enough that her short and unfinished

dialogue with Kit should leave a strong impression on her mind, and influence her dreams that night and her recollections for a long, long time. Surrounded by unfeeling creditors, and mercenary attendants upon the sick, and meeting in the height of her anxiety and sorrow with little regard or sympathy even from the women about her, it is not surprising that the affectionate heart of the child should have been touched to the quick by one kind and generous spirit, however uncouth the temple in which it dwelt. Thank Heaven that the temples of such spirits are not made with hands, and that they may be more worthily hung with poor patchwork than with purple and fine linen!

CHAPTER THE TWELFTH.

At length the crisis of the old man's disorder was past, and he began to mend. By very slow and feeble degrees his consciousness came back, but the mind was weakened and its functions were impaired. He was patient, and quiet; often sat brooding, but not despondently, for a long space; was easily amused, even by a sunbeam on the wall or ceiling; made no complaint that the days were long or the nights tedious; and appeared indeed to have lost all count of time and every sense of care or weariness. He would sit for hours together with Nell's small hand in his, playing with the fingers and stopping sometimes to smooth her hair or kiss her brow; and when he saw that tears were glistening in her eyes would look, amazed, about him for the cause, and forget his wonder even while he looked.

The child and he rode out : the old man propped up with pillows, and the child beside him. They were hand in hand as usual. The noise and motion in the streets fatigued his brain at first, but he was not surprised, or curious, or pleased, or irritated. He was asked if he remembered this, or that. "Oh yes," he said, "quite well —why not?" Sometimes he turned his head and looked with earnest gaze and outstretched neck, after some stranger in the crowd, until he disappeared from sight; but, to the question why he did this, he answered not a word.

He was sitting in his easy-chair one day, and Nell upon a stool beside him, when a man outside the door inquired if he might enter. "Yes," he said without emotion, "it was Quilp, he knew. Quilp was master there. Of course he might come in." And so he did.

"I'm glad to see you well again at last, neighbor," said the dwarf, sitting down opposite to him. "You're quite strong now?"

"Yes," said the old man feebly, "yes."

"I don't want to hurry you, you know, neighbor," said the dwarf, raising his voice, for the old man's senses were duller than they had been; "but, as soon as you *can* arrange your future proceedings, the better."

"Surely," said the old man. "The better for all parties."

"You see," pursued Quilp after a short pause, "the goods being once removed, this house would be uncomfortable; uninhabitable in fact."

"You say true," returned the old man. "Poor Nell too, what would *she* do?"

"Exactly," bawled the dwarf nodding his head; "that's very well observed. Then will you consider about it, neighbor?"

"I will, certainly," replied the old man. "We shall not stop here."

"So I supposed," said the dwarf. "I have sold the things. They have not yielded quite as much as they might have done, but pretty well—pretty well. To-day's Tuesday. When shall they be moved? There's no hurry —shall we say this afternoon?"

"Say Friday morning," returned the old man.

"Very good," said the dwarf. "So be it,—with the understanding that I can't go beyond that day, neighbor, on any account."

"Good," returned the old man. "I shall remember it."

Mr. Quilp seemed rather puzzled by the strange, even spiritless way in which all this was said; but as the old man nodded his head and repeated "on Friday morning. I shall remember it," he had no excuse for dwelling upon the subject any further, and so took a friendly leave with many expressions of good-will and many compliments to his friend on his looking so remarkably well; and went below stairs to report progress to Mr. Brass.

All that day, and all the next, the old man remained in this state. He wandered up and down the house and into

and out of the various rooms, as if with some vague intent of bidding them adieu, but he referred neither by direct allusions nor in any other manner to the interview of the morning or the necessity of finding some other shelter. An indistinct idea he had, that the child was desolate and in want of help, for he often drew her to his bosom and bade her be of good cheer, saying that they would not desert each other; but he seemed unable to contemplate their real position more distinctly, and was still the listless, passionless creature, that suffering of mind and body had left him.

We call this a state of childishness, but it is the same poor hollow mockery of it, that death is of sleep. Where, in the dull eyes of doting men, are the laughing light and life of childhood, the gaiety that has known no check, the frankness that has felt no chill, the hope that has never withered, the joys that fade in blossoming? Where, in the sharp lineaments of rigid and unsightly death, is the calm beauty of slumber, telling of rest for the waking hours that are past, and gentle hopes and loves for those which are to come? Lay death and sleep down, side by side, and say who shall find the two akin. Send forth the child and childish man together, and blush for the pride that libels our own old happy state gives and its title to an ugly and distorted image.

Thursday arrived, and there was no alteration in the old man. But, a change came upon him that evening, as he and the child sat silently together.

In a small dull yard below his window, there was a tree—green and flourishing enough, for such a place—and as the air stirred among its leaves, it threw a rippling shadow on the white wall. The old man sat watching the shadows as they trembled in this patch of light until the sun went down, and when it was night and the moon was slowly rising he still sat in the same spot.

To one who had been tossing on a restless bed so long, even these few green leaves and this tranquil light, although it languished among chimneys and house-tops, were pleasant things. They suggested quiet places afar off, and rest, and peace.

The child thought more than once that he was moved, and had forborne to speak. But now he shed tears—tears that it lightened her aching heart to see—and making as though he would fall upon his knees, besought **her** to forgive him.

"Forgive you—what?" said Nell, interposing to prevent his purpose. "Oh grandfather, what should *I* forgive?"

"All that is past, all that has come upon thee, Nell, all that was done in that uneasy dream," returned the old man.

"Do not talk so," said the child. "Pray do not. Let us speak of something else."

"Yes, yes, we will," he rejoined. "And it shall be of what we talked of long ago—many months—months is it, or weeks, or days? which is it, Nell?"

"I do not understand you"—said the child.

"It has come back upon me to-day, it has all come back since we have been sitting here. I bless thee for it, Nell?"

"For what, dear grandfather?"

"For what you said when we were first made beggars, Nell. Let us speak softly. Hush! for if they knew our purpose downstairs, they would cry that I was mad and take thee from me. We will not stop here another day. We will go far away from here."

"Yes, let us go," said the child earnestly. "Let us begone from this place, and never turn back or think of it again. Let us wander barefoot through the world, rather than linger here."

"We will"—answered the old man, "we will travel afoot through fields and woods, and by the side of rivers, and trust ourselves to God in the places where He dwells. It is far better to lie down at night beneath an open sky like that yonder—see how bright it is—than to rest in close rooms which are always full of care and weary dreams. Thou and I together, Nell, may be cheerful and happy yet, and learn to forget this time, as if it had never been."

"We will be happy," cried the child. "We never can be here."

"No, we never can again—never again—that's truly said," rejoined the old man. "Let us steal away to-morrow morning—early and softly, that we may not be seen or heard—and leave no trace or track for them to follow by. Poor Nell, thy cheek is pale and thy eyes are heavy with watching and weeping—with watching and weeping for me—I know—for me; but thou wilt be well again, and merry too, when we are far away. To-morrow morning, dear, we'll turn our faces from this scene of sorrows, and be as free and happy as the birds."

And then the old man clasped his hands above her head, and said in a few broken words that from that time forth they would wander up and down together, and never part more until Death took one or other of the twain.

The child's heart beat high with hope and confidence. She had no thought of hunger or cold, or thirst, or suffering. She saw in this, but a return of the simple pleasures they had once enjoyed, a relief from the gloomy solitude in which she had lived, an escape from the heartless people by whom she had been surrounded in her late time of trial, the restoration of the old man's health and peace, and a life of tranquil happiness. Sun, and stream, and meadow, and summer days, shone brightly in her view, and there was no dark tint in all the sparkling picture.

The old man had slept for some hours soundly in his bed, and she was yet busily engaged in preparing for their flight. There were a few articles of clothing for herself to carry, and a few for him; old garments, such as became their fallen fortunes, laid out to wear; and a staff to support his feeble steps, put ready for his use. But this was not all her task, for now she must visit the old rooms for the last time.

And how different the parting with them was from any she had expected, and most of all from that which she had oftenest pictured to herself. How could she ever have thought of bidding them farewell in triumph, when the recollection of the many hours she had passed among them rose to her swelling heart, and made her feel the wish a cruelty, lonely and sad though many of those hours had been! She sat down at the window where she had spent so many evenings—darker far than this—and every thought of hope or cheerfulness that had occurred to her in that place came vividly upon her mind, and blotted out all its dull and mournful associations in an instant.

Her own little room too, where she had so often knelt down and prayed at night—prayed for the time which she hoped was dawning now—the little room where she had slept so peacefully, and dreamed such pleasant dreams —it was hard not to be able to glance round it once more, and to be forced to leave it without one kind look or grateful tear. There were some trifles there—poor useless things—that she would have liked to take away; but that was impossible.

This brought to mind her bird, her poor bird, who hung there yet. She wept bitterly for the loss of this little creature—until the idea occurred to her—she did not know how or why it came into her head—that it might by some means fall into the hands of Kit who would keep it for her sake, and think perhaps that she had left it behind in the hope that he might have it, and as an assurance that she was grateful to him. She was calmed and comforted by the thought, and went to rest with a lighter heart.

From many dreams of rambling through light and sunny places, but with some vague object unattained which ran indistinctly through them all, she awoke to find that it was yet night, and that the stars were shining brightly in the sky. At length the day began to glimmer, and the stars to grow pale and dim. As soon as she was sure of this, she arose, and dressed herself for the journey.

The old man was yet asleep, and as she was unwilling to disturb him, she left him to slumber on until the sun rose. He was anxious that they should leave the house without a minute's loss of time, and was soon ready.

The child then took him by the hand, and they trod lightly and cautiously down the stairs, trembling whenever a board creaked, and often stopping to listen. The old man had forgotten a kind of wallet which contained the light burden he had to carry, and the going back a few steps to fetch it seemed an interminable delay.

At last they reached the passage on the ground floor, where the snoring of Mr. Quilp and his legal friend sounded more terrible in their ears than the roars of lions. The bolts of the door were rusty, and difficult to unfasten without noise. When they were all drawn back it was found to be locked, and, worst of all, the key was gone. Then the child remembered for the first time one of the nurses having told her that Quilp always locked both the house-doors at night, and kept the keys on the table in his bedroom.

It was not without great fear and trepidation that little Nell slipped off her shoes and gliding through the store-room of old curiosities, where Mr. Brass—the ugliest piece of goods in all the stock—lay sleeping on a mattress, passed into her own little chamber.

Here she stood for a few moments quite transfixed with terror at the sight of Mr. Quilp, who was hanging so far out of bed that he almost seemed to be standing

on his head, and who, either from the uneasiness of this posture or in one of his agreeable habits, was gasping and growling with his mouth wide open, and the whites (or rather the dirty yellows) of his eyes distinctly visible. It was no time, however, to ask whether anything ailed him, so possessing herself of the key after one hasty glance about the room, and repassing the prostrate Mr. Brass, she rejoined the old man in safety. They got the door open without noise, and passing into the street, stood still.

"Which way?" said the child.

The old man looked, irresolutely and helplessly, first at her, then to the right and left, then at her again, and shook his head. It was plain that she was thenceforth his guide and leader. The child felt it, but had no doubts or misgiving, and putting her hand in his, led him gently away.

It was the beginning of a day in June; the deep blue sky unsullied by a cloud, and teeming with brilliant light. The streets were as yet nearly free from passengers, the houses and shops were closed, and the healthful air of morning fell like breath from angels, on the sleeping town.

The old man and the child passed on through the glad silence, elate with hope and pleasure. They were alone together once again; every object was bright and fresh; nothing reminded them, otherwise than by contrast, of the monotony and constraint they had left behind; church towers and steeples, frowning and dark at other times, now shone and dazzled in the sun; each humble nook and corner rejoiced in light, and the sky, dimmed by excessive distance, shed its placid smile on everything beneath.

Forth from the city, while it yet slumbered, went the two poor adventurers, wandering they knew not whither.

CHAPTER THE THIRTEENTH.

DANIEL QUILP of Tower Hill, and Sampson Brass of Bevis Marks in the city of London, Gentleman, one of her Majesty's attorneys of the Courts of King's Bench and Common Pleas at Westminster and a solicitor of the High Court of Chancery, slumbered on unconscious and unsuspicious of any mischance, until a knocking at the street door, often repeated and gradually mounting up from a modest single rap into a perfect battery of knocks, fired in long discharges with a very short interval between, caused the said Daniel Quilp to struggle into a horizontal position, and to stare at the ceiling with a drowsy indifference, betokening that ne heard the noise and rather wondered at the same, but couldn't be at the trouble of bestowing any further thought upon the subject.

As the knocking, however, instead of accommodating itself to his lazy state, increased in vigor and became more importunate, as if in earnest remonstrance against his falling asleep again now that he had once opened his eyes, Daniel Quilp began by degrees to comprehend the possibility of there being somebody at the door, and thus he gradually came to recollect that it was Friday morning, and he had ordered Mrs. Quilp to be in waiting upon him at an early hour.

Mr. Brass, after writhing about in a great many strange attitudes, and often twisting his face and eyes into an expression like that which is usually produced by eating gooseberries very early in the season, was by this time awake also, and seeing that Mr. Quilp invested himself in his every-day garments, hastened to do the like, putting on his shoes before his stockings, and thrusting his legs into his coat sleeves, and making such other small mistakes as are not uncommon to those who dress in a hurry, and labor under the agitation of having been suddenly roused.

While the attorney was thus engaged, the dwarf was groping under the table, muttering desperate imprecations upon himself and mankind in general and all inanimate objects to boot, which suggested to Mr. Brass the question " what's the matter?"

" The key," said the dwarf, looking viciously at him, " the door-key,—that's the matter. D'ye know anything of it? "

" How should I know anything of it, Sir! " returned Mr. Brass.

"How should you?" repeated Quilp with a sneer. " You're a nice lawyer, an't you. Ugh, you idiot! "

Not caring to represent to the dwarf in his present humor, that the loss of a key by another person could scarcely be said to affect his (Brass's) legal knowledge in any material degree, Mr. Brass humbly suggested that it must have been forgotten over night, and was doubtless at that moment in its native key-hole. Notwithstanding that Mr. Quilp had a strong conviction to the contrary, founded on his recollection of having carefully taken it out, he was fain to admit that this was possible, and therefore went grumbling to the door where, sure enough, he found it.

Now, just as Mr. Quilp laid his hand upon the lock and saw with great astonishment that the fastenings were undone, the knocking came again with most irritating violence, and the daylight which had been shining through the key-hole was intercepted on the outside by a human eye. The dwarf was very much exasperated, and wanting somebody to wreak his ill-humor upon, determined to dart out suddenly and favor Mrs. Quilp with a gentle acknowledgment of her attention in making that hideous uproar.

With this view he drew back the lock very silently and softly, and opening the door all at once, pounced out upon the person on the other side, who had at that moment raised the knocker for another application, and at whom the dwarf ran head first, throwing out his hands and feet together, and biting the air in the fulness of his malice.

So far, however, from rushing upon somebody who offered no resistance and implored his mercy, Mr. Quilp was no sooner in the arms of the individual whom he had taken for his wife than he found himself complimented with two staggering blows on the head, and two more, of the same quality, in the chest, and closing with his assailant, such a shower of buffets rained down upon his person as sufficed to convince him that he was in skilful and experienced hands. Nothing daunted by this reception, he clung tight to his opponent, and bit and hammered away with such good-will and heartiness, that it was at least a couple of minutes before he was dislodged. Then, and not until then, Daniel Quilp found himself, all flushed and dishevelled, in the middle of the street, with Mr. Richard Swiveller performing a kind of dance round him and requiring to know "whether he wanted any more?"

"There's plenty more of it at the same shop," said Mr. Swiveller, by turns advancing and retreating in a threatening attitude, "a large and extensive assortment always on hand—country orders executed with promptitude and despatch—will you have a little more, Sir—don't say no, if you'd rather not."

"I thought it was somebody else," said Quilp rubbing his shoulders, "why didn't you say who you were?"

"Why didn't you say who *you* were?" returned Dick, "instead of flying out of the house like a Bedlamite?"

"It was you that—that knocked," said the dwarf, getting up with a short groan, "was it?"

"Yes, I am the man," replied Dick. "That lady had begun when I came, but she knocked too soft, so I relieved her." As he said this, he pointed towards Mrs. Quilp, who stood trembling at a little distance.

"Humph!" muttered the dwarf, darting an angry look at his wife, "I thought it was your fault! And you, Sir,

—don't you know there has been somebody ill here, that you knock as if you'd beat the door down?"

"Damme!" answered Dick, "that's why I did it. I thought there was somebody dead here."

"You came for some purpose, I suppose," said Quilp. "What is it you want?"

"I want to know how the old gentleman is," rejoined Mr. Swiveller, "and to hear from Nell herself, with whom I should like to have a little talk. I'm a friend of the family, Sir,—at least I'm the friend of one of the family, and that's the same thing."

" You'd better walk in then," said the dwarf.   " Go on,
Sir, go on.   Now, Mrs. Quilp—after you, ma'am."

Mrs. Quilp hesitated, but Mr. Quilp insisted.   And it
was not a contest of politeness, or by any means a matter
of form, for she knew very well that her husband wished
to enter the house in this order, that he might have a
favorable opportunity of inflicting a few pinches on her
arms, which were seldom free from impressions of his fingers in black and blue colors.   Mr. Swiveller, who was
not in the secret, was a little surprised to hear a suppressed scream, and, looking round, to see Mrs. Quilp
following him with a sudden jerk ; but he did not remark
on these appearances, and soon forgot them.

" Now, Mrs. Quilp," said the dwarf when they had
entered the shop, " go you upstairs, if you please, to
Nelly's room, and tell her that she's wanted."

" You seem to make yourself at home here," said Dick,
who was unacquainted with Mr. Quilp's authority.

" I *am* at home, young gentleman," returned the
dwarf.

Dick was pondering what these words might mean,
and still more what the presence of Mr. Brass might
mean, when Mrs. Quilp came hurrying downstairs, declaring that the rooms above were empty.

" Empty, you fool ! " said the dwarf.

" I give you my word, Quilp," answered his trembling
wife, " that I have been into every room and there's not
a soul in any of them."

" And that," said Mr. Brass, clapping his hands once,
with an emphasis, " explains the mystery of the key ! "

Quilp looked frowningly at him, and frowningly at his
wife, and frowningly at Richard Swiveller ; but, receiving no enlightenment from any of them, hurried upstairs, whence he soon hurried down again, confirming
the report which had been already made.

" It's a strange way of going," he said, glancing at
Swiveller, " very strange not to communicate with me
who am such a close and intimate friend of his !   Ah !
he'll write to me no doubt, or he'll bid Nelly write—yes,
yes, that's what he'll do.   Nelly's very fond of me.
Pretty Nell ! "

Mr. Swiveller looked, as he was, all open-mouthed
astonishment.   Still glancing furtively at him, Quilp

turned to Mr. Brass and observed with assumed careless-ness, that this need not interfere with the removal of the goods.

"For indeed," he added, "we knew that they'd go away to-day, but not that they'd go so early or so quietly. But they have their reasons, they have their reasons."

"Where in the devil's name are they gone?" said the wondering Dick.

Quilp shook his head and pursed up his lips, in a manner which implied that he knew very well, but was not at liberty to say.

"And what," said Dick, looking at the confusion about him, "what do you mean by moving the goods?"

"That I have bought 'em, Sir," rejoined Quilp. "Eh? What then?"

"Has the sly old fox made his fortune then, and gone to live in a tranquil cot in a pleasant spot with a distant view of the changing sea?" said Dick, in great bewilder-ment.

"Keeping his place of retirement very close, that he may not be visited too often by affectionate grandsons and their devoted friends, eh?" added the dwarf, rubbing his hands hard; "*I* say nothing, but is that your mean-ing, Sir?"

Richard Swiveller was utterly aghast at this unexpected alteration of circumstances, which threatened the complete overthrow of the project in which he bore so conspicuous a part, and seemed to nip his prospects in the bud. Having only received from Frederick Trent, late on the previous night, information of the old man's illness, he had come upon a visit of condolence and inquiry to Nell, prepared with the first instalment of that long train of fascinations which was to fire her heart at last. And here, when he had been thinking of all kinds of graceful and insinuating approaches, and meditating on the fearful retaliation which was slowly working against Sophy Wackles—here were Nell, the old man, and all the money gone, melted away, decamped he knew not whither, as if with a fore-knowledge of the scheme and a resolution to defeat it in the very outset, before a step was taken.

In his secret heart, Daniel Quilp was both surprised and troubled by the flight which had been made. It had not escaped his keen eye that some indispensable articles

of clothing were gone with the fugitives, and knowing
the old man's weak state of mind, he marvelled what
that course of proceeding might be in which he had so
readily procured the concurrence of the child. It must
not be supposed (or it would be a gross injustice to Mr.
Quilp) that he was tortured by any disinterested anxiety
on behalf of either. His uneasiness arose from a misgiving that the old man had some secret store of money
which he had not suspected, and the bare idea of its
escaping his clutches, overwhelmed him with mortification and self-reproach.

"In this frame of mind, it was some consolation to him
to find that Richard Swiveller was, for different reasons,
evidently irritated and disappointed by the same cause.
It was plain, thought the dwarf, that he had come there
on behalf of his friend to cajole or frighten the old man
out of some small fraction of that wealth of which they supposed him to have an abundance. Therefore it was a relief to vex his heart with a picture of the riches the old
man hoarded, and to expatiate on his cunning in removing
himself even beyond the reach of importunity.

"Well," said Dick, with a blank look, "I suppose it's
of no use my staying here."

"Not the least in the world," rejoined the dwarf.

"You'll mention that I called, perhaps?" said Dick.

Mr. Quilp nodded, and said he certainly would, the very
first time he saw them.

"And say," added Mr. Swiveller, "say, Sir, that I was
wafted here upon the pinions of concord; that I came to
remove, with the rake of friendship, the seeds of mutual
wiolence and heartburning, and to sow in their place the
germs of social harmony. Will you have the goodness
to charge yourself with that commission, Sir?"

"Certainly!" rejoined Quilp.

"Will you be kind enough to add to it, Sir," said Dick,
producing a very small limp card, "that *that* is my
address, and that I am to be found at home every morning. Two distinct knocks, Sir, will produce the slavey
at any time. My particular friends, Sir, are accustomed
to sneeze when the door is opened, to give her to understand that they *are* my friends and have no interested
motives in asking if I'm at home. I beg your pardon;
will you allow me to look at that card again?"

"Oh! by all means," rejoined Quilp.

"By a a slight and not unnatural mistake, Sir," said Dick, substituting another in its stead, "I had handed you the pass-ticket of a select convivial circle called the Glorious Apollers, of which I have the honor to be Perpetual Grand. That is the proper document, Sir. Good morning."

Quilp bade him good day; the Perpetual Grand Master of the Glorious Apollers, elevating his hat in honor of Mrs. Quilp, dropped it carelessly on the side of his head again, and disappeared with a flourish.

By this time certain vans had arrived for the conveyance of the goods, and divers strong men in carpet caps were balancing chests of drawers and other trifles of that nature upon their heads, and performing muscular feats which heightened their complexions considerably. Not to be behind-hand in the bustle, Mr. Quilp went to work with surprising vigor; hustling and driving the people about, like an evil spirit; setting Mrs. Quilp upon all kinds of arduous and impracticable tasks; carrying great weights up and down with no apparent effort; kicking the boy from the wharf whenever he could get near him; and inflicting with his loads a great many sly bumps and blows upon the shoulders of Mr. Brass, as he stood upon the doorsteps to answer all the inquiries of curious neighbors, which was his department. His presence and example diffused such alacrity among the persons employed, that in a few hours the house was emptied of everything, but pieces of matting, empty porter-pots, and scattered fragments of straw.

Seated like an African chief, on one of these pieces of matting, the dwarf was regaling himself in the parlor with bread and cheese and beer, when he observed, without appearing to do so, that a boy was prying in at the outer door. Assured that it was Kit, though he saw little more than his nose, Mr. Quilp hailed him by his name; whereupon Kit came in and demanded what he wanted.

"Come here, you Sir," said the dwarf. "Well, so your old master and young mistress have gone?"

"Where?" rejoined Kit, looking round.

"Do you mean to say you don't know where?" answered Quilp sharply. "Where have they gone, eh?"

9

"I don't know," said Kit.

"Come," retorted Quilp, "let's have no more of this? Do you mean to say that you don't know they went away by stealth, as soon as it was light this morning?"

"No," said the boy, in evident surprise.

"You don't know that?" cried Quilp. "Don't I know that you were hanging about the house the other night, like a thief, eh? Weren't you told then?"

"No," replied the boy.

"You were not?" said Quilp. "What were you told then; what were you talking about?"

Kit, who knew no particular reason why he should keep the matter secret now, related the purpose for which he had come on that occasion, and the proposal he had made.

"Oh!" said the dwarf after a little consideration. "Then, I think they'll come to you yet."

"Do you think they will?" cried Kit eagerly.

"Ay, I think they will," returned the dwarf. "Now, when they do, let me know; d'ye hear? Let me know, and I'll give you something. I want to do 'em a kindness, and I can't do 'em a kindness unless I know where they are. You hear what I say?"

Kit might have returned some answer which would not have been agreeable to his irascible questioner, if the boy from the wharf, who had been skulking about the room in search of anything that might have been left about by accident, had not happened to cry, "Here's a bird! What's to be done with this?"

"Wring its neck," rejoined Quilp.

"Oh, no, don't do that," said Kit, stepping forward. "Give it to me."

"Oh yes, I dare say," cried the other boy. "Come! You let the cage alone, and let me wring its neck, will you? He said I was to do it. You let the cage alone, will you?"

"Give it here, give it to me, you dogs," roared Quilp. "Fight for it, you dogs, or I'll wring its neck myself!"

Without further persuasion, the two boys fell upon each other tooth and nail, while Quilp, holding up the cage in one hand, and chopping the ground with his knife in an ecstasy, urged them on by his taunts and cries to fight more fiercely. They were a pretty equal match, and rolled about together, exchanging blows which were by no means child's play, until at length Kit, planting a well-directed hit in his adversary's chest, disengaged himself, sprang nimbly up, and snatching the cage from Quilp's hands made off with his prize.

He did not stop once until he reached home, where his bleeding face occasioned great consternation, and caused the elder child to howl dreadfully.

" Goodness gracious, Kit, what is the matter, what have you been doing?" cried Mrs. Nubbles.

" Never you mind, mother," answered her son, wiping his face on the jack towel behind the door. " I'm not hurt, don't you be afraid for me. I've been a fightin' for a bird and won him, that's all. Hold your noise, little Jacob. I never see such a naughty boy in all my days!"

" You have been fighting for a bird!" exclaimed his mother.

" Ah! Fightin' for a bird!" replied Kit, "and here he is —Miss Nelly's bird, mother, that they was agoin' to wring the neck of! I stopped that though—ha ha ha! They wouldn't wring his neck and me by, no no. It wouldn't do, mother, it wouldn't do at all. Ha ha ha!"

Kit laughing so heartily, with his swoln and bruised face looking out of the towel, made little Jacob laugh, and then his mother laughed, and then the baby crowed and kicked with great glee, and then they all laughed in concert, partly because of Kit's triumph, and partly because they were very fond of each other. When this fit was over, Kit exhibited the bird to both children, as a great and precious rarity—it was only a poor linnet –and looking about the wall for an old nail, made a scaffolding of a chair and table and twisted it out with great exultation.

" Let me see," said the boy, " I think I'll hang him in the winder, because it's more light and cheerful, and he can see the sky there, if he looks up very much. He's such a one to sing, I can tell you!"

So, the scaffolding was made again, and Kit, climbing up with the poker for a hammer, knocked in the nail and hung up the cage, to the immeasurable delight of the whole family. When it had been adjusted and straightened a great many times, and he had walked backwards into the fire-place in his admiration of it, the arrangement was pronounced to be perfect.

"And now, mother," said the boy, "before I rest **any** more, I'll go out and see if I can find a horse to hold, and then I can buy some birdseed, and a bit of something nice for you, into the bargain."

CHAPTER THE FOURTEENTH.

As it was very easy for Kit to persuade himself that the old house was in his way, his way being anywhere, he tried to look upon his passing it once more as a matter of imperative and disagreeable necessity, quite apart from any desire of his own, to which he could not choose but yield. It is not uncommon for people who are much better fed and taught than Christopher Nubbles had ever been, to make duties of their inclinations in matters of more doubtful propriety, and to take great credit for the self-denial with which they gratify themselves.

There was no need of any caution this time and no fear of being detained by having to pay out a return match with Daniel Quilp's boy. The place was entirely deserted, and looked as dusty and dingy as if it had been so for months. A rusty padlock was fastened on the door, ends of discolored blinds and curtains flapped drearily against the half-opened upper windows, and the crooked holes cut in the closed shutters below, were black with the darkness of the inside. Some of the glass in the window he had so often watched, had been broken in the rough hurry of the morning, and that room looked more deserted and dull than any. A group of idle urchins had taken possession of the doorsteps ; some were plying the knocker and listening with delighted dread to the hollow sounds it spread through the dismantled house ; others were clustered about the keyhole, watching half in jest and half in earnest for "the ghost," which an hour's gloom, added to the mystery that hung about the late inhabitants, had already raised. Standing all alone in the midst of the business and bustle of the street, the house looked a picture of cold desolation; and Kit, who remembered the cheerful fire that used to burn there on a winter's night and the no less cheerful laugh that made the small room ring, turned quite mournfully away.

It must be especially observed in justice to poor Kit that he was by no means of a sentimental turn, and perhaps had never heard that adjective in all his life. He was only a soft-hearted grateful fellow, and had nothing genteel or polite about him; consequently instead of going home again in his grief to kick the children and abuse his mother (for when your finely strung people are out of sorts they must have everybody else unhappy likewise), he turned his thoughts to the vulgar expedient of making them more comfortable if he could.

Bless us, what a number of gentlemen on horseback there were riding up and down, and how few of them wanted their horses held! A good city speculator or a parliamentary commissioner could have told to a fraction, from the crowds that were cantering about, what sum of money was realized in London in the course of a year, by holding horses alone. And undoubtedly it would have been a very large one, if only a twentieth part of the gentlemen without grooms had had occasion to alight; but they hadn't; and it is often an ill-natured circumstance like this, which spoils the most ingenious estimate in the world.

Kit walked about, now with quick steps and now with slow; now lingering as some rider slackened his horse's pace and looked about him; and now darting at full speed up a by-street as he caught a glimpse of some distant horseman going lazily up the shady side of the road, and promising to stop at every door. But on they all went, one after another, and there was not a penny stirring. " I wonder," thought the boy, " if one of these gentlemen knew there was nothing in the cupboard at home, whether he'd stop on purpose, and make believe that he wanted to call somewhere, that I might earn a trifle ? "

He was quite tired out with pacing the streets, to say nothing of repeated disappointments, and was sitting down upon a step to rest, when there approached towards him a little clattering jingling four-wheeled chaise, drawn by a little obstinate-looking rough-coated pony, and driven by a little fat placid-faced old gentleman. Beside the little old gentleman sat a little old lady, plump and placid like himself, and the pony was coming along at his own pace and doing exactly as he pleased with the whole concern. If the old gentleman remonstrated by shaking the reins, the pony replied by shaking his head. It was plain that the utmost the pony would consent to do, was to go in his own way up any street that the old gentleman particularly wished to traverse, but that it was an understanding between them that he must do this after his own fashion or not at all.

As they passed where he sat, Kit looked so wistfully at the little turn-out that the old gentleman looked at him, and Kit rising and putting his hand to his hat, the old gentleman intimated to the pony that he wished to stop, to which proposal the pony (who seldom objected to that part of his duty) graciously acceded.

"I beg your pardon, Sir," said Kit. "I'm sorry you stopped, Sir. I only meant did you want your horse minded."

"I'm going to get down in the next street," returned the old gentleman. "If you like to come on after us, you may have the job."

Kit thanked him, and joyfully obeyed. The pony ran off at a sharp angle to inspect a lamp-post on the opposite side of the way, and then went off at a tangent to another lamp-post on the other side. Having satisfied himself that they were of the same pattern and material, he came to a stop, apparently absorbed in meditation.

"Will you go on, Sir," said the old gentleman, gravely, "or are we to wait here for you 'till it's too late for our appointment?"

The pony remained immovable.

"Oh you naughty Whisker," said the old lady. "Fie upon you! I'm ashamed of such conduct."

The pony appeared to be touched by this appeal to his feelings, for he trotted on directly, though in a sulky manner, and stopped no more until he came to a door whereon was a brass plate with the words "Witherden —Notary." Here the old gentleman got out and helped out the old lady, and then took from under the seat a nosegay resembling in shape and dimensions a full-sized warming-pan with the handle cut short off. This, the old lady carried into the house with a staid and stately air, and the old gentleman (who had a club-foot) followed close upon her.

They went, as it was easy to tell from the sound of their voices, into the front parlor, which seemed to be a kind of office. The day being very warm and the street a quiet one, the windows were wide open, and it was easy to hear through the Venetian blinds all that passed inside.

At first there was a great shaking of hands and shuffling of feet, succeeded by the presentation of the nosegay, for a voice, supposed by the listener to be that of Mr. Witherden the Notary, was heard to exclaim a great many times, " oh, delicious ! " " oh, fragrant, indeed ! " and a nose, also supposed to be the property of that gentleman, was heard to inhale the scent with a snuffle of exceeding pleasure.

" I brought it in honor of the occasion, Sir," said the old lady.

" Ah! an occasion indeed, ma'am ; an occasion which does honor to me, ma'am, honor to me," rejoined Mr. Witherden the Notary. " I have had many a gentleman articled to me, ma'am, many a one. Some of them are now rolling in riches, unmindful of their old companion and friend, ma'am, others are in the habit of calling upon me to this day and saying, ' Mr. Witherden, some of the pleasantest hours I ever spent in my life were spent in this office—were spent, Sir, upon this very stool ;' but there was never one among the number, ma'am, attached as I have been to many of them, of whom I augured such bright things as I do of your only son."

" Oh dear ! " said the old lady. " How happy you do make us when you tell us that, to be sure ! "

" I tell you, ma'am," said Mr. Witherden, " what I think as an honest man, which, as the poet observes, is the noblest work of God. I agree with the poet in every particular, ma'am. The mountainous Alps on the one hand, or a humming-bird on the other, is nothing, in point of workmanship, to an honest man—or woman—or woman."

" Anything that Mr. Witherden can say of me," observed a small quiet voice, " I can say with interest of him, I am sure."

" It's a happy circumstance, a truly happy circumstances," said the Notary, " to happen too upon his eight-and-twentieth birthday, and I hope I know how to appreciate it. I trust, Mr. Garland, my dear Sir, that we may mutually congratulate each other upon this auspicious occasion."

To this the old gentleman replied that he felt assured they might. There appeared to be another shaking of hands in consequence, and when it was over, the old gentleman said that, though he said it who should not, he believed no son had ever been a greater comfort to his parents than Abel Garland had been to his.

"Marrying as his mother and I did, late in life, Sir, after waiting for a great many years, until we were well enough off—coming together when we were no longer young, and then being blessed with one child who has always been dutiful and affectionate—why, it's a source of great happiness to us both, Sir."

"Of course it is, I have no doubt of it," returned the Notary in a sympathizing voice. "It's the contemplation of this sort of thing, that makes me deplore my fate in being a bachelor. There was a young lady once, Sir, the daughter of an outfitting warehouse of the first respectability—but that's a weakness. Chuckster, bring in Mr. Abel's articles."

"You see, Mr. Witherden," said the old lady, "that Abel has not been brought up like the run of young men. He has always had a pleasure in our society, and always been with us. Abel has never been absent from us, for a day; has he, my dear?"

"Never, my dear," returned the old gentleman, "except when he went to Margate one Saturday with Mr. Tomkinley that had been a teacher at that school he went to, and came back upon the Monday; but he was very ill after that, you remember, my dear; it was quite a dissipation."

"He was not used to it, you know," said the old lady, "and he couldn't bear it, that's the truth. Besides he had no comfort in being there without us, and had nobody to talk to or enjoy himself with."

"That was it, you know," interposed the same small quiet voice that had spoken once before. "I was quite abroad, mother, quite desolate, and to think that the sea was between us—oh, I never shall forget what I felt when I first thought that the sea was between us!"

"Very natural under the circumstances," observed the Notary. "Mr. Abel's feelings did credit to his nature,

and credit to your nature, ma'am, and his father's nature,
and human nature. I trace the same current now, flowing through all his quiet and unobtrusive proceedings.—
I am about to sign my name, you observe, at the foot of
the articles which Mr. Chuckster will witness ; and, placing my finger upon this blue wafer with the vandyked
corners, I am constrained to remark in a distinct tone of
voice—don't be alarmed, ma'am, it is merely a form of
law—that I deliver this, as my act and deed. Mr. Abel
will place his name against the other wafer, repeating

the same cabalistic words, and the business is over. Ha
ha ha! You see how easily these things are done!"
There was a short silence, apparently, while Mr. Abel
went through the prescribed form, and then the shaking
of hands and shuffling of feet were renewed, and shortly
afterwards there was a clinking of wine-glasses and a
great talkativeness on the part of everybody. In about
a quarter of an hour Mr. Chuckster (with a pen behind
his ear and his face inflamed with wine) appeared at the
door, and condescending to address Kit by the jocose ap-

pellation of " Young Snob," informed him that the visitors were coming out.

Out they came forthwith ; Mr. Witherden, who was short, chubby, fresh-colored, brisk, and pompous, leading the old lady with extreme politeness, and the father and son following them, arm in arm. Mr. Abel, who had a quaint old-fashioned air about him, looked nearly of the same age as his father, and bore a wonderful resemblance to him in face and figure, though wanting something of his full, round cheerfulness, and substituting in its place, a timid reserve. In all other respects, in the neatness of the dress, and even in the club-foot, he and the old gentleman were precisely alike.

Having seen the old lady safely in her seat, and assisted in the arrangement of her cloak and a small basket which formed an indispensable portion of her equipage, Mr. Abel got into a little box behind which had evidently been made for his express accommodation, and smiled at everybody present by turns, beginning with his mother and ending with the pony. There was then a great to-do to make the pony hold up his head that the bearing-rein might be fastened ; at last even this was effected ; and the old gentleman, taking his seat and the reins, put his hand in his pocket to find a sixpence for Kit.

He had no sixpences, neither had the old lady, nor Mr. Abel, nor the Notary, nor Mr. Chuckster. The old gentleman thought a shilling too much, but there was no shop in the street to get change at, so he gave it to the boy.

" There," he said jokingly, " I'm coming here again next Monday at the same time, and mind you're here, my lad, to work it out."

" Thank you, Sir," said Kit. " I'll be sure to be here."

He was quite serious, but they all laughed heartily at his saying so, especially Mr. Chuckster, who roared outright and appeared to relish the joke amazingly. As the pony, with a presentiment that he was going home, or a determination that he would not go anywhere else (which was the same thing) trotted away pretty nimbly, Kit had no time to justify himself, and went his way also. Having expended his treasure in such purchases as he knew would be most acceptable at home, not forgetting some seed for the wonderful bird, he hastened back as fast as he could, so elated with his success and great good-fortune, that he more than half expected Nell and the old man would have arrived before him.

CHAPTER THE FIFTEENTH.

OFTEN, while they were yet pacing the silent streets of the town on the morning of their departure, the child trembled with a mingled sensation of hope and fear as in some far-off figure imperfectly seen in the clear distance, her fancy traced a likeness to honest Kit. But although she would gladly have given him her hand and thanked him for what he had said at their last meeting, it was always a relief to find, when they came nearer to each other, that the person who approached was not he, but a stranger; for even if she had not dreaded the effect which the sight of him might have wrought upon her fellow-traveller, she felt that to bid farewell to anybody now, and most of all to him who had been so faithful and so true, was more than she could bear. It was enough to leave dumb things behind, and objects that were insensible both to her love and sorrow. To have parted from her only other friend upon the threshold of that wild journey, would have wrung her heart indeed.

Why is it that we can better bear to part in spirit than in body, and while we have the fortitude to act farewell have not the nerve to say it? On the eve of long voyages or an absence of many years, friends who are tenderly attached will separate with the usual look, the usual pressure of the hand, planning one final interview for the morrow, while each well knows that it is but a poor feint to save the pain of uttering that one word, and that the meeting will never be. Should possibilities be worse to bear than certainties? We do not shun our dying friends; the not having distinctly taken leave of one among them, whom we left in all kindness and affection, will often embitter the whole remainder of a life.

The town was glad with morning light; places that had shown ugly and distrustful all night long, now wore a smile; and sparkling sunbeams dancing on chamber windows, and twinkling through blind and curtain before sleepers' eyes, shed light even into dreams, and chased away the shadows of the night. Birds in hot rooms, covered up close and dark, felt it was morning, and chafed and grew restless in their little cells; bright-eyed mice crept back to their tiny homes and nestled timidly together; the sleek house-cat, forgetful of her prey, sat winking at the rays of sun starting through keyhole and cranny in the door, and longed for her stealthy run and warm sleek bask outside. The nobler beasts confined in dens stood motionless behind their bars, and gazed on fluttering boughs and sunshine peeping through some little window, with eyes in which old forests gleamed—then trod impatiently the track their prisoned feet had worn—and stopped and gazed again. Men in their dungeons stretched their cramp cold limbs and cursed the stone that no bright sky could warm. The flowers that sleep by night, opened their gentle eyes and turned them to the day. The light, creation's mind, was everywhere, and all things owned its power.

The two pilgrims, often pressing each other's hands, or exchanging a smile or cheerful look, pursued their way in silence. Bright and happy as it was, there was something solemn in the long, deserted streets, from which like bodies without souls all habitual character and expression had departed, leaving but one dead uniform repose, that made them all alike. All was so still at that early hour, that the few pale people whom they met seemed as much unsuited to the scene, as the sickly lamp which had been here and there left burning was powerless and faint in the full glory of the sun.

Before they had penetrated very far into the labyrinth of men's abodes which yet lay between them and the outskirts, this aspect began to melt away, and noise and bustle to usurp its place. Some straggling carts and coaches rumbling by, first broke the charm, then others came, then others yet more active, then a crowd. The wonder was at first to see a tradesman's window open, but it was a rare thing soon to see one closed; then smoke rose slowly from the chimneys, and sashes were thrown up to let in air, and doors were opened, and servant girls, looking lazily in all directions but their brooms, scattered brown clouds of dust into the eyes of shrinking passengers, or listened disconsolately to milkmen who spoke of country fairs, and told of wagons in the mews, with awnings and all things complete and gallant swains to boot, which another hour would see upon their journey.

This quarter passed, they came upon the haunts of commerce and great traffic, where many people were resorting, and business was already rife. The old man looked about him with a startled and bewildered gaze, for these were places that he hoped to shun. He pressed his finger on his lip, and drew the child along by narrow courts and winding ways, nor did he seem at ease until they had left it far behind, often casting a backward look towards it, murmuring that ruin and self-murder were crouching in every street, and would follow if they scented them ; and that they could not fly too fast.

Again this quarter passed, they came upon a straggling neighborhood, where the mean houses parcelled off in rooms, and windows patched with rags and paper, told of the populous poverty that sheltered there. The shops sold goods that only poverty could buy, and sellers and buyers were pinched and griped alike. Here were poor streets where faded gentility essayed with scanty space and shipwrecked means to make its last feeble stand, but tax-gatherer and creditor came there as elsewhere, and the poverty that yet faintly struggled was hardly less squalid and manifest than that which had long ago submitted and given up the game.

This was a wide, wide track—for the humble followers of the camp of wealth pitch their tents round about it for many a mile—but its character was still the same. Damp rotten houses, many to let, many yet building, many half-built and mouldering away—lodgings, where it would be hard to tell which needed pity most, those who let or those who came to take—children, scantily fed and clothed, spread over every street, and sprawling in the dust—scolding mothers, stamping their slipshod feet with noisy threats upon the pavement—shabby fathers, hurrying with dispirited looks to the occupation which brought them "daily bread" and little more—mangling-women, washerwomen, cobblers, tailors, chandlers, driving their trades in parlors and kitchens and back rooms and garrets, and sometimes all of them under the same roof—brickfields, skirting gardens paled with staves of old casks, or timber pillaged from houses burnt down and blackened and blistered by the flame—mounds of dock-weed, nettles, coarse grass and oyster-shells, heaped in rank confusion—small Dissenting chapels to teach, with no lack of illustration, the miseries of Earth, and plenty of new churches, erected with a little superfluous wealth, to show the way to Heaven.

At length these streets, becoming more straggling yet, dwindled and dwindled away, until there were only small garden patches bordering the road, with many a summer-house innocent of paint and built of old timber or some fragments of a boat, green as the tough cabbage-stalks that grew about it, and grottoed at the seams with toad-stools and tight-sticking snails. To these succeeded pert cottages, two and two with plots of ground in front, laid out in angular beds with stiff box borders and narrow paths between, where footstep never strayed to make the gravel rough. Then came the public-house, freshly painted in green and white, with tea-gardens and a bowl-ing-green, spurning its old neighbor with the horse-trough where the wagons stopped; then fields; and then some houses, one by one, of goodly size with lawns, some even with a lodge where dwelt a porter and his wife. Then came a turnpike; then fields again with trees and hay-stacks; then a hill; and on the top of that the traveller might stop, and—looking back at old Saint Paul's loom-ing through the smoke, its cross peeping above the cloud (if the day were clear), and glittering in the sun; and casting his eyes upon the Babel out of which it grew until he traced it down to the furthest outposts of the invading army of bricks and mortar whose station lay for the present nearly at his feet—might feel at last that he was clear of London.

Near such a spot as this, and in a pleasant field, the old man and his little guide (if guide she were, who knew not whither they were bound) sat down to rest. She had had the precaution to furnish her basket with some slices of bread and meat, and here they made their frugal breakfast.

The freshness of the day, the singing of the birds, the beauty of the waving grass, the deep green leaves, the wild flowers, and the thousand exquisite scents and sounds that floated in the air,—deep joys to most of us, but most of all to those whose life is in a crowd or who live soli-

tarily in great cities as in the bucket of a human well,—
sank into their breasts and made them very glad. The
child had repeated her artless prayers once that morning,
more earnestly perhaps than she had ever done in all her
life, but as she felt all this, they rose to her lips again.
The old man took off his hat—he had no memory for
the words—but he said amen, and that they were very
good.

There had been an old copy of the Pilgrim's Progress,
with strange plates, upon a shelf at home, over which

she had often pored whole evenings, wondering whether
it was true in every word, and where those distant countries with the curious names might be. As she looked
back upon the place they had left, one part of it came
strongly on her mind.

"Dear grandfather," she said, "only that this place is
prettier and a great deal better than the real one, if that
in the book is like it, I feel as if we were both Christian,
and laid down on this grass all the cares and troubles we
brought with us; never to take them up again."

"No—never to return—never to return"—replied the old man, waving his hand towards the city. "Thou and I are free of it now, Nell. They shall never lure us back."

"Are you tired?" said the child, "are you sure you don't feel ill from this long walk?"

"I shall never feel ill again, now that we are once away," was his reply. "Let us be stirring, Nell. We must be further away—a long, long way further. We are too near to stop, and be at rest. Come!"

There was a pool of clear water in the field, in which the child laved her hands and face, and cooled her feet before setting forth to walk again. She would have the old man refresh himself in this way too, and making him sit down upon the grass, cast the water on him with her hands, and dried it with her simple dress.

"I can do nothing for myself, my darling," said the grandfather, "I don't know how it is, I could once, but the time's gone. Don't leave me, Nell; say that thou'lt not leave me. I loved thee all the while, indeed I did. If I lose thee too, my dear, I must die!"

He laid his head upon her shoulder and moaned piteously. The time had been, and a very few days before, when the child could not have restrained her tears and must have wept with him. But now she soothed him with gentle and tender words, smiled at his thinking they could ever part, and rallied him cheerfully upon the jest. He was soon calmed and fell asleep, singing to himself in a low voice, like a little child.

He awoke refreshed, and they continued their journey. The road was pleasant, lying between beautiful pastures and fields of corn, above which, poised high in the clear blue sky, the lark trilled out her happy song. The air came laden with the fragrance it caught upon its way, and the bees, upborne upon its scented breath, hummed forth their drowsy satisfaction as they floated by.

They were now in the open country; the houses were very few and scattered at long intervals, often miles apart. Occasionally they came upon a cluster of poor cottages, some with a chair or low board put across the open door to keep the scrambling children from the road, others shut up close while all the family were working in the fields. These were often the commencement of a little village: and after an interval came a wheelwright's shed or perhaps a blacksmith's forge; then a thriving farm with sleepy cows lying about the yard, and horses peering over the low wall and scampering away when harnessed horses passed upon the road, as though in triumph at their freedom. There were dull pigs too, turning up the ground in search of dainty food, and grunting their monotonous grumblings as they prowled about, or crossed each other in their quest; plump pigeons skimming round the roof or strutting on the eaves; and ducks and geese, far more graceful in their own conceit, waddling awkwardly about the edges of the pond or sailing glibly on its surface. The farm-yard passed, then came the little inn; the humbler beer-shop; and the village tradesman's; then the lawyer's and the parson's, at whose dread names the beer-shop trembled; the church then peeped out modestly from a clump of trees; then there were a few more cottages; then the cage, and pound, and not unfrequently, on a bank by the way-side, a deep old dusty well. Then came the trim-hedged fields on either hand, and the open road again.

They walked all day, and slept that night at a small cottage where beds were let to travellers. Next morning they were afoot again, and though jaded at first, and very tired, recovered before long and proceeded briskly forward.

They often stopped to rest, but only for a short space at a time, and still kept on, having had but slight refreshment since the morning. It was nearly five o'clock in the afternoon, when, drawing near another cluster of laborers' huts, the child looked wistfully in each, doubtful at which to ask for permission to rest awhile, and buy a draught of milk.

It was not easy to determine, for she was timid and fearful of being repulsed. Here was a crying child, and there a noisy wife. In this, the people seemed too poor; in that, too many. At length she stopped at one where the family were seated round the table—chiefly because there was an old man sitting in a cushioned chair beside the hearth, and she thought he was a grandfather and would feel for hers.

There were besides, the cottager and his wife, and three young sturdy children, brown as berries. The request

10

was no sooner preferred, than granted. The eldest boy ran out to fetch some milk, the second dragged two stools towards the door, and the youngest crept to his mother's gown, and looked at the strangers from beneath his sunburnt hand.

"God save you, master," said the old cottager in a thin piping voice; "are you travelling far?"

"Yes, Sir, a long way"—replied the child; for her grandfather appealed to her.

"From London?" inquired the old man.

The child said yes.

Ah! He had been in London many a time—used to go there often once, with wagons. It was nigh two-and-thirty year since he had been there last, and he did hear say there were great changes. Like enough! He had changed, himself, since then. Two-and-thirty year was a long time and eighty-four a great age, though there was some he had known that had lived to very hard upon a hundred—and not so hearty as he, neither—no, nothing like it.

"Sit thee down, master, in the elbow chair," said the old man, knocking his stick upon the brick floor, and trying to do so sharply. "Take a pinch out o' that box; I don't take much myself, for it comes dear, but I find it wakes me up sometimes, and ye're but a boy to me. I should have a son pretty nigh as old as you if he'd lived, but they listed him for a so'ger—he came back home though, for all he had but one poor leg. He always said he'd be buried near the sun-dial he used to climb upon when he was a baby, did my poor boy, and his words come true—you can see the place with your own eyes; we've kept the turf up, ever since."

He shook his head, and looking at his daughter with watery eyes, said she needn't be afraid that he was going to talk about that any more. He didn't wish to trouble nobody, and if he had troubled anybody by what he said, he asked pardon, that was all.

The milk arrived, and the child producing her little basket and selecting its best fragments for her grandfather, they made a hearty meal. The furniture of the room was very homely of course—a few rough chairs and a table, a corner cupboard with their little stock of crockery and delf, a gaudy tea-tray, representing a lady in bright red, walking out with a very blue parasol, a few common, colored Scripture subjects in frames upon the wall and chimney, an old dwarf clothes-press and an eight-day clock, with a few bright saucepans and a kettle, comprised the whole. But everything was clean and neat, and as the child glanced round, she felt a tranquil air of comfort and content to which she had long been unaccustomed.

" How far is it to any town or village ? " she asked of the husband.

" A matter of good five mile, my dear," was the reply, " but you're not going on to-night ? "

" Yes, yes, Nell," said the old man hastily, urging her too by signs. " Further on, further on, darling, further away if we walk 'till midnight."

" There's a good barn hard by, master," said the man, "or there's travellers' lodgings, I know, at the Plow an' Harrer. Excuse me, but you do seem a little tired, and unless you're very anxious to get on—"

" Yes, yes, we are," returned the old man fretfully, " Further away, dear Nell, pray further away."

" We must go on, indeed," said the child, yielding to his restless wish. " We thank you very much, but we cannot stop so soon. I'm quite ready, grandfather."

But the woman had observed from the young wanderer's gait, that one of her little feet was blistered and sore, and being a woman and a mother too, she would not suffer her to go until she had washed the place and applied some simple remedy, which she did so carefully and with such a gentle hand—rough-grained and hard though it was, with work—that the child's heart was too full to admit of her saying more than a fervent " God bless you ! " nor could she look back nor trust herself to speak, until they had left the cottage some distance behind. When she turned her head, she saw that the whole family, even the old grandfather, were standing in the road watching them as they went, and so, with many waves of the hand, and cheering nods, and on one side at least not without tears, they parted company.

They trudged forward, more slowly and painfully than they had done yet, for another mile or thereabouts, when they heard the sound of wheels behind them, and looking round observed an empty cart approaching pretty briskly. The driver on coming up to them stopped his horse and looked earnestly at Nell.

"Didn't you stop to rest at a cottage yonder?" he said.

"Yes, Sir," replied the child.

"Ah! They asked me to look out for you," said the man. "I'm going your way. Give me your hand—jump up, master."

This was a great relief, for they were very much fatigued and could scarcely crawl along. To them the jolting cart was a luxurious carriage, and the ride the most delicious in the world. Nell had scarcely settled herself on a little heap of straw in one corner, when she fell asleep, for the first time that day.

She was awakened by the stopping of the cart, which was about to turn up a bye-lane. The driver kindly got down to help her out, and pointing to some trees at a very short distance before them, said that the town lay there, and that they had better take the path which they would see, leading through the churchyard. Accordingly, towards this spot, they directed their weary steps.

CHAPTER THE SIXTEENTH.

THE sun was setting when they reached the wicket-gate at which the path began, and, as the rain falls upon the just and unjust alike, it shed its warm tint even upon the resting-places of the dead, and bade them be of good hope for its rising on the morrow. The church was old and gray, with ivy clinging to the walls, and round the porch. Shunning the tombs, it crept about the mounds, beneath which slept poor humble men, twining for them the first wreaths they had ever won, but wreaths less liable to wither and far more lasting in their kind, than some which were graven deep in stone and marble, and told in pompous terms of virtues meekly hidden for many a year, and only revealed at last to executors and mourning legatees.

The clergyman's horse, stumbling with a dull blunt sound among the graves, was cropping the grass; at once deriving orthodox consolation from the dead parishioners, and enforcing last Sunday's text that this was what all flesh came to; a lean ass who had sought to expound it also, without being qualified and ordained, was pricking his ears in an empty pound hard by, and looking with hungry eyes upon his priestly neighbor.

The old man and the child quitted the gravel path and strayed among the tombs; for there the ground was soft and easy to their tired feet. As they passed behind the church, they heard voices near at hand, and presently came on those who had spoken.

They were two men who were seated in easy attitudes

upon the grass, and so busily engaged as to be at first unconscious of intruders. It was not difficult to divine that they were of a class of itinerant showmen—exhibitors of the freaks of Punch—for, perched cross-legged upon a tombstone behind them, was a figure of that hero himself, his nose and chin as hooked and his face as beaming as usual. Perhaps his imperturbable character was never more strikingly developed, for he preserved his usual equable smile notwithstanding that his body was dangling in a most uncomfortable position, all loose and limp and shapeless, while his long peaked cap, unequally balanced against his exceedingly slight legs, threatened every instant to bring him toppling down.

In part scattered upon the ground at the feet of the two men, and in part jumbled together in a long flat box, were the other persons of the Drama. The hero's wife and one child, the hobby-horse, the doctor, the foreign gentleman who not being familiar with the language is unable in the representation to express his ideas otherwise than by the utterance of the word " Shallabalah " three distinct times, the Radical neighbor who will by no means admit that a tin bell is an organ, the executioner, and the Devil, were all here. Their owners had evidently come to that spot to make some needful repairs in the stage arrangements, for one of them was engaged in binding together a small gallows with thread, while the other was intent upon fixing a new black wig, with the aid of a small hammer and some tacks, upon the head of the Radical neighbor, who had been beaten bald.

They raised their eyes when the old man and his young companion were close upon them, and pausing in their work, returned their looks of curiosity. One of them, the actual exhibitor no doubt, was a little merry-faced man with a twinkling eye and a red nose, who seemed to have unconsciously imbibed something of his hero's character. The other—that was he who took the money— had rather a careful and cautious look, which was perhaps inseparable from his occupation also.

The merry man was the first to greet the strangers with a nod ; and following the old man's eyes, he observed that perhaps that was the first time he had ever seen a Punch off the stage. (Punch, it may be remarked, seemed to be pointing with the tip of his cap to a most flourishing epitaph, and to be chuckling over it with all his heart.)

" Why do you come here to do this ? " said the old man, sitting down beside them, and looking at the figures with extreme delight.

" Why you see," rejoined the little man, " we're putting up for to-night at the public-house yonder, and it wouldn't do to let 'em see the present company undergoing repair."

" No ! " cried the old man, making signs to Nell to listen, " why not, eh ? why not ? "

"Because it would destroy all the delusion, and take away all the interest, wouldn't it?" replied the little man. "Would you care a ha'penny for the Lord Chancellor if you know'd him in private and without his wig?—certainly not."

"Good!" said the old man, venturing to touch one of the puppets, and drawing away his hand with a shrill laugh. "Are you going to show 'em to-night? are you?"

"That is the intention, governor," replied the other, "and unless I'm much mistaken, Tommy Codlin is a calculating at this minute what we've lost through your coming upon us. Cheer up, Tommy, it can't be much."

The little man accompanied these latter words with a wink, expressive of the estimate he had formed of the travellers' finances.

To this Mr. Codlin, who had a surly, grumbling manner, replied, as he twitched Punch off the tombstone and flung him into the box,

"I don't care if we haven't lost a farden, but you're too free. If you stood in front of the curtain and see the public's faces as I do, you'd know human natur' better."

"Ah! it's been the spoiling of you, Tommy, your taking to that branch," rejoined his companion. "When you played the ghost in the reg'lar drama in the fairs, you believed in everything—except ghosts. But now you're a universal mistruster. *I* never see a man so changed."

"Never mind," said Mr. Codlin, with the air of a discontented philosopher. "I know better now, and p'raps I'm sorry for it."

Turning over the figures in the box like one who knew and despised them, Mr. Codlin drew one forth and held it up for the inspection of his friend:

"Look here; here's all this Judy's clothes falling to pieces again. You haven't got a needle and thread I suppose?"

The little man shook his head, and scratched it ruefully as he contemplated this severe indisposition of a principal performer. Seeing that they were at a loss, the child said timidly:

"I have a needle, Sir, in my basket, and thread too. Will you let me try to mend it for you? I think I can do it neater than you could."

Even Mr. Codlin had nothing to urge against a proposal so seasonable. Nelly, kneeling down beside the box, was soon busily engaged in her task, and accomplishing it to a miracle.

While she was thus engaged, the merry little man looked at her with an interest which did not appear to be diminished when he glanced at her helpless companion. When she had finished her work he thanked her, and inquired whither they were travelling.

" N—no further to-night, I think," said the child, looking towards her grandfather.

" If you're wanting a place to stop at," the man remarked, " I should advise you to take up at the same house with us. That's it—the long, low, white house there. It's very cheap."

The old man, notwithstanding his fatigue, would have remained in the churchyard all night if his new acquaintance had stayed there too. As he yielded to this suggestion a ready and rapturous assent, they all rose and walked away together; he keeping close to the box of puppets in which he was quite absorbed, the merry little man carrying it slung over his arm by a strap attached to it for the purpose, Nelly having hold of her grandfather's hand, and Mr. Codlin sauntering slowly behind, casting up at the church tower and neighboring trees such looks as he was accustomed in town-practice to direct to drawing-room and nursery windows, when seeking for a profitable spot on which to plant the show.

The public-house was kept by a fat old landlord and landlady who made no objection to receiving their new guests, but praised Nelly's beauty and were at once prepossessed in her behalf. There was no other company in the kitchen but the two showmen, and the child felt very thankful that they had fallen upon such good quarters. The landlady was very much astonished to learn that they had come all the way from London, and appeared to have no little curiosity touching their farther destination. The child parried her inquiries as well as she could, and with no great trouble, for finding that they appeared to give her pain, the old lady desisted.

" These two gentlemen have ordered supper in an hour's time," she said, taking her into the bar; "and your best plan will be to sup with them. Meantime you shall have a little taste of something that'll do you good, for I'm sure you must want it after all you've gone through to-day. Now, don't look after the old gentleman, because when you've drunk that, he shall have some too."

As nothing could induce the child to leave him alone, however, or to touch anything in which he was not the first and greatest sharer, the old lady was obliged to help him first. When they had been thus refreshed, the whole house hurried away into an empty stable where the show stood, and where, by the light of a few flaring candles stuck round a hoop which hung by a line from the ceiling, it was to be forthwith exhibited.

And now Mr. Thomas Codlin, the misanthrope, after blowing away at the Pan's pipes until he was intensely wretched, took his station on one side of the checked drapery which concealed the mover of the figures, and putting his hands in his pockets prepared to reply to all questions and remarks of Punch, and to make a dismal feint of being his most intimate private friend, of believing in him to the fullest and most unlimited extent, of knowing that he enjoyed day and night a merry and glorious existence in that temple, and that he was at all times and under every circumstance the same intelligent and joyful person that the spectators then beheld him. All this Mr. Codlin did with the air of a man who had made up his mind for the worst and was quite resigned; his eye slowly wandering about during the briskest rep- artee to observe the effect upon the audience, and par- ticularly the impression made upon the landlord and landlady, which might be productive of very important results in connection with the supper.

Upon this head, however, he had no cause for any anxiety, for the whole performance was applauded to the echo, and voluntary contributions were showered in with a liberality which testified yet more strongly to the gen- eral delight. Among the laughter none was more loud and frequent than the old man's. Nell's was unheard, for she, poor child, with her head drooping on his shoul- der, had fallen asleep, and slept too soundly to be roused by any of his efforts to awaken her to a participation in his glee.

The supper was very good, but she was too tired to eat, and yet would not leave the old man until she had kissed him in his bed. He, happily insensible to every care and anxiety, sat listening with a vacant smile and admiring face to all that his new friends said; and it was not until they retired yawning to their room, that he followed the child upstairs.

It was but a loft partitioned into two compartments, where they were to rest, but they were well pleased with their lodging and had hoped for none so good. The old man was uneasy when he had lain down, and begged that Nell would come and sit at his bedside as she had done for so many nights. She hastened to him, and sat there till he slept.

There was a little window, hardly more than a chink in the wall, in her room, and when she left him, she opened it, quite wondering at the silence. The sight of the old church and the graves about it in the moonlight, and the dark trees whispering among themselves, made her more thoughtful than before. She closed the window again, and sitting down upon the bed, thought of the life that was before them.

She had a little money, but it was very little, and when that was gone, they must begin to beg. There was one piece of gold among it, and an emergency might come when its worth to them would be increased a hundred fold. It would be best to hide this coin, and never produce it unless their case was absolutely desperate, and no other resource was left them.

Her resolution taken, she sewed the piece of gold into her dress, and going to bed with a lighter heart sank into a deep slumber.

CHAPTER THE SEVENTEENTH.

ANOTHER bright day shining in through the small casement, and claiming fellowship with the kindred eyes of the child, awoke her. At sight of the strange room and its unaccustomed objects she started up in alarm, wondering how she had been moved from the familiar chamber in which she seemed to have fallen asleep last night, and whither she had been conveyed. But another glance around called to her mind all that had lately passed, and she sprang from her bed, hoping and trustful.

It was yet early, and the old man being still asleep, she walked out into the churchyard, brushing the dew from the long grass with her feet, and often turning aside into places where it grew longer than in others, that she might not tread upon the graves. She felt a curious kind of pleasure in lingering among these houses of the dead, and read the inscriptions on the tombs of the good people (a great number of good people were buried there), passing on from one to another with increasing interest.

It was a very quiet place, as such a place should be, save for the cawing of the rooks who had built their nests among the branches of some tall old trees, and were calling to one another, high up in the air. First one sleek bird, hovering near his ragged house as it swung and dangled in the wind, uttered his hoarse cry, quite by chance as it would seem, and in a sober tone as though he were but talking to himself. Another answered, and he called again, but louder than before; then another spoke and then another; and each time the first, aggravated by contradiction, insisted on his case more strongly. Other voices, silent till now, struck in from boughs lower down and higher up and midway, and to the right and left, and from the tree-tops; and others, arriving hastily from the gray church turrets and old belfry window, joined the clamor which rose and fell, and swelled and dropped again, and still went on; and all this noisy contention amidst a skimming to and fro, and lighting on fresh branches, and frequent change of place, which satirized the old restlessness of those who lay so still beneath the moss and turf below, and the useless strife in which they had worn away their lives.

Frequently raising her eyes to the trees whence these sounds came down, and feeling as though they made the place more quiet than perfect silence would have done, the child loitered from grave to grave, now stopping to replace with careful hands the bramble which had started from some green mound it helped to keep in shape, and now peeping through one of the low latticed windows into the church, with its worm-eaten books upon the desks, and baize of whitened-green mouldering from the pew sides and leaving the naked wood to view. There were the seats where the poor old people sat, worn spare, and yellow like themselves; the rugged font where children had their names, the homely altar where they knelt in after life, the plain black tressels that bore their weight on their last visit to the cool old shady church. Everything told of long use and quiet slow decay ; the very bell-rope in the porch was frayed into a fringe, and hoary with old age.

She was looking at a humble stone which told of a young man who had died at twenty-three years old, fifty-five years ago, when she heard a faltering step approaching, and looking round saw a feeble woman bent with the weight of years, who tottered to the foot of that same grave and asked her to read the writing on the stone. The old woman thanked her when she had done, saying that she had had the words by heart for many a long, long year, but could not see them now.

" Were you his mother ? " said the child.

" I was his wife, my dear."

She the wife of a young man of three-and-twenty ! Ah, true ! It was fifty-five years ago.

" You wonder to hear me say that," remarked the old woman, shaking her head. " You're not the first. Older folk than you have wondered at the same thing before now. Yes, I was his wife. Death doesn't change us more than life, my dear."

" Do you come here often ? " asked the child.

" I sit here very often in the summer time," she answered ; " I used to come here once to cry and mourn, but that was a weary while ago, bless God !

" I pluck the daisies as they grow, and take them home," said the old woman after a short silence. " I like no flowers so well as these, and haven't for five-and-fifty year. It's a long time, and I'm getting very old ! "

Then growing garrulous upon a theme which was new to one listener though it were but a child, she told her how she had wept and moaned and prayed to die herself, when this happened ; and how when she first came to that place, a young creature strong in love and grief, she had hoped that her heart was breaking as it seemed to be. But that time passed by, and although she continued to be sad when she came there, still she could bear to come, and so went on until it was pain no longer, but a solemn pleasure, and a duty she had learned to like. And now that five-and-fifty years were gone, she spoke of the dead man as if he had been her son or grandson, with a kind of pity for his youth, growing out of her own old age, and an exalting of his strength and manly beauty as compared with her own weakness and decay; and yet she spoke about him as her husband too, and thinking of herself in connection with him, as she used to be and not as she was now, talked of their meeting in another world as if he were dead but yesterday, and she, separated from her former self, were thinking of the happiness of that comely girl who seemed to have died with him.

The child left her gathering the flowers that grew upon the grave, and thoughtfully retraced her steps.

The old man was by this time up and dressed. Mr. Codlin, still doomed to contemplate the harsh realities of existence, was packing among his linen the candle-ends which had been saved from the previous night's performance; while his companion received the compliments of all the loungers in the stable-yard, who, unable to separate him from the master-mind of Punch, set him down as next in importance to that merry outlaw, and loved him scarcely less. When he had sufficiently acknowledged his popularity he came in to breakfast, at which meal they all sat down together.

"And where are you going to-day?" said the little man, addressing himself to Nell.

"Indeed I hardly know,—we have not determined yet," replied the child.

"We're going on to the races," said the little man. "If that's your way and you like to have us for company, let us travel together. If you prefer going alone, only say the word and you'll find that we shan't trouble you."

"We'll go with you," said the old man, "Nell,—with them, with them."

The child considered for a moment, and reflecting that she must shortly beg, and could scarcely hope to do so at a better place than where crowds of rich ladies and gentlemen were assembled together for purposes of enjoyment and festivity, determined to accompany these men so far. She therefore thanked the little man for his offer, and said, glancing timidly towards his friend, that if there was no objection to their accompanying them as far as the race town—

" Objection ! " said the little man. " Now be gracious for once, Tommy, and say that you'd rather they went with us. I know you would. Be gracious, Tommy."

" Trotters," said Mr. Codlin, who talked very slowly and eat very greedily, as is not uncommon with philosophers and misanthropes ; " you're too free."

" Why, what harm can it do ? " urged the other.

" No harm at all in this particular case, perhaps," replied Mr. Codlin ; " but the principle's a dangerous one, and you're too free I tell you."

" Well, are they to go with us or not ? "

" Yes, they are," said Mr. Codlin ; " but you might have made a favor of it, mightn't you ? "

The real name of the little man was Harris, but it had gradually merged into the less euphonious one of Trotters, which, with the prefatory adjective, Short, had been conferred upon him by reason of the small size of his legs. Short Trotters, however, being a compound name, inconvenient of use in friendly dialogue, the gentleman on whom it had been bestowed was known among his intimates either as " Short," or " Trotters," and was seldom accosted at full length as Short Trotters, except in formal conversations and on occasions of ceremony.

Short, then, or Trotters, as the reader pleases, returned unto the remonstrance of his friend Mr. Thomas Codlin a jocose answer calculated to turn aside his discontent ; and applying himself with great relish to the cold boiled beef, the tea, and bread and butter, strongly impressed upon his companions that they should do the like. Mr. Codlin indeed required no such persuasion, as he had already eat as much as he could possibly carry and was now moistening his clay with strong ale, whereof he took deep draughts with a silent relish and invited nobody to partake,—thus again strongly indicating his misanthropical turn of mind.

Breakfast being at length over, Mr. Codlin called the bill, and charging the ale to the company generally (a practice also savoring of misanthropy) divided the sumtotal into two fair and equal parts, assigning one moiety to himself and friend, and the other to Nelly and her grandfather. These being duly discharged and all things ready for their departure, they took farewell of the landlord and landlady and resumed their journey.

And here Mr. Codlin's false position in society and the effect it wrought upon his wounded spirit, were strongly illustrated ; for whereas he had been last night accosted by Mr. Punch as "master," and had by inference left the audience to understand that he maintained that individual for his own luxurious entertainment and delight, here he was, now, painfully walking beneath the burden of that same Punch's temple, and bearing it bodily upon his shoulders on a sultry day and along a dusty road. In place of enlivening his patron with a constant fire of wit or the cheerful rattle of his quarter-staff on the heads of his relations and acquaintance, here was that beaming Punch utterly devoid of spine, all slack and drooping in a dark box, with his legs doubled up round his neck, and not one of his social qualities remaining.

Mr. Codlin trudged heavily on, exchanging a word or two at intervals with Short, and stopping to rest and growl occasionally. Short led the way ; with the flat box, the private luggage (which was not extensive) tied up in a bundle, and a brazen trumpet slung from his shoulder-blade. Nell and her grandfather walked next him on either hand, and Thomas Codlin brought up the rear.

When they came to any town or village, or even to a detached house of good appearance, Short blew a blast upon the brazen trumpet and carolled a fragment of a song in that hilarious tone common to Punches and their consorts. If people hurried to the windows, Mr. Codlin pitched the temple, and hastily unfurling the drapery and concealing Short therewith, flourished hysterically on the pipes and performed an air. Then the entertainment began as soon as might be ; Mr. Codlin having the responsibility of deciding on its length and of protracting or expediting the time for the hero's final triumph over the Enemy of mankind, according as he judged that the after-crop of half-pence would be plentiful or scant. When it had been gathered in to the last farthing, he resumed his load and on they went again.

Sometimes they played out the toll across a bridge or ferry, and once exhibited by particular desire at a turnpike, where the collector, being drunk in his solitude, paid down a shilling to have it to himself. There was one small place of rich promise in which their hopes were blighted, for a favorite character in the play having gold-

lace upon his coat and being a meddling wooden-headed
fellow was held to be a libel on the beadle, for which reason the authorities enforced a quick retreat; but they
were generally well received, and seldom left a town
without a troop of ragged children shouting at their
heels.

They made a long day's journey, despite these interruptions, and were yet upon the road when the moon was
shining in the sky. Short beguiled the time with songs
and jests, and made the best of everything that happened.
Mr. Codlin on the other hand, cursed his fate, and all the
hollow things of earth (but Punch especially), and limped
along with the theatre on his back, a prey to the bitterest
chagrin.

They had stopped to rest beneath a finger-post where
four roads met, and Mr. Codlin in his deep misanthropy
had let down the drapery and seated himself in the bottom of the show, invisible to mortal eyes and disdainful
of the company of his fellow-creatures, when two monstrous shadows were seen stalking towards them from a
turning in the road by which they had come. The child
was at first quite terrified by the sight of these gaunt
giants—for such they looked as they advanced with lofty
strides beneath the shadow of the trees—but Short, telling her there was nothing to fear, blew a blast upon the
trumpet, which was answered by a cheerful shout.

"It's Grinder's lot, an't it?" cried Mr. Short in a loud
key.

"Yes," replied a couple of shrill voices.

"Come on then," said Short. "Let's have a look at you.
I thought it was you."

Thus invited, "Grinder's lot" approached with re-
doubled speed and soon came up with the little party
Mr. Grinder's company, familiarly termed a lot, consisted
of a young gentleman and a young lady on stilts, and Mr.
Grinder himself, who used his natural legs for pedestrian
purposes and carried at his back a drum. The public
costume of the young people was of the Highland kind.
but the night being damp and cold, the young gentleman
wore over his kilt a man's pea jacket reaching to his
ankles, and a glazed hat; the young lady too was muffled
in an old cloth pelisse and had a handkerchief tied about
her head. Their Scotch bonnets, ornamented with plumes

of jet black feathers, Mr. Grinder carried on his instrument.

"Bound for the races, I see," said Mr. Grinder coming up out of breath. "So are we. How are you, Short?" With that they shook hands in a very friendly manner. The young people being too high up for the ordinary salutations, saluted Short after their own fashion. The young

gentleman twisted up his right stilt and patted him on the shoulder, and the young lady rattled her tambourine.

"Practice?" said Short, pointing to the stilts.

"No," returned Grinder. "It comes either to walkin' in 'em or carryin' of 'em, and they like walkin' in 'em best. It's wery pleasant for the prospects. Which road are you takin'? We go the nighest."

"Why, the fact is," said Short, "that we were going the longest way, because then we could stop for the night, a mile and a half on. But three or four mile gained to night is so many saved to-morrow, and if you keep on, 1 think our best way is to do the same."

"Where's your partner?" inquired Grinder.

"Here he is," cried Mr. Thomas Codlin, presenting his head and face in the proscenium of the stage, and exhibiting an expression of countenance not often seen there; "and he'll see *his* partner boiled alive before he'll go on to-night. That's what *he* says."

"Well, don't say such things as them, in a spear which is dewoted to something pleasanter," urged Short. "Respect associations, Tommy, even if you do cut up rough."

"Rough or smooth," said Mr. Codlin, beating his hand on the little footboard where Punch, when suddenly struck with the symmetry of his legs and their capacity for silk stockings, is accustomed to exhibit them to popular admiration, "rough or smooth, I won't go further than the mile and a half to-night. I put up at the Jolly Sandboys and nowhere else. If you like to come there, come there. If you like to go on by yourself, go on by yourself, and do without me if you can."

So saying, Mr. Codlin disappeared from the scene and immediately presented himself outside the theatre, took it on his shoulders at a jerk, and made off with most remarkable agility.

Any further controversy being now out of the question, Short was fain to part with Mr. Grinder and his pupils and to follow his morose companion. After lingering at the finger-post for a few minutes to see the stilts frisking away in the moonlight and the bearer of the drum toiling slowly after them, he blew a few notes upon the trumpet as a parting salute, and hastened with all speed to follow Mr. Codlin. With this view he gave his unoccupied hand to Nell, and bidding her to be of good cheer as they would soon be at the end of their journey for that night, and stimulating the old man with a similar assurance, led them at a pretty swift pace towards their destination, which he was the less unwilling to make for, as the moon was now overcast and the clouds were threatening rain.

CHAPTER THE EIGHTEENTH.

THE Jolly Sandboys was a small road-side inn of pretty ancient date, with a sign representing three Sandboys increasing their jollity with as many jugs of ale and bags of gold, creaking and swinging on its post on the opposite side of the road. As the travellers had observed that day many indications of their drawing nearer and nearer to the race town, such as gypsy camps, carts laden with gambling booths and their appurtenances, itinerant show-men of various kinds, and beggars and trampers of every degree, all wending their way in the same direction, Mr. Codlin was fearful of finding the accommodations fore-stalled ; this fear increasing as he diminished the dis-tance between himself and the hostelry, he quickened his pace, and notwithstanding the burden he had to carry, maintained a round trot until he reached the threshold. Here he had the gratification of finding that his fears were without foundation, for the landlord was leaning against the door-post looking lazily at the rain, which had by this time begun to descend heavily, and no tink-ling of cracked bell, nor boisterous shout, nor noisy chorus, gave note of company within.

" All alone ? " said Mr. Codlin, putting down his burden and wiping his forehead.

" All alone as yet," rejoined the landlord, glancing at the sky, " but we shall have more company to-night I expect. Here one of you boys, carry that show into the barn. Make haste in out of the wet, Tom ; when it came on to rain I told 'em to make the fire up, and there's a glorious blaze in the kitchen, I can tell you."

Mr. Codlin followed with a willing mind, and soon found that the landlord had not commended his prepara-tions without good reason. A mighty fire was blazing on the hearth and roaring up the wide chimney with a cheerful sound, which a large iron cauldron, bubbling and simmering in the heat, lent its pleasant aid to swell. There was a deep red ruddy blush upon the room, and when the landlord stirred the fire, sending the flames skipping and leaping up—when he took off the lid of the

iron pot and there rushed out a savory smell, while the
bubbling sound grew deeper and more rich, and an unctu-
ous steam came floating out, hanging in a delicious mist
above their heads—when he did this, Mr. Codlin's heart
was touched.   He sat down in the chimney-corner and
smiled.

Mr. Codlin sat smiling in the chimney-corner, eyeing
the landlord as with a roguish look he held the cover in
his hand, and, feigning that his doing so was needful to
the welfare of the cookery, suffered the delightful steam
to tickle the nostrils of his guest.   The glow of the fire

was upon the landlord's bald head, and upon his twinkling eye, and upon his watering mouth, and upon his pim-
pled face, and upon his round fat figure.   Mr. Codlin
drew his sleeve across his lips, and said in a murmuring
voice, "What is it?"

"It's a stew of tripe," said the landlord smacking his
lips, "and cow-heel," smacking them again, "and bacon,"
smacking them once more, "and steak," smacking them
for the fourth time, "and peas, cauliflowers, new potatoes,
and sparrow-grass, all working up together in one delicious gravy."   Having come to the climax, he smacked

his lips a great many times, and taking a long hearty sniff of the fragrance that was hovering about, put on the cover again with the air of one whose toils on earth were over.

"At what time will it be ready?" asked Mr. Codlin faintly.

"It'll be done to a turn," said the landlord looking up at the clock—and the very clock had a color in its fat white face, and looked a clock for Jolly Sandboys to consult—"it'll be done to a turn at twenty-two minutes before eleven."

"Then," said Mr. Codlin, "fetch me a pint of warm ale, and don't let anybody bring into the room even so much as a biscuit till the time arrives."

Nodding his approval of this decisive and manly course of procedure, the landlord retired to draw the beer, and presently returning with it, applied himself to warm the same in a small tin vessel shaped funnel-wise, for the convenience of sticking it far down in the fire and getting at the bright places. This was soon done, and he handed it over to Mr. Codlin with that creamy froth upon the surface which is one of the happy circumstances attendant upon mulled malt.

Greatly softened by this soothing beverage, Mr. Codlin now bethought him of his companions, and acquainted mine host of the Sandboys that their arrival might be shortly looked for. The rain was rattling against the windows and pouring down in torrents, and such was Mr. Codlin's extreme amiability of mind, that he more than once expressed his earnest hope that they would not be so foolish as to get wet.

At length they arrived, drenched with the rain and presenting a most miserable appearance, notwithstanding that Short had sheltered the child as well as he could under the skirts of his own coat, and they were nearly breathless from the haste they had made. But their steps were no sooner heard upon the road than the landlord, who had been at the outer door anxiously watching for their coming, rushed into the kitchen and took the cover off. The effect was electrical. They all came in with smiling faces, though the wet was dripping from their clothes upon the floor, and Short's first remark was, "What a delicious smell!"

It is not very difficult to forget rain and mud by the side of a cheerful fire, and in a bright room. They were furnished with slippers and such dry garments as the house or their own bundles afforded, and ensconcing themselves, as Mr. Codlin had already done, in the warm chimney-corner, soon forgot their late troubles or only remembered them as enhancing the delights of the present time. Overpowered by the warmth and comfort and the fatigue they had undergone, Nelly and the old man had not long taken their seats here, when they fell asleep.

"Who are they?" whispered the landlord.

Short shook his head, and wished he knew himself.

"Don't *you* know?" asked the host, turning to Mr. Codlin.

"Not I," he replied. "They're no good, I suppose."

"They're no harm," said Short. "Depend upon that. I tell you what—it's plain that the old man an't in his right mind—"

"If you haven't got anything newer than that to say," growled Mr. Codlin, glancing at the clock, "you'd better let us fix our minds upon the supper, and not disturb us."

"Hear me out, won't you?" retorted his friend. "It's very plain to me, besides, that they're not used to this way of life. Don't tell me that that handsome child has been in the habit of prowling about as she's done these last two or three days. I know better."

"Well, who *does* tell you she has?" growled Mr. Codlin, again glancing at the clock and from it to the cauldron, "can't you think of anything more suitable to present circumstances than saying things and then contradicting 'em?"

"I wish somebody would give you your supper," returned Short, "for there'll be no peace till you've got it. Have you seen how anxious the old man is to get on—always wanting to be furder away—furder away. Have you seen that?"

"Ah! what then?" muttered Thomas Codlin.

"This, then," said Short. "He has given his friends the slip. Mind what I say,—he has given his friends the slip, and persuaded this delicate young creetur all along of her fondness for him to be his guide and travelling companion—where to, he knows no more than the Man in the Moon. Now, I'm not a-going to stand that."

" *You're* not a-going to stand that!" cried Mr. Codlin, glancing at the clock again and pulling his hair with both hands in a kind of frenzy, but whether occasioned by his companion's observation or the tardy pace of Time, it was difficult to determine. "Here's a world to live in!"

"I," repeated Short emphatically and slowly, "am not a-going to stand it. I am not a-going to see this fair young child a-falling into bad hands, and getting among people that she's no more fit for, than they are to get among angels as their ordinary chums. Therefore when they dewelop an intention of parting company from us, I shall take measures for detaining of 'em, and restoring 'em to their friends, who I dare say have had their disconsolation pasted up on every wall in London by this time."

"Short," said Mr. Codlin, who with his head upon his hands, and his elbows on his knees, had been shaking himself impatiently from side to side up to this point and occasionally stamping on the ground, but who now looked up with eager eyes; "it's possible that there may be uncommon good sense in what you've said. If there is, and there should be a reward, Short, remember that we're partners in everything!"

His companion had only time to nod a brief assent to this position, for the child awoke at the instant. They had drawn close together during the previous whispering, and how hastily separated and were rather awkwardly endeavoring to exchange some casual remarks in their usual tone, when strange footsteps were heard without, and fresh company entered.

These were no other than four very dismal dogs, who came pattering in one after the other, headed by an old bandy dog of particularly mournful aspect, who, stopping when the last of his followers had got as far as the door, erected himself upon his hind legs and looked round at his companions, who immediately stood upon their hind legs, in a grave and melancholy row. Nor was this the only remarkable circumstance about these dogs, for each of them wore a kind of little coat of some gaudy color trimmed with tarnished spangles, and one of them had a cap upon his head, tied very carefully under his chin, which had fallen down upon his nose and completely obscured one eye; add to this, that the gaudy coats were

all wet through and discolored with rain, and that the
wearers were splashed and dirty, and some idea may be
formed of the unusual appearance of these new visitors
to the Jolly Sandboys.

Neither Short nor the landlord nor Thomas Codlin,
however, were the least surprised, merely remarking that
these were Jerry's dogs and that Jerry could not be far
behind. So there the dogs stood, patiently winking and
gaping and looking extremely hard at the boiling pot,
until Jerry himself appeared, when they all dropped down
at once and walked about the room in their natural
manner. This posture it must be confessed did not much
improve their appearance, as their own personal tails and
their coat tails—both capital things in their way—did
not agree together.

Jerry, the manager of these dancing dogs, was a tall
black-whiskered man in a velveteen coat, who seemed
well known to the landlord and his guests and accosted
them with great cordiality. Disencumbering himself of
a barrel-organ which he placed upon a chair, and retaining in his hand a small whip wherewith to awe his company of comedians, he came up to the fire to dry himself,
and entered into conversation.

"Your people don't usually travel in character, do
they?" said Short, pointing to the dresses of the dogs.
"It must come expensive if they do?"

"No," replied Jerry, "no, it's not the custom with us.
But we've been playing a little on the road to-day, and
we come out with a new wardrobe at the races, so I
didn't think it worth while to stop to undress. Down,
Pedro!"

This was addressed to the dog with the cap on, who
being a new member of the company and not quite certain
of his duty, kept his unobscured eye anxiously on his
master, and was perpetually starting upon his hind legs
when there was no occasion, and falling down again.

"I've got a animal here," said Jerry, putting his hand
into the capacious pocket of his coat, and diving into one
corner as if he were feeling for a small orange or an apple
or some such article, "a animal here, wot I think you
know something of, Short."

"Ah!" cried Short, "let's have a look at him."

"Here he is," said Jerry, producing a little terrier from

his pocket. "He was once a Toby of yours, warn't he!"

In some versions of the great drama of Punch there is a small dog—a modern innovation—supposed to be the private property of that gentleman, whose name is always Toby. This Toby has been stolen in youth from another gentleman, and fraudulently sold to the confiding hero, who having no guile himself has no suspicion that it lurks in others; but Toby, entertaining a grateful recollection of his old master, and scorning to attach himself to any new patrons, not only refuses to smoke a pipe at the bidding of Punch, but to mark his old fidelity more strongly, seizes him by the nose and wrings the same with violence, at which instance of canine attachment the spectators are deeply affected. This was the character which the little terrier in question had once sustained; if there had been any doubt upon the subject he would speedily have resolved it by his conduct; for not only did he, on seeing Short, give the strongest tokens of recognition, but catching sight of the flat-box he barked so furiously at the pasteboard nose which he knew was inside, that his master was obliged to gather him up and put him into his pocket again, to the great relief of the whole company.

The landlord now busied himself in laying the cloth, in which process Mr. Codlin obligingly assisted by setting forth his own knife and fork in the most convenient place and establishing himself behind them. When everything was ready, the landlord took off the cover for the last time, and then indeed there burst forth such a goodly promise of supper, that if he had offered to put it on again or had hinted at postponement, he would certainly have been sacrificed on his own hearth.

However, he did nothing of the kind, but instead thereof assisted a stout servant girl in turning the contents of the cauldron into a large tureen; a proceeding which the dogs, proof against various hot splashes which fell upon their noses, watched with terrible eagerness. At length the dish was lifted on the table, and mugs of ale having been previously set round, little Nell ventured to say grace, and supper began.

At this juncture the poor dogs were standing on their hind legs quite surprisingly; the child, having pity on

them, was about to cast some morsels of food to them
before she tasted it herself, hungry though she was, when
their master interposed.

" No, my dear, no, not an atom from anybody's hand
but mine if you please. That dog," said Jerry, pointing
out the old leader of the troop, and speaking in a terrible
voice, " lost a halfpenny to-day. *He* goes without his
supper."

The unfortunate creature dropped upon his fore-legs
directly, wagged his tail, and looked imploringly at his
master.

" You must be more careful, Sir," said Jerry, walking
coolly to the chair where he had placed the organ, and
setting the stop. " Come here. Now, Sir, you play away
at that, while we have supper, and leave off if you dare."

The dog immediately began to grind most mournful
music. His master having shown him the whip resumed
his seat and called up the others, who, at his directions,
formed in a row, standing upright as a file of soldiers.

" Now, gentlemen," said Jerry, looking at them attentively. " The dog whose name's called, eats. The dogs
whose names an't called, keep quiet. Carlo ! "

The lucky individual whose name was called, snapped
up the morsel thrown towards him, but none of the others
moved a muscle. In this manner they were fed at the
discretion of their master. Meanwhile the dog in disgrace ground hard at the organ, sometimes in quick time,
sometimes in slow, but never leaving off for an instant.
When the knives and forks rattled very much, or any of
his fellows got an unusually large piece of fat, he accompanied the music with a short howl, but he immediately
checked it on his master looking round, and applied himself with increased diligence to the Old Hundredth.

CHAPTER THE NINETEENTH.

Supper was not yet over, when there arrived at the
Jolly Sandboys two more travellers bound for the same
haven as the rest, who had been walking in the rain for
some hours, and came in shining and heavy with water.
One of these was the proprietor of a giant, and a little
lady without legs or arms, who had jogged forward in a

van ; the other, a silent gentleman who earned his living by showing tricks upon the cards, and who had rather deranged the natural expression of his countenance by putting small leaden lozenges into his eyes and bringing them out at his mouth, which was one of his professional accomplishments. The name of the first of these new-comers was Vuffin ; the other, probably as a pleasant satire upon his ugliness, was called Sweet William. To render them as comfortable as he could, the landlord bestirred himself nimbly, and in a very short time both gentlemen were perfectly at their ease.

" How's the Giant ? " said Short, when they all sat smok-ing round the fire.

" Rather weak upon his legs," returned Mr. Vuffin. " I begin to be afraid he's going at the knees."

" That's a bad look-out," said Short.

" Ay! Bad indeed," replied Mr. Vuffin, contemplating the fire with a sigh. " Once get a giant shaky on his legs, and the public care no more about him than they do for a dead cabbage-stalk."

" What becomes of the old giants?" said Short, turning to him again after a little reflection.

" They're usually kept in carawans to wait upon the dwarfs," said Mr. Vuffin.

" The maintaining of 'em must come expensive, when they can't be shown, eh?" remarked Short, eyeing him doubtfully.

" It's better that, than letting 'em go upon the parish or about the streets," said Mr. Vuffin. " Once make a giant common and giants will never draw again. Look at wooden legs. If there was only one man with a wooden leg what a property *he'd* be ! "

" So he would ! " observed the landlord and Short both together. " That's very true."

" Instead of which," pursued Mr. Vuffin, " if you was to advertise Shakespeare played entirely by wooden legs, it's my belief you wouldn't draw a sixpence."

" I don't suppose you would," said Short. And the land-lord said so too.

" This shows, you see," said Mr. Vuffin, waving his pipe with an argumentative air, " this shows the policy of keep-ing the used-up giants still in the carawans, where they get food and lodging for nothing, all their lives, and in general very glad they are to stop there. There was one giant—a black 'un—as left his carawan some year ago and took to carrying coach-bills about London, making himself as cheap as crossing-sweepers. He died. I make no insinuation against anybody in particular," said Mr. Vuffin, lookingly solemnly round, "but he was ruining the trade;—and he died."

The landlord drew his breath hard, and looked at the

owner of the dogs, who nodded and said gruffly that *he* remembered.

"I know you do, Jerry," said Mr. Vuffin with profound meaning. "I know you remember it, Jerry, and the universal opinion was, that it served him right. Why, I remember the time when old Maunders as had three-and-twenty wans—I remember the time when old Maunders had in his cottage in Spa Fields in the winter time when the season was over, eight male and female dwarfs setting down to dinner every day, who was waited on by eight old giants in green coats, red smalls, blue cotton stockings, and high-lows: and there was one dwarf as had grown elderly and wicious who whenever his giant wasn't quick enough to please him, used to stick pins in his legs, not being able to reach up any higher. I know that's a fact, for Maunders told it to me himself."

" What about the dwarfs, when *they* get old?" inquired the landlord.

" The older a dwarf is, the better worth he is," returned Mr. Vuffin; "a gray-headed dwarf, well wrinkled, is beyond all suspicion. But a giant weak in the legs and not standing upright!—keep him in the carawan, but never show him, never show him, for any persuasion that can be offered."

While Mr. Vuffin and his two friends smoked their pipes and beguiled the time with such conversation as this, the silent gentleman sat in a warm corner, swallowing, or seeming to swallow, sixpennyworth of halfpence for practice, balancing a feather upon his nose, and rehearsing other feats of dexterity of that kind, without paying any regard whatever to the company, who in their turn left him utterly unnoticed. At length the weary child prevailed upon her grandfather to retire, and they withdrew, leaving the company yet seated round the fire, and the dogs fast asleep at a humble distance.

After bidding the old man good-night, Nell retired to her poor garret, but had scarcely closed the door, when it was gently tapped at. She opened it directly, and was a little startled by the sight of Mr. Thomas Codlin, whom she had left, to all appearance, fast asleep downstairs.

" What is the matter?" said the child.

" Nothing's the matter, my dear," returned her visitor. "I'm your friend. Perhaps you haven't thought so, but it's me that's your friend—not him."

" Not who?" the child inquired.

" Short, my dear. I tell you what," said Codlin, "for all his having a kind of way with him that you'd be very apt to like, I'm the real, open-hearted man. I mayn't look it, but I am indeed."

The child began to be alarmed, considering that the ale had taken effect upon Mr. Codlin, and that this commendation of himself was the consequence.

" Short's very well, and seems kind," resumed the misanthrope, " but he overdoes it. Now I don't."

Certainly if there were any fault in Mr. Codlin's usual deportment, it was that he rather underdid his kindness to those about him, than overdid it. But the child was puzzled, and could not tell what to say.

" Take my advice," said Codlin ; " don't ask me why, but take it. As long as you travel with us, keep as near me as you can. Don't offer to leave us—not on any account—but always stick to me and say that I'm your friend. Will you bear that in mind, my dear, and always say that it was me that was your friend ?"

" Say so where—and when ?" inquired the child innocently.

" Oh, nowhere in particular," replied Codlin, a little put out as it seemed by the question ; " I'm only anxious that you should think me so, and do me justice. You can't think what an interest I have in you. Why didn't you tell me your little history—that about you and the poor old gentleman ? I'm the best adviser that ever was, and *so* interested in you—so much more interested than Short. I think they're breaking up downstairs ; you needn't tell Short, you know, that we've had this little talk together. God bless you. Recollect the friend. Codlin's the friend, not Short. Short's very well as far as he goes, but the real friend is Codlin—not Short."

Eking out these professions with a number of benevolent and protecting looks and great fervor of manner, Thomas Codlin stole away on tiptoe, leaving the child in a state of extreme surprise. She was still ruminating upon his curious behavior, when the floor of the crazy stairs and landing cracked beneath the tread of the other travellers who were passing to their beds. When they had all passed, and the sound of their footsteps had died away, one of them returned, and after a little hesitation and rustling in the passage, as if he were doubtful what door to knock at, knocked at hers.

" Yes ?" said the child from within.

" It's me—Short "—a voice called through the keyhole. " I only wanted to say that we must be off early to-morrow morning, my dear, because unless we get the start of the dogs and the conjurer, the villages won't be worth a penny. You'll be sure to be stirring early and go with us? I'll call you."

The child answered in the affirmative, and returning his "good-night" heard him creep away. She felt some uneasiness at the anxiety of these men, increased by the recollection of their whispering together downstairs and their slight confusion when she awoke, nor was she quite free from a misgiving that they were not the fittest companions she could have stumbled on. Her uneasiness, however, was nothing, weighed against her fatigue; and she soon forgot it in sleep.

Very early next morning Short fulfilled his promise, and knocking softly at her door, entreated that she would get up directly, as the proprietor of the dogs was still snoring, and if they lost no time they might get a good deal in advance both of him and the conjurer, who was talking in his sleep, and from what he could be heard to say, appeared to be balancing a donkey in his dreams. She started from her bed without delay, and roused the old man with so much expedition that they were both ready as soon as Short himself, to that gentleman's unspeakable gratification and relief.

After a very unceremonious and scrambling breakfast, of which the staple commodities were bacon and bread, and beer, they took leave of the landlord and issued from the door of the Jolly Sandboys. The morning was fine and warm, the ground cool to the feet after the late rain, the hedges gayer and more green, the air clear, and everything fresh and healthful. Surrounded by these influences, they walked on pleasantly enough.

They had not gone very far, when the child was again struck by the altered behavior of Mr. Thomas Codlin, who instead of plodding on sulkily by himself as he had theretofore done, kept close to her, and when he had an opportunity of looking at her unseen by his companion, warned her by certain wry faces and jerks of the head not to put any trust in Short, but to reserve all confidence for Codlin. Neither did he confine himself to looks and gestures, for when she and her grandfather were walking on beside the aforesaid Short, and that little man was talking with his accustomed cheerfulness on a variety of indifferent subjects, Thomas Codlin testified his jealousy and distrust by following close at her heels, and occasionally admonishing her ankles with the legs of the theatre in a very abrupt and painful manner.

All these proceedings naturally made the child more watchful and suspicious, and she soon observed that whenever they halted to perform outside a village ale-house or other place, Mr. Codlin while he went through his share of the entertainments kept his eye steadily upon her and the old man, or with a show of great friend-ship and consideration invited the latter to lean upon his arm, and so held him tight until the representation was over and they again went forward. Even Short seemed to change in this respect, and to mingle with his good-nature something of a desire to keep them in safe custody. This increased the child's misgivings, and made her yet more anxious and uneasy.

Meanwhile, they were drawing near the town where the races were to begin next day; for, from passing numerous groups of gypsies and trampers on the road, wending their way towards it, and straggling out from every by-way, and cross-country lane, they gradually fell into a stream of people, some walking by the side of covered carts, others with horses, others with donkeys, others toiling on with heavy loads upon their backs, but all tending to the same point. The public-houses by the wayside, from being empty and noiseless as those in the remoter parts had been, now sent out boisterous shouts and clouds of smoke; and, from the misty windows, clusters of broad red faces looked down upon the road. On every piece of waste or common ground, some small gambler drove his noisy trade, and bellowed to the idle passers-by to stop and try their chance; the crowd grew thicker and more noisy; gilt gingerbread in blanket-stalls exposed its glories to the dust; and often a four-horse carriage, dashing by, obscured all objects in the gritty cloud it raised, and left them, stunned and blinded, far behind.

It was dark before they reached the town itself, and long indeed the few last miles had been. Here all was tumult and confusion; the streets were filled with throngs of people—many strangers were there, it seemed, by the looks they cast about—the church-bells rang out their noisy peals, and flags streamed from windows and house-tops. In the large inn-yards waiters flitted to and fro and ran against each other, horses clattered on the uneven stones, carriage steps fell rattling down, and sickening smells from many dinners came in a heavy lukewarm breath upon the sense. In the smaller public-houses, fiddles with all their might and main were squeaking out the tune to staggering feet; drunken men, oblivious of the burden of their song, joined in a senseless howl, which drowned the tinkling of the feeble bell and made them savage for their drink; vagabond groups assembled round the doors to see the stroller woman dance, and add their uproar to the shrill flageolet and deafening drum.

Through this delirious scene the child, frightened and repelled by all she saw, led on her bewildered charge, clinging close to her conductor, and trembling lest in the press she should be separated from him and left to find her way alone. Quickening their steps to get clear of all the roar and riot, they at length passed through the town and made for the race-course, which was upon an open heath, situated on an eminence, a full mile distant from its furthest bounds.

Although there were many people here, none of the best favored or best clad, busily erecting tents and driving stakes into the ground, and hurrying to and fro with dusty feet and many a grumbled oath—although there were tired children cradled on heaps of straw between the wheels of carts, crying themselves to sleep—and poor lean horses and donkeys just turned loose, grazing among the men and women, and pots and kettles, and half-lighted fires, and ends of candles flaring and wasting in the air —for all this, the child felt it an escape from the town and drew her breath more freely. After a scanty supper, the purchase of which reduced her little stock so low, that she had only a few halfpence with which to buy a break-fast on the morrow, she and the old man lay down to rest in a corner of a tent, and slept, despite the busy prepara-tions that were going on around them all night long.

And now they had come to the time when they must beg their bread. Soon after sunrise in the morning she stole out from the tent, and rambling into some fields at a short distance, plucked a few wild roses and such humble flowers, proposing to make them into little nose-gays and offer them to the ladies in the carriages when the company arrived. Her thoughts were not idle

12

while she was thus employed; when she returned and was seated beside the old man in one corner of the tent, tying her flowers together, while the two men lay dozing in another corner, she plucked him by the sleeve, and slightly glancing towards them, said in a low voice—

"Grandfather, don't look at those I talk of, and don't seem as if I spoke of anything but what I am about. What was that you told me before we left the old house? That if they knew what we were going to do, they would say that you were mad, and part us?"

The old man turned to her with an aspect of wild

terror; but she checked him by a look, and bidding him hold some flowers while she tied them up, and so bringing her lips closer to his ear, said—

"I know that was what you told me. You needn't speak, dear. I recollect it very well. It was not likely that I should forget it. Grandfather, these men suspect that we have secretly left our friends, and mean to carry us before some gentleman and have us taken care of and sent back. If you let your hand tremble so, we can never get away from them, but if you're only quiet now, we shall do so, easily."

"How?" muttered the old man. "Dear Nelly, how? They will shut me up in a stone room, dark and cold, and chain me up to the wall, Nell—flog me with whips, and never let me see thee more!"

"You're trembling again," said the child. "Keep close to me all day. Never mind them, don't look at them, but me. I shall find a time when we can steal away. When I do, mind you come with me, and do not stop or speak a word. Hush! That's all."

"Halloa! what are you up to, my dear?" said Mr. Codlin, raising his head, and yawning. Then observing that his companion was fast asleep, he added in an earnest whisper, "Codlin's the friend, remember—not Short."

"Making some nosegays," the child replied; "I am going to try and sell some, these three days of the races. Will you have one—as a present I mean?"

Mr. Codlin would have risen to receive it, but the child hurried towards him and placed it in his hand. He stuck it in his buttonhole with an air of ineffable complacency for a misanthrope, and leering exultingly at the unconscious Short, muttered, as he laid himself down again, "Tom Codlin's the friend by G—!"

As the morning wore on, the tents assumed a gayer and more brilliant appearance, and long lines of carriages came rolling softly on the turf. Men who had lounged about all night in smockfrocks and leather leggings, came out in silken vests and hats and plumes, as jugglers or mountebanks; or in gorgeous liveries as soft-spoken servants at gambling booths; or in sturdy yeoman dress as decoys at unlawful games. Black-eyed gypsy girls, hooded in showy handkerchiefs, sallied forth to tell fortunes, and pale slender women with consumptive faces lingered upon the footsteps of ventriloquists and conjurers, and counted the sixpences with anxious eyes long before they were gained. As many of the children as could be kept within bounds, were stowed away, with all the other signs of dirt and poverty, among the donkeys, carts, and horses; and as many as could not be thus disposed of ran in and out in all intricate spots, crept between people's legs and carriage wheels, and came forth unharmed from under horse's hoofs. The dancing-dogs, the stilts, the little lady and the tall man, and all the other attractions, with organs out of number and bands innumerable, emerged from the holes and corners in which they had passed the night and flourished boldly in the sun.

Along the uncleared course, Short led his party, sounding the brazen trumpet and revelling in the voice of Punch; and at his heels went Thomas Codlin, bearing the show as usual, and keeping his eye on Nelly and her grandfather, as they rather lingered in the rear. The child bore upon her arm the little basket with her flowers, and sometimes stopped, with timid and modest looks, to offer them at some gay carriage; but alas! there were many bolder beggars there, gypsies who promised husbands, and other adepts in their trade, and although some ladies smiled gently as they shook their heads, and others cried to the gentlemen beside them "See, what a pretty face!" they let the pretty face pass on, and never thought that it looked tired or hungry.

There was but one lady who seemed to understand the child, and she was one who sat alone in a handsome carriage, while two young men in dashing clothes, who had just dismounted from it, talked and laughed loudly at a little distance, appearing to forget her, quite. There were many ladies all around, but they turned their backs, or looked another way, or at the young men (not unfavorably at *them*), and left her to herself. She motioned away a gypsy-woman urgent to tell her fortune, saying that it was told already and had been for some years, but called the child towards her, and taking her flowers put money into her trembling hand, and bade her go home and keep at home for God's sake.

Many a time they went up and down those long, long lines, seeing everything but the horses and the race; when the bell rang to clear the course, going back to rest among the carts and donkeys, and not coming out again until the heat was over. Many a time, too, was Punch displayed in the full zenith of his humor, but all this while the eye of Thomas Codlin was upon them, and to escape without notice was impracticable.

At length, late in the day, Mr. Codlin pitched the show in a convenient spot, and spectators were soon in the very triumph of the scene. The child, sitting down with the old man close behind it, had been thinking how strange it was that horses who were such fine honest creatures should seem to make vagabonds of all the men they drew about them, when a loud laugh at some extemporaneous witticism of Mr. Short's, having allusion to the circumstances of the day, roused her from her meditation and caused her to look around.

If they were ever to get away unseen, that was the very moment. Short was plying the quarter-stave vigorously and knocking the characters in the fury of the combat against the sides of the show, the people were looking on with laughing faces, and Mr. Codlin had relaxed into a grim smile as his roving eye detected hands going into waistcoat pockets and groping secretly for sixpences. If they were ever to get away unseen, that was the very moment. They seized it, and fled.

They made a path through booths and carriages and throngs of people, and never once stopped to look behind. The bell was ringing and the course was cleared by the time they reached the ropes, but they dashed across it insensible to the shouts and screeching that assailed them for breaking in upon its sanctity, and creeping under the brow of the hill at a quick pace, made for the open fields.

CHAPTER THE TWENTIETH.

DAY after day as he bent his steps homeward, returning from some new effort to procure employment, Kit raised his eyes to the window of the little room he had so much commended to the child, and hoped to see some indication of her presence. His own earnest wish, coupled with the assurance he had received from Quilp, filled him with the belief that she would yet arrive to claim the humble shelter he had offered, and from the death of each day's hope, another hope sprang up to live to-morrow.

"I think they must certainly come to-morrow, eh, mother?" said Kit, laying aside his hat with a weary air and sighing as he spoke. "They have been gone a week. They surely couldn't stop away more than a week, could they now?"

The mother shook her head, and reminded him how often he had been disappointed already.

"For the matter of that," said Kit, "you speak true and sensible enough, as you always do, mother. Still, I do consider that a week is quite long enough for 'em to be rambling about; don't you say so?"

"Quite long enough, Kit, longer than enough, but they may not come back for all that."

Kit was for a moment disposed to be vexed by this contradiction, and not the less so from having anticipated it in his own mind and knowing how just it was. But the impulse was only momentary, and the vexed look became a kind one before it had crossed the room.

"Then what do you think, mother, has become of 'em? You don't think they've gone to sea, anyhow?"

"Not gone for sailors, certainly," returned the mother with a smile. "But I can't help thinking they have gone to some foreign country."

"I say," cried Kit with a rueful face, "don't talk like that, mother."

"I am afraid they have, and that's the truth," she said. "It's the talk of all the neighbors, and there are some even that know of their having been seen on board ship, and can tell you the name of the place they've gone to, which is more than I can, my dear, for it's a very hard one."

"I don't believe it," said Kit. "Not a word of it. A set of idle chatterboxes, how should they know!"

"They may be wrong of course," returned the mother, "I can't tell about that, though I don't think it's at all unlikely that they're in the right, for the talk is that the old gentleman had put by a little money that nobody knew of, not even that ugly little man you talk to me about—what's his name—Quilp; and that he and Miss Nell have gone to live abroad where it can't be taken from them, and they will never be disturbed. That don't seem very far out of the way now, do it?"

Kit scratched his head mournfully, in reluctant admission that it did not, and clambering to the old nail took down the cage and set himself to clean it and to feed the bird. His thoughts reverting from his occupation to the little old gentleman who had given him the shilling, he suddenly recollected that that was the very day—nay, nearly the very hour in which the little old gentleman had said he should be at the notary's house again. He no sooner remembered this, than he hung up the cage with great precipitation, and hastily explaining the nature of his errand, went off at full speed to the appointed place.

It was some two minutes after the time when he reached the spot, which was a considerable distance from his home, but by great good luck the little old gentleman had not yet arrived; at least there was no pony-chaise to be seen, and it was not likely that he had come and gone again in so short a space. Greatly relieved to find that he was not too late, Kit leant against a lamp-post to take breath, and waited the advent of the pony and his charge.

Sure enough, before long the pony came trotting round the corner of the street, looking as obstinate as a pony might, and picking his steps as if he were spying about for the cleanest places and would by no means dirty his feet or hurry himself inconveniently. Behind the pony sat the little old gentleman, and by the old gentleman's side sat the little old lady, carrying just such a nosegay as she had brought before.

The old gentleman, the old lady, the pony, and the chaise, came up the street in perfect unanimity, until they arrived within some half a dozen doors of the notary's house, when the pony, deceived by a brass-plate beneath a tailor's knocker, came to a halt, and maintained by a sturdy silence, that that was the house they wanted.

" Now, Sir, will you have the goodness to go on ; this is *not* the place," said the old gentleman.

The pony looked with great attention into a fire-plug which was near him, and appeared to be quite absorbed in contemplating it.

" Oh dear, such a naughty Whisker ! " cried the old lady. " After being so good too, and coming along so well! I am quite ashamed of him. I don't know what we are to do with him, I really don't."

The pony having thoroughly satisfied himself as to the nature and properties of the fire-plug, looked into the air after his old enemies the flies, and as there happened to be one of them tickling his ear at that moment he shook his head and whisked his tail, after which he appeared full of thought but quite comfortable and collected. The old gentleman having exhausted his powers of persuasion, alighted to lead him ; whereupon the pony, perhaps because he held this to be a sufficient concession, perhaps because he happened to catch sight of the other brass-plate, or perhaps because he was in a spiteful humor, darted off with the old lady and stopped at the right house, leaving the old gentleman to come panting on behind.

It was then that Kit presented himself at the pony's head, and touched his hat with a smile.

" Why, bless me," cried the old gentleman, " the lad *is* here ! My dear, do you see ?"

" I said I'd be here, Sir," said Kit, patting Whisker's neck. " I hope you've had a pleasant ride, Sir. He's a very nice little pony."

" My dear," said the old gentleman. " This is an uncommon lad, a good lad, I'm sure."

" I'm sure he is," rejoined the old lady. " A very good lad, and I am sure he is a good son."

Kit acknowledged these expressions of confidence by touching his hat again and blushing very much. The old gentleman then handed the old lady out, and after looking at him with an approving smile, they went into the house—talking about him as they went, Kit could not help feeling. Presently Mr. Witherden, smelling very hard at the nosegay, came to the window and looked at him, and after that Mr. Abel came and looked at him, and after that the old gentleman and lady came and looked at him again, and after that they all came and looked at him together, which Kit, feeling very much embarrassed by, made a pretence of not observing. Therefore he patted the pony more and more; and this liberty the pony most handsomely permitted.

The faces had not disappeared from the window many moments, when Mr. Chuckster in his official coat, and with his hat hanging on his head just as it happened to fall from its peg, appeared upon the pavement, and telling him he was wanted inside, bade him go in and he would mind the chaise the while. In giving him this direction Mr. Chuckster remarked that he wished he might be blessed if he could make out whether he (Kit) was " precious raw " or " precious deep," but intimated by a distrustful shake of the head, that he inclined to the latter opinion.

Kit entered the office in a great tremor, for he was not used to going among strange ladies and gentlemen, and the tin boxes and bundles of dusty papers had in his eyes

an awful and venerable air. Mr. Witherden too was a
bustling gentleman who talked loud and fast, and all eyes
were upon him, and he was very shabby.

"Well, boy," said Mr. Witherden, "you came to work
out that shilling;—not to get another, hey?"

"No indeed, Sir," replied Kit, taking courage to look
up. "I never thought of such a thing."

"Father alive?" said the notary.

"Dead, Sir."

"Mother?"

"Yes, Sir."

"Married again—eh?"

Kit made answer, not without some indignation, that
she was a widow with three children, and that as to her
marrying again, if the gentleman knew her he wouldn't
think of such a thing. At this reply Mr. Witherden buried
his nose in the flowers again, and whispered behind the
nosegay to the old gentleman that he believed the lad was
as honest a lad as need be.

"Now," said Mr. Garland when they had made some
further inquiries of him, " I am not going to give you anything—"

"Thank you, Sir," Kit replied; and quite seriously too,
for this announcement seemed to free him from the suspicion which the notary had hinted.

"—But," resumed the old gentleman, " perhaps I may
want to know something more about you, so tell me where
you live and I'll put it down in my pocket-book."

Kit told him, and the old gentleman wrote down the
address with his pencil. He had scarcely done so, when
there was a great uproar in the street, and the old lady
hurrying to the window cried that Whisker had run away,
upon which Kit darted out to the rescue, and the others
followed.

It seemed that Mr. Chuckster had been standing with
his hands in his pockets looking carelessly at the pony,
and occasionally insulting him with such admonitions as
"Stand still,"—"Be quiet,"—"Woa-a-a," and the like,
which by a pony of spirit cannot be borne. Consequently,
the pony being deterred by no considerations of duty or
obedience, and not having before him the slightest fear of
the human eye, had at length started off, and was at that
moment rattling-down the street,—Mr. Chuckster, with

his hat off and a pen behind his ear, hanging on in the rear of the chaise and making futile attempts to draw it the other way, to the unspeakable admiration of all beholders.   Even in running away, however, Whisker was perverse, for he had not gone very far when he suddenly stopped, and before assistance could be rendered, commenced backing at nearly as quick a pace as he had gone forward.   By these means Mr. Chuckster was pushed and hustled to the office again, in a most inglorious manner, and arrived in a state of great exhaustion and discomfiture.

The old lady then stepped into her seat, and Mr. Abel (whom they had come to fetch) into his.   The old gentleman, after reasoning with the pony on the extreme impropriety of his conduct, and making the best amends in his power to Mr. Chuckster, took his place also, and they drove away, waving a farewell to the notary and his clerk, and more than once turning to nod kindly to Kit as he watched them from the road.

CHAPTER THE TWENTY-FIRST.

Kit turned away and very soon forgot the pony, and the chaise, and the little old lady, and the little old gentleman, and the little young gentleman to boot, in thinking what could have become of his late master and his lovely grandchild, who were the fountainhead of all his meditations. Still casting about for some plausible means of accounting for their non-appearance, and of persuading himself that they must soon return, he bent his steps towards home, intending to finish the task which the sudden recollection of his contract had interrupted, and then to sally forth once more to seek his fortune for the day.

When he came to the corner of the court in which he lived, lo and behold there was the pony again!   Yes, there he was, looking more obstinate than ever; and alone in the chaise, keeping a steady watch upon his every wink, sat Mr. Abel, who, lifting up his eyes by chance, and seeing Kit pass by, nodded to him as though he would have nodded his head off.

Kit wondered to see the pony again, so near his own

home too, but it never occurred to him for what purpose
the pony might have come there, or where the old lady
and the old gentleman had gone, until he lifted the latch
of the door, and walking in, found them seated in the
room in conversation with his mother, at which unexpected sight he pulled off his hat and made his best bow
in some confusion.

"We are here before you, you see, Christopher," said Mr.
Garland smiling.

"Yes, Sir," said Kit; and as he said it he looked towards his mother for an explanation of the visit.

"The gentleman's been kind enough, my dear," said
she, in reply to this mute interrogation, "to ask me
whether you were in a good place, or in any place at all,
and when I told him no, you were not in any, he was so
good as to say that—"

"That we wanted a good lad in our house," said the old
gentleman and the old lady both together, "and that
perhaps we might think of it, if we found everything as
we would wish it to be."

As this thinking of it, plainly meant the thinking of
engaging Kit, he immediately partook of his mother's anxiety and fell into a great flutter; for the little old couple
were very methodical and cautious, and asked so many
questions that he began to be afraid there was no chance of
his success.

"You see, my good woman," said Mrs. Garland to Kit's
mother, "that it's necessary to be very careful and particular in such a matter as this, for we're only three in
family, and are very quiet regular folks, and it would
be a sad thing if we made any kind of mistake, and found
things different from what we hoped and expected."

To this, Kit's mother replied, that certainly it was
quite true, and quite right, and quite proper, and Heaven
forbid that she should shrink, or have cause to shrink,
from any inquiry into her character or that of her son,
who was a very good son though she was his mother, in
which respect, she was bold to say, he took after his
father, who was not only a good son to *his* mother, but
the best of husbands and the best of fathers besides,
which Kit could and would corroborate she knew, and so
would little Jacob and the baby likewise if they were
old enough, which unfortunately they were not, though

as they didn't know what a loss they had had, perhaps it was a great deal better that they should be as young as they were; and so Kit's mother wound up a long story by wiping her eyes with her apron, and patting little Jacob's head, who was rocking the cradle and staring with all his might at the strange lady and gentleman.

When Kit's mother had done speaking, the old lady struck in again, and said that she was quite sure she was a very honest and very respectable person or she never would have expressed herself in that manner, and that certainly the appearance of the children and the cleanliness of the house deserved great praise and did her the utmost credit, whereat Kit's mother dropped a curtsey and became consoled. Then the good woman entered into a long and minute account of Kit's life and history from the earliest period down to that time, not omitting to make mention of his miraculous fall out of a back-parlor window when an infant of tender years, or his uncommon sufferings in a state of measles, which were illustrated by correct imitations of the plaintive manner in which he called for toast and water, day and night, and said "don't cry, mother, I shall soon be better;" for proof of which statements reference was made to Mrs. Green, lodger, at the cheesemonger's round the corner, and divers other ladies and gentlemen in various parts of England and Wales (and one Mr. Brown who was supposed to be then a corporal in the East Indies, and who could of course be found with very little trouble), within whose personal knowledge the circumstances had occurred. This narration ended, Mr. Garland put some questions to Kit respecting his qualifications and general acquirements, while Mrs. Garland noticed the children, and hearing from Kit's mother certain remarkable circumstances which had attended the birth of each, related certain other remarkable circumstances which had attended the birth of her own son, Mr. Abel, from which it appeared that both Kit's mother and herself had been, above and beyond all other women of what condition or age soever, peculiarly hemmed in with perils and dangers. Lastly, inquiry was made into the nature and extent of Kit's wardrobe, and a small advance being made to improve the same, he was formally hired at an annual income of Six Pounds, over and above his board and lodging, by Mr. and Mrs. Garland, of Abel Cottage, Finchley.

It would be difficult to say which party appeared most pleased with this arrangement, the conclusion of which was hailed with nothing but pleasant looks and cheerful smiles on both sides. It was settled that Kit should repair to his new abode on the next day but one, in the morning; and finally, the little old couple, after bestowing a bright half-crown on little Jacob and another on the baby, took their leaves; being escorted as far as the street by their new attendant, who held the obdurate pony by the bridle while they took their seats, and saw them drive away with a lightened heart.

" Well, mother," said Kit, hurrying back into the house, " I think my fortune's about made now."

"I should think it was indeed, Kit," rejoined his mother. " Six pound a year! Only think!"

" Ah!" said Kit, trying to maintain the gravity which the consideration of such a sum demanded, but grinning with delight in spite of himself. " There's a property!"

Kit drew a long breath when he had said this, and putting his hands deep into his pockets as if there were one year's wages at least in each, looked at his mother, as though he saw through her, and down an immense perspective of sovereigns beyond.

" Please God we'll make such a lady of you for Sundays, mother! such a scholar of Jacob, such a child of the baby, such a room of the one upstairs! Six pound a year!"

"Hem!" croaked a strange voice. " What's that about six pound a year? What about six pound a year?" And as the voice made this inquiry, Daniel Quilp walked in with Richard Swiveller at his heels.

"Who said he was to have six pound a year?" said Quilp, looking sharply round. " Did the old man say it, or did little Nell say it? And what's he to have it for, and where are they, eh?"

The good woman was so much alarmed by the sudden apparition of this unknown piece of ugliness, that she hastily caught the baby from its cradle and retreated into the furthest corner of the room; while little Jacob, sitting upon his stool with his hands on his knees, looked full at him in a species of fascination, roaring lustily all the time. Richard Swiveller took an easy observation of the family over Mr. Quilp's head, and Quilp himself, with his hands in his pockets, smiled in an exquisite enjoyment of the commotion he occasioned.

" Don't be frightened, mistress," said Quilp, after a pause. " Your son knows me; I don't eat babies; I don't like 'em. It will be as well to stop that young screamer though, in case I should be tempted to do him a mischief. Holloa, Sir! Will you be quiet?"

Little Jacob stemmed the course of two tears which he was squeezing out of his eyes, and instantly subsided into a silent horror.

" Mind you don't break out again, you villain," said Quilp, looking sternly at him, " or I'll make faces at you and throw you into fits, I will. Now you, Sir, why haven't you been to me as you promised?"

" What should I come for?" retorted Kit. " I hadn't any business with you, no more than you had with me."

" Here, mistress," said Quilp, turning quickly away, and appealing from Kit to his mother. " When did his old master come or send here last? Is he here now? If not, where's he gone?"

" He has not been here at all," she replied. " I wish we knew where they have gone, for it would make my son a good deal easier in his mind, and me too. If you're the gentleman named Mr. Quilp, I should have thought you'd have known, and so I told him only this very day."

" Humph!" muttered Quilp, evidently disappointed to believe that this was true. " That's what you tell this gentleman too, is it?"

" If the gentleman comes to ask the same question, I can't tell him anything else, Sir; and I only wish I could, for our own sakes," was the reply.

Quilp glanced at Richard Swiveller, and observed that having met him on the threshold, he assumed that he had come in search of some intelligence of the fugitives. He supposed he was right?

" Yes," said Dick, " that was the object of the present expedition. I fancied it possible—but let us go ring fancy's knell. *I'll* begin it."

" You seem disappointed," observed Quilp.

" A baffler, Sir, a baffler, that's all," returned Dick

"I have entered upon a speculation which has proved a baffler; and a Being of brightness and beauty will be offered up a sacrifice at Cheggs's altar. That's all, Sir."

The dwarf eyed Richard with a sarcastic smile, but Richard, who had been taking a rather strong lunch with a friend, observed him not, and continued to deplore his fate with mournful and despondent looks. Quilp plainly discerned that there was some secret reason for this visit and his uncommon disappointment, and, in the hope that there might be means of mischief lurking beneath it, resolved to worm it out. He had no sooner adopted this resolution, than he conveyed as much honesty into his face as it was capable of expressing, and sympathized with Mr. Swiveller exceedingly.

"I am disappointed myself," said Quilp, "out of mere friendly feeling for them; but you have real reasons, private reasons I have no doubt, for your disappointment, and therefore it comes heavier than mine."

"Why, of course it does," Dick observed, testily.

"Upon my word, I'm very sorry, very sorry. I'm rather cast down myself. As we are companions in adversity, shall we be companions in the surest way of forgetting it? If you had no particular business, now, to lead you in another direction," urged Quilp, plucking him by the sleeve and looking slyly up into his face out of the corners of his eyes, "there is a house by the water-side where they have some of the noblest Schiedam—reputed to be smuggled, but that's between ourselves—that can be got in all the world. The landlord knows me. There's a little summer-house overlooking the river, where we might take a glass of this delicious liquor with a whiff of the best tobacco—it's in this case, and of the rarest quality, to my certain knowledge—and be perfectly snug and happy, could we possibly contrive it; or is there any very particular engagement that peremptorily takes you another way, Mr. Swiveller, eh?"

As the dwarf spoke, Dick's face relaxed into a compliant smile, and his brows slowly unbent. By the time he had finished, Dick was looking down at Quilp in the same sly manner as Quilp was looking up at him, and there remained nothing more to be done but to set out

for the house in question. This they did, straig' tway.
The moment their backs were turned, little Jacob thawed,
and resumed his crying from the point where Quilp had
frozen him.

The summer-house of which Mr. Quilp had spoken
was a rugged wooden box, rotten and bare to see, which
overhung the river's mud, and threatened to slide down
into it. The tavern to which it belonged was a crazy
building, sapped and undermined by the rats and only
upheld by great bars of wood which were reared against
its walls, and had propped it up so long that even they
were decaying and yielding with their load, and of a
windy night might be heard to creak and crack as if the
whole fabric were about to come toppling down. The
house stood—if anything so old and feeble could be said
to stand—on a piece of waste ground, blighted with the
unwholesome smoke of factory chimneys, and echoing
the clank of iron wheels and rush of troubled water. Its
internal accommodations amply fulfilled the promise of
the outside. The rooms were low and damp, the clammy
walls were pierced with chinks and holes, the rotten
floors had sunk from their level, the very beams started
from their places and warned the timid stranger from
their neighborhood.

To this inviting spot, entreating him to observe its
beauties as they passed along, Mr. Quilp led Richard
Swiveller, and on the table of the summer-house, scored
deep with many a gallows and initial letter, there soon
appeared a wooden keg, full of the vaunted liquor.
Drawing it off into the glasses with the skill of a practised
hand, and mixing it with about a third part of water, Mr.
Quilp assigned to Richard Swiveller his portion, and
lighting his pipe from an end of a candle in a very old
and battered lantern, drew himself together upon a seat
and puffed away.

" Is it good?" said Quilp, as Richard Swiveller smacked
his lips, " is it strong and fiery? Does it make you wink,
and choke, and your eyes water, and your breath come
short—does it?"

"Does it?" cried Dick, throwing away part of the
contents of his glass, and filling it up with water, "why,
man, you don't mean to tell me that you drink such fire
as this?"

"No!" rejoined Quilp, "Not drink it! Look here. And here. And here again. Not drink it!"

As he spoke, Daniel Quilp drew off and drank three small glassfuls of the raw spirit, and then with a horrible grimace took a great many pulls at his pipe, and swallowing the smoke, discharged it in a heavy cloud from his nose. This feat accomplished he drew himself together in his former position, and laughed excessively.

"Give us a toast!" cried Quilp, rattling on the table in a dexterous manner with his fist and elbow alternately, in a kind of tune, "a woman, a beauty. Let's have a beauty for our toast and empty our glasses to the last drop. Her name, come!"

"If you want a name," said Dick, "here's Sophy Wackles."

"Sophy Wackles," screamed the dwarf, "Miss Sophy Wackles that is—Mrs. Richard Swiveller that shall be—that shall be—ha ha ha!"

"Ah!" said Dick, "you might have said that a few weeks ago, but it won't do now, my buck. Immolating herself upon the shrine of Cheggs—"

"Poison Cheggs, cut Cheggs's ears off," rejoined Quilp. "I won't hear of Cheggs. Her name is Swiveller or nothing. I'll drink her health again and her father's, and her mother's; and to all her sisters and brothers—the glorious family of the Wackleses—all the Wackleses in one glass—down with it to the dregs!"

"Well," said Richard Swiveller, stopping short in the act of raising the glass to his lips and looking at the dwarf in a species of stupor as he flourished his arms and legs about: "you're a jolly fellow, but of all the jolly fellows I ever saw or heard of, you have the queerest and most extraordinary way with you, upon my life you have."

This candid declaration tended rather to increase than restrain Mr. Quilp's eccentricities, and Richard Swiveller, astonished to see him in such a roystering vein, and drinking not a little himself, for company,—began imperceptibly to become more companionable and confiding, so that, being judiciously led on by Mr. Quilp, he grew at last very confiding indeed. Having once got him into this mood, and knowing now the key-note to strike whenever he was at a loss, Daniel Quilp's task was comparatively an easy one, and he was soon in possession of the whole details of the scheme contrived between the easy Dick and his more designing friend.

"Stop!" said Quilp. "That's the thing, that's the thing. It can be brought about, it shall be brought about. There's my hand upon it; I am your friend from this minute."

"What! do you think there's still a chance?" inquired Dick, in surprise at this encouragement.

"A chance!" echoed the dwarf, "a certainty! Sophy Wackles may become a Cheggs or anything else she likes, but not a Swiveller. Oh, you lucky dog! He's richer than any Jew alive; you're a made man. I see in you now nothing but Nelly's husband, rolling in gold and silver. I'll help you. It shall be done. Mind my words, it shall be done."

"But how?" said Dick.

"There's plenty of time," rejoined the dwarf, "and it shall be done. We'll sit down and talk it over again all the way through. Fill your glass while I'm gone. I shall be back directly—directly."

With these hasty words, Daniel Quilp withdrew into a dismantled skittle-ground behind the public-house, and, throwing himself upon the ground, actually screamed and rolled about in uncontrollable delight.

"Here's sport!" he cried, "sport ready to my hand, all invented and arranged, and only to be enjoyed. It was this shallow-pated fellow who made my bones ache t'other day, was it? It was his friend and fellow-plotter, Mr. Trent, that once made eyes at Mrs. Quilp, and leered and looked, was it? After laboring for two or three years in their precious scheme, to find that they've got a beggar at last, and one of them tied for life. Ha ha ha! He shall marry Nell. He shall have her, and I'll be the first man, when the knot's tied hard and fast, to tell 'em what they've gained and what I've helped 'em to. Here will be a clearing of old scores, here will be a time to remind 'em what a capital friend I was, and how I helped them to the heiress. Ha ha ha!"

In the height of his ecstasy, Mr. Quilp had like to have met with a disagreeable check, for, rolling very near a broken dog-kennel, there leapt forth a large fierce dog, who, but that his chain was of the shortest, would have given him a disagreeable salute. As it was, the dwarf remained upon his back in perfect safety, taunting the dog with hideous faces, and triumphing over him in his inability to advance another inch, though there were not a couple of feet between them.

"Why don't you come and bite me, why don't you come and tear me to pieces, you coward?" said Quilp, hissing and worrying the animal till he was nearly mad. "You're afraid, you bully, you're afraid, you know you are."

The dog tore and strained at his chain with starting

eyes and furious bark, but there the dwarf lay, snapping his fingers with gestures of defiance and contempt. When he had sufficiently recovered from his delight, he rose, and with his arms a-kimbo, achieved a kind of demon-dance round the kennel, just without the limits of the chain, driving the dog quite wild. Having by this means composed his spirits and put himself in a pleasant train, he returned to his unsuspicious companion, whom he found looking at the tide with exceeding gravity, and thinking of that same gold and silver which Mr. Quilp had men-tioned.

CHAPTER THE TWENTY-SECOND.

THE remainder of that day and the whole of the next were a busy time for the Nubbles family, to whom everything connected with Kit's outfit, and departure was matter of as great moment as if he had been about to penetrate into the interior of Africa, or to take a cruise round the world. It would be difficult to suppose that there ever was a box which was opened and shut so many times within four-and-twenty hours, as that which contained his wardrobe and necessaries; and certainly there never was one which to two small eyes presented such a mine of clothing, as this mighty chest with its three shirts and proportionate allowance of stockings and pocket-handkerchiefs, disclosed to the astonished vision of little Jacob. At last it was conveyed to the carrier's, at whose house at Finchley Kit was to find it next day; and the box being gone, there remained but two questions for consideration : firstly, whether the carrier would lose, or dishonestly feign to lose, the box upon the road; and secondly, whether Kit's mother perfectly understood how to take care of herself in the absence of her son.

"I don't think there's hardly a chance of his really losing it, but carriers are under great temptation to pretend they lose things no doubt," said Mrs. Nubbles apprehensively, in reference to the first point.

"No doubt about it," returned Kit, with a serious look ; "upon my word, mother, I don't think it was right to trust it to itself. Somebody ought to have gone with it, I'm afraid."

"We can't help it now," said his mother; "but it was foolish and wrong. People oughtn't to be tempted."

Kit inwardly resolved that he would never tempt a carrier any more, save with an empty box; and having formed this Christian determination, he turned his thoughts to the second question.

"You know you must keep up your spirits, mother, and not be lonesome because I'm not at home. I shall very often be able to look in when I come into town I dare say, and I shall send you a letter sometimes, and when the quarter comes round, I can get a holiday of course; and then see if we don't take little Jacob to the play, and let him know what oysters means."

"I hope plays mayn't be sinful, Kit, but I'm a'most afraid," said Mrs. Nubbles.

"I know who has been putting that in your head," rejoined her son disconsolately; "that's Little Bethel again. Now I say, mother, pray don't take to going there regularly, for if I was to see your good-humored face that has always made home cheerful, turned into a grievous one, and the baby trained to look grievous too, and to call itself a young sinner (bless its heart) and a child of the devil (which is calling its dead father names); if I was to see this, and see little Jacob looking grievous likewise, I should so take it to heart that I'm sure I should go and list for a soldier, and run my head on purpose against the first cannon-ball I saw coming my way."

"Oh, Kit, don't talk like that."

"I would indeed, mother, and unless you want to make me feel very wretched and uncomfortable, you'll keep that bow on your bonnet, which you'd more than half a mind to pull off last week. Can you suppose there's any harm in looking as cheerful and being as cheerful as our poor circumstances will permit? Do I see anything in the way I'm made, which calls upon me to be a snivelling, solemn, whispering chap, sneaking about as if I couldn't help it, and expressing myself in a most unpleasant snuffle? on the contrary, don't I see every reason why I shouldn't? Just hear this! Ha ha ha! An't that as nat'ral as walking, and as good for the health? Ha ha ha! An't that as nat'ral as a sheep's bleating, or a pig's grunting, or a horse's neighing, or a bird's singing? Ha ha ha! Isn't it, mother?"

There was something contagious in Kit's laugh, for his mother, who had looked grave before, first subsided into a smile, and then fell to joining in it heartily, which occasioned Kit to say that he knew it was natural, and to laugh the more. Kit and his mother, laughing together in a pretty loud key, woke the baby, who, finding that there was something very jovial and agreeable in progress, was no sooner in its mother's arms than it began to kick and laugh most vigorously. This new illustra-

tion of his argument so tickled Kit, that he fell backward
in his chair in a state of exhaustion, pointing at the baby
and shaking his sides till he rocked again. After recovering twice or thrice, and as often relapsing, he wiped his
eyes and said grace; and a very cheerful meal their scanty
supper was.

With more kisses, and hugs, and tears, than many
young gentlemen who start upon their travels, and leave
well-stocked homes behind them, would deem within the
bounds of probability (if matter so low could be herein
set down), Kit left the house at an early hour next morning, and set out to walk to Finchley; feeling a sufficient
pride in his appearance to have warranted his excom-
munication from Little Bethel from that time forth, if he
had ever been one of that mournful congregation.

Lest anybody should feel a curiosity to know how Kit
was clad, it may be briefly remarked that he wore no
livery, but was dressed in a coat of pepper-and-salt with
waistcoat of canary color, and nether garments of iron-
gray; besides these glories, he shone in the lustre of a
new pair of boots and an extremely stiff and shiny hat,
which on being struck anywhere with the knuckles,
sounded like a drum. And in this attire, rather wondering that he attracted so little attention, and attributing
the circumstance to the insensibility of those who got up
early, he made his way towards Abel Cottage.

Without encountering any more remarkable adventure
on the road, than meeting a lad in a brimless hat, the
exact counterpart of his old one, on whom he bestowed
half the sixpence he possessed, Kit arrived in course of
time at the carrier's house, where, to the lasting honor of
human nature, he found the box in safety. Receiving
from the wife of this immaculate man, a direction to Mr.
Garland's, he took the box upon his shoulder and repaired
thither directly.

To be sure, it was a beautiful little cottage with a
thatched roof and little spires at the gable-ends, and
pieces of stained glass in some of the windows, almost as
large as pocket-books. On one side of the house was a
little stable, just the size for the pony, with a little room
over it, just the size for Kit. White curtains were fluttering, and birds, in cages that looked as bright as if they
were made of gold, were singing at the windows; plants

were arranged on either side of the path, and clustered about the door ; and the garden was bright with flowers in full bloom, which shed a sweet odor all round, and had a charming and elegant appearance. Everything, within the house and without, seemed to be the perfection of neatness and order. In the garden there was not a weed to be seen, and to judge from some dapper gardening-tools, a basket, and a pair of gloves which were lying in one of the walks, old Mr. Garland had been at work in it that very morning.

Kit looked about him, and admired, and looked again, and this a great many times before he could make up his mind to turn his head another way and ring the bell. There was abundance of time to look about him again though, when he had rung it, for nobody came, so after ringing twice or thrice he sat down upon his box, and waited.

He rang the bell a great many times, and yet nobody came. But at last, as he was sitting upon the box thinking about giants' castles, and princesses tied up to pegs by the hair of their heads, and dragons bursting out from behind gates, and other incidents of the like nature, common in story-books to youths of low degree on their first visit to strange houses, the door was gently opened, and a little servant-girl, very tidy, modest, and demure, but very pretty too, appeared.

"I suppose you're Christopher, Sir," said the servant-girl.

Kit got off the box, and said yes, he was.

" I'm afraid you've rung a good many times perhaps," she rejoined, "but we couldn't hear you, because we've been catching the pony."

Kit rather wondered what this meant, but as he couldn't stop there, asking questions, he shouldered the box again and followed the girl into the hall, where through a back-door he descried Mr. Garland leading Whisker in triumph up the garden, after that self-willed pony had (as he afterwards learned) dodged the family round a small paddock in the rear, for one hour and three-quarters.

The old gentleman received him very kindly and so did the old lady, whose previous good opinion of him was greatly enhanced by his wiping his boots on the mat until the soles of his feet burnt again. He was then

taken into the parlor to be inspected in his new clothes;
and when he had been surveyed several times, and had
afforded by his appearance unlimited satisfaction, he was
taken into the stable (where the pony received him with
uncommon complaisance); and thence into the little
chamber he had already observed, which was very clean
and comfortable; and thence into the garden, in which
the old gentleman told him he would be taught to employ
himself, and where he told him, besides, what great things
he meant to do to make him comfortable, and happy, if

he found he deserved it. All these kindnesses, Kit acknowledged with various expressions of gratitude, and so many
touches of the new hat, that the brim suffered considerably. When the old gentleman had said all he had to
say in the way of promise and advice, and Kit had said
all he had to say in the way of assurance and thankfulness, he was handed over again to the old lady, who,
summoning the little servant-girl (whose name was Barbara) instructed her to take him downstairs and give
him something to eat and drink, after his walk.

Downstairs therefore, Kit went; and at the bottom of the stairs there was such a kitchen as was never before seen or heard of out of a toy-shop window, with everything in it as bright and glowing, and as precisely ordered too, as Barbara herself. And in this kitchen, Kit sat himself down at a table as white as a table-cloth, to eat cold meat, and drink small ale, and use his knife and fork the more awkwardly, because there was an unknown Barbara looking on and observing him.

It did not appear, however, that there was anything remarkably tremendous about this strange Barbara, who having lived a very quite life, blushed very much and was quite as embarrassed and uncertain what she ought to say or do, as Kit could possibly be. When he had sat for some little time, attentive to the ticking of the sober clock, he ventured to glance curiously at the dresser, and there, among the plates and dishes, were Barbara's little work-box with a sliding lid to shut in the balls of cotton, and Barbara's prayer-book, and Barbara's hymn-book, and Barbara's Bible. Barbara's little looking-glass hung in a good light near the window, and Barbara's bonnet was on a nail behind the door. From all these mute signs and tokens of her presence, he naturally' glanced at Barbara herself, who sat as mute as they, shelling peas into a dish; and just when Kit was looking at her eyelashes and wondering—quite in the simplicity of his heart—what color her eyes might be, it perversely happened that Barbara raised her head a little to look at him, when both pair of eyes were hastily withdrawn, and Kit leant over his plate, and Barbara over her pea-shells, each in extreme confusion at having been detected by the other.

CHAPTER THE TWENTY-THIRD.

MR. RICHARD SWIVELLER wending homewards from the Wilderness (for such was the appropriate name of Quilp's choice retreat), after a sinuous and corkscrew fashion, with many checks and stumbles; after stopping suddenly and staring about him, then as suddenly running forward for a few paces, and as suddenly halting again and shaking his head; doing everything with a jerk and nothing by premeditation ;—Mr. Richard Swiveller wending his way homewards after this fashion, which is considered by evil-minded men to be symbolical of intoxication, and is not held by such persons to denote that state of deep wisdom and reflection in which the actor knows himself to be, began to think that possibly he had misplaced his confidence and that the dwarf might not be precisely the sort of person to whom to entrust a secret of such delicacy and importance. And being led and tempted on by this remorseful thought into a condition which the evil-minded class before referred to would term the maudlin state or stage of drunkenness, it occurred to Mr. Swiveller to cast his hat upon the ground, and moan, crying aloud that he was an unhappy orphan, and that if he had not been an unhappy orphan things had never come to this.

" Left an infant by my parents, at an early age," said Mr. Swiveller, bewailing his hard lot, "cast upon the world in my tenderest period, and thrown upon the mercies of a deluding dwarf, who can wonder at my weakness ! Here's a miserable orphan for you. Here," said Mr. Swiveller raising his voice to a high pitch, and looking sleepily round, "is a miserable orphan !"

" Then," said somebody hard by, " let me be a father to you."

Mr. Swiveller swayed himself to and fro to preserve his balance, and, looking into a kind of haze which seemed to surround him, at last perceived two eyes dimly twinkling through the mist, which he observed after a short time were in the neighborhood of a nose and mouth. Casting his eyes down towards that quarter in which, with reference to a man's face, his legs are usually to be found, he observed that the face had a body attached ; and when he looked more intently he was satisfied that the person was Mr. Quilp, who indeed had been in his company all the time, but whom he had some vague idea of having left a mile or two behind.

" You have deceived an orphan, Sir," said Mr. Swiveller solemnly.

" I ! I'm a second father to you," replied Quilp.

" You my father, Sir ! " retorted Dick.   " Being all right myself, Sir, I request to be left alone—instantly, Sir."

" What a funny fellow you are ! " cried Quilp.

"Go, Sir," returned Dick, leaning against a post and waving his hand. "Go, deceiver, go, some day, Sir, p'r'aps you'll waken, from pleasure's dream to know, the grief of orphans forsaken. Will you go, Sir?"

The dwarf taking no heed of this adjuration, Mr. Swiveller advanced with the view of inflicting upon him condign chastisement. But forgetting his purpose or changing his mind before he came close to him, he seized his hand and vowed eternal friendship, declaring with an agreeable frankness that from that time forth they were brothers in everything but personal appearance. Then

he told his secret all over again, with the addition of being pathetic on the subject of Miss Wackles, who, he gave Mr. Quilp to understand, was the occasion of any slight incoherency he might observe in his speech at that moment, which was attributable solely to the strength of his affection and not to rosy wine or other fermented liquor. And then they went on arm-in-arm, very lovingly together.

"I'm as sharp," said Quilp to him, at parting, "as sharp as a ferret, and as cunning as a weazel. You bring Trent to me; assure him that I'm his friend though I fear he a little distrusts me (I don't know why, I have not deserved it); and you've both of you made your fortunes— in perspective."

"That's the worst of it," returned Dick. "These fortunes in perspective look such a long way off."

"But they look smaller than they really are, on that account," said Quilp pressing his arm. "You'll have no conception of the value of your prize until you draw close to it. Mark that."

"D'ye think not?" said Dick.

"Ay, I do; and I am certain of what I say, that's better," returned the dwarf. "You bring Trent to me. Tell him I am his friend and yours—why shouldn't I be?"

"There's no reason why you shouldn't, certainly," replied Dick, "and perhaps there are a great many why you should—at least there would be nothing strange in your wanting to be my friend, if you were a choice spirit, but then you know you're *not* a choice spirit."

"I not a choice spirit!" cried Quilp.

"Devil a bit, Sir," returned Dick. "A man of your appearance couldn't be. If you're any spirit at all, Sir, you're an evil spirit. Choice spirits," added Dick, smiting himself on the breast, "are quite a different looking sort of people, you may take your oath of that, Sir."

Quilp glanced at his free-spoken friend with a mingled expression of cunning and dislike, and wringing his hand almost at the same moment, declared that he was an uncommon character and had his warmest esteem. With that they parted; Mr. Swiveller to make the best of his way home and sleep himself sober; and Quilp to cogitate upon the discovery he had made, and exult in the prospect of the rich field of enjoyment and reprisal it opened to him.

It was not without great reluctance and misgiving that Mr. Swiveller, next morning, his head racked by the fumes of the renowned Schiedam, repaired to the lodging of his friend Trent (which was in the roof of an old house in an old ghostly inn), and recounted by very slow degrees what had yesterday taken place between him and Quilp. Nor was it without great surprise and much speculation on Quilp's probable motives, nor without many bitter comments on Dick Swiveller's folly, that his friend received the tale.

"I don't defend myself, Fred," said the penitent Richard; "but the fellow has such a queer way with him and is such an artful dog, that first of all he set me upon thinking whether there was any harm in telling him, and while I was thinking, screwed it out of me. If you had seen him drink and smoke, as I did, you couldn't have kept anything from him. He's a salamander you know, that's what *he* is."

Without inquiring whether salamanders were of necessity good confidential agents, or whether a fire-proof man was as a matter of course trustworthy, Frederick Trent threw himself into a chair, and, burying his head in his hands, endeavored to fathom the motives which had led Quilp to insinuate himself into Richard Swiveller's confidence;—for that the disclosure was of his seeking, and had not been spontaneously revealed by Dick, was sufficently plain from Quilp's seeking his company and enticing him away.

The dwarf had twice encountered him when he was endeavoring to obtain intelligence of the fugitives. This, perhaps, as he had not shown any previous anxiety about them, was enough to awaken suspicion in the breast of a creature so jealous and distrustful by nature, setting aside any additional impulse to curiosity that he might have derived from Dick's incautious manner. But knowing the scheme they had planned, why should he offer to assist it? This was a question more difficult of solution; but as knaves generally overreach themselves by imputing their own designs to others, the idea immediately presented itself that some circumstances of irritation between Quilp and the old man, arising out of their secret transactions and not unconnected perhaps with his sudden disappearance, now rendered the former desirous of revenging himself upon him by seeking to entrap the sole object of his love and anxiety into a connection of which he knew he had a dread and hatred. As Frederick Trent himself, utterly regardless of his sister, had this object at heart, only second to the hope of gain, it seemed to him the more likely to be Quilp's main principle of action. Once investing the dwarf with a design of his own in abetting them, which the attainment of their purpose would serve, it was easy to believe him sincere and hearty in the cause; and as there could be no doubt of his proving a powerful and useful auxiliary, Trent determined to accept his invitation and go to his house that night, and if what he said and did confirmed him in the impression he had formed, to let him share the labor of their plan, but not the profit.

Having revolved these things in his mind and arrived at this conclusion, he communicated to Mr. Swiveller as much of his meditations as he thought proper (Dick would have been perfectly satisfied with less), and giving him the day to recover himself from his late salamandering, accompanied him at evening to Mr. Quilp's house.

Mightily glad Mr. Quilp was to see them, or mightily glad he seemed to be; and fearfully polite Mr. Quilp was to Mrs. Quilp and Mrs. Jiniwin; and very sharp was the look he cast on his wife to observe how she was affected by the recognition of young Trent. Mrs. Quilp was as innocent as her own mother of any emotion, painful or pleasant, which the sight of him awakened, but as her husband's glance made her timid and confused, and uncertain what to do or what was required of her, Mr. Quilp did not fail to assign her embarrassment to the cause he had in his mind, and while he chuckled at his penetration was secretly exasperated by his jealousy.

Nothing of this appeared, however. On the contrary, Mr. Quilp was all blandness and suavity, and presided over the case-bottle of rum with extraordinary openheartedness.

"Why, let me see," said Quilp. "It must be a matter of nearly two years since we were first acquainted."

"Nearer three, I think," said Trent.

"Nearer three!" cried Quilp. "How fast time flies. Does it seem as long as that to you, Mrs. Quilp?"

"Yes, I think it seems full three years, Quilp," was the unfortunate reply.

"Oh indeed, Ma'am," thought Quilp, "you have been pining, have you? Very good, Ma'am."

"It seems to me but yesterday that you went out to Demerara in the Mary Anne," said Quilp; "but yesterday, I declare. Well, I like a little wildness. I was wild myself once."

Mr. Quilp accompanied this admission with such an awful wink, indicative of old rovings and backslidings, that Mrs. Jiniwin was indignant, and could not forbear from remarking under her breath that he might at least put off his confession until his wife was absent; for which act of boldness and insubordination Mr. Quilp first stared her out of countenance and then drank her health ceremoniously.

"I thought you'd come back directly, Fred. I always thought that," said Quilp setting down his glass. "And when the Mary Anne returned with you on board, instead of a letter to say what a contrite heart you had, and how happy you were in the situation that had been provided for you, I was amused—exceedingly amused. Ha ha ha!"

The young man smiled, but not as though the theme were the most agreeable one that could have been selected for his entertainment; and for that reason Quilp pursued it.

"I always will say," he resumed, "that when a rich relation having two young people—sisters or brothers, or brother and sister—dependent on him, attaches himself exclusively to one, and casts off the other, he does wrong."

The young man made a movement of impatience, but Quilp went on as calmly as if he were discussing some abstract question in which nobody present had the slightest personal interest.

"It's very true," said Quilp, "that your grandfather urged repeated forgiveness, ingratitude, riot, and extravagance, and all that; but as I told him 'these are common faults.' 'But he's a scoundrel,' said he. 'Granting that,' said I (for the sake of argument of course), 'a great many young noblemen and gentlemen are scoundrels too!' But he wouldn't be convinced."

"I wonder at that, Mr. Quilp," said the young man sarcastically.

"Well, so did I at the time," returned Quilp, "but he was always obstinate. He was in a manner a friend of mine, but he was always obstinate and wrong-headed. Little Nell is a nice girl, a charming girl, but you're her brother, Frederick. You're her brother after all; as you told him the last time you met, he can't alter that."

"He would if he could, confound him for that and all other kindnesses," said the young man impatiently. "But nothing can come of this subject now, and let us have done with it in the Devil's name."

"Agreed," returned Quilp, "agreed on my part readily. Why have I alluded to it? Just to show you, Frederick, that I have always stood your friend. You little knew who was your friend, and who your foe; now did you? You thought I was against you, and so there has been a coolness between us; but it was all on your side, entirely on your side. Let's shake hands again, Fred."

With his head sunk down between his shoulders, and a hideous grin overspreading his face, the dwarf stood up and stretched his short arm across the table. After a moment's hesitation, the young man stretched out his to meet it; Quilp clutched his fingers in a grip that for the moment stopped the current of the blood within them, and pressing his other hand upon his lip and frowning towards the unsuspicious Richard, released them and sat down.

This action was not lost upon Trent, who, knowing that Richard Swiveller was a mere tool in his hands and knew no more of his designs than he thought proper to communicate, saw that the dwarf perfectly understood their relative position, and fully entered into the character of his friend. It is something to be appreciated, even in knavery. This silent homage to his superior abilities, no less than a sense of the power with which the dwarf's quick perception had already invested him, inclined the young man towards that ugly worthy, and determined him to profit by his aid.

It being now Mr. Quilp's cue to change the subject with all convenient expedition, lest Richard Swiveller in his heedlessness should reveal anything which it was inexpedient for the women to know, he proposed a game at four-handed cribbage; and partners being cut for, Mrs. Quilp fell to Frederick Trent, and Dick himself to Quilp. Mrs. Jiniwin being very fond of cards was carefully excluded by her son-in-law from any participation in the game, and had assigned to her the duty of occasionally replenishing the glasses from the case-bottle; Mr. Quilp from that moment keeping one eye constantly upon her, lest she should by any means procure a taste of the same, and thereby tantalizing the wretched old lady (who was as much attached to the case-bottle as the cards) in a double degree and most ingenious manner.

But it was not to Mrs. Jiniwin alone that Mr. Quilp's attention was restricted, as several other matters required his constant vigilance. Among his various eccentric habits he had a humorous one of always cheating at cards, which rendered necessary on his part, not only a close observance of the game, and a sleight-of-hand in counting and scoring, but also involved the constant correction, by looks, and frowns, and kicks under the table, of Richard Swiveller, who being bewildered by the rapidity with which his cards were told, and the rate at which the pegs travelled down the board, could not be prevented from sometimes expressing his surprise and incredulity. Mrs. Quilp too was the partner of young Trent, and for every look that passed between them, and every word they spoke, and every card they played, the dwarf had eyes and ears; not occupied alone with what was passing above the table, but with signals that might be exchanging beneath it, which he laid all kinds of traps to detect; besides often treading on his wife's toes to see whether she cried out or remained silent under the infliction, in which latter case it would have been quite clear that Trent had been treading on her toes before. Yet, in the most of all these distractions, the one eye was upon the old lady always, and if she so much as stealthily advanced a tea-spoon towards a neighboring glass (which she often did), for the purpose of abstracting but one sup of its sweet contents, Quilp's hand would overset it in the very moment of her triumph, and Quilp's mocking voice implore her to regard her precious health. And in any one of these his many cares, from first to last, Quilp never flagged nor faltered.

At length, when they had played a great many rubbers and drawn pretty freely upon the case-bottle, Mr. Quilp warned his lady to retire to rest, and that submissive wife complying, and being followed by her indignant mother, Mr. Swiveller fell asleep. The dwarf beckoning his remaining companion to the other end of the room, held a short conference with him in whispers.

"It's as well not to say more than one can help before our worthy friend," said Quilp, making a grimace towards the slumbering Dick. "Is it a bargain between us, **Fred?** Shall he marry little rosy Nell by-and-by?"

14

"You have some end of your own to answer, of course," returned the other.

"Of course I have, dear Fred," said Quilp, grinning to think how little he suspected what the real end was. "It's retaliation perhaps; perhaps whim. I have influence, Fred, to help or oppose. Which way shall I use it? There are a pair of scales, and it goes into one."

"Throw it into mine then," said Trent.

"It's done, Fred," rejoined Quilp, stretching out his clenched hand and opening it as if he had let some weight fall out. "It's in the scale from this time, and turns it, Fred. Mind that."

"Where have they gone?" asked Trent.

Quilp shook his head, and said that point remained to be discovered, which it might be, easily. When it was, they would begin their preliminary advances. He would visit the old man, or even Richard Swiveller might visit him, and by affecting a deep concern in his behalf, and imploring him to settle in some worthy home, lead to the child's remembering him with gratitude and favor. Once impressed to this extent, it would be easy, he said, to win her in a year or two, for she supposed the old man to be poor, as it was a part of his jealous policy (in common with many other misers) to feign to be so, to those about him.

"He has feigned it often enough to me, of late," said Trent.

"Oh! and to me too!" replied the dwarf. "Which is more extraordinary, as I know how rich he really is."

"I suppose you should," said Trent.

"I think I should indeed," rejoined the dwarf; and in that, at least he spoke the truth.

After a few more whispered words, they returned to the table, and the young man rousing Richard Swiveller informed him that he was waiting to depart. This was welcome news to Dick, who started up directly. After a few words of confidence in the result of their project had been exchanged, they bade the grinning Quilp good-night.

Quilp crept to the window as they passed in the street below, and listened. Trent was pronouncing an encomium upon his wife, and they were both wondering by what enchantment she had been brought to marry such a mis-shapen wretch as he. The dwarf after watching their retreating shadows with a wider grin than his face had yet displayed, stole softly in the dark to bed.

In this hatching of their scheme, neither Trent nor Quilp had had one thought about the happiness or misery of poor innocent Nell. It would have been strange if the careless profligate, who was the butt of both, had been harassed by any such consideration; for his high opinion of his own merits and deserts rendered the project rather a laudable one than otherwise; and if he had been visited by so unwonted a guest as reflection, he would—being a brute only in the gratification of his appetites—have soothed his conscience with the plea that he did not mean to beat or kill his wife, and would therefore, after all said and done, be a very tolerable, average husband.

CHAPTER THE TWENTY-FOURTH.

IT was not until they were quite exhausted and could no longer maintain the pace at which they had fled from the race-ground, that the old man and the child ventured to stop and sit down to rest upon the borders of a little wood. Here, though the course was hidden from their view, they could yet faintly distinguish the noise of distant shouts, the hum of voices, and the beating of drums. Climbing the eminence which lay between them and the spot they had left, the child could even discern the fluttering flags and white tops of booths; but no person was approaching towards them, and their resting-place was solitary and still.

Some time elapsed before she could reassure her trembling companion, or restore him to a state of moderate tranquillity. His disordered imagination represented to him a crowd of persons stealing toward them beneath the cover of the bushes, lurking in every ditch, and peeping from the boughs of every rustling tree. He was haunted by apprehensions of being led captive to some gloomy place where he would be chained and scourged, and worse than all, where Nell could never come to see him, save through iron bars and gratings in the wall. His terrors affected the child. Separation from her grandfather was the greatest evil she could dread; and feeling for the time as though, go where they would, they were to be hunted down, and could never be safe but in hiding, her heart failed her, and her courage drooped.

In one so young, and so unused to the scenes in which she had lately moved, this sinking of the spirit was not surprising. But, Nature often enshrines gallant and noble hearts in weak bosoms—oftenest, God bless her, in female breasts—and when the child, casting her tearful eyes upon the old man, remembered how weak he was, and how destitute and helpless he would be if she failed him, her heart swelled within her, and animated her with new strength and fortitude.

"We are quite safe now, and have nothing to fear indeed, dear grandfather," she said.

"Nothing to fear!" returned the old man. "Nothing to fear if they took me from thee? Nothing to fear if they parted us! Nobody is true to me. No, not one. Not even Nell!"

"Oh! do not say that," replied the child, "for if ever anybody was true at heart, and earnest, I am. I am sure you know I am."

"Then how," said the old man, looking fearfully round, "how can you bear to think that we are safe, when they are searching for me everywhere, and may come here, and steal upon us, even while we're talking?"

"Because I'm sure we have not been followed," said the child. "Judge for yourself, dear grandfather; look round, and see how quiet and still it is. We are alone together, and may ramble where we like. Not safe! Could I feel easy—did I feel at ease—when any danger threatened you?"

"True, true," he answered, pressing her hand, but still looking anxiously about. "What noise was that?"

"A bird," said the child, "flying into the wood, and leading the way for us to follow. You remember that we said we would walk in the woods and fields, and by the side of the rivers, and how happy we would be—you remember that? But here, while the sun shines above our heads, and everything is bright and happy, we are sitting sadly down, and losing time. See what a pleasant path; and there's the bird—the same bird—now he flies to another tree, and stays to sing. Come!"

When they rose up from the ground, and took the

shady track which led them through the wood, she bounded
on before, printing her tiny footsteps in the moss, which
rose elastic from so light a pressure and gave it back
as mirrors throw off breath; and thus she lured the
old man on, with many a backward look and merry beck,
now pointing stealthily to some lone bird as it perched
and twittered on a branch that strayed across their path,
now stopping to listen to the songs that broke the happy
silence, or watch the sun as it trembled through the
leaves, and stealing in among the ivied trunks of stout
old trees, opened long paths of light. As they pressed onward, parting the boughs that clustered in their way, the
serenity which the child had first assumed, stole into her
breast in earnest; the old man cast no longer fearful
looks behind, but felt at ease and cheerful, for the further they passed into the deep green shade, the more
they felt that the tranquil mind of God was there, and
shed its peace on them.

At length, the path becoming clearer and less intricate,
brought them to the end of the wood, and into a public
road. Taking their way along it for a short distance,
they came to a lane, so shaded by the trees on either hand
that they met together overhead, and arched the narrow
way. A broken finger-post announced that this led to a
village three miles off; and thither they resolved to bend
their steps.

The miles appeared so long that they sometimes thought
they must have missed their road. But at last, to their
great joy, it led downward in a steep descent, with overhanging banks over which the footpaths led; and the
clustered houses of the village peeped out from the woody
hollow below.

It was a very small place. The men and boys were
playing at cricket on the green; and as the other folks
were looking on, they wandered up and down, uncertain
where to seek a humble lodging. There was but one old
man in the little garden before his cottage, and him they
were timid of approaching, for he was the schoolmaster,
and had " School " written up over his window in black
letters on a white board. He was a pale, simple-looking
man, of a spare and meagre habit, and sat among his
flowers and beehives, smoking his pipe, in the little porch
before his door.

"Speak to him, dear," the old man whispered.

"I am almost afraid to disturb him," said the child timidly. "He does not seem to see us. Perhaps if we wait a little, he may look this way."

They waited, but the schoolmaster cast no look towards them, and still sat, thoughtful and silent, in the little porch. He had a kind face. In his plain old suit of black, he looked pale and meagre. They fancied, too, a lonely air about him and his house, but perhaps that was

because the other people formed a merry company upon the green, and he seemed the only solitary man in all the place.

They were very tired, and the child would have been bold enough to address even a schoolmaster, but for something in his manner which seemed to denote that he was uneasy or distressed. As they stood hesitating at a little distance, they saw that he sat for a few minutes at a time like one in a brown study, then laid aside his pipe and took a few turns in his garden, then approached the gate and looked towards the green, then took up his pipe again with a sigh, and sat down thoughtfully as before.

As nobody else appeared and it would soon be dark, Nell at length took courage, and when he had resumed his pipe and seat, ventured to draw near, leading her grandfather by the hand. The slight noise they made in raising the latch of the wicket-gate, caught his attention. He looked at them kindly but seemed disappointed too, and slightly shook his head.

Nell dropped a curtsey, and told him they were poor travellers who sought a shelter for the night which they would gladly pay for, so far as their means allowed. The schoolmaster looked earnestly at her as she spoke, laid aside his pipe, and rose up directly.

"If you could direct us anywhere, Sir," said the child, "we should take it very kindly."

"You have been walking a long way," said the schoolmaster.

"A long way, Sir," the child replied.

"You're a young traveller, my child," he said, laying his hand gently on her head. "Your grandchild, friend?"

"Ay, Sir," cried the old man, "and the stay and comfort of my life."

"Come in," said the schoolmaster.

Without further preface he conducted them into his little schoolroom, which was parlor and kitchen likewise, and told them they were welcome to remain under his roof till morning. Before they had done thanking him, he spread a coarse white cloth upon the table, with knives and platters; and bringing out some bread and cold meat and a jug of beer, besought them to eat and drink.

The child looked round the room as she took her seat. There were a couple of forms, notched and cut and inked all over; a small deal desk perched on four legs, at which no doubt the master sat; a few dog's-eared books upon a high shelf; and beside them a motley collection of peg-tops, balls, kites, fishing-lines, marbles, half-eaten apples, and other confiscated property of idle urchins. Displayed on hooks upon the wall in all their terrors, were the cane and ruler; and near them, on a small shelf of its own, the dunce's cap, made of old newspapers and decorated with glaring wafers of the largest size. But, the great ornaments of the walls were certain moral sentences fairly copied in good round text, and well-worked

sums in simple addition and multiplication, evidently
achieved by the same hand, which were plentifully pasted
all round the room : for the double purpose, as it seemed,
of bearing testimony to the excellence of the school,
and kindling a worthy emulation in the bosoms of the
scholars.

"Yes," said the old schoolmaster, observing that her
attention was caught by these latter specimens. "That's
beautiful writing, my dear."

"Very, Sir," replied the child modestly, "is it yours.?"

"Mine!" he returned, taking out his spectacles and
putting them on, to have a better view of the triumphs
so dear to his heart. "*I* couldn't write like that, now-a-
days. No. They're all done by one hand; a little hand
it is, not so old as yours, but a very clever one."

As the schoolmaster said this, he saw that a small blot
of ink had been thrown on one of the copies, so he took a
penknife from his pocket, and going up to the wall, carefully scraped it out. When he had finished, he walked
slowly backward from the writing, admiring it as one
might contemplate a beautiful picture, but with something of sadness in his voice and manner which quite
touched the child, though she was unacquainted with its
cause.

"A little hand indeed," said the poor schoolmaster.
"Far beyond all his companions, in his learning and his
sports too, how did he ever come to be so fond of me!
That I should love him is no wonder, but that he should
love me—" and there the schoolmaster stopped, and took
off his spectacles to wipe them, as though they had grown
dim.

"I hope there is nothing the matter, Sir," said Nell
anxiously.

"Not much, my dear," returned the schoolmaster. "I
hoped to have seen him on the green to-night. He was
always foremost among them. But he'll be there to-
morrow."

"Has he been ill?" asked the child, with a child's
quick sympathy.

"Not very. They said he was wandering in his head
yesterday, dear boy, and so they said the day before.
But that's a part of that kind of disorder; it's not a bad
sign—not at all a bad sign."

The child was silent. He walked to the door, and looked wistfully out. The shadows of night were gathering, and all was still.

" If he could lean upon anybody's arm, he would come to me, I know," he said, returning into the room. " He always came into the garden to say good night. But perhaps his illness has only just taken a favorable turn, and it's too late for him to come out, for it's very damp and there's a heavy dew. It's much better he shouldn't come to-night."

The schoolmaster lighted a candle, fastened the window-shutter, and closed the door. But after he had done this, and sat silent a little time, he took down his hat, and said he would go and satisfy himself, if Nell would sit up till he returned. The child readily complied, and he went out.

She sat there half-an-hour or more, feeling the place very strange and lonely, for she had prevailed upon the old man to go to bed, and there was nothing to be heard but the ticking of an old clock, and the whistling of the wind among the trees. When he returned, he took his seat in the chimney-corner, but remained silent for a long time. At length he turned to her, and speaking very gently, hoped she would say a prayer that night for a sick child.

" My favorite scholar!" said the poor schoolmaster, smoking a pipe he had forgotten to light, and looking mournfully round about the walls. " It is a little hand to have done all that, and waste away with sickness. It is a very, very little hand!"

CHAPTER THE TWENTY-FIFTH.

AFTER a sound night's rest in a chamber in the thatched roof, in which it seemed the sexton had for some years been a lodger, but which he had lately deserted for a wife and a cottage of his own, the child rose early in the morning and descended to the room where she had supped last night. As the schoolmaster had already left his bed and gone out, she bestirred herself to make it neat and comfortable, and had just finished its arrangement when the kind host returned.

He thanked her many times, and said that the old dame who usually did such offices for him had gone to nurse the little scholar whom he had told her of. The child asked how he was, and hoped he was better.

"No," rejoined the schoolmaster shaking his head sorrowfully. "No better. They even say he is worse."

"I am very sorry for that, Sir," said the child.

The poor schoolmaster appeared to be gratified by her earnest manner, but yet rendered more uneasy by it, for he added hastily that anxious people often magnified an evil and thought it greater than it was; "for my part," he said, in his quiet, patient way, "I hope it's not so. I don't think he can be worse."

The child asked his leave to prepare breakfast, and her grandfather coming downstairs, they all three partook of it together. While the meal was in progress, their host remarked that the old man seemed much fatigued, and evidently stood in need of rest.

"If the journey you have before you is a long one," he said, "and don't press you for one day, you're very welcome to pass another night here. I should really be glad if you would, friend."

He saw that the old man looked at Nell, uncertain whether to accept or decline his offer; and added,

"I shall be glad to have your young companion with me for one day. If you can do a charity to a lone man, and rest yourself at the same time, do so. If you must proceed upon your journey, I wish you well through it, and will walk a little way with you before school begins."

"What are we to do, Nell?" said the old man irresolutely, "say what we're to do, dear."

It required no great persuasion to induce the child to answer that they had better accept the invitation and remain. She was happy to show her gratitude to the kind schoolmaster by busying herself in the performance of such household duties as his little cottage stood in need of. When these were done, she took some needle-work from her basket, and sat herself down upon a stool beside the lattice, where the honeysuckle and woodbine entwined their tender stems, and stealing into the room filled it with their delicious breath. Her grandfather was basking in the sun outside, breathing the perfume of the flowers, and idly watching the clouds as they floated on before the light summer wind.

As the schoolmaster, after arranging the two forms in due order, took his seat behind his desk and made other preparations for school, the child was apprehensive that she might be in the way, and offered to withdraw to her little bedroom. But this he would not allow, and as he seemed pleased to have her there, she remained, busying herself with her work.

" Have you many scholars, Sir ? " she asked.

The poor schoolmaster shook his head, and said that they barely filled the two forms.

" Are the others clever, Sir ? " asked the child, glancing at the trophies on the wall.

" Good boys," returned the schoolmaster, "good boys enough, my dear, but they'll never do like that."

A small white-headed boy with a sunburnt face appeared at the door while he was speaking, and stopping there to make a rustic bow, came in and took his seat upon one of the forms. The white-headed boy then put an open book, astonishingly dog's-eared, upon his knees, and thrusting his hands into his pockets began counting the marbles with which they were filled; displaying in the expression of his face a remarkable capacity of totally abstracting his mind from the spelling on which his eyes were fixed. Soon afterwards another white-headed little boy came straggling in, and after him a red-headed lad, and after him two more with white heads, and then one with a flaxen poll, and so on until the forms were occupied by a dozen boys or thereabouts, with heads of every color but gray, and ranging in their ages from four years old to fourteen years or more ; for the legs of the youngest were a long way from the floor when he sat upon the form, and the eldest was a heavy good-tempered foolish fellow, about half a head taller than the schoolmaster.

At the top of the first form—the post of honor in the school—was the vacant place of the little sick scholar, and at the head of the row of pegs on which those who came in hats or caps were wont to hang them up, one was left empty. No boy attempted to violate the sanctity of seat or peg, but many a one looked from the empty spaces to the schoolmaster, and whispered his idle neighbor behind his hand.

Then began the hum of conning over lessons and getting them by heart, the whispered jest and stealthy game, and all the noise and drawl of school; and in the midst of the din sat the poor schoolmaster, the very image of meekness and simplicity, vainly attempting to fix his mind upon the duties of the day, and to forget his little friend. But the tedium of his office reminded him more

strongly of the willing scholar, and his thoughts were rambling from his pupils—it was plain.

None knew this better than the idlest boys, who, growing bolder with impunity, waxed louder and more daring; playing odd-or-even under the master's eye, eating apples openly and without rebuke, pinching each other in sport or malice without the least reserve, and cutting their autographs in the very legs of his desk. The puzzled dunce, who stood beside it to say his lesson out of book, looked no longer at the ceiling for forgotten words, but drew closer to the master's elbow and boldly cast his eye upon the page; the wag of the little troop squinted and made grimaces (at the smallest boy of course), holding no book before his face, and his approving audience knew no constraint in their delight. If the master did chance to rouse himself and seem alive to what was going on, the noise subsided for a moment and no eyes met his but wore a studious and a deeply humble look; but the instant he relapsed again, it broke out afresh, and ten times louder than before.

Oh! how some of those idle fellows longed to be outside, and how they looked at the open door and window, as if they half meditated rushing violently out, plunging into the woods, and being wild boys and savages from that time forth. What rebellious thoughts of the cool river, and some shady bathing-place beneath willow trees with branches dipping in the water, kept tempting and urging that sturdy boy, who, with his shirt-collar unbuttoned and flung back as far as it could go, sat fanning his flushed face with a spelling-book, wishing himself a whale, or a tittlebat, or a fly, or anything but a boy at school on that hot, broiling day! Heat! ask that other boy, whose seat being nearest to the door gave him opportunities of gliding out into the garden and driving his companions to madness by dipping his face into the bucket of the well and then rolling on the grass—ask him if there were ever such a day as that, when even the bees were diving deep down into the cups of flowers and stopping there, as if they had made up their minds to retire from business and be manufacturers of honey no more. The day was made for laziness, and lying on one's back in green places, and staring at the sky till its brightness forced one to shut one's eyes and go to sleep; and was this a time to be poring over musty books in a dark room, slighted by the very sun itself? Monstrous!

Nell sat by the window occupied with her work, but attentive still to all that passed, though sometimes rather timid of the boisterous boys. The lessons over, writing-time began; and there being but one desk and that the master's, each boy sat at it in turn and labored at his crooked copy, while the master walked about. This was a quieter time; for he would come and look over the writer's shoulder, and tell him mildly to observe how such a letter was turned in such a copy on the wall, praise such an up-stroke here and such a down-stroke there, and bid him take it for his model. Then he would stop and tell them what the sick child had said last night, and how he had longed to be among them once again; and such was the poor schoolmaster's gentle and affectionate manner, that the boys seemed quite remorseful that they had worried him so much, and were absolutely quiet; eating no apples, cutting no names, inflicting no pinches, and making no grimaces, for full two minutes after-wards.

"I think, boys," said the schoolmaster when the clock struck twelve, "that I shall give an extra half-holiday this afternoon."

At this intelligence, the boys, led on and headed by the tall boy, raised a great shout, in the midst of which the master was seen to speak, but could not be heard. As he held up his hand, however, in token of his wish that they should be silent, they were considerate enough to leave off, as soon as the longest-winded among them were quite out of breath.

"You must promise me first," said the schoolmaster, "that you'll not be noisy, or at least, if you are, that you'll go away and be so—away out of the village I mean. I'm sure you wouldn't disturb your old playmate and companion."

There was a general murmur (and perhaps a very sincere one, for they were but boys) in the negative; and the tall boy, perhaps as sincerely as any of them, called those about him to witness that he had only shouted in a whisper.

"Then pray don't forget, there's my dear scholars," said the schoolmaster, "what I have asked you, and do it as a favor to me. Be as happy as you can, and don't be unmindful that you are blessed with health. Good-bye all!"

"Thank'ee, Sir," and "good-bye, Sir," were said a great many times in a variety of voices, and the boys went out very slowly and softly. But there was the sun shining and there were the birds singing, as the sun only shines and the birds only sing on holidays and half-holidays; there were the trees waving to all free boys to climb and nestle among their leafy branches; the hay, entreating them to come and scatter it to the pure air; the green corn, gently beckoning towards wood and stream; the smooth ground, rendered smoother still by blending lights and shadows, inviting to runs and leaps, and long walks God knows whither. It was more than boy could bear, and with a joyous whoop the whole cluster took to their heels and spread themselves about, shouting and laughing as they went.

"It's natural, thank Heaven!" said the poor schoolmaster looking after them. "I'm very glad they didn't mind me!"

It is difficult, however, to please everybody, as most of us would have discovered, even without the fable which bears that moral; and in the course of the afternoon several mothers and aunts of pupils looked in to express their entire disapproval of the schoolmaster's proceeding. A few confined themselves to hints, such as politely inquiring what red-letter day or saint's day the almanac said it was; a few (these were the profound village politicians) argued that it was a slight to the Throne and an affront to Church and State, and savored of revolutionary principles, to grant a half-holiday upon any lighter occasion than the birthday of the Monarch; but the majority expressed their displeasure on private grounds and in plain terms, arguing that to put the pupils on this short allowance of learning was nothing but an act of downright robbery and fraud: and one old lady, finding that she could not inflame or irritate the peaceable schoolmaster by talking to him, bounced out of his house and talked at him for half an-hour outside his own window, to another old lady, saying that of course he would deduct this half-holiday from his weekly charge, or of course he would naturally expect to have an opposition started against him; there was no want of idle chaps in that neighborhood (here the old lady raised her voice), and some chaps who were too idle even to be schoolmasters, might soon find that there were other chaps put over their heads, and so she would have them take care, and look pretty sharp about them. But all these taunts and vexations failed to elicit one word from the meek schoolmaster, who sat with the child by his side,—a little more dejected perhaps, but quite silent and uncomplaining.

Towards night an old woman came tottering up the garden as speedily as she could, and meeting the schoolmaster at the door, said he was to go to Dame West's directly, and had best run on before her. He and the child were on the point of going out together for a walk, and without relinquishing her hand, the schoolmaster hurried away, leaving the messenger to follow as she might.

They stopped at a cottage-door, and the schoolmaster knocked softly at it with his hand. It was opened without loss of time. They entered a room where a little group of women were gathered about one, older than the rest, who was crying very bitterly, and sat wringing her hands and rocking herself to and fro.

"Oh dame!" said the schoolmaster, drawing near her chair, "is it so bad as this?"

"He's going fast, cried the old woman; "my grandson's dying. It's all along of you. You shouldn't see him now, but for his being so earnest on it. This is what his learning has brought him to. Oh dear, dear, dear, what can I do!"

"Do not say that I am in any fault," urged the gentle schoolmaster. "I am not hurt, dame. No, no. You are in a great distress of mind, and don't mean what you say. I am sure you don't."

"I do," returned the old woman. "I mean it all. If he hadn't been poring over his books out of fear of you, he would have been well and merry now, I know he would."

The schoolmaster looked round upon the other women as if to entreat some one among them to say a kind word for him, but they shook their heads, and murmured to each other that they never thought there was much good in learning, and that this convinced them. Without saying a word in reply, or giving them a look of reproach, he followed the old woman who had summoned him (and who had now rejoined them) into another room, where his infant friend, half-dressed, lay stretched upon a bed.

He was a very young boy; quite a little child. His hair still hung in curls about his face, and his eyes were very bright; but their light was of Heaven, not earth. The schoolmaster took a seat beside him, and stooping over the pillow, whispered his name. The boy sprang up, stroked his face with his hand, and threw his wasted arms around his neck, crying out that he was his dear kind friend.

"I hope I always was. I meant to be, God knows," said the poor schoolmaster.

"Who is that?" said the boy, seeing Nell. "I am afraid

to kiss her, lest I should make her ill.   Ask her to shake hands with me."

The sobbing child came closer up, and took the little languid hand in hers.   Releasing his again after a time, the sick boy laid him gently down.

"You remember the garden, Harry," whispered the schoolmaster, anxious to rouse him, for a dulness seemed gathering upon the child, "and how pleasant it used to be in the evening time?   You must make haste to visit it again, for I think the very flowers have missed you, and are less gay than they used to be.   You will come soon, my dear, very soon now,—won't you?"

The boy smiled faintly—so very, very faintly—and put his hand upon his friend's gray head.   He moved his lips too, but no voice came from them; no, not a sound.

In the silence that ensued, the hum of distant voices borne upon the evening air came floating through the open window.   "What's that?" said the sick child, opening his eyes.

"The boys at play upon the green."

He took a handkerchief from his pillow, and tried to wave it above his head.   But the feeble arm dropped powerless down.

"Shall I do it?" said the schoolmaster.

"Please wave it at the window," was the faint reply. "Tie it to the lattice.   Some of them may see it there. Perhaps they'll think of me and look this way."

He raised his head, and glanced from the fluttering signal to his idle bat, that lay with slate and book and other boyish property upon a table in the room.   And then he laid him softly down once more, and asked if the little girl was there, for he could not see her.

She stepped forward, and pressed the passive hand that lay upon the coverlet.   The two old friends and companions—for such they were, though they were man and child—held each other in a long embrace, and then the little scholar turned his face towards the wall and fell asleep.

The poor schoolmaster sat in the same place, holding the small cold hand in his, and chafing it.   It was but the hand of a dead child.   He felt that; and yet he chafed it still, and could not lay it down.

15

CHAPTER THE TWENTY-SIXTH.

ALMOST broken-hearted, Nell withdrew with the school-master from the bedside and returned to his cottage. In the midst of her grief and tears she was yet careful to conceal their real cause from the old man, for the dead boy had been a grandchild, and left but one aged relative to mourn his premature decay.

She stole away to bed as quickly as she could, and when she was alone, gave free vent to the sorrow with which her breast was overcharged. But the sad scene she had witnessed, was not without its lesson of content and gratitude; of content with the lot which left her health and freedom ; and gratitude that she was spared to the one relative and friend she loved, and to live and move in a beautiful world, when so many young creatures —as young and full of hope as she—were stricken down and gathered to their graves. How many of the mounds in that old churchyard where she had lately strayed, grew green above the graves of children ! And though she thought as a child herself, and did not perhaps suffi-ciently consider to what a bright and happy existence those who die young are born, and how in death they lose the pain of seeing others die around them, bearing to the tomb some strong affection of their hearts (which makes the old die many times in one long life), still she thought wisely enough, to draw a plain and easy moral from what she had seen that night, and to store it deep in her mind.

Her dreams were of the little scholar: not coffined and covered up, but mingling with angels, and smiling happily. The sun darting his cheerful rays into the room, awoke her ; and now there remained but to take leave of the poor schoolmaster and wander forth once more.

By the time they were ready to depart, school had begun. In the darkened room, the din of yesterday was going on again : a little sobered and softened down, perhaps, but only a very little, if at all. The schoolmaster rose from his desk and walked with them to the gate.

It was with a trembling and reluctant hand, that the child held out to him the money which the lady had given her at the races for her flowers : faltering in her thanks as she thought how small the sum was, and blushing as she offered it. But he bade her put it up, and stooping to kiss her cheek, turned back into his house.

They had not gone half-a-dozen paces when he was at the door again ; the old man retraced his steps to shake hands, and the child did the same.

" Good fortune and happiness go with you ! " said the poor schoolmaster. " I am quite a solitary man now. If you ever pass this way again, you'll not forget the little village-school."

" We shall never forget it, Sir," rejoined Nell ; " nor ever forget to be grateful to you for your kindness to us."

" I have heard such words from the lips of children very often," said the schoolmaster, shaking his head, and smiling thoughtfully, " but they were soon forgotten. I had attached one young friend to me, the better friend for being young—but that's over—God bless you ? "

They bade him farewell very many times, and turned away, walking slowly and often looking back, until they could see him no more. At length they had left the village far behind, and even lost sight of the smoke among the trees. They trudged onward now, at a quicker pace, resolving to keep the main road, and go wherever it might lead them.

But main roads stretch a long, long way. With the exception of two or three inconsiderable clusters of cottages which they passed, without stopping, and one lonely roadside public-house where they had some bread and cheese, this highway had led them to nothing—late in the afternoon—and still lengthened out, far in the distance, the same dull, tedious, winding course, that they had been pursuing all day. As they had no resource, however, but to go forward, they still kept on, though at a much slower pace, being very weary and fatigued.

The afternoon had worn away into a beautiful evening, when they arrived at a point where the road made a sharp turn and struck across a common. On the border of this common, and close to the hedge which divided it from the cultivated fields, a caravan was drawn up to rest ; upon which, by reason of its situation, they came so suddenly that they could not have avoided it if they would.

It was not a shabby, dingy, dusty cart, but a smart little house upon wheels, with white dimity curtains festooning the windows, and window-shutters of green picked out with panels of a staring red, in which happily-contrasted colors the whole concern shone brilliant. Neither was it a poor caravan drawn by a single donkey or emaciated horse, for a pair of horses in pretty good condition were released from the shafts and grazing on the frowzy grass. Neither was it a gypsy caravan, for at the open door (graced with a bright brass knocker) sat a Christian lady, stout and comfortable to look upon, who wore a large bonnet trembling with bows. And that it was not an unprovided or destitute caravan was clear from this lady's occupation, which was the very pleasant and refreshing one of taking tea. The tea-things, including a bottle of rather suspicious character and a cold knuckle of ham, were set forth upon a drum, covered with a white napkin; and there, as if at the most convenient round-table in all the world, sat this roving lady, taking her tea and enjoying the prospect.

It happened that at that moment the lady of the caravan had her cup (which, that everything about her might be of a stout and comfortable kind, was a breakfast cup) to her lips, and that having her eyes lifted to the sky in her enjoyment of the full flavor of the tea, not unmingled possibly with just the slightest dash or gleam of something out of the suspicious bottle—but this is mere speculation and not distinct matter of history—it happened that being thus agreeably engaged, she did not see the travellers when they first came up. It was not until she was in the act of setting down the cup, and drawing a long breath after the exertion of causing its contents to disappear, that the lady of the caravan beheld an old man and a young child walking slowly by, and glancing at her proceedings with eyes of modest but hungry admiration.

"Hey!" cried the lady of the caravan, scooping the crumbs out of her lap and swallowing the same before wiping her lips. "Yes to be sure—Who won the Helter-Skelter Plate, child?"

"Won what, ma'am?" asked Nell.

"The Helter-Skelter Plate at the races, child—the plate that was run for on the second day."

"On the second day, ma'am?"

"Second day! Yes, second day," repeated the lady with an air of impatience. "Can't you say who won the Helter-Skelter Plate when you're asked the question civilly?"

"I don't know, ma'am."

"Don't know!" repeated the lady of the caravan; "why, you were there. I saw you with my own eyes."

Nell was not a little alarmed to hear this, supposing that the lady might be intimately acquainted with the

firm of Short and Codlin; but what followed tended to reassure her.

"And very sorry I was," said the lady of the caravan, "to see you in company with a Punch; a low, practical, wulgar wretch, that people should scorn to look at."

"I was not there by choice," returned the child; "we didn't know our way, and the two men were very kind to us, and let us travel with them. Do you—do you know them, ma'am?"

"Know 'em, child!" cried the lady of the caravan in a sort of shriek. "Know *them!* But you're young and inexperienced, and that's your excuse for asking sich

question.   Do I look as if I know'd 'em, does the caravan
look as if *it* know'd 'em?"

"No, ma'am, no," said the child, fearing she had committed some grievous fault.   "I beg your pardon."

It was granted immediately, though the lady still appeared much ruffled and discomposed by the degrading
supposition.   The child then explained that they had left
the races on the first day, and were travelling to the next
town on that road, where they purposed to spend the
night.   As the countenance of the stout lady began to
clear up, she ventured to inquire how far it was.   The
reply—which the stout lady did not come to, until she
had thoroughly explained that she went to the races on
the first day in a gig, and as an expedition of pleasure,
and that her presence there had no connection with any
matters of business or profit—was, that the town was
eight miles off.

This discouraging information a little dashed the child,
who could scarcely repress a tear as she glanced along
the darkening road.   Her grandfather made no complaint, but he sighed heavily as he leaned upon his staff,
and vainly tried to pierce the dusty distance.

The lady of the caravan was in the act of gathering
her tea equipage together preparatory to clearing the
table, but noting the child's anxious manner she hesitated
and stopped.   The child curtseyed, thanked her for her
information, and giving her hand to the old man had already got some fifty yards or so, away, when the lady of
the caravan called to her to return.

"Come nearer, nearer still"—said she, beckoning to
her to ascend the steps.   "Are you hungry, child?"

"Not very, but we are tired, and it's—it *is* a long
way"—

"Well, hungry or not, you had better have some tea,"
rejoined her new acquaintance.   "I suppose you are
agreeable to that, old gentleman?"

The grandfather humbly pulled off his hat and thanked
her.   The lady of the caravan then bade him come up the
steps likewise, but the drum proving an inconvenient
table for two, they descended again, and sat upon the
grass, where she handed down to them the tea-tray, the
bread and butter, the knuckle of ham, and in short everything of which she had partaken herself, except the bottle

which she had already embraced an opportunity of slipping into her pocket.

"Set 'em out near the hind wheels, child, that's the
best place"—said their friend, superintending the arrangements from above. "Now hand up the teapot for
a little more hot water, and a pinch of fresh tea, and then
both of you eat and drink as much as you can, and don't
spare anything; that's all I ask of you."

They might perhaps have carried out the lady's wish,
if it had been less freely expressed, or even if it had not
been expressed at all. But as this direction relieved them
from any shadow of delicacy or uneasiness, they made a
hearty meal and enjoyed it to the utmost.

While they were thus engaged, the lady of the caravan
alighted on the earth, and with her hands clasped behind
her, and her large bonnet trembling excessively, walked
up and down in a measured tread and very stately manner, surveying the caravan from time to time with an air
of calm delight, and deriving particular gratification from
the red panels and the brass knocker. When she had
taken this gentle exercise for some time, she sat down
upon the steps and called "George;" whereupon a man in
a carter's frock, who had been so shrouded in a hedge up to
this time as to see everything that passed without being
seen himself, parted the twigs that concealed him, and
appeared in a sitting attitude, supporting on his legs a
baking-dish and a half-gallon stone bottle, and bearing
in his right hand a knife, and in his left a fork.

"Yes, Missus "—said George.

"How did you find the cold pie, George?"

"It warn't amiss, Mum."

"And the beer," said the lady of the caravan, with an
appearance of being more interested in this question than
the last; "is it passable, George?"

"It's more flatterer than it might be," George returned,
"but it an't so bad for all that."

To set the mind of his mistress at rest, he took a sip
(amounting in quantity to a pint or thereabouts) from the
stone bottle, and then smacked his lips, winked his eye,
and nodded his head. No doubt with the same amiable
desire, he immediately resumed his knife and fork, as a
practical assurance that the beer had wrought no bad
effect upon his appetite.

The lady of the caravan looked on approvingly for some time, and then said,

"Have you nearly finished?"

"Wery nigh, Mum." And indeed, after scraping the dish all round with his knife and carrying the choice brown morsels to his mouth, and after taking such a scientific pull at the stone bottle that, by degrees almost imperceptible to the sight, his head went further and further back until he lay nearly at his full length upon the ground, this gentleman declared himself quite disengaged, and came forth from his retreat.

"I hope I haven't hurried you, George," said his mistress, who appeared to have a great sympathy with his late pursuit.

"If you have," returned the follower, wisely reserving himself for any favorable contingency that might occur, "we must make up for it next time, that's all."

"We are not a heavy load, George?"

"That's always what the ladies say," replied the man, looking a long way round, as if he were appealing to Nature in general against such monstrous propositions. "If you see a woman a driving, you'll always perceive that she never will keep her whip still; the horse can't go fast enough for her. If cattle have got their proper load, you never can persuade a woman that they'll not bear something more. What is the cause of this here?"

"Would these two travellers make much difference to the horses, if we took them with us?" asked his mistress, offering no reply to the philosophical inquiry, and pointing to Nell and the old man, who were painfully preparing to resume their journey on foot.

"They'd make a difference in course," said George doggedly.

"Would they make much difference?" repeated his mistress. "They can't be very heavy."

"The weight o' the pair, Mum," said George, eyeing them with the look of a man who was calculating within half an ounce or so, "would be a trifle under that of Oliver Cromwell."

Nell was very much surprised that the man should be so accurately acquainted with the weight of one whom she had read of in books as having lived considerably before their time, but speedily forgot the subject in the joy of hearing that they were to go forward in the caravan, for which she thanked its lady with unaffected earnestness. She helped with great readiness and alacrity to put away the tea-things and other matters that were lying about, and, the horses being by that time harnessed, mounted into the vehicle, followed by her delighted grandfather. Their patroness then shut the door and sat herself down by her drum at an open window; and, the steps being struck by George and stowed under the carriage, away they went, with a great noise of flapping and creaking and straining, and the bright brass knocker, which nobody ever knocked at, knocking one perpetual double knock of its own accord as they jolted heavily along.

CHAPTER THE TWENTY-SEVENTH.

WHEN they had travelled slowly forward for some short distance, Nell ventured to steal a look round the caravan and observe it more closely. One half of it—that moiety in which the comfortable proprietress was then seated—was carpeted, and so partitioned off at the further end as to accommodate a sleeping-place, constructed after the fashion of a berth on board ship, which was shaded, like the little windows, with fair white curtains, and looked comfortable enough, though by what kind of gymnastic exercise the lady of the caravan ever contrived to get into it, was an unfathomable mystery. The other half served for a kitchen, and was fitted up with a stove whose small chimney passed through the roof. It held also a closet or larder, several chests, a great pitcher of water, and a few cooking-utensils and articles of crockery. These latter necessaries hung upon the walls, which, in that portion of the establishment devoted to the lady of the caravan, were ornamented with such gayer and lighter decorations as a triangle and a couple of well-thumbed tambourines.

The lady of the caravan sat at one window in all the pride and poetry of the musical instruments, and little Nell and her grandfather sat at the other in all the humility of the kettle and saucepans, while the machine jogged on and shifted the darkening prospect very slowly.

At first the two travellers spoke little, and only in whispers, but as they grew more familiar with the place they ventured to converse with greater freedom, and talked about the country through which they were passing, and the different objects that presented themselves, until the old man fell asleep; which the lady of the caravan observing, invited Nell to come and sit beside her.

"Well, child," she said, "how do you like this way of travelling?"

Nell replied that she thought it was very pleasant indeed, to which the lady assented in the case of people who had their spirits. For herself, she said, she was troubled with a lowness in that respect which required a constant stimulant; though whether the aforesaid stimulant was derived from the suspicious bottle of which mention has been already made, or from other sources, she did not say.

"That's the happiness of you young people," she continued. "You don't know what it is to be low in your feelings. You always have your appetites too, and what a comfort that is."

Nell thought that she could sometimes dispense with her own appetite very conveniently; and thought, moreover, that there was nothing either in the lady's personal appearance or in her manner of taking tea, to lead to the conclusion that her natural relish for meat and drink had at all failed her. She silently assented, however, as in duty bound, to what the lady had said, and waited until she should speak again.

Instead of speaking, however, she sat looking at the child for a long time in silence, and then getting up, brought out from a corner a large roll of canvas about a yard in width, which she laid upon the floor and spread open with her foot until it nearly reached from one end of the caravan to the other.

"There, child," she said, "read that."

Nell walked down it, and read aloud in enormous black letters, the inscription, "JARLEY'S WAX-WORK."

"Read it again," said the lady, complacently.

"Jarley's Wax-Work," repeated Nell.

"That's me," said the lady. "I am Mrs. Jarley."

Giving the child an encouraging look, intended to reassure her and let her know, that, although she stood in the presence of the original Jarley, she must not allow herself to be utterly overwhelmed and borne down, the lady of the caravan unfolded another scroll, whereon was the inscription, "One hundred figures the full size of life," and then another scroll, on which was written, "The only stupendous collection of real wax-work in the world," and then several smaller scrolls with such inscriptions as "Now exhibiting within"—"The genuine and only Jarley"—"Jarley's unrivalled collection"— "Jarley is the delight of the Nobility and Gentry"— "The Royal Family are the patrons of Jarley." When she had exhibited these leviathans of public announcement to the astonished child, she brought forth specimens of the lesser fry in the shape of hand-bills, some of which were couched in the form of parodies on popular melodies, as "Believe me if all Jarley's wax-work so rare"—"I saw thy show in youthful prime"—"Over the water to Jarley;" while, to consult all tastes, others were composed with a view to the lighter and more facetious spirits, as a parody on the favorite air of "If I had a donkey," beginning

> If I know'd a donkey wot wouldn't go
> To see Mrs. JARLEY'S wax-work show,
> Do you think I'd acknowledge him?
> Oh no no !
> > Then run to Jarley's—

—besides several compositions in prose, purporting to be dialogues between the Emperor of China and an oyster, or the Archbishop of Canterbury and a Dissenter on the subject of church-rates, but all having the same moral, namely, that the reader must make haste to Jarley's, and that children and servants were admitted at half-price. When she had brought all these testimonials of her important position in society to bear upon her young companion, Mrs. Jarley rolled them up, and having put them carefully away, sat down again, and looked at the child in triumph.

"Never go into the company of a filthy Punch any more," said Mrs. Jarley, "after this."

"I never saw any wax-work, ma'am," said Nell. "Is it funnier than Punch?"

"Funnier!" said Mrs. Jarley in a shrill voice. "It is not funny at all."

"Oh!" said Nell, with all possible humility.

"It isn't funny at all," repeated Mrs. Jarley. "It's calm and—what's that word again—critical?—no—classical, that's it—it's calm and classical. No low beatings and knockings about, no jokings and squeakings like your precious Punches, but always the same, with a constantly unchanging air of coldness and gentility; and so like life, that if wax-work only spoke and walked about, you'd hardly know the difference. I won't go so far as to say, that, as it is, I've seen wax-work quite like life, but I've certainly seen some life that was exactly like wax-work."

"Is it here, ma'am?" asked Nell, whose curiosity was awakened by this description.

"Is what here, child?"

"The wax-work, ma'am."

"Why, bless you, child, what are you thinking of? How could such a collection be here, where you see everything except the inside of one little cupboard and a few boxes? It's gone on in the other wans to the assembly-rooms, and there it'll be exhibited the day after to-morrow. You are going to the same town, and you'll see it I dare say. It's natural to expect that you'll see it, and I've no doubt you will. I suppose you couldn't stop away if you was to try ever so much."

"I shall not be in town, I think, ma'am," said the child.

"Not there?" cried Mrs. Jarley. "Then where will you be?"

"I—I—don't quite know. I am not certain."

"You don't mean to say that you're travelling about the country without knowing where you're going to?" said the lady of the caravan. "What curious people you are! What line are you in? You looked to me at the races, child, as if you were quite out of your element, and had got there by accident."

"We were there quite by accident," returned Nell, confused by this abrupt questioning. "We are poor people, ma'am, and are only wandering about. We have nothing to do;—I wish we had."

"You amaze me more and more," said Mrs. Jarley, **after** remaining for some time as mute as one of her own figures. "Why, what do you call yourselves? Not beggars?"

"Indeed, ma'am, I don't know what else we are," returned the child.

"Lord bless me," said the lady of the caravan. "I never heard of such a thing. Who'd have thought it!"

She remained so long silent after this exclamation, that Nell feared she felt her having been induced to bestow her protection and conversation upon one so poor, to be an outrage upon her dignity that nothing could repair. This persuasion was rather confirmed than otherwise by the tone in which she at length broke silence and said,

"And yet you can read. And write too, I shouldn't wonder?"

"Yes, ma' am," said the child, fearful of giving new offence by the confession.

"Well, and what a thing that is," returned Mrs. Jarley. "*I* can't!"

Nell said "indeed" in a tone which might imply, either that she was reasonably surprised to find the genuine and only Jarley, who was the delight of the Nobility and Gentry and the peculiar pet of the Royal Family, destitute of these familiar arts ; or that she presumed so great a lady could scarcely stand in need of such ordinary accomplishments. In whatever way Mrs. Jarley received the response, it did not provoke her to further questioning, or tempt her into any more remarks at the time, for she relapsed into a thoughtful silence, and remained in that state so long that Nell withdrew to the other window and rejoined her grandfather, who was now awake.

At length the lady of the caravan shook off her fit of meditation, and, summoning the driver to come under the window at which she was seated, held a long conversation with him in a low tone of voice, as if she were asking his advice on an important point, and discussing the pros and cons of some very weighty matter. This conference at length concluded, she drew in her head again, and beckoned Nell to approach.

"And the old gentleman too," said Mrs. Jarley ; "for I want to have a word with him. Do you want a good situation for your grand-daughter, master ? If you do, I can put her in the way of getting one. What do you say?"

"I can't leave her," answered the old man. "We can't separate. What would become of me without her?"

"I should have thought you were old enough to take care of yourself, if you ever will be," retorted Mrs. Jarley sharply.

"But he never will be," said the child in an earnest whisper. "I fear he never will be again. Pray do not speak harshly to him. We are very thankful to you," she added aloud; "neither of us could part from the other if all the wealth of the world were halved between us."

Mrs. Jarley was a little disconcerted by this reception of her proposal, and looked at the old man, who tenderly took Nell's hand and detained it in his own, as if she could have very well dispensed with his company or even his earthly existence. After an awkward pause, she thrust her head out of the window again, and had another conference with the driver upon some point on which they did not seem to agree quite so readily as on their former topic of discussion; but they concluded at last, and she addressed the grandfather again.

"If you're really disposed to employ yourself," said Mrs. Jarley, "there would be plenty for you to do in the way of helping to dust the figures, and take the checks, and so forth. What I want your grand-daughter for, is to point 'em out to the company; they would be soon learnt, and she has a way with her that people wouldn't think unpleasant, though she does come after me; for I've been always accustomed to go round with visitors myself, which I should keep on doing now, only that my spirits make a little ease absolutely necessary. It's not a common offer, bear in mind," said the lady, rising into the tone and manner in which she was accustomed to address her audiences; "it's Jarley's wax-work, remember. The duty's very light and genteel, the company particular select, the exhibition takes place in assembly-rooms, town-halls, large rooms at inns, or auction galleries. There is none of your open-air wagrancy at Jarley's, recollect; there is no tarpaulin and sawdust at Jarley's, remember. Every expectation held out in the handbills is realized to the utmost, and the whole forms an effect of imposing brilliancy hitherto unrivalled in this kingdom.

Remember that the price of admission is only sixpence, and that this is an opportunity which may never occur again!"

Descending from the sublime when she had reached this point, to the details of common life, Mrs. Jarley remarked that with reference to salary she could pledge herself to no specific sum until she had sufficiently tested Nell's abilities, and narrowly watched her in the performance of her duties. But board and lodging, both for her and her grandfather, she bound herself to provide, and she furthermore passed her word that the board should always be good in quality, and in quantity plentiful.

Nell and her grandfather consulted together, and while they were so engaged, Mrs. Jarley with her hands behind her walked up and down the caravan, as she had walked after tea on the dull earth, with uncommon dignity and self-esteem. Nor will this appear so slight a circumstance as to be unworthy of mention, when it is remembered that the caravan was in uneasy motion all the time, and that none but a person of great natural stateliness and acquired grace could have forborne to stagger.

"Now, child?" cried Mrs. Jarley, coming to a halt as Nell turned towards her.

"We are very much obliged to you, ma'am," said Nell, "and thankfully accept your offer."

"And you'll never be sorry for it," returned Mrs. Jarley. "I'm pretty sure of that. So as that's all settled, let us have a bit of supper."

In the meanwhile, the caravan blundered on as if it too had been drinking strong beer and was drowsy, and came at last upon the paved streets of a town which were clear of passengers, and quiet, for it was by this time near midnight, and the townspeople were all abed. As it was too late an hour to repair to the exhibition room, they turned aside into a piece of waste ground that lay just within the old town-gate, and drew up there for the night, near to another caravan, which, notwithstanding that it bore on the lawful panel the great name of Jarley, and was employed besides in conveying from place to place the wax-work which was its country's pride, was designated by a grovelling stamp-office as a "Common Stage Wagon," and numbered too—seven thousand odd hundred—as though its precious freight were mere flour or coals!

This ill-used machine being empty (for it had deposited its burden at the place of exhibition, and lingered here until its services were again required) was assigned to the old man as his sleeping-place for the night; and within its wooden walls, Nell made him up the best bed she could, from the materials at hand. For herself, she was to sleep in Mrs. Jarley's own travelling-carriage, as a signal mark of that lady's favor and confidence.

She had taken leave of her grandfather and was returning to the other wagon, when she was tempted by the pleasant coolness of the night to linger for a little while in the air. The moon was shining down upon the old gateway of the town, leaving the low archway very black and dark; and with a mingled sensation of curiosity and fear, she slowly approached the gate, and stood still to look up at it, wondering to see how dark, and grim, and old, and cold, it looked.

There was an empty niche from which some old statue had fallen or been carried away hundreds of years ago, and she was thinking what strange people it must have looked down upon when it stood there, and how many hard struggles might have taken place, and how many murders might have been done, upon that silent spot, when there suddenly emerged from the black shade of the arch, a man. The instant he appeared, she recognized him—Who could have failed to recognize, in that instant, the ugly misshapen Quilp!

The street beyond was so narrow, and the shadow of the houses on one side of the way so deep, that he seemed to have risen out of the earth. But there he was. The child withdrew into a dark corner, and saw him pass close to her. He had a stick in his hand, and, when he had got clear of the shadow of the gateway, he leant upon it, looked back—directly, as it seemed, towards where she stood—and beckoned.

To her? oh no, thank God, not to her; for as she stood, in an extremity of fear, hesitating whether to scream for help, or come from her hiding-place and fly, before he should draw nearer, there issued slowly forth from the arch another figure—that of a boy—who carried on his back a trunk.

"Faster, sirrah!" said Quilp, looking up at the old
gateway, and showing in the moonlight like some monstrous image that had come down from its niche and was
casting a backward glance at its old house, "faster!"

"It's a dreadful heavy load, Sir," the boy pleaded.
"I've come on very fast, considering."

"*You* have come fast, considering!" retorted Quilp;
"you creep, you dog, you crawl, you measure distance like
a worm. There are the chimes now, half-past twelve."

He stopped to listen, and then turning upon the boy

with a suddenness and ferocity that made him start, asked
at what hour that London coach passed the corner of the
road. The boy replied, at one.

"Come on then, " said Quilp, "or I shall be too late.
Faster—do you hear me? Faster."

The boy made all the speed he could, and Quilp led
onward, constantly turning back to threaten him, and
urge him to greater haste. Nell did not dare to move
until they were out of sight and hearing, and then hurried
to where she had left her grandfather, feeling as if the
very passing of the dwarf so near him must have filled
him with alarm and terror. But he was sleeping soundly,
and she softly withdrew.

16

As she was making her way to her own bed, she determined to say nothing of this adventure, as upon whatever errand the dwarf had come (and she feared it must
have been in search of them) it was clear by his inquiry
about the London coach that he was on his way homeward, and as he had passed through that place, it was
but reasonable to suppose that they were safer from his
inquiries there, than they could be elsewhere.   These
reflections did not remove her own alarm, for she had
been too much terrified to be easily composed, and felt as
if she were hemmed in by a legion of Quilps, and the very
air itself were filled with them.

The delight of the Nobility and Gentry and the patronized of Royalty had, by some process of self-abridgment
known only to herself, got into her travelling bed, where
she was snoring peacefully, while the large bonnet, carefully disposed upon the drum, was revealing its glories
by the light of a dim lamp that swung from the roof.
The child's bed was already made upon the floor, and it
was a great comfort to her to hear the steps removed as
soon as she had entered, and to know that all easy communication between persons outside and the brass knocker
was by this means effectually prevented.   Certain gut-
tural sounds, too, which from time to time ascended
through the floor of the caravan, and a rustling of straw
in the same direction, apprised her that the driver was
couched upon the ground beneath, and gave her an additional feeling of security.

Notwithstanding these protections, she could get none
but broken sleep by fits and starts all night, for fear of
Quilp, who throughout her uneasy dreams was somehow
connected with the wax-work, or was wax-work himself,
or was Mrs. Jarley and wax-work too, or was himself,
Mrs. Jarley, wax-work, and a barrel organ all in one, and
yet not exactly any of them either.   At length, towards
break of day, that deep sleep came upon her which succeeds to weariness and over-watching, and which has no
consciousness but one of overpowering and irresistible
enjoyment.

CHAPTER THE TWENTY-EIGHTH.

SLEEP hung upon the eyelids of the child so long, that, when she awoke, Mrs. Jarley was already decorated with her large bonnet, and actively engaged in preparing breakfast. She received Nell's apology for being so late with perfect good humor, and said that she should not have roused her if she had slept on until noon.

"Because it does you good," said the lady of the caravan, "when you're tired, to sleep as long as ever you can, and get the fatigue quite off; and that's another blessing of your time of life—you can sleep so very sound."

"Have you had a bad night, ma'am?" asked Nell.

"I seldom have anything else, child," replied Mrs. Jarley, with the air of a martyr. "I sometimes wonder how I bear it."

Remembering the snores which had proceeded from that cleft in the caravan in which the proprietress of the wax-work passed the night, Nell rather thought she must have been dreaming of lying awake. However, she expressed herself very sorry to hear such a dismal account of her state of health, and shortly afterwards sat down with her grandfather and Mrs. Jarley to breakfast. The meal finished, Nell assisted to wash the cups and saucers, and put them in their proper places, and these household duties performed, Mrs. Jarley arrayed herself in an exceedingly bright shawl for the purpose of making a progress through the streets of the town.

"The wan will come on to bring the boxes," said Mrs. Jarley, "and you had better come in it, child. I am obliged to walk, very much against my will; but the people expect it of me, and public characters can't be their own masters and mistresses in such matters as these. How do I·look, child?"

Nell returned a satisfactory reply, and Mrs. Jarley, after sticking a great many pins into various parts of her figure, and making several abortive attempts to obtain a full view of her own back, was at last satisfied with her appearance, and went forth majestically.

The caravan followed at no great distance. As it went jolting through the streets, Nell peeped from the window, curious to see in what kind of place they were, and yet fearful of encountering at every turn the dreaded face of Quilp. It was a pretty large town, with an open square which they were crawling slowly across, and in the middle of which was the Town-hall, with a clock-tower and a weathercock. There were houses of stone, houses of red brick, houses of yellow brick, houses of lath and plaster; and houses of wood, many of them very old, with withered faces carved upon the beams, and staring down into the street. These had very little winking windows, and low-arched doors, and, in some of the narrower ways, quite overhung the pavement. The streets were very clean, very sunny, very empty, and very dull. A few idle men lounged about the two inns, and the empty market-place, and the tradesmen's doors, and some old people were dozing in chairs outside an almshouse wall; but scarcely any passengers who seemed bent on going anywhere, or to have any object in view, went by; and if perchance some straggler did, his footsteps echoed on the hot bright pavement for minutes afterwards. Nothing seemed to be going on but the clocks, and they had such drowsy faces, such heavy lazy hands, and such cracked voices, that they surely must have been too slow. The very dogs were all asleep, and the flies, drunk with moist sugar in the grocer's shop, forgot their wings and brisk-ness, and baked to death in dusty corners of the window.

Rumbling along with most unwonted noise, the caravan stopped at last at the place of exhibition, where Nell dismounted amidst an admiring group of children, who evidently supposed her to be an important item of the curiosities, and were fully impressed with the belief that her grandfatoer was a cunning device in wax. The chests were taken out with all convenient despatch, and taken in to be unlocked by Mrs. Jarley, who, attended by George and another man in velveteen shorts and a drab hat ornamented with turnpike tickets, were waiting to dispose their contents (consisting of red festoons and other ornamental devices in upholstery work) to the best advantage in the decoration of the room.

They all got to work without loss of time, and very busy they were. As the stupendous collection were yet concealed by cloths, lest the envious dust should injure their complexions, Nell bestirred herself to assist in the embellishment of the room, in which her grandfather also was of great service. The two men being well used to it, did a great deal in a short time; and Mrs. Jarley served out the tin tacks from a linen pocket like a toll-collector's which she wore for the purpose, and encouraged her assistants to renewed exertion.

While they were thus employed, a tallish gentleman with a hook nose and black hair, dressed in a military surtout very short and tight in the sleeves, and which had once been frogged and braided all over, but was now sadly shorn of its garniture and quite threadbare—dressed too in ancient gray pantaloons fitting tight to the leg, and a pair of pumps in the winter of their existence—looked in at the door, and smiled affably. Mrs. Jarley's back being then towards him, the military gentleman shook his forefinger as a sign that her myrmidons were not to apprise her of his presence, and stealing up close behind her, tapped her on the neck, and cried playfully "Boh!"

"What, Mr. Slum!" cried the lady of the wax-work. "Lor! who'd have thought of seeing you here!"

"'Pon my soul and honor," said Mr. Slum, "that's a good remark. 'Pon my soul and honor, that's a wise remark. Who *would* have thought it! George, my faithful feller, how are you?"

George received this advance with a surly indifference, observing that he was well enough for the matter of that, and hammering lustily all the time.

"I came here," said the military gentleman turning to Mrs. Jarley,—"'pon my soul and honor, I hardly know what I came here for. It would puzzle me to tell you, it would by Gad. I wanted a little inspiration, a little freshening up, a little change of ideas, and——'Pon my soul and honor," said the military gentleman, checking himself and looking round the room, "what a devilish classical thing this is! By Gad, it's quite Minervian!"

"It'll look well enough when it comes to be finished," observed Mrs. Jarley.

"Well enough!" said Mr. Slum. "Will you believe me when I say it's the delight of my life to have dabbled in poetry, when I think I've exercised my pen upon this charming theme? By the way—any orders? Is there any little thing I can do for you?"

"It comes so very expensive, Sir," replied Mrs. Jarley, "and I really don't think it does much good."

"Hush! No, no!" returned Mr. Slum, elevating his hand. "No fibs. I'll not hear it. Don't say it don't do good. Don't say it. I know better!"

"I don't think it does," said Mrs. Jarley.

"Ha, ha!" cried Mr. Slum, "you're giving way, you're coming down. Ask the perfumers, ask the blacking-makers, ask the hatters, ask the old lottery-office-keepers —ask any man among 'em what my poetry has done for him, and mark my words, he blesses the name of Slum. If he's an honest man, he raises his eyes to heaven, and blesses the name of Slum—mark that! You are acquainted with Westminster Abbey, Mrs. Jarley?"

"Yes, surely."

"Then upon my soul and honor, ma'am, you'll find in a certain angle of that dreary pile, called Poets' Corner, a few smaller names than Slum," retorted that gentleman, tapping himself expressively on the forehead to imply that there was some slight quantity of brains behind it. "I've got a little trifle here, now," said Mr. Slum, taking off his hat which was full of scraps of paper, "a little trifle here, thrown off in the heat of the moment, which I should say was exactly the thing you wanted to set this place on fire with. It's an acrostic—the name at this moment is Warren, but the idea's a convertible one, and a positive inspiration for Jarley. Have the acrostic."

"I suppose it's very dear," said Mrs. Jarley.

"Five shillings," returned Mr. Slum, using his pencil as a tooth-pick. "Cheaper than any prose."

"I couldn't give more than three," said Mrs. Jarley.

"—And six," retorted Slum. "Come. Three-and-six."

Mrs. Jarley was not proof against the poet's insinuating manner, and Mr. Slum entered the order in a small note-book as a three-and-sixpenny one. Mr. Slum then withdrew to alter the acrostic, after taking a most affectionate leave of his patroness, and promising to return, as soon as he possibly could, with a fair copy for the printer.

As his presence had not interfered with or interrupted the preparations, they were now far advanced, and were completed shortly after his departure. When the festoons

were all put up as tastily as they might be, the stupendous collection was uncovered, and there were displayed,
on a raised platform some two feet from the floor, running round the room and parted from the rude public by
a crimson rope breast high, divers sprightly effigies of
celebrated characters, singly and in groups, clad in glittering dresses of various climes and times, and standing
more or less unsteadily upon their legs, with their eyes
very wide open, and their nostrils very much inflated,
and the muscles of their legs and arms very strongly developed, and all their countenances expressing great surprise. All the gentlemen were very pigeon-breasted and
very blue about the beards; and all the ladies were miraculous figures; and all the ladies and all the gentlemen
were looking intensely nowhere, and staring with extraordinary earnestness at nothing.

When Nell had exhausted her first raptures at this
glorious sight, Mrs. Jarley ordered the room to be cleared
of all but herself and the child, and, sitting herself down
in an arm-chair in the centre, formally invested her with
a willow wand, long used by herself for pointing out the
characters, and was at great pains to instruct her in her
duty.

"That," said Mrs. Jarley in her exhibition tone, as
Nell touched a figure at the beginning of the platform,
" is an unfortunate Maid of Honor in the Time of Queen
Elizabeth, who died from pricking her finger in consequence of working upon a Sunday. Observe the blood
which is trickling from her finger; also the gold-eyed
needle of the period, with which she is at work."

All this Nell repeated twice or thrice, pointing to the
finger and the needle at the right times, and then passed
on to the next.

" That, ladies and gentlemen," said Mrs. Jarley, " is
Jasper Packlemerton of atrocious memory, who courted
and married fourteen wives, and destroyed them all by
tickling the soles of their feet when they was sleeping in
the consciousness of innocence and virtue. On being
brought to the scaffold and asked if he was sorry for what
he had done, he replied yes, he was sorry for having let
'em off so easy, and hoped all Christian husbands would
pardon him the offence. Let this be a warning to all
young ladies to be particular in the character of the

gentlemen of their choice. Observe that his fingers is curled as if in the act of tickling, and that his face is represented with a wink, as he appeared when committing his barbarous murders."

When Nell knew all about Mr. Packlemerton, and could say it without faltering, Mrs. Jarley passed on to the fat man, and then to the thin man, the tall man, the short man, the old lady who died of dancing at a hundred and thirty-two, the wild boy of the woods, the woman who

poisoned fourteen families with pickled walnuts, and other historical characters and interesting but misguided individuals. And so well did Nell profit by her instructions, and so apt was she to remember them, that by the time they had been shut up together for a couple of hours, she was in full possession of the history of the whole establishment, and perfectly competent to the enlightenment of visitors.

Mrs. Jarley was not slow to express her admiration at this happy result, and carried her young friend and pupil to inspect the remaining arrangements within doors, by virtue of which the passage had been already converted into a grove of green-baize hung with the inscriptions she had already seen (Mr. Slum's productions), and a highly ornamented table placed at the upper end for Mrs. Jarley herself, at which she was to preside and take the money, in company with his Majesty King George the Third, Mr. Grimaldi as clown, Mary Queen of Scots, an anonymous gentleman of the Quaker persuasion, and Mr. Pitt holding in his hand a correct model of the bill for the imposition of the window duty. The preparations without doors had not been neglected either; for a nun of great personal attractions was telling her beads on the little portico over the door; and a brigand with the blackest possible head of hair, and the clearest possible complexion, was at that moment going round the town in a cart, consulting the miniature of a lady.

It now only remained that Mr. Slum's compositions should be judiciously distributed; that the pathetic effusions should find their way to all private houses and tradespeople; and that the parody commencing "If I know'd a donkey," should be confined to the taverns, and circulated only among the lawyers' clerks and choice spirits of the place. When this had been done, and Mrs. Jarley had waited upon the boarding-schools in person, with a handbill composed expressly for them, in which it was distinctly proved that wax-work refined the mind, cultivated the taste, and enlarged the sphere of the human understanding, that indefatigable lady sat down to dinner, and drank out of the suspicious bottle to a flourishing campaign.

CHAPTER THE TWENTY-NINTH.

UNQUESTIONABLY Mrs. Jarley had an inventive genius. In the midst of the various devices for attracting visitors to the exhibition, little Nell was not forgotten. The light cart in which the Brigand usually made his perambulations being gaily dressed with flags and streamers, and the Brigand placed therein, contemplating the miniature of his beloved as usual, Nell was accommodated with a seat beside him, decorated with artificial flowers, and in this state and ceremony rode slowly through the town every morning, dispersing handbills from a basket, to the

sound of drum and trumpet. The beauty of the child,
coupled with her gentle and timid bearing, produced
quite a sensation in the little country place. The Brigand,
heretofore a source of exclusive interest in the streets,
became a mere secondary consideration, and to be important only as a part of the show of which she was the
chief attraction. Grown-up folks began to be interested
in the bright-eyed girl, and some score of little boys fell

desperately in love, and constantly left inclosures of nuts
and apples, directed in small text, at the wax-work door.
This desirable impression was not lost upon Mrs. Jarley, who, lest Nell should become too cheap, soon sent
the Brigand out alone again, and kept her in the exhibition room, where she described the figures every half-hour
to the great satisfaction of admiring audiences. And
these audiences were of a very superior description, including a great many young ladies' boarding-schools,
whose favor Mrs. Jarley had been at great pains to conciliate, by altering the face and costume of Mr. Grimaldi
as clown to represent Mr. Lindley Murray as he appeared

when engaged in the composition of his English Grammar, and turning a murderess of great renown into Mrs. Hannah More—both of which likenesses were admitted by Miss Monflathers, who was at the head of the head Boarding and Day Establishment in the town, and who condescended to take a Private View with eight chosen young ladies, to be quite startling from their extreme correctness. Mr. Pitt in a nightcap and bed-gown, and without his boots, represented the poet Cowper with perfect exactness; and Mary Queen of Scots in a dark wig, white shirt-collar, and male attire, was such a complete image of Lord Byron that the young ladies quite screamed when they saw it. Miss Monflathers, however, rebuked this enthusiasm, and took occasion to reprove Mrs. Jarley for not keeping her collection more select, observing that His Lordship had held certain free opinions quite incompatible with wax-work honors, and adding something about a Dean and Chapter, which Mrs. Jarley did not understand.

Although her duties were sufficiently laborious, Nell found in the lady of the caravan a very kind and considerate person, who had not only a peculiar relish for being comfortable herself, but for making everybody about her comfortable also; which latter taste, it may be remarked, is, even in persons who live in much finer places than caravans, a far more rare and uncommon one than the first, and is not by any means its necessary consequence. As her popularity procured her various little fees from the visitors on which her patroness never demanded any toll, and as her grandfather too was well-treated and useful, she had no cause of anxiety in connection with the wax-work, beyond that which sprang from her recollection of Quilp, and her fears that he might return and one day suddenly encounter them.

Quilp indeed was a perpetual nightmare to the child, who was constantly haunted by a vision of his ugly face and stunted figure. She slept, for their better security, in the room where the wax-work figures were, and she never retired to this place at night but she tortured herself—she could not help it—with imagining a resemblance, in some one or other of their death-like faces, to the dwarf, and this fancy would sometimes so gain upon her that she would almost believe he had removed the figure and stood within the clothes. Then there were so many of them with their great glassy eyes—and, as they stood one behind the other all about her bed, they looked so like living creatures, and yet so unlike in their grim stillness and silence, that she had a kind of terror of them for their own sakes, and would often lie watching their dusky figures until she was obliged to rise and light a candle, or go and sit at the open window and feel a companionship in the bright stars. At these times, she would recall the old house and the window at which she used to sit alone; and then she would think of poor Kit and all his kindness, until the tears came into her eyes, and she would weep and smile together.

Often and anxiously at this silent hour, her thoughts reverted to her grandfather, and she would wonder how much he remembered of their former life, and whether he was ever really mindful of the change in their condition and of their late helplessness and destitution. When they were wandering about, she seldom thought of this, but now she could not help considering what would become of them if he fell sick, or her own strength were to fail her. He was very patient and willing, happy to execute any little task, and glad to be of use; but he was in the same listless state, with no prospect of improvement—a mere child—a poor, thoughtless, vacant creature—a harmless fond old man, susceptible of tender love and regard for her, and of pleasant and painful impressions, but alive to nothing more. It made her very sad to know that this was so—so sad to see it that sometimes when he sat idly by, smiling and nodding to her when she looked round, or when he caressed some little child and carried it to and fro, as he was fond of doing by the hour together, perplexed by its simple questions, yet patient under his own infirmity, and seeming almost conscious of it too, and humbled even before the mind of an infant—so sad it made her to see him thus, that she would burst into tears, and, withdrawing into some secret place, fall down upon her knees and pray that he might be restored.

But the bitterness of her grief was not in beholding him in this condition, when he was at least content and tranquil, nor in her solitary meditations on his altered state, though these were trials for a young heart. Cause for deeper and heavier sorrow was yet to come.

One evening, a holiday night with them, Nell and her grandfather went out to walk. They had been rather closely confined for some days, and the weather being warm, they strolled a long distance. Clear of the town, they took a footpath which struck through some pleasant fields, judging that it would terminate in the road they quitted and enable them to return that way. It made, however, a much wider circuit than they had supposed, and thus they were tempted onward until sunset, when they reached the track of which they were in search, and stopped to rest.

It had been gradually getting overcast, and now the sky was dark and lowering, save where the glory of the departing sun piled up masses of gold and burning fire, decaying embers of which gleamed here and there through the black veil, and shone redly down upon the earth. The wind began to moan in hollow murmurs, as the sun went down carrying glad day elsewhere; and a train of dull clouds coming up against it, menaced thunder and lightning. Large drops of rain soon began to fall, and, as the storm clouds came sailing onward, others supplied the void they left behind and spread over all the sky. Then was heard the low rumbling of distant thunder, then the lightning quivered, and then the darkness of an hour seemed to have gathered in an instant.

Fearful of taking shelter beneath a tree or hedge, the old man and the child hurried along the high-road, hoping to find some house in which they could seek a refuge from the storm, which had now burst forth in earnest, and every moment increased in violence. Drenched with the pelting rain, confused by the deafening thunder, and bewildered by the glare of the forked lightning, they would have passed a solitary house without being aware of its vicinity, had not a man, who was standing at the door, called lustily to them to enter.

"Your ears ought to be better than other folks' at any rate, if you make so little of the chance of being struck blind," he said, retreating from the door and shading his eyes with his hands as the jagged lightning came again. "What were you going past for, eh?" he added, as he

closed the door and led the way along a passage to a room
behind.

"We didn't see the house, Sir, till we heard you calling," Nell replied.

"No wonder," said the man, "with this lightning in
one's eyes, by-the-by. You had better stand by the fire
here, and dry yourselves a bit. You can call for what
you like if you want anything. If you don't want anything, you are not obliged to give an order, don't be afraid
of that. This is a public-house, that's all. The Valiant
Soldier is pretty well known hereabouts."

"Is this house called the Valiant Soldier, Sir?" asked
Nell.

"I thought everybody knew that," replied the landlord. "Where have you come from, if you don't know
the Valiant Soldier as well as the Church catechism?
This is the Valiant Soldier, by James Groves,—Jem Groves
—honest Jem Groves, as is a man of unblemished moral
character, and has a good dry skittle-ground. If any man
has got anything to say again Jem Groves, let him say it
to Jem Groves, and Jem Groves can accommodate him
with a customer on any terms from four pounds a side to
forty."

With these words, the speaker tapped himself on the
waistcoat to intimate that he was the Jem Groves so
highly eulogized; sparred scientifically at a counterfeit
Jem Groves, who was sparring at society in general from
a black frame over the chimney-piece; and, applying
a half-emptied glass of spirits and water to his lips,
drank Jem Groves's health.

The night being warm, there was a large screen drawn
across the room, for a barrier against the heat of the fire.
It seemed as if somebody on the other side of this screen
had been insinuating doubts of Mr. Groves's prowess, and
had thereby given rise to these egotistical expressions,
for Mr. Groves wound up his defiance by giving a loud
knock upon it with his knuckles and pausing for a reply
from the other side.

"There an't many men," said Mr. Groves, no answer
being returned, "who would ventur' to cross Jem Groves
under his own roof. There's only one man, I know, that
has nerve enough for that, and that man's not a hundred
mile from here neither. But he's worth a dozen men,

and I let him say of me whatever he likes in consequence, —he knows that."

"In return for this complimentary address, a very gruff hoarse voice bade Mr. Groves "hold his noise and light a candle." And the same voice remarked that the same gentleman "needn't waste his breath in brag, for most people knew pretty well what sort of stuff he was made of."

"Nell, they're—they're playing cards," whispered the old man, suddenly interested. "Don't you hear them?"

"Look sharp with that candle," said the voice; "it's as much as I can do to see the pips on the cards as it is; and get this shutter closed as quick as you can, will you? Your beer will be the worse for to-night's thunder I expect.—Game! Seven-and-sixpence to me, old Isaac. Hand over."

"Do you hear, Nell, do you hear them?" whispered the old man again, with increased earnestness as the money chinked upon the table.

"I haven't seen such a storm as this," said a sharp cracked voice of most disagreeable quality, when a tremendous peal of thunder had died away, "since the night when old Luke Withers won thirteen times running, upon the red. We all said he had the Devil's luck and his own, and as it was the kind of night for the Devil to be out and busy, I suppose he *was* looking over his shoulder, if anybody could have seen him."

"Ah!" returned the gruff voice; "for all old Luke's winning through thick and thin of late years, I remember the time when he was the unluckiest and unfortunatest of men. He never took a dice-box in his hand, or held a card, but he was plucked, pigeoned, and cleaned out completely."

"Do you hear what he says?" whispered the old man. "Do you hear that, Nell?"

The child saw with astonishment and alarm that his whole appearance had undergone a complete change. His face was flushed and eager, his eyes were strained, his teeth set, his breath came short and thick, and the hand he laid upon her arm trembled so violently that she shook beneath its grasp.

"Bear witness," he muttered, looking upward, "that I always said it; that I knew it, dreamed of it, felt it was the truth, and that it must be so! What money have we, Nell? Come! I saw you with money yesterday. What money have we? Give it to me."

"No, no, let me keep it, grandfather," said the frightened child. "Let us go away from here. Do not mind the rain. Pray let us go."

"Give it to me, I say," returned the old man fiercely. "Hush, hush, don't cry, Nell. If I spoke sharply, dear, I didn't mean it. It's for thy good. I have wronged thee, Nell, but I will right thee yet, I will indeed. Where is the money?"

"Do not take it," said the child. "Pray do not take it, dear. For both our sakes let me keep it, or let me throw it away—better let me throw it away, than you take it now. Let us go; do let us go."

"Give me the money," returned the old man, "I must have it. There—there—that's my dear Nell. I'll right thee one day, child, I'll right thee, never fear!"

She took from her pocket a little purse. He seized it with the same rapid impatience which had characterized his speech, and hastily made his way to the other side of the screen. It was impossible to restrain him, and the trembling child followed close behind.

The landlord had placed a light upon the table, and was engaged in drawing the curtain of the window. The speakers whom they had heard were two men, who had a pack of cards and some silver money between them, while upon the screen itself the games they had played were scored in chalk. The man with the rough voice was a burly fellow of middle age, with large black whiskers, broad cheeks, a coarse wide mouth, and bull neck, which was pretty freely displayed as his shirt collar was only confined by a loose red neckerchief. He wore his hat, which was of a brownish-white, and had beside him a thick knotted stick. The other man, whom his companion had called Isaac, was of a more slender figure—stooping, and high in the shoulders—with a very ill-favored face, and a most sinister and villainous squint.

"Now, old gentleman," said Isaac, looking round. "Do you know either of us? This side of the screen is private, Sir."

"No offence, I hope," returned the old man.

"But by G—, Sir, there *is* offence," said the other, interrupting him, "when you intrude yourself upon a couple of gentlemen who are particularly engaged."

"I had no intention to offend," said the old man, looking anxiously at the cards, "I thought that—"

"But you had no right to think, Sir," retorted the other. "What the devil has a man at your time of life to do with thinking?"

"Now, bully boy," said the stout man, raising his eyes from his cards for the first time, "can't you let him speak?"

The landlord, who had apparently resolved to remain neutral until he knew which side of the question the stout man would espouse, chimed in at this place with "Ah, to be sure, can't you let him speak, Isaac List?"

"Can't I let him speak," sneered Isaac in reply, mimicking as nearly as he could, in his shrill voice, the tones of the landlord. "Yes, I can let him speak, Jemmy Groves."

"Well, then, do it, will you?" said the landlord.

Mr. List's squint assumed a portentous character, which seemed to threaten a prolongation of this controversy, when his companion, who had been looking sharply at the old man, put a timely stop to it.

"Who knows," said he, with a cunning look, "but the gentleman may have civilly meant to ask if he might have the honor to take a hand with us!"

"I did mean it," cried the old man. "That is what I mean. That is what I want now!"

"I thought so," returned the same man. "Then who knows but the gentleman, anticipating our objection to play for love, civilly desired to play for money?"

The old man replied by shaking the little purse in his eager hand, and then throwing it down upon the table, and gathering up the cards as a miser would clutch at gold.

"Oh! That indeed—" said Isaac; "if that's what the gentleman meant, I beg the gentleman's pardon. Is this the gentleman's little purse? A very pretty little purse. Rather a light purse," added Isaac, throwing it into the air and catching it dexterously, "but enough to amuse a gentleman for half an hour or so."

"We'll make a four-handed game of it, and take in Groves," said the stout man. "Come, Jemmy."

17

The landlord, who conducted himself like one who was well used to such little parties, approached the table and took his seat. The child, in a perfect agony, drew her grandfather aside, and implored him, even then to come away.

"Come; and we may be so happy," said the child.

"We *will* be happy," replied the old man hastily. "Let me go, Nell. The means of happiness are on the cards and in the dice. We must rise from little winnings to great. There's little to be won here; but great will come in time. I shall but win back my own, and it's all for thee, my darling."

"God help us!" cried the child. "Oh! what hard fortune brought us here?"

"Hush!" rejoined the old man laying his hand upon her mouth, "Fortune will not bear chiding. We must not reproach her, or she shuns us; I have found that out."

"Now, mister," said the stout man. "If you're not coming yourself, give us the cards, will you?"

"I am coming," cried the old man. "Sit thee down, Nell, sit thee down and look on. Be of good heart, it's all for thee—all—every penny. I don't tell them, no, no, or else they wouldn't play, dreading the chance that such a cause must give me. Look at them. See what they are and what thou art. Who doubts that we must win!"

"The gentleman has thought better of it, and isn't coming," said Isaac, making as though he would rise from the table. "I'm sorry the gentleman's daunted—nothing venture, nothing have—but the gentleman knows best."

"Why, I am ready. You have all been slow but me," said the old man. "I wonder who's more anxious to begin than I."

As he spoke he drew a chair to the table; and the other three closing round it at the same time, the game commenced.

The child sat by, and watched its progress with a troubled mind. Regardless of the run of luck, and mindful only of the desperate passion which had its hold upon her grandfather, losses and gains were to her alike. Exulting in some brief triumph, or cast down by a defeat, there he sat so wild and restless, so feverishly and intensely anxious, so terribly eager, so ravenous for the paltry stakes, that she could have almost better borne to see him dead. And yet she was the innocent cause of all this torture, and he, gambling with such a savage thirst for gain as the most insatiable gambler never felt, had not one selfish thought!

On the contrary, the other three—knaves and gamesters by their trade—while intent upon their game, were yet as cool and quiet as if every virtue had been centred in their breasts. Sometimes one would look up to smile to

another, or to snuff the feeble candle, or to glance at the lightning as it shot through the open window and fluttering curtain, or to listen to some louder peal of thunder than the rest, with a kind of momentary impatience, as if it put him out; but there they sat, with a calm indifference to everything but their cards, perfect philosophers in appearance, and with no greater show of passion or excitement than if they had been made of stone.

The storm had raged for full three hours; the lightning had grown fainter and less frequent; the thunder, from seeming to roll and break above their heads, had gradually died away into a deep hoarse distance; and still the game went on, and still the anxious child was quite forgotten.

CHAPTER THE THIRTIETH.

AT length the play came to an end, and **Mr. Isaac List** rose the only winner. Mat and the landlord bore their losses with professional fortitude. Isaac pocketed his gains with the air of a man who had quite made up his mind to win, all along, and was neither surprised nor pleased.

Nell's little purse was exhausted; but, although it lay empty by his side, and the other players had now risen from the table, the old man sat poring over the cards, dealing them as they had been dealt before, and turning up the different hands to see what each man would have held if they had still been playing. He was quite absorbed in this occupation, when the child drew near and laid her hand upon his shoulder, telling him it was near midnight.

"See the curse of poverty, Nell," he said, pointing to the packs he had spread out upon the table. "If I could have gone on a little longer, only a little longer, the luck would have turned on my side. Yes, it's as plain as the marks upon the cards. See here—and there—and here again."

"Put them away," urged the child. "Try to forget them."

"Try to forget them!" he rejoined, raising his haggard face to hers, and regarding her with an incredulous stare. "To forget them! How are we ever to grow rich if I forget them?"

The child could only shake her head.

"No, no, Nell," said the old man, patting her cheek; "they must not be forgotten. We must make amends for this as soon as we can. Patience—patience, and we'll right thee yet, I promise thee. Lose to-day, win to-morrow. And nothing can be won without anxiety and care—nothing. Come, I am ready."

"Do you know what the time is?" said Mr. Groves, who was smoking with his friends. "Past twelve o'clock—"

"And a rainy night," added the stout man.

"The Valiant Soldier, by James Groves. Good Beds. Cheap entertainment for man and beast," said Mr. Groves, quoting his sign-board. "Half-past twelve o'clock."

"It's very late," said the uneasy child. "I wish we had gone before. What will they think of us! It will be two o'clock by the time we get back. What would it cost, Sir, if we stopped here?"

"Two good beds, one-and-sixpence; supper and beer, one shilling; total, two shillings and sixpence," replied the Valiant Soldier.

Now, Nell had still the piece of gold sewn in her dress and when she came to consider the lateness of the hour, and the somnolent habits of Mrs. Jarley, and to imagine the state of consternation in which they would certainly throw that good lady by knocking her up in the middle of the night—and when she reflected, on the other hand' that if they remained where they were, and rose early in the morning, they might get back before she awoke, and could plead the violence of the storm by which they had been overtaken, as a good apology for their absence— she decided, after a great deal of hesitation, to remain. She therefore took her grandfather aside, and telling him that she had still enough left to defray the cost of their lodging, proposed that they should stay there for the night.

"If I had had but that money before—If I had only known of it a few minutes ago!" muttered the old man.

"We will decide to stop here, if you please," said Nell, turning hastily to the landlord.

"I think that's prudent," returned Mr. Groves. "You shall have your suppers directly."

Accordingly, when Mr. Groves had smoked his pipe out, knocked out the ashes, and placed it carefully in a corner of the fire-place, with the bowl downwards, he brought in the bread and cheese, and beer, with many high encomiums upon their excellence, and bade his guests to fall to and make themselves at home. Nell and her grandfather ate sparingly, for both were occupied with their own reflections; the other gentlemen, for whose constitutions beer was too weak and tame a liquid, consoled themselves with spirits and tobacco.

As they would leave the house very early in the morning, the child was anxious to pay for their entertainment before they retired to bed. But as she felt the necessity of concealing her little hoard from her grandfather, and had to change the piece of gold, she took it secretly from its place of concealment, and embraced an opportunity of following the landlord when he went out of the room, and tendered it to him in the little bar.

"Will you give me the change here, if you please?" said the child.

Mr. James Groves was evidently surprised, and looked at the money, and rang it and looked at the child, and at the money again, as though he had a mind to inquire how she came by it. The coin being genuine, however, and changed at his house, he probably felt, like a wise landlord, that it was no business of his. At any rate, he counted out the change, and gave it her. The child was returning to the room where they had passed the evening, when she fancied she saw a figure just gliding in at the door. There was nothing but a long dark passage between this door and the place where she had changed the money, and being very certain that no person had passed in or out while she stood there, the thought struck her that she had been watched.

But by whom? When she re-entered the room, she found its inmates exactly as she had left them. The stout fellow lay upon two chairs, resting his head on his hand, and the squinting man reposed in a similar attitude on the opposite side of the table. Between them sat her grandfather, looking intently at the winner with a kind of hungry admiration, and hanging upon his words as if he were some superior being. She was puzzled for a moment, and looked round to see if any one else were there. No. Then she asked her grandfather in a whisper whether anybody had left the room while she was absent.

"No," he said, "nobody."

It must have been her fancy then; and yet it was strange, that, without anything in her previous thoughts to lead to it, she should have imagined this figure so very distinctly. She was still wondering and thinking of it, when a girl came to light her to bed.

The old man took leave of the company at the same time, and they went upstairs together. It was a great, rambling house, with dull corridors and wide staircases which the flaring candles seemed to make more gloomy.

She left her grandfather in his chamber, and followed her guide to another, which was at the end of a passage, and approached by some half-dozen crazy steps. This was prepared for her. The girl lingered a little while to talk, and tell her grievances. She had not a good place, she said ; the wages were low, and the work was hard. She was going to leave it in a fortnight; the child couldn't recommend her to another, she supposed ? Indeed she was afraid another would be difficult to get after living there, for the house had a very indifferent character ; there was far too much card-playing, and such like. She was very much mistaken if some of the people who came there oftenest were quite as honest as they might be, but she wouldn't have it known that she had said so, for the world. Then there were some rambling allusions to a rejected sweetheart, who had threatened to go a soldiering— a final promise of knocking at the door early in the morning—and " Good night."

The child did not feel comfortable when she was left alone. She could not help thinking of the figure stealing through the passage downstairs; and what the girl had said did not tend to reassure her. The men were very ill looking. They might get their living by robbing and murdering travellers. Who could tell ?

Reasoning herself out of these fears, or losing sight of them for a little while, there came the anxiety to which the adventures of the night gave rise. Here was the old passion awakened again in her grandfather's breast, and to what further distraction it might tempt him Heaven only knew. What fears their absence might have occasioned already ! Persons might be seeking for them even then. Would they be forgiven in the morning, or turned adrift again ? Oh ! why had they stopped in that strange place ? It would have been better, under any circumstances, to have gone on !

At last, sleep gradually stole upon her—a broken, fitful sleep, troubled by dreams of falling from high towers, and waking with a start and in great terror. A deeper slumber followed this—and then——What ! That figure in the room !

A figure was there. Yes, she had drawn up the blind to admit the light when it should dawn, and there, between the foot of the bed and the dark casement, it crouched and slunk along, groping its way with noiseless hands, and stealing round the bed. She had no voice to cry for help, no power to move, but lay still, watching it.

On it came—on, silently and stealthily, to the bed's head. The breath so near her pillow, that she shrank back into it, lest those wandering hands should light upon her face. Back again it stole to the window—then turned its head towards her.

The dark form was a mere blot upon the lighter darkness of the room, but she saw the turning of the head, and felt and knew how the eyes looked and the ears listened. There it remained, motionless as she. At length, still keeping the face towards her, it busied its hands in something and she heard the chink of money.

Then, on it came again, silent and stealthy as before, and, replacing the garments it had taken from the bedside, dropped upon its hands and knees, and crawled away. How slowly it seemed to move, now that she could hear but not see it, creeping along the floor! It reached the door at last, and stood upon its feet. The steps creaked beneath its noiseless tread, and it was gone.

The first impulse of the child was to fly from the terror of being by herself in that room—to have somebody by—not to be alone—and then her power of speech would be restored. With no consciousness of having moved, she gained the door.

There was the dreadful shadow, pausing at the bottom of the steps.

She could not pass it; she might have done so, perhaps, in the darkness, without being seized, but her blood curdled at the thought. The figure stood quite still, and so did she; not boldly, but of necessity; for going back into the room was hardly less terrible than going on.

The rain beat fast and furiously without, and ran down in plashing streams from the thatched roof. Some summer insect, with no escape into the air, flew blindly to and fro, beating his body against the walls and ceiling, and filling the silent place with his murmurs. The figure moved again. The child involuntarily did the same. Once in her grandfather's room, she would be safe.

It crept along the passage until it came to the very door she longed so ardently to reach. The child, in the agony of being so near, had almost darted forward with the design of bursting into the room and closing it behind her, when the figure stopped again.

The idea flashed suddenly upon her—what if it entered there, and had a design upon the old man's life! She turned faint and sick. It did. It went in. There was a light inside. The figure was now within the chamber, and she, still dumb—quite dumb, and almost senseless—stood looking on.

The door was partly open. Not knowing what she meant to do, but meaning to preserve him or be killed herself, she staggered forward and looked in. What sight was that which met her view!

The bed had not been lain on, but was smooth and empty. And at a table sat the old man himself, the only living creature there, his white face pinched and sharpened by the greediness which made his eyes unnaturally bright, counting the money of which his hands had robbed her.

CHAPTER THE THIRTY-FIRST.

WITH steps more faltering and unsteady than those with which she had approached the room, the child withdrew from the door, and groped her way back to her own chamber. The terror she had lately felt was nothing compared with that which now oppressed her. No strange robber, no treacherous host conniving at the plunder of his guests, or stealing to their beds to kill them in their sleep, no nightly prowler, however terrible and cruel, could have awakened in her bosom half the dread which the recognition of her silent visitor inspired. The gray-headed old man gliding like a ghost into her room and acting the thief while he supposed her fast asleep, then bearing off his prize and hanging over it with the ghastly exultation she had witnessed, was worse —immeasurably worse, and far more dreadful, for the moment, to reflect upon—than anything her wildest fancy could have suggested. If he should return—there was no lock or bolt upon the door, and if, distrustful of having left some money yet behind, he should come back to seek for more—a vague awe and horror surrounded the idea of his slinking in again with stealthy tread, and turning his face toward the empty bed, while she shrank down close at his feet to avoid his touch, which was almost insupportable. She sat and listened. Hark! A footstep on the stairs, and now the door was slowly opening. It was but imagination, yet imagination had all the terrors of reality; nay, it was worse, for the reality would have come and gone, and there an end, but in imagination it was always coming, and never went away.

The feeling which beset the child was one of dim uncertain horror. She had no fear of the dear old grandfather, in whose love for her this disease of the brain had been engendered; but the man she had seen that night, wrapt in the game of chance, lurking in her room, and counting the money by the glimmering light, seemed like another creature in his shape, a monstrous distortion of his image, a something to recoil from, and be the more afraid of, because it bore a likeness to him, and kept close about her, as he did. She could scarcely connect her own affectionate companion, save by his loss, with this old man, so like yet so unlike him. She had wept to see him dull and quiet. How much greater cause she had for weeping now!

The child sat watching and thinking of these things, until the phantom in her mind so increased in gloom and terror, that she felt it would be a relief to hear the old man's voice, or, if he were asleep, even to see him, and banish some of the fears that clustered round his image. She stole down the stairs and passage again. The door was still ajar as she had left it, and the candle burning as before.

She had her own candle in her hand, prepared to say, if he were waking, that she was uneasy and could not rest, and had come to see if his were still alight. Looking into the room, she saw him lying calmly on his bed, and so took courage to enter.

Fast asleep—no passion in the face, no avarice, no anxiety, no wild desire; all gentle, tranquil, and at peace. This was not the gambler, or the shadow in her room; this was not even the worn and jaded man whose face had so often met her own in the gray morning light; this was her dear old friend, her harmless fellow-traveller, her good, kind grandfather.

She had no fear as she looked upon his slumbering

features, but she had a deep and weighty sorrow, and it found its relief in tears.

"God bless him!" said the child, stooping softly to kiss his placid cheek. "I see too well now, that they would indeed part us if they found us out, and shut him up from the light of the sun and sky. He has only me to help him. God bless us both!"

Lighting her candle, she retreated as silently as she had come, and, gaining her own room once more, sat up during the remainder of that long, long, miserable night.

At last the day turned her waning candle pale, and she fell asleep. She was quickly roused by the girl who had shown her up to bed; and, as soon as she was dressed, prepared to go down to her grandfather. But first she searched her pocket and found that her money was all gone—not a sixpence remained.

The old man was ready, and in a few seconds they were on their road. The child thought he rather avoided her eye, and appeared to expect that she would tell him of her loss. She felt she must do that, or he might suspect the truth.

"Grandfather," she said in a tremulous voice, after they had walked about a mile in silence, "do you think they are honest people at the house yonder?"

"Why?" returned the old man trembling. "Do I think them honest—yes, they played honestly."

"I'll tell you why I ask," rejoined Nell. "I lost some money last night—out of my bedroom I am sure. Unless it was taken by somebody in jest—only in jest, dear grandfather, which would make me laugh heartily if I could but know it—"

"Who would take money in jest?" returned the old man in a hurried manner. "Those who take money, take it to keep. Don't talk of jest."

"Then it was stolen out of my room, dear," said the child, whose last hope was destroyed by the manner of this reply.

"But is there no more, Nell?" said the old man; "no more anywhere? Was it all taken—every farthing of it —was there nothing left?"

"Nothing," replied the child.

"We must get more," said the old man, "we must

earn it, Nell, hoard it up, scrape it together, come by it somehow. Never mind this loss. Tell nobody of it, and perhaps we may regain it. Don't ask how;—we may regain it, and a great deal more;—but tell nobody, or trouble may come of it. And so they took it out of thy room, when thou wert asleep!" he added in a compassionate tone, very different from the secret, cunning way in which he had spoken until now. "Poor Nell, poor little Nell!"

The child hung down her head and wept. The sympathizing tone in which he spoke, was quite sincere; she was sure of that. It was not the lightest part of her sorrow to know that this was done for her.

"Not a word about it to any one but me," said the old man, "no, not even to me," he added hastily, "for it can do no good. All the losses that ever were, are not worth tears from thy eyes, darling. Why should they be, when we will win them back?"

"Let them go," said the child looking up. "Let them go, once and forever, and I would never shed another tear if every penny had been a thousand pounds."

"Well, well," returned the old man, checking himself as some impetuous answer rose to his lips, "she knows no better. I ought to be thankful for it."

"But listen to me," said the child earnestly, "will you listen to me?"

"Ay, ay, I'll listen," returned the old man, still without looking at her; "a pretty voice. It has always a sweet sound to me. It always had when it was her mother's, poor child."

"Let me persuade you, then—oh, do let me persuade you," said the child, "to think no more of gains or losses, and to try no fortune but the fortune we pursue together."

"We pursue this aim together," retorted her grandfather, still looking away and seeming to confer with himself. "Whose image sanctifies the game?"

"Have we been worse off," resumed the child, "since you forgot these cares, and we have been travelling on together? Have we not been much better and happier without a home to shelter us, than ever we were in that unhappy house, when they were on your mind?"

"She speaks the truth," murmured the old man in the

same tone as before. " It must not turn me, but it is the truth—no doubt it is."

" Only remember what we have been since that bright morning when we turned our backs upon it for the last time," said Nell, "only remember what we have been since we have been free of all those miseries—what peaceful days and quiet nights we have had—what pleasant times we have known —what happiness we have enjoyed. If we have been tired or hungry, we have been soon refreshed, and slept the sounder for it. Think what beautiful things we have seen, and how contented we have felt. And why was this blessed change?"

He stopped her with a motion of his hand, and bade her talk to him no more just then, for he was busy. After a time he kissed her cheek, still motioning her to silence, and walked on, looking far before him, and sometimes stopping and gazing with a puckered brow upon the ground, as if he were painfully trying to collect his disordered thoughts. Once she saw tears in his eyes. When he had gone on thus for some time, he took her hand in his as he was accustomed to do, with nothing of the violence or animation of his late manner; and so, by degrees so fine that the child could not trace them, settled down into his usual quiet way, and suffered her to lead him where she would.

When they presented themselves in the midst of the stupendous collection, they found, as Nell had anticipated, that Mrs. Jarley was not yet out of bed, and that, although she had suffered some uneasiness on their account overnight, and had indeed sat up for them until past eleven o'clock, she had retired in the persuasion, that, being overtaken by storm at some distance from home, they had sought the nearest shelter, and would not return before morning. Nell immediately applied herself with great assiduity to the decoration and preparation of the room, and had the satisfaction of completing her task, and dressing herself neatly, before the beloved of the Royal Family came down to breakfast.

" We haven't had," said Mrs. Jarley when the meal was over, " more than eight of Miss Monflathers's young ladies all the time we've been here, and there's twenty-six of 'em. as I was told by the cook when I asked her a question or two and put her on the free-list. We must try 'em with a parcel of new bills, and you shall take it, my dear, and see what effect that has upon 'em."

The proposed expedition being one of paramount importance, Mrs. Jarley adjusted Nell's bonnet with her own hands, and declaring that she certainly did look very pretty, and reflected credit on the establishment, dismissed her with many commendations, and certain needful directions as to the turnings on the right which she was to take, and the turnings on the left which she was to avoid. Thus instructed, Nell had no difficulty in finding out Miss Monflathers's Boarding and Day Establishment, which was a large house, with a high wall, and a large garden-gate with a large brass plate, and a small grating through which Miss Monflathers's parlor-maid inspected all visitors before admitting them; for nothing in the shape of a man—no, not even a milkman—was suffered, without special license, to pass that gate. Even the tax-gatherer, who was stout and wore spectacles and a broad-brimmed hat, had the taxes handed through the grating. More obdurate than gate of adamant or brass, this gate of Miss Monflathers's frowned on all mankind. The very butcher respected it as a gate of mystery, and left off whistling when he rang the bell.

As Nell approached the awful door, it turned slowly upon its hinges with a creaking noise, and, forth from the solemn grove beyond, came a long file of young ladies, two and two, all with open books in their hands, and some with parasols likewise. And last of the goodly procession came Miss Monflathers, bearing herself a parasol of lilac silk, and supported by two smiling teachers, each mortally envious of the other, and devoted unto Miss Monflathers.

Confused by the looks and whispers of the girls, Nell stood with downcast eyes and suffered the procession to pass on, until Miss Monflathers, bringing up the rear, approached her, when she curtseyed and presented her little packet; on receipt whereof Miss Monflathers commanded that the line should halt.

"You're the wax-work child, are you not?" said Miss Monflathers.

"Yes, ma'am," replied Nell, coloring deeply, for the young ladies had collected about her, and she was the centre on which all eyes were fixed.

"And don't you think you must be a very wicked little child," said Miss Monflathers, who was of rather uncertain temper, and lost no opportunity of impressing moral truths upon the tender minds of the young ladies, "to be a wax-work child at all?"

Poor Nell had never viewed her position in this light, and not knowing what to say, remained silent, blushing more deeply than before.

"Don't you know," said Miss Monflathers, "that it's very naughty and unfeminine, and a perversion of the properties wisely and benignantly transmitted to us, with expansive powers to be roused from their dormant state through the medium of cultivation?"

The two teachers murmured their respectful approval of this home-thrust, and looked at Nell as though they would have said that there indeed Miss Monflathers had hit her very hard. Then they smiled and glanced at Miss Monflathers, and then, their eyes meeting, they exchanged looks which plainly said that each considered herself smiler in ordinary to Miss Monflathers, and regarded the other as having no right to smile, and that her so doing was an act of presumption and impertinence.

"Don't you feel how naughty it is of you," resumed Miss Monflathers, "to be a wax-work child, when you might have the proud consciousness of assisting, to the extent of your infant powers, the manufactures of your country; of improving your mind by the constant contemplation of the steam-engine; and of earning a comfortable and independent subsistence of from two-and-ninepence to three shillings per week? Don't you know that the harder you are to work, the happier you are?"

"'How doth the little—'" murmured one of the teachers, in quotation from Doctor Watts.

"Eh?" said Miss Monflathers, turning smartly round. "Who said that?"

Of course the teacher who had not said it, indicated the rival who had, whom Miss Monflathers frowningly requested to hold her peace; by that means throwing the informing teacher into raptures of joy.

"The little busy bee," said Miss Monflathers, drawing herself up, "is applicable only to genteel children.

In books, or work, or healthful play'

is quite right as far as they are concerned; and the work means painting on velvet, fancy needle-work, or embroidery. In such cases as these," pointing to Nell, with her parasol, " and in the case of all poor people's children, we should read it thus:

> ' In work, work, work. In work alway
> Let my first years be past,
> That I may give for ev'ry day
> Some good account at last.' "

A deep hum of applause rose not only from the two teachers, but from all the pupils, who were equally astonished to hear Miss Monflathers improvising after this brilliant style; for although she had been long known as a politician, she had never appeared before as an original poet. Just then somebody happened to discover that Nell was crying, and all eyes were again turned towards her.

There were indeed tears in her eyes, and drawing out her handkerchief to brush them away, she happened to let it fall. Before she could stoop to pick it up, one young lady of about fifteen or sixteen, who had been standing a little apart from the others, as though she had no recognized place among them, sprang forward and put it in her hand. She was gliding timidly away again, when she was arrested by the governess.

" It was Miss Edwards who did that, I *know*," said Miss Monflathers predictively. "Now I am sure that was Miss Edwards."

It was Miss Edwards, and everybody said it was Miss Edwards, and Miss Edwards herself admitted that it was.

" Is it not," said Miss Monflathers, putting down her parasol to take a severer view of the offender, " a most remarkable thing, Miss Edwards, that you have an attachment to the lower classes which always draws you to their sides; or, rather, is it not a most extraordinary thing that all I say and do will not wean you from propensities which your original station in life have unhappily rendered habitual to you, you extremely vulgar-minded girl?"

" I really intended no harm, ma'am," said a sweet voice. " It was a momentary impulse, indeed."

"An impulse!" repeated Miss Monflathers scornfully. "I wonder that you presume to speak of impulses to me"—both the teachers assented—"I am astonished"—both the teachers were astonished—"I suppose it is an impulse which induces you to take the part of every grovelling and debased person that comes in your way"—both the teachers supposed so too.

"But I would have you know, Miss Edwards," resumed the governess in a tone of increased severity, "that you cannot be permitted—if it be only for the sake of pre-

serving a proper example and decorum in this establishment—that you cannot be permitted, and that you shall not be permitted, to fly in the face of your superiors in this exceedingly gross manner. If *you* have no reason to feel a becoming pride before wax-work children, there are young ladies here who have, and you must either defer to those young ladies or leave the establishment, Miss Edwards."

This young lady, being motherless and poor, was apprenticed at the school—taught for nothing—teaching others what she learnt, for nothing—boarded for nothing

18

—lodged for nothing—and set down and rated as some-thing immeasurably less than nothing, by all the dwellers in the house. The servant-maids felt her inferiority, for they were better treated; free to come and go, and re-garded in their stations with much more respect. The teachers were infinitely superior, for they had paid to go to school in their time, and were paid now. The pupils cared little for a companion who had no grand stories to tell about home; no friends to come with post-horses, and be received in all humility, with cake and wine, by the governess; no deferential servant to attend and bear her home for the holidays; nothing genteel to talk about, and nothing to display. But why was Miss Monflathers always vexed and irritated with the poor apprentice—how did that come to pass?

Why, the gayest feather in Miss Monflathers's cap, and the brightest glory of Miss Monflathers's school, was a baronet's daughter—the real live daughter of a real live baronet—who, by some extraordinary reversal of the Laws of Nature, was not only plain in features but dull in intellect, while the poor apprentice had both a ready wit, and a handsome face and figure. It seems incred-ible. Here was Miss Edwards, who only paid a small premium which had been spent long ago, every day out-shining and excelling the baronet's daughter, who learned all the extras (or was taught them all) and whose half-yearly bill came to double that of any other young lady's in the school, making no account of the honor and reputa-tion of her pupilage. Therefore, and because she was a dependant, Miss Monflathers had a great dislike to Miss Edwards, and was spiteful to her, and aggravated by her, and, when she had compassion on little Nell, verbally fell upon and maltreated her as we have already seen.

"You will not take the air to-day, Miss Edwards," said Miss Monflathers. "Have the goodness to retire to your own room, and not to leave it without permission."

The poor girl was moving hastily away, when she was suddenly, in nautical phrase, "brought to" by a subdued shriek from Miss Monflathers.

"She has passed me without any salute!" cried the governess, raising her eyes to the sky. "She has actually passed me without the slightest acknowledgment of my presence!"

The young lady turned and curtsied. Nell could see that she raised her dark eyes to the face of her superior, and that their expression, and that of her whole attitude for the instant, was one of mute but most touching appeal against this ungenerous usage. Miss Monflathers only tossed her head in reply, and the great gate closed upon a bursting heart.

"As for you, you wicked child," said Miss Monflathers, turning to Nell, "tell your mistress that if she presumes to take the liberty of sending to me any more, I will write to the legislative authorities and have her put in the stocks, or compelled to do penance in a white sheet; and you may depend upon it that you shall certainly experience the treadmill if you dare to come here again. Now ladies, on."

The procession filed off, two and two, with the books and parasols, and Miss Monflathers, calling the Baronet's daughter to walk with her and smooth her ruffled feelings, discarded the two teachers—who by this time had exchanged their smiles for looks of sympathy—and left them to bring up the rear, and hate each other a little more for being obliged to walk together.

CHAPTER THE THIRTY-SECOND.

MRS. JARLEY's wrath on first learning that she had been threatened with the indignity of Stocks and Penance, passed all description. The genuine and only Jarley exposed to public scorn, jeered by children, and flouted by beadles! The delight of the Nobility and Gentry shorn of a bonnet which a lady Mayoress might have sighed to wear, and arrayed in a white sheet as a spectacle of mortification and humility! And Miss Monflathers, the audacious creature who presumed, even in the dimmest and remotest distance of her imagination, to conjure up the degrading picture, "I am a'most inclined," said Mrs. Jarley, bursting with the fulness of her anger and the weakness of her means of revenge, "to turn atheist when I think of it!"

But instead of adopting this course of retaliation, Mrs. Jarley, on second thoughts, brought out the suspicious bottle, and ordering glasses to be set forth upon her favorite drum, and sinking into a chair behind it, called her satellites about her, and to them several times recounted, word for word, the affronts she had received. This done, she begged them in a kind of deep despair to drink; then laughed, then cried, then took a little sip herself, then laughed and cried again, and took a little more; and so by degrees the worthy lady went on, increasing in smiles and decreasing in tears, until at last she could not laugh enough at Miss Monflathers, who from being an object of dire vexation, became one of sheer ridicule and absurdity.

"For which of us is best off, I wonder," quoth Mrs. Jarley, "she or me! It's only talking, when all is said and done, and if she talks of me in the stocks, why I can talk of her in the stocks, which is a good deal funnier if we come to that. Lord, what *does* it matter, after all!"

Having arrived at this comfortable frame of mind (to which she had been greatly assisted by certain short interjectional remarks of the philosophic George), Mrs. Jarley consoled Nell with many kind words, and requested as a personal favor that whenever she thought of Miss Monflathers she would do nothing else but laugh at her, all the days of her life.

So ended Mrs. Jarley's wrath, which subsided long before the going down of the sun. Nell's anxieties, however, were of a deeper kind, and the checks they imposed upon her cheerfulness were not so easily removed.

That evening, as she had dreaded, her grandfather stole away, and did not come back until the night was far spent. Worn out as she was, and fatigued in mind and body, she sat up alone, counting the minutes, until he returned—penniless, broken-spirited, and wretched, but still hotly bent upon his infatuation.

"Get me money," he said wildly, as they parted for the night. "I must have money, Nell. It shall be paid thee back with gallant interest one day, but all the money that comes unto thy hands, must be mine—not for myself, but to use for thee. Remember, Nell, to use for thee!"

What could the child do, with the knowledge she had, but give him every penny that came into her hands, lest he should be tempted on to rob their benefactress? If she told the truth (so thought the child) he would be treated as a madman ; if she did not supply him with money, he would supply himself; supplying him, she fed the fire that burnt him up, and put him perhaps beyond recovery. Distracted by these thoughts, borne down by the weight of the sorrow which she dared not tell, tortured by a crowd of apprehensions whenever the old man was absent, and dreading alike his stay and his return, the color forsook her cheek, her eye grew dim, and her heart was oppressed and heavy. All her old sorrows had come back upon her, augmented by new fears and doubts; by day they were ever present to her mind ; by night they hovered round her pillow, and haunted her in dreams.

It was natural that, in the midst of her affliction, she should often revert to that sweet young lady of whom she had only caught a hasty glance, but whose sympathy, expressed in one slight brief action, dwelt in her memory like the kindnesses of years. She would often think, if she had such a friend as that to whom to tell her griefs, how much lighter her heart would be—that if she were but free to hear that voice, she would be happier. Then she would wish that she were something better, that she were not quite so poor and humble, that she dared address her without fearing a repulse ; and then feel that there was an immeasurable distance between them, and have no hope that the young lady thought of her any more.

It was now holiday-time at the schools, and the young ladies had gone home, and Miss Monflathers was reported to be flourishing in London and damaging the hearts of middle-aged gentlemen, but nobody said anything about Miss Edwards, whether she had gone home, or whether she had any home to go to, whether she was still at the school, or anything about her. But one evening, as Nell was returning from a lonely walk, she happened to pass the inn where the stage-coaches stopped, just as one drove up, and there was the beautiful girl she so well remembered, pressing forward to embrace a young child whom they were helping down from the roof.

Well, this was her sister, her little sister, much younger than Nell, whom she had not seen (so the story went afterwards) for five years, and to bring whom to that place on a short visit, she had been saving her poor means all that time. Nell felt as if her heart would break when she saw them meet. They went a little apart from the knot of people who had congregated about the coach, and fell upon each other's neck, and sobbed, and wept with joy. Their plain and simple dress, the distance which the child had come alone, their agitation and delight, and the tears they shed, would have told their history by themselves.

They became a little more composed in a short time, and went away, not so much hand in hand as clinging to each other. "Are you sure you're happy, sister?" said the child as they passed where Nell was standing. "Quite happy now," she answered. "But always?" said the child. "Ah, sister, why do you turn away your face?"

Nell could not help following at a little distance. They went to the house of an old nurse, where the elder sister had engaged a bedroom for the child. "I shall come to you early every morning," she said, "and we can be together all the day."—"Why not at night-time too? Dear sister, would they be angry with you for *that?*"

Why were the eyes of little Nell wet, that night, with tears like those of the two sisters? Why did she bear a grateful heart because they had met, and feel it pain to think that they would shortly part? Let us not believe that any selfish reference—unconscious though it might have been—to her own trials awoke this sympathy, but thank God that the innocent joys of others can strongly move us, and that we, even in our fallen nature, have one source of pure emotion which must be prized in Heaven!

By morning's cheerful glow, but oftener still by evening's gentle light, the child, with a respect for the short and happy intercourse of these two sisters which forbade her to approach and say a thankful word, although she yearned to do so, followed them at a distance in their walks and rambles, stopping when they stopped, sitting on the grass when they sat down, rising when they went on, and feeling it a companionship and delight to be so near them. Their evening walk was by the river's side. Here, every night, the child was too, unseen by them, unthought of, unregarded; but feeling as if they were her friends, as if they had confidences and trusts together, as if her load were lightened and less hard to bear; as if they mingled their sorrows, and found mutual consolation. It was a weak fancy perhaps, the childish fancy of a young and lonely creature; but night after night, and still the sisters loitered in the same place, and still the child followed with a mild and softened heart.

She was much startled, on returning home one night, to find that Mrs. Jarley had commanded an announcement to be prepared, to the effect that the stupendous collection would only remain in its present quarters one day longer; in fulfilment of which threat (for all announcements connected with public amusements are well known to be irrevocable and most exact), the stupendous collection shut up next day.

" Are we going from this place directly, ma'am?" said Nell.

"Look here, child," returned Mrs. Jarley. "That'll inform you." And so saying, Mrs. Jarley produced another announcement, wherein it was stated, that, in consequence of numerous inquiries at the wax-work door, and in consequence of crowds having been disappointed in obtaining admission, the Exhibition would be continued for one week longer, and would re-open next day.

" For now that the schools are gone, and the regular sightseers exhausted," said Mrs. Jarley, "we come to the General Public, and they want stimulating."

Upon the following day at noon, Mrs. Jarley established herself behind the highly-ornamented table, attended by the distinguished effigies before mentioned, and ordered the doors to be thrown open for the readmission of a discerning and enlightened public. But the first day's operations were by no means of a successful character, inasmuch as the general public, though they manifested a lively interest in Mrs. Jarley personally, and such of her waxen satellites as were to be seen for nothing, were not affected by any impulses moving them to the payment of sixpence a head. Thus, notwithstanding that a great many people continued to stare at the entry and the figures therein displayed; and remained there with great perseverance, by the hour at a time, to hear the barrel-organ played and to read the bills; and notwithstanding that they were kind enough to recommend their friends to patronize the exhibition in the like manner, until the door-way was regularly blockaded by half the population of the town, who, when they went off duty, were relieved by the other half; it was not found that the treasury was any the richer, or that the prospects of the establishment were at all encouraging.

In this depressed state of the classical market, Mrs. Jarley made extraordinary efforts to stimulate the popular taste, and whet the popular curiosity. Certain machinery in the body of the nun on the leads over the door was cleaned up and put in motion, so that the figure shook its head paralytically all day long, to the great admiration of a drunken, but very Protestant barber over the way, who looked upon the said paralytic motion as typical of the degrading effect wrought upon the human mind by

the ceremonies of the Romish Church, and discoursed upon that theme with great eloquence and morality. The two carters constantly passed in and out of the exhibition-room, under various disguises, protesting aloud that the sight was better worth the money than anything they had beheld in all their lives, and urging the bystanders, with tears in their eyes, not to neglect such a brilliant gratification. Mrs. Jarley sat in the pay-place, chinking silver moneys from noon till night, and solemnly calling upon the crowd to take notice that the price of admission was only sixpence, and that the departure of the whole collection, on a short tour among the Crowned Heads of Europe, was positively fixed for that day week.

" So be in time, be in time, be in time," said Mrs. Jarley, at the close of every such address. " Remember that this is Jarley's stupendous collection of upwards of One Hundred Figures, and that it is the only collection in the world ; all others being impostors and deceptions. Be in time, be in time, be in time! "

CHAPTER THE THIRTY-THIRD.

As the course of this tale requires that we should become acquainted, somewhere hereabouts, with a few particulars connected with the domestic economy of Mr. Sampson Brass, and as a more convenient place than the present is not likely to occur for that purpose, the historian takes the friendly reader by the hand, and springing with him into the air, and cleaving the same at a greater rate than ever Don Cleophas Leandro Perez Zambullo and his familiar travelled through that pleasant region in company, alights with him upon the pavement of Bevis Marks.

The intrepid aeronauts alight before a small dark house, once the residence of Mr. Sampson Brass.

In the parlor window of this little habitation, which is so close upon the footway that the passenger who takes the wall brushes the dim glass with his coat sleeve— much to its improvement, for it is very dirty—in this parlor window in the days of its occupation by Sampson Brass, there hung, all awry and slack, and discolored by the sun, a curtain of faded green, so threadbare from long service as by no means to intercept the view of the little dark room, but rather to afford a favorable medium through which to observe it accurately. There was not much to look at. A rickety table, with spare bundles of papers, yellow and ragged from long carriage in the pocket, ostentatiously displayed upon its top ; a couple of stools set face to face on opposite sides of this crazy piece of furniture ; a treacherous old chair by the fire-place, whose withered arms had hugged full many a client and helped to squeeze him dry ; a second-hand wig box, used as a depository for blank writs and declarations and other small forms of law, once the sole contents of the head which belonged to the wig which belonged to the box, as they were now of the box itself; two or three common books of practice; a jar of ink, a pounce box, a stunted hearth-broom, a carpet trodden to shreds but still clinging with the tightness of desperation to its tacks—these, with the yellow wainscot of the walls, the smoke-discolored ceiling, the dust and cobwebs, were among the most prominent decorations of the office of Mr. Sampson Brass.

But this was mere still-life, of no greater importance than the plate, "Brass, Solicitor," upon the door, and the bill, "First floor to let to a single gentleman," which was tied to the knocker. The office commonly held two examples of animated nature, more to the purpose of this history, and in whom it has a stronger interest and more particular concern.

Of these, one was Mr. Brass himself, who has already appeared in these pages. The other was his clerk, assistant, housekeeper, secretary, confidential plotter, adviser, intriguer, and bill of cost increaser, Miss Brass—a kind of amazon at common law, of whom it may be desirable to offer a brief description.

Miss Sally Brass, then, was a lady of thirty-five or thereabouts, of a gaunt and bony figure, and a resolute bearing, which if it repressed the softer emotions of love, and kept admirers at a distance, certainly inspired a feeling akin to awe in the breasts of those male strangers who had the happiness to approach her. In face she bore a striking resemblance to her brother, Sampson—so exact, indeed, was the likeness between them, that had it consorted with Miss Brass's maiden modesty and gentle womanhood to have assumed her brother's clothes in a frolic and sat down beside him, it would have been difficult for the oldest friend of the family to determine which was Sampson and which Sally, especially as the lady carried upon her upper lip certain reddish demonstrations, which, if the imagination had been assisted by her attire, might have been mistaken for a beard. These were, however, in all probability, nothing more than eyelashes in a wrong place, as the eyes of Miss Brass were quite free from any such natural impertinencies. In complexion Miss Brass was sallow—rather a dirty sallow, so to speak—but this hue was agreeably relieved by the healthy glow which mantled in the extreme tip of her laughing nose. Her voice was exceedingly impressive—deep and rich in quality, and once heard, not easily forgotten. Her usual dress was a green gown, in color not unlike the curtain of the office window, made tight to the figure, and terminating at the throat, where it was fastened behind by a peculiarly large and massive button. Feeling, no doubt, that simplicity and plainness are the soul of elegance, Miss Brass wore no collar or kerchief except upon her head, which was invariably ornamented with a brown gauze scarf, like the wing of the fabled vampire, and which, twisted into any form that happened to suggest itself, formed an easy and graceful head-dress.

Such was Miss Brass in person. In mind, she was of a strong and vigorous turn, having from her earliest youth devoted herself with uncommon ardor to the study of the law; not wasting her speculations upon its eagle flights, which are rare, but tracing it attentively through all the slippery and eel-like crawlings in which it commonly pursues its way. Nor had she, like many persons of great intellect, confined herself to theory, or stopped short where practical usefulness begins; inasmuch as she could ingross, fair-copy, fill up printed forms with perfect accuracy, and in short transact any ordinary duty of the office down to pouncing a skin of parchment or mending a pen. It is difficult to understand how, possessed of these combined attractions, she should remain Miss Brass; but whether she had steeled her heart against mankind, or whether those who might have wooed and won her, were deterred by fears that, being learned in the law, she might have too near her fingers' ends those particular statutes which regulate what are familiarly termed actions for breach, certain it is that she was still in a state of celibacy, and still in daily occupation of her old stool opposite to that of her brother Sampson. And equally certain it is, by the way, that between these two stools a great many people had come to the ground.

One morning Mr. Sampson Brass sat upon his stool copying some legal process, and viciously digging his pen deep into the paper, as if he were writing upon the

very heart against whom it was directed; and Miss Sally
Brass sat upon her stool making a new pen preparatory
to drawing out a little bill, which was her favorite occupation; and so they sat in silence for a long time, until
Miss Brass broke silence.

"Have you nearly done, Sammy?" said Miss Brass;
for in her mild and feminine lips, Sampson became
Sammy, and all things were softened down.

"No," returned her brother. "It would have been all
done though, if you had helped at the right time."

"Oh yes, indeed," cried Miss Sally; "you want my
help, don't you—*you*, too, that are going to keep a
clerk !"

"Am I going to keep a clerk for my own pleasure, or
because of my own wish, you provoking rascal?" said
Mr. Brass, putting his pen in his mouth, and grinning
spitefully at his sister. "What do you taunt me about
going to keep a clerk for?"

It may be observed in this place, lest the fact of Mr.
Brass calling a lady a rascal, should occasion any won-
derment or surprise, that he was so habituated to having
her near him in a man's capacity, that he had gradually
accustomed himself to talk to her as though she were
really a man. And this feeling was so perfectly recipro-
cal, that not only did Mr. Brass often call Miss Brass a
rascal, or even put an adjective before the rascal, but
Miss Brass looked upon it as quite a matter of course,
and was as little moved as any other lady would be by
being called an angel.

"What do you taunt me, after three hours' talk last
night, with going to keep a clerk for?" repeated Mr.
Brass, grinning again with the pen in his mouth, like
some nobleman's or gentleman's crest. "Is it my fault?"

"All I know is," said Miss Sally, smiling drily, for she
delighted in nothing so much as irritating her brother,
"that if every one of your clients is to force us to keep a
clerk, whether we want to or not, you had better leave
off business, strike yourself off the roll, and get taken in
execution as soon as you can."

"Have we got any other client like him?" said Brass.
"Have we got another client like him, now—will you
answer me that?"

"Do you mean in the face?" said his sister.

" Do I mean in the face!" sneered Sampson Brass, reaching over to take up the bill-book, and fluttering its leaves rapidly. "Look here—Daniel Quilp, Esquire—Daniel Quilp, Esquire—Daniel Quilp, Esquire—all through. Whether should I take a clerk that he recommends, and says 'this is the man for you,' or lose all this—eh ?"

Miss Sally deigned to make no reply, but smiled again, and went on with her work.

"But I know what it is," resumed Brass after a short silence. "You're afraid you won't have as long a finger in the business as you've been used to have. Do you think I don't see through that ?"

"The business wouldn't go on very long, I expect, without me," returned his sister composedly. "Don't you be a fool and provoke me, Sammy, but mind what you're doing, and do it."

Sampson Brass, who was at heart in great fear of his sister, sulkily bent over his writing again, and listened as she said :

"If I determined that the clerk ought not to come, of course he wouldn't be allowed to come. You know that well enough, so don't talk nonsense."

Mr. Brass received this observation with increased meekness, merely remarking, under his breath, that he didn't like that kind of joking, and that Miss Sally would be "a much better fellow" if she forbore to aggravate him. To this compliment Miss Sally replied, that she had a relish for the amusement, and had no intention to forego its gratification. Mr. Brass not caring, as it seemed, to pursue the subject any further, they both plied their pens at a great pace, and there the discussion ended.

While they were thus employed, the window was suddenly darkened, as by some person standing close against it. As Mr. Brass and Miss Sally looked up to ascertain the cause, the top sash was nimbly lowered from without, and Quilp thrust in his head.

"Hallo!" he said, standing on tip-toe on the window-sill, and looking down into the room. "Is there anybody at home? Is there any of the Devil's ware here? Is Brass at a premium, eh ?"

"Ha, ha, ha!" laughed the lawyer in an affected

ecstasy. "Oh, very good, Sir! Oh, very good indeed! Quite eccentric! Dear me, what humor he has!"

"Is that my Sally?" croaked the dwarf, ogling the fair Miss Brass. "Is it Justice with the bandage off her eyes, and without the sword and scales? Is it the Strong Arm of the Law? Is it the Virgin of Bevis?"

"What an amazing flow of spirits!" cried Brass. "Upon my word, it's quite extraordinary!"

"Open the door," said Quilp, "I've got him here. Such a clerk for you, Brass, such a prize, such an ace of

trumps. Be quick and open the door, or, if there's another lawyer near and he should happen to look out of window, he'll snap him up before your eyes, he will."

It is probable that the loss of the phœnix of clerks, even to a rival practitioner, would not have broken Mr. Brass's heart; but, pretending great alacrity, he rose from his seat, and going to the door, returned, introducing his client, who led by the hand no less a person than Mr. Richard Swiveller.

"There she is," said Quilp, stopping short at the door,

and wrinkling up his eyebrows as he looked towards Miss Sally; "there is the woman I ought to have married —there is the beautiful Sarah—there is the female who has all the charms of her sex and none of their weaknesses. Oh Sally, Sally!"

To this amorous address Miss Brass briefly responded "Bother!"

"Hard-hearted as the metal from which she takes her name," said Quilp. "Why don't she change it—melt down the brass, and take another name?"

"Hold your nonsense, Mr. Quilp, do," returned Miss Sally, with a grim smile. "I wonder you're not ashamed of yourself before a strange young man."

"The strange young man," said Quilp, handing Dick Swiveller forward, "is too susceptible himself not to understand me well. This is Mr. Swiveller, my intimate friend—a gentleman of good family and great expectations, but who, having rather involved himself by youthful indiscretion, is content for a time to fill the humble station of a clerk—humble, but here most enviable. What a delicious atmosphere!"

If Mr. Quilp spoke figuratively, and meant to imply that the air breathed by Miss Sally Brass was sweetened and rarefied by that dainty creature, he had doubtless good reason for what he said. But if he spoke of the delights of the atmosphere of Mr. Brass's office in a literal sense, he had certainly a peculiar taste, as it was of a close and earthy kind, and, besides being frequently impregnated with strong whiffs of the second-hand wearing apparel exposed for sale in Duke's Place and Houndsditch, had a decided flavor of rats and mice, and a taint of mouldiness. Perhaps some doubts of its pure delight presented themselves to Mr. Swiveller, as he gave vent to one or two short abrupt sniffs, and looked incredulously at the grinning dwarf.

"Mr. Swiveller," said Quilp, "being pretty well accustomed to the agricultural pursuits of sowing wild oats, Miss Sally, prudently considers that half a loaf is better than no bread. To be out of harm's way he prudently thinks is something too, and therefore he accepts your brother's offer. Brass, Mr. Swiveller is yours."

"I am very glad, Sir," said Mr. Brass, "very glad indeed. Mr. Swiveller, Sir, is fortunate to have your friendship. You may be very proud, Sir, to have the friendship of Mr. Quilp."

Dick murmured something about never wanting a friend or a bottle to give him, and also gasped forth his favorite allusion to the wing of friendship and its never moulting a feather; but his faculties appeared to be absorbed in the contemplation of Miss Sally Brass, at whom he stared with blank and rueful looks, which delighted the watchful dwarf beyond measure. As to the divine Miss Sally herself, she rubbed her hands as men of business do, and took a few turns up and down the office with her pen behind her ear.

"I suppose," said the dwarf, turning briskly to his legal friend, "that Mr. Swiveller enters upon his duties at once? It's Monday morning."

"At once, if you please, Sir, by all means," returned Brass.

"Miss Sally will teach him law, the delightful study of the law," said Quilp; "she'll be his guide, his friend, his companion, his Blackstone, his Coke upon Littleton, his Young Lawyer's Best Companion."

"He is exceedingly eloquent," said Brass, like a man abstracted, and looking at the roofs of the opposite houses, with his hands in his pockets; "he has an extraordinary flow of language. Beautiful, really."

"With Miss Sally," Quilp went on, "and the beautiful fictions of the law, his days will pass like minutes. Those charming creations of the poet, John Doe and Richard Roe, when they first dawn upon him, will open a new world for the enlargement of his mind and the improvement of his heart."

"Oh, beautiful, beautiful! Beau-ti-ful indeed!" cried Brass. "It's a treat to hear him!"

"Where will Mr. Swiveller sit?" said Quilp, looking round.

"Why, we'll buy another stool, Sir," returned Brass. "We hadn't any thoughts of having a gentleman with us, Sir, until you were kind enough to suggest it, and our accommodation's not extensive. We'll look about for a second-hand stool, Sir. In the meantime, if Mr. Swiveller will take my seat, and try his hand at a fair copy of this ejectment, as I shall be out pretty well all the morning——"

"Walk with me," said Quilp. "I have a word or two to say to you on points of business. Can you spare the time?"

"Can I spare the time to walk with *you*, Sir? You're joking, Sir, you're joking with me," replied the lawyer, putting on his hat. "I'm ready, Sir, quite ready. My time must be fully occupied indeed, Sir, not to leave me time to walk with you. It's not everybody, Sir, who has an opportunity of improving himself by the conversation of Mr. Quilp."

The dwarf glanced sarcastically at his brazen friend, and, with a short dry cough, turned upon his heel to bid adieu to Miss Sally. After a very gallant parting on his side, and a very cool and gentlemanly sort of one on hers, he nodded to Dick Swiveller, and withdrew with the attorney.

Dick stood at the desk in a state of utter stupefaction, staring with all his might at the beauteous Sally, as if she had been some curious animal whose like had never lived. When the dwarf got into the street, he mounted again upon the window-sill, and looked into the office for a moment with a grinning face, as a man might peep into a cage. Dick glanced upward at him, but without any token of recognition; and long after he had disappeared, still stood gazing upon Miss Sally Brass, seeing or thinking of nothing else, and rooted to the spot.

Miss Brass being by this time deep in the bill of costs, took no notice whatever of Dick, but went scratching on, with a noisy pen, scoring down the figures with evident delight, and working like a steam-engine. There stood Dick, gazing now at the green gown, now at the brown head-dress, now at the face, and now at the rapid pen, in a state of stupid perplexity, wondering how he got into the company of that strange monster, and whether it was a dream and he would ever awake. At last he heaved a deep sigh, and began slowly pulling of his coat.

Mr. Swiveller pulled off his coat, and folded it up with great elaboration, staring at Miss Sally all the time; then put on a blue jacket with a double row of gilt buttons, which he had originally ordered for aquatic expeditions, but had brought with him that morning for office purposes; and, still keeping his eye upon her, suffered himself to drop down silently upon Mr. Brass's stool. Then

;8

he underwent a relapse, and becoming powerless again, rested his chin upon his hand, and opened his eyes so wide, that it appeared quite out of the question that he coul? ever close them any more.

When he had looked so long that he could see nothing, Dick took his eyes off the fair object of his amazement, turned over the leaves of the draft he was to copy, dipped his pen into the inkstand, and at last, and by slow approaches, began to write. But he had not written half-a-dozen words when, reaching over to the inkstand to take a fresh dip, he happened to raise his eyes, and there was the intolerable brown head-dress—there was the green gown—there, in short, was Miss Sally Brass, arrayed in all her charms, and more tremendous than ever.

This happened so often, that Mr. Swiveller by degrees began to feel strange influences creeping over him—horrible desires to annihilate this Sally Brass—mysterious promptings to knock her head-dress off and try how she looked without it. There was a very large ruler on the table—a large, black shining ruler. Mr. Swiveller took it up and began to rub his nose with it.

From rubbing his nose with the ruler, to poising it in his hand and giving it an occasional flourish after the tomahawk manner, the transition was easy and natural. In some of these flourishes it went close to Miss Sally's head; the ragged edges of the head-dress fluttered with the wind it raised; advance it but an inch, and that great brown knot was on the ground; yet still the unconscious maiden worked away, and never raised her eyes.

Well, this was a great relief. It was a good thing to write doggedly and obstinately until he was desperate, and then snatch up the ruler and whirl it about the brown head-dress with the consciousness that he could have it off if he liked. It was a good thing to draw it back, and rub his nose very hard with it, if he thought Miss Sally was going to look up, and to recompense himself with more hardy flourishes when he found she was still absorbed. By these means Mr. Swiveller calmed the agitation of his feelings, until his applications to the ruler became less fierce and frequent, and he could even write as many as half-a-dozen consecutive lines without having recourse to it,—which was a great victory.

CHAPTER THE THIRTY-FOURTH.

In course of time, that is to say, after a couple of hours or so, of diligent application, Miss Brass arrived at the conclusion of her task, and recorded the fact by wiping her pen upon the green gown, and taking a pinch of snuff from a little round tin box which she carried in her pocket. Having disposed of this temperate refreshment, she arose from her stool, tied her papers into a formal packet with red tape, and taking them under her arm, marched out of the office.

Mr. Swiveller had scarcely sprung off his seat and commenced the performance of a maniac hornpipe, when he was interrupted, in the fulness of his joy at being again alone, by the opening of the door, and the reappearance of Miss Sally's head.

"I am going out," said Miss Brass.

"Very good, ma'am," returned Dick. "And don't hurry yourself on my account to come back, ma'am," he added inwardly.

"If anybody comes on office business, take their messages, and say that the gentleman who attends to that matter isn't in at present, will you?" said Miss Brass.

"I will, ma'am," replied Dick.

"I shan't be very long," said Miss Brass, retiring.

"I'm sorry to hear it, ma'am," rejoined Dick when she had shut the door. "I hope you may be unexpectedly detained, ma'am. If you could manage to be run over, ma'am, but not seriously, so much the better."

Uttering these expressions of good-will with extreme gravity, Mr. Swiveller sat down in the client's chair and pondered; then took a few turns up and down the room and fell into the chair again.

"So I'm Brass's clerk, am I?" said Dick. "Brass's clerk, eh? And the clerk of Brass's sister—clerk to a female Dragon. Very good, very good! What shall I be next? Shall I be a convict in a felt hat and a gray suit, trotting about a dockyard with my number neatly embroidered on my uniform, and the order of the garter on my leg, restrained from chafing my ankle by a twisted

Belcher handkerchief? Shall I be that? Will that do, or is it too genteel? Whatever you please, have it your own way of course."

As he was entirely alone, it may be presumed that, in these remarks, Mr. Swiveller addressed himself to his fate or destiny, whom, as we learn by the precedents, it is the custom of heroes to taunt in a very bitter and ironical manner when they find themselves in situations of an unpleasant nature. This is the more probable from the circumstance of Mr. Swiveller directing his observations to the ceiling, which these bodily personages are usually supposed to inhabit—except in theatrical cases, when they live in the heart of the great chandelier.

"Quilp offers me this place, which he says he can insure me," resumed Dick after a thoughtful silence, and telling off the circumstances of his position, one by one, upon his fingers; "Fred, who, I could have taken my affidavit, would not have heard of such a thing, backs Quilp to my astonishment, and urges me to take it also —staggerer, number one. My aunt in the country stops the supplies, and writes an affectionate note to say that she has made a new will, and left me out of it—staggerer, number two. No money ; no credit; no support from Fred, who seems to turn steady all at once; notice to quit the old lodging—staggerers three, four, five, and six. Under an accumulation of staggerers, no man can be considered a free agent. No man knocks himself down ; if his destiny knocks him down, his destiny must pick him up again. Then I'm very glad that mine has brought all this upon itself, and I shall be as careless as I can, and make myself quite at home to spite it. So go on, my buck," said Mr. Swiveller, taking his leave of the ceiling with a significant nod, "and let us see which of us will be tired first!"

Dismissing the subject of his downfall with these reflections, which were no doubt very profound, and are indeed not altogether unknown in certain systems of moral philosophy, Mr. Swiveller shook off his despondency and assumed the cheerful ease of an irresponsible clerk.

As a means towards his composure and self-possession, he entered into a more minute examination of the office than he had yet had time to make ; looked into the wig-box, the books, and ink-bottle; untied and inspected all the papers; carved a few devices on the table with the sharp blade of Mr. Brass's penknife; and wrote his name on the inside of the wooden coal-scuttle. Having, as it were, taken formal possession of his clerkship in virtue of these proceedings, he opened the window and leaned negligently out of it until a beer-boy happened to pass, whom he commanded to set down his tray and to serve him with a pint of mild porter, which he drank upon the spot and promptly paid for, with the view of breaking ground for a system of future credit and opening a correspondence tending thereto, without loss of time. Then three or four little boys dropped in, on legal errands from three or four attorneys of the Brass grade: whom Mr. Swiveller received and dismissed with about as profes sional a manner, and as correct and comprehensive an understanding of their business, as would have been shown by a clown in a pantomime under similar circumstances. These things done and over, he got upon his stool again and tried his hand at drawing caricatures of Miss Brass with a pen and ink, whistling very cheerfully all the time.

He was occupied in this diversion when a coach stopped near the door, and presently afterwards there was a loud double-knock. As this was no business of Mr. Swiveller's, the person not ringing the office bell, he pursued his diversion with perfect composure, notwithstanding that he rather thought there was nobody else in the house.

In this, however, he was mistaken; for, after the knock had been repeated with increased impatience, the door was opened, and somebody with a very heavy tread went up the stairs and into the room above. Mr. Swiveller was wondering whether this might be another Miss Brass, twin sister to the Dragon, when there came a rapping of knuckles at the office door.

"Come in!" said Dick. "Don't stand upon ceremony. The business will get rather complicated if I've many more customers. Come in!"

"Oh, please," said a little voice very low down in the doorway, "will you come and show the lodgings?"

Dick leant over the table, and descried a small slipshod girl in a dirty coarse apron and bib, which left nothing

of her visible but her face and feet. She might as well
have been dressed in a violin-case.

" Why, who are you ? " said Dick.

To which the only reply was, " Oh, please will you
come and show the lodgings ? "

There never was such an old-fashioned child in her
looks and manner. She must have been at work from
her cradle. She seemed as much afraid of Dick as Dick
was amazed at her.

" I hav'n't got anything to do with the lodgings," said
Dick. " Tell 'em to call again."

" Oh, but please will you come and show the lodgings,"
returned the girl ; " it's eighteen shillings a week and us
finding plate and linen. Boots and clothes is extra, and
fires in winter-time is eightpence a day."

" Why don't you show 'em yourself ? You seem to
know all about 'em," said Dick.

" Miss Sally said I wasn't to, because people wouldn't
believe the attendance was good if they saw how small I
was first."

" Well, but they'll see how small you are afterwards,
won't they ? " said Dick.

" Ah ! But then they'll have taken 'em for a fortnight
certain," replied the child with a shrewd look ; " and
people don't like moving when they're once settled."

" This is a queer sort of thing," muttered Dick, rising.
" What do you mean to say you are—the cook ? "

" Yes, I do plain cooking ; " replied the child. " I'm
housemaid too ; I do all the work of the house."

" I suppose Brass and the Dragon and I, do the dirtiest
part of it," thought Dick. And he might have thought
much more, being in a doubtful and hesitating mood, but
that the girl again urged her request, and certain mysterious bumping sounds on the passage and staircase seemed
to give note of the applicant's impatience. Richard
Swiveller, therefore, sticking a pen behind each ear, and
carrying another in his mouth as a token of his great importance and devotion to business, hurried out to meet
and treat with the single gentleman.

He was a little surprised to perceive that the bumping
sounds were occasioned by the progress upstairs of the
single gentleman's trunk, which, being nearly twice as
wide as the staircase, and exceedingly heavy withal, it

was no easy matter for the united exertions of the single gentleman and the coachman to convey up the steep ascent. But there they were, crushing each other, and pushing and pulling with all their might, and getting the trunk tight and fast in all kinds of impossible angles, and to pass them was out of the question; for which sufficient reason, Mr. Swiveller followed slowly behind, entering a new protest on every stair against the house of Mr. Sampson Brass being thus taken by storm.

To these remonstrances, the single gentleman answered not a word, but when the trunk was at last got into the bedroom, sat down upon it and wiped his bald head and face with his handkerchief. He was very warm, and well he might be; for, not to mention the exertion of getting the trunk upstairs, he was closely muffled up in winter garments, though the thermometer had stood all day at eighty-one in the shade.

" I believe, Sir," said Richard Swiveller, taking his pen out of his mouth, " that you desire to look at these apartments. They are very charming apartments, Sir. They command an uninterrupted view of—of over the way, and they are within one minute's walk of—of the corner of the street. There is exceedingly mild porter, Sir, in the immediate vicinity, and the contingent advantages are extraordinary."

" What's the rent?" said the single gentleman.

" One pound per week," replied Dick, improving on the terms.

" I'll take 'em."

" The boots and clothes are extras," said Dick; "and the fires in winter time are——"

" Are all agreed to," answered the single gentleman.

" Two weeks certain," said Dick, " are the——"

" Two weeks!" cried the single gentleman gruffly, eyeing him from top to toe. " Two years. I shall live here for two years. Here. Ten pounds down. The bargain's made."

" Why, you see," said Dick, " my name is not Brass, and——"

" Who said it was? *My* name's not Brass. What then?"

" The name of the master of the house is," said Dick.

" I'm glad of it," returned the single gentleman; " it's

a good name for a lawyer. Coachman, you may go. So may you, Sir."

Mr. Swiveller was so much confounded by the single gentleman riding rough-shod over him at this rate, that he stood looking at him almost as hard as he had looked at Miss Sally. The single gentleman, however, was not in the slightest degree affected by this circumstance, but proceeded with perfect composure to unwind the shawl which was tied round his neck, and then to pull off his boots. Freed of these encumbrances, he went on to divest himself of his other clothing, which he folded up piece by

piece and ranged in order upon the trunk. Then he pulled down the window-blinds, drew the curtains, wound up his watch, and, quite leisurely and methodically, got into bed.

"Take down the bill," were his parting words, as he looked out from between the curtains; "and let nobody call me till I ring the bell."

With that the curtains closed, and he seemed to snore immediately.

"This is a most remarkable and supernatural sort of house!" said Mr. Swiveller, as he walked into the office

with the bill in his hand. " She-dragons in the business, conducting themselves like professional gentlemen; plain cooks of three feet high appearing mysteriously from under ground; strangers walking in and going to bed without leave or license in the middle of the day! If he should be one of the miraculous fellows that turn up, now and then, and has gone to sleep for two years, I shall be in a pleasant situation. It's my destiny, however, and I hope Brass may like it. I shall be sorry if he don't. But it's no business of mine—I have nothing whatever to do with it!"

CHAPTER THE THIRTY-FIFTH.

MR. BRASS on returning home received the report of his clerk with much complacency and satisfaction, and was particular in inquiring after the ten-pound note, which, proving on examination to be a good and lawful note of the Governor and Company of the Bank of England, increased his good-humor considerably. Indeed he so overflowed with liberality and condescension that in the fulness of his heart he invited Mr. Swiveller to partake of a bowl of punch with him at that remote and indefinite period which is currently denominated " one of these days," and paid him many handsome compliments on the uncommon aptitude for business which his conduct on the first day of his devotion to it had so plainly evinced.

It was a maxim with Mr. Brass that the habit of paying compliments kept a man's tongue oiled without any expense; and as that useful member ought never to grow rusty or creak in turning on its hinges in the case of a practitioner of the law, in whom it should be always glib and easy, he lost few opportunities of improving himself by the utterance of handsome speeches and eulogistic expressions. And this had passed into such a habit with him, that, if he could not be correctly said to have his tongue at his fingers' ends, he might certainly be said to have it anywhere but in his face: which being as we have already seen, of a harsh and repulsive character, was not oiled so easily, but frowned above all the smooth speeches —one of nature's beacons, warning off those who navigated the shoals and breakers of the World, or of that dangerous strait the Law, and admonishing them to seek less treacherous harbors and try their fortunes elsewhere.

While Mr. Brass by turns overwhelmed his clerk with compliments and inspected the ten-pound note, Miss Sally showed little emotion and that of no pleasurable kind, for as the tendency of her legal practice had been to fix her thoughts on small gains and gripings, and to whet and sharpen her natural wisdom, she was not a little disappointed that the single gentleman had obtained the lodgings at such an easy rate, arguing that when he was seen to have set his mind upon them, he should have been at the least charged double or treble the usual terms, in exact proportion as he pressed forward, Mr. Swiveller should have hung back. But neither the good opinion of Mr. Brass, nor the dissatisfaction of Miss Sally, wrought any impression upon that young gentleman, who, throwing the responsibility of this and all other acts and deeds thereafter to be done by him, upon his unlucky destiny, was quite resigned and comfortable: fully prepared for the worst, and philosophically indifferent to the best.

"Good-morning, Mr. Richard," said Brass, on the second day of Mr. Swiveller's clerkship. "Sally found you a second-hand stool, Sir, yesterday evening in Whitechapel. She's a rare fellow at a bargain, I can tell you, Mr. Richard. You'll find that a first-rate stool, Sir, take my word for it."

"It's rather a crazy one to look at," said Dick.

"You'll find it a most amazing stool to sit down upon, you may depend," returned Mr. Brass. "It was bought in the open street just opposite the hospital, and as it has been standing there a month or two, it has got rather dusty and a little brown from being in the sun, that's all."

"I hope it hasn't got any fevers or anything of that sort in it," said Dick, sitting himself down discontentedly between Mr. Sampson and the chaste Sally. "One of the legs is longer than the others."

"Then we get a bit of timber in, Sir," retorted Brass. "Ha, ha, ha! We get a bit of timber in, Sir, and that's another advantage of my sister's going to market for us. Miss Brass, Mr. Richard, is the——"

"Will you keep quiet?" interrupted the fair subject of

these remarks, looking up from her papers. "How am I to work if you keep on chattering?"

"What an uncertain chap you are!" returned the lawyer. "Sometimes you're all for a chat. At another time you're all for work. A man never knows what humor he'll find you in."

"I'm in a working humor now," said Miss Sally, "so don't disturb me, if you please. And don't take him," Miss Sally pointed with the feather of her pen to Richard, "off his business. He won't do more than he can help, I dare say."

Mr Brass had evidently a strong inclination to make an angry reply, but was deterred by prudent or timid considerations, as he only muttered something about aggravation and a vagabond; not associating the terms with any individual, but mentioning them as connected with some abstract ideas which happened to occur to him. They went on writing for a long time in silence after this —in such a dull silence that Mr. Swiveller (who required excitement) had several times fallen asleep, and written divers strange words in an unknown character with his eyes shut, when Miss Sally at length broke in upon the monotony of the office by pulling out the little tin box, taking a noisy pinch of snuff, and then expressing her opinion that Mr. Richard Swiveller had "done it."

"Done what, ma'am?" said Richard.

"Do you know," returned Miss Brass, "that the lodger isn't up yet—that nothing has been seen or heard of him since he went to bed yesterday afternoon?"

"Well, ma'am," said Dick, "I suppose he may sleep his ten pound out, in peace and quietness, if he likes."

"Ah! I begin to think he'll never wake," observed Miss Sally.

"It's a very remarkable circumstance," said Brass, laying down his pen; "really, very remarkable. Mr. Richard, you'll remember, if this gentleman should be found to have hung himself to the bed-post, or any unpleasant accident of that kind should happen—you'll remember, Mr. Richard, that this ten-pound note was given to you in part payment of two years' rent? You'll bear that in mind, Mr. Richard; you had better make a note of it, Sir, in case you should ever be called upon to give evidence."

Mr. Swiveller took a large sheet of foolscap, and with a

countenance of profound gravity, began to make a very small note in one corner.

"We can never be too cautious," said Mr. Brass. "There is a deal of wickedness going about the world, a deal of wickedness. Did the gentleman happen to say, Sir—— but never mind that at present, Sir; finish that little memorandum first."

Dick did so, and handed it to Mr. Brass, who had dismounted from his stool and was walking up and down the office.

"Oh, this is the memorandum, is it?" said Brass, running his eye over the document. "Very good. Now, Mr. Richard, did the gentleman say anything else?"

"No."

"Are you sure, Mr. Richard," said Brass, solemnly, "that the gentleman said nothing else?"

"Devil a word, Sir," replied Dick.

"Think again, Sir," said Brass; "it's my duty, Sir, in the position in which I stand, and as an honorable member of the legal profession—the first profession in this country, Sir, or in any other country, or in any of the planets that shine above us at night and are supposed to be inhabited—it's my duty, Sir, as an honorable member of that profession, not to put to you a leading question in a matter of this delicacy and importance. Did the gentleman, Sir, who took the first floor of you yesterday afternoon, and who brought with him a box of property—a box of property—say anything more than is set down in this memorandum?"

"Come, don't be a fool," said Miss Sally.

Dick looked at her, and then at Brass, and then at Miss Sally again, and still said "No."

"Pooh, pooh! Deuce take it, Mr. Richard, how dull you are!" cried Brass, relaxing into a smile. "Did he say anything about his property?—there!"

"That's the way to put it," said Miss Sally, nodding to her brother.

"Did he say, for instance," added Brass, in a kind of comfortable, cozy tone—"I don't assert that he did say so, mind; I only ask you, to refresh your memory—did he say, for instance, that he was a stranger in London— that it was not his humor or within his ability to give any references—that he felt we had a right to require them—and that, in case anything should happen to him, at any time, he particularly desired that whatever property he had upon the premises should be considered mine, as some slight recompense for the trouble and annoyance I should sustain—and were you, in short," added Brass, still more comfortably and cozily than before, "were you induced to accept him on my behalf, as a tenant, upon those conditions?"

"Certainly not," replied Dick.

"Why then, Mr. Richard," said Brass, darting at him a supercilious and reproachful look, "it's my opinion that you've mistaken your calling, and will never make a lawyer."

"Not if you live a thousand years," added Miss Sally. Whereupon the brother and sister took each a noisy pinch of snuff from the little tin box, and fell into a gloomy thoughtfulness.

Nothing further passed up to Mr. Swiveller's dinner-time, which was at three o'clock, and seemed about three weeks in coming. At the first stroke of the hour, the new clerk disappeared. At the last stroke of five, he reappeared, and the office, as if by magic, became fragrant with the smell of gin and water and lemon-peel.

"Mr. Richard," said Brass, "this man's not up yet. Nothing will wake him, Sir. What's to be done?"

"I should let him have his sleep out," returned Dick.

"Sleep out!" cried Brass; "why he has been asleep now, six-and-twenty hours. We have been moving chests of drawers over his head, we have knocked double knocks at the street-door, we have made the servant-girl fall downstairs several times (she's a light weight, and it don't hurt her much), but nothing wakes him."

"Perhaps a ladder," suggested Dick, "and getting in at the first-floor window——"

"But then there's a door between; besides, the neighborhood would be up in arms," said Brass.

"What do you say to getting on the roof of the house through the trap-door, and dropping down the chimney?" suggested Dick.

"That would be an excellent plan," said Brass, if anybody would be—" and here he looked very hard at Mr. Swiveller—"would be kind, and friendly, and generous

enough, to undertake it. I dare say it would not be anything like as disagreeable as one supposes."

Dick had made the suggestion, thinking that the duty
might possibly fall within Miss Sally's department. As
he said nothing further, and declined taking the hint, Mr.
Brass was fain to propose that they should go upstairs
together, and make a last effort to awaken the sleeper
by some less violent means, which, if they failed on this
last trial, must positively be succeeded by stronger
measures. Mr. Swiveller, assenting, armed himself with
his stool and the large ruler, and repaired with his employer to the scene of action, where Miss Brass was
already ringing a hand-bell with all her might, and yet
without producing the smallest effect upon their mysterious lodger.

"There are his boots, Mr. Richard," said Brass.

"Very obstinate-looking articles they are too," quoth
Richard Swiveller. And truly they were as sturdy and
bluff a pair of boots as one would wish to see; as firmly
planted on the ground as if their owner's legs and feet
had been in them, and seeming, with their broad soles
and blunt toes, to hold possession of their place by main
force.

"I can't see anything but the curtain of the bed," said
Brass, applying his eye to the keyhole of the door. "Is
he a strong man, Mr. Richard?"

"Very," answered Dick.

"It would be an extremely unpleasant circumstance if
he was to bounce out suddenly," said Brass. "Keep the
stairs clear. I should be more than a match for him, of
course, but I'm the master of the house, and the laws
of hospitality must be respected.—Hallo there! Hallo,
hallo!"

While Mr. Brass, with his eye curiously twisted into
the keyhole, uttered these sounds as a means of attracting the lodger's attention, and while Miss Brass plied the
hand-bell, Mr. Swiveller put his stool close against the
wall by the side of the door, and mounting on the top
and standing bolt upright, so that if the lodger did make
a rush, he would most probably pass him in its onward
fury, began a violent battery with the ruler upon the
upper panels of the door. Captivated with his own ingenuity, and confident in the strength of his position,

which he had taken up after the method of those hardy individuals who open the pit and gallery doors of theatres on crowded nights, Mr. Swiveller rained down such a shower of blows that the noise of the bell was drowned; and the small servant, who lingered on the stairs below, ready to fly at a moment's notice, was obliged to hold her ears lest she should be rendered deaf for life.

Suddenly the door was unlocked on the inside and flung violently open. The small servant fled to the coal-cellar; Miss Sally dived into her own bedroom; Mr. Brass, who

was not remarkable for personal courage, ran into the next street, and finding that nobody followed him, armed with a poker or other offensive weapon, put his hands in his pockets, walked very slowly all at once, and whistled.

Meanwhile Mr. Swiveller, on the top of the stool, drew himself into as flat a shape as possible against the wall and looked, not unconcernedly, down upon the single gentleman, who appeared at the door growling and cursing in a very awful manner, and, with the boots in his hand, seemed to have an intention of hurling them downstairs on speculation. This idea, however, he abandoned, and he was turning into his room again, still growling vengefully, when his eyes met those of the watchful Richard.

"Have *you* been making that horrible noise?" said the single gentleman.

"I have been helping, Sir," returned Dick, keeping his eye upon him, and waving the ruler gently in his right hand, as an indication of what the single gentleman had to expect if he attempted any violence.

"How dare you then," said the lodger, "Eh?"

To this, Dick made no other reply than by inquiring whether the lodger held it to be consistent with the conduct and character of a gentleman to go to sleep for six-and-twenty hours at a stretch, and whether the peace of an amiable and virtuous family was to weigh as nothing in the balance.

"Is my peace nothing?" said the single gentleman.

"Is their peace nothing, Sir?" returned Dick. "I don't wish to hold out any threats, Sir—indeed the law does not allow of threats, for to threaten is an indictable offence—but if ever you do that again, take care you're not sat upon by the coroner and buried in a cross road before you wake. We have been distracted with fears that you were dead, Sir," said Dick, gently sliding to the ground, "and the short and the long of it is, that we cannot allow single gentlemen to come into this establishment and sleep like double gentlemen without paying extra for it."

"Indeed!" cried the lodger.

"Yes, Sir, indeed," returned Dick, yielding to his destiny and saying whatever came uppermost; "an equal quantity of slumber was never got out of one bed and bedstead, and if you're going to sleep in that way, you must pay for a double-bedded room."

Instead of being thrown into a greater passion by these remarks, the lodger lapsed into a broad grin and looked at Mr. Swiveller, with twinkling eyes. He was a brown-faced sun-burnt man, and appeared browner and more sun-burnt from having a white night-cap on. As it was clear that he was a choleric fellow in some respects, Mr. Swiveller was relieved to find him in such good humor, and, to encourage him in it, smiled himself.

The lodger, in the testiness of being so rudely roused,

had pushed his nightcap very much on one side of his bald head. This gave him a rakish eccentric air which, now that he had leisure to observe it, charmed Mr. Swiveller exceedingly; therefore, by way of propitiation, he expressed his hope that the gentleman was going to get up, and further that he would never do so any more.

"Come here, you impudent rascal!" was the lodger's answer as he re-entered his room.

Mr. Swiveller followed him in, leaving the stool outside, but reserving the ruler in case of a surprise. He rather congratulated himself upon his prudence when the single gentleman, without notice or explanation of any kind, double-locked the door.

"Can you drink anything?" was his next inquiry.

Mr. Swiveller replied that he had very recently been assuaging the pangs of thirst, but that he was still open to "a modest quencher," if the materials were at hand. Without another word spoken on either side, the lodger took from his great trunk a kind of temple, shining as of polished silver, and placed it carefully on the table.

Greatly interested in his proceedings, Mr. Swiveller observed him closely. Into one little chamber of this temple he dropped an egg, into another some coffee, into a third a compact piece of raw steak from a neat tin case, into a fourth he poured some water. Then, with the aid of a phosphorus-box and some matches, he procured a light and applied it to a spirit-lamp which had a place of its own below the temple; then he shut down the lids of all the little chambers; then he opened them; and then, by some wonderful and unseen agency, the steak was done, the egg was boiled, the coffee was accurately prepared, and his breakfast was ready.

"Hot water—" said the lodger, handing it to Mr. Swiveller with as much coolness as if he had a kitchen fire before him—"extraordinary rum—sugar—and a travelling glass. Mix for yourself And make haste."

Dick complied, his eyes wandering all the time from the temple on the table which seemed to do everything, to the great trunk which seemed to hold everything. The lodger took his breakfast like a man who was used to work these miracles, and thought nothing of them.

"The man of the house is a lawyer, is he not?" said the lodger.

20

Dick nodded. The rum was amazing.

"The woman of the house—what's she?"

"A dragon," said Dick.

The single gentleman, perhaps because he had met with such things in his travels, or perhaps because he *was* a single gentleman, evinced no surprise, but merely inquired "Wife or sister?"   "Sister," said Dick.—"So much the better," said the single gentleman, "he can get rid of her when he likes."

"I want to do as I like, young man," he added after a short silence; "to go to bed when I like, get up when I like, come in when I like, go out when I like,—to be asked no questions and be surrounded by no spies. In this last respect, servants are the devil. There's only one here."

"And a very little one," said Dick.

"And a very little one," repeated the lodger. "Well, the place will suit me, will it?"

"Yes," said Dick.

"Sharks, I suppose?" said the lodger.

Dick nodded assent, and drained his glass.

"Let them know my humor," said the single gentleman, rising. "If they disturb me, they lose a good tenant. If they know me to be that, they know enough. If they try to know more, it's a notice to quit. It's better to understand these things at once. Good day."

"I beg your pardon," said Dick, halting in the passage to the door, which the lodger prepared to open. "When he who adores thee has left but the name—"

"What do you mean?"

"—But the name," said Dick—"has left but the name —in case of letters or parcels—"

"I never have any," returned the lodger.

"Or in case anybody should call."

"Nobody ever calls on me."

"If any mistake should arise from not having the name, don't say it was my fault, Sir," added Dick, still lingering.—"Oh blame not the bard—"

"I'll blame nobody," said the lodger, with such irascibility that in a moment Dick found himself on the staircase, and the locked door between them.

Mr. Brass and Miss Sally were lurking hard by, having been, indeed, only routed from the keyhole by Mr. Swiveller's abrupt exit. As their utmost exertions had not enabled them to overhear a word of the interview, however, in consequence of a quarrel for precedence, which, though limited of necessity to pushes and pinches and such quiet pantomime, had lasted the whole time, they hurried him down to the office to hear his account of the conversation.

This Mr. Swiveller gave them—faithfully as regarded the wishes and character of the single gentleman, and poetically as concerned the great trunk, of which he gave a description more remarkable for brilliancy of imagination then a strict adherence to truth; declaring, with many strong asseverations, that it contained a specimen of every kind of rich food and wine known in these times, and in particular that it was of a self-acting kind and served up whatever was required, as he supposed by clock-work. He also gave them to understand that the cooking apparatus roasted a fine piece of sirloin of beef, weighing about six pounds avoirdupois, in two minutes and a quarter, as he had himself witnessed, and proved by his sense of taste; and further that, however the effect was produced, he had distinctly seen water boil and bubble up when the single gentleman winked; from which facts he (Mr. Swiveller) was led to infer that the lodger was some great conjurer or chemist, or both, whose residence under that roof could not fail at some future day to shed a great credit and distinction upon the name of Brass, and add a new interest to the history of Bevis Marks.

There was one point which Mr. Swiveller deemed it unnecessary to enlarge upon, and that was the fact of the modest quencher, which, by reason of its intrinsic strength and its coming close upon the heels of the temperate beverage he had discussed at dinner, awakened a slight degree of fever, and rendered necessary two or three other modest quenchers at the public-house in the course of the evening.

CHAPTER THE THIRTY-SIXTH.

As the single gentleman, after some weeks' occupation of his lodgings, still declined to correspond by word or gesture either with Mr. Brass or his sister Sally, but invariably chose Richard Swiveller as his channel of communication; and as he proved himself in all respects a highly desirable inmate, paying for everything beforehand, giving very little trouble, making no noise, and keeping early hours; Mr. Richard imperceptibly rose to an important position in the family, as one who had influence over this mysterious lodger, and could negotiate with him, for good or evil, when nobody else durst approach his person.

If the truth must be told, even Mr. Swiveller's approaches to the single gentleman were of a very distant kind, and met with small encouragement; but as he never returned from a monosyllabic conference with the unknown, without quoting such expressions as " Swiveller, I know I can rely upon you,"—" I have no hesitation in saying, Swiveller, that I entertain a regard for you,"—" Swiveller, you are my friend, and will stand by me I am sure," with many other short speeches of the same familiar and confiding kind, purporting to have been addressed by the single gentleman to himself, and to form the staple of their ordinary discourse, neither Mr. Brass nor Miss Sally for a moment questioned the extent of his influence, but accorded to him their fullest and most unqualified belief.

But quite apart from and independent of this source of popularity, Mr. Swiveller had another, which promised to be equally enduring, and to lighten his position considerably.

He found favor in the eyes of Miss Sally Brass. Let not the light scorners of female fascination erect their ears to listen to a new tale of love which shall serve them for a jest; for Miss Brass, however accurately formed to be beloved, was not of the loving kind. That amiable virgin, having clung to the skirts of the Law from her earliest youth—having sustained herself by their aid, as it were, in her first running alone, and maintained a firm grasp upon them ever since—had passed her life in a kind of legal childhood. She had been remarkable, when a tender prattler, for an uncommon talent in counterfeiting the walk and manner of a bailiff : in which character she had learned to tap her little playfellows on the shoulder, and to carry them off to imaginary sponging-houses, with a correctness of imitation which was the surprise and delight of all who witnessed her performances, and which was only to be exceeded by her exquisite manner of putting an execution into her doll's house, and taking an exact inventory of the chairs and tables. These artless sports had naturally soothed and cheered the decline of her widowed father : a most exemplary gentleman (called " old Foxey " by his friends from his extreme sagacity), who encouraged them to the utmost, and whose chief regret on finding that he drew near to Houndsditch Churchyard was, that his daughter could not take out an attorney's certificate and hold a place upon the roll. Filled with this affectionate and touching sorrow, he had solemnly confided her to his son Sampson as an invaluable auxiliary ; and from the old gentleman's decease to the period of which we treat, Miss Sally Brass had been the prop and pillar of his business.

It is obvious that, having devoted herself from infancy to this one pursuit and study, Miss Brass could know but little of the world, otherwise than in connection with the law ; and that from a lady gifted with such high tastes, proficiency in those gentler and softer arts in which women usually excel, was scarcely to be looked for. Miss Sally's accomplishments were all of a masculine and strictly legal kind. They began with the practice of an attorney and they ended with it. She was in a state of lawful innocence, so to speak. The law had been her nurse, and, as bandy-legs, or such physical deformities in children are held to be the consequence of bad nursing, so, if in a mind so beautiful any moral twist or bandiness could be found, Miss Sally Brass's nurse was alone to blame.

It was upon this lady, then, that Mr. Swiveller burst in full freshness as something new and hitherto undreamed of, lighting up the office with scraps of song and merriment, conjuring with inkstands and boxes of wafers, catching three oranges in one hand, balancing stools **upon** his chin and penknives on his nose, and constantly performing a hundred other feats of equal ingenuity; for with such unbendings did Richard, in Mr. Brass's absence, relieve the tedium of his confinement. These social qualities, which Miss Sally first discovered by accident, gradually made such an impression upon her, that she would entreat Mr. Swiveller to relax as though she were not by, which Mr. Swiveller, nothing loth, would readily consent to do. By these means a friendship sprang up between them. Mr. Swiveller gradually came to look upon her as her brother Sampson did, and as he would have looked upon any other clerk. He imparted to her the mystery of going the odd man or plain Newmarket for fruit, ginger-beer, baked potatoes, or even a modest quencher, of which Miss Brass did not scruple to partake. He would often persuade her to undertake his share of writing in addition to her own; nay, he would sometimes reward her with a hearty slap on the back, and protest that she was a devilish good fellow, a jolly dog, and so forth; all of which compliments Miss Sally would receive in entire good part and with perfect satisfaction.

One circumstance troubled Mr. Swiveller's mind very much, and that was that the small servant always remained somewhere in the bowels of the earth under Bevis Marks, and never came to the surface unless the single gentleman rang his bell, when she would answer it and immediately disappear again. She never went out, or came into the office, or had a clean face, or took off the coarse apron, or looked out of any one of the windows, or stood at the street-door for a breath of air, or had any rest or enjoyment whatever. Nobody ever came to see her, nobody spoke of her, nobody cared about her. Mr. Brass had said once, that he believed she was a "love-child" (which means anything but a child of love), and that was all the information Richard Swiveller could obtain.

"It's of no use asking the dragon," thought Dick one day, as he sat contemplating the features of Miss Sally Brass. "I suspect if I asked any questions on that head, our alliance would be at an end. I wonder whether she *is* a dragon by the bye, or something in the mermaid way. She has rather a scaly appearance. But mermaids **are** fond of looking at themselves in the glass, which she can't be. And they have a habit of combing their hair, which she hasn't. No, she's a dragon."

"Where are you going, old fellow?" said Dick aloud, as Miss Sally wiped her pen as usual on the green dress, and uprose from her seat..

"To dinner," answered the dragon.

"To dinner!" thought Dick, "that's another circumstance. I don't believe that small servant ever has anything to eat."

"Sammy won't be home," said Miss Brass. "Stop 'till I come back. I shan't be long."

Dick nodded, and followed Miss Brass—with his eyes to the door, and with his ears to a little back parlor, where she and her brother took their meals.

"Now," said Dick, walking up and down with his hands in his pockets, "I'd give something—if I had it—to know how they use that child, and where they keep her. My mother must have been a very inquisitive woman; I have no doubt I'm marked with a note of interrogation somewhere. My feelings I smother, but thou hast been the cause of this anguish, my—upon my word," said Mr. Swiveller, checking himself and falling thoughtfully into the client's chair, "I should like to know how they use her!"

After running on in this way for some time, Mr. Swiveller softly opened the office door, with the intention of darting across the street for a glass of the mild porter. At that moment he caught a parting glimpse of the brown head-dress of Miss Brass flitting down the kitchen stairs. "And by Jove!" thought Dick, "she's going to feed the servant. Now or never!"

First peeping over the handrail and allowing the head-dress to disappear in the darkness below, he groped his way down, and arrived at the door of a back kitchen immediately after Miss Brass had entered the same, bearing in her hand a cold leg of mutton. It was a very dark miserable place, very low and very damp: the walls disfigured by a thousand rents and blotches. The water was trickling out of a leaky butt, and a most wretched cat was lapping up the drops with the sickly eagerness of starvation. The grate, which was a wide one, was wound and screwed up tight, so as to hold no more than a little thin sandwich of fire. Everything was locked up ; the coal-cellar, the candle-box, the salt-box, the meat-safe, were all padlocked. There was nothing that a beetle could have lunched upon. The pinched and meagre aspect of the place would have killed a chameleon. He would have known at the first mouthful that the air was not eatable, and must have given up the ghost in despair.—The small servant stood with humility in presence of Miss Sally, and hung her head.

"Are you there?" said Miss Sally.

"Yes, ma'am," was the answer in a weak voice.

"Go further away from the leg of mutton, or you'll be picking it, I know," said Miss Sally.

The girl withdrew into a corner, while Miss Brass took a key from her pocket, and opening the safe, brought from it a dreary waste of cold potatoes, looking as eatable as Stonehenge. This she placed before the small servant, ordering her to sit down before it, and then, taking up a great carving-knife, made a mighty show of sharpening it upon the carving-fork.

"Do you see this?" said Miss Brass, slicing off about two square inches of cold mutton, after all this preparation, and holding it out on the point of the fork.

The small servant looked hard enough at it with her hungry eyes to see every shred of it, small as it was, and answered, "yes."

"Then don't you ever go and say," retorted Miss Sally, "that you hadn't meat here. There, eat it up."

This was soon done. "Now, do you want any more?" said Miss Sally.

The hungry creature answered with a faint "No." They were evidently going through an established form.

"You've been helped once to meat," said Miss Brass, summing up the facts; "you have had as much as you can eat, you're asked if you want any more, and you answer, 'no!' Then don't you ever go and say you were allowanced, mind that."

With those words, Miss Sally put the meat away and locked the safe, and then drawing near to the small servant, overlooked her while she finished the potatoes.

It was plain that some extraordinary grudge was working in Miss Brass's gentle breast, and that it was this which impelled her, without the smallest present cause, to rap the child with the blade of the knife, now on her hand, now on her head, and now on her back, as if she found it quite impossible to stand so close to her without administering a few slight knocks. But Mr. Swiveller was not a little surprised to see his fellow-clerk, after walking slowly backwards towards the door, as if she were trying to withdraw herself from the room but could not accomplish it, dart suddenly forward, and falling on the small servant give her some hard blows with her clenched hand. The victim cried, but in a subdued manner as if she feared to raise her voice, and Miss Sally, comforting herself with a pinch of snuff, ascended the stairs, just as Richard had safely reached the office.

CHAPTER THE THIRTY-SEVENTH.

THE single gentleman among his other peculiarities— and he had a very plentiful stock, of which he every day furnished some new specimen—took a most extraordinary and remarkable interest in the exhibition of Punch. If the sound of a Punch's voice, at ever so remote a dis-

tance, reached Bevis Marks, the single gentleman, though
in bed and asleep, would start up, and, hurrying on his
clothes, make for the spot with all speed, and presently
return at the head of a long procession of idlers, having
in the midst the theatre and its proprietors. Straightway, the stage would be set up in front of Mr. Brass's
house; the single gentleman would establish himself at
the first-floor window; and the entertainment would proceed with all its exciting accompaniments of fife and
drum and shout, to the excessive consternation of all
sober votaries of business in that silent thoroughfare. It
might have been expected that when the play was done,
both players and audience would have dispersed; but the
epilogue was as bad as the play, for no sooner was the
Devil dead, than the manager of the puppets and his
partner were summoned by the single gentleman to his
chamber, where they were regaled with strong waters
from his private store, and where they held with him
long conversations, the purport of which no human being
could fathom. But the secret of these discussions was
of little importance. It was sufficient to know that while
they were proceeding, the concourse without still lingered
round the house; that boys beat upon the drum with
their fists, and imitated Punch with their tender voices ;
that the office-window was rendered opaque by flattened
noses, and the key-hole of the street-door luminous with
eyes; that every time the single gentleman or either of
his guests was seen at the upper window, or so much as
the end of one of their noses was visible, there was a
great shout of execration from the excluded mob, who
remained howling and yelling, and refusing consolation,
until the exhibitors were delivered up to them to be attended elsewhere. It was sufficient, in short, to know that
Bevis Marks was revolutionized by these popular move-
ments, and that peace and quietness fled from its precincts.

Nobody was rendered more indignant by these proceedings than Mr. Sampson Brass, who, as he could by no
means afford to lose so profitable an inmate, deemed it
prudent to pocket his lodger's affront along with his cash,
and to annoy the audiences who clustered round his door
by such imperfect means of retaliation as were open to
him, and which were confined to the trickling down of

foul water on their heads from unseen watering-pots, pelting them with fragments of tile and mortar from the roof of the house, and bribing the drivers of hackney cabriolets to come suddenly round the corner and dash in among them precipitately. It may at first sight be matter of surprise to the thoughtless few that Mr. Brass, being a professional gentleman, should not have legally indicted some party or parties, active in the promotion of the nuisance; but they will be good enough to remember that as Doctors seldom take their own prescriptions, and Divines do not always practise what they preach, so Lawyers are shy of meddling with the Law on their own account, knowing it to be an edged tool of uncertain application, very expensive in the working, and rather remarkable for its properties of close shaving, than for its always shaving the right person.

"Come," said Mr. Brass one afternoon, "this is two days without a Punch. I'm in hopes he has run through 'em all, at last."

"Why are you in hopes?" returned Miss Sally. "What harm do they do?"

"Here's a pretty sort of fellow!" cried Brass, laying down his pen in despair. "Now here's an aggravating animal!"

"Well, what harm do they do?" retorted Sally.

"What harm!" cried Brass. "Is it no harm to have a constant hallooing and hooting under one's very nose, distracting one from business, and making one grind one's teeth with vexation? Is it no harm to be blinded and choked up, and have the King's highway stopped with a set of screamers and roarers whose throats must be made of—of—"

"Brass," suggested Mr. Swiveller.

"Ah! of brass," said the lawyer, glancing at his clerk, to assure himself that he had suggested the word in good faith and without any sinister intention. "Is that no harm?"

The lawyer stopped short in his invective, and listening for a moment, and recognizing the well-known voice, rested his headed upon his hand, raised his eyes to the ceiling and muttered faintly, "There's another!"

Up went the single gentleman's window directly.

"There's another," repeated Brass; "and if I could get

a break and four blood horses to cut into the Marks when the crowd is at its thickest, I'd give eighteen-pence and never grudge it!"

The distant squeak was heard again. The single gentleman's door burst open. He ran violently down the stairs, out into the street, and so past the window, without any hat, towards the quarter whence the sound proceeded—bent, no doubt, upon securing the strangers' services directly.

"I wish I only knew who his friends were," muttered Sampson, filling his pocket with papers; "if they'd just get up a pretty little Commission *de lunatico* at the Gray's Inn Coffee House and give me the job, I'd be content to have the lodgings empty for one while, at all events."

With which words, and knocking his hat over his eyes as if for the purpose of shutting out even a glimpse of the dreadful visitation, Mr Brass rushed from the house and hurried away.

As Mr. Swiveller was decidedly favorable to these performances, upon the ground that looking at a Punch, or indeed looking at anything out of window, was better than working; and as he had been for this reason at some pains to awaken in his fellow-clerk a sense of their beauties and manifold deserts; both he and Miss Sally rose as with one accord and took up their positions at the window: upon the sill whereof, as in a post of honor, sundry young ladies and gentlemen who were employed in the dry nurture of babies, and who made a point of being present, with their young charges, on such occasions, had already established themselves as comfortably as the circumstances would allow.

The glass being dim, Mr. Swiveller, agreeably to a friendly custom which he had established between them, hitched off the brown head-dress from Miss Sally's head, and dusted it carefully therewith. By the time he had handed it back, and its beautiful wearer had put it on again (which she did with perfect composure and indifference), the lodger returned with the show and showmen at his heels, and a strong addition to the body of spectators. The exhibitor disappeared with all speed behind the drapery, and his partner, stationing himself by the side of the Theatre, surveyed the audience with a remarkable expression of melancholy, which became more remarkable still when he breathed a hornpipe tune into that sweet musical instrument which is popularly termed a mouth-organ, without at all changing the mournful expression of the upper part of his face, though his mouth and chin were, of necessity, in lively spasms.

The drama proceeded to its close, and held the spectators enchained in the customary manner. The sensation which kindles in large assemblies, when they are relieved from a state of breathless suspense and are again free to speak and move, was yet rife, when the lodger, as usual, summoned the men upstairs.

"Both of you," he called from the window; for only the actual exhibitor—a little fat man—prepared to obey the summons. "I want to talk to you. Come, both of you."

"Come, Tommy," said the little man.

"I an't a talker," replied the other. "Tell him so. What should I go and talk for?"

"Don't you see the gentleman's got a bottle and glass up there?" returned the little man.

"And couldn't you have said so, at first?" retorted the other with sudden alacrity. "Now, what are you waiting for? Are you going to keep the gentleman expecting us all day? haven't you *no* manners?"

With this remonstrance, the melancholy man, who was no other than Mr. Thomas Codlin, pushed past his friend and brother in the craft, Mr. Harris, otherwise Short or Trotters, and hurried before him to the single gentleman's apartment.

"Now, my men," said the single gentleman; "you have done very well. What will you take? Tell that little man behind, to shut the door."

"Shut the door, can't you?" said Mr. Codlin, turning gruffly to his friend. "You might have knowed that the gentleman wanted the door shut, without being told, I think."

Mr. Short obeyed, observing under his breath that his friend seemed unusually "cranky," and expressing a hope that there was no dairy in the neighborhood, or his temper would certainly spoil its contents.

The gentleman pointed to a couple of chairs, and intimated by an emphatic nod of his head that he expected them to be seated. Messrs. Codlin and Short, after looking at each other with considerable doubt and indecision, at length sat down—each on the extreme edge of the chair pointed out to him—and held their hats very tight, while the single gentleman filled a couple of glasses from a bottle on the table beside him, and presented them in due form.

" You're pretty well browned by the sun, both of you," said their entertainer. " Have you been travelling?"

Mr. Short replied in the affirmative with a nod and a smile. Mr. Codlin added a corroborative nod and a short

groan, as if he still felt the weight of the Temple upon his shoulders.

" To fairs, markets, races, and so forth, I suppose?" pursued the single gentleman.

" Yes, Sir," returned Short, "pretty nigh all over the West of England."

" I have talked to men of your craft from North, East, and South," returned their host, in rather a hasty manner ; " but I never lighted on any from the West before."

" It's our reg'lar summer circuit is the West, master,"

said Short; "that's where it is. We take the East of London in the spring and winter, and the West of England in the summer time. Many's the hard day's walking in rain and mud, and with never a penny earned, we've had down in the West."

"Let me fill your glass again."

"Much obleeged to you, Sir, I think I will," said Mr. Codlin, suddenly thrusting in his own and turning Short's aside. "I'm the sufferer, Sir, in all the travelling, and in all the staying at home. In town or country, wet or dry, hot or cold, Tom Codlin suffers. But Tom Codlin isn't to complain for all that. Oh, no! Short may complain, but if Codlin grumbles by so much as a word —oh dear, down with him, down with *him* directly. It isn't *his* place to grumble. That's quite out of the question."

"Codlin an't without his usefulness," observed Short with an arch look, "but he don't always keep his eyes open. He falls asleep sometimes, you know. Remember them last races, Tommy."

"Will you never leave off aggravating a man?" said Codlin. "It's very likely I was asleep when five-and-tenpence was collected, in one round, isn't it? I was attending to my business, and couldn't have my eyes in twenty places at once, like a peacock, no more than you could. If I an't a match for an old man and a young child, you an't neither, so don't throw that out against me, for the cap fits your head quite as correct as it fits mine."

"You may as well drop the subject, Tom," said Short. "It isn't particular agreeable to the gentleman, I dare say."

"Then you shouldn't have brought it up," returned Mr. Codlin; "and I ask the gentleman's pardon on your account, as a giddy chap that likes to hear himself talk, and don't much care what he talks about, so that he does talk."

Their entertainer had sat perfectly quiet in the beginning of this dispute, looking first at one man and then at the other, as if he were lying in wait for an opportunity of putting some further question, or reverting to that from which the discourse had strayed. But, from the point where Mr. Codlin was charged with sleepiness, he

had shown an increasing interest in the discussion:
which now attained a very high pitch.

"You are the two men I want," he said, "the two men
I have been looking for, and searching after. Where are
that old man and that child you speak of?"

"Sir?" said Short, hesitating, and looking towards his
friend.

"The old man and his grandchild who travelled with
you—where are they? It will be worth your while to
speak out, I assure you; much better worth your while
than you believe. They left you, you say,—at those

races, as I understand. They have been traced to that
place, and there lost sight of. Have you no clue, can
you suggest no clue, to their recovery?"

"Did I always say, Thomas," cried Short, turning with
a look of amazement to his friend, "that there was sure
to be an inquiry after them two travellers?"

"*You* said!" returned Mr. Codlin. "Did I always say
that that 'ere blessed child was the most interesting I ever
see? Did I always say I loved her, and doted on her?
Pretty creetur, I think I hear her now. 'Codlin's my
friend,' she says, with a tear of gratitude a trickling down
her little eye; 'Codlin's my friend,' she says—'not Short.

Short's very well,' she says; ' I've no quarrel with Short; he means to be kind, I dare say; but Codlin,' she says, ' has the feelings for my money, though he mayn't look it.' "

Repeating these words with great emotion, Mr. Codlin rubbed the bridge of his nose with his coat-sleeve, and shaking his head mournfully from side to side, left the single gentleman to infer that, from the moment when he lost sight of his dear young charge, his peace of mind and happiness had fled.

"Good God!" said the single gentleman, pacing up and down the room, " have I found these men at last, only to discover that they can give me no information or assistance! It would have been better to have lived on in hope from day to day, and never to have lighted on them, than to have my expectations scattered."

" Stay a minute," said Short. " A man of the name of Jerry—you know Jerry, Thomas?"

" Oh, don't talk to me of Jerrys," replied Mr. Codlin. " How can I care a pinch of snuff for Jerrys, when I think of that 'ere darling child? ' Codlin's my friend,' she says, ' dear, good, kind Codlin, as is always a devising pleasures for me! I don't object to Short,' she says, ' but I cotton to Codlin.' Once," said that gentleman reflectively, " she called me Father Codlin. I thought I should have bust! "

" A man of the name of Jerry, Sir," said Short, turning from his selfish colleague to their new acquaintance, " wot keeps a company of dancing dogs, told me in a accidental sort of way that he had seen the old gentleman in connection with a travelling wax-work, unbeknown to him. As they'd given us the slip, and nothing had come of it, and this was down in the country that he'd been seen I took no measures about it, and asked no questions—But I can, if you like."

" Is this man in town?" said the impatient single gentleman. " Speak faster."

" No he isn't, but he will be to morrow, for he lodges in our house," replied Mr. Short rapidly.

" Then bring him here," said the single gentleman. " Here's a sovereign a-piece. If I can find these people through your means, it is but a prelude to twenty more. Return to me to-morrow, and keep your own counsel upon this subject—though I need hardly tell you that, for you'll do so for your own sakes. Now, give me your address, and leave me."

The address was given, the two men departed, the crowd went with them, and the single gentleman for two mortal hours walked in uncommon agitation up and down his room, over the wondering heads of Mr. Swiveller and Miss Sally Brass.

CHAPTER THE THIRTY-EIGHTH.

KIT—for it happens at this juncture, not only that we have breathing time to follow his fortunes, but that the necessity of these adventures so adapt themselves to our ease and inclination as to call upon us imperatively to pursue the track we most desire to take—Kit, while the matters treated of in the last fifteen chapters were yet in progress, was, as the reader may suppose, gradually familiarizing himself more and more with Mr. and Mrs. Garland, Mr. Abel, the pony, and Barbara, and gradually coming to consider them one and all as his particular private friends, and Abel Cottage, Finchley, as his own proper home.

Stay—the words are written, and may go, but if they convey any notion that Kit, in the plentiful board and comfortable lodging of his new abode, began to think slightingly of the poor fare and furniture of his old dwelling, they do their office badly and commit injustice. Who so mindful of those he left at home—albeit they were but a mother and two young babies—as Kit? What boastful father in the fulness of his heart ever related such wonders of his infant prodigy, as Kit never wearied of telling Barbara in the evening time, concerning little Jacob? Was there ever such a mother as Kit's mother, on her son's showing; or was there ever such comfort in poverty as in the poverty of Kit's family, if any correct judgment might be arrived at, from his own glowing account!

And let us linger in this place for an instant to remark that if ever household affections and loves are graceful things, they are graceful in the poor. The ties that bind the wealthy and the proud to home may be forged on earth,

but those which link the poor man to his humble hearth
are of the true metal and bear the stamp of Heaven.
The man of high descent may love the halls and lands of
his inheritance as part of himself, as trophies of his birth
and power ; his associations with them are associations
of pride and wealth and triumph ; the poor man's attachment to the tenements he holds, which strangers have
held before, and may to-morrow occupy again, has a worth-
ier root, struck deep into a purer soil. His household
gods are of flesh and blood, with no alloy of silver, gold,
or precious stones ; he has no property but in the affections of his own heart ; and when they endear bare floors
and walls, despite of rags and toil and scanty meals, that
man has his love of home from God, and his rude hut
becomes a solemn place.

Oh! if those who rule the destinies of nations would
but remember this—if they would but think how hard it
is for the very poor to have engendered in their hearts
that love of home from which all domestic virtues spring,
when they live in dense and squalid masses where social
decency is lost, or rather never found,—if they would but
turn aside from the wide thoroughfares and great houses,
and strive to improve the wretched dwellings in bye-
ways where only Poverty may walk,—many low roofs
would point more truly to the sky, than the loftiest steeple
that now rears proudly up from the midst of guilt, and
crime, and horrible disease, to mock them by its contrast.
In hollow voices from Workhouse, Hospital, and Jail,
this truth is preached from day to day, and has been proclaimed for years. It is no light matter—no outcry from
the working vulgar—no mere question of the people's
health and comforts that may be whistled down on
Wednesday nights. In love of home, the love of country
has its rise ; and who are truer patriots or the best in
time of need—those who venerate the land, owning its
wood, and stream, and earth, and all that they produce?
or those who love their country, boasting not a foot of
ground in all its wide domain.

Kit knew nothing about such questions, but he knew
that his old home was a very poor place and that his new
one was very unlike it, and yet he was constantly looking
back with grateful satisfaction and affectionate anxiety,
and often indited square-folded letters to his mother,

inclosing a shilling or eighteen-pence or such other small remittance, which Mr. Abel's liberality enabled him to make. Sometimes, being in the neighborhood, he had leisure to call upon her, and then great was the joy and pride of Kit's mother, and extremely noisy the satisfaction of little Jacob and the baby, and cordial the congratulations of the whole court, who listened with admiring ears to the accounts of Abel Cottage, and could never be told too much of its wonders and magnificence.

Although Kit was in the very highest favor with the old lady and gentleman, and Mr. Abel, and Barbara, it is certain that no member of the family evinced such a remarkable partiality for him as the self-willed pony, who, from being the most obstinate and opinionated pony on the face of the earth, was in his hands the meekest and most tractable of animals. It is true that in exact proportion as he became manageable by Kit he became utterly ungovernable by anybody else (as if he had determined to keep him in the family at all risks and hazards), and that, even under the guidance of his favorite, he would sometimes perform a great variety of strange freaks and capers, to the extreme discomposure of the old lady's nerves ; but as Kit always represented that this was only his fun, or a way he had of showing his attachment to his employers, Mrs. Garland gradually suffered herself to be persuaded into the belief, in which she at last became so strongly confirmed that if in one of these ebullitions he had overturned the chaise, she would have been quite satisfied that he did it with the very best intentions.

Besides becoming in a short time a perfect marvel in all stable matters, Kit soon made himself a very tolerable gardener, a handy fellow within doors, and an indispensable attendant on Mr. Abel, who every day gave him some new proof of his confidence and approbation. Mr. Witherden the notary, too, regarded him with a friendly eye ; and even Mr. Chuckster would sometimes condescend to give him a slight nod, or to honor him with that peculiar form of recognition which is called "taking a sight," or to favor him with some other salute combining pleasantry with patronage.

One morning Kit drove Mr. Abel to the Notary's office, as he sometimes did, and having set him down at the house, was about to drive off to a livery stable hard by, when this same Mr. Chuckster emerged from the office-door, and cried " Woa-a-a-a-a ! "—dwelling upon the note a long time, for the purpose of striking terror into the pony's heart, and asserting the supremacy of man over the inferior animals.

" Pull up, Snobby," cried Mr. Chuckster, addressing himself to Kit. " You're wanted inside here."

" Has Mr. Abel forgotten anything, I wonder ? " said Kit as he dismounted.

" Ask no questions, Snobby," returned Mr. Chuckster, " but go and see. Woa-a-a then, will you ? If that pony was mine, *I*'d break him."

"You must be very gentle with him, if you please," said Kit "or you'll find him troublesome. You'd better not keep on pulling his ears, please. I know he won't like it."

To this remonstrance Mr. Chuckster deigned no other answer, than addressing Kit with a lofty and distant air as " young feller," and requesting him to cut and come again with all speed. The " young feller " complying, Mr. Chuckster put his hands in his pockets, and tried to look as if he were not minding the pony, but happened to be lounging there by accident.

Kit scraped his shoes very carefully (for he had not yet lost his reverence for the bundles of papers and the tin boxes), and tapped at the office-door, which was quickly opened by the Notary himself.

" Oh ! come in, Christopher," said Mr. Witherden.

" Is that the lad ? " asked an elderly gentleman, but of a stout, bluff figure—who was in the room.

" That's the lad," said Mr. Witherden. " He fell in with my client, Mr. Garland, Sir, at this very door. I have reason to think he is a good lad, Sir, and that you may believe what he says. Let me introduce Mr. Abel Garland, Sir—his young master; my articled pupil, Sir, and most particular friend. My most particular friend, Sir," repeated the Notary, drawing out his silk handkerchief and flourishing it about his face.

" Your servant, Sir," said the stranger gentleman.

" Yours, Sir, I'm sure," replied Mr. Abel mildly. " You were wishing to speak to Christopher, Sir ? "

" Yes, I was. Have I your permission ? "

" By all means."

"My business is no secret; or I should rather say if need be no secret *here*," said the stranger, observing that Mr. Abel and the Notary were preparing to retire. "It relates to a dealer in curiosities with whom he lived, and in whom I am earnestly and warmly interested. I have been a stranger to this country, gentlemen, for very many years, and if I am deficient in form and ceremony, I hope you will forgive me."

"No forgiveness is necessary, Sir;—none whatever," replied the Notary, and so said Mr. Abel.

"I have been making inquiries in the neighborhood in which his old master lived," said the stranger, "and I learnt that he had been served by this lad. I found out his mother's house, and was directed by her to this place as the nearest in which I should be likely to find him. That's the cause of my presenting myself here this morning."

"I am very glad of any cause, Sir," said the Notary, "which procures me the honor of this visit."

"Sir," retorted the stranger, "you speak like a mere man of the world, and I think you something better. Therefore, pray do not sink your real character in paying unmeaning compliments to me."

"Hem!" coughed the Notary. "You're a plain speaker, Sir."

"And a plain dealer," returned the stranger. "It may be my long absence and inexperience that lead me to the conclusion, but if plain speakers are scarce in this part of the world, I fancy that plain dealers are still scarcer. If my speaking should offend you, Sir, my dealing, I hope, will make amends."

Mr. Witherden seemed a little disconcerted by the elderly gentleman's mode of conducting the dialogue; and as for Kit, he looked at him in open-mouthed astonishment, wondering what kind of language he would address to him, if he talked in that free and easy way to a Notary. It was with no harshness, however, though with something of constitutional irritability and haste, that he turned to Kit and said:

"If you think, my lad, that I am pursuing these inquiries with any other view than that of serving and reclaiming those I am in search of, you do me a very great wrong, and deceive yourself. Don't be deceived, I beg of you, but rely upon my assurance. The fact is, gentlemen," he added, turning again to the Notary and his pupil, "that I am in a very painful and wholly unexpected position. I came to this city with a darling object at my heart, expecting to find no obstacle or difficulty in the way of its attainment. I find myself suddenly checked and stopped short in the execution of my design, by a mystery which I cannot penetrate. Every effort I have made to penetrate it, has only served to render it darker and more obscure; and I am afraid to stir openly in the matter, lest those whom I anxiously pursue should fly still farther from me. I assure you that if you could give me any assistance, you would not be sorry to do so, if you knew how greatly I stand in need of it, and what a load it would relieve me from."

There was a simplicity in this confidence which occasioned it to find a quick response in the breast of the good-natured Notary, who replied, in the same spirit, that the stranger had not mistaken his desire, and that if he could be of service to him, he would most readily.

Kit was then put under examination and closely questioned by the unknown gentleman touching his old master and the child, their lonely way of life, their retired habits, and strict seclusion. The nightly absence of the old man, the solitary existence of the child at those times, his illness and recovery, Quilp's possession of the house, and their sudden disappearance, were all the subjects of much questioning and answer. Finally, Kit informed the gentleman that the premises were now to let, and that a board upon the door referred all inquirers to Mr. Sampson Brass, Solicitor, of Bevis Marks, from whom he might perhaps learn some further particulars.

"Not by inquiry," said the gentleman shaking his head. "I live there."

"Live at Brass's the attorney's!" cried Mr. Witherden in some surprise, having professional knowledge of the gentleman in question.

"Ay," was the reply. "I entered upon his lodgings t'other day, chiefly because I had seen this very board. It matters little to me where I live, and I had a desperate hope that some intelligence might be cast in my way there, which would not reach me elsewhere. Yes, I live at Brass's—more shame for me, I suppose?"

"That's a mere matter of opinion," said the Notary, shrugging his shoulders. "He is looked upon as rather a doubtful character."

"Doubtful?" echoed the other. "I am glad to hear there's any doubt about it. I supposed that had been thoroughly settled, long ago. But will you let me speak a word or two with you in private?"

Mr. Witherden consenting, they walked into that gentleman's private closet, and remained there in close conversation for some quarter of an hour, when they returned into the outer office. The stranger had left his hat in Mr. Witherden's room, and seemed to have established himself in this short interval on quite a friendly footing.

"I'll not detain you any longer now," he said, putting a crown into Kit's hand, and looking towards the Notary. "You shall hear from me again. Not a word of this, you know, except to your master and mistress."

"Mother, Sir, would be glad to know—" said Kit, faltering.

"Glad to know what?"

"Anything—so that it was no harm—about Miss Nell."

"Would she? Well then, you may tell her if she can keep a secret. But mind, not a word of this to anybody else. Don't forget that. Be particular."

"I'll take care, Sir," said Kit. "Thankee, Sir, and good morning."

Now, it happened that the gentleman, in his anxiety to impress upon Kit that he was not to tell anybody what had passed between them followed him up to the door to repeat his caution, and it further happened that at that moment the eyes of Mr. Richard Swiveller were turned in that direction, and beheld his mysterious friend and Kit together.

It was quite an accident, and the way in which it came about was this. Mr. Chuckster, being a gentleman of a cultivated taste and refined spirit, was one of that Lodge of Glorious Apollos whereof Mr. Swiveller was Perpetual Grand. Mr. Swiveller, passing through the street in the execution of some Brazen errand, and beholding one of his Glorious Brotherhood intently gazing on a pony, crossed over to give him that fraternal greeting with which Perpetual Grands are, by the very constitution of their office, bound to cheer and encourage their disciples. He had scarcely bestowed upon him his blessing, and followed it with a general remark touching the present state and prospects of the weather, when lifting up his eyes he beheld the single gentleman of Bevis Marks in earnest conversation with Christopher Nubbles.

"Hallo!" said Dick, "who *is* that?"

"He called to see my Governor this morning," replied Mr. Chuckster; "and beyond that I don't know him from Adam."

"At least you know his name?" said Dick.

To which Mr. Chuckster replied, with an elevation of speech becoming a Glorious Apollo, that he was "ever-lastingly blessed" if he did.

"All I know, my dear feller," said Mr. Chuckster, running his fingers through his hair, "is, that he is the cause of my having stood here twenty minutes, for which I hate him with a mortal and undying hatred, and would pursue him to the confines of eternity, if I could afford the time."

While they were thus discoursing, the subject of their conversation (who had not appeared to recognize Mr. Richard Swiveller) re-entered the house, and Kit came down the steps and joined them; to whom Mr. Swiveller again propounded his inquiry with no better success.

"He is a very nice gentleman, Sir," said Kit, "and that's all *I* know about him."

Mr. Chuckster waxed wroth at this answer, and without applying the remark to any particular case, mentioned as a general truth that it was expedient to break the heads of Snobs, and to tweak their noses. Without expressing his concurrence in this sentiment, Mr. Swiveller after a few moments of abstraction inquired which way Kit was driving, and, being informed, declared it was his way, and that he would trespass on him for a lift. Kit would gladly have declined the proffered honor, but as Mr. Swiveller was already established in the seat beside him, he had no means of doing so otherwise than by a forcible ejectment, and therefore drove briskly off—so briskly indeed as to cut short the leave-taking between Mr. Chuckster and his Grand Master, and to occasion the former gentleman some inconvenience from having his corns squeezed by the impatient pony.

As Whisker was tired of standing, and **Mr. Swiveller** was kind enough to stimulate him still futher by shrill whistles, and various sporting cries, they rattled off at too sharp a pace to admit of much conversation, especially as the pony, incensed by Mr. Swiveller's admonitions, took a particular fancy for the lamp-posts and cart-wheels, and evinced a strong desire to run on the pavement and rasp himself against brick walls. It was not, therefore, until they had arrived at the stable, and the chaise had been extricated from a very small doorway, into which the pony dragged it under the impression that he would take it along with him into his usual stall, that Mr. Swiveller found time to talk.

" It's hard work," said Richard. " What do you say to some beer?"

Kit at first declined, but presently consented, and they adjourned to the neighboring bar together.

" We'll drink our friend what's-his-name," said Dick, holding up the bright frothy pot; "—that was talking to you this morning, you know—*I* know him—a good fellow, but eccentric—very—here's what's-his-name!"

Kit pledged him.

" He lives in my house," said Dick; "at least in the house occupied by the firm in which I'm a sort of a—of a managing partner—a difficult fellow to get anything out of, but we like him—we like him."

" I must be going, Sir, if you please," said Kit, moving away.

" Don't be in a hurry, Christopher," replied his patron, " we'll drink your mother."

" Thank you, Sir."

" An excellent woman that mother of yours, Christopher," said Mr. Swiveller. " Who ran to catch me when I fell, and kissed the place to make it well? My mother A charming woman. He's a liberal sort of fellow. We must get him to do something *for* your mother. Does he know her, Christopher?"

Kit shook his head, and glancing slyly at his questioner, thanked him, and made off before he could say another word.

" Humph!" said Mr. Swiveller pondering, " this is queer. Nothing but mysteries in connection with Brass's house. I'll keep my own counsel, however. Everybody

and anybody has been in my confidence as yet, but now I
think I'll set up in business for myself. Queer—very
queer!"

After pondering deeply and with a face of exceeding
wisdom for some time, Mr. Swiveller drank some more
of the beer, and summoning a small boy who had been
watching his proceedings, poured forth the few remaining drops as a libation upon the gravel, and bade him

carry the empty vessel to the bar with his compliments,
and above all things to lead a sober and temperate life,
and abstain from all intoxicating and exciting liquors.
Having given him this piece of moral advice for his
trouble (which, as he wisely observed, was far better than
half-pence) the Perpetual Grand Master of the Glorious
Apollos thrust his hands into his pockets and sauntered
away; still pondering as he went.

CHAPTER THE THIRTY-NINTH.

ALL that day, though he waited for Mr. Abel until evening, Kit kept clear of his mother's house, determined not to anticipate by the slightest approach the pleasures of the morrow, but to let them come in their full rush of delight ; for to-morrow was the great and long looked-for epoch in his life—to-morrow was the end of his first quarter—the day of receiving for the first time one-fourth part of his annual income of Six Pounds in one vast sum of Thirty Shillings—to-morrow was to be a half-holiday devoted to a whirl of entertainments, and little Jacob was to know what oysters meant, and to see a play.

All manner of incidents combined in favor of the occasion : not only had Mr. and Mrs. Garland forewarned him that they intended to make no deduction for his outfit from the great amount, but to pay it him unbroken in all its gigantic grandeur ; not only had the unknown gentleman increased the stock by the sum of five shillings, which was a perfect godsend and in itself a fortune; not only had these things come to pass which nobody could have calculated upon, or in their wildest dreams have hoped ; but it was Barbara's quarter too—Barbara's quarter, that very day—and Barbara had a half-holiday as well as Kit, and Barbara's mother, was going to make one of the party, and to take tea with Kit's mother, and cultivate her acquaintance.

To be sure Kit looked out of his window very early that morning to see which way the clouds were flying, and to be sure Barbara would have been at hers too if she had not sat up so late over-night, starching and iron-ing small pieces of muslin, and crimping them into frills, and sewing them on to other pieces to form magnificent wholes for next day's wear. But they were both up very early for all that, and had small appetites for break-fast and less for dinner, and were in a state of great ex-citement when Barbara's mother came in with astonish-ing accounts of the fineness of the weather out of doors (but with a very large umbrella notwithstanding, for people like Barbara's mother seldom make holiday without one), and when the bell rang for them to go upstairs and receive their quarter's money in gold and silver.

Well, wasn't Mr. Garland kind when he said "Christopher, here's your money, and you have earned it well;" and wasn't Mrs. Garland kind when she said "Barbara, here's yours, and I'm much pleased with you;" and didn't Kit sign his name bold to his receipt, and didn't Barbara sign her name all a trembling to hers; and wasn't it beautiful to see how Mrs. Garland poured out Barbara's mother a glass of wine; and didn't Barbara's mother speak up when she said "Here's blessing you, ma'am, as a good lady, and you, Sir, as a good gentleman, and Barbara, my love to you, and here's towards you, Mr. Christopher;" and wasn't she as long drinking it as if it been a tumblerful; and didn't she look genteel, standing there with her gloves on; and wasn't there plenty of laughing and talking among them as they reviewed all these matters upon the top of the coach; and didn't they pity the people who hadn't got a holiday!

But Kit's mother, again—wouldn't anybody have supposed she had come of a good stock and been a lady all her life? There she was, quite ready to receive them, with a display of tea-things that might have warmed the heart of a china-shop; and little Jacob and the baby in such a state of perfection that their clothes looked as good as new, though Heaven knows they were old enough! Didn't she say before they had sat down five minutes that Barbara's mother was exactly the sort of lady she expected, and didn't Barbara's mother say that Kit's mother was the very picture of what *she* had expected, and didn't Kit's mother compliment Barbara's mother on Barbara, and didn't Barbara's mother compliment Kit's mother on Kit, and wasn't Barbara herself quite fascinated with little Jacob, and did ever a child show off when he was wanted, as that child did, or make such friends as he made?

"And we are both widows too!" said Barbara's mother. "We must have been made to know each other."

"I haven't a doubt about it," returned Mrs. Nubbles. "And what a pity it is we didn't know each other sooner."

"But then you know it's such a pleasure," said Barbara's mother, "to have it brought about by one's son and daughter, that it's fully made up for, now, an't it?"

To this, Kit's mother yielded her full assent, and tracing things back from effects to causes, they naturally reverted to their deceased husbands, respecting whose lives, deaths, and burials, they compared notes, and discovered sundry circumstances that tallied with wonderful exactness; such as Barbara's father having been exactly four years and ten months older than Kit's father, and one of them having died on a Wednesday and the other on a Thursday, and both of them having been of a very fine make and remarkably good-looking, with other extraordinary coincidences. These recollections being of a kind calculated to cast a shadow on the brightness of the holiday, Kit diverted the conversation to general topics, and they were soon in great force again, and as merry as before. Among other things, Kit told them about his old place, and the extraordinary beauty of Nell (of whom he had talked to Barbara a thousand times already); but the last-named circumstance failed to interest his hearers to anything like the extent he had supposed, and even his mother said (looking accidentally at Barbara at the same time) that there was no doubt Miss Nell was very pretty, but she was but a child after all, and there were many young women quite as pretty as she; and Barbara mildly observed that she should think so, and that she never could help believing Mr. Christopher must be under a mistake—which Kit wondered at very much, not being able to conceive what reason she had for doubting him. Barbara's mother too observed that it was very common for young folks to change at about fourteen or fifteen, and whereas they had been very pretty before, to grow up quite plain; which truth she illustrated by many forcible examples, especially one of a young man who, being a builder with great prospects, had been particular in his attentions to Barbara, but whom Barbara would have nothing to say to; which (though everything happened for the best) she almost thought was a pity. Kit said he thought so too, and so he did honestly, and he wondered what made Barbara so silent all at once, and why his mother looked at him as if he shouldn't have said it.

However, it was high time now to be thinking of the play; for which great preparation was required in the way of shawls and bonnets, not to mention one handker-

chief full of oranges and another of apples, which took
some time tying up, in consequence of the fruit having a
tendency to roll out at the corners. At length everything was ready, and they went off very fast; Kit's
mother carrying the baby, who was dreadfully wide
awake, and Kit holding little Jacob in one hand, and
escorting Barbara with the other—a state of things
which occasioned the two mothers, who walked behind,
to declare that they looked quite family folks, and caused
Barbara to blush and say, "Now don't, mother!" But
Kit said she had no call to mind what they said; and indeed she need not have had, if she had known how
very far from Kit's thoughts any love-making was. Poor
Barbara!

At last they got to the theatre, which was Astley's :
and in some two minutes after they had reached the yet
unopened door, little Jacob was squeezed flat, and the
baby had received divers concussions, and Barbara's
mother's umbrella had been carried several yards off and
passed back to her over the shoulders of the people, and
Kit had hit a man on the head with the handkerchief of
apples for "scrowdging" his parent with unnecessary
violence, and there was a great uproar. But when they
were once past the pay-place and tearing away for very
life with their checks in their hands; and above all, when
they were fairly in the theatre, and seated in such places
that they couldn't have had better if they had picked
them out and taken them beforehand; all this was looked
upon as quite a capital joke, and an essential part of the
entertainment.

Dear, dear, what a place it looked, that Astley's! with
all the paint, gilding, and looking-glass; the vague smell
of horses suggestive of coming wonders; the curtain
that hid such gorgeous mysteries; the clean white sawdust down in the circus; the company coming in and
taking their places; the fiddlers looking carelessly up at
them while they tuned their instruments, as if they didn't
want the play to begin, and knew it all beforehand!
What a glow was that which burst upon them all, when
that long, clear, brilliant row of lights came slowly up;
and what the feverish excitement when the little bell
rang and the music began in good earnest, with strong
parts for the drums, and sweet effects for the triangles!

Well might Barbara's mother say to Kit's mother that the gallery was the place to see from, and wonder it wasn't much dearer than the boxes; and well might Barbara feel doubtful whether to laugh or cry, in her flutter of delight.

Then the play itself! the horses which little Jacob believed from the first to be alive, and the ladies and gentlemen of whose reality he could be by no means persuaded, having never seen or heard anything at all like them—the firing, which made Barbara wink—the forlorn lady, who made her cry—the tyrant, who made her tremble—the man who sang the song with the lady's-maid and danced the chorus, who made her laugh—the pony who reared up on his hind legs when he saw the murderer, and wouldn't hear of walking on all fours again until he was taken into custody—the clown who ventured on such familiarities with the military man in boots—the lady who jumped over the nine-and-twenty ribbons and came down safe upon the horse's back—everything was delightful, splendid, and surprising. Little Jacob applauded till his hands were sore; Kit cried "an-kor" at the end of everything, the three-act piece included; and Barbara's mother beat her umbrella on the floor, in her ecstasies, until it was nearly worn down to the gingham.

In the midst of all these fascinations, Barbara's thoughts seemed to have been still running upon what Kit had said at tea-time; for when they were coming out of the play, she asked him, with an hysterical simper, if Miss Nell was as handsome as the lady who jumped over the ribbons.

"As handsome as *her?*" said Kit. "Double as handsome."

"Oh Christopher! I'm sure she was the beautifullest creature ever was," said Barbara.

"Nonsense!" returned Kit. "She was well enough, I don't deny that; but think how she was dressed and painted, and what a difference that made. Why *you* are a good deal better-looking than her, Barbara."

"Oh Christopher!" said Barbara, looking down.

"You are, any day," said Kit,—"and so's your mother."

Poor Barbara!

What was all this though—even all this—to the extraordinary dissipation that ensued, when Kit, walking into an oyster-shop as bold as if he lived there, and not so much as looking at the counter or the man behind it, led his party into a box—a private box, fitted up with red curtains, white table-cloth, and cruet-stand complete—and ordered a fierce gentleman with whiskers, who acted as waiter and called him, him, Christopher Nubbles, "Sir," to bring three dozen of his largest-sized oysters, and to look sharp about it! Yes, Kit told this gentle-

man to look sharp, and he not only said he would look sharp, but he actually did, and presently came running back with the newest loaves, and the freshest butter, and the largest oysters, ever seen. Then said Kit to this gentleman, "a pot of beer"—just so—and the gentleman, instead of replying, "Sir, did you address that language to me?" only said, "Pot o' beer, Sir? Yes, Sir," and went off and fetched it, and put it on the table in a small decanter-stand, like those which blind men's dogs carry about the streets in their mouths to catch the halfpence in; and both Kit's mother and Barbara's mother declared

22

as he turned away that he was one of the slimmest and gracefullest young men she had ever looked upon.

Then they fell to work upon the supper in earnest; and there was Barbara, that foolish Barbara, declaring that she couldn't eat more than two, and wanting more pressing than you would believe before she would eat four; though her mother and Kit's mother made up for it pretty well, and ate and laughed and enjoyed themselves so thoroughly that it did Kit good to see them, and made him laugh and eat likewise from strong sympathy. But the greatest miracle of the night was little Jacob, who ate oysters as if he had been born and bred to the business, sprinkled the pepper and the vinegar with a discretion beyond his years, and afterwards built a grotto on the table with the shells. There was the baby too, who had never closed an eye all night, but had sat as good as gold, trying to force a large orange into his mouth, and gazing intently at the lights in the chandelier—there he was, sitting up in his mother's lap, staring at the gas without winking, and making indentations in his soft visage with an oyster-shell, to that degree that a heart of iron must have loved him! In short, there never was a more successful supper; and when Kit ordered in a glass of something hot to finish with, and proposed Mr. and Mrs. Garland before sending it round, there were not six happier people in all the world.

But all happiness has an end—hence the chief pleasure of its next beginning—and as it was now growing late, they agreed it was time to turn their faces homewards. So, after going a little out of their way to see Barbara and Barbara's mother safe to a friend's house where they were to pass the night, Kit and his mother left them at the door, with an early appointment for returning to Finchley next morning, and a great many plans for next quarter's enjoyment. Then Kit took little Jacob on his back, and giving his arm to his mother, and a kiss to the baby, they all trudged merrily home together.

CHAPTER THE FORTIETH.

FULL of that vague kind of penitence which holidays awaken next morning, Kit turned out at sunrise, and, with his faith in last night's enjoyments a little shaken by cool daylight and the return to every-day duties and occupations, went to meet Barbara and her mother at the appointed place. And being careful not to awaken any of the little household, who were yet resting from their unusual fatigues, Kit left his money on the chimney-piece, with an inscription in chalk calling his mother's attention to the circumstance, and informing her that it came from her dutiful son; and went his way, with a heart something heavier than his pockets, but free from any very great oppression notwithstanding.

Oh these holidays! why will they leave us some regret! why cannot we push them back only a week or two in our memories, so as to put them at once at that convenient distance whence they may be regarded either with a calm indifference or a pleasant effort of recollection! why will they hang about us like the flavor of yesterday's wine, suggestive of headaches and lassitude, and those good intentions for the future, which under the earth form the everlasting pavement of a large estate, and upon it usually endure until dinner-time or thereabouts!

, Who will wonder that Barbara had a headache, or that Barbara's mother was disposed to be cross, or that she slightly underrated Astley's and thought the clown was older than they had taken him to be last night? Kit was not surprised to hear her say so—not he. He had already had a misgiving that the inconstant actors in that dazzling vision had been doing the same thing the night before last, and would do it again that night, and the next, and for weeks and months to come, though he would not be there. Such is the difference between yesterday and to-day. We are all going to the play, or coming home from it.

However, the Sun himself is weak when he first rises, and gathers strength and courage as the day gets on.

By degrees, they began to recall circumstances more and more pleasant in their nature, until, what between talking, walking, and laughing, they reached Finchley in such good heart, that Barbara's mother declared she never felt less tired or in better spirits, and so said Kit. Barbara had been silent all the way, but she said so too. Poor little Barbara! she was very quiet.

They were at home in such good time that Kit had rubbed down the pony and made him as spruce as a race-horse, before Mr. Garland came down to breakfast; which punctual and industrious conduct the old lady, and the old gentleman, and Mr. Abel, highly extolled. At his usual hour (or rather at his usual minute and second, for he was the soul of punctuality) Mr. Abel walked out, to be overtaken by the London coach, and Kit and the old gentleman went to work in the garden.

This was not the least pleasant of Kit's employments, for on a fine day they were quite a family party; the old lady sitting hard by with her work-basket on a little table; the old gentleman digging, or pruning, or clipping about with a large pair of shears, or helping Kit in some way or other with great assiduity; and Whisker looking on from his paddock in placid contemplation of them all. To-day they were to trim the grape-vine, so Kit mounted half-way up a short ladder, and began to snip and hammer away, while the old gentleman, with a great interest in his proceedings, handed up the nails and shreds of cloth as he wanted them. The old lady and Whisker looked on as usual.

"Well, Christopher," said Mr. Garland, "and so you have made a new friend, eh?"

"I beg your pardon, Sir?" returned Kit, looking down from the ladder.

"You have made a new friend, I hear from Mr. Abel," said the old gentleman, "at the office?"

"Oh—yes, Sir, yes. He behaved very handsome, Sir."

"I'm glad to hear it," returned the old gentleman with a smile. "He is disposed to behave more handsomely still though, Christopher."

"Indeed, Sir! It's very kind in him, but I don't want him to, I'm sure," said Kit, hammering stoutly at an obdurate nail.

"He is rather anxious," pursued the old gentleman,

"to have you in his own service—take care what you're doing, or you will fall down and hurt yourself."

"To have me in his service, Sir!" cried Kit, who had stopped short in his work and faced about upon the ladder like some dexterous tumbler. "Why, Sir, I don't think he can be in earnest when he says that."

"Oh! But he is indeed," said Mr. Garland. "And he has told Mr. Abel so."

"I never heard of such a thing!" muttered Kit, look-

ing ruefully at his master and mistress. "I wonder at him; that I do."

"You see, Christopher," said Mr. Garland, "this is a point of much importance to you, and you should understand and consider it in that light. This gentleman is able to give you more money than I—not, I hope, to carry through the various relations of master and servant, more kindness and confidence, but certainly, Christopher, to give you more money."

"Well," said Kit, "after that, Sir—"

"Wait a moment," interposed Mr. Garland. "That is not all. You were a very faithful servant to your old employers, as I understand, and should this gentleman recover them, as it is his purpose to attempt doing by every means in his power, I have no doubt that you, being in his service, would meet with your reward. Besides," added the old gentleman with stronger emphasis, "besides having the pleasure of being again brought into communication with those to whom you seem to be so very strongly and disinterestedly attached. You must think of all this, Christopher, and not be rash or hasty in your choice."

Kit did suffer one twinge, one momentary pang in keeping the resolution he had already formed, when this last argument passed swiftly into his thoughts, and conjured up the realization of all his hopes and fancies. But it was gone in a minute, and he sturdily rejoined that the gentleman must look out for somebody else, as he did think he might have done at first.

"He has no right to think that I'd be led away to go to him, Sir," said Kit, turning round again after half a minute's hammering. "Does he think I'm a fool?"

"He may perhaps, Christopher, if you refuse his offer," said Mr. Garland gravely.

"Then let him, Sir," retorted Kit; "what do I care, Sir, what he thinks? why should I care for his thinking, Sir, when I know that I should be a fool, and worse than a fool, Sir, to leave the kindest master and mistress that ever wasor can be, who took me out of the streets a very poor and hungry lad indeed— poorer and hungrier perhaps than ever you think for, Sir— to go to him or anybody? If Miss Nell was to come back, ma'am," added Kit, turning suddenly to his mistress, "why that would be another thing, and perhaps if *she* wanted me, I might ask you now and then to let me work for her when all was done at home. But when she comes back, I see now that she'll be rich as old master always said she would, and being a rich young lady, what could she want of me? No, no," added Kit, shaking his head sorrowfully, "she'll never want me any more, and bless her, I hope she never may, though I *should* like to see her too!"

Here Kit drove a nail into the wall, very hard—much harder than was necessary—and having done so, faced about again.

"There's the pony, Sir," said Kit—" Whisker, ma'am (and he knows so well I'm talking about him that he begins to neigh directly, Sir),—would he let anybody come near him but me, ma'am? Here's the garden, Sir, and Mr. Abel, ma'am. Would Mr. Abel part with me, Sir, or is there anybody that could be fonder of the garden, ma'am? It would break mother's heart, Sir, and even little Jacob would have sense enough to cry his eyes out, ma'am, if he thought that Mr. Abel could wish to part with me so soon, after having told me only the other day, that he hoped we might be together for years to come—"

There is no telling how long Kit might have stood upon the ladder, addressing his master and mistress by turns, and generally turning towards the wrong person, if Barbara had not at that moment come running up to say that a messenger from the office had brought a note, which, with an expression of some surprise at Kit's oratorical appearance, she put into her master's hand.

"Oh!" said the old gentleman after reading it, "ask the messenger to walk this way."

Barbara tripping off to do as she was bid, he turned to Kit and said that they would not pursue the subject any further, and that Kit could not be more unwilling to part with them, than they would be to part with Kit; a sentiment which the old lady very generously echoed.

"At the same time, Christopher," added Mr. Garland, glancing at the note in his hand, "if the gentleman should want to borrow you now and then for an hour or so, or even a day or so, at a time, we must consent to lend you, and you must consent to be lent.—Oh! here is the young gentleman. How do you do, Sir?"

This salutation was addressed to Mr. Chuckster, who, with his hat extremely on one side, and his hair a long way beyond it, came swaggering up the walk.

"Hope I see you well, Sir," returned that gentleman. "Hope I see *you* well, ma'am. Charming box this, Sir. Delicious country, to be sure."

"You want to take Kit back with you, I find?" observed Mr. Garland.

· "I've got a chariot-cab waiting on purpose," replied the clerk. "A very spanking gray in that cab, Sir, if you're a judge of horseflesh."

Declining to inspect the spanking gray, on the plea that he was but poorly acquainted with such matters, and would but imperfectly appreciate his beauties, Mr. Garland invited Mr. Chuckster to partake of a slight repast in the way of lunch, and that gentleman readily consenting, certain cold viands, flanked with ale and wine, were speedily prepared for his refreshment.

At this repast, Mr. Chuckster exerted his utmost abilities to enchant his entertainers, and impress them with a conviction of the mental superiority of those who dwelt in town; with which view he led the discourse to the small scandal of the day, in which he was justly considered by his friends to shine prodigiously. Thus he was in a condition to relate the exact circumstances of the difference between the Marquis of Mizzler and Lord Bobby, which it appeared originated in a disputed bottle of champagne, and not in a pigeon-pie, as erroneously reported in the newspapers; neither had Lord Bobby said to the Marquis of Mizzler, "Mizzler, one of us two tells a lie, and I'm not the man," as incorrectly stated by the same authorities; but "Mizzler, you know where I'm to be found, and damme, Sir, find me if you want me"—which, of course, entirely changed the aspect of this interesting question, and placed it in a very different light. He also acquainted them with the precise amount of income guaranteed by the Duke of Thigsberry to Violetta Stetta of the Italian Opera, which it appeared was payable quarterly, and not half-yearly, as the public had been given to understand, and which was *ex*clusive, and not *in*clusive (as had been monstrously stated), of jewelry, perfumery, hair-powder for five footmen, and two daily changes of kid-gloves for a page. Having entreated the old lady and gentleman to set their minds at rest upon these absorbing points, for they might rely on his statement being the correct one, Mr. Chuckster entertained them with theatrical chit-chat and the court circular; and so wound up a brilliant and fascinating conversation which he had maintained alone, and without any assistance whatever, for upwards of the three-quarters of an hour.

"And now that the nag has got his wind again," said

Mr. Chuckster, rising in a graceful manner, " I'm afraid I must cut my stick."

Neither Mr. nor Mrs. Garland offered any opposition to his tearing himself away (feeling, no doubt, that such a man could ill be spared from his proper sphere of action), and therefore Mr. Chuckster and Kit were shortly afterwards upon their way to town; Kit being perched upon the box of the cabriolet beside the driver, and Mr. Chuckster seated in solitary state inside, with one of his boots sticking out at each of the front windows.

When they reached the Notary's house, Kit followed into the office, and was desired by Mr. Abel to sit down and wait, for the gentleman who wanted him had gone out, and perhaps might not return for some time. This anticipation was strictly verified, for Kit had had his dinner, and his tea, and had read all the lighter matter in the Law-List, and the Post-Office Directory, and had fallen asleep a great many times, before the gentleman whom he had seen before, came in; which he did at last in a very great hurry.

He was closeted with Mr. Witherden for some little time, and Mr. Abel had been called in to assist at the conference, before Kit, wondering very much what he was wanted for, was summoned to attend them.

" Christopher," said the gentleman, turning to him directly he entered the room, " I have found your old master and young mistress."

" No, Sir ! Have you, though ? " returned Kit, his eyes sparkling with delight. " Where are they, Sir ? How are they, Sir ? Are they—are they near here ? "

" A long way from here," returned the gentleman, shaking his head. " But I am going away to-night to bring them back, and I want you to go with me."

" Me, Sir ? " cried Kit, full of joy and surprise.

" The place," said the strange gentleman, turning thoughtfully to the Notary, " indicated by this man of the dogs, is—how far from here—sixty miles ? "

" From sixty to seventy."

" Humph ! If we travel post all night, we shall reach there in good time to-morrow morning. Now, the only question is, as they will not know me, and the child, God bless her, would think that any stranger pursuing them had a design upon her grandfather's liberty,—can I do better than take this lad, whom they both know and will readily remember, as an assurance to them of my friendly intentions?"

"Certainly not," replied the Notary. "Take Christopher by all means."

"I beg your pardon, Sir," said Kit, who had listened to this discourse with a lengthening countenance, "but if that's the reason, I'm afraid I should do more harm than good—Miss Nell, Sir, *she* knows me, and would trust in me, I am sure; but old master—I don't know why, gentlemen; nobody does—would not bear me in his sight after he had been ill, and Miss Nell herself told me that I must not go near him or let him see me any more. I should spoil all that you were doing if I went, I'm afraid. I'd give the world to go, but you had better not take me, Sir."

"Another difficulty!" cried the impetuous gentleman. "Was ever man so beset as I? Is there nobody else that knew them, nobody else in whom they had any confidence? Solitary as their lives were, is there no one person who would serve my purpose?"

"*Is* there, Christopher?" said the Notary.

"Not one, Sir," replied Kit.—"Yes, though—there's my mother."

"Did they know her?" said the single gentleman.

"Know her, Sir! why, she was always coming backwards and forwards. They were as kind to her as they were to me. Bless you, Sir, she expected they'd come back to her house."

"Then where the devil is the woman?" said the impatient gentleman, catching up his hat. "Why isn't she here? Why is that woman always out of the way when she is most wanted?"

In a word, the single gentleman was bursting out of the office, bent upon laying violent hands on Kit's mother, forcing her into a post-chaise, and carrying her off, when this novel kind of abduction was with some difficulty prevented by the joint efforts of Mr. Abel and the Notary, who restrained him by dint of their remonstrances, and persuaded him to sound Kit upon the probability of her being able and willing to undertake such a journey on so short a notice.

This occasioned some doubts on the part of Kit, and

some violent demonstrations on that of the single gentleman, and a great many soothing speeches on that of the Notary and Mr. Abel. The upshot of the business was, that Kit, after weighing the matter in his mind and considering it carefully, promised, on behalf of his mother, that she should be ready within two hours from that time to undertake the expedition, and engaged to produce her in that place, in all respects equipped and prepared for the journey, before the specified period had expired.

Having given this pledge, which was rather a bold one, and not particularly easy of redemption, Kit lost no time in sallying forth, and taking measures for its immediate fulfilment.

CHAPTER THE FORTY-FIRST.

KIT made his way through the crowded streets, dividing the stream of people, dashing across the busy roadways, diving into lanes and alleys, and stopping or turning aside for nothing, until he came in front of the Old Curiosity Shop, when he came to a stand ; partly from habit and partly from being out of breath.

It was a gloomy autumn evening, and he thought the old place had never looked so dismal as in its dreary twilight. The windows broken, the rusty sashes rattling in their frames, the deserted house a dull barrier dividing the glaring lights and bustle of the street into two long lines, and standing in the midst, cold, dark, and empty,—presented a cheerless spectacle which mingled harshly with the bright prospects the boy had been building up for its late inmates, and came like a disappointment or misfortune. Kit would have had a good fire roaring up the empty chimneys, lights sparkling and shining through the windows, people moving briskly to and fro, voices in cheerful conversation, something in unison with the new hopes that were astir. He had not expected that the house would wear any different aspect —had known indeed that it could not—but coming upon it in the midst of eager thoughts and expectations it checked the current in its flow, and darkened it with a mournful shadow.

Kit, however, fortunately for himself, was not learned enough or contemplative enough to be troubled with presages of evil afar off, and, having no mental spectacles to assist his vision in this respect, saw nothing but the dull house, which jarred uncomfortably upon his previous thoughts. So, almost wishing that he had not passed it, though hardly knowing why, he hurried on again, making up by his increased speed for the few moments he had lost.

"Now, if she should be out," thought Kit, as he approached the poor dwelling of his mother, "and I not able to find her, this impatient gentleman would be in a pretty taking. And sure enough there's no light, and the door's fast. Now, God forgive me for saying so, but if this is Little Bethel's doing, I wish Little Bethel was —was farther off," said Kit checking himself, and knocking at the door.

A second knock brought no reply from within the house; but caused a woman over the way to look out and inquire who that was, wanting Mrs. Nubbles.

"Me," said Kit. "She's at—at Little Bethel, I suppose?"—getting out the name of the obnoxious conventicle with some reluctance, and laying a spiteful emphasis upon the words.

The neighbor nodded assent.

"Then pray tell me where it is," said Kit, "for I have come on a pressing matter, and must fetch her out, even if she was in the pulpit."

It was not very easy to procure a direction to the fold in question, as none of the neighbors were of the flock that resorted thither, and few knew anything more of it than the name. At last a gossip of Mrs. Nubbles's, who had accompanied her to chapel on one or two occasions when a comfortable cup of tea had preceded her devotions, furnished the needful information, which Kit had no sooner obtained than he started off again.

Little Bethel might have been nearer, and might have been in a straighter road, though in that case the reverend gentleman who presided over its congregation would have lost his favorite allusion to the crooked ways by which it was approached, and which enabled him to liken it to Paradise itself, in contradistinction to the parish church and the broad thoroughfare leading thereunto.

Kit found it at last after some trouble, and pausing at the door to take breath that he might enter with becoming decency, passed into the chapel.

It was not badly named in one respect, being in truth a particularly little Bethel—a Bethel of the smallest dimensions—with a small number of small pews, and a small pulpit, in which a small gentleman (by trade a Shoemaker, and by calling a Divine) was delivering in a by no means small voice, a by no means small sermon, judging of its dimensions by the condition of his audience which, if their gross amount were but small, comprised a still smaller number of hearers, as the majority were slumbering.

Among these was Kit's mother, who, finding it matter of extreme difficulty to keep her eyes open after the fatigues of last night, and feeling their inclination to close strongly backed and seconded by the arguments of the preacher, had yielded to the drowsiness that overpowered her and fallen asleep; though not so soundly but that she could from time to time utter a slight and almost inaudible groan, as if in recognition of the orator's doctrines. The baby in her arms was as fast asleep as she; and little Jacob, whose youth prevented him from recognizing in this prolonged spiritual nourishment anything half as interesting as oysters, was alternately very fast asleep and very wide awake, as his inclination to slumber, or his terror of being personally alluded to in the discourse, gained the mastery over him.

"And now I'm here," thought Kit, gliding into the nearest empty pew which was opposite his mother's, and on the other side of the little aisle, "how am I ever to get at her, or persuade her to come out! I might as well be twenty miles off. She'll never wake till it's all over, and there goes the clock again! If he would but leave off for a minute, or if they'd only sing!"—

But there was little encouragement to believe that either event would happen for a couple of hours to come. The preacher went on telling them what he meant to convince them of before he had done, and it was clear that if he only kept to one half of his promises and forgot the other, he was good for that time at least.

In his desperation and restlessness Kit cast his eyes about the chapel, and happening to let them fall upon a

little seat in front of the clerk's desk, could scarcely believe them when they showed him—Quilp!

He rubbed them twice or thrice, but still they insisted
that Quilp was there, and there indeed he was, sitting
with his hand upon his knees, and his hat between them
on a little wooden bracket, with the accustomed grin
upon his dirty face, and his eyes fixed upon the ceiling.
He certainly did not glance at Kit or at his mother, and
appeared utterly unconscious of their presence; still Kit
could not help feeling directly that the attention of the
sly little fiend was fastened upon them, and upon nothing
else.

But astounded as he was by the apparition of the dwarf
among the Little Bethelites, and not free from a misgiving that it was the forerunner of some trouble or annoyance, he was compelled to subdue his wonder and to take
active measures for the withdrawal of his parent, as the
evening was now creeping on, and the matter grew serious.
Therefore the next time little Jacob woke, Kit set himself to attract his wandering attention, and this not being
a very difficult task (one sneeze effected it), he signed to
him to rouse his mother.

Ill-luck would have it, however, that just then the
preacher, in a forcible exposition of one head of his discourse, leaned over upon the pulpit desk so that very
little more of him than his legs remained inside; and,
while he made vehement gestures with his right hand,
and held on with his left, stared, or seemed to stare,
straight into little Jacob's eyes, threatening him by his
strained look and attitude—so it appeared to the child—
that if he so much as moved a muscle, he, the preacher,
would be literally, and not figuratively, "down upon
him" that instant. In this fearful state of things, distracted by the sudden appearance of Kit, and fascinated
by the eyes of the preacher, the miserable Jacob sat bolt
upright, wholly incapable of motion, strongly disposed to
cry but afraid to do so, and returning his pastor's gaze
until his infant eyes seemed starting from their sockets.

"If I must do it openly, I must," thought Kit. With
that, he walked softly out of his pew and into his
mother's, and as Mr. Swiveller would have observed if
he had been present, "collared" the baby without speaking a word.

"Hush, mother!" whispered Kit. "Come along with me, I've got something to tell you."

"Where am I?" said Mrs. Nubbles.

"In this blessed Little Bethel," returned her son, peevishly.

"Blessed indeed!" cried Mrs. Nubbles, catching at the word. "Oh, Christopher, how have I been edified this night!"

"Yes, yes, I know," said Kit hastily; "but come along mother, everybody's looking at us. Don't make a noise —bring Jacob—that's right."

"Stay, Satan, stay!" cried the preacher, as Kit was moving off.

"The gentleman says you're to stay, Christopher," whispered his mother.

"Stay, Satan, stay!" roared the preacher again. "Tempt not the woman that doth incline her ear to thee, but hearken to the voice of him that calleth. He hath a lamb from the fold!" cried the preacher, raising his voice still higher and pointing to the baby. "He beareth off a lamb, a precious lamb! He goeth about like a wolf in the night season, and inveigleth the tender lambs!"

Kit was the best-tempered fellow in the world, but considering this strong language, and being somewhat excited by the circumstances in which he was placed, he faced round to the pulpit with the baby in his arms, and replied aloud,

"No, I don't. He's my brother."

"He's *my* brother!" cried the preacher.

"He isn't," said Kit indignantly. "How can you say such a thing?—And don't call me names, if you please; what harm have I done? I shouldn't have come to take 'em away unless *I* was obliged, you may depend upon that; and I wanted to do it very quiet, but you wouldn't let me. Now, you have the goodness to abuse Satan and them as much as you like, Sir, and to let me alone if you please."

So saying, Kit marched out of the chapel, followed by his mother and little Jacob, and found himself in the open air, with an indistinct recollection of having seen the people wake up and look surprised, and of Quilp having remained throughout the interruption in his old attitude, without moving his eyes from the ceiling, or appearing to take the smallest notice of anything that passed.

"Oh Kit!" said his mother, with her handkerchief to her eyes, "what have you done! I never can go there again—never!"

"I'm glad of it, mother. What was there in the little bit of pleasure you took last night that made it necessary for you to be low-spirited and sorrowful to-night? That's the way you do. If you're happy or merry ever, you come here to say, along with that chap, that you're sorry for it. More shame for you, mother, I was going to say."

"Hush, dear!" said Mrs. Nubbles; "you don't mean what you say I know, but you're talking sinfulness."

"Don't mean it? But I do mean it!" retorted Kit. "I don't believe, mother, that harmless cheerfulness and good humor are thought greater sins in Heaven than shirt-collars are, and that those chaps are just about as right and sensible in putting down the one as in leaving off the other—that's my belief. But I won't say anything more about it, if you'll promise not to cry, that's all; and you take the baby that's a lighter weight, and give me little Jacob; and as we go along (which we must do pretty quick) I'll tell you the news I bring, which will surprise you a little, I can tell you. There—that's right. Now you look as if you'd never seen Little Bethel in all your life, as I hope you never will again; and here's the baby; and little Jacob, you get atop of my back and catch hold of me tight round the neck, and wherever a Little Bethel parson calls you a precious lamb or says your brother's one, you tell him it's the truest things he's said for a twelvemonth, and that if he'd got a little more of the lamb himself, and less of the mint-sauce—not being quite so sharp and sour over it—I should like him all the better. That's what you've got to say to *him*, Jacob."

Talking on in this way, half in jest and half in earnest, and cheering up his mother, the children, and himself, by the one simple process of determining to be in a good humor, Kit led them briskly forward; and on the road home he related what had passed at the Notary's house, and the purpose with which he had intruded on the solemnities of Little Bethel.

His mother was not a little startled on learning what service was required of her, and presently fell into a confusion of ideas, of which the most prominent were that it was a great honor and dignity to ride in a post-chaise, and that it was a moral impossibility to leave the children behind. But this objection, and a great many others, founded upon certain articles of dress being at the wash, and certain other articles having no existence in the wardrobe of Mrs. Nubbles, were overcome by Kit, who opposed to each and every of them, the pleasure of re-covering Nell, and the delight it would be to bring her back in triumph.

"There's only ten minutes now, mother "—said Kit

when they reached home. "There's a bandbox. Throw in what you want, and we'll be off directly."

To tell how Kit then hustled into the box all sorts of things which could by no remote contingency be wanted, and how he left out everything likely to be of the smallest use ; how a neighbor was persuaded to come and stop with the children, and how the children at first cried dismally, and then laughed heartily on being promised all kinds of impossible and unheard-of toys ; how Kit's mother wouldn't leave off kissing them, and how Kit couldn't make up his mind to be vexed with her for doing

23

it ; would take more time and room than we can spare.
So, passing over all such matters, it is sufficient to say
that within a few minutes after the two hours had expired,
Kit and his mother arrived at the Notary's door, where
a post-chaise was already waiting.

" With four horses I declare ! " said Kit, quite aghast
at the preparations. " Well you *are* going to do it,
mother ! Here she is, Sir. Here's my mother. She's
quite ready, Sir."

" That's well "—returned the gentleman. " Now, don't
be in a flutter, ma'am ; you'll be taken great care of.
Where's the box with the new clothing and necessaries
for them ? "

" Here it is," said the Notary. " In with it, Christopher."

" All right, Sir," replied Kit. " Quite ready now, Sir."

" Then come along," said the single gentleman. And
thereupon he gave his arm to Kit's mother, handed her
into the carriage as politely as you please, and took his
seat beside her.

Up went the steps, bang went the door, round whirled
the wheels, and off they rattled, with Kit's mother hanging out at one window waving a damp pocket-handkerchief and screaming out a great many messages to little
Jacob and the baby, of which nobody heard a word.

Kit stood in the middle of the road, and looked after
them with tears in his eyes—not brought there by the
departure he witnessed, but by the return to which he
looked forward. " They went away," he thought, " on
foot with nobody to speak to them or say a kind word at
parting, and they'll come back, drawn by four horses,
with this rich gentleman for their friend, and all their
troubles over ! She'll forget that she taught me to
write—"

Whatever Kit thought about after this, took some
time to think of, for he stood gazing up the lines of shining lamps, long after the chaise had disappeared, and
did not return into the house until the Notary and Mr.
Abel, who had themselves lingered outside till the sound
of the wheels was no longer distinguishable had several
times wondered what could possibly detain him.

CHAPTER THE FORTY-SECOND.

IT behoves us to leave Kit for a while, thoughtful and expectant, and to follow the fortunes of little Nell; resuming the thread of the narrative at the point where it was left. some chapters back.

In one of those wanderings in the evening time, when, following the two sisters at a humble distance, she felt, in her sympathy with them and her recognition in their trials of something akin to her own loneliness of spirit, a comfort and consolation which made such moments a time of deep delight, though the softened pleasure they yielded was of that kind which lives and dies in tears— in one of those wanderings at the quiet hour of twilight, when sky, and earth, and air, and rippling water, and sound of distant bells, claimed kindred with the emotions of the solitary child, and inspired her with soothing thoughts, but not of a child's world or its easy joys—in one of those rambles which had now become her only pleasure or relief from care, light had faded into darkness and evening deepened into night, and still the young creature lingered in the gloom ; feeling a companionship in Nature so serene and still, when noise of tongues and glare of garish lights would have been solitude indeed.

The sisters had gone home, and she was alone. She raised her eyes to the bright stars looking down so mildly from the wide worlds of air, and, gazing on them, found new stars, burst upon her view, and more beyond, and more beyond again, until the whole great expanse sparkled with shining spheres, rising higher and higher in immeasurable space, eternal in their numbers as in their changeless and incorruptible existence. She bent over the calm river, and saw them shining in the same majestic order as when the dove beheld them gleaming through the swollen waters, upon the mountain tops down far below, and dead mankind, a million fathoms deep.

The child sat silently beneath a tree, hushed in her very breath by the stillness of the night, and all its attendant wonders. The time and place awoke reflection, and she thought with a quiet hope—less hope, perhaps, than resignation—on the past, and present, and what was yet before her. Between the old man and herself there had come a gradual separation, harder to bear than any former sorrow. Every evening, and often in the day-time too, he was absent, alone; and although she well knew where he went, and why—too well from the constant drain upon her scanty purse and from his haggard looks—he evaded all inquiry, maintained a strict reserve, and even shunned her presence.

She sat meditating sorrowfully upon this change, and mingled it, as it were, with everything about her, when the distant church-clock bell struck nine. Rising at the sound, she retraced her steps, and turned thoughtfully towards the town.

She had gained a little wooden bridge, which, thrown across the stream, led into a meadow in her way, when she came suddenly upon a ruddy light, and looking forward more attentively, discerned that it proceeded from what appeared to be an encampment of gypsies, who had made a fire in one corner at no great distance from the path, and were sitting or lying round it. As she was too poor to have any fear of them, she did not alter her course (which, indeed, she could not have done without going a long way round), but quickened her pace a little, and kept straight on.

A movement of timid curiosity impelled her, when she approached the spot, to glance towards the fire. There was a form between it and her, the outline strongly developed against the light, which caused her to stop abruptly. Then, as if she had reasoned with herself and were assured that it could not be, or had satisfied herself that it was not that of the person she had supposed, she went on again.

But at that instant the conversation, whatever it was, which had been carrying on near this fire was resumed, and the tones of the voice that spoke—she could not distinguish words—sounded as familiar to her as her own.

She turned, and looked back. The person had been seated before, but was now in a standing posture, and leaning forward upon a stick on which he rested both hands. The attitude was no less familiar to her than the tone of voice had been. It *was* her grandfather.

Her first impulse was to call to him; her next to won-der who his associates could be, and for what purpose they were together. Some vague apprehension succeeded, and yielding to the strong inclination it awakened, she drew nearer to the place; not advancing across the open field, however, but creeping towards it by the hedge.

In this way she advanced within a few feet of the fire, and standing among a few young trees, could both see and hear, without much danger of being observed.

There were no women or children, as she had seen in other gypsy camps they had passed in their wayfaring, and but one gypsy—a tall athletic man, who stood with his arms folded, leaning against a tree at a little distance off, looking now at the fire, and now, under his black eye-lashes, at three other men who were there, with a watch-ful but half-concealed interest in their conversation. Of these her grandfather was one; the others she recognized as the first card-players at the public-house on the event-ful night of the storm—the man whom they had called Isaac List, and his gruff companion. One of the low, arched gypsy-tents, common to that people, was pitched hard by, but it either was, or appeared to be, empty.

"Well, are you going?" said the stout man, looking up from the ground where he was lying at his ease, into her grandfather's face. "You were in a mighty hurry a minute ago. Go, if you like. You're your own master, I hope?"

"Don't vex him," returned Isaac List, who was squat-ting like a frog on the other side of the fire, and had so screwed himself up that he seemed to be squinting all over; "he didn't mean any offence."

"You keep me poor, and plunder me, and make a sport and jest of me besides," said the old man, turning from one to the other. "Ye'll drive me mad among ye."

The utter irresolution and feebleness of the gray-haired child, contrasted with the keen and cunning looks of those in whose hands he was, smote upon the little listener's heart. But she constrained herself to attend to all that passed, and to note each look and word.

"Confound you, what do you mean?" said the stout man rising a little, and supporting himself upon his elbow. "Keep you poor! You'd keep us poor if you could, wouldn't you? That's the way with you whining, puny, pitiful players. When you lose, you're martyrs; but I don't find that when you win, you look upon the other losers in that light. As to plunder!" cried the fellow, raising his voice—"Damme, what do you mean by such ungentlemanly language as plunder, eh?"

The speaker laid himself down again at full length, and gave one or two short, angry kicks, as if in further expression of his unbounded indignation. It was quite plain that he acted the bully, and his friend the peace-maker, for some particular purpose; or rather, it would

have been to any one but the weak old man; for they exchanged glances quite openly, both with each other and with the gypsy, who grinned his approval of the jest un-til his white teeth shone again.

The old man stood helplessly among them for a little time, and then said, turning to his assailant:

"You yourself were speaking of plunder just now, you know. Don't be so violent with me. You were, were you not?"

"Not of plundering among present company. Honor among—among gentlemen, Sir," returned the other, who seemed to have been very near giving an awkward termination to the sentence.

"Don't be hard upon him, Jowl," said Isaac List. "He's very sorry for giving offence. There—go on with what you were saying—go on."

"I'm a jolly old tender-hearted lamb, I am," cried Mr. Jowl, "to be sitting here at my time of life giving advice when I know it won't be taken, and that I shall get nothing but abuse for my pains. But that's the way I've gone through life. Experience has never put a chill upon my warm-heartedness."

"I tell you he's very sorry, don't I?" remonstrated Isaac List, "and that he wishes you'd go on."

"*Does* he wish it?" said the other.

"Ay," groaned the old man sitting down, and rocking himself to and fro. "Go on, go on. It's in vain to fight with it; I can't do it; go on."

"I go on then," said Jowl, "where I left off, when you got up so quick. If you're persuaded that it's time for luck to turn, as it certainly is, and find that you haven't means enough to try it (and that's where it is, for you know yourself that you never have the funds to keep on long enough at a sitting), help yourself to what seems put in your way on purpose. Borrow it, I say, and, when you're able, pay it back again."

"Certainly," Isaac List struck in, "if this good lady as keeps the wax-works has money, and does keep it in a tin box when she goes to bed, and doesn't lock her door for fear of fire, it seems a easy thing; quite a Providence, *I* should call it—but then I've been religiously brought up."

"You see, Isaac," said his friend, growing more eager, and drawing himself closer to the old man, while he signed to the gypsy not to come between them; "you see, Isaac, strangers are going in and out every hour of the day; nothing would be more likely than for one of these strangers to get under the good lady's bed, or lock himself in the cupboard; suspicion would be very wide, and would fall a long way from the mark, no doubt. I'd give him his revenge to the last farthing he brought, whatever the amount was."

"But could you?" urged Isaac List. "Is your bank strong enough?"

"Strong enough!" answered the other, with assumed disdain. "Here, you Sir, give me that box out of the straw!"

This was addressed to the gypsy, who crawled into the low tent on all fours, and after some rummaging and rustling returned with a cash-box, which the man who had spoken opened with a key he wore about his person.

"Do you see this?" he said, gathering up the money in his hand and letting it drop back into the box, between his fingers, like water. "Do you hear it? Do you know the sound of gold? There, put it back—and don't talk about banks again, Isaac, till you've got one of your own."

Isaac List, with great apparent humility, protested that he had never doubted the credit of a gentleman so notorious for his honorable dealing as Mr. Jowl, and that he had hinted at the production of the box, not for the satisfaction of his doubts, for he could have none, but with a view to being regaled with a sight of so much wealth, which, though it might be deemed by some but an unsubstantial and visionary pleasure, was to one in his circumstances a source of extreme delight, only to be surpassed by its safe depository in his own personal pockets. Although Mr. List and Mr. Jowl addressed themselves to each other, it was remarkable that they both looked narrowly at the old man, who, with his eyes fixed upon the fire, sat brooding over it, yet listening eagerly—as it seemed from a certain involuntary motion of the head, or twitching of the face from time to time—to all they said.

"My advice," said Jowl, lying down again with a careless air, "is plain—I have given it, in fact. I act as a friend. Why should I help a man to the means perhaps of winning all I have, unless I considered him my friend? It's foolish, I dare say, to be so thoughtful of the welfare of other people, but that's my constitution, and I can't help it; so don't blame me, Isaac List."

"*I* blame you!" returned the person addressed; "not for the world, Mr. Jowl. I wish I could afford to be as liberal as you; and, as you say, he might pay it back if he won—and if he lost——"

"You're not to take that into consideration at all," said Jowl. "But suppose he did (and nothing's less likely, from all I know of chances), why, it's better to lose other people's money than one's own I hope?"

"Ah!" cried Isaac List rapturously, "the pleasures of winning! The delight of picking up the money—the bright, shining yellow-boys—and sweeping 'em into one's pocket! The deliciousness of having a triumph at last, and thinking that one didn't stop short and turn back, but went half-way to meet it! The——but you're not going, old gentleman?"

"I'll do it," said the old man, who had risen and taken two or three hurried steps away, and now returned as hurriedly. "I'll have it, every penny."

"Why, that's brave," cried Isaac, jumping up and slapping him on the shoulder; "and I respect you for having so much young blood left. Ha, ha, ha! Joe Jowl's half sorry he advised you now. We've got the laugh against him. Ha, ha, ha!"

"He gives me my revenge, mind," said the old man, pointing to him eagerly with his shrivelled hand: "mind—he stakes coin against coin, down to the last one in the box, be there many or few. Remember that!"

"I'm witness," returned Isaac. I'll see fair between you."

"I have passed my word," said Jowl with feigned reluctance, and I'll keep it. When does this match come off? I wish it was over.—To-night?"

"I must have the money first," said the old man; "and that I'll have to-morrow—"

"Why not to-night?" urged Jowl.

"It's late now, and I should be flushed and flurried," said the old man. "It must be softly done. No, to-morrow night."

"Then to-morrow be it," said Jowl. "A drop of comfort here. Luck to the best man! Fill!"

The gypsy produced three tin cups, and filled them to the brim with brandy. The old man turned aside and muttered to himself before he drank. Her own name struck upon the listener's ear, coupled with some wish so fervent, that he seemed to breathe it in an agony of supplication.

"God be merciful to us!" cried the child within herself, "and help us in this trying hour! What shall I do to save him!"

The remainder of their conversation was carried on in a lower tone of voice, and was sufficiently concise ; relating merely to the execution of the project, and the best precautions for diverting suspicion. The old man then shook hands with his tempters, and withdrew.

They watched his bowed and stooping figure as it retreated slowly, and when he turned his head to look back, which he often did, waved their hands, or shouted some brief encouragement. It was not until they had seen him gradually diminish into a mere speck upon the distant road, that they turned to each other, and ventured to laugh aloud.

"So," said Jowl, warming his hands at the fire, "it's done at last. He wanted more persuading than I expected. It's three weeks ago since we first put this in his head. What'll he bring, do you think ? "

" Whatever he brings, it's halved between us," returned Isaac List.

The other man nodded. "We must make quick work of it," he said, "and then cut his acquaintance, or we may be suspected. Sharp's the word."

List and the gypsy acquiesced. When they had all three amused themselves a little with their victim's infatuation, they dismissed the subject as one which had been sufficiently discussed, and began to talk in a jargon which the child did not understand. As their discourse appeared to relate to matters in which they were warmly interested, however, she deemed it the best time for escaping unobserved ; and crept away with slow and cautious steps, keeping in the shadow of the hedges, or forcing a path through them or the dry ditches, until she could emerge upon the road at a point beyond their range of vision. Then she fled homewards as quickly as she could, torn and bleeding from the wounds of thorns and briers, but more lacerated in mind, and threw herself upon her bed, distracted.

The first idea that flashed upon her mind was flight, instant flight; dragging him from that place, and rather dying of want upon the roadside, than ever exposing him again to such terrible temptations. Then she remembered that the crime was not to be committed until next night, and there was the intermediate time for thinking, and resolving what to do. Then she was distracted with a horrible fear that he might be committing it at that moment; with a dread of hearing shrieks and cries piercing the silence of the night; with fearful thoughts of what he might be tempted and led on to do, if he were detected in the act, and had but a woman to struggle with. It was impossible to bear such torture. She stole to the room where the money was, opened the door, and looked in. God be praised! He was not there, and she was sleeping soundly.

She went back to her own room, and tried to prepare herself for bed. But who could sleep—sleep! who could lie passively down, distracted by such terrors? They came upon her more and more strongly yet. Half undressed, and with her hair in wild disorder, she flew to the old man's bedside, clasped him by the wrist, and roused him from his sleep.

"What's this!" he cried, starting up in bed, and fixing his eyes upon her spectral face.

"I have had a dreadful dream," said the child, with an energy that nothing but such terrors could have inspired. "A dreadful, horrible dream. I have had it once before. It is a dream of gray-haired men like you, in darkened rooms by night, robbing the sleepers of their gold. Up, up!" The old man shook in every joint, and folded his hands like one who prays.

"Not to me," said the child, "not to me—to Heaven, to save us from such deeds! This dream is too real. I cannot sleep, I cannot stay here, I cannot leave you alone under the roof where such dreams come. Up! We must fly."

He looked at her as if she were a spirit—she might have been, for all the look of earth she had—and trembled more and more.

"There is no time to lose; I will not lose one minute," said the child. "Up! and away with me!"

"To-night!" murmured the old man.

"Yes, to-night," replied the child. "To-morrow night will be too late. The dream will have come again. Nothing but flight can save us. Up!"

The old man rose from his bed, his forehead bedewed with the cold sweat of fear, and, bending before the child as if she had been an angel messenger sent to lead him where she would, made ready to follow her. She took him by the hand and led him on. As they passed the door of the room he had proposed to rob, she shuddered and looked up into his face. What a white face was that, and with what a look did he meet hers!

She took him to her own chamber, and, still holding him by the hand as if she feared to lose him for an instant, gathered together the little stock she had, and hung her basket on her arm. The old man took his wallet from her hands and strapped it on his shoulders—his staff, too, she had brought away—and then she led him forth.

Through the strait streets, and narrow crooked outskirts, their trembling feet passed quickly. Up the steep hill too, crowned by the old gray castle, they toiled with rapid steps, and had not once looked behind.

But as they drew nearer the ruined walls, the moon rose in all her gentle glory, and, from their venerable age, garlanded with ivy, moss, and waving grass, the child looked back upon the sleeping town, deep in the valley's shade, and on the far-off river with its winding track of light, and on the distant hills; and as she did so, she clasped the hand she held, less firmly, and bursting into tears, fell upon the old man's neck.

CHAPTER THE FORTY-THIRD.

HER momentary weakness past, the child again summoned the resolution which had until now sustained her, and, endeavoring to keep steadily in her view the one idea that they were flying from disgrace and crime, and that her grandfather's preservation must depend solely upon her firmness, unaided by one word of advice or any helping hand, urged him onward and looked back no more.

While he, subdued and abashed, seemed to crouch before her, and to shrink and cower down as if in the presence of some superior creature, the child herself was sensible of a new feeling within her, which elevated her nature, and inspired her with an energy and confidence she had never known. There was no divided responsibility now; the whole burden of their two lives had fallen upon her, and henceforth she must think and act for both.

"I have saved him," she thought. "In all dangers and distresses, I will remember that."

At any other time the recollection of having deserted the friend who had shown them so much homely kindness, without a word of justification—the thought that they were guilty, in appearance, of treachery and ingratitude—even the having parted from the two sisters—would have filled her with sorrow and regret. But now, all other considerations were lost in the new uncertainties and anxieties of their wild and wandering life; and the very desperation of their condition roused and stimulated her.

In the pale moonlight, which lent a wanness of its own, the delicate face where thoughtful care already mingled with the winning grace and loveliness of youth, the too bright eye, the spiritual head, the lips that pressed each other with such high resolve and courage of the heart, the slight figure firm in its bearing and yet so very weak, told their silent tale; but told it only to the wind that rustled by, which, taking up its burden, carried, perhaps to some mother's pillow, faint dreams of childhood fading in its bloom, and resting in the sleep that knows no waking.

The night crept on apace, the moon went down, the stars grew pale and dim, and morning, cold as they, slowly approached. Then, from behind a distant hill, the noble sun rose up, driving the mists in phantom shapes before it, and clearing the earth of their ghostly forms till darkness came again. When it had climbed higher into the sky, and there was warmth in its cheerful beams, they laid them down to sleep, upon a bank, hard by some water.

But Nell retained her grasp upon the old man's arm, and long after he was slumbering soundly, watched him with untiring eyes. Fatigue stole over her at last; her grasp relaxed, tightened, relaxed again, and they slept side by side.

A confused sound of voices mingling with her dreams, awoke her. A man of very uncouth and rough appearance was standing over them, and two of his companions were looking on from a long heavy boat which had come close to the bank while they were sleeping. The boat had neither oar nor sail, but was towed by a couple of horses, who, with the rope to which they were harnessed slack and dripping in the water, were resting on the path.

"Holloa!" said the man roughly. "What's the matter here, eh?"

"We were only asleep, Sir," said Nell. "We have been walking all night."

"A pair of queer travellers to be walking all night," observed the man who had first accosted them. "One of you is a trifle too old for that sort of work, and the other a trifle too young. Where are you going?"

Nell faltered, and pointed at hazard towards the West, upon which the man inquired if she meant a certain town which he named. Nell, to avoid further questioning, said "Yes, that was the place."

"Where have you come from?" was the next question; and this being an easier one to answer, Nell mentioned the name of the village in which their friend the schoolmaster dwelt, as being less likely to be known to the men or to provoke further inquiry.

"I thought somebody had been robbing and ill-using you, might be," said the man. "That's all. Good-day."

Returning his salute and feeling greatly relieved by his departure, Nell looked after him as he mounted one of the horses, and the boat went on. It had not gone very far, when it stopped again, and she saw the men beckoning to her.

"Did you call to me?" said Nell, running up to them.

"You may go with us if you like," replied one of those in the boat. "We're going to the same place."

The child hesitated for a moment, and thinking, as she had thought with great trepidation more than once before, that the men whom she had seen with her grandfather might perhaps, in their eagerness for the booty, follow them, and, regaining their influence over him, set hers at naught; and that if they went with these men, all traces of them must surely be lost at that spot; determined to accept the offer. The boat came close to the bank again, and before she had had any time for further consideration, she and her grandfather were on board, and gliding smoothly down the canal.

The sun shone pleasantly upon the bright water, which was sometimes shaded by trees, and sometimes open to a wide extent of country, intersected by running streams, and rich with wooded hills, cultivated land, and sheltered farms. Now and then a village with its modest spire, thatched roofs, and gable-ends, would peep out from among the trees; and more than once a distant town, with great church towers looming through its smoke, and high factories or workshops rising above the mass of houses would come in view, and, by the length of time it lingered in the distance, show them how slowly they travelled. Their way lay for the most part through the low grounds, and open plains; and except these distant places, and occasionally some men working in the fields, or lounging on the bridges under which they passed, to see them creep along, nothing encroached on their monotonous and secluded track.

Nell was rather disheartened, when they stopped at a kind of wharf late in the afternoon, to learn from one of the men that they would not reach their place of destination until next day, and that if she had no provision with her she had better buy it there. She had but a few pence, having already bargained with them for some bread, but even of these it was necessary to be very careful, as they were on their way to an utterly strange place, with no resource whatever. A small loaf and a morsel of cheese, therefore, were all she could afford, and with these she took her place in the boat again, and, after half an hour's delay, during which the men were drinking at the public-house, proceeded on the journey.

They brought some beer and spirits into the boat with them, and what with drinking freely before, and again now, were soon on a fair way of being quarrelsome and intoxicated. Avoiding the small cabin, therefore, which was very dark and filthy, and to which they often invited both her and her grandfather, Nell sat in the open air with the old man by her side, listening to their boisterous hosts with a palpitating heart, and almost wishing herself safe on shore again though she should have to walk all night.

They were in truth very rugged, noisy fellows, and quite brutal among themselves, though civil enough to their two passengers. Thus, when a quarrel arose between the man who was steering and his friend in the cabin, upon the question who had first suggested the propriety of offering Nell some beer, and when the quarrel led to a scuffle in which they beat each other fearfully, to her inexpressible terror, neither visited his displeasure upon her, but each contented himself with venting it on his adversary, on whom, in addition to blows, he bestowed, a variety of compliments, which, happily for the child, were conveyed in terms, to her quite unintelligible. The difference was finally adjusted, by the man who had come out of the cabin knocking the other into it head first, and taking the helm into his own hands, without evincing the least discomposure himself, or causing any in his friend, who, being of a tolerably strong constitution and perfectly inured to such trifles, went to sleep as he was, with his heels upwards, and in a couple of minutes or so was snoring comfortably.

By this time it was night again, and though the child felt cold, being but poorly clad, her anxious thoughts were far removed from her own suffering or uneasiness, and busily engaged in endeavoring to devise some scheme for their joint subsistence. The same spirit which had supported her on the previous night, upheld and sustained her now. Her grandfather lay sleeping safely at her side, and the crime to which his madness urged him, was not committed. That was her comfort.

How every circumstance of her short, eventful life, came thronging into her mind as they travelled on! Slight incidents, never thought of or remembered until now; faces seen once and ever since forgotten; words spoken and scarcely heeded at the time; scenes of a year ago and those of yesterday mixing up and linking themselves together; familiar places shaping themselves out in the darkness from things which, when approached, were of all others the most remote and most unlike them; sometimes a strange confusion in her mind relative to the occasion of her being there, and the place to which she was going, and the people she was with; and imagination suggesting remarks and questions which sounded so plainly in her ears, that she would start, and turn, and be almost tempted to reply;—all the fancies and contradictions common in watching and excitement and restless change of place, beset the child.

She happened, while she was thus engaged, to encounter the face of the man on deck, in whom the sentimental stage of drunkenness had now succeeded to the boisterous,

and who, taking from his mouth a short pipe, quilted over with string for its longer preservation, requested that she would oblige him with a song.

"You've got a very pretty voice, a very soft eye, and a very strong memory," said this gentleman; "the voice and eye I've got evidence for, and the memory's an opinion of my own. And I'm never wrong. Let me hear a song this minute."

"I don't think I know one, Sir," returned Nell.

"You know forty-seven songs," said the man, with a

gravity which admitted of no altercation on the subject. "Forty-seven's your number. Let me here one of 'em—the best. Give me a song this minute."

Not knowing what might be the consequences of irritating her friend, and trembling with the fear of doing so, poor Nell sang him some little ditty which she had learned in happier times, and which was so agreeable to his ear, that on its conclusion he in the same peremptory manner requested to be favored with another, to which he was so obliging as to roar a chorus to no particular tune, and with no words at all, but which amply made

24

up in its amazing energy for its deficiency in other respects. The noise of this vocal performance awakened the other man who, staggering upon deck and shaking his late opponent by the hand, swore that singing was his pride and joy and chief delight, and that he desired no better entertainment. With a third call, more imperative than either of the two former, Nell felt obliged to comply, and this time a chorus was maintained not only by the two men together, but also by the third man on horseback, who, being by his position debarred from a nearer participation in the revels of the night, roared when his companions roared, and rent the very air. In this way, with little cessation, and singing the same songs again and again, the tired and exhausted child kept them in good humor all that night; and many a cottager, who was roused from his soundest sleep by the discordant chorus as it floated away upon the wind, hid his head beneath the bed-clothes and trembled at the sounds.

At length the morning dawned. It was no sooner light than it began to rain heavily. As the child could not endure the intolerable vapors of the cabin, they covered her, in return for her exertions, with some pieces of sail-cloth and ends of tarpaulin, which sufficed to keep her tolerably dry and to shelter her grandfather besides. As the day advanced the rain increased. At noon it poured down more hopelessly and heavily than ever, without the faintest promise of abatement.

They had for some time been gradually approaching the place for which they were bound. The water had become thicker and dirtier; other barges coming from it passed them frequently; the paths of coal-ash and huts of staring brick, marked the vicinity of some great manufacturing town; while scattered streets and houses, and smoke from distant furnaces, indicated that they were already in the outskirts. Now, the clustered roofs, and piles of buildings trembling with the working of engines, and dimly resounding with their shrieks and throbbings; the tall chimneys vomiting forth a black vapor, which hung in a dense ill-favored cloud above the housetops and filled the air with gloom; the clank of hammers beating upon iron, the roar of busy streets and noisy crowds, gradually augmenting until all the various sounds blended into one and none was distinguishable for itself, announced the termination of their journey.

The boat floated into the wharf to which it belonged. The men were occupied directly. The child and her grandfather, after waiting in vain to thank them, or ask them whither they should go, passed through a dirty lane into a crowded street, and stood amid its din and tumult, and in the pouring rain, as strange, bewildered, and confused, as if they had lived a thousand years before, and were raised from the dead and placed there by a miracle.

CHAPTER THE FORTY-FOURTH.

THE throng of people hurried by, in two opposite streams, with no symptom of cessation or exhaustion; intent upon their own affairs; and undisturbed in their business speculations, by the roar of carts and wagons laden with clashing wares, the slipping of horses' feet upon the wet and greasy pavement, the rattling of the rain on windows and umbrella-tops, the jostling of the more impatient passengers, and all the noise and tumult of a crowded street in the high tide of its occupation: while the two poor strangers, stunned and bewildered by the hurry they beheld but had no part in, looked mournfully on; feeling amidst the crowd a solitude which has no parallel but in the thirst of the shipwrecked mariner, who, tossed to and fro upon the billows of a mighty ocean, his red eyes blinded by looking on the water which hems him in on every side, has not one drop to cool his burning tongue.

They withdrew into a low archway for shelter from the rain, and watched the faces of those who passed, to find in one among them a ray of encouragement or hope. Some frowned, some smiled, some muttered to themselves, some made slight gestures, as if anticipating the conversation in which they would shortly be engaged, some wore the cunning look of bargaining and plotting, some were anxious and eager, some slow and dull; in some countenances were written gain; in others loss. It was like being in the confidence of all these people to stand quietly there, looking into their faces as they flitted

past. In busy places, where each man has an object of
his own, and feels assured that every other man has his, his
character and purpose are written broadly in his face.
In the public walks and lounges of a town, people go to
see and to be seen, and there the same expression, with
little variety, is repeated a hundred times. The working-
day faces come nearer to the truth, and let it out more
plainly.

Falling into that kind of abstraction which such a solitude awakens, the child continued to gaze upon the passing crowd with a wondering interest, amounting almost
to a temporary forgetfulness of her own condition. But
cold, wet, hunger, want of rest, and lack of any place in
which to lay her aching head, soon brought her thoughts
back to the point whence they had strayed. No one
passed who seemed to notice them, or to whom she durst
appeal. After some time, they left their place of refuge
from the weather, and mingled with the concourse.

Evening came on. They were still wandering up and
down, with fewer people about them, but with the same
sense of solitude in their own breasts, and the same indifference from all around. The lights in the streets and
shops made them feel yet more desolate, for with their
help, night and darkness seemed to come on faster.
Shivering with the cold and damp, ill in body, and sick
to death at heart, the child needed her utmost firmness
and resolution even to creep along.

Why had they ever come to this noisy town, when
there were peaceful country places, in which, at least,
they might have hungered and thirsted, with less suffering than in its squalid strife! They were but an atom,
here, in a mountain heap of misery, the very sight of
which increased their hopelessness and suffering.

The child had not only to endure the accumulated hard-
ships of their destitute condition, but to bear the reproaches of her grandfather, who began to murmur at
having been led away from their late abode, and demand
that they should return to it. Being now penniless, and
no relief or prospect of relief appearing, they retraced
their steps through the deserted streets, and went back
to the wharf, hoping to find the boat in which they had
come, and to be allowed to sleep on board that night.
But here again they were disappointed, for the gate was

closed, and some fierce dogs, barking at their approach, obliged them to retreat.

" We must sleep in the open air to-night, dear," said the child in a weak voice, as they turned away from this last repulse; " and to-morrow we will beg our way to some quiet part of the country, and try to earn our bread in very humble work."

" Why did you bring me here?" returned the old man fiercely. "I cannot bear these close eternal streets. We came from a quiet part. Why did you force me to leave it?"

" Because I must have that dream I told you of, no more," said the child, with a momentary firmness that lost itself in tears ; " and we must live among poor people, or it will come again. Dear grandfather, you are old and weak, I know ; but look at me. I never will complain if you will not, but I have some suffering indeed."

" Ah, poor, houseless, wandering, motherless child ! " cried the old man, clasping his hands and gazing as if for the first time upon her anxious face, her travel-stained dress, and bruised and swollen feet ; " has all my agony of care brought her to this at last ! Was I a happy man once, and have I lost happiness and all I had, for this ! "

" If we were in the country now," said the child, with assumed cheerfulness, as they walked on looking about them for a shelter, " we should find some good old tree, stretching out his green arms as if he loved us, and nodding and rustling as if he would have us fall asleep, thinking of him while he watched. Please God, we shall be there soon—to-morrow or next day at the farthest—and in the meantime let us think, dear, that it was a good thing we came here ; for we are lost in the crowd and hurry of this place, and if any cruel people should pursue us, they could surely never trace us further. There's comfort in that. And here's a deep old doorway—very dark, but quite dry, and warm too, for the wind don't blow in here—What's that ! "

Uttering a half shriek, she recoiled from a black figure which came suddenly out of the dark recess in which they were about to take refuge, and stood still looking at them.

" Speak again," it said ; " do I know the voice? "

"No," replied the child timidly; "we are strangers, and having no money for a night's lodging, were going to rest here."

There was a feeble lamp at no great distance; the only one in the place, which was a kind of square yard, but sufficient to show how poor and mean it was. To this, the figure beckoned them; at the same time drawing within its rays, as if to show that it had no desire to conceal itself or take them at an advantage.

The form was that of a man, miserably clad and begrimed with smoke, which, perhaps by its contrast with the natural color of his skin, made him look paler than he really was. That he was naturally of a very wan and pallid aspect, however, his hollow cheeks, sharp features, and sunken eyes, no less than a certain look of patient endurance, sufficiently testified. His voice was harsh by nature, but not brutal; and though his face, besides possessing the characteristics already mentioned, was overshadowed by a quantity of long dark hair, its expression was neither ferocious nor cruel.

"How came you to think of resting there?" he said. "Or how," he added, looking more attentively at the child, "do you come to want a place of rest at this time of night?"

"Our misfortunes," the grandfather answered, "are the cause."

"Do you know," said the man, looking still more earnestly at Nell, "how wet she is, and that the damp streets are not a place for her?"

"I know it well, God help me," he replied. "What can I do!"

The man looked at Nell again, and gently touched her garments, from which the rain was running off in little streams. "I can give you warmth," he said, after a pause; "nothing else. Such lodging as I have is in that house," pointing to the doorway from which he had emerged, "but she is safer and better there than here. The fire is in a rough place, but you can pass the night beside it safely, if you'll trust yourselves to me. You see that red light yonder?"

They raised their eyes, and saw a lurid glare hanging in the dark sky; the dull reflection of some distant fire.

"It's not far," said the man. "Shall I take you there?

You were going to sleep upon cold bricks; I can give you a bed of warm ashes—nothing better."

Without waiting for any further reply than he saw in their looks, he took Nell in his arms, and bade the old man follow.

Carrying her as tenderly, and as easily too, as if she had been an infant, and showing himself both swift and sure of foot, he led the way through what appeared to be the poorest and most wretched quarter of the town; not turning aside to avoid the overflowing kennels or running waterspouts, but holding his course, regardless of such obstructions, and making his way straight through them. They had proceeded thus in silence for some quarter of an hour, and had lost sight of the glare to which he had pointed, in the dark and narrow ways by which they had come, when it suddenly burst upon them again, streaming up from the high chimney of a building close before them.

"This is the place," he said, pausing at a door to put Nell down and take her hand. "Don't be afraid. There's nobody here will harm you."

It needed a strong confidence in this assurance to induce them to enter, and what they saw inside did not diminish their apprehension and alarm. In a large and lofty building, supported by pillars of iron, with great black apertures in the upper walls, open to the external air; echoing to the roof with the beating of hammers and roar of furnaces, mingled with the hissing of red-hot metal plunged in water, and a hundred strange unearthly noises never heard elsewhere; in this gloomy place, moving like demons among the flame and smoke, dimly and fitfully seen, flushed and tormented by the burning fires, and wielding great weapons, a faulty blow from any one of which must have crushed some workman's skull, a number of men labored like giants. Others, reposing upon heaps of coals or ashes with their faces turned to the black vault above, slept or rested from their toil. Others again, opening the white-hot furnace-doors, cast fuel on the flames, which came rushing and roaring forth to meet it, and licked it up like oil. Others drew forth, with clashing noise upon the ground, great sheets of glowing steel, emitting an insupportable heat, and a dull deep light like that which reddens in the eyes of savage beasts.

Through these bewildering sights and deafening sounds, their conductor led them to where, in a dark portion of the building, one furnace burnt by night and day—so at least they gathered from the motion of his lips, for as yet they could only see him speak : not hear him.   The man who had been watching this fire and whose task was ended for the present, gladly withdrew; and left them with their friend, who, spreading Nell's little cloak upon a heap of ashes, and showing her where she could hang her outer clothes to dry, signed to her and the old man to lie down and sleep.   For himself, he took his station on a rugged mat before the furnace-door, and resting his

chin upon his hands, watched the flames as it shone through the iron chinks, and the white ashes as they fell into their bright hot grave below.

The warmth of her bed, hard and humble as it was, combined with the great fatigue she had undergone, soon caused the tumult of the place to fall with a gentler sound upon the child's tired ears, and was not long in lulling her to sleep.   The old man was stretched beside her, and with her hand upon his neck she lay and dreamed.

It was yet night when she awoke, nor did she know

how long, or for how short a time, she had slept. But she found herself protected, both from any cold air that might find its way into the building, and from the scorching heat, by some of the workmen's clothes; and glancing at their friend saw that he sat in exactly the same attitude, looking with a fixed earnestness of attention towards the fire, and keeping so very still that he did not even seem to breathe. She lay in the state between sleeping and waking, looking so long at his motionless figure that at length she almost feared he had died as he sat there; and, softly rising and drawing close to him, ventured to whisper in his ear.

He moved, and glancing from her to the place she had lately occupied, as if to assure himself that it was really the child so near him, looked inquiringly into her face.

"I feared you were ill," she said. "The other men are all in motion, and you are so very quiet."

"They leave me to myself," he replied. "They know my humor. They laugh at me, but don't harm me in it. See yonder there—that's *my* friend."

"The fire?" said the child.

"It has been alive as long as I have," the man made answer. "We talk and think together all night long."

The child glanced quickly at him in her surprise, but he had turned his eyes in their former direction, and was musing as before.

"It's like a book to me," he said—"the only book I ever learned to read; and many an old story it tells me. It's music, for I should know its voice among a thousand, and there are other voices in its roar. It has its pictures too. You don't know how many strange faces and different scenes I trace in the red-hot coals. It's my memory, that fire, and shows me all my life."

The child, bending down to listen to his words, could not help remarking with what brightened eyes he continued to speak and muse.

"Yes," he said, with a faint smile, "it was the same when I was quite a baby, and crawled about it, till I fell asleep. My father watched it then."

"Had you no mother?" asked the child.

"No, she was dead. Women work hard in these parts. She worked herself to death they told me, and, as they said so then, the fire has gone on saying the same thing

ever since. I suppose it was true. I have always believed it."

"Were you brought up here, then?" said the child.

"Summer and winter," he replied. "Secretly at first,
but when they found it out, they let him keep me here.
So the fire nursed me—the same fire. It has never gone
out."

"You are fond of it?" said the child.

"Of course I am. He died before it. I saw him fall
down—just there, where those ashes are burning
now—and wondered, I remember, why it didn't help
him."

"Have you been here ever since?" asked the child.

"Ever since I came to watch it; but there was a while
between, and a very cold dreary while it was. It burned
all the time though, and roared and leaped when I came
back, as it used to do in our play days. You may guess
from looking at me what kind of child I was, but for all
the difference between us I was a child, and when I saw
you in the street to-night, you put me in mind of myself
as I was after he died, and made me wish to bring you to
the old fire. I thought of those old times again when I
saw you sleeping by it. You should be sleeping now.
Lie down again, poor child, lie down again."

With that he led her to her rude couch, and covering
her with the clothes with which she had found herself
enveloped when she woke, returned to his seat, whence
he moved no more unless to feed the furnace, but remained motionless as a statue. The child continued to
watch him for a little time, but soon yielded to the drowsiness that came upon her, and, in the dark strange place
and on the heap of ashes, slept as peacefully as if the
room had been a palace chamber, and the bed, a bed of
down.

When she awoke again, broad day was shining through
the lofty openings in the walls, and, stealing in slanting
rays but midway down, seemed to make the building
darker than it had been at night. The clang and tumult
were still going on, and the remorseless fires were burning fiercely as before; for few changes of night and day
brought rest or quiet there.

Her friend parted his breakfast—a scanty mess of coffee and some coarse bread—with the child and her grand-

father, and inquired whither they were going. She told him that they sought some distant country place remote from towns or even other villages, and with a faltering tongue inquired what road they would do best to take.

"I know little of the country," he said, shaking his head, "for such as I pass all our lives before our furnace doors, and seldom go forth to breathe. But there *are* such places yonder."

"And far from here?" said Nell.

"Ay surely. How could they be near us, and be green and fresh? The road lies too, through miles and miles, all lighted up by fires like ours—a strange black road, and one that would frighten you by night."

"We are here and must go on," said the child boldly; for she saw that the old man listened with anxious ears to this account.

"Rough people—paths never made for little feet like yours—a dismal, blighted way—is there no turning back, my child?"

"There is none," cried Nell, pressing forward. "If you can direct us, do. If not, pray do not seek to turn us from our purpose. Indeed you do not know the danger that we shun, and how right and true we are in flying from it, or you would not try to stop us, I am sure you would not."

"God forbid, if it is so!" said their uncouth protector, glancing from the eager child to her grandfather, who hung his head and bent his eyes upon the ground. "I'll direct you from the door, the best I can. I wish I could do more."

He showed them, then, by which road they must leave the town, and what course they should hold when they had gained it. He lingered so long on these instructions, that the child, with a fervent blessing, tore herself away, and stayed to hear no more.

But before they had reached the corner of the lane, the man came running after them, and, pressing her hand, left something in it—two old, battered, smoke-encrusted penny pieces. Who knows but they shone as brightly in the eyes of angels as golden gifts that have been chronicled on tombs?

And thus they separated; the child to lead her sacred

charge farther from guilt and shame ; and the laborer
to attach a fresh interest to the spot where his guests
had slept, and read new histories in his furnace fire.

CHAPTER THE FORTY-FIFTH.

In all their journeying, they had never longed so ardently, they had never so pined and wearied, for the freedom of pure air and open country, as now.   No, not even
on that memorable morning, when, deserting their old
home, they abandoned themselves to the mercies of a
strange world, and left all the dumb and senseless things
they had known and loved, behind—not even then, had
they so yearned for the fresh solitudes of wood, hillside,
and field, as now ; when the noise and dirt and vapor of
the great manufacturing town, reeking with lean misery
and hungry wretchedness, hemmed them in on every side,
and seemed to shut out hope, and render escape impossible.

" Two days and nights ! " thought the child.   " He said
two days and nights we should have to spend among such
scenes as these.   Oh ! if we live to reach the country
once again, if we get clear of these dreadful places, though
it is only to lie down and die, with what a grateful heart
I shall thank God for so much mercy ! "

With thoughts like this, and with some vague design
of travelling to a great distance among streams and mountains, where only very poor and simple people lived, and
where they might maintain themselves by very humble
helping work in farms, free from such terrors as that from
which they fled,—the child, with no resource but the poor
man's gift, and no encouragement but that which flowed
from her own heart, and its sense of the truth and right
of what she did, nerved herself to this last journey and
boldly pursued her task.

" We shall be very slow to-day, dear," she said, as they
toiled painfully through the streets ; " my feet are sore,
and I have pains in all my limbs from the wet of yesterday.   I saw that he looked at us and thought of that,
when he said how long we should be upon the road."

" It was a dreary way he told us of," returned her

grandfather, piteously. "Is there no other road? Will you not let me go some other way than this?"

"Places lie beyond these," said the child, firmly, "where we may live in peace, and be tempted to do no harm. We will take the road that promises to have that end, and we would not turn out of it, if it were a hundred times worse than our fears lead us to expect. We would not, dear, would we?"

"No," replied the old man, wavering in his voice, no less than in his manner. "No. Let us go on. I am ready. I am quite ready, Nell."

The child walked with more difficulty than she had led her companion to expect, for the pains that racked her joints were of no common severity, and every exertion increased them. But they wrung from her no complaint, or look of suffering; and, though the two travellers proceeded very slowly, they did proceed; and clearing the town in course of time, began to feel that they were fairly on their way.

A long suburb of red brick houses,—some with patches of garden-ground, where coal-dust and factory smoke darkened the shrinking leaves, and coarse rank flowers; and where the struggling vegetation sickened and sank under the hot breath of kiln and furnace, making them by its presence seem yet more blighting and unwholesome than in the town itself,—a long, flat, straggling suburb passed, they came by slow degrees upon a cheerless region, where not a blade of grass was seen to grow; where not a bud put forth its promise in the spring; where nothing green could live but on the surface of the stagnant pools, which here and there lay idly sweltering by the black roadside.

Advancing more and more into the shadow of this mournful place, its dark depressing influence stole upon their spirits, and filled them with a dismal gloom. On every side, and far as the eye could see into the heavy distance, tall chimneys, crowding on each other, and presenting that endless repetition of the same dull, ugly form, which is the horror of oppressive dreams, poured out their plague of smoke, obscured the light, and made foul the melancholy air. On mounds of ashes by the wayside, sheltered only by a few rough boards, or rotten pent-house roofs, strange engines spun and writhed like tortured creatures; clanking their iron chains, shrieking

in their rapid whirl from time to time as though in tor-
ment unendurable, and making the ground tremble with
their agonies. Dismantled houses here and there appeared, tottering to the earth, propped up by fragments
of others that had fallen down, unroofed, windowless,
blackened, desolate, but yet inhabited. Men, women,
children, wan in their looks and ragged in attire, tended
the engines, fed their tributary fires, begged upon the
road, or scowled half-naked from the doorless houses.
Then came more of the wrathful monsters, whose like

they almost seemed to be in their wildness and their un-
tamed air, screeching and turning round and round again ;
and still, before, behind, and to the right and left, was
the same interminable perspective of brick towers, never
ceasing in their black vomit, blasting all things living or
inanimate, shutting black out the face of day, and closing in on all these horrors with a dense dark cloud.

But night-time in this dreadful spot !—night, when the
smoke was changed to fire ; when every chimney spirted
up its flame ; and places, that had been dark vaults all

day, now shone red-hot, with figures moving to and fro within their blazing jaws, and calling to one another with hoarse cries—night, when the noise of every strange machine was aggravated by the darkness; when the people near them looked wilder and more savage; when bands of unemployed laborers paraded in the roads, or clustered by torch-light round their leaders, who told them in stern language of their wrongs, and urged them on to frightful cries and threats; when maddened men, armed with sword and firebrand, spurning the tears and prayers of women who would restrain them, rushed forth on errands of terror and destruction, to work no ruin half so surely as their own—night, when carts came rumbling by, filled with rude coffins (for contagious disease and death had been busy with the living crops); when orphans cried, and distracted women shrieked and followed in their wake—night, when some called for bread, and some for drink to drown their cares; and some with tears, and some with staggering feet, and some with bloodshot eyes, went brooding home—night, which, unlike the night that Heaven sends on earth, brought with it no peace, nor quiet, nor signs of blessed sleep—who shall tell the terrors of the night to that young wandering child!

And yet she lay down, with nothing between her and the sky; and, with no fear for herself, for she was past it now, put up a prayer for the poor old man. So very weak and spent she felt, so very calm and unresisting, that she had no thought of any wants of her own, but prayed that God would raise up some friend for *him*. She tried to recall the way they had come, and to look in the direction where the fire by which they had slept last night was burning. She had forgotten to ask the name of the poor man, their friend, and when she had remembered him in her prayers, it seemed ungrateful not to turn one look towards the spot where he was watching.

A penny loaf was all they had had that day. It was very little, but even hunger was forgotten in the strange tranquillity that crept over her senses. She lay down very gently, and, with a quiet smile upon her face, fell into a slumber. It was not like sleep—and yet it must have been, or why those pleasant dreams of the little scholar all night long!

Morning came. Much weaker, diminished powers even of sight and hearing, and yet the child made no complaint—perhaps would have made none, even if she had not that inducement to be silent, travelling by her side. She felt a hopelessness of their ever being extricated together from that forlorn place, a dull conviction that she was very ill, perhaps dying; but no fear or anxiety.

A loathing of food, that she was not conscious of until they expended their last penny in the purchase of another loaf, prevented her partaking even of this poor repast. Her grandfather ate greedily, which she was glad to see.

Their way lay through the same scenes as yesterday, with no variety or improvement. There was the same thick air, difficult to breathe; the same blighted ground, the same hopeless prospect, the same misery and distress. Objects appeared more dim, the noise less, the path more rugged and uneven, for sometimes she stumbled, and became roused, as it were, in the effort to prevent herself from falling. Poor child! the cause was in her tottering feet.

Towards the afternoon, her grandfather complained bitterly of hunger. She approached one of the wretched hovels by the way-side, and knocked with her hand upon the door.

" What would you have here?" said a gaunt miserable man, opening it.

"Charity. A morsel of bread."

" Do you see that?" returned the man hoarsely, pointing to a kind of bundle on the ground. " That's a dead child. I and five hundred other men were thrown out of work three months ago. That is my third dead child, and last. Do you think I have charity to bestow, or a morsel of bread to spare?"

The child recoiled from the door, and it closed upon her. Impelled by strong necessity, she knocked at another: a neighboring one, which, yielding to the slight pressure of her hand, flew open.

It seemed that a couple of poor families lived in this hovel, for two women, each among children of her own, occupied different portions of the room. In the centre stood a grave gentleman in black who appeared to have just entered, and who held by the arm a boy.

" Here, woman," he said, " here's your deaf and dumb

son. You may thank me for restoring him to you. He was brought before me this morning, charged with theft; and with any other boy it would have gone hard, I assure you. But as I had compassion on his infirmities, and thought he might have learnt no better, I have managed to bring him back to you. Take more care of him for the future."

"And won't you give me back *my* son!" said the other woman, hastily rising and confronting him. "Won't you give me back *my* son, Sir, who was transported for the same offence!"

"Was *he* deaf and dumb, woman?" asked the gentleman sternly.

"Was he not, Sir?"

"You know he was not."

"He was," cried the woman. "He was deaf, dumb, and blind, to all that was good and right, from his cradle. Her boy may have learnt no better! where did mine learn better? where could he? who was there to teach him better, or where was it to be learnt?"

"Peace, woman," said the gentleman, "your boy was in possession of all his senses."

"He was," cried the mother; "and he was the more easy to be led astray because he had them. If you save this boy because he may not know right from wrong, why did you not save mine who was never taught the difference? You gentlemen have as good a right to punish her boy, that God has kept in ignorance of sound and speech, as you have to punish mine, that you kept in ignorance yourselves. How many of the girls and boys—ah, men and women too—that are brought before you and you don't pity, are deaf and dumb in their minds, and go wrong in that state, and are punished in that state, body and soul, while you gentleman are quarrelling among yourselves whether they ought to learn this or that?—Be a just man, Sir, and give me back my son."

"You are desperate," said the gentleman, taking out his snuff-box, "and I am sorry for you."

"I *am* desperate," returned the woman, "and you have made me so. Give me back my son, to work for these helpless children. Be a just man, Sir, and for God's sake as you have had mercy upon this boy, give me back my son!"

The child had seen and heard enough to know that this was not a place at which to ask for alms. She led the old man softly from the door, and they pursued their journey.

With less and less of hope or strength, as they went on, but with an undiminished resolution not to betray by any word or sign her sinking state, so long as she had energy to move, the child throughout the remainder of that hard day compelled herself to proceed: not even stopping to rest as frequently as usual, to compensate in some measure for the tardy pace at which she was obliged to walk. Evening was drawing on, but had not closed in, when—still travelling among the same dismal objects —they came to a busy town.

Faint and spiritless as they were, its streets were insupportable. After humbly asking for relief at some few doors and being repulsed, they agreed to make their way out of it as speedily as they could, and try if the inmates of any lone house beyond, would have more pity on their exhausted state.

They were dragging themselves along through the last street, and the child felt that the time was close at hand when her enfeebled powers would bear no more. There appeared before them, at this juncture, going in the same direction as themselves, a traveller on foot, who, with a portmanteau strapped to his back, leant upon a stout stick as he walked, and read from a book which he held in his other hand.

It was not an easy matter to come up with him, and beseech his aid, for he walked fast, and was a little distance in advance. At length he stopped to look more attentively at some passage in his book. Animated with a ray of hope, the child shot on before her grandfather, and, going close to the stranger without rousing him by the sound of her footsteps, began in a few faint words to implore his help.

He turned his head, the child clapped her hands together, uttered a wild shriek, and fell senseless at his feet.

CHAPTER THE FORTY-SIXTH.

IT was the poor schoolmaster. No other than the poor schoolmaster. Scarcely less moved and surprised by the sight of the child than she had been on recognizing him, he stood for a moment silent and confounded by this unexpected apparition, without even the presence of mind to raise her from the ground.

But quickly recovering his self-possession, he threw down his stick and book, and dropping on one knee beside her, endeavored, by such simple means as occurred to him, to restore her to herself; while her grandfather, standing idly by, wrung his hands, and implored her with many endearing expressions to speak to him, were it only a word.

" She is quite exhausted," said the schoolmaster, glancing upward into his face. " You have taxed her powers too far, friend."

" She is perishing of want," rejoined the old man. " I never thought how weak and ill she was, till now."

Casting a look upon him, half-reproachful and half-compassionate, the schoolmaster took the child in his arms, and, bidding the old man gather up her little basket and follow him directly, bore her away at his utmost speed.

There was a small inn within sight, to which it would seem he had been directing his steps when so unexpectedly overtaken. Towards this place he hurried with his unconscious burden, and rushing into the kitchen, and calling upon the company there assembled to make way for God's sake, deposited it on a chair before the fire.

The company, who rose in confusion upon the schoolmaster's entrance, did as people usually do under such circumstances. Everybody called for his or her favorite remedy, which nobody brought; each cried for more air, at the same time carefully excluding what air there was, by closing round the object of sympathy; and all wondered why somebody else didn't do what it never appeared to occur to them might be done by themselves.

The landlady, however, who possessed more readiness and activity than any of them, and who had withal a quicker perception of the merits of the case, soon came running in, with a little hot brandy and water, followed by her servant-girl, carrying vinegar, hartshorn, smelling-salts, and such other restoratives; which, being duly administered, recovered the child so far as to enable her to thank them in a faint voice, and to extend her hand to the poor schoolmaster, who stood with an anxious face, hard by. Without suffering her to speak another word, or so much as to stir a finger any more, the women

straightway carried her off to bed; and having covered her up warm, bathed her cold feet, and wrapped them in flannel, they despatched a messenger for the doctor.

The doctor, who was a red-nosed gentleman with a great bunch of seals dangling below a waistcoat of ribbed black satin, arrived with all speed, and taking his seat by the bedside of poor Nell, drew out his watch, and felt her pulse. Then he looked at her tongue, then he felt her pulse again, and while he did so, he eyed the half-emptied wine-glass as if in profound abstraction.

"I should give her—" said the doctor at length, "a

teaspoonful, every now and then, of hot **brandy and water.**"

"Why, that's exactly what we've done, Sir!" said the delighted landlady.

"I should also," observed the doctor, who had passed the foot-bath on the stairs, "I should also," said the doctor, in the voice of an oracle, "put her feet in hot water, and wrap them up in flannel. "I should likewise," said the doctor with increased solemnity, "give her something light for supper—the wing of a roasted fowl now—"

"Why, goodness gracious me, Sir, it's cooking at the kitchen fire this instant!" cried the landlady. And so indeed it was, for the schoolmaster had ordered it to be put down, and it was getting on so well that the doctor might have smelt it if he had tried—perhaps he did.

"You may then," said the doctor, rising gravely, "give her a glass of hot mulled port wine, if she likes wine—"

"And a toast, Sir?" suggested the landlady.

"Ay," said the doctor, in the tone of a man who makes a dignified concession. "And a toast—of bread. But be very particular to make it of bread, if you please, ma'am."

With which parting injunction, slowly and portentously delivered, the doctor departed, leaving the whole house in admiration of that wisdom which tallied so closely with their own. Everybody said he was a very shrewd doctor indeed, and knew perfectly what people's constitutions were; which there appears some reason to suppose he did.

While her supper was preparing, the child fell into a refreshing sleep, from which they were obliged to rouse her when it was ready. As she evinced extraordinary uneasiness on learning that her grandfather was below stairs, and as she was greatly troubled at the thought of their being apart, he took his supper with her. Finding her still very restless on this head, they made him up a bed in an inner room, to which he presently retired. The key of this chamber happened by good fortune to be on that side of the door which was in Nell's room; she turned it on him when the landlady had withdrawn, and crept to bed again with a thankful heart.

The schoolmaster sat for a long time smoking his pipe by the kitchen fire, which was now deserted, thinking, with a very happy face, on the fortunate chance which had brought him so opportunely to the child's assistance, and parrying, as well as in his simple way he could, the inquisitive cross-examination of the landlady, who had a great curiosity to be made acquainted with every particular of Nell's life and history. The poor schoolmaster was so open-hearted, and so little versed in the most ordinary cunning or deceit, that she could not have failed to succeed in the first five minutes, but that he happened to be unacquainted with what she wished to know; and so he told her. The landlady, by no means satisfied with this assurance, which she considered an ingenious evasion of the question, rejoined that he had his reasons of course. Heaven forbid that she should wish to pry into the affairs of her customers, which indeed were no business of hers, who had so many of her own. She had merely asked a civil question, and to be sure she knew it would meet with a civil answer. She was quite satisfied—quite. She had rather perhaps that he would have said at once that he didn't choose to be communicative, because that would have been plain and intelligible. However, she had no right to be offended of course. He was the best judge, and had a perfect right to say what he pleased ; nobody could dispute that, for a moment. Oh dear, no !

"I assure you, my good lady," said the mild schoolmaster, "that I have told you the plain truth—as I hope to be saved, I have told you the truth."

"Why then, I do believe you are in earnest," rejoined the landlady, with ready good-humor, "and I'm very sorry I have teased you. But curiosity you know is the curse of our sex, and that's the fact."

The landlord scratched his head, as if he thought the curse sometimes involved the other sex likewise ; but he was prevented from making any remark to that effect, if he had it in contemplation to do so, by the schoolmaster's rejoinder.

"You should question me for half-a-dozen hours at a sitting, and welcome, and I would answer you patiently for the kindness of heart you have shown to-night, if I could," he said. "As it is, please to take care of her in the morning, and let me know early how she is ; and to understand that I am paymaster for the three."

So, parting with them on most friendly terms, not the

less cordial perhaps for this last direction, the schoolmaster went to his bed, and the host and hostess to theirs.

The report in the morning was that the child was better, but was extremely weak, and would at least require a day's rest, and careful nursing, before she could proceed upon her journey, The schoolmaster received this communication with perfect cheerfulness, observing that he had a day to spare—two days for that matter—and could very well afford to wait. As the patient was to sit up in the evening, he appointed to visit her in her room at a certain hour, and rambling out with his book, did not return until the hour arrived.

Nell could not help weeping when they were left alone; whereat, and at sight of her pale face and wasted figure, the simple schoolmaster shed a few tears himself, at the same time showing in very energetic language how foolish it was to do so, and how very easily it could be avoided, if one tried.

"It makes me unhappy even in the midst of all this kindness," said the child, "to think that we should be a burden upon you. How can I ever thank you? If I had not met you so far from home, I must have died, and he would have been left alone."

"We'll not talk about dying," said the schoolmaster; "and as to burdens, I have made my fortune since you slept at my cottage."

"Indeed!" cried the child joyfully.

"Oh yes," returned her friend. "I have been appointed clerk and schoolmaster to a village a long way from here —and a long way from the old one as you may suppose —at five-and-thirty pounds a year. Five-and-thirty pounds!"

"I am very glad," said the child—"so very, very glad."

"I am on my way there now," resumed the schoolmaster. "They allowed me the stage-coach hire—outside stage-coach hire all the way. Bless you, they grudge me nothing. But as the time at which I am expected there, left me ample leisure, I determined to walk instead. How glad I am, to think I did so!"

"How glad should we be!"

"Yes, yes," said the schoolmaster, moving restlessly in his chair, "certainly, that's very true. But you— where are you going, where are you coming from, what

have you been doing since you left me, what had you
been doing before? Now, tell me—do tell me. I know
very little of the world, and perhaps you are better fitted
to advise me in its affairs than I am qualified to give
advice to you; but I am very sincere, and I have a reason
(you have not forgotten it) for loving you. I have felt
since that time as if my love for him who died had been
transferred to you who stood beside his bed. If this,"
he added, looking upwards, " is the beautiful creation
that springs from ashes, let its peace prosper with me,
as I deal tenderly and compassionately by this young
child ! "

The plain, frank kindness of the honest schoolmaster,
the affectionate earnestness of his speech and manner,
the truth which was stamped upon his every word and
look, gave the child a confidence in him, which the
utmost arts of treachery and dissimulation could never
have awakened in her breast. She told him all—that
they had no friend or relative—that she had fled with the
old man, to save him from a mad-house and all the
miseries he dreaded—that she was flying now, to save
him from himself—and that she sought an asylum in
some remote and primitive place, where the temptation
before which he fell would never enter, and her late
sorrows and distresses could have no place.

The schoolmaster heard her with astonishment. " This
child ! "—he thought—" Has this child heroically per-
severed under all doubts and dangers, struggled with
poverty and suffering, upheld and sustained by strong
affection and the consciousness of rectitude alone ! And
yet the world is full of such heroism. Have I yet to
learn that the hardest and best-borne trials are those
which are never chronicled in any earthly record, and
are suffered every day ! And should I be surprised to
hear the story of this child ! "

What more he thought or said, matters not. It was
concluded that Nell and her grandfather should accompany him to the village whither he was bound, and that
he should endeavor to find them some humble occupation by which they could subsist. " We shall be sure to
succeed," said the schoolmaster, heartily. " The cause is
too good a one to fail."

They arranged to proceed upon their journey next

evening, as a stage-wagon, which travelled for some distance on the same road as they must take, would stop at the inn to change horses, and the driver for a small gratuity would give Nell a place inside. A bargain was soon struck when the wagon came; and in due time it rolled away; with the child comfortably bestowed among the softer packages, her grandfather and the schoolmaster walking on beside the driver, and the landlady and all the good folks of the inn screaming out their good wishes and farewells.

What a soothing, luxurious, drowsy way of travelling, to lie inside that slowly-moving mountain, listening to the tinkling of the horses' bells, the occasional smacking of the carter's whip, the smooth rolling of the great broad wheels, the rattle of the harness, the cheery good-nights of passing travellers jogging past on little short-stepped horses—all made pleasantly indistinct by the thick awning, which seemed made for lazy listening under, till one fell asleep! The very going to sleep, still with an indistinct idea, as the head jogged to and fro upon the pillow, of moving onward with no trouble or fatigue, and hearing all these sounds like dreamy music, lulling to the senses—and the slow waking up, and finding one's self staring out through the breezy curtain half-opened in the front, far up into the cold bright sky with its countless stars, and downward at the driver's lantern dancing on like its namesake Jack of the swamps and marshes, and sideways at the dark grim trees, and forward at the long bare road rising up, up, up, until it stopped abruptly at a sharp high ridge as if there were no more road, and all beyond was sky—and the stopping at the inn to bait, and being helped out, and going into a room with fire and candles, and winking very much, and being agreeably reminded that the night was cold, and anxious for very comfort's sake to think it colder than it was!—What a delicious journey was that journey in the wagon!

Then the going on again—so fresh at first, and shortly afterwards so sleepy. The waking from a sound nap as the mail came dashing past like a highway comet, with gleaming lamps and rattling hoofs, and visions of a guard behind, standing up to keep his feet warm, and of a gentleman in a fur cap opening his eyes and looking wild and

stupefied—the stopping at the turnpike where the man
was gone to bed, and knocking at the door until he answered with a smothered shout from under the bedclothes
in the little room above, where the faint light was burning, and presently came down, night-capped and shivering, to throw the gate wide open, and wish all wagons off
the road except by day. The cold sharp interval between
night and morning—the distant streak of light widening
and spreading, and turning from gray to white, and from
white to yellow, and from yellow to burning red—the
presence of day, with all its cheerfulness and life—men
and horses at the plough—birds in the trees and hedges,
and boys in solitary fields, frightening them away with
rattles. The coming to a town—people busy in the
markets; light carts and chaises round the tavern yard;
tradesmen standing at their doors; men running horses
up and down the street for sale; pigs plunging and grunting in the dirty distance, getting off with long strings at
their legs, running into clean chemists' shops and being
dislodged with brooms by 'prentices; the night coach
changing horses—the passengers cheerless, cold, ugly, and
discontented, with three months' growth of hair in one
night—the coachman fresh as from a bandbox, and exquisitely beautiful by contrast:—so much bustle, so many
things in motion, such a variety of incidents—when was
there a journey with so many delights as that journey in
the wagon!

Sometimes walking for a mile or two while her grandfather rode inside, and sometimes even prevailing upon
the schoolmaster to take her place and lie down to rest,
Nell travelled on very happily until they came to a large
town, where the wagon stopped, and where they spent a
night. They passed a large church; and in the streets
were a number of old houses, built of a kind of earth or
plaster, crossed and re-crossed in a great many directions
with black beams, which gave them a remarkable and
very ancient look. The doors, too, were arched and low,
some with oaken portals and quaint benches, where the
former inhabitants had sat on summer evenings. The
windows were latticed in little diamond panes, that
seemed to wink and blink upon the passengers as if
they were dim of sight. They had long since got clear
of the smoke and furnaces, except in one or two solitary

instances, where a factory planted among fields withered
the space about it, like a burning mountain. When they
had passed through this town they entered again upon
the country, and began to draw near their place of destination.

It was not so near, however, but that they spent another
night upon the road; not that their doing so was quite
an act of necessity, but that the schoolmaster, when they
approached within a few miles of his village, had a fidgety
sense of his dignity as the new clerk, and was unwilling
to make his entry in dusty shoes, and travel-disordered
dress. It was a fine, clear, autumn morning, when they
came upon the scene of his promotion, and stopped to contemplate its beauties.

" See—here's the church!" cried the delighted schoolmaster, in a low voice; "and that old building close beside it, is the school-house, I'll be sworn. Five-and-thirty
pounds a year in this beautiful place!"

They admired everything—the old gray porch, the mul-
lioned windows, the venerable gravestones dotting the
green churchyard, the ancient tower, the very weathercock; the brown thatched roofs of cottage, barn, and
homestead, peeping from among the trees; the stream that
rippled by the distant watermill; the blue Welsh mountains far away. It was for such a spot the child had
wearied in the dense, dark, miserable haunts of labor.
Upon her bed of ashes, and amidst the squalid horrors
through which they had forced their way, visions of such
scenes—beautiful indeed, but not more beautiful than
this sweet reality—had been always present to her mind.
They had seemed to melt into a dim and airy distance, as
the prospect of ever beholding them again grew fainter;
but, as they receded, she had loved and panted for them
more.

" I must leave you somewhere for a few minutes," said
the schoolmaster, at length breaking the silence into which
they had fallen in their gladness. "I have a letter to
present, and inquiries to make, you know. Where shall
I take you? To the little inn yonder?"

" Let us wait here," rejoined Nell. "The gate is open.
We will sit in the church porch till you come back."

" A good place too," said the schoolmaster, leading the
way towards it, disencumbering himself of his portman-

teau, and placing it on the stone seat. "Be sure that I
come back with good news, and am not long gone."

So, the happy schoolmaster put on a bran-new pair of
gloves which he had carried in a little parcel in his
pocket all the way, and hurried off, full of ardor and excitement.

The child watched him from the porch until the intervening foliage hid him from her view, and then stepped
softly out into the old churchyard—so solemn and
quiet, that every rustle of her dress upon the fallen

leaves, which strewed the path and made her footsteps
noiseless, seemed an invasion of its silence. It was a
very aged, ghostly place; the church had been built many
hundreds of years ago, and had once had a convent or
monastery attached; for arches in ruins, remains of oriel
windows, and fragments of blackened walls, were yet
standing; while other portions of the old building, which
had crumbled away and fallen down, were mingled with
the churchyard earth and overgrown with grass, as if
they too claimed a burying-place and sought to mix their

ashes with the dust of men. Hard by these gravestones of dead years, and forming a part of the ruin which some pains had been taken to render habitable in modern times, were two small dwellings with sunken windows and oaken doors, fast hastening to decay, empty and desolate.

Upon these tenements, the attention of the child became exclusively riveted. She knew not why. The church, the ruin, the antiquated graves, had equal claims at least upon a stranger's thoughts, but from the moment when her eyes first rested on these two dwellings, she could turn to nothing else. Even when she had made the circuit of the inclosure, and, returning to the porch, sat pensively waiting for their friend, she took her station where she could still look upon them, and felt as if fascinated towards that spot.

CHAPTER THE FORTY-SEVENTH.

Kit's mother and the single gentleman—upon whose track it is expedient to follow with hurried steps, lest this history should be chargeable with inconstancy, and the offence of leaving its characters in situations of uncertainty and doubt—Kit's mother and the single gentleman, speeding onward in the post-chaise-and-four whose departure from the Notary's door we have already witnessed, soon left the town behind them, and struck fire from the flints of the broad highway.

The good woman, being not a little embarrassed by the novelty of her situation, and certain maternal apprehensions that perhaps by this time little Jacob, or the baby, or both, had fallen into the fire, or tumbled downstairs, or had been squeezed behind doors, or had scalded their windpipes in endeavoring to allay their thirst at the spouts of tea-kettles, preserved an uneasy silence; and meeting from the window the eyes of turnpike-men, omnibus-drivers, and others, felt in the new dignity of her position like a mourner at a funeral, who, not being greatly afflicted by the loss of the departed, recognizes his every-day acquaintance from the window of the mourning-coach, but is constrained to preserve a decent solemnity, and the appearance of being indifferent to all external objects.

To have been indifferent to the companionship of the single gentleman would have been tantamount to being gifted with nerves of steel. Never did chaise inclose, or horses draw, such a restless gentleman as he. He never sat in the same position for two minutes together, but was perpetually tossing his arms and legs about, pulling up the sashes and letting them violently down, or thrusting his head out of one window to draw it in again and thrust it out of another. He carried in his pocket, too, a fire-box of mysterious and unknown construction; and as sure as ever Kit's mother closed her eyes, so surely—whisk, rattle, fizz—there was the single gentleman consulting his watch by a flame of fire, and letting the sparks fall down among the straw as if there were no such thing as a possibility of himself and Kit's mother being roasted alive before the boys could stop their horses. Whenever they halted to change, there he was—out of the carriage without letting down the steps, bursting about the inn-yard like a lighted cracker, pulling out his watch by lamplight and forgetting to look at it before he put it up again, and in short committing so many extravagances that Kit's mother was quite afraid of him. Then, when the horses were to, in he came like a harlequin, and before they had gone a mile, out came the watch and the fire-box together, and Kit's mother was wide awake again, with no hope of a wink of sleep for that stage.

" Are you comfortable ? " the single gentleman would say after one of these exploits, turning sharply round.

" Quite, Sir, thank you."

" Are you sure ! An't you cold ? "

" It is a little chilly, Sir," Kit's mother would reply.

" I knew it ! " cried the single gentleman, letting down one of the front glasses. " She wants some brandy and water! Of course she does. How could I forget it? Hallo! Stop at the next inn, and call out for a glass of hot brandy and water."

It was in vain for Kit's mother to protest that she stood in need of nothing of the kind. The single gentleman was inexorable; and whenever he had exhausted all other modes and fashions of restlessness, it invariably occurred to him that Kit's mother wanted brandy and water.

In this way they travelled on until near midnight, when

they stopped to supper, for which meal the single gentleman ordered everything eatable that the house contained; and because Kit's mother didn't eat everything at once, and eat it all, he took it into his head that she must be ill.

"You're faint," said the single gentleman, who did nothing himself but walk about the room. "I see what's the matter with you, ma'am. You're faint."

"Thank you, Sir, I'm not indeed."

"I know you are. I'm sure of it. I drag this poor woman from the bosom of her family at a minute's notice, and she goes on getting fainter and fainter before my eyes. I'm a pretty fellow! How many children have you got, ma'am?"

"Two, Sir, besides Kit."

"Boys, ma'am?"

"Yes, Sir."

"Are they christened!"

"Only half baptized, as yet, Sir."

"I'm godfather to both of 'em. Remember that, if you please, ma'am. You had better have some mulled wine."

"I couldn't touch a drop indeed, Sir."

"You must," said the single gentleman. "I see you want it. I ought to have thought of it before."

Immediately flying to the bell, and calling for mulled wine as impetuously as if it had been wanted for instant use in the recovery of some person apparently drowned, the single gentleman made Kit's mother swallow a bumper of it at such a high temperature that the tears ran down her face, and then hustled her off to the chaise again, where—not impossibly from the effects of this agreeable sedative—she soon became insensible to his restlessness, and fell fast asleep. Nor were the happy effects of this prescription of a transitory nature, as, notwithstanding that the distance was greater, and the journey longer, than the single gentleman had anticipated, she did not awake until it was broad day, and they were clattering over the pavement of a town.

"This is the place!" cried her companion, letting down all the glasses. "Drive to the wax-work!"

The boy on the wheeler touched his hat, and setting spurs to his horse, to the end that they might go in brilliantly, all four broke into a smart canter, and dashed through the streets with a noise that brought the good folks wondering to their doors and windows, and drowned the sober voices of the town-clocks as they chimed out half-past eight. They drove up to a door round which a crowd of persons were collected, and there stopped.

" What's this ? " said the single gentleman thrusting out his head. " Is anything the matter here ? "

" A wedding, Sir, a wedding ! " cried several voices. " Hurrah ! "

The single gentleman, rather bewildered by finding himself the centre of this noisy throng, alighted with the assistance of one of the postilions, and handed out Kit's mother, at sight of whom the populace cried out, " Here's another wedding ! " and roared and leaped for joy.

" The world has gone mad, I think," said the single gentleman, pressing through the concourse with his supposed bride. " Stand back here, will you, and let me knock."

Anything that makes a noise is satisfactory to a crowd. A score of dirty hands were raised directly to knock for him, and seldom has a knocker of equal powers been made to produce more deafening sounds than this particular engine on the occasion in question. Having rendered these voluntary services, the throng modestly retired a little, preferring that the single gentleman should bear their consequences alone.

" Now, Sir, what do you want ? " said a man with a large white bow at his button-hole, opening the door, and confronting him with a very stoical aspect.

" Who has been married here, my friend ? " said the single gentleman.

" I have."

" You ! and to whom in the devil's name ? "

What right have you to ask ? " returned the bridegroom, eyeing him from top to toe.

" What right ! " cried the single gentleman, drawing the arm of Kit's mother more tightly through his own, for that good woman evidently had it in contemplation to run away. " A right you little dream of. Mind, good people, if this fellow has been marrying a minor—tut, tut, that can't be. Where is the child you have here, my good fellow. You call her Nell. Where is she ? "

As he propounded this question, which Kit's mother

echoed, somebody in a room near at hand uttered a great shriek, and a stout lady in a white dress came running to the door, and supported herself upon the bridegroom's arm.

"Where is she!" cried this lady. "What news have you brought me? What has become of her ? "

The single gentleman started back, and gazed upon the face of the late Mrs. Jarley (that morning wedded to the philosophic George, to the eternal wrath and despair of Mr. Slum the poet), with looks of conflicting apprehension, disappointment, and incredulity. At length he stammered out,

"I ask *you* where she is? What do you mean?"

"Oh Sir!" cried the bride, "If you have come here to do her any good, why weren't you here a week ago?"

"She is not—not dead?" said the person to whom she addressed herself, turning very pale.

"No, not so bad as that."

"I thank God!" cried the single gentleman feebly "Let me come in."

They drew back to admit him, and when he had entered, closed the door.

"You see in me, good people," he said, turning to the newly-married couple, "one to whom life itself is not dearer than the two persons whom I seek. They would not know me. My features are strange to them, but if they or either of them are here, take this good woman with you, and let them see her first, for her they both know. If you deny them from any mistaken regard or fear for them, judge of my intentions by their recognition of this person as their old humble friend."

"I always said it!" cried the bride, "I knew she was not a common child! Alas, Sir! we have no power to help you, for all that we could do has been tried in vain."

With that, they related to him, without disguise or concealment, all that they knew of Nell and her grandfather, from their first meeting with them, down to the time of their sudden disappearance; adding (which was quite true) that they had made every possible effort to trace them, but without success; having been at first in great alarm for their safety, as well as on account of the suspicions to which they themselves might one day be exposed in consequence of their abrupt departure. They

26

dwelt upon the old man's imbecility of mind, upon the uneasiness the child had always testified when he was absent, upon the company he had been supposed to keep, and upon the increased depression which had gradually crept over her and changed her both in health and spirits. Whether she had missed the old man in the night, and, knowing or conjecturing whither he had bent his steps, had gone in pursuit, or whether they had left the house together, they had no means of determining. Certain they considered it, that there was but slender prospect left of hearing of them again, and that whether their flight originated with the old man, or with the child, there was now no hope of their return.

To all this, the single gentleman listened with the air of a man quite borne down by grief and disappointment. He shed tears when he spoke of the grandfather, and appeared in deep affliction.

Not to protract this portion of our narrative, and to make short work of a long story, let it be briefly written that before the interview came to a close, the single gentleman deemed he had sufficient evidence of having been told the truth, and that he endeavored to force upon the bride and bridegroom an acknowledgment of their kindness to the unfriended child, which, however, they steadily declined accepting. In the end, the happy couple jolted away in the caravan to spend their honeymoon in a country excursion; and the single gentleman and Kit's mother stood ruefully before their carriage-door.

"Where shall we drive you, Sir?" said the post-boy.

"You may drive me," said the single gentleman, to the—" He was not going to add "inn," but he added it for the sake of Kit's mother; and to the inn they went.

Rumors had already got abroad that the little girl who used to show the wax-work, was the child of great people who had been stolen from her parents in infancy, and had only just been traced. Opinion was divided whether she was the daughter of a prince, a duke, an earl, a viscount, or a baron, but all agreed upon the main fact, and that the single gentleman was her father; and all bent forward to catch a glimpse, though it were only of the tip of his noble nose, as he rode away, desponding, in his four-horse chaise.

What would he have given to know, and what sorrow would have been saved if he had only known, that at that moment both child and grandfather were seated in the old church porch, patiently awaiting the schoolmaster's return!

CHAPTER THE FORTY-EIGHTH.

POPULAR rumor concerning the single gentleman and his errand, travelling from mouth to mouth, and waxing stronger in the marvellous as it was bandied about—for your popular rumor, unlike the rolling stone of the proverb, is one which gathers a deal of moss in its wanderings up and down,—occasioned his dismounting at the inn-door to be looked upon as an exciting and attractive spectacle, which could scarcely be enough admired; and drew together a large concourse of idlers, who having recently been, as it were, thrown out of employment by the closing of the wax-work and the completion of the nuptial ceremonies, considered his arrival as little else than a special providence, and hailed it with demonstrations of the liveliest joy.

Not at all participating in the general sensation, but wearing the depressed and wearied look of one who sought to meditate on his disappointment in silence and privacy, the single gentleman alighted, and handed out Kit's mother with a gloomy politeness which impressed the lookers-on extremely. That done, he gave her his arm and escorted her into the house, while several active waiters ran on before as a skirmishing party, to clear the way and to show the room which was ready for their reception.

"Any room will do," said the single gentleman. "Let it be near at hand, that's all."

"Close here, Sir, if you please to walk this way."

"Would the gentleman like this room?" said a voice, as a little out-of-the-way door at the foot of the well-staircase flew briskly open and a head popped out. "He's quite welcome to it. He's as welcome as flowers in May, or coals at Christmas. *Would* you like this room, Sir? Honor me by walking in. Do me the favor, pray."

"Goodness gracious me!" cried Kit's mother, falling back in extreme surprise, "only think of this!"

She had some reason to be astonished, for the person who proffered the gracious invitation was no other than Daniel Quilp. The little door out of which he had thrust his head was close to the inn larder; and there he stood, bowing with grotesque politeness; as much at his ease as if the door were that of his own house; blighting all the legs of mutton and cold roast fowls by his close companionship, and looking like the evil genius of the cellars come from under ground upon some work of mischief.

"Would you do me the honor?" said Quilp.

"I prefer being alone," replied the single gentleman.

"Oh!" said Quilp. And with that, he darted in again with one jerk and clapped the little door to, like a figure in a Dutch clock when the hour strikes.

"Why it was only last night, Sir," whispered Kit's mother, "that I left him in Little Bethel."

"Indeed!" said her fellow-passenger. "When did that person come here, waiter?"

"Come down by the night-coach this morning, Sir."

"Humph! And when is he going?"

"Can't say, Sir, really. When the chambermaid asked

him just now if he should want a bed, Sir, he first made faces at her, and then wanted to kiss her."

"Beg him to walk this way," said the single gentleman. "I should be glad to exchange a word with him, tell him. Beg him to come at once, do you hear?"

The man stared on receiving these instructions, for the single gentleman had not only displayed as much astonishment as Kit's mother at sight of the dwarf, but standing in no fear of him, had been at less pains to conceal his dislike and repugnance. He departed on his errand, however, and immediately returned, ushering in its object.

"Your servant, Sir," said the dwarf. "I encountered your messenger half-way. I thought you'd allow me to pay my compliments to you. I hope you're well. I hope you're very well."

There was a short pause, while the dwarf, with half-shut eyes and puckered face, stood waiting for an answer. Receiving none, he turned towards his more familiar acquaintance.

"Christopher's mother!" he cried. "Such a dear lady, such a worthy woman, so blest in her honest son! How is Christopher's mother? Have change of air and scene improved her? Her little family too, and Christopher? Do they thrive? Do they flourish? Are they growing into worthy citizens, eh?"

Making his voice ascend in the scale with every succeeding question, Mr. Quilp finished in a shrill squeak, and subsided into the panting look which was customary with him, and which, whether it were assumed or natural, had equally the effect of banishing all expression from his face, and rendering it, as far as it afforded any index to his mood or meaning, a perfect blank.

"Mr. Quilp," said the single gentleman.

"The dwarf put his hand to his great flapped ear, and counterfeited the closest attention.

"We two have met before—"

"Surely," cried Quilp, nodding his head. "Oh surely, Sir. Such an honor and pleasure—it's both, Christopher's mother, it's both—is not to be forgotten so soon. By no means!"

"You may remember that the day I arrived in London, and found the house to which I drove, empty and deserted,

I was directed by some of the neighbors to you, and waited upon you without stopping for rest or refreshment?"

"How precipitate that was, and yet what an earnest and vigorous measure!" said Quilp, conferring with himself, in imitation of his friend Mr. Sampson Brass.

"I found," said the single gentleman, "you, most unaccountably, in possession of everything that had so recently belonged to another man, and that other man, who up to the time of your entering upon his property had been looked upon as affluent, reduced to sudden beggary, and driven from house and home."

"We had warrant for what we did, my good Sir," rejoined Quilp, "we had our warrant. Don't say driven either. He went of his own accord—vanished in the night, Sir."

"No matter," said the single gentleman angrily. "He was gone."

"Yes, he was gone," said Quilp, with the same exasperating composure. "No doubt he was gone. The only question was, where. And it's a question still."

"Now, what am I to think," said the single gentleman, sternly regarding him, "of you, who, plainly indisposed to give me any information then—nay, obviously holding back, and sheltering yourself with all kinds of cunning, trickery, and evasion,—are dogging my footsteps now?"

"I dogging!" cried Quilp.

"Why, are you not?" returned his questioner, fretted into a state of the utmost irritation. "Were you not a few hours since, sixty miles off, and in the chapel to which this good woman goes to say her prayers?"

"She was there too, I think?" said Quilp, still perfectly unmoved. "I might say, if I was inclined to be rude, how do I know but you are dogging *my* footsteps. Yes, I was at chapel. What then? I've read in books that pilgrims were used to go to chapel before they went on journeys, to put up petitions for their safe return. Wise men! journeys are very perilous—especially outside the coach. Wheels come off, horses take fright, coachmen drive too fast, coaches overturn. I always go to chapel before I start on journeys. It's the last thing I do on such occasions, indeed."

That Quilp lied most heartily in this speech, it needed

no very great penetration to discover, although for any-thing that he suffered to appear in his face, voice, or manner, he might have been clinging to the truth with the quiet constancy of a martyr.

"In the name of all that's calculated to drive one crazy, man," said the unfortunate single gentleman, "have you not, for some reason of your own, taken upon yourself my errand? don't you know with what object I have come here, and if you do know, can you throw no light upon it?"

"You think I'm a conjurer, Sir," replied Quilp, shrug-ging up his shoulders. "If I was, I should tell my own fortune—and make it."

"Ah! we have said all we need say, I see," returned the other, throwing himself impatiently upon a sofa. "Pray leave us, if you please."

"Willingly," returned Quilp. "Most willingly. Chris-topher's mother, my good soul, farewell. A pleasant journey—*back*, Sir. Ahem!"

With these parting words, and with a grin upon his features altogether indescribable, but which seemed to be compounded of every monstrous grimace of which men or monkeys are capable, the dwarf slowly retreated and closed the door behind him.

"Oho!" he said when he had regained his own room, and sat himself down in a chair with his arms akimbo. "Oho! Are you there, my friend? In-deed!"

Chuckling as though in very great glee, and recompens-ing himself for the restraint he had lately put upon his countenance by twisting it into all imaginable varie-ties of ugliness, Mr. Quilp, rocking himself to and fro in his chair and nursing his left leg at the same time, fell into certain meditations, of which it may be necessary to relate the substance.

First, he reviewed the circumstances which had led to his repairing to that spot, which were briefly these. Drop-ping in at Mr. Sampson Brass's office on the previous even-ing, in the absence of that gentleman and his learned sister, he had lighted upon Mr. Swiveller, who chanced at the moment to be sprinkling a glass of warm gin and water on the dust of the law, and to be moistening his clay, as the phrase goes, rather copiously. But as clay in the abstract, when too much moistened, becomes of a

weak and uncertain consistency, breaking down in unex·
pected places, retaining impressions but faintly, and preserving no strength or steadiness of character, so Mr.
Swiveller's clay, having imbibed a considerable quantity
of moisture, was in a very loose and slippery state, in-
somuch that the various ideas impressed upon it were
fast losing their distinctive character and running into
each other. It is not uncommon for human clay in this
condition to value itself above all things upon its great
prudence and sagacity; and Mr. Swiveller, especially
prizing himself upon these qualities, took occasion to
remark that he had made strange discoveries in connection
with the single gentleman who lodged above, which he
had determined to keep within his own bosom, and which
neither tortures nor cajolery should ever induce him to
reveal. Of this determination Mr. Quilp expressed his
nigh approval, and setting himself in the same breath to
goad Mr. Swiveller on to further hints, soon made out
that the single gentleman had been seen in communication with Kit, and that this was the secret which was
never to be disclosed.

Possessed of this piece of information, Mr. Quilp directly supposed that the single gentleman above stairs
must be the same individual who had waited on him, and
having assured himself by further inquiries that this sur-
mise was correct, had no difficulty in arriving at the conclusion that the intent and object of his correspondence
with Kit was the recovery of his old client and the child.
Burning with curiosity to know what proceedings were
afoot, he resolved to pounce upon Kit's mother as the
person least able to resist his arts, and consequently the
most likely to be entrapped into such revelations as he
sought; so taking an abrupt leave of Mr. Swiveller, he
hurried to her house. The good woman being from home,
he made inquiries of a neighbor, as Kit himself did soon
afterwards, and being directed to the chapel betook himself there, in order to waylay her, at the conclusion of the
service.

He had not sat in the chapel more than a quarter of an
hour, and with his eyes piously fixed upon the ceiling
was chuckling inwardly over the joke of his being there
at all, when Kit himself appeared. Watchful as a lynx,
one glance showed the dwarf that he had come on busi-

ness. Absorbed in appearance, as we have seen, and feigning a profound abstraction, he noted every circumstance of his behavior, and when he withdrew with his family, shot out after him. In fine, he traced them to the Notary's house; learned the destination of the carriage from one of the postilions; and knowing that a fast night-coach started for the same place, at the very hour which was on the point of striking, from a street hard by, darted round to the coach-office without more ado, and took his seat upon the roof. After passing and repassing the carriage on the road, and being passed and repassed by it sundry times in the course of the night, according as their stoppages were longer or shorter, or their rate of travelling varied, they reached the town almost together. Quilp kept the chaise in sight, mingled with the crowd, learnt the single gentleman's errand, and its failure, and having possessed himself of all that it was material to know, hurried off, reached the inn before him, had the interview just now detailed, and shut himself up in the little room in which he hastily reviewed all these occurrences.

"You are there, are you, my friend?" he repeated, greedily biting his nails. "I am suspected and thrown aside, and Kit's the confidential agent, is he? I shall have to dispose of him, I fear. If we had come up with them this morning," he continued, after a thoughtful pause, "I was ready to prove a pretty good claim. I could have made my profit. But for these canting hypocrites, the lad and his mother, I could get this fiery gentleman as comfortable into my net as our old friend —our mutual friend, ha! ha!—and chubby, rosy Nell. At the worst, it's a golden opportunity, not to be lost. Let us find them first, and I'll find means of draining you of some of your superfluous cash, Sir, while there are prison bars, and bolts, and locks, to keep your friend or kinsman safely. I hate your virtuous people!" said the dwarf, throwing off a bumper of brandy, and smacking his lips, "ah! I hate 'em every one!"

This was not a mere empty vaunt, but a deliberate avowal of his real sentiments; for Mr. Quilp, who loved nobody, had by little and little come to hate everybody nearly or remotely connected with his ruined client:— the old man himself, because he had been able to deceive him and elude his vigilance—the child, because she was the object of Mrs. Quilp's commiseration and constant self-reproach—the single gentleman, because of his unconcealed aversion to himself—Kit and his mother, most mortally, for the reasons already shown. Above and beyond that general feeling of opposition to them, which would have been inseparable from his ravenous desire to enrich himself by these altered circumstances, Daniel Quilp hated them every one.

In this amiable mood, Mr. Quilp enlivened himself and his hatreds with more brandy, and then, changing his quarters, withdrew to an obscure alehouse, under cover of which seclusion he instituted all possible inquiries that might lead to the discovery of the old man and his grandchild. But all was in vain. Not the slightest trace or clue could be obtained. They had left the town by night; no one had seen them go; no one had met them on the road; the driver of no coach, cart, or wagon, had seen any travellers answering their description; nobody had fallen in with them, or heard of them. Convinced at last that for the present all such attempts were hopeless, he appointed two or three scouts, with promises of large rewards in case of their forwarding him any intelligence, and returned to London by the next day's coach.

It was some gratification to Mr. Quilp to find, as he took his place upon the roof, that Kit's mother was alone inside; from which circumstance he derived in the course of the journey much cheerfulness of spirit, inasmuch as her solitary condition enabled her to terrify her with many extraordinary annoyances; such as hanging over the side of the coach at the risk of his life, and staring in with his great goggle eyes, which seemed in hers the more horrible from his face being upside down; dodging her in this way from one window to another; getting nimbly down whenever they changed horses and thrusting his head in at the window with a dismal squint: which ingenious tortures had such an effect upon Mrs. Nubbles, that she was quite unable for the time to resist the belief that Mr. Quilp did in his own person represent and embody that Evil power, who was so vigorously attacked at Little Bethel, and who, by reason of her backslidings in respect of Astley's and oysters, was now frolicsome and rampart.

Kit, having been apprised by letter of his mother's

intended return, was waiting for her at the coach-office; and great was his surprise when he saw, leering over the coachman's shoulder like some familiar demon invisible to all eyes but his, the well-known face of Quilp.

"How are you, Christopher?" croaked the dwarf from the coach-top. "All right, Christopher. Mother's inside."

"Why, how did he come here, mother?" whispered Kit.

"I don't know how he came or why, my dear," rejoined Mrs. Nubbles, dismounting with her son's assistance, "but he has been a terrifying of me out of my seven senses all this blessed day."

"He has?" cried Kit.

"You wouldn't believe it, that you wouldn't," replied his mother; "but don't say a word to him, for I really don't believe he's human. Hush! Don't turn round as if I was talking of him, but he's a squinting at me now in the full blaze of the coach-lamp, quite awful!"

In spite of his mother's injunction, Kit turned sharply round to look. Mr. Quilp was serenely gazing at the stars, quite absorbed in celestial contemplation.

"Oh, he's the artfullest creetur!" cried Mrs. Nubbles. "But come away. Don't speak to him for the world."

"Yes I will, mother. What nonsense. I say, Sir—"

Mr. Quilp affected to start, and looked smilingly around.

"You let my mother alone, will you?" said Kit. "How dare you tease a poor lone woman like her, making her miserable and melancholy as if she hadn't got enough to make her so, without you. An't you ashamed of yourself, you little monster?"

"Monster!" said Quilp inwardly, with a smile. "Ugliest dwarf that could be seen anywhere for a penny—monster—ah!"

"You show her any of your impudence again," resumed Kit, shouldering the bandbox, "and I tell you what, Mr. Quilp, I won't bear with you any more. You have no right to do it; I'm sure we never interfered with you. This isn't the first time; and if ever you worry or frighten her again, you'll oblige me (though I should be very sorry to do it, on account of your size) to beat you."

Quilp said not a word in reply, but walking up so close to Kit as to bring his eyes within two or three inches of his face, looked fixedly at him, retreated a little distance without averting his gaze, approached again, again withdrew, and so on for half-a-dozen times, like a head in a phantasmagoria. Kit stood his ground as if in expectation of an immediate assault, but finding that nothing came of these gestures, snapped his fingers and walked away; his mother dragging him off as fast as she could, and, even in the midst of his news of little Jacob and the baby, looking anxiously over her shoulder to see if Quilp were following.

CHAPTER THE FORTY-NINTH.

Kit's mother might have spared herself the trouble of looking back so often, for nothing was further from Mr. Quilp's thoughts than any intention of pursuing her and her son, or renewing the quarrel with which they had parted. He went his way, whistling from time to time some fragments of a tune; and with a face quite tranquil and composed, jogged pleasantly towards home; entertaining himself as he went with visions of the fears and terrors of Mrs. Quilp, who, having received no intelligence of him for three whole days and two nights, and having had no previous notice of his absence, was doubtless by that time in a state of distraction, and constantly fainting away with anxiety and grief.

This facetious probability was so congenial to the dwarf's humor, and so exquisitely amusing to him, that he laughed as he went along until the tears ran down his cheeks; and more than once, when he found himself in a bye street, vented his delight in a shrill scream, which greatly terrifying any lonely passenger, who happened to be walking on before him expecting nothing so little, increased his mirth, and made him remarkably cheerful and lighthearted.

In this happy flow of spirits Mr. Quilp reached Tower Hill, when, gazing up at the window of his own sitting-room, he thought he descried more light than is usual in a house of mourning. Drawing nearer, and listening attentively, he could hear several voices in earnest conversation, among which he could distinguish, not only those of his wife and mother-in-law, but the tongues of men.

"Ha!" cried the jealous dwarf. "What's this! Do they entertain such visitors while I'm away!"

A smothered cough from above, was the reply. He felt in his pockets for his latch-key, but had forgotten it. There was no resource but to knock at the door.

"A light in the passage," said Quilp, peeping through the keyhole. "A very soft knock; and, by your leave, my lady, I may yet steal upon you unawares. Soho!"

A very low and gentle rap received no answer from within. But after a second application to the knocker, no louder than the first, the door was softly opened by the boy from the wharf, whom Quilp instantly gagged with one hand, and dragged into the street with the other.

"You'll throttle me, master," whispered the boy. "Let go, will you."

"Who's upstairs, you dog?" retorted Quilp in the same tone. "Tell me. And don't speak above your breath, or I'll choke you in good earnest."

The boy could only point to the window, and reply with a stifled giggle, expressive of such intense enjoyment, that Quilp clutched him by the throat again and might have carried his threat into execution, or at least have made very good progress towards that end, but for the boy's nimbly extricating himself from his grasp, and fortifying himself behind the nearest post, at which, after some fruitless attempts to catch him by the hair of his head, his master was obliged to come to a parley.

"Will you answer me?" said Quilp. "What's going on, above?"

"You won't let one speak," replied the boy. "They— ha ha ha!—they think you're—you're dead. Ha ha ha!"

"Dead!" cried Quilp, relaxing into a grim laugh himself. "No. Do they? Do they really, you dog?"

"They think you're—you're drowned," replied the boy, who in his malicious nature had a strong infusion of his master. "You was last seen on the brink of the wharf, and they think you tumbled over. Ha ha!"

The prospect of playing the spy under such delicious circumstances, and of disappointing them all by walking in alive, gave more delight to Quilp than the greatest stroke of good fortune could possibly have inspired him with. He was no less tickled than his hopeful assistant, and they both stood for some seconds, grinning and gasping, and wagging their heads at each other, on either side of the post, like an unmatchable pair of Chinese idols.

"Not a word," said Quilp, making towards the door on tiptoe. "Not a sound, not so much as a creaking board, or a stumble against a cobweb. Drowned, eh, Mrs. Quilp? Drowned!"

So saying, he blew out the candle, kicked off his shoes, and groped his way upstairs ; leaving his delighted young friend in an ecstasy of summersets on the pavement.

The bedroom-door on the staircase being unlocked, Mr. Quilp slipped in, and planted himself behind the door of communication between that chamber and the sitting-room, which standing ajar to render both more airy, and having a very convenient chink (of which he had often availed himself for purposes of espial, and had indeed enlarged with his pocket-knife), enabled him not only to hear, but to see distinctly, what was passing.

Applying his eye to this convenient place, he descried Mr. Brass seated at the table with pen, ink, and paper, and the case-bottle of rum—his own case bottle, and his own particular Jamaica—convenient to his hand; with hot water, fragrant lemons, white lump sugar, and all things fitting ; from which choice materials, Sampson, by no means insensible to their claims upon his attention, had compounded a mighty glass of punch reeking hot; which he was at that very moment stirring up with a teaspoon, and contemplating with looks in which a faint assumption of sentimental regret struggled but weakly with a bland and comfortable joy. At the same table, with both her elbows upon it, was Mrs. Jiniwin; no longer sipping other people's punch feloniously with teaspoons, but taking deep draughts from a jorum of her own ; while her daughter —not exactly with ashes on her head, or sackcloth on her back, but preserving a very decent and becoming appearance of sorrow nevertheless—was reclining in an easy-chair, and soothing her grief with a smaller allowance of the same glib liquid. There were also present a couple of water-side men, bearing between them certain machines called drags ; even these fellows were accommodated with a stiff glass a-piece ; and as they drank with a great relish, and were naturally of a red-nosed, pimple-faced, convivial look, their presence rather increased than detracted from that decided appearance of comfort, which was the great characteristic of the party.

"If I could poison that dear old lady's rum and water," murmured Quilp, "I'd die happy."

"Ah!" said Mr. Brass, breaking the silence, and raising his eyes to the ceiling with a sigh, "Who knows but he may be looking down upon us now! Who knows but he may be surveying of us from—from somewheres or another, and contemplating us with a watchful eye! Oh Lor!"

Here Mr. Brass stopped to drink half his punch, and then resumed; looking at the other half, as he spoke, with a dejected smile.

"I can almost fancy," said the lawyer shaking his head, "that I see his eye glistening down at the very bottom of my liquor. When shall we look upon his like again? Never, never! One minute we are here"—holding his tumbler before his eyes—"the next we are there"—gulping down its contents, and striking himself emphatically a little below the chest—"in the silent tomb. To think that I should be drinking his very rum! It seems like a dream."

With the view, no doubt, of testing the reality of his position, Mr. Brass pushed his tumbler as he spoke towards Mrs. Jiniwin for the purpose of being replenished; and turned towards the attendant mariners.

"The search has been quite unsuccessful then?"

"Quite, master. But I should say that if he turns up anywhere, he'll come ashore somewhere about Grinidge to-morrow, at ebb tide, eh, mate?"

The other gentleman assented, observing that he was expected at the Hospital, and that several pensioners would be ready to receive him whenever he arrived.

"Then we have nothing for it but resignation," said Mr. Brass; "nothing but resignation, and expectation. It would be a comfort to have his body; it would be a dreary comfort."

"Oh, beyond a doubt," assented Mrs. Jiniwin hastily; "if we once had that, we should be quite sure."

"With regard to the descriptive advertisement," said Sampson Brass, taking up his pen. "It is a melancholy pleasure to recall his traits. Respecting his legs now——?"

"Crooked, certainly," said Mrs. Jiniwin.

"Do you think they *were* crooked?" said Brass, in an insinuating tone. "I think I see them now coming up the street very wide apart, in nankeen pantaloons a little shrunk and without straps. Ah! what a vale of tears we live in. Do we say crooked?"

"I think they were a little so," observed Mrs. Quilp with a sob.

"Legs crooked," said Brass, writing as he spoke. "Large head, short body, legs crooked—"

"Very crooked," suggested Mrs. Jiniwin.

"We'll not say very crooked, ma'am," said Brass piously. "Let us not bear hard upon the weaknesses of the deceased. He is gone, ma'am, to where his legs will never come in question.—We will content ourselves with crooked, Mrs. Jiniwin."

"I thought you wanted the truth," said the old lady "That's all."

"Bless your eyes, how I love you," muttered Quilp. "There she goes again. Nothing but punch!"

"This is an occupation," said the lawyer laying down his pen and emptying his glass, "which seems to bring him before my eyes like the Ghost of Hamlet's father, in the very clothes that he wore on work-a-days. His coat, his waistcoat, his shoes and stockings, his trousers, his hat, his wit and humor, his pathos and his umbrella, all come before me like visions of my youth. His linen!" said Mr. Brass smiling fondly at the wall, "his linen which was always of a particular color, for such was his whim and fancy—how plain I see his linen now!"

"You had better go on, Sir," said Mrs. Jiniwin impatiently.

"True, ma'am, true," cried Mr. Brass. "Our faculties must not freeze with grief. I'll trouble you for a little more of that, ma'am. A question now arises, with relation to his nose."

"Flat," said Mrs. Jiniwin.

"Aquiline!" cried Quilp, thrusting in his head, and striking the feature with his fist. "Aquiline, you hag. Do you see it? Do you call this flat? Do you? Eh?"

"Oh capital, capital!" shouted Brass, from the mere force of habit. "Excellent! How very good he is! He's a most remarkable man—so extremely whimsical! Such an amazing power of taking people by surprise!"

Quilp paid no regard whatever to these compliments, nor to the dubious and frightened look into which the lawyer gradually subsided, nor to the shrieks of his wife and mother-in-law, nor to the latter's running from the room, nor to the former's fainting away. Keeping his eye fixed on Sampson Brass, he walked up to the table, and beginning with his glass, drank off the contents, and went regularly round until he had emptied the other two, when he seized the case-bottle, and hugging it under his arm, surveyed him with a most extraordinary leer.

"Not yet, Sampson," said Quilp. "Not just yet!"

"Oh very good indeed!" cried Brass, recovering his spirits a little. "Ha ha ha! Oh exceedingly good! There's not another man alive who could carry it off like that. A most difficult position to carry off. But he has such a flow of good-humor, such an amazing flow!"

"Good-night," said the dwarf, nodding expressively.

"Good-night, Sir, good-night," cried the lawyer, retreating backwards towards the door. "This is a joyful occasion indeed, extremely joyful. Ha ha ha! oh very rich. very rich indeed, re-markably so!"

Waiting until Mr. Brass's ejaculations died away in the distance (for he continued to pour them out, all the way downstairs), Quilp advanced towards the two men, who yet lingered in a kind of stupid amazement.

"Have you been dragging the river all day, gentlemen?" said the dwarf, holding the door open with great politeness.

"And yesterday too, master."

"Dear me, you've had a deal of trouble. Pray consider everything yours that you find upon the—upon the body. Good-night!"

The men looked at each other, but had evidently no inclination to argue the point just then, and shuffled out of the room. This speedy clearance effected, Quilp locked the doors; and, still embracing the case-bottle with shrugged-up shoulders and folded arms, stood looking at his insensible wife like a dismounted nightmare.

CHAPTER THE FIFTIETH.

MATRIMONIAL differences are usually discussed by the parties concerned in the form of dialogue, in which the lady bears at least her full half share. Those of Mr. and Mrs. Quilp, however, were an exception to the general rule; the remarks which they occasioned being limited to a long soliloquy on the part of the gentleman, with perhaps a few deprecatory observations from the lady, not extending beyond a trembling monosyllable uttered at long intervals, and in a very submissive and humble tone. On the present occasion, Mrs. Quilp did not for a long time venture even upon this gentle defence, but when she had recovered from her fainting-fit sat in a tearful silence, meekly listening to the reproaches of her lord and master.

Of these Mr. Quilp delivered himself with the utmost animation and rapidity, and with so many distortions of limb and feature, that even his wife, although tolerably well accustomed to his proficiency in these respects, was wellnigh beside herself with alarm. But the Jamaica rum, and the joy of having occasioned a heavy disappointment, by degrees cooled Mr. Quilp's wrath; which, from being at savage heat, dropped slowly to the bantering or chuckling point, at which it steadily remained.

"So you thought I was dead and gone, did you?" said Quilp. "You thought you were a widow, eh? Ha, ha, ha, you jade!"

"Indeed, Quilp," returned his wife. "I'm very sorry——"

"Who doubts it!" cried the dwarf. "You very sorry! to be sure you are. Who doubts that you're *very* sorry!"

"I don't mean sorry that you have come home again alive and well," said his wife, "but sorry that I should have been led into such a belief. I am glad to see you, Quilp; indeed I am."

In truth Mrs. Quilp did seem a great deal more glad to behold her lord than might have been expected, and did evince a degree of interest in his safety which, all things considered, was rather unaccountable. Upon Quilp, however, this circumstance made no impression, further than as it moved him to snap his fingers close to his wife's eyes, with divers grins of triumph and derision.

"How could you go away so long without saying a word to me or letting me hear of you or know anything about you?" asked the poor little woman, sobbing. "How could you be so cruel, Quilp?"

"How could I be so cruel! cruel!" cried the dwarf. "Because I was in the humor. I'm in the humor now, I shall be cruel when I like. I'm going away again."

"Not again!"

"Yes again. I'm going away now. I'm off directly. I mean to go and live wherever the fancy seizes me, at the wharf—at the counting-house—and be a jolly bachelor. You were a widow in anticipation. Damme," screamed the dwarf, "I'll be a bachelor in earnest."

"You can't be serious, Quilp," sobbed his wife.

"I tell you," said the dwarf, exulting in his project, "that I'll be a bachelor, a devil-may-care bachelor; and I'll have my bachelor's hall at the counting-house, and at such times come near it if you dare. And mind too that I don't pounce in upon you at unseasonable hours again, for I'll be a spy upon you, and come and go like a mole or a weazel. Tom Scott—where's Tom Scott?"

"Here I am, master," cried the voice of the boy, as Quilp threw up the window.

" Wait there, you dog," returned the dwarf, **" to carry** a bachelor's portmanteau. Pack it up, Mrs. Quilp. Knock up the dear old lady to help; knock her up. Hallo there! Hallo! "

With these exclamations, Mr. Quilp caught up the poker, and hurrying to the door of the good lady's sleeping-closet beat upon it therewith until she awoke in inexpressible terror, thinking that her amiable son-in-law surely intended to murder her in justification of the legs she had slandered. Impressed with this idea, she was no sooner fairly awake than she screamed violently, and would have quickly precipitated herself out of the window and through a neighboring skylight, if her daughter had not hastened in to undeceive her, and implore her assistance. Somewhat reassured by her account of the service she was required to render, Mrs. Jiniwin made her appearance in a flannel dressing-gown; and both mother and daughter, trembling with terror and cold—for the night was now far advanced—obeyed Mr. Quilp's directions in submissive silence. Prolonging his preparations as much as possible, for their greater comfort, that eccentric gentleman superintended the packing of his wardrobe, and having added to it with his own hands, a plate, knife and fork, spoon, teacup and saucer, and other small household matters of that nature, strapped up the portmanteau, took it on his shoulders, and actually marched off without another word, and with the case-bottle (which he had never once put down) still tightly clasped under his arm. Consigning his heavier burden to the care of Tom Scott when he reached the street, taking a dram from the bottle for his own encouragement, and giving the boy a rap on the head with it as a small taste for himself, Quilp very deliberately led the way to the wharf, and reached it at between three and four o'clock in the morning.

" Snug! " said Quilp, when he had groped his way to the wooden counting-house, and opened the door with a key he carried about with him. " Beautifully snug! Call me at eight, you dog."

With no more formal leave-taking or explanation, he clutched the portmanteau, shut the door upon his attendant, and climbing on the desk, and rolling himself up as round as a hedgehog, in an old boat-cloak, fell fast asleep.

Being roused in the morning at the appointed time, and roused with difficulty, after his late fatigues, Quilp instructed Tom Scott to make a fire in the yard of sundry pieces of old timber, and to prepare some coffee for breakfast; for the better furnishing of which repast he entrusted him with certain small moneys, to be expended in the purchase of hot rolls, butter, sugar, Yarmouth bloaters, and other articles of housekeeping; so that in a few minutes a savory meal was smoking on the board. With this substantial comfort, the dwarf regaled himself to his heart's content; and being highly satisfied with this free and gypsy mode of life (which he had often meditated, as offering, whenever he chose to avail himself of it, an agreeable freedom from the restraints of matrimony, and a choice means of keeping Mrs. Quilp and her mother in a state of incessant agitation and suspense), bestirred himself to improve his retreat, and render it more commodious and comfortable.

With this view, he issued forth to a place hard by, where such stores were sold; purchased a second-hand hammock, and had it slung in seamanlike fashion from the ceiling of the counting-house. He also caused to be erected, in the same mouldy cabin, an old ship's stove with a rusty funnel to carry the smoke through the roof; and these arrangements completed, surveyed them with ineffable delight.

"I've got a country-house like Robinson Crusoe—" said the dwarf, ogling the accommodations; a solitary, sequestered, desolate-island sort of spot, where I can be quite alone when I have business on hand, and be secure from all spies and listeners. Nobody near me here, but rats, and they are fine stealthy secret fellows. I shall be as merry as a grig among these gentry. I'll look out for one like Christopher, and poison him—ha, ha, ha! Business though—business—we must be mindful of business in the midst of pleasure, and the time has flown this morning, I declare."

Enjoining Tom Scott, to await his return, and not to stand upon his head, or throw a summerset, or so much as walk upon his hands meanwhile, on pain of lingering torments, the dwarf threw himself into a boat, and crossing to the other side of the river, and then speeding away on foot, reached Mr. Swiveller's usual house of entertainment in Bevis Marks, just as that gentleman sat down alone to dinner in its dusky parlor.

"Dick"—said the dwarf, thrusting his head in at the door, "my pet, my pupil, the apple of my eye, hey, hey!"

"Oh you're there, are you?" returned Mr. Swiveller; "*how* are you?"

"How's Dick?" retorted Quilp. "How's the cream of clerkship, eh?"

"Why, rather sour, Sir," replied Mr. Swiveller. "Beginning to border upon cheesiness, in fact."

"What's the matter?" said the dwarf, advancing. "Has Sally proved unkind? 'Of all the girls that are so smart, there's none like—' eh, Dick!"

"Certainly not," replied Mr. Swiveller, eating his dinner with great gravity, "none like her. She's the sphynx of private life is Sally B."

"You're out of spirits," said Quilp, drawing up a chair. "What's the matter?"

"The law don't agree with me," returned Dick. "It isn't moist enough, and there's too much confinement. I have been thinking of running away."

"Bah!" said the dwarf. "Where would you run to, Dick?"

"I don't know," returned Mr. Swiveller. "Towards Highgate, I suppose. Perhaps the bells might strike up 'Turn again Swiveller, Lord Mayor of London.' Whittington's name was Dick. I wish cats were scarcer."

Quilp looked at his companion with his eyes screwed up into a comical expression of curiosity, and patiently awaited his further explanation; upon which, however, Mr. Swiveller appeared in no hurry to enter, as he ate a very long dinner in profound silence, and finally pushed away his plate, threw himself back into his chair, folded his arms, and stared ruefully at the fire, in which some ends of cigars were smoking on their own account, and sending up a fragrant odor.

"Perhaps you'd like a bit of cake"—said Dick, at last turning to the dwarf. "You're quite welcome to it. You ought to be, for it's of your making."

"What do you mean?" said Quilp.

Mr. Swiveller replied by taking from his pocket a small and very greasy parcel, slowly unfolding it, and displaying a little slab of plum cake extremely indigestible in appearance, and bordered with a paste of white sugar an inch and a half deep.

"What should you say this was?" demanded Mr. Swiveller.

"It looks like bride-cake," replied the dwarf, grinning.

"And whose should you say it was?" inquired Mr. Swiveller, rubbing the pastry against his nose with a dreadful calmness. "Whose?"

"Not—"

"Yes," said Dick, "the same. You needn't mention her name. There's no such name now. Her name is Cheggs now, Sophy Cheggs. Yet loved I as man never loved that hadn't wooden legs, and my heart, my heart is breaking for the love of Sophy Cheggs."

With this extemporary adaptation of a popular ballad to the distressing circumstances of his own case, Mr. Swiveller folded up the parcel again, beat it very flat between the palms of his hands, thrust it into his breast, buttoned his coat over it, and folded his arms upon the whole.

"Now I hope you're satisfied, Sir," said Dick; "and I hope Fred's satisfied. You went partners in the mischief, and I hope you like it. This is the triumph I was to have, is it? It's like the old country-dance of that name, where there are two gentlemen to one lady, and one has her, and the other hasn't, but comes limping up behind to make out the figure. But it's Destiny, and mine's a crusher!"

Disguising his secret joy in Mr. Swiveller's defeat, Daniel Quilp adopted the surest means of soothing him, by ringing the bell, and ordering in a supply of rosy wine, (that is to say, of its usual representative), which he put about with great alacrity, calling upon Mr. Swiveller to pledge him in various toasts derisive of Cheggs, and eulogistic of the happiness of single men. Such was their impression on Mr. Swiveller, coupled with the reflection that no man could oppose his destiny, that in a very short space of time his spirits rose surprisingly, and he was enabled to give the dwarf an account of the receipt of the cake, which, it appeared, had been brought to Bevis Marks by the two surviving Miss Wackleses in person, and delivered at the office door with much giggling and joyfulness.

"Ha!" said Quilp. "It will be our turn to giggle soon. And that reminds me—-you spoke of young Trent—where is he?"

Mr. Swiveller explained that his respectable friend had recently accepted a responsible situation in a locomotive gaming-house, and was at that time absent on a professional tour among the adventurous spirits of Great Britain.

"That's unfortunate," said the dwarf, "for I came, in fact, to ask you about him. A thought has occurred to me, Dick; your friend over the way—"

"Which friend?"

"In the first floor."

"Yes?"

"Your friend in the first floor, Dick, may know him."

"No, he don't," said Mr. Swiveller, shaking his head.

"Don't! No, because he has never seen him," rejoined Quilp; "but if we were to bring them together, who knows, Dick, but Fred, properly introduced, would serve his turn almost as well as little Nell or her grandfather —who knows but it might make the young fellow's fortune, and, through him, yours, eh?"

"Why, the fact is, you see," said Mr. Swiveller, "that they *have been* brought together."

"Have been!" cried the dwarf, looking suspiciously at his companion. "Through whose means?"

"Through mine," said Dick, slightly confused. "Didn't I mention it to you the last time you called over yonder?"

"You know you didn't," returned the dwarf.

"I believe you're right," said Dick. "No. I didn't, I recollect. Oh yes, I brought 'em together that very day. It was Fred's suggestion."

"And what came of it?"

"Why, instead of my friend's bursting into tears when he knew who Fred was, embracing him kindly, and telling him that he was his grandfather, or his grandmother in disguise (which we fully expected), he flew into a tremendous passion; called him all manner of names; said it was in a great measure his fault that little Nell and the old gentleman had ever been brought to poverty; didn't hint at our taking anything to drink; and—and in short rather turned us out of the room than otherwise."

"That's strange," said the dwarf, musing.

"So we remarked to each other at the time," returned Dick coolly, "but quite true."

Quilp was plainly staggered by this intelligence, over which he brooded for some time in moody silence, often raising his eyes to Mr. Swiveller's face, and sharply scanning its expression. As he could read in it, however, no additional information or anything to lead him to believe he had spoken falsely ; and as Mr. Swiveller, left to his own meditations, sighed deeply, and was evidently growing maudlin on the subject of Mrs. Cheggs; the dwarf soon broke up the conference and took his departure, leaving the bereaved one to his melancholy ruminations.

"Have been brought together, eh?" said the dwarf as he walked the streets alone. "My friend has stolen a march upon me. It led him to nothing, and therefore is no great matter, save in the intention. I'm glad he has lost his mistress. Ha ha! The blockhead mustn't leave the law at present. I'm sure of him where he is, whenever I want him for my own purposes, and, besides, he's a good unconscious spy on Brass, and tells, in his cups, all that he sees and hears. You're useful to me, Dick, and cost nothing but a little treating now and then. I am not sure that it may not be worth while, before long, to take credit with the stranger, Dick, by discovering your designs upon the child ; but for the present, we'll remain the best friends in the world, with your good leave."

Pursuing these thoughts, and gasping as he went along, after his own peculiar fashion, Mr. Quilp once more crossed the Thames and shut himself up in his Bachelor's Hall, which by reason of its newly-erected chimney depositing the smoke inside the room and carrying none of it off, was not quite so agreeable as more fastidious people might have desired. Such inconveniences, however, instead of disgusting the dwarf with his new abode, rather suited his humor ; so, after dining luxuriously from the public-house, he lighted his pipe, and smoked against the chimney until nothing of him was visible through the mist but a pair of red and highly inflamed eyes, with sometimes a dim vision of his head and face, as, in a violent fit of coughing, he slightly stirred the smoke and scattered the heavy wreaths by which they were obscured. In the midst of this atmosphere, which must infallibly have

smothered any other man, Mr. Quilp passed the evening
with great cheerfulness; solacing himself all the time
with the pipe and the case-bottle; and occasionally entertaining himself with a melodious howl, intended for a
song, but bearing not the faintest resemblance to any
scrap of any piece of music, vocal or instrumental ever
invented by man. Thus he amused himself until nearly
midnight, when he turned into his hammock with the
utmost satisfaction.

The first sound that met his ears in the morning—as
he half opened his eyes, and, finding himself so unusually
near the ceiling, entertained a drowsy idea that he must
have been transformed into a fly or blue-bottle in the
course of the night,—was that of a stifled sobbing and
weeping in the room. Peeping cautiously over the side
of his hammock, he descried Mrs. Quilp, to whom, after
contemplating her for some time in silence, he communicated a violent start by suddenly yelling out,

"Halloa!"

"Oh, Quilp!" cried his poor little wife, looking up.
"How you frightened me!"

"I meant to, you jade," returned the dwarf. "What
do you want here? I'm dead, ain't I?"

"Oh, please come home, do come home," said Mrs.
Quilp, sobbing; "we'll never do so any more, Quilp, and
after all it was only a mistake that grew out of our
anxiety."

"Out of your anxiety," grinned the dwarf. "Yes, I
know that—out of your anxiety for my death. I shall
come home when I please, I tell you. I shall come home
when I please, and go when I please. I'll be a Will o' the
Wisp, now here, now there, dancing about you always,
starting up when you least expect me, and keeping you
in a constant state of restlessness and irritation. Will
you begone?"

Mrs. Quilp durst only make a gesture of entreaty.

"I tell you no," cried the dwarf. "No. If you dare
to come here again unless you're sent for, I'll keep watch-
dogs in the yard that'll growl and bite—I'll have man-
traps, cunningly altered and improved for catching women
—I'll have spring guns, that shall explode when you tread
upon the wires, and blow you into little pieces. Will you
begone?"

"Do forgive me. Do come back," said his wife, earnestly.

"No-o-o-o-o!" roared Quilp. "Not till my own good time, and then I'll return again as often as I choose, and be accountable to nobody for my goings or comings. You see the door there. Will you go?"

Mr. Quilp delivered this last command in such a very energetic voice, and moreover accompanied it with such

a sudden gesture, indicative of an intention to spring out of his hammock, and, night-capped as he was, bear his wife home again through the public streets, that she sped away like an arrow. Her worthy lord stretched his neck and eyes until she had crossed the yard, and then, not at all sorry to have had this opportunity of carrying his point, and asserting the sanctity of his castle, fell into an immoderate fit of laughter, and laid himself down to sleep again.

CHAPTER THE FIFTY-FIRST.

THE bland and open-hearted proprietor of Bachelor's Hall slept on amidst the congenial accompaniments of rain, mud, dirt, damp, fog, and rats, until late in the day; when, summoning his valet Tom Scott to assist him to rise, and to prepare breakfast, he quitted his couch, and made his toilet. This duty performed, and his repast ended, he again betook himself to Bevis Marks.

This visit was not intended for Mr. Swiveller, but for his friend and employer Mr. Sampson Brass. Both gentlemen however were from home, nor was the life and light of law, Miss Sally, at her post either. The fact of their joint desertion of the office was made known to all comers by a scrap of paper in the handwriting of Mr. Swiveller, which was attached to the bell-handle, and which, giving the reader no clue to the time of day when it was first posted, furnished him with the rather vague and unsatisfactory information that that gentleman would "return in an hour."

"There's a servant, I suppose," said the dwarf, knocking at the house-door. "She'll do."

After a sufficiently long interval, the door was opened, and a small voice immediately accosted him with, "Oh please will you leave a card or message?"

"Eh?" said the dwarf, looking down (it was something quite new to him) upon the small servant.

To this, the child, conducting her conversation as upon the occasion of her first interview with Mr. Swiveller, again replied, "Oh please will you leave a card or message?"

"I'll write a note," said the dwarf, pushing past her into the office; "and mind your master has it directly he comes home." So Mr. Quilp climbed up to the top of a tall stool to write the note, and the small servant, carefully tutored for such emergencies, looked on with her eyes wide open, ready, if he so much as abstracted a wafer, to rush into the street and give the alarm to the police.

As Mr. Quilp folded his note (which was soon written;

being a very short one) he encountered the gaze of the small servant. He looked at her long and earnestly.

"How are you?" said the dwarf, moistening a wafer with horrible grimaces.

The small servant, perhaps frightened by his looks, returned no audible reply; but it appeared from the motion of her lips that she was inwardly repeating the same form of expression concerning the note or message.

"Do they use you ill here? is your mistress a tartar?" said Quilp with a chuckle.

In reply to the last interrogation, the small servant, with a look of infinite cunning mingled with fear, screwed up her mouth very tight and round, and nodded violently.

Whether there was anything in the peculiar slyness of her action which fascinated Mr. Quilp, or anything in the expression of her features at the moment which attracted his attention for some other reason; or whether it merely occurred to him as a pleasant whim to stare the small servant out of countenance; certain it is, that he planted his elbows square and firmly on the desk, and squeezing up his cheeks with his hands, looked at her fixedly.

"Where do you come from?" he said after a long pause, stroking his chin.

"I don't know."

"What's your name?"

"Nothing."

"Nonsense!" retorted Quilp. "What does your mistress call you when she wants you?"

"A little devil," said the child.

She added in the same breath, as if fearful of any further questioning, "But please will you leave a card or message?"

These unusual answers might naturally have provoked some more inquiries, Quilp, however, without uttering another word, withdrew his eyes from the small servant, stroked his chin more thoughtfully than before, and then, bending over the note as if to direct it with scrupulous, and hair-breadth nicety, looked at her, covertly but very narrowly, from under his bushy eyebrows. The result of this secret survey was, that he shaded his face with his hands, and laughed slyly and noiselessly, until every vein in it was swollen almost to bursting. Pulling his hat over his brow to conceal his mirth and its effects, he tossed the letter to the child, and hastily withdrew.

Once in the street, moved by some secret impulse, he laughed, and held his sides, and laughed again, and tried to peer through the dusty area railings as if to catch another glimpse of the child, until he was quite tired out. At last, he travelled back to the Wilderness, which was within rifle-shot of his bachelor retreat, and ordered tea in the wooden summer-house that afternoon for three persons; an invitation to Miss Sally Brass and her brother to partake of that entertainment at that place, having been the object both of his journey and his note.

It was not precisely the kind of weather in which people usually take tea in summer-houses, far less in summer-houses in an advanced state of decay, and overlooking the slimy banks of a great river at low water. Nevertheless, it was in this choice retreat that Mr. Quilp ordered a cold collation to be prepared, and it was beneath its cracked and leafy roof that he in due course of time received Mr. Sampson and his sister Sally.

"You're fond of the beauties of nature," said Quilp with a grin. "Is this charming, Brass? Is it unusual, unsophisticated, primitive?"

"It's delightful indeed, Sir," replied the lawyer.

"Cool?" said Quilp.

"N-not particularly so, I think, Sir," rejoined Brass, with his teeth chattering in his head.

"Perhaps a little damp and ague-ish?" said Quilp.

"Just damp enough to be cheerful, Sir," rejoined Brass. "Nothing more, Sir, nothing more."

"And Sally?" said the delighted dwarf. "Does *she* like it?"

"She'll like it better," returned that strong-minded lady, "when she has tea; so let us have it, and don't bother."

"Sweet Sally?" cried Quilp, extending his arms as if about to embrace her. "Gentle, charming, overwhelming Sally."

"He's a very remarkable man indeed!" soliloquized Mr. Brass. "He's quite a Troubadour, you know; quite a Troubadour!"

These complimentary expressions were uttered in a

somehow absent and distracted manner; for the unfortunate lawyer, besides having a bad cold in his head, had got wet in coming, and would have willingly borne some pecuniary sacrifice if he could have shifted his present raw quarters to a warm room, and have dried himself at a fire. Quilp, however,—who, beyond the gratification of his demon whims, owed Sampson some acknowledgment of the part he had played in the mourning scene of which he had been a hidden witness, marked these symptoms of uneasiness with a delight past all expression,

and derived from them a secret joy which the costliest banquet could never have afforded him.

It is worthy of remark, too, as illustrating a little feature in the character of Miss Sally Brass, that, although on her own account she would have borne the discomforts of the Wilderness with a very ill grace, and would probably, indeed, have walked off before the tea appeared, she no sooner beheld the latent uneasiness and misery of her brother than she developed a grim satisfaction, and began to enjoy herself after her own manner. Though the wet came stealing through the roof and trickling down upon their heads, Miss Brass uttered no complaint, but presided over the tea equipage with imperturbable composure. While Mr. Quilp, in his uproarious hospitality, seated himself upon an empty beer-barrel, vaunted the place as the most beautiful and comfortable in the three kingdoms, and elevating his glass, drank to their next merry-meeting in that jovial spot; and Mr. Brass, with the rain plashing down into his tea-cup, made a dismal attempt to pluck up his spirits and appear at his ease; and Tom Scott, who was in waiting at the door under an old umbrella, exulted in his agonies and bade fair to split his sides with laughing; while all this was passing, Miss Sally Brass, unmindful of the wet which dripped down upon her own feminine person and fair apparel, sat placidly behind the tea-board, erect and grizzly, contemplating the unhappiness of her brother with a mind at ease, and content, in her amiable disregard of self, to sit there all night, witnessing the torments which his avaricious and grovelling nature compelled him to endure and forbade him to resent. And this, it must be observed, or the illustration would be incomplete, although in a business point of view she had the strongest sympathy with Mr. Sampson, and would have been beyond measure indignant if he had thwarted their client in any one respect.

In the height of his boisterous merriment, Mr. Quilp, having on some pretence dismissed his attendant sprite for the moment, resumed his usual manner all at once, dismounted from his cask, and laid his hand upon the lawyer's sleeve.

"A word," said the dwarf, "before we go further. Sally, hark'ee for a minute."

Miss Sally drew closer, as if accustomed to business conferences with their host which were the better for not having air.

"Business," said the dwarf, glancing from brother to sister. "Very private business. Lay your heads together when you're by yourselves."

"Certainly, Sir," returned Brass, taking out his pocket-book and pencil. "I'll take down the heads if you please, Sir. Remarkable documents," added the lawyer, raising his eyes to the ceiling, "most remarkable documents. He states his points so clearly that it's a treat to have 'em! I don't know any Act of Parliament that's equal to him in clearness."

"I shall deprive you of a treat," said Quilp. "Put up your book. We don't want any documents. So. There's a lad named Kit—"

Miss Sally nodded, implying that she knew of him.

"Kit!" said Mr. Sampson.—"Kit! Ha! I've heard the name before, but I don't exactly call to mind—I don't exactly—"

"You're as slow as a tortoise, and more thick-headed than a rhinoceros," returned his obliging client with an impatient gesture.

"He's extremely pleasant!" cried the obsequious Sampson. "His acquaintance with Natural History too is surprising. Quite a Buffoon, quite!"

There is no doubt that Mr. Brass intended some compliment or other; and it has been argued with show of reason that he would have said Buffon, but made use of a superfluous vowel. Be this as it may, Quilp gave him no time for correction, as he performed that office himself by more than tapping him on the head with the handle of his umbrella.

"Don't let's have any wrangliug," said Miss Sally, staying his hand. "I've showed you that I know him, and that's enough."

"She's always foremost!" said the dwarf, patting her on the back and looking contemptuously at Sampson. "I don't like Kit, Sally."

"Nor I," rejoined Miss Brass.

"Nor I," said Sampson.

"Why, that's right!" cried Quilp. "Half our work is done already. This Kit is one of your honest people; one of your fair characters; a prowling prying hound; a hypocrite; a double-faced, white-livered, sneaking spy; a crouching cur to those that feed and coax him, and a barking, yelping dog to all besides."

"Fearfully eloquent!" cried Brass with a sneeze. "Quite appalling!"

"Come to the point," said Miss Sally, "and don't talk so much."

"Right again!" exclaimed Quilp, with another contemptuous look at Sampson, "always foremost! I say, Sally, he is a yelping, insolent dog to all besides, and most of all, to me. In short, I owe him a grudge."

"That's enough, Sir," said Sampson.

28

" No, it's not enough, Sir," sneered Quilp; "will you hear me out? Besides that I owe him a grudge on that account, he thwarts me at this minute, and stands between me and an end which might otherwise prove a golden one to us all. Apart from that, I repeat that he crosses my humor, and I hate him. Now, you know the lad, and can guess the rest. Devise your own means of putting him out of my way, and execute them. Shall it be done?"

" It shall, Sir," said Sampson.

" Then give me your hand," retorted Quilp. "Sally, girl, yours. I rely as much or more, on you than him. Tom Scott comes back. Lantern, pipes, more grog, and a jolly night of it!"

No other word was spoken, no other look exchanged, which had the slightest reference to this, the real occasion of their meeting. The trio were well accustomed to act together, and were linked to each other by ties of mutual interest and advantage, and nothing more was needed. Resuming his boisterous manner with the same ease with which he had thrown it off, Quilp was in an instant the same uproarious, reckless little savage he had been a few seconds before. It was ten o'clock at night before the amiable Sally supported her beloved and loving brother from the Wilderness, by which time he needed the utmost support her tender frame could render; his walk being for some unknown reason anything but steady, and his legs constantly doubling up in unexpected places.

Overpowered, notwithstanding his late prolonged slumbers, by the fatigues of the last few days, the dwarf lost no time in creeping to his dainty house, and was soon dreaming in his hammock. Leaving him to visions, in which perhaps the quiet figures we quitted in the old church porch were not without their share, be it our task to rejoin them as they sat and watched.

CHAPTER THE FIFTY-SECOND.

AFTER a long time, the schoolmaster appeared at the wicket-gate of the church-yard, and hurried towards them, jingling in his hand, as he came along, a bundle of rusty keys. He was quite breathless with pleasure and haste when he reached the porch, and at first could only point towards the old building which the child had been contemplating so earnestly.

" You see those two old houses," he said at last.

" Yes surely," replied Nell. " I have been looking at them nearly all the time you have been away."

" And you would have looked at them more curiously yet, if you could have guessed what I have to tell you," said the friend. " One of those houses is mine."

Without saying any more, or giving the child time to reply, the schoolmaster took her hand, and, his honest face quite radiant with exultation, led her to the place of which he spoke.

They stopped before its low arched door. After trying several of the keys in vain, the schoolmaster found one to fit the huge lock, which turned back, creaking, and admitted them into the house.

The room into which they entered was a vaulted chamber once nobly ornamented by cunning architects, and still retaining, in its beautiful groined roof and rich stone tracery, choice remnants of its ancient splendor. Foliage carved in the stone, and emulating the mastery of Nature's hand, yet remained to tell how many times the leaves outside had come and gone, while it lived on unchanged. The broken figures supporting the burden of the chimney-piece, though mutilated, were still distinguishable for what they had been—far different from the dust without—and showed sadly by the empty hearth, like creatures who had outlived their kind, and mourned their own too slow decay.

In some old time—for even change was old in that old place—a wooden partition had been constructed in one part of the chamber to form a sleeping closet, into which the light was admitted at the same period by a rude window, or rather niche, cut in the solid wall. This screen, together with two seats in the broad chimney, had at some forgotten date been part of the church or convent; for the oak, hastily appropriated to its present purpose, had been little altered from its former shape, and presented to the eye a pile of fragments of rich carving from old monkish stalls.

An open door leading to a small room or cell, dim with the light that came through leaves of ivy, completed the

interior of this portion of the ruin. It was not quite
destitute of furniture. A few strange chairs, whose
arms and legs looked as though they had dwindled away
with age; a table, the very spectre of its race: a great
old chest that had once held records in the church, with
other quaintly-fashioned domestic necessaries, and store
of firewood for the winter, were scattered around, and
gave evident tokens of its occupation as a dwelling-place
at no very distant time.

The child looked around her, with that solemn feeling
with which we contemplate the work of ages that have
become but drops of water in the great ocean of eternity.
The old man had followed them, but they were all three
hushed for a space, and drew their breath softly, as if they
feared to break the silence even by so slight a sound.

"It is a very beautiful place!" said the child, in a low
voice.

"I almost feared you thought otherwise," returned the
schoolmaster. "You shivered when we first came in, as
if you felt it cold or gloomy."

"It was not that," said Nell, glancing round with a

slight shudder. "Indeed I cannot tell you what it was, but when I saw the outside, from the church porch, the same feeling came over me. It is its being so old and gray perhaps."

"A peaceful place to live in, don't you think so?" said her friend.

"Oh yes," rejoined the child, clasping her hands earnestly. "A quiet, happy place—a place to live and learn to die in!" She would have said more, but that the energy of her thoughts caused her voice to falter, and come in trembling whispers from her lips.

"A place to live, and learn to live, and gather health of mind and body in," said the schoolmaster; "for this old house is yours."

"Ours!" cried the child.

"Ay," returned the schoolmaster gayly, "for many a merry year to come, I hope. I shall be a close neighbor—only next door—but this house is yours."

Having now disburdened himself of his great surprise, the schoolmaster sat down, and drawing Nell to his side, told her how he had learnt that that ancient tenement had been occupied for a very long time by an old person, nearly a hundred years of age, who kept the keys of the church, opened and closed it for the services, and showed it to strangers; how she had died not many weeks ago, and nobody had yet been found to fill the office; how, learning all this in an interview with the sexton, who was confined to his bed by rheumatism, he had been bold to make mention of his fellow-traveller, which had been so favorably received by that high authority, that he had taken courage, acting on his advice, to propound the matter to the clergyman. In a word, the result of his exertions was, that Nell and her grandfather were to be carried before the last-named gentleman next day; and, his approval of their conduct and appearance reserved as a matter of form, that they were already appointed to the vacant post.

"There's a small allowance of money," said the schoolmaster. "It is not much, but still enough to live upon in this retired spot. By clubbing our funds together, we shall do bravely; no fear of that."

"Heaven bless and prosper you!" sobbed the child.

"Amen, my dear," returned her friend cheerfully;

"and all of us, as it will, and has, in leading us through sorrow and trouble to this tranquil life. But we must look at *my* house now. Come!"

They repaired to the other tenement; tried the rusty keys as before; at length found the right one; and opened the worm-eaten door. It led into a chamber, vaulted and old, like that from which they had come, but not so spacious, and having only one other little room attached. It was not difficult to divine that the other house was of right the schoolmaster's, and that he had chosen for himself the least commodious, in his care and regard for them. Like the adjoining habitation, it held such old articles of furniture as were absolutely necessary, and had its stack of fire-wood.

To make these dwellings as habitable and full of comfort as they could, was now their pleasant care. In a short time, each had its cheerful fire glowing and crackling on the hearth, and reddening the pale old wall with a hale and healthy blush. Nell, busily plying her needle, repaired the tattered window-hangings, drew together the rents that time had worn in the threadbare scraps of carpet, and made them whole and decent. The schoolmaster swept and smoothed the ground before the door, trimmed the long grass, trained the ivy and creeping plants which hung their drooping heads in melancholy neglect; and gave to the outer walls a cheery air of home. The old man, sometimes by his side and sometimes with the child, lent his aid to both, went here and there on little patient services, and was happy. Neighbors too, as they came from work, proffered their help; or sent their children with such small presents or loans as the strangers needed most. It was a busy day; and night came on, and found them wondering that there was yet so much to do, and that it should be dark so soon.

They took their supper together, in the house which may be henceforth called the child's; and when they had finished their meal drew round the fire, and almost in whispers—their hearts were too quiet and glad for loud expression—discussed their future plans. Before they separated, the schoolmaster read some prayers aloud; and then, full of gratitude and happiness, they parted for the night.

At that silent hour, when her grandfather was sleeping

peacefully in his bed, and every sound was hushed, the child lingered before the dying embers, and thought of her past fortunes as if they had been a dream and she only now awoke. The glare of the sinking flame, reflected in the oaken panels whose carved tops were dimly seen in the gloom of the dusky roof—the aged walls, where strange shadows came and went with every flickering of the fire—the solemn presence, within, of that decay which falls on senseless things the most enduring in their nature: and, without, and round about on every side, of Death—filled her with deep and thoughtful feelings, but with none of terror or alarm. A change had been gradually stealing over her, in the time of her loneliness and sorrow. With failing strength and heightening resolution, there had sprung up a purified and altered mind; there had grown in her bosom blessed thoughts and hopes, which are the portion of few but the weak and drooping. There were none to see the frail, perishable figure, as it glided from the fire and leaned pensively at the open casement; none but the stars, to look into the upturned face and read its history. The old church bell rang out the hour with a mournful sound, as if it had grown sad from so much communing with the dead and unheeded warning to the living; the fallen leaves rustled; the grass stirred upon the graves; all else was still and sleeping.

Some of those dreamless sleepers lay close within the shadow of the church—touching the wall, as if they clung to it for comfort and protection. Others had chosen to lie beneath the changing shade of trees; others by the path, that footsteps might come near them; others among the graves of little children. Some had desired to rest beneath the very ground they had trodden in their daily walks; some where the setting sun might shine upon their beds; some where its light would fall upon them when it rose. Perhaps not one of the imprisoned souls had been able quite to separate itself in living thought from its old companion. If any had, it had still felt for it a love like that which captives have been known to bear towards the cell in which they have been long confined, and even at parting hung upon its narrow bounds affectionately.

It was long before the child closed the window, and approached her bed. Again something of the same sensation as before—an involuntary chill—a momentary feeling akin to fear—but vanishing directly, and leaving no alarm behind. Again too, dreams of the little scholar; of the roof opening, and a column of bright faces, rising far away into the sky, as she had seen in some old Scriptural picture once, and looking down on her, asleep. It was a sweet and happy dream. The quiet spot, outside, seemed to remain the same, saving that there was music in the air, and a sound of angels' wings. After a time the sisters came there hand in hand, and stood among the graves. And then the dream grew dim, and faded.

With the brightness and joy of morning, came the renewal of yesterday's labors, the revival of its pleasant thoughts, the restoration of its energies, cheerfulness, and hope. They worked gayly in ordering and arranging their houses until noon, and then went to visit the clergyman.

He was a simple-hearted old gentleman, of a shrinking, subdued spirit, accustomed to retirement, and very little acquainted with the world, which he had left many years before to come and settle in that place. His wife had died in the house in which he still lived, and he had long since lost sight of any earthly cares or hopes beyond it.

He received them very kindly, and at once showed an interest in Nell; asking her name, and age, her birthplace, the circumstances which had led her there, and so forth. The schoolmaster had already told her story. They had no other friends or home to leave, he said, and had come to share his fortunes. He loved the child as though she were his own.

" Well, well," said the clergyman. " Let it be as you desire. She is very young."

" Old in adversity and trial, Sir," replied the schoolmaster.

" God help her! Let her rest, and forget them," said the old gentleman. " But an old church is a dull and gloomy place for one so young as you, my child."

" Oh no, Sir," returned Nell. " I have no such thoughts, indeed."

" I would rather see her dancing on the green at nights," said the old gentleman, laying his hand upon her head, and smiling sadly, " than have her sitting in the shadow of our mouldering arches. You must look to this, and see that her heart does not grow heavy among these solemn ruins. Your request is granted, friend."

After more kind words, they withdrew, and repaired to the child's house; where they were yet in conversation on their happy fortune, when another friend appeared.

This was a little old gentleman, who lived in the parsonage-house, and had resided there (so they learnt soon afterwards) ever since the death of the clergyman's wife, which had happened fifteen years before. He had been his college friend and always his close companion; in the first shock of his grief had come to console and comfort him; and from that time they had never parted company. The little old gentleman was the active spirit of the place; the adjuster of all differences, the promoter of all merry-makings, the dispenser of his friend's bounty, and of no small charity of his own besides; the universal mediator, comforter, and friend. None of the simple villagers had cared to ask his name, or, when they knew it, to store it in their memory. Perhaps from some vague rumor of his college honors which had been whispered abroad on his first arrival, perhaps because he was an unmarried, unencumbered gentleman, he had been called the Bachelor. The name pleased him, or suited him as well as any other, and the Bachelor he had ever since remained. And the bachelor it was, it may be added, who with his own hands had laid in the stock of fuel which the wanderers had found in their new habitation.

The bachelor, then—to call him by his usual appellation—lifted the latch, showed his little round mild face for a moment at the door, and stepped into the room like one who was no stranger to it.

"You are Mr. Marton, the new schoolmaster?" he said, greeting Nell's kind friend.

"I am, Sir."

"You come well recommended, and I am glad to see you. I should have been in the way yesterday, expecting you, but I rode across the country to carry a message from a sick mother to her daughter in service some miles off, and have but just now returned. This is our young church-keeper? You are not the *less* welcome, friend,

for her sake, or for this old man's ; nor the worse teacher
for having learnt humanity."

"She has been ill, Sir, very lately," said the schoolmaster, in answer to the look with which their visitor
regarded Nell when he had kissed her cheek.

"Yes, yes. I know she has," he rejoined. "There
have been suffering and heartache here."

"Indeed there have, Sir."

The little old gentleman glanced at the grandfather,
and back again at the child, whose hand he took tenderly
in his, and held.

"You will be happier here," he said; "we will try, at
least, to make you so. You have made great improvements here already. Are they the work of your hands?"

"Yes, Sir."

"We may make some others—not better in themselves,
but with better means perhaps," said the bachelor. "Let
us see now, let us see."

Nell accompanied him into the other little rooms, and
over both the houses, in which he found various small
comforts wanting, which he engaged to supply from a certain collection of odds and ends he had at home, and
which must have been a very miscellaneous and extensive one, as it comprehended the most opposite articles
imaginable. They all came, however, and came without
loss of time ; for the little old gentleman, disappearing
for some five or ten minutes, presently returned, laden
with old shelves, rugs, blankets, and other household gear,
and followed by a boy bearing a similar load. These being
cast on the floor in a promiscuous heap, yielded a quantity
of occupation in arranging, erecting, and putting away ;
the superintendence of which task evidently afforded the
old gentleman extreme delight, and engaged him for some
time with great briskness and activity. When nothing
more was left to be done, he charged the boy to run off
and bring his schoolmates to be marshalled before their
new master, and solemnly reviewed.

"As good a set of fellows, Marton, as you'd wish to
see," he said, turning to the schoolmaster when the boy
was gone; "but I don't let 'em know I think so. That
wouldn't do, at all."

The messenger soon returned at the head of a long row
of urchins, great and small, who, being confronted by the

bachelor at the house door, fell into various convulsions of politeness ; clutching their hats and caps, squeezing them into the smallest possible dimensions, and making all manner of bows and scrapes, which the little old gentleman contemplated with excessive satisfaction, and expressed his approval of by a great many nods and smiles. Indeed, his approbation of the boys was by no means so scrupulously disguised as he had led the schoolmaster to suppose, inasmuch as it broke out in sundry loud whispers and confidential remarks which were perfectly audible to them every one.

" This first boy, schoolmaster," said the bachelor, " is John Owen ; a lad of good parts, Sir, and frank, honest temper ; but too thoughtless, too playful, too light-headed by far. That boy, my good Sir, would break his neck with pleasure, and deprive his parents of their chief comfort—and between ourselves, when you come to see him at hare and hounds, taking the fence and ditch by the finger-post, and sliding down the face of the little quarry, you'll never forget it. It's beautiful ! "

John Owen having been thus rebuked, and being in perfect possession of the speech aside, the bachelor singled out another boy.

" Now, look at that lad, Sir," said the bachelor. " You see that fellow ? Richard Evans his name is, Sir. An amazing boy to learn, blessed with a good memory, and a ready understanding, and moreover with a good voice and ear for psalm-singing, in which he is the best among us. Yet, Sir, that boy will come to a bad end ; he'll never die in his bed ; he's always falling asleep in church in sermon-time—and to tell you the truth, Mr Marton, I always did the same at his age, and feel quite certain that it was natural to my constitution and I couldn't help it."

This hopeful pupil edified by the above terrible reproval, the bachelor turned to another.

" But if we talk of examples to be shunned," said he, " if we come to boys that should be a warning and a beacon to all their fellows, here's the one, and I hope you won't spare him. This is the lad, Sir ; this one with the blue eyes and light hair. This is a swimmer, Sir, this fellow —a diver, Lord save us ! This is a boy, Sir, who had a fancy for plunging into eighteen feet of water, with his clothes on, and bringing up a blind man's dog, who was being drowned by the weight of his chain and collar, while his master stood wringing his hands upon the bank, bewailing the loss of his guide and friend. I sent the boy two guineas anonymously, Sir," added the bachelor, in his peculiar whisper, "directly I heard of it; but never mention it on any account, for he hasn't the least idea that it came from me."

Having disposed of this culprit, the bachelor turned to another, and from him to another, and so on through the whole array, laying, for their wholesome restriction within due bounds, the same cutting emphasis on such of their propensities as were dearest to his heart and were unquestionably referable to his own precept and example. Thoroughly persuaded, in the end, that he had made them miserable by his severity, he dismissed them with a small present, and an admonition, to walk quietly home, without any leapings, scufflings, or turnings out of the way; which injunction (he informed the schoolmaster in the same audible confidence) he did not think he could have obeyed when he was a boy, had his life depended on it.

Hailing these little tokens of the bachelor's disposition as so many assurances of his own welcome course from that time, the schoolmaster parted from him with a light heart and joyous spirits, and deemed himself one of the happiest men on earth. The windows of the two old houses were ruddy again that night with the reflection of the cheerful fires that burnt within; and the bachelor and his friend, pausing to look upon them as they returned from their evening walk, spoke softly together of the beautiful child, and looked round upon the churchyard with a sigh.

CHAPTER THE FIFTY-THIRD.

NELL was stirring early in the morning; and having discharged her household tasks, and put everything in order for the good schoolmaster (though sorely against his will, for he would have spared her the pains), took down, from its nail by the fireside, a little bundle of keys with which the bachelor had formally invested her on the previous day, and went out alone to visit the old church.

The sky was serene and bright, the air clear, perfumed with the fresh scent of newly-fallen leaves, and grateful to every sense. The neighboring stream sparkled, and rolled onward with a tuneful sound; the dew glistened on the green mounds, like tears shed by Good Spirits over the dead.

Some young children sported among the tombs, and hid from each other, with laughing faces. They had an infant with them, and had laid it down asleep upon a child's grave, in a little bed of leaves. It was a new grave —the resting-place, perhaps, of some little creature, who, meek and patient in its illness, had often sat and watched them; and now seemed to their minds scarcely changed.

She drew near and asked one of them whose grave it was. The child answered that that was not its name; it was a garden—his brother's. It was greener, he said, than all the other gardens, and the birds loved it better because he had been used to feed them. When he had done speaking, he looked at her with a smile, and kneeling down and nestling for a moment with his cheek against the turf, bounded merrily away.

She passed the church, gazing upward at its old tower, went through the wicket-gate, and so into the village. The old sexton, leaning on a crutch, was taking the air at his cottage door, and gave her good morrow.

"You are better?" said the child, stopping to speak with him.

"Ay surely," returned the old man. "I'm thankful to say, much better."

"You will be quite well soon."

"With Heaven's leave, and a little patience. But come in, come in."

The old man limped on before, and warning her of the downward step, which he achieved himself with no small difficulty, led the way into his little cottage.

"It is but one room you see. There is another up above, but the stair has got harder to climb o' late years, and I never use it. I'm thinking of taking to it again next summer though."

The child wondered how a gray-headed man like him —one of his trade too—could talk of time so easily. He saw her eyes wandering to the tools that hung upon the wall, and smiled.

"I warrant now," he said, "that you think all those are used in making graves."

"Indeed, I wondered that you wanted so many."

"And well you might. I am a gardener. I dig the ground, and plant things that are to live and grow. My works don't all moulder away and rot in the earth. You see that spade in the centre?"

"The very old one—so notched and worn? Yes."

"That's the sexton's spade, and it's a well-used one, as you see. We're healthy people here, but it has done a power of work. If it could speak now, that spade, it would tell you tell of many an unexpected job that it and I have done together; but I forget 'em, for my memory's a poor one. That's nothing new," he added hastily. "It always was."

"There are flowers and shrubs to speak to your other work," said the child.

"Oh yes. And tall trees. But they are not so separated from the sexton's labors as you think."

"No!"

"Not in my mind, and recollection—such as it is," said the old man. "Indeed they often help it. For say that I planted such a tree for such a man. There it stands to remind me that he died. When I look at its broad shadow, and remember what it was in his time, it helps me to the age of my other work, and I can tell you pretty nearly when I made his grave."

"But it may remind you of one who is still alive," said the child.

"Of twenty that are dead, in connection with that one who lives, then," rejoined the old man; "wife, husband, parents, brothers, sisters, children, friends—a score at least. So it happens that the sexton's spade gets worn and battered. I shall need a new one—next summer."

The child looked quickly towards him, thinking that he jested with his age and infirmity: but the unconscious sexton was quite in earnest.

"Ah!" he said, after a brief silence. "People never learn. They never learn. It's only we who turn up the ground, where nothing grows and everything decays, who think of such things as these—who think of them properly, I mean. You have been into the church?"

"I am going there now," the child replied.

"There's an old well there," said the sexton, "right underneath the belfry; a deep, dark, echoing well. Forty year ago, you had only to let down the bucket till the first knot in the rope was free of the windlass, and you heard it splashing in the cold dull water. By little and little the water fell away, so that in ten year after that, a second knot was made, and you must unwind so much rope, or the bucket swung tight and empty at the end. In ten years' time, the water fell again, and a third knot was made. In ten years more the well dried up; and now, if you lower the bucket till your arms are tired and let out nearly all the cord, you'll hear it of a sudden clanking and rattling on the ground below, with a sound of being so deep and so far down, that your heart leaps into your mouth, and you start away as if you were falling in."

"A dreadful place to come on in the dark!" exclaimed the child, who had followed the old man's looks and words until she seemed to stand upon its brink.

"What is it but a grave!" said the sexton. "What else! And which of our old folks, knowing all this, thought, as the spring subsided, of their own failing strength, and lessening life? Not one!"

"Are you very old yourself?" asked the child, involuntarily.

"I shall be seventy-nine—next summer."

"You still work when you are well?"

"Work! To be sure. You shall see my gardens hereabout. Look at the window there. I made, and have kept, that plot of ground entirely with my own hands. By this time next year I shall hardly see the sky, the boughs will have grown so thick. I have my winter work at night besides."

He opened, as he spoke, a cupboard close to where he sat, and produced some miniature boxes, carved in a homely manner and made of old wood.

"Some gentlefolks who are fond of ancient days, and what belongs to them," he said, "like to buy these keepsakes from our church and ruins. Sometimes, I make them of scraps of oak, that turn up here and there; sometimes of bits of coffins which the vaults have long preserved. See here—this is a little chest of the last kind, clasped at the edges with fragments of brass plates that had writing on 'em once, though it would be hard to read it now. I haven't many by me at this time of year, but these shelves will be full—next summer."

The child admired and praised his work, and shortly afterwards departed; thinking as she went, how strange it was, that this old man, drawing from his pursuits, and everything around him, one stern moral, never contemplated its application to himself; and, while he dwelt upon the uncertainty of human life, seemed both in word and deed to deem himself immortal. But her musings did not stop here, for she was wise enough to think that by a good and merciful adjustment this must be human nature, and that the old sexton, with his plans for next summer, was but a type of all mankind.

Full of these meditations, she reached the church. It was easy to find the key belonging to the outer door, for each was labelled on a scrap of yellow parchment. Its very turning in the lock awoke a hollow sound, and when she entered with a faltering step, the echoes that it raised in closing made her start.

Everything in our lives, whether of good or evil, affects us most by contrast. If the peace of the simple village had moved the child more strongly, because of the dark and troubled ways that lay beyond and through which she had journeyed with such failing feet, what was the deep impression of finding herself alone in that solemn building; where the very light, coming through sunken windows, seemed old and gray, and the air, redolent of earth and mould, seemed laden with decay, purified by time of all its grosser particles, and sighing through arch and aisle, and clustered pillars, like the breath of ages gone! Here was the broken pavement, worn so long ago by pious feet, that Time, stealing on the pilgrim's steps, had trodden out their track, and left but crumbling stones. Here were the rotten beam, the sinking arch, the sapped and mouldering wall, the lowly trench of earth, the stately tomb on which no epitaph remained,—all,—marble, stone, iron, wood, and dust, one common monument of ruin. The best work and the worst, the plainest and the richest, the stateliest and the least imposing—both of Heaven's work and Man's—all found one common level here, and told one common tale.

Some part of the edifice had been a baronial chapel,

and here were effigies of warriors stretched upon **their**
beds of stone with folded hands, cross-legged—those who
had fought in the Holy Wars—girded with their swords,
and cased in armor as they had lived. Some of these
knights had their own weapons, helmets, coats of **mail,**
hanging upon the walls hard by, and dangling from rusty
hooks. Broken and dilapidated as they were, they **yet**
retained their ancient form, and something of their an-

cient aspect. Thus violent deeds live after men upon the
earth, and traces of war and bloodshed will survive in
mournful shapes, long after those who worked the desolation are but atoms of earth themselves.

The child sat down in this old, silent place, among the
stark figures on the tombs—they made it more quiet
there, than elsewhere, to her fancy—and gazing round
with a feeling of awe, tempered with a calm delight, felt
that now she was happy, and at rest. She took a Bible
from the shelf, and read; then, laying it down, **thought**

29

of the summer days and the bright spring-time that would come—of the rays of sun that would fall in aslant upon the sleeping forms—of the leaves that would flutter at the window, and play in glistening shadows on the pavement—of the songs of birds, and growth of buds and blossoms out of doors—of the sweet air, that would steal in and gently wave the tattered banners overhead. What if the spot awakened thoughts of death! Die who would, it would still remain the same; these sights and sounds would still go on as happily as ever. It would be no pain to sleep amidst them.

She left the chapel—very slowly and often turning back to gaze again—and coming to a low door, which plainly led into the tower, opened it, and climbed the winding stair in darkness; save where she looked down through narrow loopholes on the place she had left, or caught a glimmering vision of the dusty bells. At length she gained the end of the ascent and stood upon the turret top.

Oh! the glory of the sudden burst of light; the freshness of the fields and woods, stretching away on every side and meeting the bright blue sky; the cattle grazing in the pasturage; the smoke, that, coming from among the trees, seemed to rise upward from the green earth; the children yet at their gambols down below—all, everything, so beautiful and happy! It was like passing from death to life; it was drawing nearer Heaven.

The children were gone by the time she emerged into the porch, and locked the door. As she passed the schoolhouse she could hear the busy hum of voices. Her friend had begun his labors only that day. The noise grew louder, and, looking back, she saw the boys come trooping out and disperse themselves with merry shouts and play. "It's a good thing," thought the child, "I am very glad they pass the church." And then she stopped, to fancy how the noise would sound inside, and how gently it would seem to die away upon the ear.

Again that day, yes, twice again, she stole back to the old chapel, and in her former seat read from the same book, or indulged the same quiet train of thought. Even when it had grown dusk, and the shadows of coming night made it more solemn still, the child remained like one rooted to the spot, and had no fear, or thought of stirring

They found her there at last, and took her home. She looked pale but very happy, until they separated for the night; and then, as the poor schoolmaster stooped down to kiss her cheek, he thought he felt a tear upon his face.

CHAPTER THE FIFTY-FOURTH.

THE bachelor, among his various occupations, found in the old church a constant source of interest and amusement. Taking that pride in it which men conceived for the wonders of their own little world, he had made its history his study; and many a summer day within its walls, and many a winter's night beside the parsonage fire, had found the bachelor still poring over and adding to his goodly store of tale and legend.

As he was not one of those rough spirits who would strip fair Truth of every little shadowy vestment in which time and teeming fancies love to array her—and some of which become her pleasantly enough, serving, like the waters of her well, to add new graces to the charms they half conceal and half suggest, and to awaken interest and pursuit rather than languor and indifference—as, unlike this stern and obdurate class, he loved to see the goddess crowned with those garlands of wild flowers which tradition wreathes for her gentle wearing, and which are often freshest in their homeliest shapes,—he trod with a light step and bore with a light hand upon the dust of centuries, unwilling to demolish any of the airy shrines that had been ra'sed above it, if one good feeling or affection of the human heart were hiding thereabouts. Thus, in the case of an ancient coffin of rough stone, supposed for many generations to contain the bones of a certain baron, who, after ravaging, with cut, and thrust, and plunder, in foreign lands, came back with a penitent and sorrowing heart to die at home, but which had been lately shown by learned antiquaries to be no such thing as the baron in question (so they contended) had died hard in battle, gnashing his teeth and cursing with his latest breath,—the bachelor stoutly maintained that the old tale was the true one; that the baron, repenting him of the evil, had done great charities and meekly given up the ghost; and that, if ever baron went to heaven, that baron was then at peace. In like manner, when the aforesaid antiquaries did argue and contend that a certain secret vault was not the tomb of a gray-haired lady who had been hanged and drawn and quartered by glorious Queen Bess for succoring a wretched priest who fainted of thirst and hunger at her door, the bachelor did solemnly maintain against all comers that the church was hallowed by the said poor lady's ashes; that her remains had been collected in the night from four of the city's gates, and thither in secret brought, and there deposited; and the bachelor did further (being highly excited at such times) deny the glory of Queen Bess, and assert the immeasurably greater glory of the meanest woman in her realm who had a merciful and tender heart. As to the assertion that the flat stone near the door was not the grave of the miser who had disowned his only child and left a sum of money to the church to buy a peal of bells, the bachelor did readily admit the same, and that the place had given birth to no such man. In a word, he would have had every stone, and plate of brass, the monument only of deeds whose memory should survive. All others he was willing to forget. They might be buried in consecrated ground, but he would have had them buried deep, and never brought to light again.

It was from the lips of such a tutor, that the child learnt her easy task. Already impressed, beyond all telling, by the silent building and the peaceful beauty of the spot in which it stood—majestic age surrounded by perpetual youth—it seemed to her, when she heard these things, sacred to all goodness and virtue. It was another world, where sin and sorrow never came; a tranquil place of rest, where nothing evil entered.

When the bachelor had given her in connection with almost every tomb and flat grave-stone some history of its own, he took her down into the old crypt, now a mere dull vault, and showed her how it had been lighted up in the time of the monks, and how, amid lamps depending from the roof, and swinging censers exhaling scented odors, and habits glittering with gold and silver, and pictures, and precious stuffs, and jewels all flashing and glistening through the low arches, the chant of aged voices had been many a time heard there at midnight in old days, while hooded figures knelt and prayed around, and told their rosaries of beads. Thence, he took her above ground again, and showed her, high up in the old walls, small galleries, where the nuns had been wont to glide along—dimly seen in their dark dresses so far off—or to pause like gloomy shadows, listening to the prayers. He showed her too, how the warriors, whose figures rested on the tombs, had worn those rotting scraps of armor up above—how this had been a helmet, and that a shield, and that a gauntlet—and how they had wielded the great two-handed swords, and beaten men down with yonder iron mace. All that he told the child she treasured in her mind; and sometimes, when she woke at night from dreams of those old times, and rising from her bed looked out at the dark church, she almost hoped to see the windows lighted up, and hear the organ's swell, and sound of voices, on the rushing wind.

The old sexton soon got better, and was about again. From him the children learnt many other things, though of a different kind. He was not able to work, but one day there was a grave to be made, and he came to overlook the man who dug it. He was in a talkative mood; and the child, at first standing by his side, and afterwards sitting on the grass at his feet, with her thoughtful face raised towards his, began to converse with him.

Now the man who did the sexton's duty was a little older than he, though much more active. But he was deaf; and when the sexton (who peradventure, on a pinch, might have walked a mile with great difficulty in half-a-dozen hours) exchanged a remark with him about his work, the child could not help noticing that he did so with an impatient kind of pity for his infirmity, as if he were himself the strongest and the heartiest man alive.

"I'm sorry to see there is this to do," said the child, when she approached. "I heard of no one having died."

"She lived in another hamlet, my dear," returned the sexton. "Three mile away."

"Was she young?"

"Ye—yes," said the sexton; "not more than sixty-four, I think. David, was she more than sixty-four?"

David who was digging hard, heard nothing of the question. The sexton, as he could not reach to touch him with his crutch, and was too infirm to rise without assistance, called his attention by throwing a little mould upon his red night-cap.

"What's the matter now?" said David, looking up.

"How old was Becky Morgan?" asked the sexton.

"Becky Morgan?" repeated David.

"Yes," replied the sexton; adding in a half compassionate, half irritable tone, which the old man couldn't hear, "you're getting very deaf, Davy, very deaf to be sure!"

The old man stopped in his work, and cleansing his spade with a piece of slate he had by him for the purpose —and scraping off, in the process, the essence of Heaven knows how many Becky Morgans—set himself to consider the subject.

"Let me think," quoth he. "I saw last night what they had put upon the coffin—was it seventy-nine?"

"No, no," said the sexton.

"Ah yes, it was though," returned the old man with a sigh. "For I remember thinking she was very near our age. Yes, it was seventy-nine."

"Are you sure you didn't mistake a figure, Davy?" asked the sexton, with signs of some emotion.

"What?" said the old man. "Say that again."

"He's very deaf. He's very deaf indeed," cried the sexton petulantly; "are you sure you're right about the figures?"

"Oh quite," replied the old man. "Why not?"

"He's exceedingly deaf," muttered the sexton to himself. "I think he's getting foolish."

The child rather wondered what had led him to this belief, as to say the truth the old man seemed quite as sharp as he, and was infinitely more robust. As the sexton said nothing more just then, however, she forgot it for the time, and spoke again.

"You were telling me," she said, "about your gardening. Do you ever plant things here?"

"In the churchyard?" returned the sexton, "Not I."

"I have seen some flowers and little shrubs about," the child rejoined; "there are some over there, you see. I thought they were of your rearing, though indeed they grow but poorly."

"They grow as Heaven wills," said the old man; "and it kindly ordains that they shall never flourish here."

"I do not understand you."

"Why, this it is," said the sexton. "They mark the graves of those who had very tender, loving friends."

"I was sure they did!" the child exclaimed. "I am very glad to know they do!"

"Ay," returned the old man, "but stay. Look at them. See how they hang their heads, and droop, and wither. Do you guess the reason?"

"No," the child replied.

"Because the memory of those who lie below, passes away so soon. At first they tend them, morning, noon, and night; they soon begin to come less frequently; from once a day, to once a week; from once a week to once a month; then, at long and uncertain intervals; then, not at all. Such tokens seldom flourish long. I have known the briefest summer flowers to outlive them."

"I grieve to hear it," said the child.

"Ah! so say the gentlefolks who come down here to look about them," returned the old man, shaking his head, "but I say otherwise. 'It's a pretty custom you have in this part of the country,' they say to me sometimes, 'to plant the graves, but it's melancholy to see these things all withering or dead.' I crave their pardon and tell them that, as I take it, 'tis a good sign for the happiness of the living. And so it is. It's nature."

"Perhaps the mourners learn to look to the blue sky by day, and to the stars by night, and to think that the dead are there, and not in graves," said the child in an earnest voice.

"Perhaps so," replied the old man doubtfully. "It may be."

"Whether it be as I believe it is, or no," thought the child within herself, "I'll make this place my garden. It will be no harm at least to work here day by day, and pleasant thoughts will come of it, I am sure."

Her glowing cheek and moistened eye passed unnoticed by the sexton, who turned towards old David, and called him by his name. It was plain that Becky Morgan's age still troubled him; though why, the child could scarcely understand.

The second or third repetition of his name attracted the old man's attention. Pausing from his work, he leant upon his spade, and put his hand to his dull ear.

"Did you call?" he said.

"I have been thinking, Davy," replied the sexton, "that she," he pointed to the grave, "must have been a deal older than you or me."

"Seventy-nine," answered the old man with a sorrowful shake of the head, "I tell you that I saw it."

"Saw it?" replied the sexton; "ay, but, Davy, women don't always tell the truth about their age."

"That's true indeed," said the other old man, with a sudden sparkle in his eye. "She might have been older."

"I'm sure she must have been. Why, only think how old she looked. You and I seemed but boys to her."

"She did look old," rejoined David. "You're right. She did look old."

"Call to mind how old she looked for many a long, long year, and say if she could be but seventy-nine at last —only our age," said the sexton.

"Five year older at the very least!" cried the other.

"Five!" retorted the sexton. "Ten. Good eighty-nine. I call to mind the time her daughter died. She was eighty-nine if she was a day, and tries to pass upon us now, for ten year younger. Oh! human vanity!"

The other old man was not behindhand with some moral reflections on this fruitful theme, and both adduced a mass of evidence, of such weight as to render it doubtful—not whether the deceased was of the age suggested, but whether she had not almost reached the patriarchal term of a hundred. When they had settled this question to their mutual satisfaction, the sexton, with his friend's assistance, rose to go.

"It's chilly, sitting here, and I must be careful—till the summer," he said, as he prepared to limp away.

"What?" asked old David.

"He's very deaf, poor fellow!" cried the sexton. "Good-bye."

"Ah!" said old David, looking after him. "He's failing very fast. He ages every day."

And so they parted: each persuaded that the other had less life in him than himself; and both greatly consoled and comforted by the little fiction they had agreed upon, respecting Becky Morgan, whose decease was no longer a precedent of uncomfortable application, and would be no business of theirs for half a score of years to come.

The child remained for some minutes, watching the deaf old man as he threw out the earth with his shovel, and, often stopping to cough and fetch his breath, still muttered to himself, with a kind of sober chuckle, that the sexton was wearing fast. At length she turned away, and walking thoughtfully through the churchyard, came unexpectedly upon the schoolmaster, who was sitting on a green grave in the sun, reading.

"Nell here?" he said cheerfully, as he closed his book. "It does me good to see you in the air and light. I feared you were again in the church, where you so often are."

"Feared!" replied the child, sitting down beside him. "Is it not a good place?"

"Yes, yes," said the schoolmaster. "But you must be gay sometimes—nay, don't shake your head and smile so very sadly."

"Not sadly, if you knew my heart. Do not look at me as if you thought me sorrowful. There is not a happier creature on the earth than I am now."

Full of grateful tenderness, the child took his hand, and folded it between her own. "It's God's will!" she said, when they had been silent for some time.

"What?"

"All this," she rejoined; "all this about us. But which of us is sad now? You see that *I* am smiling."

"And so am I," said the schoolmaster; "smiling to think how often we shall laugh in this same place. Were you not talking yonder?"

"Yes," the child rejoined.

"Of something that has made you sorrowful?"

There was a long pause.

"What was it?" said the schoolmaster, tenderly. "Come. Tell me what it was."

"I rather grieve—I *do* rather grieve to think," said the child, bursting into tears, "that those who die about us, are so soon forgotten."

"And do you think," said the schoolmaster, marking the glance she had thrown around, "that an unvisited grave, a withered tree, a faded flower or two, are tokens of forgetfulness or cold neglect? Do you think there are no deeds far away from here, in which these dead may be best remembered? Nell, Nell, there may be people busy in the world at this instant, in whose good actions and good thoughts these very graves—neglected as they look to us—are the chief instruments."

"Tell me no more," said the child quickly. "Tell me no more. I feel, I know it. How could I be unmindful of it, when I thought of you?"

"There is nothing," cried her friend, "no, nothing innocent or good, that dies, and is forgotten. Let us hold to that faith, or none. An infant, a prattling child, dying in its cradle, will live again in the better thoughts of those who loved it, and play its part, through them, in the redeeming actions of the world, though its body be burnt to ashes or drowned in the deepest sea. There is not an angel added to the Host of Heaven but does its blessed work on earth in those that loved it here. Forgotten! oh, if the good deeds of human creatures could be traced to their source, how beautifully would even death appear; for how much charity, mercy, and purified affection, would be seen to have their growth in dusty graves!"

"Yes," said the child, "it is the truth; I know it is. Who should feel its force so much as I, in whom your little scholar lives again! Dear, dear good friend, if you knew the comfort you have given me!"

The poor schoolmaster made her no answer, but bent over her in silence; for his heart was full.

They were yet seated in the same place, when the grandfather approached. Before they had spoken many words together, the church clock struck the hour of school, and their friend withdrew.

"A good man," said the grandfather, looking after him; "a kind man. Surely *he* will never harm us, Nell. We are safe here, at last—eh? We will never go away from here?"

The child shook her head and smiled.

"She needs rest," said the old man, patting her cheek; "too pale—too pale. She is not like what she was."

"When?" asked the child.

"Ha!" said the old man, "to be sure—when? How many weeks ago? Could I count them on my fingers? Let them rest though; they're better gone."

"Much better, dear," replied the child. "We will forget them; or, if we ever call them to mind, it shall be only as some uneasy dream that has passed away."

"Hush!" said the old man, motioning hastily to her with his hand and looking over his shoulder; "no more talk of the dream, and all the miseries it brought. There are no dreams here. 'Tis a quiet place, and they keep away. Let us never think about them, lest they should pursue us again. Sunken eyes and hollow cheeks—wet, cold, and famine—and horrors before them all, that were

even worse—we must forget such things if we would be tranquil here."

"Thank Heaven!" inwardly exclaimed the child, "for this most happy change!"

"I will be patient," said the old man, "humble, very thankful and obedient, if you will let me stay. But do not hide from me; do not steal away alone; let me keep beside you. Indeed, I will be very true and faithful, Nell."

"I steal away alone! why that," replied the child, with assumed gayety, "would be a pleasant jest indeed. See here, dear grandfather, we'll make this place our garden —why not? It is a very good one—and to-morrow we'll begin, and work together, side by side."

"It is a brave thought!" cried her grandfather. "Mind, darling—we begin to-morrow!"

Who so delighted as the old man, when they next day began their labor! Who so unconscious of all associations connected with the spot, as he! They plucked the long grass and nettles from the tombs, thinned the poor shrubs and roots, made the turf smooth, and cleared it of the leaves and weeds. They were yet in the ardor of their work, when the child, raising her head from the ground over which she bent, observed that the bachelor was sitting on the stile close by, watching them in silence.

"A kind office," said the little gentleman, nodding to Nell as she curtseyed to him. "Have you done all that, this morning?"

"It is very little, Sir," returned the child, with downcast eyes, "to what we mean to do."

"Good work, good work," said the bachelor. "But do you only labor at the graves of children, and young people?"

"We shall come to the others in good time, Sir," replied Nell, turning her head aside, and speaking softly.

It was a slight incident, and might have been design or accident, or the child's unconscious sympathy with youth. But it seemed to strike upon her grandfather, though he had not noticed it before. He looked in a hurried manner at the graves, then anxiously at the child, then pressed her to his side, and bade her stop to rest. Something he had long forgotten appeared to struggle faintly in his mind. It did not pass away, as weightier things had done; but came uppermost again, and yet again, and many times that day, and often afterwards. Once, while they were yet at work, the child, seeing that he often turned and looked uneasily at her, as though he were trying to resolve some painful doubts or collect some scattered thoughts, urged him to tell the reason. But he said it was nothing—nothing—and, laying her head upon his arm, patted her fair cheek with his hand, and muttered that she grew stronger every day, and would be a woman soon.

CHAPTER THE FIFTY-FIFTH.

FROM that time, there sprang up in the old man's mind, a solicitude about the child which never slept or left him. There are chords in the human heart—strange, varying strings—which are only struck by accident; which will remain mute and senseless to appeals the most passionate and earnest, and respond at last to the slightest casual touch. In the most insensible or childish minds, there is some train of reflection which art can seldom lead, or skill assist, but which will reveal itself, as great truths have done, by chance, and when the discoverer has the plainest and simplest end in view. From that time, the old man never for a moment forgot the weakness and devotion of the child : from the time of that slight incident, he, who had seen her toiling by his side through so much difficulty and suffering, and had scarcely thought of her otherwise than as the partner of miseries which he felt severely in his own person, and deplored for his own sake at least as much as hers, awoke to a sense of what he owed her, and what those miseries had made her. Never, no, never once, in one unguarded moment from that time to the end, did any care for himself, any thought of his own comfort, any selfish consideration or regard distract his thoughts from the gentle object of his love.

He would follow her up and down, waiting till she should tire and lean upon his arm—he would sit opposite to her in the chimney-corner, content to watch, and look, until she raised her head and smiled upon him as of old —he would discharge, by stealth, those household duties which tasked her powers too heavily—he would rise, in the cold dark nights, to listen to her breathing in her sleep, and sometimes crouch for hours by her bedside only to touch her hand. He Who knows all, can only know what hopes, and fears, and thoughts of deep affection, were in that one disordered brain, and what a change had fallen on the poor old man.

Sometimes—weeks had crept on, then—the child, exhausted though with little fatigue, would pass whole evenings on a couch beside the fire.   At such times, the schoolmaster would bring in books, and read to her aloud; and seldom an evening passed, but the bachelor came in, and took his turn of reading.   The old man sat and listened, —with little understanding for the words, but with his eyes fixed upon the child,—and if she smiled or brightened with the story, he would say it was a good one, and conceive a fondness for the very book.   When, in their evening talk, the bachelor told some tale that pleased her (as his tales were sure to do), the old man would painfully try to store it in his mind; nay, when the bachelor left them, he would sometimes slip out after him, and humbly beg that he would tell him such a part again, that he might learn to win a smile from Nell.

But these were rare occasions, happily; for the child yearned to be out of doors, and walking in her solemn garden.   Parties, too, would come to see the church; and those who came, speaking to others of the child sent more; so that even at that season of the year they had visitors almost daily.   The old man would follow them at a little distance through the building, listening to the voice he loved so well; and when the strangers left, and parted from Nell, he would mingle with them to catch up fragments of their conversation; or he would stand for the same purpose, with his gray head uncovered, at the gate, as they passed through.   They always praised the child, her sense and beauty, and he was proud to hear them!   But what was that, so often added, which wrung his heart, and made him sob and weep alone, in some dull corner!   Alas! even careless strangers—they who had no feeling for her, but the interest of the moment—they who would go away and forget next week that such a being lived—even they saw it—even they pitied her—even they bade him good-day compassionately, and whispered as they passed.

The people of the village, too, of whom there was not one but grew to have a fondness for poor Nell; even among them, there was the same feeling; a tenderness towards her—a compassionate regard for her, increasing every day.   The very schoolboys, light-hearted and thoughtless as they were, even they cared for her.   The roughest among them was sorry if he missed her in the usual place upon his way to school, and would turn out of the path to ask for her at the latticed window. If she were sitting in the church, they perhaps might peep in softly at the open door; but they never spoke to her, unless she rose and went to speak to them. Some feeling was abroad which raised the child above them all.

So, when Sunday came. They were all poor country people in the church, for the castle in which the old family had lived, was an empty ruin, and there were none but humble folks for seven miles around. There, as elsewhere, they had an interest in Nell. They would gather round her in the porch, before and after service; young children would cluster at her skirts; and aged men and women forsake their gossips, to give her kindly greeting. None of them, young or old, thought of passing the child without a friendly word. Many who came from three or four miles distant, brought her little presents; the humblest and rudest had good wishes to bestow.

She had sought out the young children whom she first saw playing in the churchyard. One of these—he who had spoken of his brother—was her little favorite and friend, and often sat by her side in the church, or climbed with her to the tower-top. It was his delight to help her, or to fancy that he did so, and they soon became close companions.

It happened, that, as she was reading in the old spot by herself one day, this child came running in with his eyes full of tears, and after holding her from him and looking at her eagerly for a moment, clasped his little arms passionately about her neck.

"What now?" said Nell, soothing him. "What is the matter?"

"She is not one yet!" cried the boy, embracing her still more closely. "No, no. Not yet."

She looked at him wonderingly, and putting his hair back from his face, and kissing him, asked what he meant.

"You must not be one, dear Nell," cried the boy. "We can't see them. They never come to play with us, or talk to us. Be what you are. You are better so."

"I do not understand you," said the child. "Tell me what you mean."

"Why, they say," replied the boy, looking up into her face, "that you will be an angel, before the birds sing again. But you won't be, will you? Don't leave us, Nell, though the sky *is* bright. Do not leave us!"

The child drooped her head, and put her hands before her face.

"She cannot bear the thought!" cried the boy, exulting through his tears. "You will not go. You know how sorry we should be. Dear Nell, tell me that you'll stay amongst us. Oh! Pray, pray, tell me that you will."

The little creature folded his hands, and knelt down at her feet.

"Only look at me, Nell," said the boy, "and tell me that you'll stop, and then I shall know that they are wrong, and will cry no more. Won't you say yes, Nell?"

Still the drooping head and hidden face, and the child quite silent—save for her sobs.

"After a time," pursued the boy, trying to draw away her hand, "the kind angels will be glad to think that you are not among them, and that you stayed here to be with us. Willy went away, to join them; but if he had known how I should miss him in our little bed at night, he never would have left me, I am sure."

Yet the child could make him no answer, and sobbed as though her heart were bursting.

"Why would you go, dear Nell? I know you would not be happy when you heard that we were crying for your loss. They say that Willy is in Heaven now, and that it's always summer there, and yet I'm sure he grieves when I lie down upon his garden bed, and he cannot turn to kiss me. But if you do go, Nell," said the boy, caressing her, and pressing his face to hers, "be fond of him, for my sake. Tell him how I love him still, and how much I loved you; and when I think that you two are together, and are happy, I'll try to bear it, and never give you pain by doing wrong—indeed I never will!"

The child suffered him to move her hands, and put them round his neck. There was a tearful silence, but it was not long before she looked upon him with a smile, and promised him, in a very gentle, quiet voice, that she would stay, and be his friend, as long as Heaven would let her. He clapped his hands for joy and thanked her many times ; and being charged to tell no person what had passed between them, gave her an earnest promise that he never would.

Nor did he, so far as the child could learn; but was her quiet companion in all her walks and musings, and never again adverted to the theme, which he felt had given her pain although he was unconscious of its cause. Something of distrust lingered about him still; for he would often come, even in the dark evenings, and call in a timid voice outside the door to know if she were safe within; and being answered yes, and bidden to enter, would take his station on a low stool at her feet, and sit there patiently until they came to seek, and take him home. Sure as the morning came, it found him lingering near the house to ask if she were well; and, morning, noon, or night, go where she would, he would forsake his playmates and his sports to bear her company.

"And a good little friend he is, too," said the old sexton to her once. "When his elder brother died—elder seems a strange word, for he was only seven year old—I remember this one took it sorely to heart."

The child thought of what the schoolmaster had told her, and felt how its truth was shadowed out even in this inant.

"It has given him something of a quiet way, I think," said the old man, "though for that he is merry enough at times. I'd wager now that you and he have been listening by the old well."

"Indeed we have not," the child replied. "I have been afraid to go near it; for I am not often down in that part of the church, and do not know the ground."

"Come down with me," said the old man. "I have known it from a boy. Come!"

They descended the narrow steps which led into the crypt, and paused among the gloomy arches, in a dim and murky spot.

"This is the place," said the old man. "Give me your hand while you throw back the cover, lest you should stumble and fall in. I am too old—I mean rheumatic—to stoop, myself."

"A black and dreadful place!" exclaimed the child.

"Look in," said the old man, pointing downward with his finger.

The child complied, and gazed down into the pit.

"It looks like a grave, itself," said the old man.

"It does," replied the child.

30

"I have often had the fancy," said the sexton, "that it might have been dug at first to make the old place more gloomy, and the old monks more religious.   It's to be closed up, and built over."

The child still stood, looking thoughtfully into the vault

"We shall see," said the sexton, "on what gay heads other earth will have closed, when the light is shut out from here.   God knows!   They'll close it up, **next spring**."

" The birds sing again in spring," thought the child, as she leant at her casement window, and gazed at the declining sun. " Spring! a beautiful and happy time!"

CHAPTER THE FIFTY-SIXTH.

A DAY or two after the Quilp tea-party at the Wilderness, Mr. Swiveller walked into Sampson Brass's office at the usual hour, and being alone in that Temple of Probity, placed his hat upon the desk, and taking from his pocket a small parcel of black crape, applied himself to folding and pinning the same upon it, after the manner of a hatband. Having completed the construction of this appendage, he surveyed his work with great complacency, and put his hat on again—very much over one eye, to increase the mournfulness of the effect. These arrangements perfected to his entire satisfaction, he thrust his hands into his pockets, and walked up and down the office with measured steps.

" It has always been the same with me," said Mr. Swiveller, " always. 'Twas ever thus—from childhood's hour I've seen my fondest hopes decay, I never loved a tree or flower but 'twas the first to fade away. I never nursed a dear Gazelle, to glad me with its soft black eye, but when it came to know me well, and love me, it was sure to marry a market-gardener."

Overpowered by these reflections, Mr. Swiveller stopped short at the clients' chair, and flung himself into its open arms.

" And this," said Mr. Swiveller, with a kind of bantering composure, " is life, I believe. Oh, certainly. Why not! I'm quite satisfied. I shall wear," added Richard, taking off his hat again and looking hard at it, as if he were only deterred by pecuniary considerations from spurning it with his foot, " I shall wear this emblem of woman's perfidy, in remembrance of her with whom I shall never again thread the windings of the mazy; whom I shall never more pledge in the rosy; who, during the short remainder of my existence, will murder the balmy. Ha, ha, ha!"

It may be necessary to observe, lest there should

appear any incongruity in the close of his soliloquy, that Mr. Swiveller did not wind up with a cheerful hilarious laugh, which would have been undoubtedly at variance with his solemn reflections, but that, being in a theatrical mood, he merely achieved that performance which is designated in melodramas "laughing like a fiend,"—for it seems that your fiends always laugh in syllables, and always in three syllables, never more or less, which is a remarkable property in such gentry, and one worthy of remembrance.

The baleful sounds had hardly died away, and Mr. Swiveller was still sitting in a very grim state in the clients' chair, when there came a ring—or, if we may adapt the sound to his then humor, a knell—at the office bell.   Opening the door with all speed, he beheld the expressive countenance of Mr. Chuckster, between whom and himself a fraternal greeting ensued.

" You're devilish early at this pestiferous old slaughter-house," said that gentleman, poising himself on one leg, and shaking the other in an easy manner.

"Rather," returned Dick.

"Rather!" retorted Mr. Chuckster, with that air of graceful trifling which so well became him.   "*I* should think so.   Why, my good feller, do you know what o'clock it is—half-past nine a. m. in the morning?"

" Won't you come in?" said Dick.   "All alone.   Swiveller solus.   ' 'Tis now the witching—' "

" ' Hour of night!' "

" ' When churchyards yawn,' "

" ' And the graves give up their dead.' "

At the end of this quotation in dialogue, each gentleman struck an attitude, and immediately subsiding into prose walked into the office.   Such morsels of enthusiasm were common among the Glorious Apollos, and were indeed the links that bound them together, and raised them above the cold dull earth.

" Well, and how are you, my buck?" said Mr. Chuckster, taking a stool.   " I was forced to come into the City upon some little private matters of my own, and couldn't pass the corner of the street without looking in, but upon my soul I didn't expect to find you.   It is so everlastingly early."

Mr. Swiveller expressed his acknowledgments ; and it

appearing on further conversation that he was in good health, and that Mr. Chuckster was in the like enviable condition, both gentlemen, in compliance with a solemn custom of the ancient Brotherhood to which they belonged, joined in a fragment of the popular duet of " All's Well," with a long shake at the end.

" And what's the news ? " said Richard.

" The town's as flat, my dear feller," replied Mr. Chuckster, " as the surface of a Dutch oven. There's no news. By-the-bye, that lodger of yours is a most extraordinary person. He quite eludes the most vigorous comprehension, you know. Never was such a feller ! "

" What has he been doing now ? " said Dick.

" By Jove, Sir," returned Mr. Chuckster, taking out an oblong snuff-box, the lid whereof was ornamented with a fox's head curiously carved in brass, " that man is an unfathomable. Sir, that man has made friends with our articled clerk. There's no harm in him, but he is so amazingly slow and soft. Now, if he wanted a friend, why couldn't he have one that knew a thing or two, and could do him some good by his manners and conversation. I have my faults, Sir," said Mr. Chuckster.—

" No, no," interposed Mr. Swiveller.

" Oh yes I have, I have my faults, no man knows his faults better than I know mine. But," said Mr. Chuckster, " I'm not meek. My worst enemies—every man has his enemies, Sir, and I have mine—never accused me of being meek. And I tell you what, Sir, if I hadn't more of these qualities that commonly endear man to man, than our articled clerk has, I'd steal a Cheshire cheese, tie it round my neck, and drown myself. I'd die degraded, as I have lived. I would upon my honor."

Mr. Chuckster paused, rapped the fox's head exactly on the nose with the knuckle of the forefinger, took a pinch of snuff, and looked steadily at Mr. Swiveller, as much as to say that if he thought he was going to sneeze, he would find himself mistaken.

" Not contented, Sir," said Mr. Chuckster, " with making friends with Abel, he has cultivated the acquaintance of his father and mother. Since he came home from that wild-goose chase he has been there—actually been there. He patronizes young Snobby besides ; you'll find, Sir, that

he'll be constantly coming backwards and forwards to
this place : yet I don't suppose that beyond the common
forms of civility, he has ever exchanged half-a-dozen
words with *me.* Now, upon my soul, you know," said
Mr. Chuckster, shaking his head gravely as men are wont
to do when they consider things are going a little too far,
"this is altogether such a low-minded affair, that if I
didn't feel for the governor, and know that he could never
get on without me, I should be obliged to cut the connection.   I should have no alternative."

Mr. Swiveller, who sat on another stool opposite to his
friend, stirred the fire in an excess of sympathy, but said
nothing.

"As to young Snob, Sir," pursued Mr. Chuckster with
a prophetic look, "you'll find he'll turn out bad.   In our
profession we know something of human nature, and take
my word for it, that the feller that came back to work
out that shilling, will show himself one of these days in
his true colors.   He's a low thief, Sir.   He must be."

Mr. Chuckster being roused, would probably have pursued this subject further, and in more emphatic language, but for a tap at the door, which seeming to announce the arrival of somebody on business, caused him to assume a greater appearance of meekness than was perhaps quite consistent with his late declaration. Mr. Swiveller, hearing the same sound, caused his stool to revolve rapidly on one leg until it brought him to his desk, into which, having forgotten in the sudden flurry of his spirits to part with the poker, he thrust it as he cried " Come in ! "

Who should present himself but that very Kit who had been the theme of Mr. Chuckster's wrath ! Never did man pluck up his courage so quickly, or look so fierce, as Mr. Chuckster when he found it was he. Mr. Swiveller stared at him for a moment, and then leaping from his stool, and drawing out the poker from its place of concealment, performed the broad-sword exercise with all the cuts and guards complete, in a species of frenzy.

" Is the gentleman at home ? " said Kit, rather astonished by this uncommon reception.

Before Mr. Swiveller could make any reply, Mr. Chuckster took occasion to enter his indignant protest against this form of inquiry ; which he held to be of a disrespectful and snobbish tendency, inasmuch as the inquirer, seeing two gentlemen then and there present, should have spoken of the other gentleman ; or rather (for it was not impossible that the object of his search might be of inferior quality) should have mentioned his name, leaving it to his hearers to determine his degree as they thought proper. Mr. Chuckster further remarked, that he had some reason to believe this form of address was personal to himself, and that he was not a man to be trifled with, as certain snobs (whom he did not more particularly mention or describe) might find, to their cost.

" I mean the gentleman upstairs," said Kit, turning to Richard Swiveller. " Is he at home ? "

" Why ? " rejoined Dick.

" Because if he is, I have a letter for him."

" From whom ? " said Dick.

" From Mr. Garland."

" Oh ! " said Dick, with extreme politeness. " Then you may hand it over, Sir. And if you're to wait for an answer, Sir, you may wait in the passage, Sir, which is an airy and well-ventilated apartment, Sir."

"Thank you," returned Kit. "But I am to give it to himself, if you please."

The excessive audacity of this retort so overpowered Mr. Chuckster, and so moved his tender regard for his friend's honor, that he declared, if he were not restrained by official considerations, he must certainly have annihilated Kit upon the spot; a resentment of the affront which he did consider, under the extraordinary circumstances of aggravation attending it, could but have met with the proper sanction and approval of a jury of Englishmen, who, he had no doubt would have returned a verdict of Justifiable Homicide, coupled with a high testimony to the morals and character of the Avenger. Mr. Swiveller, without being quite so hot upon the matter, was rather shamed by his friend's excitement and not a little puzzled how to act (Kit being quite cool and good-humored), when the single gentleman was heard to call violently down the stairs.

"Didn't I see somebody for me, come in?" cried the lodger.

"Yes, Sir," replied Dick. "Certainly, Sir."

"Then where is he?" roared the single gentleman.

"He's here, Sir," rejoined Mr. Swiveller. "Now young man, don't you hear you're to go upstairs? Are you deaf?"

Kit did not appear to think it worth his while to enter into any further altercation, but hurried off and left the Glorious Apollos gazing at each other in silence.

"Didn't I tell you so?" said Mr. Chuckster. "What do you think of that?"

Mr. Swiveller being in the main a good-natured fellow, and not perceiving in the conduct of Kit any villainy of enormous magnitude, scarcely knew what answer to return. He was relieved from his perplexity, however, by the entrance of Mr. Sampson and his sister, Sally, at sight of whom Mr. Chuckster precipitately retired.

Mr. Brass and his lovely companion appeared to have been holding a consultation over their temperate breakfast, upon some matter of great interest and importance. On the occasion of such conferences, they generally appeared in the office some half an hour after their usual time, and in a very smiling state, as though their late plots and designs had tranquillized their minds and shed a light upon their toilsome way. In the present instance, they seemed particularly gay; Miss Sally's aspect being of a most oily kind, and Mr. Brass rubbing his hands in an exceedingly jocose and light-hearted manner.

"Well, Mr. Richard," said Brass. "How are we this morning? Are we pretty fresh and cheerful, Sir—eh, Mr. Richard?"

"Pretty well, Sir," replied Dick.

"That's well," said Brass. "Ha ha! We should be gay as larks, Mr. Richard—why not? It's a pleasant world we live in, Sir, a very pleasant world. There are bad people in it, Mr. Richard, but if there were no bad people, there would be no good lawyers. Ha ha! Any letters by the post this morning, Mr. Richard?"

Mr. Swiveller answered in the negative.

"Ha!" said Brass, "no matter. If there's little business to-day, there'll be more to-morrow. A contented spirit, Mr. Richard, is the sweetness of existence. Anybody been here, Sir?"

"Only my friend"—replied Dick. "'May we ne'er want a—'"

"'Friend,'" Brass chimed in quickly, "'or a bottle to give him.' Ha ha! That's the way the song runs, isn't it? A very good song, Mr. Richard, very good. I like the sentiment of it. Ha ha! Your friend's the young man from Witherden's office, I think—yes—'May we ne'er want a—' Nobody else at all, sir, Mr. Richard?"

"Only somebody to the lodger," replied Mr. Swiveller.

"Oh indeed!" cried Brass. "Somebody to the lodger, eh? Ha ha! 'May we ne'er want a friend or a—' Somebody to the lodger, eh, Mr. Richard?"

"Yes," said Dick, a little disconcerted by the excessive buoyancy of spirits which his employer displayed. "With him now."

"With him now!" cried Brass; "Ha ha! There let 'em be, merry and free, toor rul lol le. Eh, Mr. Richard? Ha ha!"

"Oh certainly," replied Dick.

"And who," said Brass, shuffling among his papers, "who is the lodger's visitor—not a lady visitor, I hope, eh Mr. Richard? The morals of the Marks you know, Sir—'when lovely woman stoops to folly'—and all that —eh, Mr. Richard?"

"Another young man, who belongs to Witherden's too, or half belongs there," returned Richard. "Kit, they call him."

"Kit, eh!" said Brass. "Strange name—name of a dancing-master's fiddle, eh, Mr. Richard? Ha ha! Kit's there, is he? Oh!"

Dick looked at Miss Sally, wondering that she didn't check this uncommon exuberance on the part of Mr Sampson; but as she made no attempt to do so, and rather appeared to exhibit a tacit acquiescence in it, he concluded that they had just been cheating somebody, and receiving the bill.

"Will you have the goodness, Mr. Richard," said Brass, taking a letter from his desk, "just to step over to Peckham Rye with that? There's no answer, but it's rather particular and should go by hand. Charge the office with your coach-hire back, you know; don't spare the office; get as much out of it as you can—clerk's motto—Eh, Mr. Richard? Ha ha!"

Mr. Swiveller solemnly doffed the aquatic jacket, put on his coat, took down his hat from its peg, pocketed the letter, and departed. Directly he was gone, up rose Miss Sally Brass, and smiling sweetly at her brother (who nodded and smote his nose in return) withdrew also.

Sampson Brass was no sooner left alone, than he set the office-door wide open, and establishing himself at his desk directly opposite, so that he could not fail to see anybody who came downstairs and passed out at the street door, began to write with extreme cheerfulness and assiduity; humming as he did so, in a voice that was anything but musical, certain vocal snatches which appeared to have reference to the union between Church and State, inasmuch as they were compounded of the Evening Hymn and God save the King.

"Thus, the attorney of Bevis Marks sat, and wrote, and hummed, for a long time, except when he stopped to listen with a very cunning face, and hearing nothing, went on humming louder, and writing slower than ever. At length, 'n one of these pauses, he heard his lodger's door opened and shut, and footsteps coming down the stairs. Then Mr. Brass left off writing entirely, and with his pen in his hand hummed his very loudest; shaking his head meanwhile from side to side like a man whose whole soul was in the music, and smiling in a manner quite seraphic.

It was towards this moving spectacle that the staircase and the sweet sounds guided Kit, on whose arrival before his door, Mr. Brass stopped his singing, but not his smiling, and nodded affably, at the same time beckoning to him with his pen.

"Kit," said Mr. Brass, in the pleasantest way imaginable, "how do you do?"

Kit, being rather shy of his friend, made a suitable reply, and had his hand upon the lock of the street door when Mr. Brass called him softly back.

"You are not to go, if you please, Kit," said the attorney in a mysterious and yet business-like way. "You are to step in here, if you please. Dear me, dear me! When I look at you," said the lawyer, quitting his stool, and standing before the fire with his back towards it, "I am reminded of the sweetest little face that ever my eyes beheld. I remember your coming there twice or thrice when we were in possession. Ah Kit, my dear fellow, gentlemen in my profession have such painful duties to perform sometimes, that you needn't envy us— you needn't indeed!"

"I don't, Sir," said Kit, "though it isn't for the like of me to judge."

"Our only consolation, Kit," pursued the lawyer, looking at him in a sort of pensive abstraction, "is, that although we cannot turn away the wind, we can soften it; we can temper it, if I may say so, to the shorn lambs."

"Shorn indeed!" thought Kit. "Pretty close!" But he didn't say so.

"On that occasion, Kit," said Mr. Brass, "on that occasion that I have just alluded to, I had a hard battle with Mr. Quilp (for Mr. Quilp is a very hard man) to obtain them the indulgence they had. It might have cost me a client. But suffering virtue inspired me, and I prevailed."

"He's not so bad after all," thought honest Kit, as the attorney pursed up his lips and looked like a man who was struggling with his better feelings.

"I respect *you*, Kit," said Brass with emotion. "I saw enough of your conduct at that time to respect you, though your station is humble, and your fortune lowly.

It isn't the waistcoat that I look at. It is the heart. The checks in the waistcoat are but the wires of the cage. But the heart is the bird. Ah! How many sich birds are perpetually moulting, and putting their beaks through the wires to peck at all mankind!"

This poetic figure, which Kit took to be in special allusion to his own checked waistcoat, quite overcame him; Mr. Brass's voice and manner added not a little to its effect, for he discoursed with all the mild austerity of a hermit, and wanted but a cord round the waist of his rusty surtout, and a skull on the chimney-piece, to be completely set up in that line of business.

"Well, well," said Sampson, smiling as good men smile when they compassionate their own weakness or that of their fellow-creatures, "this is wide of the bull's-eye. You're to take that, if you please." As he spoke, he pointed to a couple of half-crowns upon the desk.

Kit looked at the coins, and then at Sampson, and hesitated.

"For yourself," said Brass.

"From——"

"No matter about the person they came from," replied the lawyer.—"Say me, if you like. We have eccentric friends overhead, Kit, and we mustn't ask questions or talk too much—you understand. You're to take them, that's all; and between you and me, I don't think they'll be the last you'll have to take from the same place. I hope not. Good-bye, Kit. Good-bye!"

With many thanks, and many more self-reproaches for having on such slight grounds suspected one who in their very first conversation turned out such a different man from what he had supposed,·Kit took the money and made the best of his way home. Mr. Brass remained airing himself at the fire, and resumed his vocal exercise, and his seraphic smile, simultaneously.

"May I come in?" said Miss Sally, peeping.

"Oh yes, you may come in," returned her brother.

"Ahem?" coughed Miss Brass interrogatively.

"Yes," returned Sampson, "I should say as good as done."

CHAPTER THE FIFTY-SEVENTH.

MR. CHUCKSTER'S indignant apprehensions were not without foundation. Certainly the friendship between the single gentleman and Mr. Garland was not suffered to cool, but had a rapid growth and flourished exceedingly. They were soon in habits of constant intercourse and communication; and the single gentleman laboring at this time under a slight attack of illness—the consequence most probably of his late excited feelings and subsequent disappointment—furnished a reason for their holding yet more frequent correspondence; so that some one of the inmates of Abel Cottage, Finchley, came backwards and forwards between that place and Bevis Marks, almost every day.

As the pony had now thrown off all disguise, and without any mincing of the matter or beating about the bush, sturdily refused to be driven by anybody but Kit, it generally happened that whether old Mr. Garland came, or Mr. Abel, Kit was of the party. Of all messages and inquiries, Kit was in right of his position the bearer; thus it came about that, while the single gentleman remained indisposed, Kit turned into Bevis Marks every morning with nearly as much regularity as the General Postman.

Mr. Sampson Brass, who no doubt had his reasons for looking sharply about him, soon learnt to distinguish the pony's trot and the clatter of the little chaise at the corner of the street. Whenever this sound reached his ears, he would immediately lay down his pen and fall to rubbing his hands and exhibiting the greatest glee.

"Ha ha!" he would cry. "Here's the pony again. Most remarkable pony, extremely docile, eh Mr. Richard, eh Sir?"

Dick would return some matter-of-course reply, and Mr. Brass, standing on the bottom rail of his stool, so as to get a view of the street over the top of the window-blind, would take an observation of the visitors.

"The old gentleman again!" he would exclaim, "a very prepossessing old gentleman, Mr. Richard—charming countenance, Sir—extremely calm—benevolence **in** every feature, Sir. He quite realizes my idea of King Lear, as he appeared when in possession of his kingdom, Mr. Richard—the same good humor, the same white hair and partial baldness, the same liability to be imposed upon. Ah! A sweet subject for contemplation, Sir, **very** sweet!"

Then, Mr. Garland having alighted and gone upstairs, Sampson would nod and smile to Kit from the window, and presently walk out into the street to greet him, when some such conversation as the following would ensue.

"Admirably groomed, Kit"—Mr. Brass is patting the pony—"does you great credit—amazingly sleek and bright to be sure. He literally looks as if he had been varnished all over."

Kit touches his hat, smiles, pats the pony himself, and expresses his conviction, "that Mr. Brass will not find many like him."

"A beautiful animal indeed!" cries Brass. "Sagacious too!"

"Bless you!" replies Kit, "he knows what you say to him as well as a Christian does."

"Does he indeed!" cried Brass, who has heard the same thing in the same place from the same person in the same words a dozen times, but is paralyzed with astonishment notwithstanding. "Dear me!"

"I little thought the first time I saw him, Sir," says Kit, pleased with the attorney's strong interest in his favorite, "that I should come to be as intimate with him as I am now."

"Ah!" rejoins Mr. Brass, brim-full of moral precepts and love of virtue. "A charming subject of reflection for you, very charming. A subject of proper pride and congratulation, Christopher. Honesty is the best policy. —I always find it so myself. I lost forty-seven pound ten by being honest this morning. But it's all gain, it's gain!"

Mr. Brass slyly tickles his nose with his pen and looks at Kit with the water standing in his eyes. Kit thinks that if ever there was a good man who belied his appearance, that man is Sampson Brass.

"A man," says Sampson, "who loses forty-seven pound ten in one morning by his honesty, is a man to be envied.

If it had been eighty pound, the luxuriousness of feeling would have been increased. Every pound lost, would have been a hundredweight of happiness gained. The still, small voice, Christopher," cries Brass smiling, and tapping himself on the bosom, "is a singing comic songs within me, and all is happiness and joy!"

Kit is so improved by the conversation, and finds it go so completely home to his feelings, that he is considering what he shall say, when Mr. Garland appears. The old gentleman is helped into the chaise with great obsequiousness by Mr. Sampson Brass; and the pony, after shaking his head several times, and standing for three or four minutes with all his four legs planted firmly on the ground as if he had made up his mind never to stir from that spot, but there to live and die, suddenly darts off without the smallest notice, at the rate of twelve English miles an hour. Then Mr. Brass and his sister (who has joined him at the door) exchange an odd kind of smile—not at all a pleasant one in its expression—and return to the society of Mr. Richard Swiveller, who during their absence has been regaling himself with various feats of pantomime, and is discovered at his desk, in a very flushed and heated condition, violently scratching out nothing with half a penknife.

Whenever Kit came alone, and without the chaise, it always happened that Sampson Brass was reminded of some mission, calling Mr. Swiveller, if not to Peckham Rye again, at all events to some pretty distant place from which he could not be expected to return for two or three hours, or in all probability a much longer period, as that gentleman was not, to say the truth, renowned for using great expedition on such occasions, but rather for protracting and spinning out the time to the very utmost limit of possibility. Mr. Swiveller out of sight, Miss Sally immediately withdrew. Mr. Brass would then set the office-door wide open, hum his old tune with great gaiety of heart, and smile seraphically as before. Kit coming downstairs would be called in; entertained with some moral and agreeable conversation; perhaps entreated to mind the office for an instant while Mr. Brass stepped over the way; and afterwards presented with one or two half-crowns as the case might be. This occurred so often, that Kit, nothing doubting but that they came from the single gentleman, who had already rewarded his mother with great liberality, could not enough admire his generosity; and brought so many cheap presents for her, and for little Jacob, and for the baby, and for Barbara to boot, that one or other of them was having some new trifle every day of their lives.

While these acts and deeds were in progress in and out of the office of Sampson Brass, Richard Swiveller, being often left alone therein, began to find the time hang heavy on his hands. For the better preservation of his cheerfulness therefore, and to prevent his faculties from rusting, he provided himself with a cribbage-board and pack of cards, and accustomed himself to play at cribbage with a dummy, for twenty, thirty, or sometimes even fifty thousand pounds aside, besides many hazardous bets to a considerable amount.

As these games were very silently conducted, notwithstanding the magnitude of the interests involved, Mr. Swiveller began to think that on those evenings when Mr. and Miss Brass were out (and they often went out now) he heard a kind of snorting or hard breathing sound in the direction of the door, which it occurred to him, after some reflection, must proceed from the small servant, who always had a cold from damp living. Looking intently that way one night, he plainly distinguished an eye gleaming and glistening at the keyhole; and having now no doubt that his suspicions were correct, he stole softly to the door, and pounced upon her before she was aware of his approach.

"Oh! I didn't mean any harm indeed. Upon my word I didn't," cried the small servant, struggling like a much larger one. "It's so very dull, downstairs. Please don't you tell upon me; please don't."

"Tell upon you!" said Dick. "Do you mean to say you were looking through the keyhole for company?"

"Yes, upon my word I was," replied the small servant.

"How long have you been cooling your eye there?" said Dick.

"Oh ever since you first began to play them cards, and long before."

Vague recollections of several fantastic exercises with which he had refreshed himself after the fatigues of business, and to all of which, no doubt, the small servant was a party, rather disconcerted Mr. Swiveller; but he was not very sensitive on such points, and recovered himself speedily.

" Well,—come in "—he said, after a little consideration. " Here—sit down, and I'll teach you how to play."

" Oh! I durstn't do it," rejoined the small servant; " Miss Sally 'ud kill me, if she know'd I came up here."

" Have you got a fire downstairs ? " said Dick.

" A very little one," replied the small servant.

" Miss Sally couldn't kill me if she know'd I went down there, so I'll come," said Richard, putting the cards into his pocket. " Why, how thin you are! What do you mean by it ?"

" It ain't my fault."

" Could you eat any bread and meat ?" said Dick, taking down his hat. " Yes? Ah! I thought so. Did you ever taste beer ? "

" I had a sip of it once," said the small servant.

" Here's a state of things! " cried Mr. Swiveller, raising his eyes to the ceiling. " She *never* tasted it—it can't be tasted in a sip! Why, how old are you ? "

" I don't know."

Mr Swiveller opened his eyes very wide, and appeared thoughtful for a moment; then, bidding the child mind the door until he came back, vanished straightway.

Presently he returned, followed by the boy from the public-house, who bore in one hand a plate of bread and beef, and in the other a great pot, filled with some very fragrant compound, which sent forth a grateful steam, and was indeed choice purl, made after a particular recipe which Mr. Swiveller had imparted to the landlord at a period when he was deep in his books and desirous to conciliate his friendship. Relieving the boy of his burden at the door, and charging his little companion to fasten it to prevent surprise, Mr. Swiveller followed her into the kitchen.

" There ! " said Richard, putting the plate before her. " First of all, clear that off, and then you'll see what's next."

The small servant needed no second bidding, and the plate was soon empty.

" Next," said Dick, handing the purl, " take a pull at

31

that; but moderate your transports, you know, for you're not used to it. Well, is it good?"

"Oh! isn't it?" said the small servant.

Mr. Swiveller appeared gratified beyond all expression by this reply, and took a long draught himself, steadfastly regarding his companion while he did so. These preliminaries disposed of, he applied himself to teaching her the game, which she soon learnt tolerably well, being both sharp-witted and cunning.

"Now," said Mr. Swiveller, putting two sixpences into a saucer, and trimming the wretched candle, when the

cards had been cut and dealt, "those are the stakes. If you win, you get 'em all. If I win, I get 'em. To make it seem more real and pleasant, I shall call you the Marchioness, do you hear?"

The small servant nodded.

"Then, Marchioness," said Mr. Swiveller, "fire away!"

The Marchioness, holding her cards very tight in both hands, considered which to play, and Mr. Swiveller, assuming the gay and fashionable air which such society required, took another pull at the tankard, and waited for the lead.

CHAPTER THE FIFTY-EIGHTH.

MR. SWIVELLER and his partner played several rubbers with varying success, until the loss of three sixpences, the gradual sinking of the purl, and the striking of ten o'clock, combined to render that gentleman mindful of the flight of Time, and the expediency of withdrawing before Mr. Sampson and Miss Sally Brass returned.

"With which object in view, Marchioness," said Mr. Swiveller gravely, "I shall ask your ladyship's permission to put the board in my pocket, and to retire from the presence when I have finished this tankard ; merely observing, Marchioness, that since life like a river is flowing, I care not how fast it rolls on, ma'am, on, while such purl on the bank still is growing, and such eyes light the waves as they run. Marchioness, your health. You will excuse my wearing my hat, but the palace is damp, and the marble floor is—if I may be allowed the expression—sloppy."

As a precaution against this latter inconvenience, Mr. Swiveller had been sitting for some time with his feet on the hob, in which attitude he now gave utterance to these apologetic observations, and slowly sipped the last choice drops of nectar.

"The Baron Sampsono Brasso and his fair sister are (you tell me) at the Play?" said Mr. Swiveller, leaning his left arm heavily upon the table, and raising his voice and his right leg after the manner of a theatrical bandit.

The Marchioness nodded.

"Ha!" said Mr. Swiveller, with a portentous frown. "'Tis well. Marchioness!—but no matter. Some wine there. Ho!" He illustrated these melodramatic morsels by handing the tankard to himself with great humility, receiving it haughtily, drinking from it thirstily, and smacking his lips fiercely.

The small servant, who was not so well acquainted with theatrical conventionalities as Mr. Swiveller (having indeed never seen a play, or heard one spoken of, except by chance through chinks of doors and in other forbidden

places), was rather alarmed by demonstrations so novel
in their nature, and showed her concern so plainly in her
looks, that Mr. Swiveller felt it necessary to discharge
his brigand manner for one more suitable to private life,
as he asked,

"Do they often go where glory waits 'em, and leave
you here?"

"Oh, yes; I believe you they do," returned the small
servant.   "Miss Sally's such a one-er for that, she is."

"Such a what?" said Dick.

"Such a one-er," returned the Marchioness.

After a moment's reflection, Mr. Swiveller determined
to forego his responsible duty of setting her right, and to
suffer her to talk on; as it was evident that her tongue
was loosened by the purl, and her opportunities for conversation were not so frequent as to render a momentary
check of little consequence.

"They sometimes go to see Mr. Quilp," said the small
servant with a shrewd look; "they go to a many places,
bless you."

"Is Mr. Brass a wunner?" said Dick.

"Not half what Miss Sally is, he isn't," replied the
small servant, shaking her head.   "Bless you, he'd never
do anything without her."

"Oh! He wouldn't, wouldn't he?" said Dick.

"Miss Sally keeps him in such order," said the small
servant; "he always asks her advice, he does; and he
catches it sometimes. Bless you, you wouldn't believe
how much he catches it."

"I suppose," said Dick, "that they consult together a
good deal, and talk about a great many people—about me
for instance, sometimes, eh, Marchioness?"

The Marchioness nodded amazingly.

"Complimentary?" said Mr. Swiveller.

The Marchioness changed the motion of her head,
which had not yet left off nodding, and suddenly began to
shake it from side to side with a vehemence which threatened to dislocate her neck.

"Humph!" Dick muttered.   "Would it be any breach
of confidence, Marchioness, to relate what they say of the
humble individual who has now the honor to—?"

"Miss Sally says you're a funny chap," replied his
friend.

" Well, Marchioness," said Mr. Swiveller, "that's not uncomplimentary. Merriment, Marchioness, is not a bad or degrading quality. Old King Cole was himself a merry old soul, if we may put any faith in the pages of history."

" But she says," pursued his companion, " that you an't to be trusted."

" Why, really, Marchioness," said Mr. Swiveller, thoughtfully ; "several ladies and gentlemen—not exactly professional persons, but tradespeople, ma'am, tradespeople—have made the same remark. The obscure citizen who keeps the hotel over the way, inclined strongly to that opinion to-night when I ordered him to prepare the banquet. It's a popular prejudice, Marchioness ; and yet I am sure I don't know why, for I have been trusted in my time to a considerable amount, and I can safely say that I never forsook my trust until it deserted me—never. Mr. Brass is of the same opinion, I suppose ? "

His friend nodded again, with a cunning look which seemed to hint that Mr. Brass held stronger opinions on the subject than his sister ; and seeming to recollect herself, added imploringly, " But don't you ever tell upon me, or I shall be beat to death."

" Marchioness," said Mr. Swiveller, rising, " the word of a gentleman is as good as his bond—sometimes better ; as in the present case, where his bond might prove but a doubtful sort of security. I am your friend, and I hope we shall play many more rubbers together in this same saloon. But, Marchioness," added Richard, stopping in his way to the door, and wheeling slowly round upon the small servant, who was following with the candle ; " it occurs to me that you must be in the constant habit of airing your eye at keyholes, to know all this."

" I only wanted," replied the trembling Marchioness, " to know where the key of the safe was hid ; that was all ; and I wouldn't have taken much, if I had found it— only enough to squench my hunger."

" You didn't find it then ? " said Dick. " But of course you didn't, or you'd be plumper. Good-night, Marchioness. Fare thee well, and if forever, then forever fare thee well—and put up the chain, Marchioness, in case of accidents."

With this parting injunction, Mr. Swiveller emerged

from the house; and feeling that he had by this time taken quite as much to drink as promised to be good for his constitution (purl being a rather strong and heady compound), wisely resolved to betake himself to his lodgings, and to bed at once. Homeward he went therefore; and his apartments (for he still retained the plural fiction) being at no great distance from the office, he was soon seated in his own bed-chamber, where, having pulled off one boot and forgotten the other, he fell into deep cogitation.

"This Marchioness," said Mr. Swiveller, folding his arms, "is a very extraordinary person—surrounded by mysteries, ignorant of the taste of beer, unacquainted with her own name (which is less remarkable), and taking a limited view of society though the keyholes of doors —can these things be her destiny, or has some unknown person started an opposition to the decrees of fate? It is a most inscrutable and unmitigated staggerer!"

When his meditations had attained this satisfactory point, he became aware of his remaining boot, of which, with unimpaired solemnity, he proceeded to divest himself; shaking his head with exceeding gravity all the time, and sighing deeply.

"These rubbers," said Mr. Swiveller, putting on his nightcap in exactly the same style as he wore his hat, "remind me of the matrimonial fireside. Cheggs's wife plays cribbage; all-fours likewise. She rings the changes on 'em now. From sport to sport they hurry her, to banish her regrets, and when they win a smile from her, they think that she forgets—but she don't. By this time, I should say," added Richard, getting his left cheek into profile, and looking complacently at the reflection of a very little scrap of whisker in the looking-glass; "by this time, I should say, the iron has entered into her soul. It serves her right!"

Melting from this stern and obdurate, into the tender and pathetic mood, Mr. Swiveller groaned a little, walked wildly up and down, and even made a show of tearing his hair, which however he thought better of, and wrenched the tassel from his night-cap instead. At last, undressing himself with a gloomy resolution, he got into bed.

Some men in his blighted position would have taken to

drinking; but as Mr. Swiveller had taken to that before, he only took, on receiving the news that Sophy Wackles was lost to him forever, to playing the flute; thinking after mature consideration that it was a good, sound, dismal occupation, not only in unison with his own sad thoughts, but calculated to awaken a fellow-feeling in the bosoms of his neighbors. In pursuance of this resolution, he now drew a little table to his bedside, and arranging the light and a small oblong music-book to the best advantage, took his flute from its box, and began to play most mournfully.

The air was "Away with melancholy"—a composition, which, when it is played very slowly on the flute in bed, with the further disadvantage of being performed by a gentleman but imperfectly acquainted with the instrument, who repeats one note a great many times before he can find the next, has not a lively effect. Yet for half the night, or more, Mr. Swiveller, lying sometimes on his back with his eyes upon the ceiling, and sometimes half out of bed to correct himself by the book, played this unhappy tune over and over again; never leaving off, save for a minute or two at a time to take breath and soliloquize about the Marchioness, and then beginning again with renewed vigor. It was not until he had quite exhausted his several subjects of meditation, and had breathed into the flute the whole sentiment of the purl down to its very dregs, and had nearly maddened the people of the house, and at both the next doors, and over the way,—that he shut up the music-book, extinguished the candle, and finding himself greatly lightened and relieved in his mind, turned round and fell asleep.

He awoke in the morning, much refreshed ; and having taken half an hour's exercise at the flute, and graciously received a notice to quit from his landlady, who had been in waiting on the stairs for that purpose since the dawn of day, repaired to Bevis Marks; where the beautiful Sally was already at her post, bearing in her looks a radiance, mild as that which beameth from the virgin moon.

Mr. Swiveller acknowledged her presence by a nod, and exchanged his coat for the aquatic jacket ; which usually took some time fitting on, for in consequence of a tightness in the sleeves, it was only to be got into by a series of struggles. This difficulty overcome, he took his seat at the desk.

"I say "—quoth Miss Brass, abruptly breaking the silence, "you haven't seen a silver pencil-case this morning, have you ? "

"I didn't meet many in the street," rejoined Mr. Swiveller. "I saw one—a stout pencil-case of respectable appearance—but as he was in company with an elderly penknife and a young toothpick, with whom he was in earnest conversation, I felt a delicacy in speaking to him."

"No, but have you ?" returned Miss Brass. "Seriously, you know."

"What a dull dog you must be to ask me such a question seriously," said Mr. Swiveller. "Haven't I this moment come ? "

"Well, all I know is," replied Miss Sally, "that it's not to be found, and that it disappeared one day this week, when I left it on the desk."

"Halloa ! " thought Richard, "I hope the Marchioness hasn't been at work here."

"There was a knife too," said Miss Sally, "of the same pattern. They were given to me by my father, years ago, and are both gone. You haven't missed anything yourself, have you?"

Mr. Swiveller involuntarily clapped his hands to the jacket to be quite sure that it *was* a jacket and not a skirted coat; and having satisfied himself of the safety of this, his only movable in Bevis Marks, made answer in the negative.

"It's a very unpleasant thing, Dick—" said Miss Brass, pulling out the tin box and refreshing herself with a pinch of snuff; "but between you and me—between friends you know, for if Sammy knew it, I should never hear the last of it—some of the office money, too, that has been left about, has gone in the same way. In particular, I have missed three half-crowns at three different times."

"You don't mean that?" cried Dick. "Be careful what you say, old boy, for this is a serious matter. Are you quite sure? Is there no mistake?"

"It is so, and there can't be any mistake at all," rejoined Miss Brass emphatically.

"Then by Jove," thought Richard, laying down his pen, "I'm afraid the Marchioness is done for!"

The more he discussed the subject in his thoughts, the more probable it appeared to Dick that the miserable little servant was the culprit. When he considered on what a spare allowance of food she lived, how neglected and untaught she was, and how her natural cunning had been sharpened by necessity and privation, he scarcely doubted it. And yet he pitied her so much, and felt so unwilling to have a matter of such gravity disturbing the oddity of their acquaintance, that he thought, and thought truly, that rather than receive fifty pounds down, he would have the Marchioness proved innocent.

While he was plunged in very profound and serious meditation upon this theme, Miss Sally sat shaking her head with an air of great mystery and doubt; when the voice of her brother Sampson, carolling a cheerful strain, was heard in the passage, and that gentleman himself, beaming with virtuous smiles, appeared.

"Mr. Richard, Sir, good-morning! Here we are again, Sir, entering upon another day, with our bodies strengthened by slumber and breakfast, and our spirits fresh and flowing. Here we are, Mr. Richard, rising with the sun to run our little course,—our course of duty, Sir—and like him, get through our day's work with credit to ourselves and advantage to our fellow-creatures. A charming reflection, Sir, very charming!"

While he addressed his clerk in these words, Mr. Brass was somewhat ostentatiously engaged in minutely examining and holding up against the light a five-pound bank note, which he had brought in, in his hand.

Mr. Richard not receiving his remarks with anything like enthusiasm, his employer turned his eyes to his face, and observed that it wore a troubled expression.

"You're out of spirits, Sir," said Brass. "Mr. Richard, Sir, we should fall to work cheerfully, and not in a despondent state. It becomes us, Mr. Richard, Sir, to——"

Here the chaste Sarah heaved a loud sigh.

"Dear me!" said Mr. Sampson, "you too! Is anything the matter? Mr. Richard, Sir—"

Dick, glancing at Miss Sally, saw that she was making signals to him, to acquaint her brother with the subject of their recent conversation. As his own position was not a very pleasant one until the matter was set at rest one way or other, he did so; and Miss Brass, plying her snuff-box at a most wasteful rate, corroborated his account.

The countenance of Sampson fell, and anxiety over-spread his features. Instead of passionately bewailing the loss of his money, as Miss Sally had expected, he walked on tiptoe to the door, opened it, looked outside, shut it softly, returned on tiptoe, and said in a whisper,

"This is a most extraordinary and painful circumstance—Mr. Richard, Sir, a most painful circumstance. The fact is, that I myself have missed several small sums from the desk of late, and have refrained from mentioning it, hoping that accident would discover the offender; but it has not done so—it has not done so. Sally—Mr. Richard, Sir—this is a particularly distressing affair!"

As Sampson spoke, he laid the bank-note upon the desk among some papers, in an absent manner, and thrust his hands into his pockets. Richard Swiveller pointed to it, and admonished him to take it up.

"No, Mr. Richard, Sir," rejoined Brass with emotion. "I will not take it up. I will let it lie there, Sir. To take it up, Mr. Richard, Sir, would imply a doubt of you; and in you, Sir, I have unlimited confidence. We will let it lie there, Sir, if you please, and we will not take it up by any means." With that, Mr. Brass patted him twice or thrice upon the shoulder, in a most friendly manner, and entreated him to believe that he had as much faith in his honesty as he had in his own.

Although at another time Mr. Swiveller might have looked upon this as a doubtful compliment, he felt it, under the then-existing circumstances, a great relief to be assured that he was not wrongfully suspected. When he had made a suitable reply, Mr. Brass wrung him by the hand, and fell into a brown study, as did Miss Sally likewise. Richard too remained in a thoughtful state; fearing every moment to hear the Marchioness impeached, and unable to resist the conviction that she must be guilty.

When they had severally remained in this condition for some minutes, Miss Sally all at once gave a loud rap upon the desk with her clenched fist, and cried, " I've hit it ! "— as indeed she had, and chipped a piece out of it too; but that was not her meaning.

" Well," cried Brass anxiously. " Go on, will you ? "

"Why," replied his sister with an air of triumph, "hasn't there been somebody always coming in and out of this office for the last there or four weeks; hasn't that some-body been left alone in it sometimes—thanks to you; and do you mean to tell me that that somebody isn't the thief ! "

" What somebody ? " blustered Brass.

" Why, what do you call him—Kit ! "

" Mr. Garland's young man ? "

" To be sure."

" Never ! " cried Brass. " Never. I'll not hear of it. Don't tell me—" said Sampson, shaking his head, and working with both his hands as if he were clearing away ten thousand cobwebs. " I'll never believe it of him. Never ! "

" I say," repeated Miss Brass, taking another pinch of snuff, " that he's the thief."

" I say," returned Sampson violently, " that he is *not*. What do you mean ? How dare you ? Are characters to be whispered away like this ? Do you know that he's the honestest and faithfullest fellow that ever lived, and that he has an irreproachable good name ? Come in, come in ! "

These last words were not addressed to Miss Sally, though they partook of the tone in which the indignant remonstrances that preceded them had been uttered. They were addressed to some person who had knocked at the office-door; and they had hardly passed the lips of Mr. Brass, when this very Kit himself looked in.

" Is the gentleman upstairs, Sir, if you please ? "

" Yes, Kit," said Brass, still fired with an honest in-dignation, and frowning with knotted brows upon his sister " Yes, Kit, he is. I am glad to see you, Kit, I am rejoiced to see you. Look in again, as you come down-stairs, Kit. *That* lad a robber ! " cried Brass when he had withdrawn, " with that frank and open countenance ! I'd trust him with untold gold. Mr. Richard, Sir, have the goodness to step directly to Wrasp and Co.'s in Broad Street, and inquire if they have had instructions to ap-pear in Carkem and Painter. *That* lad a robber," sneered Sampson, flushed and heated with his wrath. " Am I blind, deaf, silly ; do I know nothing of human nature when I see it before me ? Kit a robber ! Bah ! "

Flinging this final interjection at Miss Sally with im-measurable scorn and contempt, Sampson Brass thrust his head into his desk as if to shut the base world from his view, and breathed defiance from under its half-closed lid.

CHAPTER THE FIFTY-NINTH.

When Kit, having discharged his errand, came down-stairs from the single gentleman's apartment after the lapse of a quarter of an hour or so, Mr. Sampson Brass was alone in the office. He was not singing as usual, nor was he seated at his desk. The open door showed him standing before the fire with his back towards it, and looking so very strange that Kit supposed he must have been suddenly taken ill.

" Is anything the matter, Sir ? " said Kit.

" Matter ! " cried Brass. " No. Why anything the matter ? "

" You are so very pale," said Kit, " that I should hardly have known you."

" Pooh pooh ! mere fancy," cried Brass, stooping to

throw up the cinders. "Never better, Kit, never better in all my life. Merry too. Ha ha! How's our friend above-stairs, eh?"

"A great deal better," said Kit.

"I'm glad to hear it," rejoined Brass; "thankful, I may say. An excellent gentleman—worthy, liberal, generous, gives very little trouble—an admirable lodger. Ha ha! Mr. Garland—he's well, I hope, Kit—and the pony—my friend, my particular friend, you know. Ha ha!"

Kit gave a satisfactory account of all the little household at Abel Cottage. Mr. Brass, who seemed remarkably inattentive and impatient, mounted on his stool, and beckoning him to come nearer, took him by the button-hole.

"I have been thinking, Kit," said the lawyer, "that I could throw some little emoluments into your mother's way—You have a mother, I think? If I recollect right, you told me—"

"Oh yes, Sir, yes certainly."

"A widow, I think? an industrious widow?"

"A harder-working woman or a better mother never lived, Sir,"

"Ah!" cried Brass. "That's affecting, truly affecting. A poor widow struggling to maintain her orphans in decency and comfort, is a delicious picture of human goodness.—Put down your hat, Kit."

"Thank you, Sir, I must be going directly."

"Put it down while you stay, at any rate," said Brass, taking it from him and making some confusion among the papers, in finding a place for it on the desk. "I was thinking, Kit, that we have often houses to let for people we are concerned for, and matters of that sort. Now you know we're obliged to put people into those houses to take care of 'em—very often undeserving people that we can't depend upon. What's to prevent our having a person that we *can* depend upon, and enjoying the delight of doing a good action at the same time? I say, what's to prevent our employing this worthy woman, your mother? What with one job and another, there's lodging—and good lodging too—pretty well all the year round, rent free, and a weekly allowance besides, Kit, that would provide them with a great many comforts they don't at present enjoy. Now what do you think of that? Do you see any objection? My only desire is to serve you, Kit; therefore if you do, say so freely."

As Brass spoke, he moved the hat twice or thrice, and shuffled among the papers again, as if in search of something.

"How can I see any objection to such a kind offer, Sir?" replied Kit with his whole heart. "I don't know how to thank you, Sir, I don't indeed."

"Why then," said Brass, suddenly turning upon him and thrusting his face close to Kit's with such a repulsive smile that the latter, even in the very height of his gratitude, drew back quite startled. "Why then, *it's done.*"

Kit looked at him in some confusion.

"Done, I say—" added Sampson, rubbing his hands and veiling himself again in his usual oily manner. "Ha ha! and so you shall find, Kit, so you shall find. But dear me," said Brass, "what a time Mr. Richard is gone! A sad loiterer to be sure! Will you mind the office one minute, while I run upstairs? Only one minute. I'll not detain you an instant longer, on any account, Kit."

Talking as he went, Mr. Brass bustled out of the office, and in a very short time returned. Mr. Swiveller came back almost at the same instant; and as Kit was leaving the room hastily to make up for lost time, Miss Brass herself encountered him in the doorway.

"Oh!" sneered Sally, looking after him as she entered. "There goes your pet, Sammy, eh?"

"Ah! There he goes," replied Brass. "My pet, if you please. An honest fellow, Mr. Richard, Sir—a worthy fellow indeed!"

"Hem!" coughed Miss Brass.

"I tell you, you aggravating vagabond," said the angry Sampson, "that I'd stake my life upon his honesty. Am I never to hear the last of this? Am I always to be baited, and beset, by your mean suspicions? Have you no regard for true merit, you malignant fellow? If you come to that, I'd sooner suspect your honesty than his."

Miss Sally pulled out the tin snuff-box, and took a long, slow pinch: regarding her brother with a steady gaze all the time.

"She drives me wild, Mr. Richard, Sir," said Brass, "she exasperates me beyond all bearing. I am heated and excited, Sir, I know I am. These are not business manners, Sir, nor business looks, but she carries me out of myself."

"Why don't you leave him alone?" said Dick.

"Because she can't, Sir," retorted Brass; "because to chafe and vex me is a part of her nature, Sir, and she will and must do it, or I don't believe she'd have her health. But never mind," said Brass, "never mind. I've carried my point. I've shown my confidence in the lad. He has minded the office again. Ha ha! Ugh, you viper!"

The beautiful virgin took another pinch, and put the snuff-box in her pocket; still looking at her brother with perfect composure.

"He has minded the office again," said Brass triumphantly; "he has had my confidence, and he shall continue to have it; he—why, where's the—"

"What have you lost?" inquired Mr. Swiveller.

"Dear me!" said Brass, slapping all his pockets one after another, and looking into his desk, and under it, and upon it, and wildly tossing the papers about, "the note, Mr. Richard, Sir, the five-pound note—what can have become of it? I laid it down here—God bless me!"

"What!" cried Miss Sally, starting up, clapping her hands, and scattering the papers on the floor. "Gone! Now, who's right? Now, who's got it? Never mind five pounds—what's five pounds? He's honest you know, quite honest. It would be mean to suspect him. Don't run after him. No, no, not for the world!"

"Is it really gone though?" said Dick, looking at Brass with a face as pale as his own.

"Upon my word, Mr. Richard, Sir," replied the lawyer, feeling in all his pockets with looks of the greatest agitation, "I fear this is a black business. It's certainly gone, Sir. What's to be done?"

"Don't run after him," said Miss Sally, taking more snuff. "Don't run after him on any account. Give him time to get rid of it, you know. It would be cruel to find him out!"

Mr. Swiveller and Sampson Brass looked from Miss Sally to each other in a state of utter bewilderment, and then, as by one impulse, caught up their hats and rushed out into the street—darting along in the middle of the road, and dashing aside all obstructions as though they were running for their lives.

It happened that Kit had been running too, though not so fast, and having the start of them by some few minutes, was a good distance ahead. As they were pretty certain of the road he must have taken, however, and kept on at a great pace, they came up with him, at the very moment when he had taken breath, and was breaking into a run again.

"Stop!" cried Sampson, laying his hand on one shoulder, while Mr. Swiveller pounced upon the other. "Not so fast, Sir. You're in a hurry?"

" Yes, I am," said Kit, looking from one to the other in great surprise.

"I—I—can hardly believe it," panted Sampson, "but something of value is missing from the office. I hope you don't know what."

"Know what! good Heaven, Mr. Brass!" cried Kit, trembling from head to foot ; " you don't suppose—"

" No, no," rejoined Brass quickly, "I don't suppose anything. Don't say *I* said you did. You'll come back quietly, I hope?"

"Of course I will," returned Kit. "Why not?"

" To be sure!" said Brass. "Why not? I hope there may turn out to be no why not. If you knew the trouble I've been in this morning through taking your part, Christopher, you'd be sorry for it."

"And I am sure you'll be sorry for having suspected me, Sir," replied Kit. "Come. Let us make haste back."

"Certainly!" cried Brass, "the quicker, the better. Mr. Richard—have the goodness, Sir, to take that arm. I'll take this one. It's not easy walking three abreast, but under these circumstances it must be done, Sir; there's no help for it."

Kit did turn from white to red, and from red to white again, when they secured him thus, and for a moment seemed disposed to resist. But, quickly recollecting himself, and remembering that if he made any struggle, he would perhaps be dragged by the collar through the public streets, he only repeated, with great earnestness and with the tears standing in his eyes, that they would be sorry for this—and suffered them to lead him off. While they were on the way back, Mr. Swiveller, upon whom his present functions sat very irksomely, took an opportunity of whispering in his ear that if he would confess his guilt, even by so much as a nod, and promise not to do so any more, he would connive at his kicking Sampson Brass on the shins and escaping up a court; but Kit indignantly rejecting this proposal, Mr. Richard had nothing for it, but to hold him tight until they reached Bevis Marks, and ushered him into the presence of the charming Sarah, who immediately took the precaution of locking the door.

"Now, you know," said Brass, "if this is a case of innocence, it is a case of that description, Christopher, where the fullest disclosure is the best satisfaction for everybody. Therefore if you'll consent to an examination," he demonstrated what kind of examination he meant by turning back the cuffs of his coat, "it will be a comfortable and pleasant thing for all parties."

"Search me," said Kit, proudly, holding up his arms. "But mind, Sir—I know you'll be sorry for this, to the last day of your life."

"It is certainly a very painful occurrence," said Brass with a sigh, as he dived into one of Kit's pockets, and fished up a miscellaneous collection of small articles; "very painful. Nothing here, Mr. Richard, Sir, all perfectly satisfactory. Not here, Sir. Nor in the waistcoat, Mr. Richard, nor in his coat tails. So far, I am rejoiced, I am sure."

Richard Swiveller, holding Kit's hat in his hand, was watching the proceedings with great interest, and bore upon his face the slightest possible indication of a smile, as Brass, shutting one of his eyes, looked with the other up the inside of one of the poor fellow's sleeves as if it were a telescope, when Sampson turning hastily to him, bade him search the hat.

"Here's a handkerchief," said Dick.

"No harm in that, Sir," rejoined Brass, applying his eye to the other sleeve, and speaking in the voice of one who was contemplating an immense extent of prospect. "No harm in a handkerchief, Sir, whatever. The faculty don't consider it a healthy custom, I believe, Mr. Richard, to carry one's handkerchief in one's hat—I have heard that it keeps the head too warm—but in every other point

3²

of view, its being there, is extremely satisfactory—extremely so."

An exclamation, at once from Richard Swiveller, Miss Sally, and Kit himself, cut the lawyer short. He turned his head, and saw Dick standing with the bank-note in his hand.

" In the hat?" cried Brass, in a sort of shriek.

" Under the handkerchief, and tucked beneath the lining," said Dick, aghast at the discovery.

Mr. Brass looked at him, at his sister, at the walls, at the ceiling, at the floor—everywhere but at Kit, who stood quite stupefied and motionless.

" And this," cried Sampson, clasping his hands, " is the world that turns upon its own axis, and has Lunar influences, and revolutions round Heavenly Bodies, and various games of that sort! This is human natur, is it! Oh natur, natur! This is the miscreant that I was going to benefit with all my little arts, and that even now I feel so much for, as to wish to let him go! But," added Mr. Brass with greater fortitude, " I am myself a lawyer, and bound to set an example in carrying the laws of my happy country into effect. Sally my dear, forgive me, and catch hold of him on the other side. Mr. Richard, Sir, have the goodness to run and fetch a constable. The weakness is past and over, Sir, and moral strength returns. A constable, Sir, if *you* please! "

CHAPTER THE SIXTIETH.

KIT stood as one entranced, with his eyes opened wide and fixed upon the ground, regardless alike of the tremulous hold which Mr. Brass maintained on one side of his cravat, and of the firmer grasp of Miss Sally upon the other; although this latter detention was in itself no small inconvenience, as that fascinating woman, besides screwing her knuckles rather inconveniently into his throat from time to time, had fastened upon him in the first instance with so tight a grip that even in the disorder and distraction of his thoughts he could not divest himself of an uneasy sense of choking. Between the brother and sister he remained in this posture, quite un-

resisting and passive, until Mr. Swiveller returned with a police constable at his heels.

This functionary, being of course well used to such scenes, looking upon all kinds of robbery from petty larceny up to housebreaking or ventures on the highway as matters in the regular course of business, and regarding the perpetrators in the light of so many customers coming to be served at the wholesale and retail shop of criminal law where he stood behind the counter, received Mr. Brass's statement of facts with about as much interest and surprise, as an undertaker might evince if required to listen to a circumstantial account of the last illness of a person whom he was called in to wait upon professionally; and took Kit into custody with a decent indifference.

"We had better," said this subordinate minister of justice, "get to the office while there's a magistrate sitting. I shall want you to come along with us, Mr. Brass, and the—" he looked at Miss Sally as if in some doubt whether she might not be a griffin or other fabulous monster.

"The lady, eh?" said Sampson.

"Ah!" replied the constable. "Yes—the lady. Likewise the young man that found the property."

"Mr. Richard, Sir," said Brass in a mournful voice. "A sad necessity. But the altar of our country, Sir—"

"You'll have a hackney-coach, I suppose?" interrupted the constable, holding Kit (whom his other captors had released) carelessly by the arm, a little above the elbow. "Be so good as send for one, will you?"

"But hear me speak a word," cried Kit, raising his eyes and looking imploringly about him. "Hear me speak a word. I am no more guilty than any one of you. Upon my soul I am not. I a thief! Oh, Mr. Brass, you know me better. I am sure you know me better. This is not right of you, indeed."

"I give you my word, constable—" said Brass. But here the constable interposed with the constitutional principle "words be blowed;" observing that words were but spoonmeat for babes and sucklings, and that oaths were the food for strong men.

"Quite true, constable," assented Brass in the same mournful tone. "Strictly correct. I give you my oath, constable, that down to a few minutes ago, when this

fatal discovery was made, I had such confidence in that
lad, that I'd have trusted him with—a hackney-coach,
Mr. Richard, Sir; you're very slow, Sir."

"Who is there that knows me," cried Kit, "that would
not trust me—that does not? ask anybody whether they
have ever doubted me; whether I have ever wronged
them of a farthing. Was I ever once dishonest when I
was poor and hungry, and is it likely I would begin now!
Oh consider what you do. How can I meet the kindest
friends that ever human creature had, with this dreadful
charge upon me!"

Mr. Brass rejoined that it would have been well for the
prisoner if he had thought of that before, and was about
to make some other gloomy observations, when the voice
of the single gentleman was heard demanding from above-
stairs what was the matter, and what was the cause of
all that noise and hurry. Kit made an involuntary start
towards the door in his anxiety to answer for himself,
but being speedily detained by the constable, had the
agony of seeing Sampson Brass run out alone to tell the
story in his own way.

"And he can hardly believe it either," said Sampson,
when he returned, "nor nobody will. I wish I could
doubt the evidence of my senses, but their depositions
are unimpeachable. It's of no use cross-examining my
eyes," cried Sampson, winking and rubbing them, "they
stick to their first account, and will. Now, Sarah, I hear
the coach in the Marks; get on your bonnet, and we'll
be off. A sad errand! a moral funeral, quite!"

"Mr. Brass," said Kit, "do me one favor. Take me to
Mr. Witherden's first."

Sampson shook his head irresolutely.

"Do," said Kit. "My master's there. For Heaven's
sake, take me there first."

"Well, I don't know," stammered Brass, who perhaps
had his reasons for wishing to show as fair as possible
in the eyes of the notary. "How do we stand in point
of time, constable, eh?"

The constable, who had been chewing a straw all this
while with great philosophy, replied that if they went
away at once they would have time enough, but that if
they stood shilly-shallying there any longer they must
go straight to the Mansion House; and finally expressed

his opinion that that was where it was, and that was all about it.

Mr. Richard Swiveller having arrived inside the coach, and still remaining immovable in the most commodious corner with his face to the horses, Mr. Brass instructed the officer to remove his prisoner, and declared himself quite ready. Therefore the constable, still holding Kit in the same manner, and pushing him on a little before him, so as to keep him at about three-quarters of an arm's length in advance (which is the professional mode), thrust him into the vehicle and followed himself. Miss Sally entered next; and there being now four inside, Sampson Brass got upon the box, and made the coachman drive on.

Still completely stunned by the sudden and terrible change which had taken place in his affairs, Kit sat gazing out of the coach window, almost hoping to see some monstrous phenomenon in the streets which might give him reason to believe he was in a dream. Alas! Everything was too real and familiar: the same succession of turnings, the same houses, the same streams of people running side by side in different directions upon the pavement, the same bustle of carts and carriages in the road, the same well-remembered objects in the shop windows: a regularity in the very noise and hurry which no dream ever mirrored. Dreamlike as the story was, it was true. He stood charged with robbery; the note had been found upon him, though he was innocent in thought and deed; and they were carrying him back, a prisoner.

Absorbed in these painful ruminations, thinking with a drooping heart of his mother and little Jacob, feeling as though even the consciousness of innocence would be insufficient to support him in the presence of his friends if they believed him guilty, and sinking in hope, and courage more and more as they drew nearer to the notary's, poor Kit was looking earnestly out of the window, observant of nothing,—when all at once, as though it had been conjured up by magic, he became aware of the face of Quilp.

And what a leer there was upon the face! It was from the open window of a tavern that it looked out; and the dwarf had so spread himself over it, with his elbows on the window-sill and his head resting on both his hands, that what between this attitude and his being swoln with suppressed laughter, he looked puffed and bloated into twice his usual breadth. Mr. Brass on recognizing him immediately stopped the coach. As it came to a halt directly opposite to where he stood, the dwarf pulled off his hat, and saluted the party with a hideous and grotesque politeness.

"Aha!" he cried. "Where now, Brass? where now? Sally with you too? Sweet Sally! And Dick? Pleasant Dick! And Kit? Honest Kit!"

"He's extremely cheerful!" said Brass to the coach-

man. "Very much so! Ah, Sir—a sad business! Never believe in honesty any more, Sir."

"Why not?" returned the dwarf. "Why not, you rogue of a lawyer, why not?"

"Bank-note lost in our office, Sir," said Brass, shaking his head. "Found in his hat, Sir—he previously left alone there—no mistake at all, Sir—chain of evidence complete—not a link wanting."

"What!" cried the dwarf, leaning half his body out of window. "Kit a thief! Kit a thief! Ha ha ha! Why, he's an uglier-looking thief than can be seen anywhere for a penny. Eh, Kit—eh? Ha ha ha! Have you taken Kit into custody before he had time and opportunity to beat me! Eh, Kit—eh?" And with that, he burst into a yell of laughter, manifestly to the great terror of the coachman, and pointed to a dyer's pole hard by, where a dangling suit of clothes bore some resemblance to a man upon a gibbet.

"Is it coming to that, Kit!" cried the dwarf, rubbing his hands violently. "Ha ha ha ha! What a disappointment for little Jacob, and for his darling mother! Let him have the Bethel minister to comfort and console him, Brass. Eh, Kit—eh? Drive on, coachey, drive on. Bye bye, Kit; all good go with you; keep up your spirits; my love to the Garlands—the dear old lady and gentleman. Say I inquired after 'em, will you? Blessings on 'em, on you, and on everybody, Kit. Blessings on all the world!"

With such good wishes and farewells, poured out in a rapid torrent until they were out of hearing, Quilp suffered them to depart; and when he could see the coach no longer, drew in his head, and rolled upon the ground in an ecstasy of enjoyment.

When they reached the notary's, which they were not long in doing, for they had encountered the dwarf in a bye street at a very little distance from the house, Mr. Brass dismounted; and opening the coach-door with a melancholy visage, requested his sister to accompany him into the office, with the view of preparing the good people within for the mournful intelligence that awaited them. Miss Sally complying, he desired Mr. Swiveller to accompany them. So, into the office they went; Mr. Sampson and his sister arm-in-arm; and Mr. Swiveller following, alone.

The notary was standing before the fire in the outer office, talking to Mr. Abel and the elder Mr. Garland, while Mr. Chuckster sat writing at the desk, picking up such crumbs of their conversation as happened to fall in his way. This posture of affairs Mr. Brass observed through the glass-door as he was turning the handle, and seeing that the notary recognized him, he began to shake his head and sigh deeply while that partition yet divided them.

"Sir," said Sampson, taking off his hat, and kissing

the two forefingers of his right-hand beaver glove, "my name is Brass—Brass of Bevis Marks, Sir. I have had the honor and pleasure, Sir, of being concerned against you in some little testamentary matters. How do you do, Sir?"

"My clerk will attend to any business you may have come upon, Mr. Brass," said the notary, turning away.

"Thank you, Sir," said Brass, "thank you, I am sure. Allow me, Sir, to introduce my sister—quite one of us, Sir, although of the weaker sex—of great use in my business, Sir, I assure you. Mr. Richard, Sir, have the goodness to come forward if you please—No really," said Brass, stepping between the notary and his private office (towards which he had begun to retreat), and speaking in the tone of an injured man, "really, Sir, I must, under favor, request a word two with you, indeed."

"Mr. Brass," said the other, in a decided tone, "I am engaged. You see that I am occupied with these gentlemen. If you will communicate your business to Mr. Chuckster yonder, you will receive every attention."

"Gentlemen," said Brass, laying his right hand on his waistcoat, and looking towards the father and son with a smooth smile—"Gentlemen, I appeal to you—really, gentlemen—consider, I beg of you. I am of the law. I am styled 'gentleman' by Act of Parliament. I maintain the title by the annual payment of twelve pound sterling for a certificate. I am not one of your players of music, stage actors, writers of books, or painters of pictures, who assume a station that the laws of their country don't recognize. I am none of your strollers or vagabonds. If any man brings his action against me, he must describe me as a gentleman, or his action is null and void. I appeal to you—is this quite respectful? Really, gentlemen—"

"Well, will you have the goodness to state your business then, Mr. Brass?" said the notary.

"Sir," rejoined Brass, "I will. Ah, Mr. Witherden! you little know the—but I will not be tempted to travel from the point, Sir. I believe the name of one of these gentlemen is Garland."

"Of both," said the notary.

"Indeed!" rejoined Brass, cringing excessively. "But I might have known that, from the uncommon likeness.

Extremely happy, I am sure, to have the honor of an introduction to two such gentlemen, although the occasion is a most painful one. One of you gentlemen has a servant called Kit ? "

" Both," replied the notary.

" Two Kits ? " said Brass smiling. " Dear me ! "

" One Kit, Sir," returned Mr. Witherden angrily, " who is employed by both gentlemen. What of him ? "

" This of him, Sir," rejoined Brass, dropping his voice impressively. " That young man, Sir, that I have felt unbounded and unlimited confidence in, and always behaved to as if he was my equal—that young man has this morning committed a robbery in my office, and been taken almost in the fact."

" This must be some falsehood ! " cried the notary.

" It is not possible," said Mr. Abel.

" I'll not believe one word of it," exclaimed the old gentleman.

Mr. Brass looked mildly round upon them, and rejoined.

" Mr. Witherden, Sir, *your* words are actionable, and if I was a man of low and mean standing, who couldn't afford to be slandered, I should proceed for damages. Hows'ever, Sir, being what I am, I merely scorn such expressions. The honest warmth of the other gentleman I respect, and I am truly sorry to be the messenger of such unpleasant news. I shouldn't have put myself in this painful position, I assure you, but that the lad himself desired to be brought here in the first instance, and I yielded to his prayers. Mr. Chuckster, Sir, will you have the goodness to tap at the window for the constable that's waiting in the coach ? "

The three gentleman looked at each other with blank faces when these words were uttered, and Mr. Chuckster, doing as he was desired, and leaping off his stool with something of the excitement of an inspired prophet whose foretellings had in the fulness of time been realized, held the door open for the entrance of the wretched captive.

Such a scene as there was, when Kit came in, and bursting into the rude eloquence with which Truth at length inspired him, called Heaven to witness that he was innocent, and that how the property came to be found upon him he knew not ! Such a confusion of tongues, before the circumstances were related, and the proofs dis-closed! Such a dead silence when all was told, and his three friends exchanged looks of doubt and amazement!

"Is it not possible," said Mr. Witherden, after a long pause, "that this note may have found its way into the hat by some accident,—such as the removal of papers on the desk, for instance?"

But this was clearly shown to be quite impossible. Mr. Swiveller, though an unwilling witness, could not help proving to demonstration, from the position in which it was found, that it must have been designedly secreted.

"It's very distressing," said Brass, "immensely dis-tressing, I am sure. When he comes to be tried, I shall be very happy to recommend him to mercy on account of his previous good character. I did lose money before, certainly, but it doesn't quite follow that he took it. The presumption's against him—strongly against him—but we're Christians, I hope?"

"I suppose," said the constable, looking round, "that no gentleman here can give evidence as to whether he's been flush of money of late. Do you happen to know, Sir?"

"He has had money from time to time, certainly," re-turned Mr. Garland, to whom the man had put the ques-tion. "But that, as he always told me, was given him by Mr. Brass himself."

"Yes, to be sure," said Kit eagerly. "You can bear me out in that, Sir?"

"Eh?" cried Brass, looking from face with an expres-sion of stupid amazement.

"The money you know, the half-crowns, that you gave me—from the lodger," said Kit.

"Oh dear me!" cried Brass, shaking his head and frowning heavily. "This is a bad case, I find; a very bad case indeed."

"What! Did you give him no money on account of anybody, Sir?" asked Mr. Garland, with great anxiety.

"*I* give him money, Sir!" returned Sampson. "Oh, come you know, this is too barefaced. Constable, my good fellow, we had better be going."

"What!" shrieked Kit. "Does he deny that he did? ask him, somebody, pray. Ask him to tell you whether he did or not!"

" Did you, Sir?" asked the notary.

"I tell you what, gentlemen," replied Brass, in a very grave manner, "he'll not serve his case this way, and really, if you feel any interest in him, you had better advise him to go upon some other tack. Did I, Sir? Of course I never did."

"Gentlemen," cried Kit, on whom a light broke suddenly, "Master, Mr. Abel, Mr. Witherden, every one of you—he did it! What I have done to offend him I don't know, but this is a plot to ruin me. Mind, gentlemen, it's a plot, and whatever comes of it, I will say with my dying breath that he put that note in my hat himself! Look at him, gentlemen! see how he changes color. Which of us looks the guilty person—he, or I?"

"You hear him, gentlemen?" said Brass, smiling, "you hear him. Now, does this case strike you as assuming rather a black complexion, or does it not? Is it at all a treacherous case, do you think, or is it one of mere ordinary guilt? Perhaps, gentlemen, if he had not said this in your presence and I had reported it, you'd have held this to be impossible likewise, eh?"

With such pacific and bantering remarks did Mr. Brass refute the foul aspersion on his character; but the virtuous Sarah, moved by stronger feelings, and having at heart, perhaps, a more jealous regard for the honor of her family, flew from her brother's side, without any previous intimation of her design, and darted at the prisoner with the utmost fury. It would undoubtedly have gone hard with Kit's face, but that the wary constable, foreseeing her design, drew him aside at the critical moment, and thus placed Mr. Chuckster in circumstances of some jeopardy; for that gentleman happening to be next the object of Miss Brass's wrath; and rage being, like Love and Fortune, blind; was pounced upon by the fair enslaver, and had a false collar plucked up by the roots, and his hair very much dishevelled, before the exertions of the company could make her sensible of her mistake.

The constable, taking warning by this desperate attack, and thinking perhaps that it would be more satisfactory to the ends of justice if the prisoner was taken before a magistrate, whole, rather than in small pieces, led him back to the hackney-coach without more ado, and further insisted on Miss Brass becoming an outside passenger;

to which proposal the charming creature, after a little angry discussion, yielded her consent; and so took her brother Sampson's place upon the box: Mr. Brass with some reluctance agreeing to occupy her seat inside. These arrangements perfected, they drove to the justice-room with all speed, followed by the notary and his two friends in another coach.   Mr. Chuckster alone was left behind—greatly to his indignation; for he held the evidence he could have given, relative to Kit's returning to work out the shilling, to be so very material as bearing upon his hypocritical and designing character, that he considered its suppression little better than a compromise of felony.

At the justice-room, they found the single gentleman, who had gone straight there, and was expecting them with desperate impatience.   But not fifty single gentlemen rolled into one could have helped poor Kit, who in half an hour afterwards was committed for trial, and was assured by a friendly officer on his way to prison that there was no occasion to be cast down, for the sessions would soon be on, and he would in all likelihood get his little affair disposed of, and be comfortably transported, in less than a fortnight.

CHAPTER THE SIXTY-FIRST.

LET moralists and philosophers say what they may, it is very questionable whether a guilty man would have felt half as much misery that night, as Kit did, being innocent.   The world, being in the constant commission of vast quantities of injustice, is a little too apt to comfort itself with the idea that if the victim of its falsehood and malice have a clear conscience, he cannot fail to be sustained under his trials, and somehow or other to come right at last; "in which case," say they who have hunted him down, " —though we certainly don't expect it—nobody will be better pleased than we."   Whereas, the world would do well to reflect, that injustice is in itself, to every generous and properly constituted mind, an injury, of all others the most insufferable, the most torturing, and the most hard to bear; and that many clear consciences have gone to their account elsewhere, and many sound hearts have broken, because of this very reason ; the knowledge of their own deserts only aggravating their sufferings, and rendering them the less endurable.

The world, however, was not in fault in Kit's case. But Kit was innocent; and knowing this, and feeling that his best friends deemed him guilty—that Mr. and Mrs. Garland would look upon him as a monster of ingratitude—that Barbara would associate him with all that was bad and criminal—that the pony would consider himself forsaken—and that even his own mother might perhaps yield to the strong appearances against him, and believe him to be the wretch he seemed—knowing and feeling all this, he experienced at first an agony of mind which no words can describe, and walked up and down the little cell in which he was locked up for the night, almost beside himself with grief.

Even when the violence of these emotions had in some degree subsided, and he was beginning to grow more calm, there came into his mind a new thought, the anguish of which was scarcely less. The child—the bright star of the simple fellow's life—she, who always came back upon him like a beautiful dream,—who had made the poorest part of his existence, the happiest and best —who had ever been so gentle, and considerate, and good —if she were ever to hear of this, what would she think ! As this idea occurred to him, the walls of the prison seemed to melt away, and the old place to reveal itself in their stead, as it was wont to be on winter nights—the fireside, the little supper-table, the old man's hat and coat, and stick—the half-opened door, leading to her little room—they were all there. And Nell herself was there, and he—both laughing heartily as they had often done— and when he had got as far as this, Kit could go no farther, but flung himself upon his poor bedstead and wept.

It was a long night, which seemed as though it would have no end ; but he slept too, and dreamed—always of being at liberty, and roving about, now with one person and now with another, but ever with a vague dread of being recalled to prison ; not that prison, but one which was in itself a dim idea, not of a place, but of a care and sorrow : of something oppressive and always present, and yet impossible to define. At last the morning dawned, and there was the jail itself—cold, black, and dreary, and very real indeed.

He was left to himself, however, and there was comfort in that. He had liberty to walk in a small paved yard at a certain hour, and learnt from the turnkey, who came to unlock his cell and show him where to wash, that there was a regular time for visiting, every day, and that if any of his friends came to see him, he would be fetched down to the gate. When he had given him this information, and a tin porringer containing his breakfast, the man locked him up again ; and went clattering along the stone passage, opening and shutting a great many other doors, and raising numberless loud echoes which resounded through the building for a long time, as if they were in prison too, and unable to get out.

This turnkey had given him to understand that he was lodged, like some few others in the jail, apart from the mass of prisoners ; because he was not supposed to be utterly depraved and irreclaimable, and had never occupied apartments in that mansion before. Kit was thankful for this indulgence, and sat reading the Church Catechism very attentively (though he had known it by heart from a little child), until he heard the key in the lock, and the man entered again.

" Now then," he said, " come on ! "

" Where to, Sir ? " asked Kit.

The man contented himself by briefly replying " Wisitors ; " and taking him by the arm in exactly the same manner as the constable had done the day before, led him through several winding ways and strong gates into a passage, where he placed him at a grating, and turned upon his heel. Beyond this grating, at the distance of about four or five feet, was another exactly like it. In the space between, sat a turnkey reading a newspaper ; and outside the further railing, Kit saw, with a palpitating heart, his mother with the baby in her arms ; Barbara's mother with her never-failing umbrella ; and poor little Jacob, staring in with all his might, as though he were looking for the bird, or the wild beast, and thought the men were mere accidents with whom the bars could have no possible concern.

But directly little Jacob saw his brother, and, thrusting his arms between the rails to hug him, found that he came no nearer, but still stood afar off with his head resting on the arm by which he held to one of the bars, he began to cry most piteously; whereupon, Kit's mother and Barbara's mother, who had restrained themselves as much as possible, burst out sobbing and weeping afresh. Poor Kit could not help joining them, and not one of them could speak a word.

During this melancholy pause, the turnkey read his

newspaper with a waggish look (he had evidently got among the facetious paragraphs) until, happening to take his eyes off it for an instant as if to get by dint of contemplation at the very marrow of some joke of a deeper sort than the rest, it appeared to occur to him for the first time that somebody was crying.

"Now, ladies, ladies," he said, looking round with surprise, "I'd advise you not to waste time like this. It's allowanced here, you know. You mustn't let that child make that noise either. It's against all rules."

"I'm his poor mother, Sir," sobbed Mrs. Nubbles, curt-seying humbly, "and this is his brother, Sir. Oh dear me, dear me!"

"Well!" replied the turnkey, folding the paper on his knee, so as to get with greater convenience at the top of the next column. "It can't be helped, you know. He ain't the only one in the same fix. You mustn't make a noise about it!"

With that, he went on reading. The man was not un-naturally cruel or hard-hearted. He had come to look upon felony as a kind of disorder, like the scarlet fever or erysipelas: some people had it—some hadn't—just as it might be.

"Oh! my darling Kit—" said his mother, whom Bar-bara's mother had charitably relieved of the baby—"that I should see my poor boy here!"

"You don't believe that I did what they accuse me of, mother dear?" cried Kit, in a choking voice.

"*I* believe it!" exclaimed the poor woman, "*I* that never knew you tell a lie, or do a bad action from your cradle—that have never had a moment's sorrow on your account, except it was for the poor meals that you have taken with such good-humor and content, that I forgot how little there was when I thought how kind and thoughtful you were, though you were but a child!—*I* believe it of the son that's been a comfort to me from the hour of his birth to this time, and that I never laid down one night in anger with! *I* believe it of you, Kit!—"

"Why then, thank God!" said Kit, clutching the bars with an earnestness that shook them, "and I can bear it, mother. Come what may, I shall always have one drop of happiness in my heart when I think that you said that."

At this the poor woman fell a-crying again, and Bar-bara's mother too. And little Jacob, whose disjointed thoughts had by this time resolved themselves into a pretty distinct impression that Kit couldn't go out for a walk if he wanted, and that there were no birds, lions, tigers or other natural curiosities behind those bars—nothing indeed, but a caged brother—added his tears to theirs with as little noise as possible.

Kit's mother, drying her eyes (and moistening them, poor soul, more than she dried them), now took from the ground a small basket, and submissively addressed herself to the turnkey, saying, would he please to listen to her for a minute? The turnkey, being in the very crisis and passion of a joke, mentioned to her with his hand to keep silent one minute longer, for her life. Nor did he remove his hand into its former posture, but kept it in the same warning attitude until he had finished the paragraph, when he paused for a few seconds, with a smile upon his face, as who should say "this editor is a comical blade—a funny dog," and then asked her what she wanted.

"I have brought him a little something to eat," said the good woman. "If you please, Sir, might he have it?"

"Yes,—he may have it. There's no rule against that. Give it to me when you go, and I'll take care he has it."

"No, but if you please, Sir—don't be angry with me, Sir—I am his mother, and you had a mother once—if I might only see him eat a little bit, I should go away so much more satisfied that he was all comfortable."

And again the tears of Kit's mother burst forth, and of Barbara's mother, and of little Jacob. As to the baby, it was crowing and laughing with all its might—under the idea, apparently, that the whole scene had been invented and got up for its particular satisfaction.

The turnkey looked as if he thought the request a strange one and rather out of the common way, but nevertheless he laid down his paper, and coming round to where Kit's mother stood, took the basket from her, and after inspecting its contents, handed it to Kit, and went back to his place. It may be easily conceived that the prisoner had no great appetite, but he sat down upon the ground, and ate as hard as he could, while, at every morsel he put into his mouth, his mother sobbed and wept afresh, though with a softened grief that bespoke the satisfaction the sight afforded her.

While he was thus engaged, Kit made some anxious inquiries about his employers, and whether they had expressed any opinion about him; but all he could learn was that Mr. Abel had himself broken the intelligence to his mother with great kindness and delicacy late on the previous night, but had himself expressed no opinion of his innocence or guilt. Kit was on the point of mustering

courage to ask Barbara's mother about Barbara, when
the turnkey who had conducted him re-appeared, a
second turnkey appeared behind his visitors, and the
third turnkey with the newspaper cried "Time's up!"—
adding in the same breath "Now for the next party!"
and then plunging deep into his newspaper again. Kit
was taken off in an instant, with a blessing from his
mother, and a scream from little Jacob, ringing in his
ears. As he was crossing the next yard with the basket
in his hand, under the guidance of his former conductor,
another officer called to them to stop, and came up with
a pint-pot of porter in his hand.

"This is Christopher Nubbles, isn't it, that come in
last night for felony?" said the man.

His comrade replied that this was the chicken in question.

"Then here's your beer," said the other man to Christopher. "What are you looking at? There ain't a discharge in it."

"I beg your pardon," said Kit. "Who sent it me?"

"Why, your friend," replied the man. "You're to
have it every day, he says. And so you will, if he pays
for it."

"My friend!" repeated Kit.

"You're all abroad, seemingly," returned the other
man. "There's his letter. Take hold!"

Kit took it, and when he was locked up again, read as
follows.

"Drink of this cup. You'll find there's a spell in its
every drop 'gainst the ills of mortality. Talk of the
cordial that sparkled for Helen! *Her* cup was a fiction,
but this is reality (Barclay and Co.'s). If they ever send
it in a flat state, complain to the Governor. Yours.
R. S."

"R. S.!" said Kit, after some consideration. "It must
be Mr. Richard Swiveller. Well, it's very kind of him,
and I thank him heartily."

CHAPTER THE SIXTY-SECOND.

.A faint light, twinkling from the window of the counting-house on Quilp's wharf, and looking inflamed and red
through the night-fog, as though it suffered from it like
an eye, forewarned Mr. Sampson Brass, as he approached
the wooden cabin with a cautious step, that the excellent
proprietor, his esteemed client, was inside, and probably
waiting with his accustomed patience and sweetness of
temper the fulfilment of the appointment which now
brought Mr. Brass within his fair domain.

"A treacherous place to pick one's steps in of a dark night
muttered," Sampson, as he stumbled for the twentieth
time over some stray lumber, and limped in pain. "I
believe that boy strews the ground differently every day,
on purpose to bruise and maim one; unless his master
does it with his own hands, which is more than likely. I
hate to come to this place without Sally. She's more
protection than a dozen men."

As he paid this compliment to the merit of the absent
charmer, Mr. Brass came to a halt; looking doubtfully
towards the light, and over his shoulder.

"What's he about, I wonder?" murmured the lawyer,
standing on tiptoe and endeavoring to obtain a glimpse of
what was pasing inside, which at that distance was impossible—" drinking, I suppose,—making himself more
fiery and furious, and heating his malice and mischiev-
ousness till they boil. I'm always afraid to come here by
myself, when his account's a pretty large one. I don't
believe he'd mind throttling me and dropping me softly
into the river when the tide was at its strongest, any
more than he'd mind killing a rat—indeed I don't know
whether he wouldn't consider it a pleasant joke. Hark!
Now he's singing!"

Mr. Quilp was certainly entertaining himself with
vocal exercise, but it was rather a kind of chant than a
song; being a monotonous repetition of one sentence in
a very rapid manner, with a long stress upon the last
word, which he swelled into a dismal roar. Nor did the
burden of this performance bear any reference to love, or

war, or wine, or loyalty, or any other, the standard topics of song, but to a subject not often set to music or generally known in ballads; the words being these:—" The worthy magistrate, after remarking that the prisoner would find some difficulty in persuading a jury to believe his tale, committed him to take his trial at the approaching sessions; and directed the customary recognizances to be entered into for the pros-e-cu-tion."

Every time he came to this concluding word, and had exhausted all possible stress upon it, Quilp burst into a shriek of laughter, and began again.

"He's dreadfully imprudent," muttered Brass, after he had listened to two or three repetitions of the chant. "Horribly imprudent. I wish he was dumb. I wish he was deaf. I wish he was blind. Hang him," cried Brass, as the chant began again, "I wish he was dead!"

Giving utterance to these friendly aspirations in behalf of his client, Mr. Sampson composed his face into its usual state of smoothness, and waiting until the shriek came again and was dying away, went up to the wooden house, and knocked at the door.

"Come in!" cried the dwarf.

"How do you do to-night, Sir?" said Sampson, peeping in. "Ha ha ha! How do you do, Sir? Oh dear me, how very whimsical! Amazingly whimsical to be sure!"

"Come in, you fool!" returned the dwarf, "and don't stand there shaking your head and showing your teeth. Come in, you false witness, you perjurer, you suborner of evidence, come in!"

"He has the richest humor!" cried Brass, shutting the door behind him; "the most amazing vein of comicality! But isn't it *rather* injudicious, Sir—?"

"What?" demanded Quilp, "What, Judas?"

"Judas!" cried Brass. "He has such extraordinary spirits! His humor is so extremely playful! Judas! Oh yes—dear me, how very good! Ha ha ha!"

All this time, Sampson was rubbing his hands, and staring, with ludicrous surprise and dismay, at a great, goggle-eyed, blunt-nosed figurehead of some old ship, which was reared up against the wall in a corner near the stove, looking like a goblin or hideous idol whom the dwarf worshipped. A mass of timber on its head, carved into the dim and distant semblance of a cocked hat, to-

gether with a representation of a star on the left breast
and epaulettes on the shoulders, denoted that it was intended for the effigy of some famous admiral; but, without those helps, any observer might have supposed it the
authentic portrait of a distinguished merman, or great
sea-monster. Being originally much too large for the
apartment which it was now employed to decorate, it had
been sawn short off at the waist. Even in this state it
reached from floor to ceiling; and thrusting itself forward with that excessively wide-awake aspect, and air of
somewhat obtrusive politeness, by which figure-heads are
usually characterized, seemed to reduce everything else
to mere pigmy proportions.

"Do you know it?" said the dwarf, watching Sampson's eyes. "Do you see the likeness?"

"Eh?" said Brass, holding his head on one side, and
throwing it a little back, as connoisseurs do. "Now I
look at it again, I fancy I see a—yes, there certainly is
something in the smile that reminds me of—and yet upon
my word I—"

Now, the fact was, that Sampson, having never seen
anything in the smallest degree resembling this substantial phantom, was much perplexed; being uncertain
whether Mr. Quilp considered it like himself, and had
therefore bought it for a family portrait; or whether he
was pleased to consider it as the likeness of some enemy.
He was not very long in doubt; for, while he was surveying it with that knowing look which people assume when
they are contemplating for the first time portraits which
they ought to recognize but don't, the dwarf threw down
the newspaper from which he had been chanting the
words already quoted, and seizing a rusty iron bar, which
he used in lieu of poker, dealt the figure such a stroke on
the nose that it rocked again.

"Is it like Kit—is it his picture, his image, his very
self?" cried the dwarf, aiming a shower of blows at the
insensible countenance, and covering it with deep dimples.
"Is it the exact model and counterpart of the dog—is it—
is it—is it?" And with every repetition of the question,
he battered the great image until the perspiration
streamed down his face with the violence of the exercise.

Although this might have been a very comical thing to
look at from a secure gallery, as a bull-fight is found to

be a comfortable spectacle by those who are not in the
arena, and a house on fire is better than a play to people
who don't live near it, there was something in the earnestness of Mr. Quilp's manner which made his legal adviser feel that the counting-house was a little too small,
and a great deal too lonely, for the due enjoyment of these
humors. Therefore he stood as far off as he could while
the dwarf was thus engaged; whimpering out but feeble
applause; and when he left off and sat down again from
pure exhaustion, approached with more obsequiousness
than ever.

"Excellent indeed!" cried Brass. "He he! Oh, very
good, Sir. You know," said Sampson, looking round as
if in appeal to the bruised admiral, "he's quite a remarkable man—quite!"

"Sit down," said the dwarf. "I bought the dog yesterday. I've been screwing gimlets into him, and sticking
forks in his eyes, and cutting my name on him. I mean
to burn him at last."

"Ha ha!" cried Brass. "Extremely entertaining, indeed!"

" Come here! " said Quilp, beckoning him to draw near.
" What's injudicious, hey ? "

"Nothing, Sir—nothing. Scarcely worth mentioning,
Sir; but I thought that song—admirably humorous in
itself you know—was perhaps rather—"

" Yes," said Quilp, " rather what ? "

" Just bordering, or as one may say remotely verging
upon the confines of injudiciousness perhaps, Sir," returned Brass, looking timidly at the dwarf's cunning
eyes, which were turned towards the fire and reflected
its red light.

" Why ? " inquired Quilp, without looking up.

" Why, you know, Sir," returned Brass, venturing to
be more familiar : "—the fact is, Sir, that any allusion to
these little combinings together of friends for objects in
themselves extremely laudable, but which the law terms
conspiracies, are—you take me, Sir ?—best kept snug and
among friends, you know."

" Eh ! " said Quilp, looking up with a perfectly vacant
countenance. " What do you mean ? "

" Cautious, exceedingly cautious, very right and proper ! " cried Brass, nodding his head. " Mum, Sir, even
here—my meaning, Sir, exactly."

" *Your* meaning exactly, you brazen scarecrow,—what's
your meaning ? " retorted Quilp. " Why do you talk to
me of combining together ? Do *I* combine ? Do I know
anything about your combinings ? "

"No no, Sir—certainly not; not by any means," returned Brass.

"If you so wink and nod at me," said the dwarf, looking
about him as if for his poker, " I'll spoil the expression
of your monkey's face, I will."

" Don't put yourself out of the way I beg, Sir." rejoined
Brass, checking himself with great alacrity. "You're
quite right, Sir, quite right. I shouldn't have mentioned
the subject, Sir. It's much better not to. You're quite
right, Sir. Let us change it, if you please. You were
asking, Sir, Sally told me, about our lodger. He has not
returned, Sir."

" No ? " said Quilp, heating some rum in a little saucepan, and watching it to prevent its boiling over. " Why
not ? "

" Why, Sir," returned Brass, " he—dear me, Mr. Quilp
Sir "—

"What's the matter?" said the dwarf, stopping his hand in the act of carrying the saucepan to his mouth.

"You have forgotten the water, Sir," said Brass. "And —excuse me, Sir—but it's burning hot."

Deigning no other that a practical answer to this remonstrance, Mr. Quilp raised the hot saucepan to his lips, and deliberately drank off all the spirit it contained, which might have been in quantity about half a pint, and had been but a moment before, when he took it off the fire, bubbling and hissing fiercely. Having swallowed this gentle stimulant, and shaken his fist at the admiral, he bade Mr Brass proceed.

"But first," said Quilp, with his accustomed grin, "have a drop yourself—a nice drop—a good, warm, fiery drop."

"Why, Sir," replied Brass, "if there was such a thing as a mouthful of water that could be got without trouble—"

"There's no such thing to be had here," cried the dwarf. "Water for lawyers! Melted lead and brimstone, you mean, nice hot blistering pitch and tar—that's the thing for them—eh, Brass, eh?"

"Ha ha ha!" laughed Mr. Brass. "Oh very biting! and yet it's like being tickled—there's a pleasure in it too, Sir!"

"Drink that," said the dwarf, who had by this time heated some more. "Toss it off, don't leave any heeltap, scorch your throat and be happy."

The wretched Sampson took a few short sips of the liquor, which immediately distilled itself into burning tears, and in that form came rolling down his cheeks into the pipkin again, turning the color of his face and eyelids to a deep red, and giving rise to a violent fit of coughing, in the midst of which he was still heard to declare, with the constancy of a martyr, that it was "beautiful indeed!" While he was yet in unspeakable agonies, the dwarf renewed their conversation.

"The lodger," said Quilp,—"what about him?"

"He is still, Sir," returned Brass, with intervals of coughing, "stopping with the Garland family. He has only been home once, Sir, since the day of the examination of that culprit. He informed Mr. Richard, Sir, that he couldn't bear the house after what had taken place; that he was wretched in it; and that he looked upon himself as being in a certain kind of way the cause of the occurrence. —A very excellent lodger, Sir. I hope we may not lose him."

"Yah!" cried the dwarf. "Never thinking of anybody but yourself—why don't you retrench then—scrape up, hoard, economize, eh?"

"Why, Sir," replied Brass, "upon my word I think Sarah's as good an economizer as any going. I do indeed, Mr. Quilp."

"Moisten your clay, wet the other eye, drink, man!" cried the dwarf. "You took a clerk to oblige me."

"Delighted, Sir, I am sure, at any time," replied Sampson. "Yes, Sir, I did."

"Then, now you may discharge him," said Quilp. "There's a means of retrenchment for you at once."

"Discharge Mr. Richard, Sir?" cried Brass.

"Have you more than one clerk, you parrot, that you ask the question? Yes."

"Upon my word, Sir," said Brass, "I wasn't prepared for this—"

"How could you be?" sneered the dwarf, "when *I* wasn't? How often am I to tell you that I brought him to you that I might always have my eye on him and know where he was—and that I had a plot, a scheme, a little quiet piece of enjoyment afoot, of which the very cream and essence was, that this old man and grandchild who have sunk underground I think) should be, while he and his precious friend believed them rich, in reality as poor as frozen rats!"

"I quite understood that, Sir," rejoined Brass. "Thoroughly."

"Well, Sir," retorted Quilp, "and do you understand now, that they're *not* poor—that they can't be, if they have such men as your lodger searching for them and scouring the country far and wide?"

"Of course I do, Sir," said Sampson.

"Of course you do," retorted the dwarf, viciously snapping at his words. "Of course do you understand then, that it's no matter what comes of this fellow? of course do you understand that for any other purpose he's no man for me, nor for you?"

"I have frequently said to Sarah, Sir," returned Brass,

"that he was of no use at all in the business. You can't put any confidence in him, Sir. If you'll believe me I've found that fellow, in the commonest little matters of the office that have been trusted to him, blurting out the truth, though expressly cautioned. The aggravation of that chap, Sir, has exceeded anything you can imagine, it has indeed. Nothing but the respect and obligation I owe to you, Sir—"

As it was plain that Sampson was bent on a complimentary harangue, unless he received a timely interruption, Mr. Quilp politely tapped him on the crown of his head with the little saucepan, and requested that he would be so obliging as to hold his peace.

"Practical, Sir, practical," said Brass, rubbing the place and smiling; "but still extremely pleasant—immensely so!"

"Hearken to me, will you?" returned Quilp, "or I'll be a little more pleasant, presently. There's no chance of his comrade and friend returning. The scamp has been obliged to fly, as I learn, for some knavery, and has found his way abroad. Let him rot there."

"Certainly, Sir. Quite proper.—Forcible!" cried Brass, glancing at the admiral again, as if he made a third in company. "Extremely forcible!"

"I hate him," said Quilp between his teeth, "and have always hated him, for family reasons. Besides, he was an intractable ruffian; otherwise *he* would have been of use. This fellow is pigeon-hearted, and light-headed. I don't want him any longer. Let him hang or drown—starve—go to the devil."

"By all means, Sir," returned Brass. "When would you wish him, Sir, to—ha, ha!—to make that little excursion?"

"When this trial's over," said Quilp. "As soon as that's ended, send him about his business."

"It shall be done, Sir," returned Brass; "by all means. It will be rather a blow to Sarah, Sir, but she has all her feelings under control. Ah, Mr. Quilp, I often think, Sir, if it had only pleased Providence to bring you and Sarah together in earlier life, what blessed results would have flowed from such a union! You never saw our dear father, Sir?—A charming gentleman. Sarah was his pride and joy, Sir. He would have closed his eyes in bliss, would

Foxey, Mr. Quilp, if he could have found her such a partner. You esteem her, Sir?"

"I love her," croaked the dwarf.

"You're very good, Sir," returned Brass, "I am sure. Is there any other order, Sir, that I can take a note of, besides this little matter of Mr. Richard?"

"None," replied the dwarf, seizing the saucepan. "Let us drink the lovely Sarah."

"If we could do it in something, Sir, that wasn't quite boiling," suggested Brass humbly, "perhaps it would be better. I think it will be more agreeable to her feelings, when she comes to hear from me of the honor you have done her, if she learns it was in liquor rather cooler than the last, Sir."

But to these remonstrances Mr. Quilp turned a deaf ear. Sampson Brass, who was by this time anything but sober, being compelled to take further draughts of the same strong bowl, found that, instead of at all contributing to his recovery, they had the novel effect of making the counting-house spin round and round with extreme velocity, and causing the floor and ceiling to heave in a very distressing manner. After a brief stupor, he awoke to a consciousness of being partly under the table and partly under the grate. This position not being the most comfortable one he could have chosen for himself, he managed to stagger to his feet, and, holding on by the admiral, looked round for his host.

Mr. Brass's first impression was, that his host was gone and had left him there alone—perhaps locked him in for the night. A strong smell of tobacco, however, suggested a new train of ideas, he looked upwards, and saw that the dwarf was smoking in his hammock.

"Good-bye, Sir," cried Brass faintly. "Good-bye, Sir."

"Won't you stop all night?" said the dwarf, peeping out. "Do stop all night."

"I couldn't indeed, Sir," replied Brass, who was almost dead from nausea and the closeness of the room. "If you'd have the goodness to show me a light, so that I may see my way across the yard, Sir—"

Quilp was out in an instant; not with his legs first, or his head first, or his arms first, but bodily—altogether.

"To be sure," he said, taking up a lantern, which was now the only light in the place. "Be careful how you go, my dear friend. Be sure to pick your way among the timber, for all the rusty nails are upwards. There's a dog in the lane. He bit a man last night, and a woman the night before, and last Tuesday he killed a child—but that was in play. Don't go too near him."

" Which side of the road is he, Sir ?" asked Brass, in great dismay.

He lives on the right hand," said Quilp, " but sometimes he hides on the left, ready for a spring. He's uncertain in that respect. Mind you take care of yourself. I'll never forgive you if you don't. There's the light out—never mind—you know the way—straight on !"

Quilp had slyly shaded the light by holding it against his breast, and now stood chuckling and shaking from head to foot in a rapture of delight, as he heard the lawyer stumbling up the yard, and now and then falling heavily down. At length, however, he got quit of the place, and was out of hearing.

The dwarf shut himself up again, and sprang once more into his hammock.

CHAPTER THE SIXTY-THIRD.

THE professional gentleman who had given Kit that consolatory piece of information relative to the settlement of his trifle of business at the Old Bailey, and the probability of its being very soon disposed of, turned out to be quite correct in his prognostications. In eight days' time, the sessions commenced. In one day afterwards, the Grand Jury found a True Bill against Christoper Nubbles for felony ; and in two days from that finding, the aforesaid Christopher Nubbles was called upon to plead Guilty or Not Guilty to an Indictment for that he the said Christopher did feloniously abstract and steal from the dwelling-house and office of one Sampson Brass, gentleman, one Bank Note for Five Pounds issued by the Governor and Company of the Bank of England ; in contravention of the Statutes in that case made and provided, and against the peace of our Sovereign Lord the King, his crown, and dignity.

To this indictment, Christopher Nubbles, in a low and

trembling voice, pleaded Not Guilty : and here let those
who are in the habit of forming hasty judgments from
appearances, and who would have had Christopher, if innocent, speak out very strong and loud, observe, that
confinement and anxiety will subdue the stoutest hearts;
and that to one who has been close shut up, though it be
only for ten or eleven days, seeing but stone walls and a
very few stony faces, the sudden entrance into a great
hall filled with life is a rather disconcerting and startling
circumstance. To this it must be added, that life in a
wig is to a large class of people much more terrifying and
impressive than life with its own head of hair; and if,
in addition of these considerations, there be further taken
into account Kit's natural emotion on seeing the two Mr.
Garlands and the little Notary looking on with pale and
anxious faces, it will perhaps seem matter of no very
great wonder that he should have been rather out of sorts,
and unable to make himself exactly at home.

Although he had never seen either of the Mr. Garlands,
or Mr. Witherden, since the time of his arrest, he had
been given to understand that they had employed counsel for him. Therefore, when one of the gentlemen in
wigs got up and said " I am for the prisoner, my Lord,"
Kit made him a bow; and when another gentleman in a
wig got up and said "And I'm against him, my Lord,"
Kit trembled very much, and bowed to him too. And
didn't he hope in his own heart that his gentleman was
a match for the other gentleman, and would make him
ashamed of himself in no time!

The gentleman who was against him had to speak first,
and being in dreadfully good spirits (for he had, in the
last trial, very nearly procured the acquittal of a young
gentleman who had had the misfortune to murder his
father) he spoke up you may be sure; telling the Jury
that if they acquitted this prisoner they must expect to
suffer no less pangs and agonies than he had told the
other Jury they would certainly undergo if they convicted
that prisoner. And when he had told them all about
the case, and that he had never known a worse case, he
stopped a little while, like a man who had something
terrible to tell them, and then said that he understood
an attempt would be made by his learned friend (and
here he looked sideways at Kit's gentleman) to impeach

the testimony of those immaculate witnesses whom he should call before them; but he did hope and trust that his learned friend would have a greater respect and veneration for the character of the prosecutor; than whom, as he well knew, there did not exist, and never had existed, a more honorable member of that most honorable profession to which he was attached. And then he said, did the Jury know Bevis Marks? And if they did know Bevis Marks (as he trusted, for their own characters, they did) did they know the historical and elevating associations connected with that most remarkable spot? Did they believe that a man like Brass could reside in a place like Bevis Marks, and not be a virtuous and most upright character? And when he had said a great deal to them on this point, he remembered that it was an insult to their understandings to make any remarks on what they must have felt so strongly without him, and therefore called Sampson Brass into the witness-box, straightway.

Then up comes Mr. Brass, very brisk and fresh; and, having bowed to the judge, like a man who has had the pleasure of seeing him before and who hopes he has been pretty well since their last meeting, folds his arms, and looks at his gentleman as much as to say "Here I am—full of evidence—Tap me!" And the gentleman does tap him presently, and with great discretion too; drawing off the evidence by little and little, and making it run quite clear and bright in the eyes of all present. Then Kit's gentleman takes him in hand, but can make nothing of him; and after a great many very long questions and very short answers, Mr. Sampson Brass goes down in glory.

To him succeeds Sarah, who in like manner is easy to be managed by Mr. Brass's gentleman, but very obdurate to Kit's. In short, Kit's gentleman can get nothing out of her but a repetition of what she has said before (only a little stronger this time, as against his client), and therefore lets her go, in some confusion. Then Mr. Brass's gentleman calls Richard Swiveller, and Richard Swiveller appears accordingly.

Now, Mr. Brass's gentleman has it whispered in his ear that this witness is disposed to be friendly to the prisoner—which, to say the truth, he is rather glad to

hear, as his strength is considered to lie in what is familiarly termed badgering. Wherefore, he begins by re-
questing the officer to be quite sure that this witness
kisses the book, and then goes to work at him, tooth and
nail.

"Mr. Swiveller," says this gentleman to Dick, when
he has told his tale with evident reluctance and a desire
to make the best of it : "Pray, Sir, where did you dine
yesterday ? "—" Where did I dine yesterday ? "—" Ay,
Sir, where did you dine yesterday—was it near here, Sir ? "
—" Oh to be sure—yes—just over the way."—" To be
sure. Yes. Just over the way," repeats Mr. Brass's
gentleman, with a glance at the Court—" Alone, Sir ? "—
"I beg your pardon," says Mr. Swiveller, who has not
caught the question—" *Alone*, Sir ? " repeats Mr. Brass's
gentleman in a voice of thunder, " did you dine alone?
Did you treat anybody, Sir ? Come ! "—" Oh yes, to be
sure—yes, I did," says Mr. Swiveller with a smile.
" Have the goodness to banish a levity, Sir, which is very
ill-suited to the place in which you stand (though perhaps you have reason to be thankful that it's only that
place)," says Mr. Brass's gentleman, with a nod of the
head insinuating that the dock is Mr. Swiveller's legitimate sphere of action; "and attend to me. You were
waiting about here yesterday in expectation that this
trial was coming on. You dined over the way. You
treated somebody. Now, was that somebody brother
to the prisoner at the bar ? "—Mr. Swiveller is proceeding to explain—" Yes or No, Sir," cries Mr. Brass's gentleman—" But will you allow me—"—" Yes or No, Sir,"—
" Yes it was, but—"—" Yes it was," cries the gentleman, taking him up short—" And a very pretty witness
you are ! "

Down sits Mr. Brass's gentleman. Kit's gentleman,
not knowing how the matter really stands, is afraid to
pursue the subject. Richard Swiveller retires abashed.
Judge, jury, and spectators have visions of his lounging
about with an ill-looking, large-whiskered, dissolute
young fellow of six feet high. The reality is, little Jacob,
with the calves of his legs exposed to the open air, and
himself tied up in a shawl. Nobody knows the truth,
everybody believes a falsehood—and all because of the
ingenuity of Mr. Brass's gentleman!

Then come the witnesses to character, and here Mr
Brass's gentleman shines again. It turns out that Mr.
Garland has had no character with Kit, no recommenda-
tion of him but from his own mother, and that he was
suddenly dismissed by his former master for unknown
reasons. " Really, Mr. Garland," says Mr. Brass's gentleman, " for a person who has arrived at your time of life,
you are, to say the least of it, singularly indiscreet, I
think." The Jury think so too, and find Kit guilty. He
is taken off, humbly protesting his innocence. The spectators settle themselves in their places with renewed
attention, for there are several female witnesses to be

examined in the next case, and it has been rumored that
Mr. Brass's gentleman will make great fun in cross-examining them for the prisoner.

Kit's mother, poor woman, is waiting at the grate below
stairs, accompanied by Barbara's mother (who, honest
soul! never does anything but cry, and hold the baby),
and a sad interview ensues. The newspaper-reading
turnkey has told them all. He don't think it will be
transportation for life, because there's time to prove the
good character yet, and that is sure to serve him. He
wonders what he did it for. "He never did it!" cries

Kit's mother. "Well," says the turnkey, "I won't contradict you. It's all one now, whether he did or not."

Kit's mother can reach his hand through the bars, and clasps it—God, and those to whom he has given such tenderness, only know in how much agony. Kit bids her keep a good heart, and, under pretence of having the children lifted up to kiss him, prays Barbara's mother in a whisper to take her home.

"Some friend will rise up for us, mother," cries Kit, "I am sure. If not now, before long. My innocence will come out, mother, and I shall be brought back again; I feel confidence in that. You must teach little Jacob and the baby how all this was, for if they thought I had ever been dishonest, when they grow old enough to understand, it would break my heart to know it, if I was thousands of miles away.—Oh! is there no good gentleman here, who will take care of her!"

The hand slips out of his, for the poor creature sinks down upon the earth, insensible. Richard Swiveller comes hastily up, elbows the bystanders out of the way, takes her (after some trouble) in one arm after the manner of theatrical ravishers, and nodding to Kit, and commanding Barbara's mother to follow, for he has a coach waiting, bears her swiftly off.

Well; Richard took her home. And what astonishing absurdities in the way of quotation from song and poem he perpetrated on the road, no man knows. He took her home, and stayed till she was recovered; and, having no money to pay the coach, went back in state to Bevis Marks, bidding the driver (for it was Saturday night) wait at the door while he went in for "change."

"Mr. Richard, Sir," said Brass cheerfully, "Good-evening."

Monstrous as Kit's tale had appeared at first, Mr. Richard did, that night, half suspect his affable employer of some deep villainy. Perhaps it was but the misery he had just witnessed which gave his careless nature this impulse; but, be that as it may, it was very strong upon him, and he said in as few words as possible, what he wanted.

"Money!" cried Brass, taking out his purse. "Ha ha! To be sure, Mr. Richard, to be sure, Sir. All men

34

must live. You haven't change for a five-pound note, have you, Sir?"

"No," returned Dick, shortly.

"Oh!" said Brass, "here's the very sum. That saves trouble. You're very welcome I'm sure.—Mr. Richard, Sir—"

Dick, who had by this time reached the door, turned round.

"You needn't," said Brass, "trouble yourself to come back any more, Sir."

"Eh?"

"You see, Mr. Richard," said Brass, thrusting his hands in his pockets and rocking himself to and fro upon his stool, "the fact is, that a man of your abilities is lost, Sir, quite lost, in our dry and mouldy line. It's terrible drudgery—shocking. I should say now that the stage, or the—or the army, Mr. Richard—or something very superior in the license victualling way—was the kind of thing that would call out the genius of such a man as you. I hope you'll look in to see us now and then. Sally, Sir, will be delighted I'm sure. She's extremely sorry to lose you, Mr. Richard, but a sense of her duty to society reconciles her.—An amazing creature that, Sir! You'll find the money quite correct, I think. There's a cracked window, Sir, but I've not made any deduction on that account. Whenever we part with friends, Mr. Richard, let us part liberally. A delightful sentiment, Sir!"

To all these rambling observations, Mr. Swiveller answered not one word, but, returning for the aquatic jacket, rolled it into a tight round ball, looking steadily at Brass meanwhile as if he had some intention of bowling him down with it. He only took it under his arm, however, and marched out of the office in profound silence. Directly he had closed the door, he opened it, stared in again, for a few moments with the same portentous gravity; and nodding his head once, in a slow and ghost-like manner, vanished.

He paid the coachman and turned his back on Bevis Marks, big with great designs for the comforting of Kit's mother and the aid of Kit himself.

But the lives of gentlemen devoted to such pleasures as Richard Swiveller, are extremely precarious. The spiritual excitement of the last fortnight, working upon a

system affected in no slight degree by the spirituous excitement of some years, proved a little too much for him.
That very night, Mr. Richard was seized with an alarming illness, and in twenty-four hours was stricken with
a raging fever.

CHAPTER THE SIXTY-FOURTH.

TOSSING to and fro upon his hot, uneasy bed; tormented
by a fierce thirst which nothing could appease; unable to
find, in any change of posture, a moment's peace or ease;
and rambling ever through deserts of thought where
there was no resting-place, no sight or sound suggestive
of refreshment or repose, nothing but a dull eternal weariness, with no change but the restless shiftings of his miserable body, and the weary wanderings of his mind, constant still to one ever-present anxiety—to a sense of something left undone, of some fearful obstacle to be surmounted, of some carking care that would not be driven away,
and haunted the distempered brain, now in this form, now
in that—always shadowy and dim, but recognizable for
the same phantom in every shape it took, darkening
every vision like an evil conscience, and making slumber
horrible; in these slow tortures of his dread disease, the
unfortunate Richard lay wasting and consuming inch by
inch, until at last, when he seemed to fight and struggle
to rise up, and to be held down by devils, he sank into a
deep sleep, and dreamed no more.

He awoke; and, with a sensation of most blissful rest,
better than sleep itself, began gradually to remember
something of these sufferings, and to think what a long
night it had been, and whether he had not been delirious
twice or thrice. Happening in the midst of these cogita-
tions to raise his hand, he was astonished to find how
heavy it seemed, and yet how thin and light it really was.
Still he felt indifferent and happy; and having no curiosity to pursue the subject, remained in the same waking
slumber until his attention was attracted by a cough.
This made him doubt whether he had locked his door last
night, and feel a little surprised at having a companion
in the room. Still, he lacked energy to follow up this

train of thought; and unconsciously fell, in a luxury of repose, to staring at some green stripes upon the bed-furniture, and associating them strangely with patches of fresh turf, while the yellow ground between made gravel-walks, and so helped out a long perspective of trim gardens.

He was rambling in imagination upon these terraces, and had quite lost himself among them indeed, when he heard the cough once more. The walks shrank into stripes again at the sound; and raising himself a little in the bed, and holding the curtain open with one hand, he looked out.

The same room certainly, and still by candle-light; but with what unbounded astonishment did he see all those bottles, and basins, and articles of linen airing by the fire, and such-like furniture of a sick chamber—all very clean and neat, but all quite different from anything he had left there, when he went to bed! The atmosphere, too, filled with a cool smell of herbs and vinegar; the floor newly sprinkled; the—the what? The Marchioness? Yes; playing cribbage with herself at the table. There she sat, intent upon her game, coughing now and then in a subdued manner as if she feared to disturb him—shuffling the cards, cutting, dealing, playing, counting, pegging—going through all the mysteries of cribbage as though she had been in full practice from her cradle!

Mr. Swiveller contemplated these things for a short time, and suffering the curtain to fall into its former position, laid his head upon the pillow again.

"I'm dreaming," thought Richard, "that's clear. When I went to bed, my hands were not made of egg-shells; and now I can almost see through 'em. If this is not a dream, I have woke up by mistake in an Arabian Night, instead of a London one. But I have no doubt I'm asleep. Not the least."

Here the small servant had another cough.

"Very remarkable!" thought Mr. Swiveller. "I never dreamt such a real cough as that before. I don't know, indeed, that I ever dreamt either a cough or a sneeze. Perhaps it's part of the philosophy of dreams that one never does. There's another—and another—I say,—I'm dreaming rather fast!"

For the purpose of testing his real condition, Mr.

Swiveller, after some reflection, pinched himself in the arm.

"Queerer still!" he thought. "I came to bed rather plump than otherwise, and now there's nothing to lay hold of. I'll take another survey."

The result of this further inspection was, to convince Mr. Swiveller that the objects by which he was surrounded were real, and that he saw them, beyond all question, with his waking eyes.

"It's an Arabian Night, that's what it is," said Richard. "I'm in Damascus or Grand Cairo. The Marchioness is a Genie, and having had a wager with another Genie about who is the handsomest young man alive, and the worthiest to be the husband of the Princess of China, has brought me away, room and all, to compare us together. Perhaps," said Mr. Swiveller, turning languidly round upon his pillow, and looking on that side of his bed which was next the wall, "the Princess may be still—No, she's gone."

Not feeling quite satisfied with this explanation, as, even taking it to be the correct one, it still involved a little mystery and doubt, Mr. Swiveller raised the curtain again, determined to take the first favorable opportunity of addressing his companion. An occasion soon presented itself. The Marchioness dealt, turned up a knave, and omitted to take the usual advantage; upon which Mr. Swiveller called out as loud as he could—"Two for his heels!"

The Marchioness jumped up quickly, and clapped her hands. "Arabian Night, certainly," thought Mr. Swiveller; "they always clap their hands instead of ringing the bell. Now for the two thousand black slaves, with jars of jewels on their heads!"

It appeared, however, that she had only clapped her hands in joy; for directly afterwards she began to laugh, and then to cry; declaring, not in choice Arabic but in familiar English, that she was "so glad, she didn't know what to do."

"Marchioness," said Mr. Swiveller, thoughtfully, "be pleased to draw nearer. First of all, will you have the goodness to inform me where I shall find my voice; and secondly, what has become of my flesh?"

The Marchioness only shook her head mournfully, and

cried again ; whereupon Mr. Swiveller (being **very weak**) felt his own eyes affected likewise.

"I begin to infer, from your manner and these appearances, Marchioness,"—said Richard after a pause, and smiling with a trembling lip, "that I have been ill."

"You just have!" replied the small servant, wiping her eyes. "And haven't you been a talking nonsense!"

"Oh!" said Dick. "Very ill, Marchioness, have I been?"

"Dead, all but," replied the small servant. "I never thought you'd get better. Thank Heaven you have!"

Mr. Swiveller was silent for a long while. By and by, he began to talk again—inquiring how long he had been there.

"Three weeks to-morrow," replied the small servant.

"Three what?" said Dick.

"Weeks," returned the Marchioness emphatically ; "three long, slow weeks."

The bare thought of having been in such extremity caused Richard to fall into another silence, and to lie flat down again at his full length. The Marchioness, having arranged the bed-clothes more comfortably, and felt that his hands and forehead were quite cool—a discovery that filled her with delight—cried a little more, and then applied herself to getting tea ready, and making some thin dry toast.

While she was thus engaged, Mr. Swiveller looked on with a grateful heart, very much astonished to see how thoroughly at home she made herself, and attributing this attention, in its origin, to Sally Brass, whom, in his own mind, he could not thank enough. When the Marchioness had finished her toasting, she spread a clean cloth on a tray, and brought him some crisp slices and a great basin of weak tea, with which (she said) the doctor had left word he might refresh himself when he awoke. She propped him up with pillows, if not as skilfully as if she had been a professional nurse all her life, at least as tenderly ; and looked on with unutterable satisfaction while the patient—stopping every now and then to shake her by the hand—took his poor meal with an appetite and relish, which the greatest dainties of the earth, under any other circumstances, would have failed to provoke. Having cleared away, and disposed everything comfortably about him again, she sat down at the table to take her own tea.

"Marchioness," said Mr. Swiveller, "how's Sally!"

The small servant screwed her face into an expression of the very uttermost entanglement of slyness, and shook her head.

"What, haven't you seen her lately?" said Dick.

"Seen her!" cried the small servant. "Bless you, I've run away!"

Mr. Swiveller immediately laid himself down again quite flat, and so remained for about five minutes. By slow degrees he resumed his sitting posture after that lapse of time, and inquired:

"And where do you live, Marchioness?"

"Live!" cried the small servant. "Here!"

"Oh!" said Mr. Swiveller.

And with that he fell down flat again, as suddenly as if he had been shot. Thus he remained, motionless and bereft of speech, until she had finished her meal, put everything in its place, and swept the hearth; when he motioned her to bring a chair to the bedside, and being propped up again, opened a farther conversation.

"And so," said Dick, "you have run away?"

"Yes," said the Marchioness, "and they've been a tizing of me."

"Been—I beg your pardon," said Dick—"what have they been doing?"

"Been a tizing of me—tizing you know—in the news-papers," rejoined the Marchioness.

"Ay, ay," said Dick, "advertising?"

The small servant nodded and winked. Her eyes were so red with waking and crying, that the Tragic Muse might have winked with greater consistency. And so Dick felt.

"Tell me," said he, "how it was that you thought of coming here."

"Why, you see," returned the Marchioness, "when you was gone, I hadn't any friend at all, because the lodger he never come back, and I didn't know where either him or you was to be found, you know. But one morn-ing, when I was—"

"Was near a keyhole?" suggested Mr. Swiveller, observing that she faltered.

" Well then," said the small servant, nodding; " when I was near the office keyhole—as you see me through, you know—I heard somebody saying that she lived here, and was the lady whose house you lodged at, and that you was took very bad, and wouldn't nobody come and take care of you. Mr. Brass, he says, ' It's no business of mine;' and Miss Sally, she says, ' He's a funny chap, but it's no business of mine;' and the lady went away, and slammed the door to, when she went out, I can tell you. So I run away that night, and come here, and told 'em you was my brother, and they believed me, and I've been here ever since."

" This poor little Marchioness has been wearing herself to death! " cried Dick.

" No I haven't," she returned, " not a bit of it. Don't you mind about me. I like sitting up, and I've often had a sleep, bless you, in one of them chairs. But if you could have seen how you tried to jump out o' winder, and if you could have heard how you used to keep on singing and making speeches, you wouldn't have believed it—I'm so glad you're better, Mr. Liverer."

"Liverer indeed! " said Dick thoughtfully. " It's well I *am* a liverer. I strongly suspect I should have died, Marchioness, but for you."

At this point, Mr. Swiveller took the small servant's hand in his again, and being, as we have seen, but poorly, might in struggling to express his thanks have made his eyes as red as hers, but that she quickly changed the theme by making him lie down, and urging him to keep very quiet.

"The doctor," she told him, " said you was to be kept quite still, and there was to be no noise nor nothing. Now, take a rest, and then we'll talk again. I'll sit by you, you know. If you shut your eyes, perhaps you'll go to sleep. You'll be all the better for it if you do."

The Marchioness, in saying these words, brought a little table to the bedside, took her seat at it, and began to work away at the concoction of some cooling drink, with the address of a score of chemists. Richard Swiveller, being indeed fatigued, fell into a slumber, and waking in about half an hour, inquired what time it was.

"Just gone half after six," replied his small friend, helping him to sit up again.

"Marchioness," said Richard, passing his hand over his forehead and turning suddenly round, as though the subject but that moment flashed upon him, "what has become of Kit?"

He had been sentenced to transportation for a great many years, she said.

"Has he gone?" asked Dick—"his mother—how is she, —what has become of her?"

His nurse shook her head, and answered that she knew nothing about them.

"But, if I thought," said she, very slowly, "that you'd keep quiet, and not put yourself into another fever, I could tell you—but I won't now."

"Yes, do," said Dick. "It will amuse me."

"Oh! would it though!" rejoined the small servant, with a horrified look. "I know better than that. Wait till you're better and then I'll tell you."

Dick looked very earnestly at his little friend : and his eyes, being large and hollow from illness assisted the expression so much, that she was quite frightened, and besought him not to think any more about it. What had already fallen from her, however, had not only piqued his curiosity, but seriously alarmed him, wherefore he urged her to tell him the worst at once.

"Oh! there's no worst in it," said the small servant. "It hasn't anything to do with you."

"Has it anything to do with—is it anything you heard through chinks or keyholes—and that you were not intended to hear?" asked Dick, in a breathless state.

"Yes," replied the small servant.

"In—in Bevis Marks?" pursued Dick hastily. "Conversations between Brass and Sally?"

"Yes," cried the small servant again.

Richard Swiveller thrust his lank arm out of bed, and, gripping her by the wrist and drawing her close to him, bade her out with it, and freely too, or he would not answer for the consequences ; being wholly unable to endure that state of excitement and expectation. She, seeing that he was greatly agitated, and that the effects of postponing her revelation might be much more injurious than any that were likely to ensue from its being made at once, promised compliance, on condition that the patient kept himself perfectly quiet, and abstained from starting up or tossing about.

"But if you begin to do that," said the small servant, "I'll leave off. And so I tell you."

"You can't leave off till you have gone on," said Dick. "And do go on, there's a darling. Speak, sister, speak, Pretty Polly say—Oh tell me when, and tell me where, pray Marchioness, I beseech you!"

Unable to resist these fervent adjurations, which Richard Swiveller poured out as passionately as if they had been of the most solemn and tremendous nature, his companion spoke thus:

"Well! Before I run away, I used to sleep in the kitchen—where we played cards, you know. Miss Sally used to keep the key of the kitchen door in her pocket, and she always come down at night to take away the candle and rake out the fire. When she had done that, she left me to go to bed in the dark, locked the door on the outside, put the key in her pocket again, and kept me locked up till she come down in the morning—very early I can tell you—and let me out. I was terrible afraid of being kept like this, because if there was a fire, I thought they might forget me and only take care of themselves, you know. So whenever I see an old rusty key anywhere, I picked it up and tried if it would fit the door, and at last I found in the dust cellar a key that *did* fit it."

Here, Mr. Swiveller made a violent demonstration with his legs. But the small servant immediately pausing in her talk, he subsided again, and, pleading a momentary forgetfulness of their compact, entreated her to proceed.

"They kept me very short," said the small servant. "Oh! you can't think how short they kept me! So I used to come out at night after they'd gone to bed, and feel about in the dark for bits of biscuit, or sangwitches that you'd left in the office, or even pieces of orange peel to put into cold water and make believe it was wine. Did you ever taste orange peel and water?"

Mr. Swiveller replied that he had never tasted that ardent liquor; and once more urged his friend to resume the thread of her narrative.

"If you make believe very much, it's quite nice," said

the small servant; "but if you don't, you know, it seems as if it would bear a little more seasoning, certainly. Well, sometimes I used to come out after they'd gone to bed, and sometimes before, you know; and one or two nights before there was all that precious noise in the office—when the young man was took, I mean—I come upstairs while Mr. Brass and Miss Sally was a sittin' at the office fire; and I'll tell you the truth, that I come to listen again about the key of the safe."

Mr. Swiveller gathered up his knees so as to make a great cone of the bed-clothes, and conveyed into his countenance an expression of the utmost concern. But the small servant pausing, and holding up her finger, the cone gently disappeared, though the look of concern did not.

"There was him and her," said the small servant, "a sittin' by the fire, and talking softly together. Mr. Brass says to Miss Sally, 'Upon my word,' he says, 'it's a dangerous thing, and it might get us into a world of trouble, and I don't half like it.' She says—you know her way—she says, 'You're the chickenest-hearted, feeblest, faintest man I ever see, and I think,' she says, 'that I ought to have been the brother, and you the sister. Isn't Quilp,' she says, 'our principal support?' 'He certainly is,' says Mr. Brass. 'And an't we,' she says, 'constantly ruining somebody or other in the way of business?' 'We certainly are,' says Mr. Brass. 'Then does it signify,' she says, 'about ruining this Kit when Quilp desires it?' 'It certainly does not signify,' says Brass. Then, they whispered and laughed for a long time about there being no danger if it was well done, and then Mr. Brass pulls out his pocket-book, and says, 'Well,' he says, 'here it is—Quilp's own five-pound note. We'll agree that way, then,' he says. 'Kit's coming to-morrow morning, I know. While he's upstairs, you'll get out of the way, and I'll clear off Mr. Richard. Having Kit alone, I'll hold him in conversation, and put this property in his hat. I'll manage so besides,' he says, 'that Mr. Richard shall find it there, and be the evidence. And if that don't get Christopher out of Mr. Quilp's way, and satisfy Mr. Quilp's grudges,' he says, 'the Devil's in it.' Miss Sally laughed, and said that was the plan, and as they seemed to be moving away, and I was afraid to stop any longer, I went downstairs again.—There!"

The small servant had gradually worked herself into as much agitation as Mr. Swiveller, and therefore made no effort to restrain him when he sat up in bed and hastily demanded whether this story had been told to anybody.

"How could it be?" replied his nurse. "I was almost afraid to think about it, and hoped the young man would be let off. When I heard 'em say they had found him guilty of what he didn't do, you was gone, and so was the lodger—though I think I should have been frightened to tell him, even if he'd been there. Ever since I come here, you've been out of your senses, and what would have been the good of telling you then?"

"Marchioness," said Mr. Swiveller, plucking off his nightcap and flinging it to the other end of the room; "if you'll do me the favor to retire for a few minutes and see what sort of a night it is, I'll get up."

"You mustn't think of such a thing," cried his nurse.

"I must indeed," said the patient, looking round the room. "Whereabouts are my clothes?"

"Oh, I'm so glad—you haven't got any," replied the Marchioness.

"Ma'am!" said Mr. Swiveller, in great astonishment.

"I've been obliged to sell them, every one, to get the things that was ordered for you. But don't take on about that," urged the Marchioness, as Dick fell back upon his pillow. "You're too weak to stand indeed."

"I am afraid," said Richard dolefully, "that you're right. What ought I to do! what is to be done!"

It naturally occurred to him on very little reflection, that the first step to take would be to communicate with one of the Mr. Garlands instantly. It was very possible that Mr. Abel had not yet left the office. In as little time as it takes to tell it, the small servant had the address in pencil on a piece of paper; a verbal description of father and son, which would enable her to recognize either without difficulty; and a special caution to be shy of Mr. Chuckster, in consequence of that gentleman's known antipathy to Kit. Armed with these slender powers, she hurried away, commissioned to bring either old Mr. Garland or Mr. Abel, bodily, to that apartment.

"I suppose," said Dick, as she closed the door slowly, and peeped into the room again to make sure that he was

comfortable, " I suppose there's nothing left—not so much
as a waistcoat even ? "

" No, nothing."

" It's embarrassing," said Mr. Swiveller, " in case of fire
—even an umbrella would be something—but you did
quite right, dear Marchioness. I should have died without you ! "

CHAPTER THE SIXTY-FIFTH.

IT was well for the small servant that she was of a
sharp, quick nature, or the consequence of sending her
out alone, from the very neighborhood in which it was
most dangerous for her to appear, would probably have
been the restoration of Miss Sally Brass to the supreme
authority over her person. Not unmindful of the risk
she ran, however, the Marchioness no sooner left the house
than she dived into the first dark by-way that presented
itself, and, without any present reference to the point to
which her journey tended, made it her first business to
put two good miles of brick and mortar between herself
and Bevis Marks.

When she had accomplished this object, she began to
shape her course for the notary's office, to which—
shrewdly inquiring of apple-women and oyster-sellers at
street-corners, rather than in lighted shops or of well-
dressed people, at the hazard of attracting notice—she
easily procured a direction. As carrier-pigeons, on being
first let loose in a strange place beat the air at random
for a short time, before darting off towards the spot for
which they are designed, so did the Marchioness flutter
round and round until she believed herself in safety, and
then bear swiftly down upon the port for which she was
bound.

She had no bonnet—nothing on her head but a great
cap which in some old time had been worn by Sally Brass,
whose taste in head-dresses was, as we have seen, peculiar—and her speed was rather retarded than assisted by
her shoes, which, being extremely large and slipshod,
flew off every now and then, and were difficult to find
again, among the crowd of passengers. Indeed, the poor
little creature experienced so much trouble and delay

from having to grope for these articles of dress in mud and kennel, and suffered in these researches so much jostling, pushing, squeezing, and bandying from hand to hand, that by the time she reached the street in which the notary lived, she was fairly worn out and exhausted, and could not refrain from tears.

But to have got there at last was a great comfort, especially as there were lights still burning in the office window, and therefore some hope that she was not too late. So, the Marchioness dried her eyes with the backs of her hands, and, stealing softly up the steps, peeped in through the glass door.

Mr. Chuckster was standing behind the lid of his desk, making such preparations towards finishing off for the night as pulling down his wristbands and pulling up his shirt-collar, settling his neck more gracefully in his stock, and secretly arranging his whiskers by the aid of a little triangular bit of looking-glass. Before the ashes of the fire stood two gentlemen, one of whom she rightly judged to be the notary, and the other (who was buttoning his great-coat, and was evidently about to depart immediately, Mr. Abel Garland.

Having made these observations, the small spy took counsel with herself, and resolved to wait in the street until Mr. Abel came out, as there would be then n fear of having to speak before Mr. Chuckster, and less difficulty in delivering her message. With this purpose she slipped out again, and crossing the road, sat down upon a door-step just opposite.

She had hardly taken this position, when there came dancing up the street, with his legs all wrong, and his head everywhere by turns, a pony. This pony had a little phaeton behind him, and a man in it; but neither man nor phaeton seemed to embarrass him in the least, as he reared up on his hind legs, or stopped, or went on, or stood still again, or backed, or went sideways, without the smallest reference to them,—just as the fancy seized him, and as if he were the freest animal in creation. When they came to the notary's door, the man called out in a very respectful manner, "Woa then,"—intimating that if he might venture to express a wish, it would be that they stopped there. The pony made a moment's pause; but as if it occurred to him that to stop when he was required might be to establish an inconvenient and dangerous precedent, he immediately started off again, rattled at a fast trot to the street-corner, wheeled round, came back, and then stopped of his own accord.

"Oh! you're a precious creatur!" said the man—who didn't venture by the bye to come out in his true colors until he was safe on the pavement. "I wish I had the rewarding of you,—I do."

"What has he been doing?" said Mr. Abel, tying a shawl round his neck as he came down the steps.

"He's enough to fret a man's heart out," replied the hostler. "He is the most wicious rascal—woa then, will you?"

"He'll never stand still, if you call him names," said Mr. Abel, getting in, and taking the reins. "He's a very good fellow if you know how to manage him. This is the first time he has been out, this long while, for he has lost his old driver and wouldn't stir for anybody else, till this morning. The lamps are right, are they? That's well. Be here to take him to-morrow, if you please. Goodnight!"

And after one or two strange plunges, quite of his own invention, the pony yielded to Mr. Abel's mildness, and trotted gently off.

All this time Mr. Chuckster had been standing at the door, and the small servant had been afraid to approach. She had nothing for it now, therefore, but to run after the chaise, and to call to Mr. Abel to stop. Being out of breath when she came up with it, she was unable to make him hear. The case was desperate; for the pony was quickening his pace. The Marchioness hung on behind for a few moments, and, feeling that she could go no farther, and must soon yield, clambered by a vigorous effort into the hinder seat, and in so doing lost one of the shoes forever.

Mr. Abel being in a thoughtful frame of mind, and having quite enough to do to keep the pony going, went jogging on without looking round: little dreaming of the strange figure that was close behind him, until the Marchioness, having in some degree recovered her breath, and the loss of her shoe, and the novelty of her position, uttered close into his ear, the words—

"I say, Sir"—

He turned his head quickly enough then, and stopping the pony, cried, with some trepidation, "God bless me, what is this!"

"Don't be frightened, Sir," replied the still panting messenger. "Oh, I've run such a way after you!"

"What do you want with me?" said Mr. Abel. "How did you come here?"

"I got in behind," replied the Marchioness. "Oh please drive on, Sir—don't stop—and go towards the City, will you? And oh do please make haste, because it's of consequence. There's somebody wants to see you

there. He sent me to say would you come directly, and that he knowed all about Kit, and could save him yet, and prove his innocence."

"What do you tell me, child?"

"The truth, upon my word and honor I do. But please to drive on—quick, please? I've been such a time gone, he'll think I'm lost."

Mr. Abel involuntarily urged the pony forward. The pony, impelled by some secret sympathy or some new caprice, burst into a great pace, and neither slackened it, nor indulged in any eccentric performances, until they arrived at the door of Mr. Swiveller's lodging, where, marvellous to relate, he consented to stop when Mr. Abel checked him.

" See ! It's that room up there," said the Marchioness, pointing to one where there was a faint light. " Come ! "

Mr. Abel, who was one of the simplest and most retiring creatures in existence, and naturally timid withal, hesitated ; for he had heard of people being decoyed into strange places to be robbed and murdered, under circumstances very like the present, and, for anything he knew to the contrary, by guides very like the Marchioness. His regard for Kit, however, overcame every other consideration. So, entrusting Whisker to the charge of a man who was lingering hard by in expectation of the job, he suffered his companion to take his hand and to lead him up the dark and narrow stairs.

He was not a little surprised to find himself conducted into a dimly-lighted sick chamber, where a man was sleeping tranquilly in bed.

" An't it nice to see him lying there so quiet ? " said his guide, in an earnest whisper. " Oh ! you'd say it was, if you had only seen him two or three days ago."

Mr. Abel made no answer, and, to say the truth, kept a long way from the bed and very near the door. His guide, who appeared to understand his reluctance, trimmed the candle, and taking it in her hand, approached the bed. As she did so, the sleeper started up, and he recognized in the wasted face the features of Richard Swiveller.

" Why, how is this ? " said Mr. Abel kindly, as he hurried towards him. " You have been ill ? "

" Very," replied Dick. " Nearly dead. You might have chanced to hear of your Richard on his bier, but for the friend I sent to fetch you. Another shake of the hand, Marchioness, if you please. Sit down, Sir."

Mr. Abel seemed rather astonished to hear of the quality of his guide, and took a chair by the bedside.

" I have sent for you, Sir," said Dick—" but she told you on what account ? "

" She did. I am quite bewildered by all this. I really don't know what to say or think," replied Mr. Abel.

" You'll say that presently," retorted Dick. " Marchioness, take a seat on the bed, will you? Now, tell

35

this gentleman all that you told me; and be particular.
Don't you speak another word, Sir."

The story was repeated; it was, in effect, exactly the
same as before, without any deviation or omission. Richard Swiveller kept his eyes fixed on his visitor during its
narration, and directly it was concluded, took the word
again.

"You have heard it all, and you'll not forget it. I'm
too giddy and too queer to suggest anything; but you
and your friends will know what to do. After this long
delay, every minute is an age. If ever you went home
fast in your life, go home fast to-night. Don't stop to
say one word to me, but go. She will be found here,
whenever she's wanted; and as to me, you're pretty sure
to find me at home, for a week or two. There are more
reasons than one for that. Marchioness, a light! If you
lose another minute in looking at me, Sir, I'll never forgive you!"

Mr. Abel needed no more remonstrance or persuasion.
He was gone in an instant; and the Marchioness, returning from lighting him downstairs, reported that the
pony, without any preliminary objection whatever, had
dashed away at full gallop.

"That's right!" said Dick; "and hearty of him; and
I honor him from this time. But get some supper and a
mug of beer, for I am sure you must be tired. Do have a
mug of beer. It will do me as much good to see you take
it as if I might drink it myself."

Nothing but this assurance could have prevailed upon
the small nurse to indulge in such a luxury. Having
eaten and drunk to Mr. Swiveller's extreme contentment,
given him his drink, and put everything in neat order, she
wrapped herself in an old coverlet and lay down upon
the rug before the fire.

Mr. Swiveller was by that time murmuring in his sleep,
"Strew then, oh strew, a bed of rushes. Here will we
stay. till morning blushes. Good-night. Marchioness!"

CHAPTER THE SIXTY-SIXTH.

On awaking in the morning, Richard Swiveller became conscious by slow degrees of whispering voices in his room. Looking out between the curtains, he espied Mr. Garland, Mr. Abel, the notary, and the single gentleman, gathered round the Marchioness, and talking to her with great earnestness but in very subdued tones—fearing, no doubt, to disturb him. He lost no time in letting them know that this precaution was unnecessary, and all four gentlemen directly approached his bedside. Old Mr. Garland was the first to stretch out his hand, and inquire how he felt.

Dick was about to answer that he felt much better, though still as weak as need be, when his little nurse, pushing the visitors aside and pressing up to his pillow as if in jealousy of their interference, set his breakfast before him, and insisted on his taking it before he underwent the fatigue of speaking or of being spoken to. Mr. Swiveller, who was perfectly ravenous, and had had, all night, amazingly distinct and consistent dreams of mutton chops, double stout, and similar delicacies, felt even the weak tea and dry toast such irresistible temptations, that he consented to eat and drink upon one condition.

"And that is," said Dick, returning the pressure of Mr. Garland's hand, "that you answer me this question truly, before I take a bit or drop. Is it too late?"

"For completing the work you began so well last night?" returned the old gentleman. "No. Set your mind at rest upon that point. It is not, I assure you."

Comforted by this intelligence, the patient applied himself to his food with a keen appetite, though evidently not with a greater zest in the eating than his nurse appeared to have in seeing him eat. The manner of his meal was this:—Mr. Swiveller, holding the slice of toast or cup of tea in his left hand, and taking a bite or drink as the case might be, constantly kept, in his right, one palm of the Marchioness tight locked; and to shake, or even to kiss this imprisoned hand, he would stop every now and then, in the very act of swallowing, with perfect seriousness of intention, and the utmost gravity. As often as he put anything into his mouth, whether for eating or drinking, the face of the Marchioness lighted up beyond all description; but whenever he gave her one or other of these tokens of recognition, her countenance became overshadowed, and she began to sob. Now, whether she was in her laughing joy, or in her crying one, the Marchioness could not help turning to the visitors with an appealing look, which seemed to say, "You see this fellow—can I help this?"—and they being thus made, as it were, parties to the scene, as regularly answered by another look, "No. Certainly not." This dumb-show taking place during the whole time of the invalid's breakfast, and the invalid himself, pale and emaciated, performing no small part in the same, it may be fairly questioned whether at any meal, where no word, good or bad, was spoken from beginning to end, so much was expressed by gestures in themselves so slight and unimportant.

At length—and to say the truth before very long—Mr. Swiveller had despatched as much toast and tea as in that stage of his recovery it was discreet to let him have. But the cares of the Marchioness did not stop here; for, disappearing for an instant and presently returning with a basin of fair water, she laved his face and hands, brushed his hair, and in short made him as spruce and smart as anybody under such circumstances could be made; and all this in as brisk and business like a manner, as if he were a very little boy, and she his grown-up nurse. To these various attentions, Mr. Swiveller submitted in a kind of grateful astonishment beyond the reach of language. When they were at last brought to an end, and the Marchioness had withdrawn into a distant corner to take her own poor breakfast (cold enough by that time), he turned his face away for some few moments, and shook hands heartily with the air.

"Gentlemen," said Dick, rousing himself from this pause, and turning round again, "you'll excuse me. Men who have been brought so low as I have been, are easily fatigued. I am fresh again now, and fit for talking. We're short of chairs here, among other trifles, but if you'll do me the favor to sit upon the bed——"

"What can we do for you?" said Mr. Garland, kindly.

"If you could make the Marchioness yonder, a Marshioness in real, sober earnest," returned Dick, " I'd thank you to get it done off-hand. But as you can't, and as the question is not what you will do for me, but what you will do for somebody else who has a better claim upon you, pray, Sir, let me know what you intend doing."

" It's chiefly on that account that we have come just now," said the single gentleman, " for you will have another visitor presently. We feared you would be anxious unless you knew from ourselves what steps we intended to take, and therefore came to you before we stirred in the matter."

" Gentlemen," returned Dick, " I thank you. Anybody in the helpless state that you see me in, is naturally anxious. Don't let me interrupt you, Sir."

" Then, you see, my good fellow," said the single gentleman, " that while we have no doubt whatever of the truth of this disclosure, which has so providentially come to light—"

" Meaning hers ?" said Dick, pointing towards the Marchioness.

" —Meaning hers, of course. While we have no doubt of that, or that a proper use of it would procure the poor lad's immediate pardon and liberation, we have a great doubt whether it would, by itself, enable us to reach Quilp, the chief agent in this villainy. I should tell you that this doubt has been confirmed into something very nearly approaching certainty by the best opinions we have been enabled, in this short space of time, to take upon the subject. You'll agree with us, that to give him even the most distant chance of escape, if we could help it, would be monstrous. You say with us, no doubt, if somebody must escape, let it be any one but he."

" Yes," returned Dick, " certainly. That is if somebody *must*—but upon my word, I'm unwilling that anybody should. Since laws were made for every degree, to curb vice in others as well as in me—and so forth you know— doesn't it strike you in that light ? "

The single gentleman smiled as if the light in which Mr. Swiveller had put the question were not the clearest in the world, and proceeded to explain that they contemplated proceeding by stratagem in the first instance ; and that their design was to endeavor to extort a confession from the gentle Sarah.

"When she finds how much we know, and how we know it," he said, "and that she is clearly compromised already, we are not without strong hopes that we may be enabled through her means to punish the other two effectually. If we could do that, she might go scot-free for aught I cared."

Dick received this project in anything but a gracious manner, representing with as much warmth as he was then capable of showing, that they would find the old buck (meaning Sarah) more difficult to manage than Quilp himself—that for any tampering, terrifying, or cajolery, she was a very unpromising and unyielding subject—that she was of a kind of brass not easily melted or moulded into shape—in short, that they were no match for her, and would be signally defeated. But, it was in vain to urge them to adopt some other course. The single gentleman has been described as explaining their joint intentions, but it should have been written that they all spoke together; that if any one of them by chance held his peace for a moment, he stood gasping and panting for an opportunity to strike in again; in a word, that they had reached that pitch of impatience and anxiety where men can neither be persuaded nor reasoned with; and that it would have been easier to turn the most impetuous wind that ever blew, than to prevail on them to reconsider their determination. So, after telling Mr. Swiveller how they had not lost sight of Kit's mother and the children; how they had never once even lost sight of Kit himself, but had been unremitting in their endeavors to procure a mitigation of his sentence; how they had been perfectly distracted between the strong proofs of his guilt, and their own fading hopes of his innocence; and how he, Richard Swiveller, might keep his mind at rest, for everything should be happily adjusted between that time and night;—after telling him all this, and adding a great many kind and cordial expressions, personal to himself, which it is unnecessary to recite, Mr. Garland, the Notary, and the single gentleman, took their leaves at a very critical time, or Richard Swiveller must assuredly have been driven into another fever, whereof the results might have been fatal.

Mr. Abel remained behind, very often looking at his watch and at the room door, until Mr. Swiveller was

roused from a short nap, by the setting-down on the land-
ing-place outside, as from the shoulders of a porter, of
some giant load, which seemed to shake the house, and
make the little physic bottles on the mantel-shelf ring
again. Directly this sound reached his ears, Mr. Abel
started up, and hobbled to the door, and opened it; and
behold! there stood a strong man, with a mighty hamper, which, being hauled into the room and presently un-
packed, disgorged such treasures of tea, and coffee, and
wine, and rusks, and oranges, and grapes, and fowls ready

trussed for boiling, and calves'-foot jelly, and arrow-root,
and sago, and other delicate restoratives, that the small
servant, who had never thought it possible that such
things could be, except in shops, stood rooted to the spot
in her one shoe, with her mouth and eyes watering in unison, and her power of speech quite gone. But not so Mr.
Abel; or the strong man who emptied the hamper, big as
it was, in a twinkling; and not so the nice old lady, who
appeared so suddenly that she might have come out of the
hamper too (it was quite large enough), and who, bustling
about on tiptoe and without noise—now here, now there,

now everywhere at once—began to fill out the jelly in tea-cups, and to make chicken broth in small saucepans, and to peel oranges for the sick man and to cut them up in little pieces, and to ply the small servant with glasses of wine and choice bits of everything until more substantial meat could be prepared for her refreshment. The whole of which appearances were so unexpected and bewilder-ing, that Mr. Swiveller, when he had taken two oranges and a little jelly, and had seen the strong man walk off with the empty basket, plainly leaving all that abundance for his use and benefit, was fain to lie down and fall asleep again, from sheer inability to entertain such won-ders in his mind.

Meanwhile the single gentleman, the Notary, and Mr. Garland, repaired to a certain coffee-house, and from that place indited and sent a letter to Miss Sally Brass, re-questing her, in terms mysterious and brief, to favor an un-known friend who wished to consult her, with her company there, as speedily as possible. The communication per-formed its errand so well, that within ten minutes of the messenger's return and report of its delivery, Miss Brass herself was announced.

"Pray, ma'am," said the single gentleman, whom she found alone in the room, "take a chair."

Miss Brass sat herself down in a very stiff and frigid state, and seemed—as indeed she was—not a little aston-ished to find that the lodger and her mysterious corre-spondent were one and the same person.

"You did not expect to see me?" said the single gentleman.

"I didn't think much about it," returned the beauty. "I supposed it was business of some kind or other. If it's about the apartments, of course you'll give my brother regular notice, you know—or money. That's very easily settled. You're a responsible party, and in such a case lawful money and lawful notice are pretty much the same."

"I am obliged to you for your good opinion," retorted the single gentleman, "and quite concur in those senti-ments. But that is not the subject on which I wish to speak with you."

"Oh!" said Sally. "Then just state the particulars, will you? I suppose it's professional business?"

" Why, it *is* connected with the law, certainly."

"Very well," returned Miss Brass. "My brother and I are just the same. I can take any instructions, or give you any advice."

"As there are other parties interested besides myself," said the single gentleman, rising and opening the door of an inner room, "we had better confer together. Miss Brass is here, gentlemen!"

Mr. Garland and the Notary walked in, looking very grave; and drawing up two chairs, one on each side of the single gentleman, formed a kind of fence round the gentle Sarah, and penned her into a corner. Her brother Sampson under such circumstances would certainly have evinced some confusion or anxiety, but she—all composure—pulled out the tin box and calmly took a pinch of snuff.

"Miss Brass," said the Notary, taking the word at this crisis, "we professional people understand each other, and, when we choose, can say what we have to say, in very few words. You advertised a runaway servant, the other day?"

"Well," returned Miss Sally, with a sudden flush overspreading her features, "what of that?"

"She is found, ma'am," said the Notary, pulling out his pockethandkerchief with a flourish. "She is found."

"Who found her?" demanded Sarah hastily.

"We did, ma'am—we three. Only last night, or you would have heard from us before."

"And now I *have* heard from you," said Miss Brass, folding her arms resolutely, as though she were about to deny something to the death, "what have you got to say? Something you have got into your heads about her, of course. Prove it, will you—that's all. Prove it. You have found her, you say. I can tell you (if you don't know it) that you have found the most artful, lying, pilfering, and devilish little minx that was ever born.—Have you got her here?" she added, looking sharply around.

"No, she is not here at present," returned the Notary. "But she is quite safe."

"Ha!" cried Sally, twitching a pinch of snuff out of her box, as spitefully as if she were in the very act of wrenching off the small servant's nose; "she shall be safe enough from this time, I warrant you."

"I hope so," replied the Notary.—"Did it occur to you for the first time when you found she had run away, that there were two keys to your kitchen door?"

Miss Sally took another pinch, and putting her head on one side, looked at her questioner with a curious kind of spasm about her mouth, but with a cunning aspect of immense expression.

"Two keys," repeated the Notary; "one of which gave her the opportunities of roaming through the house at nights when you supposed her fast locked up, and of overhearing confidential consultations—among others, that particular conference to be described to-day before a justice, which you will have an opportunity of hearing her relate; that conference which you and Mr. Brass held together on the night before that most unfortunate and innocent young man was accused of robbery by a horrible device of which I will only say that it may be characterized by the epithets you have applied to this wretched little witness, and by a few stronger ones besides."

Sally took another pinch. Although her face was wonderfully composed, it was apparent that she was wholly taken by surprise, and that what she had expected to be taxed with, in connection with her small servant, was something very different from this.

"Come, come, Miss Brass," said the Notary, "you have great command of feature, but you feel, I see, that by a chance which never entered your imagination, this base design is revealed, and two of its plotters must be brought to justice. Now, you know the pains and penalties you are liable to, and so I need not dilate upon them, but I have a proposal to make to you. You have the honor of being sister to one of the greatest scoundrels unhung; and, if I may venture to say so to a lady, you are in every respect quite worthy of him. But, connected with you two is a third party, a villain of the name of Quilp, the prime mover of the whole diabolical device, who I believe to be worse than either. For his sake, Miss Brass, do us the favor to reveal the whole history of this affair. Let me remind you that your doing so at our instance will place you in a safe and comfortable position—your present one is not desirable—and cannot injure your brother, for against him and you we have quite sufficient evidence (as you hear) already. I will not say to you that we suggest this course in mercy (for, to tell you the truth, we do not entertain any regard for you), but it is a necessity to which we are reduced, and I recommend it to you as a matter of the very best policy. Time," said Mr. Witherden, pulling out his watch, "in a business like this, is exceedingly precious. Favor us with your decision as speedily as possible, ma'am."

With a smile upon her face, and looking at each of the three by turns, Miss Brass took two or three more pinches of snuff, and having by this time very little left, travelled round and round the box with her forefinger and thumb, scraping up another. Having disposed of this likewise and put the box carefully in her pocket, she said,—

"I am to accept or reject at once, am I?"

"Yes," said Mr. Witherden.

The charming creature was opening her lips to speak in reply, when the door was hastily opened too, and the head of Sampson Brass was thrust into the room.

"Excuse me," said that gentleman hastily. "Wait a bit!"

So saying, and quite indifferent to the astonishment his presence occasioned, he crept in, shut the door, kissed his greasy glove as servilely as if it were the dust, and made a most abject bow.

"Sarah," said Brass, "hold your tongue if you please, and let me speak. Gentlemen, if I could express the pleasure it gives me to see three such men in a happy unity of feeling and concord of sentiment, I think you would hardly believe me. But though I am unfortunate —nay, gentlemen, criminal, if we are to use harsh expressions in a company like this—still I have my feelings like other men. I have heard of a poet, who remarked that feelings were the common lot of all. If he could have been a pig, gentlemen, and have uttered that sentiment, he would still have been immortal."

"If you're not an idiot," said Miss Brass harshly, "hold your peace."

"Sarah, my dear," returned her brother, "thank you. But I know what I am about, my love, and will take the liberty of expressing myself accordingly. Mr. Witherden, Sir, your handkerchief is hanging out of your pocket —would you allow me to—"

As Mr. Brass advanced to remedy this accident, the
Notary shrank from him with an air of great disgust.
Brass, who over and above his usual prepossessing qualities, had a scratched face, a green shade over one eye, and
a hat grievously crushed, stopped short, and looked
round with a pitiful smile.

"He shuns me," said Sampson, "even when I would,
as I may say, heap coals of fire upon his head. Well!
Ah! But I am a falling house, and the rats (if I may be
allowed the expression in reference to a gentleman that I
respect and love beyond everything) fly from me! Gen-

tlemen—regarding your conversation just now, I happened to see my sister on her way here, and, wondering
where she could be going to, and being—may I venture
to say?—naturally of a suspicious turn, followed her.
Since then, I have been listening."

"If you're not mad," interposed Miss Sally, "stop there,
and say no more."

"Sarah, my dear," rejoined Brass with undiminished
politeness, "I thank you kindly, but will still proceed. Mr. Witherden, Sir, as we have the honor to be
members of the same profession—to say nothing of that

other gentleman having been my lodger, and having partaken, as one may say, of the hospitality of my roof—I think you might have given me the refusal of this offer in the first instance. I do indeed. Now, my dear Sir," cried Brass, seeing that the notary was about to interrupt him, "suffer me to speak, I beg."

Mr. Witherden was silent, and Brass went on.

"If you will do me the favor," he said, holding up the green shade, and revealing an eye most horribly discolored, "to look at this, you will naturally inquire in your own minds how did I get it. If you look from that, to my face, you will wonder what could have been the cause of all these scratches. And if from them to my hat, how it came into the state in which you see it. Gentlemen," said Brass, striking the hat fiercely with his clenched hand, "to all these questions I answer—Quilp!"

The three gentlemen looked at each other, but said nothing.

"I say," pursued Brass, glancing aside at his sister, as though he were talking for her information, and speaking with a snarling malignity, in violent contrast to his usual smoothness, "that I answer to all these questions,—Quilp—Quilp, who deludes me into his infernal den, and takes a delight in looking on and chuckling while I scorch, and burn, and bruise, and maim myself—Quilp, who never once no, never once in all our communications together, has treated me otherwise than as a dog—Quilp, whom I have always hated with my whole heart, but never so much as lately. He gives me the cold shoulder on this very matter as if he had had nothing to do with it, instead of being the first to propose it. I can't trust him. In one of his howling, raving, blazing humors, I believe he'd let it out if it was murder, and never think of himself so long as he could terrify me. Now," said Brass, picking up his hat again, replacing the shade over his eye, and actually crouching down, in the excess of his servility, "What does all this lead me to?—what should you say it led me to, gentlemen? —could you guess at all near the mark?"

Nobody spoke. Brass stood smirking for a little while as if he had propounded some choice conundrum; and then said:

"To be short with you, then, it leads me to this. If the truth has come out, as it plainly has in a manner that there's no standing up against—and a very sublime and grand thing is Truth, gentlemen, in its way, though like other sublime and grand things, such as thunder-storms and that, we're not always over and above glad to see it— I had better turn upon this man than let this man turn upon me. It's clear to me that I am done for. Therefore, if anybody is to split, I had better be the person and have the advantage of it. Sarah, my dear, comparatively speaking, you're safe. I relate these circumstances for my own profit."

With that Mr. Brass, in a great hurry, revealed the whole story; bearing as heavily as possible on his amiable employer, and making himself out to be rather a saint-like and holy character, though subject—he acknowledged —to human weaknesses. He concluded thus:

"Now, gentlemen, I am not a man who does things by halves. Being in for a penny, I am ready as the saying is, to be in for a pound. You must do with me what you please, and take me where you please. If you wish to have this in writing, we'll reduce it into manuscript immediately. You will be tender with me, I am sure. I am quite confident you will be tender with me. You are men of honor, and have feeling hearts. I yielded from necessity to Quilp, for though necessity has no law, she has her lawyers. I yield to you from necessity too; from policy besides; and because of feelings that have been a pretty long time working within me, Punish Quilp, gentlemen. Weigh heavily upon him. Grind him down. Tread him under foot. He has done as much by me, for many and many a day."

Having now arrived at the conclusion of his discourse, Sampson checked the current of his wrath, kissed his glove again, and smiled as only parasites and cowards can.

"And this," said Miss Brass, raising her head, with which she had hitherto sat resting on her hands, and surveying him from head to foot with a bitter sneer, "this is my brother, is it! This is my brother, that I have worked and toiled for, and believed to have had something of the man in him!"

"Sarah, my dear," returned Sampson, rubbing his hands feebly; "you disturb our friends. Besides you— you're disappointed, Sarah, and, not knowing what you say, expose yourself."

"Yes, you pitiful dastard," retorted the lovely damsel, "I understand you. You feared, that I should be beforehand with you. But do you think that *I* would have been enticed to say a word! I'd have scorned it, if they had tried and tempted me for twenty years."

"He he!" simpered Brass, who in his deep debasement really seemed to have changed sexes with his sister, and to have made over to her any spark of manliness he might have possessed. "You think so, Sarah, you think so perhaps; but you would have acted quite different, my good fellow. You will not have forgotten that it was a maxim with Foxey—our revered father, gentlemen— 'Always suspect everybody.' That's the maxim to go through life with! If you were not actually about to purchase your own safety when I showed myself, I suspect you'd have done it by this time. And therefore I've done it myself, and spared you the trouble as well as the shame. The shame, gentlemen," added Brass, allowing himself to be slightly overcome, "if there is any, is mine. It's better that a female should be spared it."

With deference to the better opinion of Mr. Brass, and more particularly to the authority of his Great Ancestor, it may be doubted with humility whether the elevating principle laid down by the latter gentleman, and acted upon by his descendant, is always a prudent one, or attended in practice with the desired results. This is beyond question a bold and presumptuous doubt, inasmuch as many distinguished characters, called men of the world, long-headed customers, knowing dogs, shrewd fellows, capital hands at business, and the like, have made, and do daily make, this axiom their polar star and compass. Still the doubt may be gently insinuated. And in illustration it may be observed, that if Mr. Brass, not being over-suspicious, had, without prying and listening, left his sister to manage the conference on their joint behalf, or prying and listening, had not been in such a mighty hurry to anticipate her (which he would not have been, but for his distrust and jealousy), he would probably have found himself much better off in the end. Thus it will always happen that these men of the world, who go through it in armor, defend themselves from quite as much good as evil; to say nothing of the inconvenience and absurdity of mounting guard with a microscope at all times, and of wearing a coat of mail on the most innocent occasions.

The three gentlemen spoke together apart for a few moments. At the end of their consultation, which was very brief, the Notary pointed to the writing-materials on the table, and informed Mr. Brass that if he wished to make any statement in writing, he had the opportunity of doing so. At the same time he felt bound to tell him that they would require his attendance presently before a Justice of the Peace, and that in what he did or said, he was guided entirely by his own discretion.

"Gentlemen," said Brass, drawing off his gloves, and crawling in spirit upon the ground before them, "I will justify the tenderness with which I know I shall be treated; and as, without tenderness, I should, now that this discovery has been made, stand in the worst position of the three, you may depend upon it I will make a clean breast. Mr. Witherden, Sir, a kind of faintness is upon my spirits—if you would do me the favor to ring the bell and order up a glass of something warm and spicy, I shall, notwithstanding what has passed, have a melancholy pleasure in drinking your good health. I had hoped," said Brass, looking round with a mournful smile, "to have seen you three gentlemen one day or another with your legs under the mahogany in my humble parlor in the Marks. But hopes are fleeting. Dear me!"

Mr. Brass found himself so exceedingly affected at this point that he could say or do nothing more until some refreshment arrived. Having partaken of it, pretty freely for one in his agitated state, he sat down to write.

The lovely Sarah, now with her arms folded, and now with her hands clasped behind her, paced the room with manly strides while her brother was thus employed, and sometimes stopped to pull out her snuff-box and bite the lid. She continued to pace up and down until she was quite tired, and then fell asleep on a chair near the door.

It has been since supposed with some reason that this slumber was a sham or feint, as she contrived to slip away unobserved in the dusk of the afternoon. Whether this was an intentional and waking departure, or a somnambulistic leave-taking and walking in her sleep, may remain a subject of contention; but on one point (and indeed the main one) all parties are agreed. In whatever state she walked away, she certainly did not walk back again.

Mention having been made of the dusk of the afternoon, it will be inferred that Mr. Brass's task occupied some time in the completion. It was not finished until evening; but being done at last, that worthy person and the three friends adjourned in a hackney-coach to the private office of a Justice, who, giving Mr. Brass a warm reception and detaining him in a secure place that he might insure to himself the pleasure of seeing him on the morrow, dismissed the others with the cheering assurance that a warrant could not fail to be granted next day for the apprehension of Mr. Quilp, and that a proper application and statement of all the circumstances to the Secretary of State (who was fortunately in town), would no doubt procure Kit's free pardon and liberation without delay.

And now indeed it seemed that Quilp's malignant career was drawing to a close, and that retribution, which often travels slowly—especially when heaviest, had tracked his footstops with a sure and certain scent and was gaining on him fast. Unmindful of her stealthy tread, her victim holds his course in fancied triumph. Still at his heels she comes, and once afoot, is never turned aside.

Their business ended, the three gentlemen hastened back to the lodgings of Mr. Swiveller, whom they found progressing so favorably in his recovery as to have been able to sit up for half an hour, and to have conversed with cheerfulness. Mrs. Garland had gone home some time since, but Mr. Abel was still sitting with him. After telling him all they had done, the two Mr. Garlands and the single gentleman, as if by some previous understanding, took their leaves for the night, leaving the invalid alone with the Notary and the small servant.

"As you are so much better," said Mr. Witherden, sitting down at the bedside, "I may venture to communicate to you a piece of news which has come to me professionally."

The idea of any professional intelligence from a gentleman connected with legal matters appeared to afford Richard anything but a pleasing anticipation. Perhaps he connected it in his own mind with one or two outstand-

36

ing accounts, in reference to which he had already received divers threatening letters. His countenance fell as he replied,

"Certainly, Sir. I hope it's not anything of a very disagreeable nature, though?"

"If I thought it so, I should choose some better time for communicating it," replied the Notary. "Let me tell you, first, that my friends who have been here to-day, know nothing of it, and that their kindness to you has been quite spontaneous, and with no hope of return. It may do a thoughtless, careless man good to know that."

Dick thanked him, and said he hoped it would.

"I have been making some inquiries about you," said Mr. Witherden, "little thinking that I should find you under such circumstances as those which have brought us together. You are the nephew of Rebecca Swiveller, spinster, deceased, of Cheselbourne in Dorsetshire."

"Deceased!" cried Dick.

"Deceased. If you had been another sort of nephew, you would have come into possession (so says the will, and I see no reason to doubt it) of five-and-twenty thousand pounds. As it is, you have fallen into an annuity of one hundred and fifty pounds a year; but I think I may congratulate you even upon that."

"Sir," said Dick, sobbing and laughing together, "you may. For, please God, we'll make a scholar of the poor Marchioness yet! And she shall walk in silk attire, and siller have to spare, or may I never rise from this bed again!"

CHAPTER THE SIXTY-SEVENTH.

UNCONSCIOUS of the proceedings faithfully narrated in the last chapter, and little dreaming of the mine which had been sprung beneath him (for, to the end that he should have no warning of the business afoot, the profoundest secrecy was observed in the whole transaction), Mr. Quilp remained shut up in his hermitage, undisturbed by any suspicion, and extremely well satisfied with the result of his machinations. Being engaged in the adjustment of some accounts—an occupation to which the silence and solitude of his retreat were very favorable—he had not strayed from his den for two whole days. The third day of his devotion to this pursuit found him still hard at work, and little disposed to stir abroad.

It was the day next after Mr. Brass's confession, and consequently that which threatened the restriction of Mr. Quilp's liberty, and the abrupt communication to him of some very unpleasant and unwelcome facts. Having no intuitive perception of the cloud which lowered upon his house, the dwarf was in his ordinary state of cheerfulness; and, when he found he was becoming too much engrossed by business with a due regard to his health and spirits, he varied its monotonous routine with a little screeching, or howling, or some other innocent relaxation of that nature.

He was attended, as usual, by Tom Scott, who sat crouching over the fire after the manner of a toad, and from time to time, when his master's back was turned, imitated his grimaces with a fearful exactness. The figure-head had not yet disappeared, but remained in its old place. The face, horribly seared by the frequent application of the red-hot poker, and further ornamented by the insertion in the tip of the nose of a tenpenny nail, yet smiled blandly in its less lacerated parts, and seemed, like a sturdy martyr, to provoke its tormentor to the commission of new outrages and insults.

The day, in the highest and brightest quarters of the town, was damp, dark, cold, and gloomy. In that low and marshy spot, the fog filled every nook and corner with a thick dense cloud. Every object was obscured at one or two yards' distance. The warning lights and fires upon the river were powerless beneath this pall, and, but for a raw and piercing chillness in the air, and now and then the cry of some bewildered boatman as he rested on his oars and tried to make out where he was, the river itself might have been miles away.

The mist, though sluggish and slow to move, was of a keenly searching kind. No muffling up in furs and broadcloth kept it out. It seemed to penetrate into the very bones of the shrinking wayfarers, and to rack them with cold and pains. Everything was wet, and clammy to the touch. The warm blaze alone defied it, and leaped and sparkled merrily. It was a day to be at home, crowding about the fire, telling stories of travellers who had lost their way in such weather on heaths and moors; and to love a warm hearth more than ever.

The dwarf's humor, as we know, was to have a fireside to himself; and when he was disposed to be convivial, to enjoy himself alone. By no means insensible to the comfort of being within doors, he ordered Tom Scott to pile the little stove with coals, and, dismissing his work for that day, determined to be jovial.

To this end, he lighted up fresh candles and heaped more fuel on the fire; and having dined off a beefsteak, which he cooked himself in somewhat of a savage and cannibal-like manner, brewed a great bowl of hot punch, lighted his pipe, and sat down to spend the evening.

At this moment, a low knocking at the cabin door arrested his attention. When it had been twice or thrice repeated, he softly opened the little window, and thrusting his head out, demanded who was there.

"Only me, Quilp," replied a woman's voice.

"Only you!" cried the dwarf, stretching his neck to obtain a better view of his visitor. "And what brings you here, you jade? How dare you approach the ogre's castle, eh!"

"I have come with some news," rejoined his spouse. "Don't be angry with me."

"Is it good news, pleasant news, news to make a man skip and snap his fingers?" said the dwarf. "Is the dear old lady dead?"

"I don't know what news it is, or whether it's good or bad," rejoined his wife.

"Then she's alive," said Quilp, "and there's nothing the matter with her. Go home again, you bird of evil note, go home!"

"I have brought a letter—" cried the meek little woman.

"Toss it in at the window here, and go your ways," said Quilp, interrupting her, "or I'll come out and scratch you."

"No, but please, Quilp—do hear me speak," urged his submissive wife, in tears. "Please do!"

"Speak then," growled the dwarf, with a malicious grin. "Be quick and short about it. Speak, will you?"

"It was left at our house this afternoon," said Mrs. Quilp, trembling, "by a boy who said he didn't know from whom it came, but that it was given to him to leave, and that he was told to say it must be brought on to you directly, for it was of the very greatest consequence.— But please," she added, as her husband stretched out his hand for it, " please let me in. You don't know how wet and cold I am, or how many times I have lost my way in coming here through this thick fog. Let me dry myself at the fire for five minutes. I'll go away directly you tell me to, Quilp. Upon my word I will."

Her amiable husband hesitated for a few moments; but bethinking himself that the letter might require some answer, of which she could be the bearer, closed the window, opened the door, and bade her enter. Mrs. Quilp obeyed right willingly, and, kneeling down before the fire to warm her hands, delivered into his a little packet.

"I'm glad you're wet," said Quilp, snatching it, and squinting at her. " I'm glad you're cold. I'm glad you've lost your way. I'm glad your eyes are red with crying. It does my heart good to see your little nose so pinched and frosty."

"Oh Quilp!" sobbed his wife. " How cruel it is of you!"

" Did she think I was dead!" said Quilp, wrinkling his face into a most extraordinary series of grimaces. " Did she think she was going to have all the money, and to marry somebody she liked! Ha ha ha! Did she?"

These taunts elicited no reply from the poor little woman, who remained on her knees, warming her hands, and sobbing, to Mr. Quilp's great delight. But as he was contemplating her, and chuckling excessively, he happened to observe that Tom Scott was delighted too; wherefore, that he might have no presumptuous partner in his glee, the dwarf instantly collared him, dragged him to the door, and after a short scuffle, kicked him into the yard In return for this mark of attention, Tom immediately walked upon his hands to the window, and—if the expression be allowable—looked in with his shoes: besides rattling his feet upon the glass like a Banshee upside down. As a matter of course, Mr. Quilp lost no time in resorting to the infallible poker, with which, after some dodging and lying in ambush, he paid his young friend one or two such unequivocal compliments that he vanished precipitately, and left him in quiet possession of the field.

"So! That little job being disposed of," said the dwarf, coolly, "I'll read my letter. Humph!" he muttered, looking at the direction. "I ought to know this writing. Beautiful Sally!"

Opening it, he read, in a fair, round, legal hand, as follows:

"Sammy has been practised upon, and has broken confidence. It has all come out. You had better not be in the way, for strangers are going to call upon you. They have been very quiet as yet, because they mean to surprise you. Don't lose time. I didn't. I am not to be found anywhere. If I was you, I wouldn't be, either. S. B., late of B. M."

To describe the changes that passed over Quilp's face as he read this letter half-a-dozen times, would require some new language; such, for power of expression, as was never written, read, or spoken. For a long time he did not utter one word; but after a considerable interval, during which Mrs. Quilp was almost paralyzed with the alarm his looks engendered, he contrived to gasp out,

"—If I had him here. If I only had him here——"

"Oh, Quilp!" said his wife, "what's the matter? Who are you angry with?"

"—I should drown him," said the dwarf, not heeding her. "Too easy a death, too short, too quick—but the river runs close at hand. Oh! if I had him here! Just to take him to the brink, coaxingly and pleasantly,— holding him by the buttonhole—joking with him,—and, with a sudden push, to send him splashing down! Drowning men come to the surface three times, they say. Ah! To see him those three times, and mock him as his face came bobbing up,—oh, what a rich treat that would be!"

"Quilp!" stammered his wife, venturing at the same time to touch him on the shoulder; "what has gone wrong?"

She was so terrified by the relish with which he pictured this pleasure to himself, that she could scarcely make herself intelligible.

"Such a bloodless cur!" said Quilp, rubbing his hands very slowly and pressing them tight together. "I

thought his cowardice and servility were the best guarantee for his keeping silence. Oh Brass, Brass—my dear,
good, affectionate, faithful, complimentary, charming
friend—if I only had you here ! "

His wife, who had retreated lest she should seem to
listen to these mutterings, ventured to approach him
again, and was about to speak, when he hurried to the
door and called Tom Scott, who, remembering his late
gentle admonition, deemed it prudent to appear immediately.

"There ! " said the dwarf, pulling him in. "Take her
home. Don't come here to-morrow, for this place will be
shut up. Come back no more till you hear from me or
see me. Do you mind ? "

Tom nodded sulkily, and beckoned Mrs. Quilp to lead
the way.

"As for you," said the dwarf, addressing himself to her,
"ask no questions about me, make no search for me, say
nothing concerning me. I shall not be dead, Mistress,
and that'll comfort you. He'll take care of you."

"But, Quilp? What is the matter? Where are you
going ? Do say something more."

"I'll say that," said the dwarf, seizing her by the arm,
"and do that too, which undone and unsaid would be
best for you unless you go directly."

"Has anything happened ? " cried his wife. "Oh ! Do
tell me that."

"Yes," snarled the dwarf. "No. What matter which ?
I have told you what to do. Woe betide you if you fail
to do it, or disobey me by a hair's breadth. Will you
go ! "

"I am going, I'll go directly ; but," faltered his wife,
"answer me one question first. Has this letter any connection with dear little Nell ? I must ask you that—I
must indeed, Quilp. You cannot think what days and
nights of sorrow I have had through having once deceived
that child. I don't know what harm I may have brought
about, but, great or little, I did it for you, Quilp. My
conscience misgave me when I did it. Do answer me
this question, if you please."

The exasperated dwarf returned no answer, but turned
round and caught up his usual weapon with such vehemence, that Tom Scott dragged his charge away by main

force, and as swiftly as he could. It was well he did so, for Quilp, who was nearly mad with rage, pursued them to the neighboring lane, and might have prolonged the chase but for the dense mist which obscured them from his view, and appeared to thicken every moment.

"It will be a good night for travelling anonymously," he said, as he returned slowly, being pretty well breathed with his run. "Stay. We may look better here. This is too hospitable and free."

By a great exertion of strength, he closed the two old gates which were deeply sunken in the mud, and barred them with a heavy beam. That done, he shook his matted hair from about his eyes, and tried them.—Strong and fast.

"The fence between this wharf and the next is easily climbed," said the dwarf, when he had taken these precautions. "There's a back lane too from there. That shall be my way out. A man need know his road well, to find it in this lovely place to-night. I need fear no unwelcome visitors while this lasts, I think."

Almost reduced to the necessity of groping his way with his hands (it had grown so dark and the fog had so much increased), he returned to his lair; and, after musing for some time over the fire, busied himself in preparations for a speedy departure.

While he was collecting a few necessaries and cramming them into his pockets, he never once ceased communing with himself in a low voice, or unclenched his teeth, which he had ground together on finishing Miss Brass's note.

"Oh Sampson!" he muttered, "good, worthy creature—if I could but hug you! If I could only fold you in my arms, and squeeze your ribs, as I *could* squeeze them if I once had you tight, what a meeting there would be between us! If we ever do cross each other again, Sampson, we'll have a greeting not easily to be forgotten, trust me. This time, Sampson, this moment when all had gone on so well, was no nicely chosen! It was so thoughtful of you, so penitent, so good. Oh, if we were face to face in this room again, my white-livered man of law, how well contented one of us would be!"

There he stopped; and raising the bowl of punch to his lips, drank a long deep draught, as if it were fair water and cooling to his parched mouth. Setting it down abruptly, and resuming his preparations, he went on with his soliloquy.

"There's Sally," he said with flashing eyes; "the woman has spirit, determination, purpose—was she asleep, or petrified? She could have stabbed him—poisoned him safely. She might have seen this coming on. Why does she give me notice when it's too late? When he sat there,—yonder there, over there,—with his white face, and red head, and sickly smile, why didn't I know what was passing in his heart? It should have stopped beating that night, if I had been in his secret; or there are no drugs to lull a man to sleep, and no fire to burn him!"

Another draught from the bowl; and, cowering over the fire with a ferocious aspect, he muttered to himself again.

"And this, like every other trouble and anxiety I have had of late times, springs from that old dotard and his darling child—two wretched feeble wanderers! I'll be their evil genius yet. And you, sweet Kit, honest Kit, virtuous, innocent Kit, look to yourself. Where I hate I bite. I hate you, my darling fellow, with good cause, and proud as you are to-night, I'll have my turn.—What's that!"

A knocking at the gate he had closed. A loud and violent knocking. Then a pause; as if those who knocked had stopped to listen. Then the noise again, more clamorous and importunate than before.

"So soon!" said the dwarf. "And so eager! I am afraid I shall disappoint you. It's well I'm quite prepared. Sally, I thank you!"

As he spoke, he extinguished the candle. In his impetuous attempts to subdue the brightness of the fire, he overset the stove, which came tumbling forward, and fell with a crash upon the burning embers it had shot forth in its descent, leaving the room in pitchy darkness. The noise at the gate still continuing, he felt his way to the door, and stepped into the open air.

At that moment the knocking ceased. It was about eight o'clock; but the dead of the darkest night would have been as noon-day, in comparison with the thick cloud which then rested upon the earth, and shrouded everything from view. He darted forward for a few paces, as if into the mouth of some dim, yawning cavern; then, thinking he had gone wrong, changed the direction of his steps; then stood still, not knowing where to turn.

"If they would knock again," said Quilp, trying to peer into the gloom by which he was surrounded, "the sound might guide me. Come. Batter the gate once more!"

He stood listening intently, but the noise was not renewed. Nothing was to be heard in that deserted place, but at intervals the distant barking of dogs. The sound was far away—now in one quarter, now answered in another—nor was it any guide, for it often came from shipboard, as he knew.

"If I could find a wall or fence," said the dwarf, stretching out his arms, and walking slowly on, "I should know which way to turn. A good, black, devil's night this, to have my dear friend here! If I had but that wish, it might, for anything I cared, never be day again."

As the word passed his lips, he staggered and fell; and next moment was fighting with the cold dark water.

For all its bubbling up and rushing in his ears, he could hear the knocking at the gate again—could hear a shout that followed it—could recognize the voice. For all his struggling and plashing, he could understand that they had lost their way, and had wandered back to the point from which they started; that they were all but looking on while he was drowned; that they were close at hand, but could not make an effort to save him; that he himself had shut and barred them out. He answered the shout—with a yell, which seemed to make the hundred fires that danced before his eyes tremble and flicker as if a gust of wind had stirred them. It was of no avail. The strong tide filled his throat, and bore him on, upon its rapid current.

Another mortal struggle, and he was up again, beating the water with his hands, and looking out with wild and glaring eyes that showed him some black object he was drifting close upon. The hull of a ship! He could touch its smooth and slippery surface with his hand. One loud cry now—but the resistless water bore him down before he could give it utterance, and, driving him under it, carried away a corpse.

It toyed and sported with its ghastly freight, now bruising it against the slimy piles, now hiding it in mud or long rank grass, now dragging it heavily over rough stones and gravel, now feigning to yield to its own element, and in the same action luring it away, until, tired of the ugly plaything, it flung it on a swamp—a dismal place where pirates had swung in chains, through many a wintry night—and left it there to bleach.

And there it lay alone. The sky was red with flame and the water that bore it there had been tinged with the sullen light as it flowed along. The place the deserted carcass had left so recently, a living man, was now a blazing ruin. There was something of the glare upon its face. The hair, stirred by the damp breeze, played in a kind of mockery of death—such a mockery as the dead man himself would have revelled in when alive—about its head, and its dress fluttered idly in the night wind.

CHAPTER THE SIXTY-EIGHTH.

LIGHTED rooms, bright fires, cheerful faces, the music of glad voices, words of love and welcome, warm hearts, and tears of happiness—what a change is this! But it is to such delights that Kit is hastening. They are awaiting him, he knows. He fears he will die of joy before he gets among them.

They have prepared him for this, all day. He is not to be carried off to-morrow with the rest, they tell him first. By degrees they let him know that doubts have arisen, that inquiries are to be made, and perhaps he may be pardoned after all. At last, the evening being come, they bring him to a room where some gentlemen are assembled. Foremost among them is his good old master, who comes and takes him by the hand. He hears that his innocence is established, and that he is pardoned. He cannot see the speaker, but he turns towards the voice, and in trying to answer, falls down insensible.

They recover him again, and tell him he must be composed, and bear this like a man. Somebody says he must think of his poor mother. It is because he does think of her so much that the happy news has overpowered him. They crowd about him, and tell him that the truth has gone abroad, and that all the town and country ring with sympathy for his misfortunes. He has no ears for this. His thoughts as yet have no wider range than home. Does *she* know it? what did she say? who told her? He can speak of nothing else.

They make him drink a little wine, and talk kindly to him for a while, until he is more collected, and can listen, and thank them. He is free to go. Mr. Garland thinks, if he feels better, it is time they went away. The gentlemen cluster round him, and shake hands with him. He feels very grateful to them for the interest they have in him, and for the kind promises they make; but the power of speech is gone again, and he has much ado to keep his feet, even though leaning on his master's arm.

As they pass through the dismal passages, some officers of the jail who are waiting there congratulate him in their rough way on his release. The newsmonger is of the number, but his manner is not quite hearty—there is something of surliness in his compliments. He looks upon Kit as an intruder, as one who has obtained admission to that place on false pretences, who has enjoyed a privilege without being duly qualified. He may be a very good sort of young man, he thinks, but he has no business there, and the sooner he is gone, the better.

The last door shuts behind them. They have passed the outer wall, and stand in the open air—in the street he has so often pictured to himself when hemmed in by those gloomy stones, and which has been in all his dreams. It seems wider and more busy than it used to be. The night is bad, and yet how cheerful and gay in his eyes! One of the gentlemen, in taking leave of him, pressed some money into his hand. He has not counted it; but when they have gone a few paces beyond the box for poor Prisoners, he hastily returns and drops it in.

Mr. Garland has a coach waiting in a neighboring street, and, taking Kit inside with him, bids the man drive home. At first they can only travel at a foot pace, and then with torches going on before, because of the heavy fog. But as they get farther from the river, and leave the closer portions of the town behind, they are able to dispense with this precaution and to proceed at a brisker rate. On the road hard galloping would be too slow for Kit; but when they are drawing near their journey's end, he begs they may go more slowly, and when the house appears in sight, that they may stop—only for a minute or two, to give him time to breathe.

But there is no stopping then, for the old gentleman speaks stoutly to him, the horses mend their pace, and they are already at the garden-gate. Next minute they are at the door. There is a noise of tongues, and tread of feet, inside. It opens. Kit rushes in, and finds his mother clinging round his neck.

And there, too, is the ever faithful Barbara's mother, still holding the baby as if she had never put it down since that sad day when they little hoped to have such joy as this—there she is, Heaven bless her, crying her eyes out, and sobbing as never woman sobbed before; and there is little Barbara—poor little Barbara, so much thinner and so much paler, and yet so very pretty—trembling like a leaf and supporting herself against the wall; and there is Mrs. Garland, neater and nicer than ever, fainting away stone dead with nobody to help her; and there is Mr. Abel, violently blowing his nose, and wanting to embrace everybody; and there is the single gentleman hovering round them all, and constant to nothing for an instant; and there is that good, dear, thoughtful little Jacob, sitting all alone by himself on the bottom stair, with his hands on his knees like an old man, roaring fearfully without giving any trouble to anybody; and each and all of them are for the time clean out of their wits, and do jointly and severally commit all manner of follies.

And even when the rest have in some measure come to themselves again, and can find words and smiles, Barbara —that soft-hearted, gentle foolish little Barbara—is suddenly missed, and found to be in a swoon by herself in the back parlor, from which swoon she falls into hysterics, and from which hysterics into a swoon again, and is, indeed, so bad, that despite a mortal quantity of vinegar and cold water she is hardly a bit better at last than she was at first. Then Kit's mother comes in and says, will he come and speak to her; and Kit says " Yes," and goes; and he says in a kind voice " Barbara!" and Barbara's mother tells her that "it's only Kit;" and Barbara says (with her eyes closed all the time) "Oh! but is it him indeed?" and Barbara's mother says "To be sure it is, my dear; there's nothing the matter now." And in further assurance that he's safe and sound, Kit speaks to her again; and then Barbara goes off into another fit of laughter, and then into another fit of crying; and then Barbara's mother and Kit's mother nod to each other and pretend to scold her—but only to bring her to herself the faster, bless you—and being experienced matrons, and acute at perceiving the first dawning symptoms of recovery, they comfort Kit with the assurance that "she'll do now," and so dismiss him to the place from whence he came.

Well! In that place (which is the next room) there are decanters of wine, and all that sort of thing, set out as grand as if Kit and his friends were first-rate company; and there is little Jacob, walking, as the popular phrase is, into a home-made plum-cake at a most surprising pace, and keeping his eye on the figs and oranges which are to follow, and making the best use of his time, you may believe. Kit no sooner comes in, than that single gentleman (never was such a busy gentleman) charges all the glasses—bumpers—and drinks his health, and tells him he shall never want a friend while he lives; and so does Mr. Garland, and so does Mrs. Garland, and so does Mr. Abel. But even this honor and distinction is not all, for the single gentleman forthwith pulls out of his pocket a massive silver watch—going hard, and right to half a second—and upon the back of this watch is engraved Kit's name, with flourishes all over; and in short it is Kit's watch, bought expressly for him, and presented to him on the spot. You may rest assured that Mr. and Mrs. Garland can't help hinting about their present in store, and that Mr. Abel tells outright that he has his; and that Kit is the happiest of the happy.

There is one friend he has not seen yet, and as he cannot be conveniently introduced into the family circle, by reason of his being an iron-shod quadruped, Kit takes the first opportunity of slipping away and hurrying to the stable. The moment he lays his hand upon the latch, the pony neighs the loudest pony's greeting; before he has crossed the threshold, the pony is capering about his loose box (for he brooks not the indignity of a halter), mad to give him welcome; and when Kit goes up to caress and pat him, the pony rubs his nose against his coat, and fondles him more lovingly than ever pony fondled man. It is the crowning circumstance of his earnest, heartfelt reception; and Kit fairly puts his arm round Whisker's neck and hugs him.

But how comes Barbara to trip in there? and how smart she is again! she has been at her glass since she recovered. How comes Barbara in the stable, of all places in the world? Why, since Kit has been away, the pony would take his food from nobody but her, and Barbara, you see, not dreaming Christopher was there, and just looking in to see that everything was right, has come upon him unawares. Blushing little Barbara!

It may be that Kit has caressed the pony enough; it may be that there are even better things to caress than ponies. He leaves him for Barbara at any rate, and hopes

she is better. Yes. Barbara is a great deal better.
She is afraid—and here Barbara looks down and blushes
more—that he must have thought her very foolish.
"Not at all," says Kit. Barbara is glad of that, and
coughs—Hem!—just the slightest cough possible—not
more than that.

What a discreet pony, when he chooses! He is as
quiet now, as if he were of marble. He has a very knowing look, but that he always has. "We have hardly
had time to shake hands, Barbara," says Kit. Barbara

gives him hers. Why, she is trembling now! Foolish,
fluttering Barbara!

Arm's length! The length of an arm is not much.
Barbara's was not a long arm by any means, and besides,
she didn't hold it out straight, but bent a little. Kit was
so near her when they shook hands, that he could see a
small tiny tear, yet trembling on an eyelash. It was
natural that he should look at it, unknown to Barbara.
It was natural that Barbara should raise her eyes unconsciously, and find him out. Was it natural that at that

instant, without any previous impulse or design, Kit should kiss Barbara? He did it, whether or no. Barbara said "for shame," but let him do it too—twice. He might have done it thrice, but the pony kicked up his heels and shook his head, as if he were suddenly taken with convulsions of delight, and Barbara being frightened, ran away—not straight to where her mother and Kit's mother were, though, lest they should see how red her cheeks were, and should ask her why. Sly little Barbara!

When the first transports of the whole party had subsided, and Kit and his mother, and Barbara and her mother, with little Jacob and the baby to boot, had had their suppers together—which there was no hurrying over, for they were going to stop there all night—Mr. Garland called Kit to him, and taking him into a room where they could be alone, told him that he had something yet to say, which would surprise him greatly. Kit looked so anxious and turned so pale on hearing this, that the old gentleman hastened to add, he would be agreeably surprised; and asked him if he would be ready next morning for a journey.

"For a journey, Sir!" cried Kit.

"In company with me and my friend in the next room. Can you guess its purpose?"

Kit turned paler yet, and shook his head.

"Oh yes. I think you do already," said his master. "Try."

Kit murmured something rather rambling and unintelligible, but he plainly pronounced the words "Miss Nell," three or four times—shaking his head while he did so, as if he would add there was no hope of that.

But Mr. Garland, instead of saying "Try again," as Kit had made sure he would, told him very seriously that he had guessed right.

"The place of their retreat is indeed discovered," he said, "at last. And that is our journey's end."

Kit faltered out such questions as, where was it, and how had it been found, and how long since, and was she well, and happy.

"Happy she is, beyond all doubt," said Mr. Garland. "And well, I—I trust she will be soon. She has been weak and ailing, as I learn, but she was better when I heard this morning, and they were full of hope. Sit you down, and you shall hear the rest."

Scarcely venturing to draw his breath, Kit did as he was told. Mr. Garland then related to him, how he had a brother (of whom he would remember to have heard him speak, and whose picture, taken when he was a young man, hung in the best room), and how this brother lived a long way off in a country-place, with an old clergyman who had been his early friend. How, although they loved each other as brothers should, they had not met for many years, but had communicated by letter from time to time, always looking forward to some period when they would take each other by the hand once more, and still letting the Present time steal on, as it was the habit of men to do, and suffering the Future to melt into the Past. How this brother, whose temper was very mild and quiet and retiring—such as Mr. Abel's—was greatly beloved by the simple people among whom he dwelt, who quite revered the Bachelor (for so they called him), and had every one experienced his charity and benevolence. How even those slight circumstances had come to his knowledge, very slowly and in course of years, for the Bachelor was one of those whose goodness shuns the light, and who have more pleasure in discovering and extolling the good deeds of others, than in trumpeting their own, be they never so commendable. How, for that reason, he seldom told them of his village friends; but how, for all that, his mind had become so full of two among them—a child and an old man, to whom he had been very kind—that, in a letter received a few days before, he had dwelt upon them from first to last, and had told there such a tale of their wanderings, and mutual love, that few could read it without being moved to tears. How he, the recipient of that letter, was directly led to the belief that these must be the very wanderers for whom so much search had been made, and whom Heaven had directed to his brother's care. How he had written for such further information as would put the fact beyond all doubt; how it had that morning arrived; had confirmed his first impression into a certainty; and was the immediate cause of that journey being planned, which they were to take to-morrow.

"In the meantime," said the old gentleman rising, and

laying his hand on Kit's shoulder, "you have great need of rest, for such a day as this would wear out the strongest man. Good-night and Heaven send our journey may have a prosperous ending!"

CHAPTER THE SIXTY-NINTH.

KIT was no sluggard next morning, but, springing from his bed some time before day, began to prepare for his welcome expedition. The hurry of spirits consequent upon the events of yesterday, and the unexpected intelligence he had heard at night, had troubled his sleep through the long dark hours, and summoned such uneasy dreams about his pillow that it was rest to rise.

But had it been the beginning of some great labor with the same end in view—had it been the commencement of a long journey, to be performed on foot in that inclement season of the year; to be pursued under every privation and difficulty; and to be achieved only with great distress, fatigue, and suffering—had it been the dawn of some painful enterprise, certain to task his utmost powers of resolution and endurance, and to need his utmost fortitude, but only likely to end, if happily achieved, in good fortune and delight to Nell—Kit's cheerful zeal would have been as highly roused, Kit's ardor and impatience would have been at least the same.

Nor was he alone excited and eager. Before he had been up a quarter of an hour the whole house were astir and busy. Everybody hurried to do something towards facilitating the preparations. The single gentleman, it is true, could do nothing himself, but he overlooked everybody else and was more locomotive than anybody. The work of packing and making ready went briskly on, and by daybreak every preparation for the journey was completed. Then Kit began to wish they had not been quite so nimble; for the travelling-carriage which had been hired for the occasion was not to arrive until nine o'clock, and there was nothing but breakfast to fill up the intervening blank of one hour and a half.

Yes there was, though. There was Barbara. Barbara was busy, to be sure, but so much the better—Kit could

help her, and that would pass away the time better than
any means that could be devised. Barbara had no objection to this arrangement, and Kit, tracking out the idea
which had come upon him so suddenly overnight, began
to think that surely Barbara was fond of him, and surely
he was fond of Barbara.

Now, Barbara, if the truth must be told—as it must
and ought to be—Barbara seemed, of all the little household, to take least pleasure in the bustle of the occasion ;
and when Kit, in the openness of his heart, told her how
glad and overjoyed it made him, Barbara became more
downcast still, and seemed to have even less pleasure in
it than before!

"You have not been home so long, Christopher," said
Barbara—and it is impossible to tell how carelessly she
said it—"You have not been home so long, that you need
be glad to go away again, I should think."

"But for such a purpose," returned Kit. "To bring
back Miss Nell! To see her again! Only think of that!
I am so pleased too to think that you will see her, Barbara, at last."

Barbara did not absolutely say that she felt no great
gratification on this point, but she expressed the sentiment so plainly by one little toss of her head, that
Kit was quite disconcerted, and wondered in his simplicity why she was so cool about it.

"You'll say she has the sweetest and beautifullest face
you ever saw, I know," said Kit, rubbing his hands.
"I'm sure you'll say that!"

Barbara tossed her head again.

"What's the matter, Barbara?" said Kit.

"Nothing," cried Barbara. And Barbara pouted—not
sulkily, or in an ugly manner, but just enough to make
her look more cherry-lipped than ever.

There is no school in which a pupil gets on so fast, as
that in which Kit became a scholar when he gave Barbara the kiss. He saw what Barbara meant now—he
had his lesson by heart all at once—she was the book—
there it was before him as plain as print.

"Barbara," said Kit, "you're not cross with me?"

Oh dear no! Why should Barbara be cross? And
what right had she to be cross? And what did it matter
whether she was cross or no? Who minded *her!*

" Why, *I* do," said Kit. " Of course I do."

Barbara didn't see why it was of course, at all.

Kit was sure she must. Would she think again?

Certainly, Barbara would think again. No, she didn't see why it was of course. She didn't understand what Christopher meant. And besides she was sure they wanted her upstairs by this time, and she must go, indeed——

" No, but Barbara," said Kit, detaining her gently, " let us part friends. I was always thinking of you, in my troubles. I should have been a great deal more miserable than I was, if it hadn't been for you."

Goodness gracious, how pretty Barbara was when she colored—and when she trembled, like a little shrinking bird!

" I am telling you the truth, Barbara, upon my word, but not half so strong as I could wish," said Kit, earnestly. " When I want you to be pleased to see Miss Nell, it's only because I like you to be pleased with what pleases me—that's all. As to her, Barbara, I think I could almost die to do her service, but you would think so too if you knew her as I do. I am sure you would."

Barbara was touched, and sorry to have appeared indifferent.

" I have been used, you see," said Kit, " to talk and think of her, almost as if she was an angel. When I look forward to meeting her again, I think of her smiling as she used to do, and being glad to see me, and putting out her hand and saying, ' It's my own old Kit,' or some such words as those—like what she used to say. I think of seeing her happy, and with friends about her, and brought up as she deserves, and as she ought to be. When I think of myself, it's as her old servant, and one that loved her dearly, as his kind, good, gentle mistress; and who would have gone—yes, and still would go—through any harm to serve her. Once I couldn't help being afraid that if she came back with friends about her she might forget, or be ashamed of having known, a humble lad like me, and so speak coldly, which would have cut me, Barbara, deeper than I can tell. But when I came to think again, I felt sure that I was doing her wrong in this; and so I went on as I did at first, hoping to see her once more, just as she used to be. Hoping this, and remembering what she was, has made me feel as if I would always try to please her, and always be what I should like to seem to her if I was still her servant. If I'm the better for that—and I don't think I'm the worse —I am grateful to her for it, and love and honor her the more. That's the plain honest truth, dear Barbara, upon my word it is!"

Little Barbara was not of a wayward or capricious nature, and, being full of remorse, melted into tears. To what further conversation this might have led, we need not stop to inquire; for the wheels of the carriage were heard at that moment, and, being followed by a smart ring at the garden gate, caused the bustle in the house, which had lain dormant for a short time, to burst again into tenfold life and vigor.

Simultaneously with the travelling equipage, arrived Mr. Chuckster in a hackney cab, with certain papers and supplies of money for the single gentleman, into whose hands he delivered them. This duty discharged, he subsided into the bosom of the family; and entertaining himself with a strolling or peripatetic breakfast, watched with a genteel indifference the process of loading the carriage.

"Snobby's in this I see, Sir?" he said to Mr. Abel Garland. "I thought he wasn't in the last trip because it was expected that his presence wouldn't be very acceptable to the ancient buffalo."

"To whom, Sir?" demanded Mr. Abel.

"To the old gentleman," returned Mr. Chuckster, slightly abashed.

"Our client prefers to take him now," said Mr. Abel, dryly. "There is no longer any need for that precaution, as my father's relationship to a gentleman in whom the objects of his search have full confidence, will be a sufficient guarantee for the friendly nature of their errand."

"Ah!" thought Mr. Chuckster, looking out of window, "anybody but me! Snobby before me, of course. He didn't happen to take that particular five-pound note, but I have not the smallest doubt that he's always up to something of that sort. I always said it, long before this came out. Devilish pretty girl that! 'Pon my soul, an amazing little creature!"

Barbara was the subject of Mr. Chuckster's commendations ; and as she was lingering near the carriage (all being now ready for its departure), that gentleman was suddenly seized with a strong interest in the proceedings, which impelled him to swagger down the garden, and take up his position at a convenient ogling distance. Having had great experience of the sex, and being perfectly acquainted with all those little artifices which find the readiest road to their hearts, Mr. Chuckster, on taking his ground, planted one hand on his hip, and with the other adjusted his flowing hair. This is a favorite at-

titude in the polite circles, and accompanied with a graceful whistling has been known to do immense execution.

Such, however, is the difference between town and country, that nobody took the smallest notice of this insinuating figure ; the wretches being wholly engaged in bidding the travellers farewell, in kissing hands to each other, waving handkerchiefs, and the like tame and vulgar practices. For now the single gentleman and Mr. Garland were in the carriage, and the postboy was in the saddle, and Kit, well wrapped and muffled up, was in the rumble behind; and Mrs. Garland was there, and Mr. Abel was there, and Kit's mother was there, and little Jacob was there, and Barbara's mother was visible in remote perspective, nursing the ever-wakeful baby; and all were nodding, beckoning, curtseying, or crying out "Goodbye!" with all the energy they could express. In another minute, the carriage was out of sight; and Mr. Chuckster remained alone upon the spot where it had lately been, with a vision of Kit standing up in the rumble waving his hand to Barbara, and of Barbara in the full light and lustre of his eyes—*his* eyes—Chuckster's—Chuckster the successful—on whom ladies of quality had looked with favor from phaetons in the parks on Sundays—waving hers to Kit!

How Mr. Chuckster, entranced by this monstrous fact, stood for some time rooted to the earth, protesting within himself that Kit was the Prince of felonious characters, and very Emperor or Great Mogul of Snobs, and how he clearly traced this revolting circumstance back to that old villany of the shilling, are matters foreign to our purpose; which is to track the rolling wheels, and bear the travellers company on their cold, bleak journey.

It was a bitter day. A keen wind was blowing, and rushed against them fiercely: bleaching the hard ground, shaking the white frost from the trees and hedges, and whirling it away like dust. But little cared Kit for weather. There was a freedom and freshness in the wind, as it came howling by, which, let it cut never so sharp, was welcome. As it swept on with its cloud of frost, bearing down the dry twigs and boughs and withered leaves, and carrying them away pell-mell, it seemed as though some general sympathy had got abroad, and everything was in a hurry like themselves. The harder the gusts, the better progress they appeared to make. It was a good thing to go struggling and fighting forward, vanquishing them one by one; to watch them driving up, gathering strength and fury as they came along; to bend for a moment, as they whistled past; and then to look back and see them speed away, their hoarse noise dying in the distance, and the stout trees cowering down before them.

All day long it blew without cessation. The night was clear and starlight, but the wind had not fallen, and the cold was piercing. Sometimes—towards the end of a long stage—Kit could not help wishing it were a little warmer : but when they stopped to change horses, and he had had a good run ; and what with that, and the bustle of paying the old postilion, and rousing the new one, and running to and fro again until the horses were put to, he was so warm that the blood tingled and smarted in his fingers' ends ; then he felt as if to have it one degree less cold would be to lose half the delight and glory of the journey : and up he jumped again right cheerily, singing to the merry music of the wheels as they rolled away, and, leaving the townspeople in their warm beds, pursued their course along the lonely road.

Meantime the two gentlemen inside, who were little disposed to sleep, beguiled the time with conversation. As both were anxious and expectant, it naturally turned upon the subject of their expedition, on the manner in which it had been brought about, and on the hopes and fears they entertained respecting it. Of the former they had many, of the latter few—none perhaps beyond that indefinable uneasiness which is inseparable from suddenly awakened hope, and protracted expectation.

In one of the pauses of their discourse, and when half the night had worn away, the single gentleman, who had gradually become more and more silent and thoughtful, turned to his companion and said abruptly :

" Are you a good listener ? "

" Like most other men, I suppose," returned Mr. Garland, smiling. " I can be, if I am interested ; and if not interested I should still try to appear so. Why do you ask ? "

" I have a short narrative on my lips," rejoined his friend, " and will try you with it. It is very brief."

Pausing for no reply, he laid his hand on the old gentleman's sleeve, and proceeded thus :

" There were once two brothers, who loved each other dearly. There was a disparity in their ages—some twelve years. I am not sure but they may insensibly have loved each other the better for that reason. Wide as the interval between them was, however, they became rivals too soon. The deepest and strongest affection of both their hearts settled upon one object.

" The youngest—there were reasons for *his* being sensitive and watchful—was the first to find this out. I will not tell you what misery he underwent, what agony of soul he knew, how great his mental struggle was. He had been a sickly child. His brother, patient and considerate in the midst of his own high health and strength, had many and many a day denied himself the sports he loved, to sit beside his couch, telling him old stories till his pale face lighted up with an unwonted glow; to carry him in his arms to some green spot, where he could tend the poor pensive boy as he looked upon the bright summer day, and saw all nature healthy but himself; to be in any way his fond and faithful nurse. I may not dwell on all he did, to make the poor, weak creature love him, or my tale would have no end. But when the time of trial came, the younger brother's heart was full of those old days. Heaven strengthened it to repay the sacrifices of inconsiderate youth by one of thoughtful manhood. He left his brother to be happy. The truth never passed his lips, and he quitted the country, hoping to die abroad.

"The elder brother married her. She was in Heaven before long, and left him with an infant daughter.

"If you have seen the picture gallery of any one old family, you will remember how the same face and figure —often the fairest and slightest of them all—come upon you in different generations; and how you trace the same sweet girl through a long line of portraits—never growing old or changing—the Good Angel of the race—abiding by them in all reverses—redeeming all their sins—

"In this daughter the mother lived again. You may judge with what devotion he who lost that mother almost in the winning, clung to this girl, her breathing image. She grew to womanhood, and gave her heart to one who could not know its worth. Well! Her fond father could not see her pine and droop. He might be more deserving than he thought him. He surely might become so with a wife like her. He joined their hands, and they were married.

"Through all the misery that followed this union; through all the cold neglect and undeserved reproach; through all the poverty he brought upon her; through all the struggles of their daily life, too mean and pitiful to tell, but dreadful to endure; she toiled on, in the deep devotion of her spirit, and in her better nature, as only

women can. Her means and substance wasted; her
father nearly beggared by her husband's hand, and the
hourly witness (for they lived now under one roof) of her
ill-usage and unhappiness,—she never, but for him, be-
wailed her fate. Patient, and upheld by strong affection
to the last, she died a widow of some three weeks' date,
leaving to her father's care two orphans; one a son of
ten or twelve years old; the other a girl—such another
infant child—the same in helplessness, in age, in form,
in feature—as she had been herself when her young
mother died.

"The elder brother, grandfather to these two children,
was now a broken man; crushed and borne down, less by
the weight of years than by the heavy hand of sorrow.
With the wreck of his possessions, he began to trade—
in pictures first, and then in curious ancient things. He
had entertained a fondness for such matters from a boy,
and the tastes he had cultivated were now to yield him
an anxious and precarious subsistence.

"The boy grew like his father in mind and person;
the girl so like her mother, that when the old man had
her on his knee, and looked into her mild blue eyes, he
felt as if awakening from a wretched dream, and his
daughter were a little child again. The wayward boy
soon spurned the shelter of his roof, and sought associates more congenial to his taste. The old man and the
child dwelt alone together.

"It was then, when the love of two dead people who
had been nearest and dearest to his heart, was all transferred to this slight creature; when her face, constantly
before him, reminded him from hour to hour of the too
early change he had seen in such another—of all the
suffering he had watched and known, and all his child
had undergone; when the young man's profligate and
hardened course drained him of money as his father's
had, and even sometimes occasioned them temporary privation and distress; it was then that there began to beset
him, and to be ever in his mind, a gloomy dread of poverty and want. He had no thought for himself in this.
His fear was for the child. It was a spectre in his house,
and haunted him night and day.

"The younger brother had been a traveller in many
countries, and had made his pilgrimage through life

alone. His voluntary banishment had been misconstrued, and he had borne (not without pain) reproach and slight for doing that which had wrung his heart, and cast a mournful shadow on his path. Apart from this, communication between him and the elder was difficult, and uncertain, and often failed; still it was not so wholly broken off but that he learnt—with long blanks and gaps between each interval of information—all that I have told you now.

"Then dreams of their young, happy life—happy to him though laden with pain and early care—visited his pillow yet oftener than before; and every night, a boy again, he was at his brother's side. With the utmost speed he could exert, he settled his affairs; converted into money all the goods he had; and, with honorable wealth enough for both, with open heart and hand, with limbs that trembled as they bore him on, with emotion such as men can hardly bear and live, arrived one evening at his brother's door!"

The narrator, whose voice had faltered lately, stopped. "The rest," said Mr. Garland, pressing his hand, "I know."

"Yes," rejoined his friend, after a pause, "We may spare ourselves the sequel. You know the poor result of all my search. Even when, by dint of such inquiries as the utmost vigilance and sagacity could set on foot, we found they had been seen with two poor travelling showmen; and in time discovered the men themselves—and in time, the actual place of their retreat; even then, we were too late. Pray God we are not too late again!"

"We cannot be," said Mr. Garland. "This time we must succeed."

"I have believed and hoped so," returned the other. "I try to believe and hope so still. But a heavy weight has fallen on my spirits, my good friend, and the sadness that gathers over me, will yield to neither hope nor reason."

"That does not surprise me," said Mr. Garland; "it is a natural consequence of the events you have recalled; of this dreary time and place; and above all, of this wild and dismal night. A dismal night, indeed! Hark! how the wind is howling!"

CHAPTER THE SEVENTIETH.

DAY broke and found them still upon their way. Since leaving home, they had halted here and there for necessary refreshment, and had been frequently delayed, especially in the night time, by waiting for fresh horses. They had made no other stoppages, but the weather continued rough, and the roads were often steep and heavy. It would be night again before they reached their place of destination.

Kit, all bluff and hardened with the cold, went on manfully; and having enough to do to keep his blood circulating, to picture to himself the happy end of this adventurous journey and to look about him and be amazed at everything, had little spare time for thinking of discomforts. Though his impatience, and that of his fellow-travellers, rapidly increased as the day waned, the hours did not stand still. The short daylight of winter soon faded away, and it was dark again when they had yet many miles to travel.

As it grew dusk, the wind fell; its distant moanings were more low and mournful; and as it came creeping up the road, and rattling covertly among the dry brambles on either hand, it seemed like some great phantom for whom the way was narrow, whose garments rustled as it stalked along. By degrees it lulled and died away; and then it came on to snow.

The flakes fell fast and thick, soon covering the ground some inches deep, and spreading abroad a solemn stillness. The rolling wheels were noiseless; and the sharp ring and clatter of the horses' hoofs, became a dull, muffled tramp. The life of their progress seemed to be slowly hushed, and something death-like to usurp its place.

Shading his eyes from the falling snow, which froze upon their lashes and obscured his sight, Kit often tried to catch the earliest glimpse of twinkling lights denoting their approach to some not distant town. He could descry objects enough at such times, but none correctly. Now a tall church-spire appeared in view, which presently became a tree, a barn, a shadow on the ground, thrown on it by their own bright lamps. Now there were horsemen, foot-passengers, carriages, going on before, or meeting them in narrow ways; which, when they were close upon them, turned to shadows too. A wall, a ruin, a sturdy gable-end, would rise up in the road; and when they were plunging headlong at it, would be the road itself. Strange turnings too, bridges, and sheets of water, appeared to start up here and there, making the way doubtful and uncertain; and yet they were on the same bare road, and these things, like the others, as they were passed, turned into dim illusions.

He descended slowly from his seat—for his limbs were numbed—when they arrived at a lone posting-house, and inquired how far they had to go to reach their journey's end. It was a late hour in such by-places, and the people were abed; but a voice answered from an upper window, Ten miles. The ten minutes that ensued appeared an hour; but at the end of that time, a shivering figure led out the horses they required, and after another brief delay they were again in motion.

It was a cross-country road, full, after the first three or four miles, of holes and cart ruts, which being covered by the snow, were so many pitfalls to the trembling horses, and obliged them to keep a footpace. As it was next to impossible for men so much agitated as they were by this time, to sit still and move so slowly, all three got out and plodded on behind the carriage. The distance seemed interminable, and the walk was most laborious. As each was thinking within himself that the driver must have lost his way, a church bell, close at hand, struck the hour of midnight, and the carriage stopped. It had moved softly enough, but when it ceased to crunch the snow, the silence was as startling as if some great noise had been replaced by perfect stillness.

"This is the place, gentlemen," said the driver, dismounting from his horse, and knocking at the door of a little inn. "Halloa! Past twelve o'clock is the dead of night here."

The knocking was loud and long, but it failed to rouse the drowsy inmates. All continued dark and silent as before. They fell back a little, and looked up at the windows, which were mere black patches in the whitened house front. No light appeared. The house might have been deserted, or the sleepers dead, for any air of life it had about it.

They spoke together, with a strange inconsistency, in whispers; unwilling to disturb again the dreary echoes they had just now raised.

" Let us go on," said the younger brother, "and leave this good fellow to wake them, if he can. I cannot rest until I know that we are not too late. Let us go on, in the name of heaven ! "

They did so, leaving the postilion to order such accommodation as the house afforded, and to renew his knocking. Kit accompanied them with a little bundle, which he had hung in the carriage when they left home, and had not forgotten since—the bird in his old cage—just as she had left him. She would be glad to see her bird, he knew.

The road wound gently downward. As they proceeded, they lost sight of the church whose clock they had heard, and of the small village clustering round it. The knocking, which was now renewed, and which in that stillness they could plainly hear, troubled them. They wished the man would forbear, or that they had told him not to break the silence until they returned.

The old church-tower, clad in a ghostly garb of pure cold white, again rose up before them, and a few moments brought them close beside it. A venerable building—gray, even in the midst of the hoary landscape. An ancient sun-dial on the belfry wall was nearly hidden by the snow-drift, and scarcely to be known for what it was. Time itself seemed to have grown dull and old, as if no day were ever to displace the melancholy night.

A wicket gate was close at hand, but there was more than one path across the churchyard to which it led, and, uncertain which to take, they came to a stand again.

The village street—if street that could be called which was an irregular cluster of poor cottages of many heights and ages, some with their fronts, some with their backs, and some with gable-ends towards the road, with here and there a signpost, or a shed encroaching on the path —was close at hand. There was a faint light in a chamber window not far off, and Kit ran towards that house to ask their way.

His first shout was answered by an old man within, who presently appeared at the casement, wrapping some garment round his throat as a protection from the cold, and demanded who was abroad at that unseasonable hour, wanting him.

"'Tis hard weather this," he grumbled, "and not a night to call me up in. My trade is not of that kind that I need be roused from bed. The business on which folks want me, will keep cold, especially at this season. What do you want?"

"I would not have roused you, if I had known you were old and ill," said Kit.

"Old!" repeated the other peevishly. "How do you know I am old? Not so old as you think, friend, perhaps. As to being ill, you will find many young people in worse case than I am. More's the pity that it should be so— not that I should be strong and hearty for my years, I mean, but that they should be weak and tender. I ask your pardon though," said the old man, "if I spoke rather rough at first. My eyes are not good at night—that's neither age nor illness; they never were—and I didn't see you were a stranger."

"I am sorry to call you from your bed," said Kit, "but those gentlemen you may see by the churchyard gate, are strangers too, who have just arrived from a long journey, and seek the parsonage-house. You can direct us?"

"I should be able to," answered the old man, in a trembling voice, "for come next summer I have been sexton here good fifty years. The right-hand path, friend, is the road.—There is no ill news for our good gentleman, I hope?"

Kit thanked him, and made him a hasty answer in the negative; he was turning back, when his attention was caught by the voice of a child. Looking up, he saw a very little creature at a neighboring window.

"What is that?" cried the child, earnestly. "Has my dream come true? Pray speak to me, whoever that is, awake and up."

"Poor boy!" said the sexton, before Kit could answer, "how goes it, darling?"

"Has my dream come true?" exclaimed the child again, in a voice so fervent that it might have thrilled to the heart of any listener. "But no, that can never be. How could it be—Oh! how could it!"

"I guess his meaning," said the sexton. "To thy bed again, dear boy!"

"Ay!" cried the child, in a burst of despair, "I knew it could never be, I felt too sure of that, before I asked. But, all to-night and last night too, it was the same. I never fall asleep, but that cruel dream comes back."

"Try to sleep again," said the old man, soothingly. "It will go, in time."

"No no, I would rather that it stayed—cruel as it is, I would rather that it stayed," rejoined the child. "I am not afraid to have it in my sleep, but I am so sad—so very, very sad."

The old man blessed him, the child in tears replied Good-night, and Kit was again alone.

He hurried back, moved by what he had heard, though more by the child's manner than by anything he had said, as his meaning was hidden from him. They took the path indicated by the sexton, and soon arrived before the parsonage wall. Turning round to look about them when

38

they had got thus far, they saw, among some ruined buildings at a distance, one single solitary light.

It shone from what appeared to be an old oriel window. and being surrounded by the deep shadows of overhanging walls, sparkled like a star. Bright and glimmering as the stars above their heads, lonely and motionless as they, it seemed to claim some kindred with the eternal lamps of Heaven, and to burn in fellowship with them.

"What light is that!" exclaimed the younger brother.

"It is surely," said Mr. Garland, "in the ruin where they live. I see no other ruin hereabouts."

"They cannot," returned the brother hastily, "be waking at this late hour—"

Kit interposed directly, and begged that, while they rang and waited at the gate, they would let him make his way to where this light was shining and try to ascertain if any people were about. Obtaining the permission he desired, he darted off with breathless eagerness, and, still carrying the bird-cage in his hand, made straight towards the spot.

It was not easy to hold that pace among the graves, and at another time he might have gone more slowly, or round by the path. Unmindful of all obstacles, however, he pressed forward without slackening his speed, and soon arrived within a few yards of the window.

He approached as softly as he could, and advancing so near the wall as to brush the whitened ivy with his dress, listened. There was no sound inside. The church itself was not more quiet. Touching the glass with his cheek, he listened again. No. And yet there was such a silence all round, that he felt sure he could have heard even the breathing of a sleeper, if there had been one there.

A strange circumstance, a light in such a place at that time of night, with no one near it.

A curtain was drawn across the lower portion of the window, and he could not see into the room. But there was no shadow thrown upon it from within. To have gained a footing on the wall and tried to look in from above, would have been attended with some danger—certainly with some noise, and the chance of terrifying the child, if that really were her habitation. Again and again he listened; again and again the same wearisome blank.

Leaving the spot with slow and cautious steps, and skirting the ruin for a few paces, he came at length to a door. He knocked. No answer. But there was a curious noise inside. It was difficult to determine what it was. It bore a resemblance to the low moaning of one in pain, but it was not that, being far too regular and constant. Now it seemed a kind of song, now a wail—seemed, that is, to his changing fancy, for the sound itself was never changed or checked It was unlike anything he had ever heard, and, in its tone there was something fearful, chilling, and unearthly.

The listener's blood ran colder now than ever it had done in frost and snow, but he knocked again. There was no answer, and the sound went on without any interruption. He laid his hand softly upon the latch, and put his knee against the door. It was not secured on the inside, but yielded to the pressure, and turned upon its hinges. He saw the glimmering of a fire upon the old walls, and entered.

CHAPTER THE SEVENTY-FIRST.

THE dull, red glow of a wood fire—for no lamp or candle burnt within the room—showed him a figure, seated on the hearth with its back towards him, bending over the fitful light. The attitude was that of one who sought the heat. It was, and yet was not. The stooping posture and the cowering form were there, but no hands were stretched out to meet the grateful warmth, no shrug or shiver compared its luxury with the piercing cold outside. With limbs huddled together, head bowed down, arms crossed upon the breast, and fingers tightly clenched, it rocked to and fro upon its seat without a moment's pause, accompanying the action with the mournful sound he had heard.

The heavy door had closed behind him on his entrance, with a crash that made him start. The figure neither spoke nor turned to look, nor gave in any other way the faintest sign of having heard the noise. The form was that of an old man, his white head akin in color to the mouldering embers upon which he gazed. He, and the failing light and dying fire, the time-worn room, the soliwide, the wasted life, and gloom, were all in fellowship. Ashes, and dust, and ruin!

Kit tried to speak, and did pronounce some words, though what they were he scarcely knew. Still the same terrible low cry went on—still the same rocking in the chair—the same stricken figure was there, unchanged and heedless of his presence.

He had his hand upon the latch, when something in the form—distinctly seen as one log broke and fell, and, as it fell, blazed up—arrested it. He returned to where he had stood before—advanced a pace—another—another still. Another, and he saw the face. Yes! Changed as it was, he knew it well.

"Master!" he cried, stooping on one knee and catching at his hand. "Dear master. Speak to me!"

The old man turned slowly towards him; and muttered, in a hollow voice,

"This is another!—How many of these spirits there have been to-night!"

"No spirit, master. No one but your old servant. You know me now, I am sure? Miss Nell—where is she—where is she?"

"They all say that!" cried the old man. "They all ask the same question. A spirit!"

"Where is she?" demanded Kit. "Oh tell me but that —but that, dear master!"

"She is asleep—yonder—in there."

"Thank God!"

"Ay! Thank God!" returned the old man. "I have prayed to Him, many, and many, and many a livelong night, when she has been asleep, He knows. Hark! Did she call?"

"I heard no voice."

"You did. You hear her now. Do you tell me that you don't hear *that?*"

He started up, and listened again.

"Nor that?" he cried, with a triumphant smile. "Can anybody know that voice so well as I! Hush! hush!"

Motioning to him to be silent, he stole away into another chamber. After a short absence (during which he could be heard to speak in a softened soothing tone) he returned, bearing in his hand a lamp.

"She is still asleep," he whispered. "You were right.

She did not call—unless she did so in her slumber. She has called to me in her sleep before now, Sir; as I sat by, watching, I have seen her lips move, and have known, though no sound came from them, that she spoke of me. I feared the light might dazzle her eyes and wake her, so I brought it here."

He spoke rather to himself than to the visitor, but when he had put the lamp upon the table, he took it up, as if impelled by some momentary recollection or curiosity, and held it near his face. Then, as if forgetting his motive in the very action, he turned away and put it down again.

"She is sleeping soundly," he said; "but no wonder. Angel hands have strewn the ground deep with snow, that the lightest footstep may be lighter yet; and the very birds are dead, that they may not wake her. She used to feed them, Sir. Though never so cold and hungry, the timid things would fly from us. They never flew from her!"

Again he stopped to listen, and scarcely drawing breath, listened for a long, long time. That fancy past, he opened an old chest, took out some clothes as fondly as if they had been living things, and began to smooth and brush them with his hand.

"Why dost thou lie so idle there, dear Nell," he murmured, "when there are bright red berries out of doors waiting for thee to pluck them! Why dost thou lie so idle there, when thy little friends come creeping to the door, crying ' where is Nell—sweet Nell ?'—and sob, and weep, because they do not see thee. She was always gentle with children. The wildest would do her bidding —she had a tender way with them, indeed she had!"

Kit had no power to speak. His eyes were filled with tears.

"Her little homely dress,—her favorite!" cried the old man, pressing it to his breast, and patting it with his shrivelled hand. "She will miss it when she wakes. They have hid it here in sport, but she shall have it—she shall have it. I would not vex my darling, for the wide world's riches. See here—these shoes—how worn they are—she kept them to remind her of our last long journey. You see where the little feet were bare upon the ground. They told me, afterwards, that the stones had cut and bruised them. *She* never told me that. No, no,

God bless her! and, I have remembered since, she walked
behind me, Sir, that I might not see how lame she was—
but yet she had my hand in hers, and seemed to lead me
still."

He pressed them to his lips, and having carefully put
them back again, went on communing with himself—looking wistfully from time to time towards the chamber he
had lately visited.

"She was not wont to be a lie-abed; but she was well
then. We must have patience. When she is well again,
she will rise early, as she used to do, and ramble abroad
in the healthy morning time. I often tried to track the
way she had gone, but her small fairy footstep left no
print upon the dewy ground, to guide me. Who is that?
Shut the door. Quick!—Have we not enough to do to
drive away that marble cold, and keep her warm!"

The door was indeed opened, for the entrance of Mr.
Garland and his friend, accompanied by two other persons. These were the schoolmaster, and the bachelor.
The former held a light in his hand. He had, it seemed,
but gone to his own cottage to replenish the exhausted
lamp, at the moment when Kit came up and found the
old man alone.

He softened again at sight of these two friends, and,
laying aside the angry manner—if to anything so feeble
and so sad the term can be applied—in which he had
spoken when the door opened, resumed his former seat,
and subsided, by little and little, into the old action, and
the old dull, wandering sound.

Of the strangers he took no heed whatever. He had
seen them, but appeared quite incapable of interest or
curiosity. The younger brother stood apart. The bachelor drew a chair towards the old man, and sat down close
beside him. After a long silence, he ventured to speak.

"Another night, and not in bed!" he said softly; "I
hoped you would be more mindful of your promise to me.
Why do you not take some rest?"

"Sleep has left me," returned the old man. "It is all
with her!"

"It would pain her very much to know that you were
watching thus," said the bachelor. "You would not give
her pain?"

"I am not so sure of that, if it would only rouse her.

She has slept so very long. And yet I am rash to say so. It is a good and happy sleep—eh?"

"Indeed it is," returned the bachelor. "Indeed, indeed, it is!"

"That's well!—and the waking,"—faltered the old man.

"Happy too. Happier than tongue can tell, or heart of man conceive."

They watched him as he rose and stole on tiptoe to the other chamber where the lamp had been replaced. They listened as he spoke again within its silent walls. They looked into the faces of each other, and no man's cheek was free from tears. He came back, whispering that she was still asleep, but that he thought she had moved. It was her hand, he said—a little—a very, very little—but he was pretty sure she had moved it—perhaps in seeking his. He had known her do that before now, though in the deepest sleep the while. And when he had said this, he dropped into his chair again, and clasping his hands above his head, uttered a cry never to be forgotten.

The poor schoolmaster motioned to the bachelor that he would come upon the other side, and speak to him. They gently unlocked his fingers, which he had twisted in his gray hair, and pressed them in their own.

"He will hear me," said the schoolmaster, "I am sure. He will hear either me or you if we beseech him. She would, at all times."

"I will hear any voice she liked to hear," cried the old man. "I love all she loved!"

"I know you do," returned the schoolmaster. "I am certain of it. Think of her; think of all the sorrows and afflictions you have shared together; of all the trials, and all the peaceful pleasures, you have jointly known."

"I do. I do. I think of nothing else."

"I would have you think of nothing else to-night—of nothing but those things which will soften your heart, dear friend, and open it to old affections and old times. It is so that she would speak to you herself, and in her name it is that I speak now."

"You do well to speak softly," said the old man. "We will not wake her. I should be glad to see her eyes again, and to see her smile. There is a smile upon her young face now, but it is fixed and changeless. I would have it come and go. That shall be in Heaven's good time. We will not wake her."

"Let us not talk of her in her sleep, but as she used to be when you were journeying together, far away—as she was at home, in the old house from which you fled together—as she was in the old cheerful time," said the schoolmaster.

"She was always cheerful—very cheerful," cried the old man, looking steadfastly at him. "There was ever something mild and quiet about her, I remember, from the first; but she was of a happy nature."

"We have heard you say," pursued the schoolmaster, "that in this, and in all goodness, she was like her mother. You can think of, and remember her?"

He maintained his steadfast look, but gave no answer.

"Or even one before her," said the bachelor. "It is many years ago, and affliction makes the time longer, but you have not forgotten her whose death contributed to make this child so dear to you even before you knew her worth or could read her heart? Say, that you could carry back your thoughts to very distant days—to the time of your early life—when, unlike this fair flower, you did not pass your youth alone. Say, that you could remember, long ago, another child who loved you dearly, you being but a child yourself. Say, that you had a brother, long forgotten, long unseen, long separated from you, who now, at last, in your utmost need came back to comfort and console you "—

"To be to you what you were once to him," cried the younger, falling on his knee before him; "to repay your old affection, brother dear, by constant care, solicitude, and love; to be, at your right hand, what he never ceased to be when oceans rolled between us; to call to witness his unchanging truth and mindfulness of bygone days, whole years of desolation. Give me but one word of recognition, brother—and never—no never, in the brightest moment of our youngest days, when, poor silly boys, we thought to pass our lives together—have we been half as dear and precious to each other as we shall be from this time hence!"

The old man looked from face to face, and his lips moved; but no sound came from them in reply.

"If we were knit together then," pursued the younger

brother, "what will be the bond between us now! Our
love and fellowship began in childhood, when life was all
before us, and will be resumed when we have proved it,
and are but children at the last. As many restless spirits,
who have hunted fortune, fame, or pleasure through the
world, retire in their decline to where they first drew
breath, vainly seeking to be children once again before
they die, so we, less fortunate than they in early life, but
happier in its closing scenes, will set up our rest again

among our boyish haunts; and going home with no hope
realized, that had its growth in manhood—carrying back
nothing that we brought away, but our old yearnings to
each other—saving no fragment from the wreck of life,
but that which first endeared it—may be indeed but children as at first. And even," he added in an altered voice,
"even if what I dread to name has come to pass—even
if that be so, or is to be (which Heaven forbid and spare
us!)—still, dear brother, we are not apart, and have that
comfort in our great affliction."

By little and little, the old man had drawn back towards the inner chamber, while these words were spoken. He pointed there, as he replied, with trembling lips,

"You plot among you to wean my heart from her. You never will do that—never while I have life. I have no relative or friend but her—I never had—I never will have. She is all in all to me. It is too late to part us now."

Waving them off with his hand, and calling softly to her as he went, he stole into the room. They who were left behind, drew close together, and after a few whispered words—not unbroken by emotion, or easily uttered —followed him. They moved so gently, that their footsteps made no noise; but there were sobs from among the group, and sounds of grief and mourning.

For she was dead. There, upon her little bed, she lay at rest. The solemn stillness was no marvel now.

She was dead. No sleep so beautiful and calm, so free from trace of pain, so fair to look upon. She seemed a creature fresh from the hand of God, and waiting for the breath of life; not one who had lived and suffered death.

Her couch was dressed with here and there some winter berries and green leaves, gathered in a spot she had been used to favor. "When I die, put near me something that has loved the light, and had the sky above it always." Those were her words.

She was dead. Dear, gentle, patient, noble Nell was dead. Her little bird—a poor slight thing the preasure of a finger would have crushed—was stirring nimbly in its cage; and the strong heart of its child-mistress was mute and motionless forever.

Where were the traces of her early cares, her sufferings, and fatigues? All gone. Sorrow was dead indeed in her, but peace and perfect happiness were born; imaged in her tranquil beauty and profound repose.

And still her former self lay there, unaltered in this change. Yes. The old fireside had smiled upon that same sweet face; it had passed like a dream through haunts of misery and care; at the door of the poor schoolmaster on the summer evening, before the furnace fire upon the cold wet night, at the still bedside of the dying boy, there had been the same mild lovely look. So shall we know the angels in their majesty, after death.

The old man held one languid arm in his, and had the small hand tight folded to his breast, for warmth. It was the hand she had stretched out to him with her last smile—the hand that had led him on through all their wanderings. Ever and anon he pressed it to his lips; then hugged it to his breast again, murmuring that it was warmer now; and as he said it he looked, in agony, to those who stood around, as if imploring them to help her.

She was dead, and past all help, or need of it. The ancient rooms she had seemed to fill with life, even while her own was waning fast—the garden she had tended— the eyes she had gladdened—the noiseless haunts of many a thoughtful hour—the paths she had trodden as it were but yesterday—could know her no more.

" It is not," said the schoolmaster, as he bent down to kiss her on the cheek, and gave his tears free vent, " it is not on earth that Heaven's justice ends. Think what it is, compared with the World to which her young spirit has winged its early flight, and say, if one deliberate wish expressed in solemn terms above this bed could call her back to life, which of us would utter it ! "

CHAPTER THE SEVENTY-SECOND.

WHEN morning came, and they could speak more calmly on the subject of their grief, they heard how her life had closed.

She had been dead two days. They were all about her at the time, knowing that the end was drawing on. She died soon after daybreak. They had read and talked to her in the earlier portion of the night, but as the hours crept on, she sank to sleep. They could tell, by what she faintly uttered in her dreams, that they were of her journeyings with the old man; they were of no painful scenes, but of those who had helped and used them kindly, for she often said " God bless you ! " with great fervor. Waking, she never wandered in her mind but once, and that was of beautiful music which she said was in the air. God knows. It may have been.

Opening her eyes at last, from a very quiet sleep, she

begged that they would kiss her once again. That done, she turned to the old man with a lovely smile upon her face—such, they said, as they had never seen, and never could forget—and clung with both her arms about his neck. They did not know that she was dead, at first.

She had spoken very often of the two sisters, who, she said, were like dear friends to her. She wished they could be told how much she thought about them, and how she had watched them as they walked together, by the river side at night. She would like to see poor Kit, she had often said of late. She wished there was somebody to take her love to Kit. And even then, she never thought or spoke about him, but with something of her old, clear, merry laugh.

For the rest, she had never murmured or complained; but, with a quiet mind, and manner quite unaltered—save that she every day became more earnest and more grateful to them—faded like the light upon a summer's evening.

The child who had been her little friend came there almost as soon as it was day, with an offering of dried flowers which he begged them to lay upon her breast. It was he who had come to the window overnight and spoken to the sexton, and they saw in the snow traces of small feet, where he had been lingering near the room in which she lay before he went to bed. He had a fancy, it seemed, that they had left her there alone; and could not bear the thought.

He told them of his dream again, and that it was of her being restored to them, just as she used to be. He begged hard to see her, saying that he would be very quiet, and that they need not fear his being alarmed, for he had sat alone by his young brother all day long, when *he* was dead, and had felt glad to be so near him. They let him have his wish; and indeed he kept his word, and was in his childish way a lesson to them all.

Up to that time, the old man had not spoken once—except to her—or stirred from the bedside. But when he saw her little favorite, he was moved as they had not seen him yet, and made as though he would have him come nearer. Then pointing to the bed, he burst into tears for the first time, and they who stood by, knowing that the sight of this child had done him good, left them alone together.

Soothing him with his artless talk of her, the child persuaded him to take some rest, to walk abroad, to do almost as he desired him. And when the day came on, which must remove her in her earthly shape from earthly eyes forever, he led him away, that he might not know when she was taken from him.

They were to gather fresh leaves and berries for her bed. It was Sunday—a bright, clear, wintry afternoon —and as they traversed the village street, those who were walking in their path drew back to make way for them, and gave them a softened greeting. Some shook the old man kindly by the hand, some stood uncovered while he tottered by, and many cried, "God help him!" as he passed along.

"Neighbor!" said the old man, stopping at the cottage where his young guide's mother dwelt, "how is it that the folks are nearly all in black to-day? I have seen a mourning ribbon or a piece of crape on almost every one."

She could not tell, the woman said.

"Why, you yourself—you wear the color too!" he cried. "Windows are closed that never used to be by day. What does this mean?"

Again the woman said she could not tell.

"We must go back," said the old man, hurriedly. "We must see what this is."

"No, no," cried the child, detaining him. "Remember what you promised. Our way is to the old green lane, where she and I so often were, and where you found us more than once making those garlands for her garden. Do not turn back!"

"Where is she now?" said the old man. "Tell me that."

"Do you not know?" returned the child. "Did we not leave her, but just now?"

"True. True. It *was* her we left—was it!"

He pressed his hand upon his brow, looked vacantly round, and as if impelled by a sudden thought, crossed the road, and entered the sexton's house. He and his deaf assistant were sitting before the fire. Both rose up, on seeing who it was.

The child made a hasty sign to them with his hand. It

was the action of an instant, but that, and the old man's look, were quite enough.

"Do you—do you bury any one to-day?" he said, eagerly.

"No, no! Who should we bury, Sir?" returned the sexton.

"Ay, who indeed! I say with you, who indeed?"

"It is a holiday with us, good Sir," returned the sexton mildly. "We have no work to do to-day."

"Why then, I'll go where you will," said the old man, turning to the child. "You're sure of what you tell me? You would not deceive me? I am changed even in the little time since you last saw me."

"Go thy ways with him, Sir," cried the sexton, "and Heaven be with ye both!"

"I am quite ready," said the old man, meekly. "Come, boy, come—" and so submitted to be led away.

And now the bell—the bell she had so often heard by night and day, and listened to with solemn pleasure almost as a living voice—rang its remorseless toll for her, so young, so beautiful, so good. Decrepit age, and vigorous life, and blooming youth, and helpless infancy, poured forth—on crutches, in the pride of strength and health, in the full blush of promise, in the mere dawn of life—to gather round her tomb. Old men were there, whose eyes were dim and senses failing—grandmothers, who might have died ten years ago, and still been old— the deaf, the blind, the lame, the palsied, the living dead in many shapes and forms, to see the closing of that early grave. What was the death it would shut in, to that which still could crawl and creep above it!

Along the crowded path they bore her now; pure as the newly-fallen snow that covered it; whose day on earth had been as fleeting. Under that porch, where she had sat when Heaven in its mercy brought her to that peaceful spot, she passed again, and the old church received her in its quiet shade.

They carried her to one old nook, where she had many and many a time sat musing, and laid their burden softly on the pavement. The light streamed on it through the colored window—a window, were the boughs of trees were ever rustling in the summer, and where the birds sang sweetly all day long. With every breath of air that stirred among those branches in the sunshine, some trembling, changing light would fall upon her grave.

Earth to earth, ashes to ashes, dust to dust. Many a young hand dropped in its little wreath, many a stifled sob was heard. Some—and they were not a few—knelt down. All were sincere and truthful in their sorrow.

The service done, the mourners stood apart, and the villagers closed round to look into the grave before the pavement-stone should be replaced. One called to mind how he had seen her sitting on that very spot, and how her book had fallen on her lap, and she was gazing with a pensive face upon the sky. Another told how he had wondered much that one so delicate as she, should be so bold; how she had never feared to enter the church alone at night, but had loved to linger there when all was quiet, and even to climb the tower stair, with no more light than that of the moon rays stealing through the loopholes in the thick old wall. A whisper went about among the oldest there, that she had seen and talked with angels; and when they called to mind how she had looked, and spoken, and her early death, some thought it might be so, indeed. Thus, coming to the grave in little knots, and glancing down, and giving place to others, and falling off in whispering groups of three or four, the church was cleared in time of all but the sexton and the mourning friends.

They saw the vault covered and the stone fixed down. Then, when the dusk of evening had come on, and not a sound disturbed the sacred stillness of the place—when the bright moon poured in her light on tomb and monument, on pillar, wall, and arch, and most of all (it seemed to them) upon her quiet grave—in that calm time, when all outward things and inward thoughts teem with assurances of immortality, and worldly hopes and fears are humbled in the dust before them—then, with tranquil and submissive hearts they turned away, and left the child with God.

Oh! it is hard to take to heart the lesson that such deaths will teach, but let no man reject it, for it is one that all must learn, and is a mighty, universal Truth. When Death strikes down the innocent and young, for every fragile form from which he lets the panting spirit free, a hundred virtues rise, in shapes of mercy, charity, and love, to walk the world, and bless it. Of every tear that sorrowing mortals shed on such green graves, some good is born, some gentler nature comes. In the Destroyer's steps there spring up bright creations that defy his power, and his dark path becomes a way of light to Heaven.

It was late when the old man came home. The boy had led him to his own dwelling, under some pretence, on their way back; and, rendered drowsy by his long ramble and late want of rest, he had sunk into a deep sleep by the fireside. He was perfectly exhausted, and they were careful not to rouse him. The slumber held him a long time, and when he at length awoke the moon was shining.

The younger brother, uneasy at his protracted absence, was watching at the door for his coming, when he appeared in the pathway with his little guide. He advanced to meet them, and tenderly obliging the old man to lean upon his arm, conducted him with slow and trembling steps towards the house.

He repaired to her chamber, straight. Not finding what he had left there, he returned with distracted looks to the room in which they were assembled. From that, he rushed into the schoolmaster's cottage, calling her name. They followed close upon him, and when he had vainly searched it, brought him home.

With such persuasive words as pity and affection could suggest, they prevailed upon him to sit among them and hear what they should tell him. Then, endeavoring by every little artifice to prepare his mind for what must come, and dwelling with many fervent words upon the happy lot to which she had been removed, they told him, at last, the truth. The moment it had passed their lips he fell down among them like a murdered man.

For many hours, they had little hope of his surviving; but grief is strong, and he recovered.

If there be any who have never known the blank that follows death—the weary void—the sense of desolation that will come upon the strongest minds, when something familiar and beloved is missed at every turn—the connection between inanimate and senseless things, and the object of recollection, when every household god becomes a monument and every room a grave—if there be any who have not known this, and proved it by their own experience, they can never faintly guess how, for many days, the old man pined and moped away the time, and wandered here and there as seeking something, and had no comfort.

Whatever power of thought or memory he retained, was all bound up in her. He never understood or seemed to care to understand, about his brother. To every endearment and attention he continued listless. If they spoke to him on this, or any other theme—save one—he would hear them patiently for awhile, then turn away, and go on seeking as before.

On that one theme, which was in his and all their minds, it was impossible to touch. Dead! He could not hear or bear the word. The slightest hint of it would throw him into a paroxysm, like that he had had when it was first spoken. In what hope he lived, no man could tell; but that he had some hope of finding her again— some faint and shadowy hope, deferred from day to day, and making him from day to day more sick and sore at heart—was plain to all.

They bethought them of a removal from the scene of this last sorrow; of trying whether change of place would rouse or cheer him. His brother sought the advice of those who were accounted skilful in such matters, and they came and saw him. Some of the number stayed upon the spot, conversed with him when he would converse, and watched him as he wandered up and down, alone and silent. Move him where they might, they said, he would ever seek to get back there. His mind would run upon that spot. If they confined him closely, and kept a strict guard upon him, they might hold him prisoner, but if he could by any means escape, he would surely wander back to that place, or die upon the road.

The boy, to whom he had submitted at first, had no longer any influence with him. At times he would suffer the child to walk by his side, or would even take such notice of his presence as giving him his hand, or would stop to kiss his cheek, or pat him on the head. At other times, he would entreat him—not unkindly—to be gone, and would not brook him near. But whether alone; or

39

with this pliant friend; or with those who would have given him, at any cost or sacrifice, some consolation or some peace of mind, if happily the means could have been devised; he was at all times the same—with no love or care for anything in life—a broken-hearted man.

At length they found one day that he had risen early, and, with his knapsack on his back, his staff in hand, her own straw hat, and little basket full of such things as she had been used to carry, was gone.   As they were making

ready to pursue him far and wide, a frightened schoolboy came who had seen him, but a moment before, sitting in the church—upon her grave, he said.

They hastened there, and going softly to the door, espied him in the attitude of one who waited patiently. They did not disturb him then, but kept a watch upon him all that day.   When it grew quite dark, he rose and returned home, and went to bed, murmuring to himself, "She will come to-morrow!"

Upon the morrow he was there again from sunrise until night; and still at night he laid him down to rest, and muttered, " She will come to-morrow!"

And henceforth, every day, and all day long, he waited at her grave for her. How many pictures of new journeys over pleasant country, of resting-places under the free broad sky, of rambles in the fields and woods, and paths not often trodden—how many tones of that one well-remembered voice—how many glimpses of the form, the fluttering dress, the hair that waved so gaily in the wind—how many visions of what had been, and what he hoped was yet to be—rose up before him, in the old, dull, silent church! He never told them what he thought, or where he went. He would sit with them at night, pondering with a secret satisfaction, they could see, upon the flight that he and she would take before night came again; and still they would hear him whisper in his prayers, "Oh! Let her come to-morrow!"

The last time was on a genial day in spring. He did not return at the usual hour, and they went to seek him. He was lying dead upon the stone.

They laid him by the side of her whom he had loved so well; and, in the church where they had often prayed, and mused, and lingered hand in hand, the child and the old man slept together.

CHAPTER THE LAST.

THE magic reel, which, rolling on before, has lead the chronicler thus far, now slackens in its pace, and stops. It lies before the goal; the pursuit is at an end.

It remains but to dismiss the leaders of the little crowd who have borne us company upon the road, and so to close the journey.

Foremost among them, smooth Sampson Brass and Sally, arm in arm, claim our polite attention.

Mr. Sampson, then, being detained, as already has been shown, by the Justice upon whom he called, and being so strongly pressed to protract his stay that he could by no means refuse, remained under his protection for a considerable time, during which the great attention of his entertainer kept him so extremely close, that he was quite lost to society, and never even went abroad for exercise

saving into a small paved yard. So well, indeed, was his
modest and retiring temper understood by those with
whom he had to deal, and so jealous were they of his
absence, that they required a kind of friendly bond to be
entered into by two substantial housekeepers, in the sum
of fifteen hundred pounds a-piece, before they would suffer him to quit their hospitable roof—doubting it appeared,
that he would return, if once let loose, on any other terms.
Mr. Brass, struck with the humor of his jest, and carrying out its spirit to the utmost, sought from his wide connection a pair of friends whose joint possessions fell some
halfpence short of fifteen pence, and proffered them as
bail—for that was the merry word agreed upon on both
sides. These gentlemen being rejected after twenty-four
hours' pleasantry Mr. Brass consented to remain, and did
remain, until a club of choice spirits called a Grand Jury
(who were in the joke) summoned him to a trial before
twelve other wags for perjury and fraud, who in their
turn found him guilty with a most facetious joy,—nay, the
very populace entered into the whim, and when Mr. Brass
was moving in a hackney-coach towards the building where
these wags assembled, saluted him with rotten eggs and
carcasses of kittens, and feigned to wish to tear him in o
shreds, which greatly increased the comicality of the
thing, and made him relish it the more, no doubt.

To work this sportive vein still further, Mr. Brass by
his counsel, moved in arrest of judgment that he had been
led to criminate himself, by assurances of safety and
promises of pardon, and claimed the leniency which the
law extends to such confiding natures as are thus deluded.
After solemn argument, this point (with others of a tech-
nical nature, whose humorous extravagance it would be
difficult to exaggerate) was referred to the judges for
their decision, Sampson being meantime removed to his
former quarters. Finally, some of the points were given
in Sampson's favor, and some against him; and the upshot was that, instead of being desired to travel for a
time in foreign parts, he was permitted to grace the
mother country under certain insignificant restrictions.

These were that he should, for a term of years, reside
in a spacious mansion where several other gentlemen
were lodged and boarded at the public charge, who went
clad in a sober uniform of gray turned up with yellow,

had their hair cut extremely short, and chiefly **lived** on gruel and light soup. It was also required of him that he should partake their exercise of constantly ascending an endless flight of stairs; and lest his legs, unused to such exertion, should be weakened by it, that he should wear upon one ankle an amulet or charm of iron. These conditions being arranged, he was removed one evening to his new abode, and enjoyed, in common with nine other gentlemen and two ladies, the privilege of being taken to his place of retirement in one of Royalty's own carriages.

Over **and above** these trifling penalties, his name was erased and blotted out from the roll of attorneys; which erasure has been always held in these latter times to be a great degradation and reproach, and to imply the commission of some amazing villiany—as indeed would seem to be the case, when so many worthless names remain among its better records, unmolested.

Of Sally Brass, conflicting rumors went abroad. Some said with confidence that she had gone down to the docks in male attire, and had become a female sailor; others darkly whispered that she had enlisted as a private in the second regiment of Foot Guards, and had been seen in uniform and on duty, to wit, leaning on her musket and looking out of a sentry-box in St. James's Park, one evening. There were many such whispers as these in circulation; but the truth appears to be that, after a lapse of some five years (during which there is no direct evidence of her having been seen at all), two wretched people were more than once observed to crawl at dusk from the inmost recesses of St. Giles's, and to take their way along the streets, with shuffling steps and cowering, shivering forms, looking into the roads and kennels as they went in search of refuse food or disregarded offal. These forms were never beheld but in those nights of cold and gloom, when the terrible spectres, who lie at all other times in the obscene hiding-places of London, in archways, dark vaults and cellars, venture to creep into the streets; the embodied spirits of Disease, and Vice, and Famine. It was whispered by those who should have known, that these were Sampson and his sister Sally; and to this day, it is said, they sometimes pass, on bad nights, in the same loathsome guise, close at the elbow of the shrinking passenger.

The body of Quilp being found—though not until some days had elapsed—an inquest was held on it near the spot where it had been washed ashore. The general supposition was that he had committed suicide, and, this appearing to be favored by all the circumstances of his death, the verdict was to that effect. He was left to be buried with a stake through his heart in the centre of four lonely roads.

It was rumored afterwards that this horrible and barbarous ceremony had been dispensed with, and that the remains had been secretly given up to Tom Scott. But even here, opinion was divided; for some said Tom had dug them up at midnight, and carried them to a place indicated to him by the widow. It is probable that both these stories may have had their origin in the simple fact of Tom's shedding tears upon the inquest—which he certainly did, extraordinary as it may appear. He manifested, besides, a strong desire to assault the jury; and being restrained and conducted out of court, darkened its only window by standing on his head upon the sill, until he was dexterously tilted upon his feet again by a cautious beadle.

Being cast upon the world by his master's death, he determined to go through it upon his head and hands, and accordingly began to tumble for his bread. Finding, however, his English birth an insurmountable obstacle to his advancement in this pursuit (notwithstanding that his art was in high repute and favor), he assumed the name of an Italian image lad, with whom he had become acquainted; and afterwards tumbled with extraordinary success, and to overflowing audiences.

Little Mrs. Quilp never quite forgave herself the one deceit that lay so heavy on her conscience, and never spoke or thought of it but with bitter tears. Her husband had no relations, and she was rich. He had made no will, or she would probably have been poor. Having married the first time at her mother's instigation, she consulted in her second choice nobody but herself. It fell upon a smart young fellow enough; and as he made it a preliminary condition that Mrs. Jiniwin should be thenceforth an out-pensioner, they lived together after marriage with no more than the average amount of quarrelling, and led a merry life upon the dead dwarf's money.

Mr. and Mrs. Garland, and Mr. Abel, went on as usual (except that there was a change in their household, as will be seen presently), and in due time the latter went into partnership with his friend the notary, on which occasion there was a dinner, and a ball, and great extent of dissipation. Unto this ball there happened to be invited the most bashful young lady that was ever seen, with whom Mr. Abel happened to fall in love. *How* it happened, or how they found it out, or which of them first communicated the discovery to the other, nobody knows. But certain it is that in course of time they were married; and equally certain it is that they were the happiest of the happy; and no less certain it is that they deserved to be so. And it is pleasant to write down that they reared a family; because any propagation of goodness and benevolence is no small addition to the aristocracy of nature, and no small subject of rejoicing for mankind at large.

The pony preserved his character for independence and principle down to the last moment of his life; which was an unusually long one, and caused him to be looked upon, indeed as the very Old Parr of ponies. He often went to and fro with the little phaeton between Mr. Garland's and his son's, and, as the old people and the young were frequently together, had a stable of his own at the new establishment, into which he would walk of himself with surprising dignity. He condescended to play with the children, as they grew old enough to cultivate his friendship, and would run up and down the little paddock with them like a dog; but though he relaxed so far, and allowed them such small freedoms as caresses, or even to look at his shoes or hang on by his tail, he never permitted any one among them to mount his back or drive him; thus showing that even their familiarity must have its limits, and that there were points between them far too serious for trifling.

He was not unsusceptible of warm attachments in his latter life, for when the good bachelor came to live with Mr. Garland upon the clergyman's decease, he conceived a friendship for him, and amiably submitted to be driven by his hands without the least resistance. He did no work for two or three years before he died, but lived in clover; and his last act (like a choleric old gentleman) was to kick his doctor.

Mr. Swiveller, recovering very slowly from his illness, and entering into the receipt of his annuity, bought for the Marchioness a handsome stock of clothes, and put her to school forthwith, in redemption of the vow he had made upon his fevered bed. After casting about for some time for a name which should be worthy of her, he decided in favor of Sophronia Sphynx, as being euphonious and genteel, and furthermore indicative of mystery. Under this title the Marchioness repaired, in tears, to the school of his selection, from which, as she soon distanced all competitors, she was removed before the lapse of many quarters to one of a higher grade. It is but bare justice to Mr. Swiveller to say, that, although the expenses of her education kept him in straitened circumstances for half a dozen years, he never slackened in his zeal and always held himself sufficiently repaid by the accounts he heard (with great gravity) of her advancement, on his monthly visits to the governess, who looked upon him as a literary gentleman of eccentric habits, and of a most prodigious talent in quotation.

In a word, Mr. Swiveller kept the Marchioness at this establishment until she was, at a moderate guess, full nineteen years of age—good-looking, clever, and good-humored ; when he began to consider seriously what was to be done next, On one of his periodical visits, while he was revolving this question in his mind, the Marchioness came down to him, alone, looking more smiling and more fresh than ever. Then it occurred to him, but not for the first time, that if she would marry him, how comfortable they might be! So Richard asked her; whatever she said, it wasn't No; and they were married in good earnest that day week, which gave Mr. Swiveller frequent occasion to remark at divers subsequent periods that there had been a young lady saving up for him after all.

A little cottage at Hampstead being to let, which had in its garden a smoking-box, the envy of the civilized world, they agreed to become its tenants; and when the honeymoon was over, entered upon its occupation. To this retreat Mr. Chuckster repaired regularly every Sunday to spend the day—usually beginning with breakfast; and here he was the great purveyor of general news and fashionable intelligence. For some years he continued a deadly foe to Kit, protesting that he had a better opinion of him when he was supposed to have stolen the five-pound note, than when he was shown to be perfectly free of the crime; inasmuch as his guilt would have had in it something daring and bold, whereas his innocence was but another proof of a sneaking and crafty disposition. By slow degrees, however, he was reconciled to him in the end; and even went so far as to honor him with his patronage, as one who had in some measure reformed, and was therefore to be forgiven. But he never forgot or pardoned that circumstance of the shilling; holding that if he had come back to get another he would have done well enough, but that his returning to work out of the former gift was a stain upon his moral character which no penitence or contrition could ever wash away.

Mr. Swiveller, having always been in some measure of a philosophic and reflective turn, grew immensely contemplative, at times, in the smoking-box, and was accustomed at such periods to debate in his own mind the mysterious question of Sophronia's parentage. Sophronia herself supposed she was an orphan; but Mr. Swiveller, putting various slight circumstances together, often thought Miss Brass must know better than that; and, having heard from his wife of her strange interview with Quilp, entertained sundry misgivings whether that person, in his lifetime, might not also have been able to solve the riddle, had he chosen. These speculations, however, gave him no uneasiness; for Sophronia was ever a most cheerful, affectionate, and provident wife to him; and Dick (excepting for an occasional outbreak with Mr. Chuckster, which she had the good sense rather to encourage than oppose) was to her an attached and domesticated husband. And they played many hundred thousand games of cribbage together. And let it be added, to Dick's honor, that, though we have called her Sophronia, he called her the Marchioness from first to last; and that upon every anniversary of the day on which he found her in his sick room Mr. Chuckster came to dinner, and there was great glorification.

The gamblers, Isaac List and Jowl, with their trusty confederate Mr. James Groves of unimpeachable memory, pursued their course with varying success, until the failure of a spirited enterprise in the way of their profession, dispersed them in various directions, and caused their career to receive a sudden check from the long and strong arm of the law. This defeat had its origin in the untoward detection of a new associate—young Frederick Trent—who thus became the unconscious instrument of their punishment and his own.

For the young man himself, he rioted abroad for a brief term, living by his wits—which means by the abuse of every faculty that worthily employed raises man above the beasts, and so degraded, sinks him far below them. It was not long before his body was recognized by a stranger, who chanced to visit that hospital in Paris where the drowned are laid out to be owned; despite the bruises and disfigurements which were said to have been occasioned by some previous scuffle. But the stranger kept his own counsel until he returned home, and it was never claimed or cared for.

The younger brother, or the single gentleman, for that designation is more familiar, would have drawn the poor schoolmaster from his lone retreat, and made him his companion and friend. But the humble village-teacher was timid of venturing into the noisy world, and had become fond of his dwelling in the old churchyard. Calmly happy in his school, and in the spot, and in the attachment of Her little mourner, he pursued his quiet course in peace; and was, through the righteous gratitude of his friend—let this brief mention suffice for that—a *poor* schoolmaster no more.

That friend—single gentleman, or younger brother, which you will, had at his heart a heavy sorrow; but it bred in him no misanthropy or monastic gloom. He went forth into the world, a lover of his kind. For a long, long time, it was his chief delight to travel in the steps of the old man and the child (so far as he could trace them from her last narrative), to halt where they had halted, sympathize where they had suffered, and rejoice where they had been made glad. Those who had been kind to them, did not escape his search. The sisters at the school—they who were her friends, because themselves so friendless—Mrs. Jarley of the wax-work, Codlin, Short—he found them all; and trust me, that the man who fed the furnace fire was not forgotten.

Kit's story having got abroad, raised him up a host of friends, and many offers of provision for his future life.

He had no idea at first of ever quitting Mr. Garland's service; but, after serious remonstrance and advice from that gentleman, began to contemplate the possibility of such a change being brought about in time. A good post was procured for him, with a rapidity which took away his breath, by some of the gentlemen who had believed him guilty of the offence laid to his charge, and who had acted upon that belief. Through the same kind agency, his mother was secured from want, and made quite happy. Thus, as Kit often said, his great misfortune turned out to be the source of all his subsequent prosperity.

Did Kit live a single man all his days, or did he marry; Of course he married, and who should be his wife but Barbara? And the best of it was, he married so soon that little Jacob was an uncle, before the calves of his legs, already mentioned in this history, had ever been encased in broadcloth pantaloons,—though that was not quite the best either, for of necessity the baby was an uncle too. The delight of Kit's mother and of Barbara's mother upon the great occasion is past all telling; finding they agreed so well on that, and on all other subjects, they took up their abode together, and were a most harmonious pair of friends from that time forth. And hadn't Astley's cause to bless itself for their all going together once a quarter—to the pit—and didn't Kit's mother always say, when they painted the outside, that Kit's last treat had helped to that, and wonder what the manager would feel if he but knew it as they passed his house!

When Kit had children six and seven years old, there was a Barbara among them, and a pretty Barbara she was. Nor was there wanting an exact fac-simile and copy of little Jacob as he appeared in those remote times when they taught him what oysters meant. Of course there was an Abel, own godson to the Mr. Garland of that name; and there was a Dick, whom Mr. Swiveller did especially favor. The little group would often gather round him of a night and beg him to tell again that story of good Miss Nell who died. This Kit would do; and when they cried to hear it, wishing it longer too, he would teach them how she had gone to Heaven, as all good people did; and how, if they were good like her, they might hope to be there too one day, and to see and know her as he had done

when he was quite a boy. Then he would relate to them
how needy he used to be, and how she had taught him
what he was otherwise too poor to learn, and how the
old man had been used to say "she always laughs at
Kit;" at which they would brush away their tears, and
laugh themselves to think that she had done so, and be
again quite merry.

He sometimes took them to the street where she had
lived; but new improvements had altered it so much, it
was not like the same. The old house had been long ago
pulled down, and a fine broad road was in its place. At
first he would draw with his stick a square upon the
ground to show them where it used to stand. But he
soon became uncertain of the spot, and could only say
it was thereabouts, he thought, and that these alterations
were confusing.

Such are the changes which a few years bring about,
and so do things pass away, like a tale is that told!

HARD TIMES

HARD TIMES.

BOOK THE FIRST, SOWING.

CHAPTER I.

THE ONE THING NEEDFUL.

"Now, what I want is, Facts. Teach these boys and girls nothing but Facts. Facts alone are wanted in life. Plant nothing else, and root out everything else. You can only form the minds of reasoning animals upon Facts: nothing else will ever be of any service to them. This is the principle on which I bring up my own children, and this is the principle on which I bring up these children. Stick to Facts, sir!"

The scene was a plain, bare, monotonous vault of a schoolroom, and the speaker's square forefinger emphasized his observations by underscoring every sentence with a line on the schoolmaster's sleeve. The emphasis was helped by the speaker's square wall of a forehead, which had his eyebrows for its base, while his eyes found commodious cellarage in two dark caves, overshadowed by the wall. The emphasis was helped by the speaker's mouth, which was wide, thin, and hard set. The emphasis was helped by the speaker's voice, which was inflexible, dry, and dictatorial. The emphasis was helped by the speaker's hair, which bristled on the skirts of his bald head, a plantation of firs to keep the wind from its shining surface, all covered with knobs, like the crust of a plum pie, as if the head had scarcely warehouse-room for the hard facts stored inside. The speaker's obstinate carriage, square coat, square legs, square shoulders,—nay,

5

his very neckcloth, trained to take him by the throat with an unaccommodating grasp, like a stubborn fact, as it was, —all helped the emphasis.

"In this life, we want nothing but Facts, sir ; nothing but Facts!"

The speaker, and the schoolmaster, and the third grown person present, all backed a little, and swept with their eyes the inclined plane of little vessels then and there arranged in order, ready to have imperial gallons of facts poured into them until they were full to the brim.

CHAPTER II.

MURDERING THE INNOCENTS.

THOMAS GRADGRIND, sir. A man of realities. A man of facts and calculations. A man who proceeds upon the principle that two and two are four and nothing over, and who is not to be talked into allowing for anything over. Thomas Gradgrind, sir—peremptory Thomas— Thomas Gradgrind. With a rule and a pair of scales, and the multiplication table always in his pocket, sir, ready to weigh and measure any parcel of human nature, and tell you exactly what it comes to. It is a mere question of figures, a case of simple arithmetic. You might hope to get some other nonsensical belief into the head of George Gradgrind, or Augustus Gradgrind, or John Gradgrind, or Joseph Gradgrind (all supposititious, non-existent persons), but into the head of Thomas Gradgrind—no, sir!

In such terms Mr. Gradgrind always mentally introduced himself, whether to his private circle of acquaintance, or to the public in general. In such terms, no doubt, substituting the words "boys and girls," for "sir," Thomas Gradgrind now presented Thomas Gradgrind to the little pitchers before him, who were to be filled so full of facts.

Indeed, as he eagerly sparkled at them from the cellarage before mentioned, he seemed a kind of cannon loaded to the muzzle with facts, and prepared to blow them clean out of the regions of childhood at one discharge. He seemed a galvanizing apparatus, too, charged with a grim mechanical substitute for the tender young imaginations that were to be stormed away.

"Girl number twenty," said Mr. Gradgrind, squarely pointing with his square forefinger, "I don't know that girl. Who is that girl?"

"Sissy Jupe, sir," explained number twenty, blushing, standing up, and curtseying.

"Sissy is not a name," said Mr. Gradgrind. "Don't call yourself Sissy. Call yourself Cecilia."

"It's father as calls me Sissy, sir," returned the young girl in a trembling voice, and with another curtsey.

"Then he has no business to do it," said Mr. Gradgrind. "Tell him he mustn't. Cecilia Jupe. Let me see. What is your father?"

"He belongs to the horse-riding, if you please, sir."

Mr. Gradgrind frowned, and waved off the objectionable calling with his hand.

"We don't want to know anything about that, here. You mustn't tell us about that, here. Your father breaks horses, don't he?"

"If you please, sir, when they can get any to break, they do break horses in the ring, sir."

"You mustn't tell us about the ring, here. Very well, then. Describe your father as a horsebreaker. He doctors sick horses, I dare say?"

"Oh yes, sir."

"Very well, then. He is a veterinary surgeon, a farrier, and horsebreaker. Give me your definition of a horse."

(Sissy Jupe thrown into the greatest alarm by this demand.)

"Girl number twenty unable to define a horse!" said Mr. Gradgrind, for the general behoof of all the little pitchers. "Girl number twenty possessed of no facts, in reference to one of the commonest of animals! Some boy's definition of a horse. Bitzer, yours."

The square finger, moving here and there, lighted suddenly on Bitzer, perhaps because he chanced to sit in the same ray of sunlight which, darting in at one of the bare windows of the intensely whitewashed room, irradiated Sissy. For, the boys and girls sat on the face of the inclined plane in two compact bodies, divided up the centre by a narrow interval; and Sissy, being on the corner of a row on the sunny side, came in for the beginning of a sunbeam, of which Bitzer, being at the corner of a row on the other side, a few rows in advance, caught the end. But, whereas the girl was so dark-eyed and dark-haired, that she seemed to receive a deeper and more lustrous color from the sun, when it shone upon her, the boy was so light-eyed and light-haired that the self-same rays appeared to draw out of him what little color he ever possessed. His cold eyes would hardly have been eyes, but for the short ends of lashes which, by bringing them into immediate contrast with something paler than themselves, expressed their form. His short-cropped hair might have been a mere continuation of the sandy freckles on his forehead and face. His skin was so unwholesomely deficient in the natural tinge, that he looked as though, if he were cut, he would bleed white.

"Bitzer," said Thomas Gradgrind. "Your definition of a horse."

"Quadruped. Graminivorous. Forty teeth, namely twenty-four grinders, four eye-teeth, twelve incisive. Sheds coat in the spring; in marshy countries, sheds hoofs, too. Hoofs hard, but requiring to be shod with iron. Age known by marks in mouth. Thus (and much more) Bitzer.

"Now girl number twenty," said Mr. Gradgrind. "You know what a horse is."

She curtseyed again, and would have blushed deeper, if she could have blushed deeper than she had blushed all this time. Bitzer, after rapidly blinking at Thomas Gradgrind with both eyes at once, and so catching the light upon his quivering ends of lashes that they looked like the antennæ of busy insects, put his knuckles to his freckled forehead, and sat down again.

The third gentleman now stepped forth. A mighty man at cutting and drying, he was; a government officer; in his way (and in most other people's too), a professed pugilist; always in training, always with a system to force down the general throat like a bolus, always to be heard of at the bar of his little Public-office, ready to fight all England. To continue in fistic phraseology, he had a genius for coming up to the scratch, wherever and whatever it was, and proving himself an ugly customer. He would go in and damage any subject whatever with his right, follow up with his left, stop, exchange, counter, bore his opponent (he always fought All England) to the ropes, and fall upon him neatly. He was certain to knock the wind out of common sense, and render that unlucky adversary deaf to the call of time. And he had it in charge from high authority to bring about the great public-office millennium, when Commissioners should reign upon earth.

"Very well," said this gentleman, briskly smiling and folding his arms. "That's a horse. Now, let me ask you girls and boys, Would you paper a room with representations of horses?"

After a pause one half of the children cried in chorus, "Yes, sir!" Upon which the other half, seeing in the gentleman's face that Yes was wrong, cried out in chorus, "No, sir!"—as the custom is, in these examinations.

"Of course, No. Why wouldn't you?"

A pause. One corpulent slow boy, with a wheezy manner of breathing, ventured the answer, Because he wouldn't paper a room at all, but would paint it.

"You *must* paper it," said the gentleman, rather warmly.

"You must paper it," said Thomas Gradgrind, "whether you like it or not. Don't tell *us* you wouldn't paper it. What do you mean, boy?"

"I'll explain to you then," said the gentleman, after another and a dismal pause, "why you wouldn't paper a room with representations of horses. Do you ever see horses walking up and down the sides of rooms in reality —in fact? Do you?"

"Yes, sir!" from one half. "No, sir!" from the other.

"Of course no," said the gentleman, with an indignant look at the wrong half. "Why then, you are not to see anywhere, what you don't see in fact; you are not to have anywhere, what you don't have in fact. What is called Taste, is only another name for Fact."

Thomas Gradgrind nodded his approbation.

"This is a new principle, a discovery, a great discovery," said the gentleman. "Now, I'll try you again. Suppose you were going to carpet a room. Would you use a carpet having a representation of flowers upon it!"

There being a general conviction by this time that "No, sir!" was always the right answer to this gentleman, the chorus of No was very strong. Only a few feeble stragglers said Yes; among them Sissy Jupe.

"Girl number twenty," said the gentleman, smiling in the calm strength of knowledge.

Sissy blushed, and stood up.

"So you would carpet your room—or your husband's room, if you were a grown woman, and had a husband—with representations of flowers, would you," said the gentleman. "Why would you?"

"If you please, sir, I am very fond of flowers," returned the girl.

"And is that why you would put tables and chairs upon them, and have people walking over them with heavy boots?"

"It wouldn't hurt them, sir. They wouldn't crush and wither, if you please, sir. They would be the pictures of what was very pretty and pleasant, and I would fancy——"

"Ay, ay, ay! But you mustn't fancy," cried the gentleman, quite elated by coming so happily to his point. "That's it! You are never to fancy."

"You are not, Cecilia Jupe," Thomas Gradgrind solemnly repeated, "to do anything of that kind."

"Fact, fact, fact!" said the gentleman. And "Fact, fact, fact!" repeated Thomas Gradgrind,

"You are to be in all things regulated and governed," said the gentleman, "by fact. We hope to have, before long, a board of fact, composed of commissioners of fact, who will force the people to be a people of fact, and of nothing but fact. You must discard the word Fancy altogether. You have nothing to do with it. You are not to have, any object of use or ornament, what would be a contradiction in fact. You don't walk upon flowers in fact; you cannot be allowed to walk upon flowers in carpets. You don't find that foreign birds and butterflies come and perch upon your crockery; you cannot be permitted to paint foreign birds and butterflies upon your crockery. You never meet with quadrupeds going up and down walls; you must not have quadrupeds represented upon walls. You must use," said the gentleman, "for all these purposes, combinations and modifications (in primary colors) of mathematical figures which are susceptible of proof and demonstration. This is the new discovery. This is fact. This is taste."

The girl curtseyed, and sat down. She was very young, and she looked as if she were frightened by the matter of fact prospect the world afforded.

"Now, if Mr. M'Choakumchild," said the gentleman, "will proceed to give his first lesson here, Mr. Gradgrind, I shall be happy, at your request, to observe his mode of procedure."

Mr. Gradgrind was much obliged. "Mr. M'Choakumchild, we only wait for you."

So, Mr. M'Choakumchild began in his best manner. He and some one hundred and forty other schoolmasters, had been lately turned at the same time, in the same factory, on the same principles, like so many pianoforte legs. He had been put through an immense variety of paces, and had answered volumes of head-breaking questions. Orthography, etymology, syntax, and prosody, biography, astronomy, geography, and general cosmography, the sciences of compound proportion, algebra, land-surveying and levelling, vocal music, and drawing from models, were all at the ends of his ten chilled fingers. He had worked his stony way into Her Majesty's most Honorable Privy Council's Schedule B, and had taken the bloom off the higher branches of mathematics and physical science, French, German, Latin, and Greek. He knew all about all the Water Sheds of all the world (whatever they are), and all the histories of all the peoples, and all the names of all the rivers and mountains, and all the productions, manners, and customs of all the countries, and all their boundaries and bearings on the two and thirty points of the compass. Ah, rather overdone, M'Choakumchild. If he had only learnt a little less, how infinitely better he might have taught much more!

He went to work in this preparatory lesson, not unlike Morgiana in the Forty Thieves : looking into all the vessels ranged before him, one after another, to see what they contained. Say, good M'Choakumchild. When from thy boiling store, thou shalt fill each jar brim full by-and-by, dost thou think that thou wilt always kill outright the robber Fancy lurking within—or sometimes only maim him and distort him!

CHAPTER III.

A LOOPHOLE.

MR. GRADGRIND walked homeward from the school, in a state of considerable satisfaction. It was his school, and he intended it to be a model. He intended every child in it to be a model—just as the young Gradgrinds were all models.

There were five young Gradgrinds, and they were models every one. They had been lectured at, from their tenderest years; coursed, like little hares. Almost as soon as they could run alone, they had been made to run to the lecture-room. The first object with which they had an association, or of which they had a remembrance, was a large black board with a dry Ogre chalking ghastly white figures on it.

Not that they knew, by name or nature, anything about an Ogre. Fact forbid! I only use the word to express a monster in a lecturing castle, with Heaven knows how many heads manipulated into one, taking childhood captive, and dragging it into gloomy statistical dens by the hair.

No little Gradgrind had ever seen a face in the moon; it was up in the moon before it could speak distinctly. No little Gradgrind had ever learnt the silly jingle, Twinkle, twinkle little star; how I wonder what you are! No little Gradgrind had ever known wonder on the subject, each little Gradgrind having at five years old dissected the Great Bear like a Professor Owen, and driven Charles's Wain like a locomotive engine-driver. No little Gradgrind had ever associated a cow in a field with that famous cow with the crumpled horn who tossed the dog who worried the cat who killed the rat who ate the malt, or with that yet more famous cow who swallowed Tom Thumb: it had never heard of those celebrities, and had only been introduced to a cow as a graminivorous ruminating quadruped with several stomachs.

To his matter of fact home, which was called Stone

Lodge, Mr. Gradgrind directed his steps. He had virtu-ally retired from the wholesale hardware trade before he built Stone Lodge, and was now looking about for a suit-able opportunity of making an arithmetical figure in Parliament. Stone Lodge was situated on a moor within a mile or two of a great town—called Coketown in the present faithful guide-book.

A very regular feature on the face of the country, Stone Lodge was. Not the least disguise toned down or shaded off that uncompromising fact in the landscape. A great square house, with a heavy portico darkening the principal windows, as its master's heavy brows over-shadowed his eyes. A calculated, cast up, balanced, and proved house. Six windows on this side of the door, six on that side; a total of twelve in this wing, a total of twelve in the other wing; four-and-twenty carried over to the back wings. A lawn and garden and an infant avenue, all ruled straight like a botanical account-book. Gas and ventilation, drainage and water-service, all of the primest quality. Iron clamps and girders, fireproof from top to bottom ; mechanical lifts for the housemaids, with all their brushes and brooms ; everything that heart could desire.

Everything? Well, I suppose so. The little Grad-grinds had cabinets in various departments of science too. They had a little conchological cabinet, and a little metallurgical cabinet, and a little mineralogical cabinet; and the specimens were all arranged and labelled, and the bits of stone and ore looked as though they might have been broken from the parent substances by those tremendously hard instruments their own names ; and, to paraphrase the idle legend of Peter Piper, who had never found his way into their nursery—If the greedy little Gradgrinds grasped at more than this, what was it for good gracious goodness sake, that the greedy little Grad-grinds grasped at !

Their father walked on in a hopeful and satisfied frame of mind. He was an affectionate father, after his man-ner ; but he would probably have described himself (if he had been put, like Sissy Jupe, upon a definition) as " an eminently practical father. He had a particular pride in the phrase eminently practical," which was considered to have special application to him. Whatsoever the public meeting held in Coketown, and what oever the subject of such meeting, some Coketowner was sure to seize the occasion of alluding to his eminently practical friend Gradgrind. This always pleased the eminently practical friend. He knew it to be his due, but his due was acceptable.

He had reached the neutral ground upon the outskirts of the town, which was neither town nor country, and yet was either spoiled, when his ears were invaded by the sound of music. The clashing and banging band attached to the horse-riding establishment which had there set up its rest in a wooden pavilion was in full bray. A flag, floating from the summit of the temple, proclaimed to mankind that it was "Sleary's Horse-riding" which claimed their suffrages. Sleary himself, a stout modern statue with a money-box at his elbow, in an ecclesiastical niche of early Gothic architecture, took the money. Miss Josephine Sleary, as some very long and very narrow strips of printed bill announced, was then inaugurating the entertainments with her graceful equestrian Tyrolean flower-act. Among the other pleasing but always strictly moral wonders which must be seen to be believed, Signor Jupe was that afternoon to "elucidate the diverting accomplishments of his highly trained performing dog Merrylegs." He was also to exhibit "his astounding feat of throwing seventy-five hundred-weight in rapid succession backhanded over his head, thus forming a fountain of solid iron in mid-air, a feat never before attempted in this or any other country, and which having elicited such rapturous plaudits from enthusiastic throngs it cannot be withdrawn." The same Signor Jupe was to "enliven the varied performances at frequent intervals with his chaste Shakesperean quips and retorts." Lastly, he was to wind them up by appearing in his favorite character of Mr. William Button, of Tooley Street, in "the highly novel and laughable hippo-comedietta of "The Tailor's Journey to Brentford."

Thomas Gradgrind took no heed of these trivialities of course, but passed on as a practical man ought to pass on, either brushing the noisy insects from his thoughts, or consigning them to the House of Correction. But, the turning of the road took him by the back of the booth, and at the back of the booth a number of children were congregated in a number of stealthy attitudes, **striving** to peep in at the hidden glories of the place.

This brought him to a stop. "Now, to think of these vagabonds," said he, "attracting the young rabble from a model school."

A space of stunted grass and dry rubbish being between him and the young rabble, he took his eyeglass out of his waistcoat to look for any child he knew by name, and might order off. Phenomenon almost incredible through distinctly seen, what did he then behold but his own metallurgical Louisa, peeping with all her might through a hole in a deal board, and his own mathematical Thomas abasing himself on the ground to catch but a hoof of the graceful equestrian Tyrolean flower-act!

Dumb with amazement, Mr. Gradgrind crossed to the spot where his family was thus disgraced, laid his hand upon each erring child, and said:

"Louisa!! Thomas!!"

Both rose, red and disconcerted. But, Louisa looked at her father with more boldness than Thomas did. Indeed, Thomas did not look at him, but gave himself up to be taken home like a machine.

"In the name of wonder, idleness, and folly!" said Mr. Gradgrind, leading each away by a hand; "what do you do here?"

"Wanted to see what it was like," returned Louisa, shortly.

"What it was like?"

"Yes, father."

There was an air of jaded sullenness in them both, and particularly in the girl: yet, struggling through the dissatisfaction of her face, there was a light with nothing to rest upon, a fire with nothing to burn, a starved imagination keeping life in itself somehow, which brightened its expression. Not with the brightness natural to cheerful youth, but with uncertain, eager, doubtful flashes, which had something painful in them, analogous to the changes on a blind face groping its way.

She was a child now, of fifteen or sixteen; but at no distant day would seem to become a woman all at once. Her father thought so as he looked at her. She was pretty. Would have been self-willed (he thought in his eminently practical way) but for her bringing-up.

" Thomas, though I have the fact before me, I find it difficult to believe that you, with your education and resources, should have brought your sister to a scene like this ! "

" I brought *him*, father," said Louisa, quickly. " I asked him to come."

"I am sorry to hear it. I am very sorry indeed to hear it. It makes Thomas no better, and it makes you worse, Louisa."

She looked at her father again, but no tear fell down her cheek.

" You! Thomas and you, to whom the circle of the sciences is open; Thomas and you, who may be said to be replete with facts ; Thomas and you, who have been trained to mathematical exactness ; Thomas and you, here!" cried Mr. Gradgrind. "In this degraded position ! I am amazed."

"I was tired, father. I have been tired a long time," said Louisa.

" Tired ? Of what ? " asked the astonished father.

" I don't know of what—of everything I think."

" Say not another word," returned Mr. Gradgrind. "You are childish. I will hear no more." He did not speak again until they had walked some half-a-mile in silence, when he gravely broke out with : " What would your best friends say, Louisa? Do you attach no value to their good opinion ? What would Mr. Bounderly say ? "

At the mention of this name, his daughter stole a look at him, remarkable for its intense and searching character. He saw nothing of it, for before he looked at her, she had again cast down her eyes !

" What," he repeated presently, " would Mr. Bounderby say ? " All the way to Stone Lodge, as with grave indignation he led the two delinquents home, he repeated at intervals. " What would Mr. Bounderby say ! "—as if Mr. Bounderby had been Mrs. Grundy.

CHAPTER IV.

MR. BOUNDERBY.

NOT being Mrs. Grundy, who was Mr. Bounderby!

Why Mr. Bounderby was as near being Mr. Gradgrind's bosom friend, as a man perfectly devoid of sentiment can approach that spiritual relationship towards another man perfectly devoid of sentiment. So near was Mr. Bounderby—or, if the reader should prefer it, so far off.

He was a rich man, banker, merchant, manufacturer, and what not. A big, loud man, with a stare, and a metallic laugh. A man made out of coarse material, which seemed to have been stretched to make so much of him. A man with a great puffed head and forehead, swelled veins in his temples, and such a strained skin to his face that it seemed to hold his eyes open, and lift his eyebrows up. A man with a pervading appearance on him of being inflated like a balloon, and ready to start; A man who could never sufficiently vaunt himself a self-made man. A man who was always proclaiming, through that brassy speaking-trumpet of a voice of his, his old ignorance and his old poverty. A man who was the Bully of humility.

A year or two younger than his eminently practical friend, Mr. Bounderby looked older; his seven or eight and forty might have had the seven or eight added to it again, without surprising anybody. He had not much hair. One might have fancied he had talked it off; and that what was left, all standing up in disorder, was in that condition from being constantly blown about by his windy boastfulness.

In the formal drawing-room of Stone Lodge, standing on the hearthrug, warming himself before the fire, Mr. Bounderby delivered some observations to Mrs. Gradgrind on the circumstance of its being his birthday. He stood before the fire partly because it was a cool spring afternoon, though the sun shone; partly because the shade of

2

Stone Lodge was always haunted by the ghost of damp
mortar; partly because he thus took up a commanding
position, from which to subdue Mrs. Gradgrind.

"I hadn't a shoe to my foot. As to a stocking, I didn't
know such a thing by name. I passed the day in a ditch,
and the night in a pigsty. That's the way I spent my
tenth birthday. Not that a ditch was new to me, for I
was born in a ditch."

Mrs. Gradgrind, a little, thin, white, pink-eyed bundle
of shawls of surpassing feebleness, mental and bodily;
who was always taking physic without any effect, and
who, whenever she showed a symptom of coming to life,
was invariably stunned by some weighty piece of fact
tumbling on her; Mrs. Gradgrind hoped it was a dry
ditch?

"No! As wet as a sop. A foot of water in it," said
Mr. Bounderby.

"Enough to give a baby a cold," Mrs. Gradgrind considered.

"Cold? I was born with inflammation of the lungs,
and of everything else, I believe, that was capable of
inflammation," returned Mr. Bounderby. "For years,
ma'am, I was one of the most miserable little wretches ever
seen. I was so sickly, that I was always moaning and
groaning. I was so ragged and dirty, that you wouldn't
have touched me with a pair of tongs."

Mrs. Gradgrind faintly looked at the tongs, as the most
appropriate thing her imbecility could think of doing.

"How I fought through it, *I* don't know," said Bounderby. "I was determined, I suppose. I have been a
determined character in later life, and I suppose I was
then. Here I am, Mrs. Gradgrind, anyhow, and nobody
to thank for my being here, but myself."

Mrs. Gradgrind meekly and weakly hoped that his
mother—

"*My* mother? Bolted, ma'am!" said Bounderby.

Mrs. Gradgrind, stunned, as usual collapsed and gave
it up.

"My mother left me to my grandmother," said Bounderby; "and, according to the best of my remembrance,
my grandmother was the wickedest and the worst old
woman that ever lived. If I got a little pair of shoes by
any chance, she would take 'em off and sell 'em for

drink. Why, I have known that grandmother of mine lie in her bed and drink her fourteen glasses of liquor before breakfast!"

Mrs. Gradgrind, weakly smiling, and giving no other sign of vitality, looked (as she always did) like an indifferently executed transparency of a small female figure, without enough light behind it.

"She kept a chandler's shop," pursued Bounderby, "and kept me in an egg-box. That was the cot of *my* infancy; an old egg-box. As soon as I was big enough to run away, of course I ran away. Then I became a young vagabond; and instead of one old woman knocking me about and starving me, everybody of all ages knocked me about and starved me. They were right; they had no business to do anything else. I was a nuisance, an incumbrance, and a pest. I know that very well."

His pride in having at any time of his life achieved such a great social distinction as to be a nuisance, an incumbrance, and a pest, was only to be satisfied by three sonorous repetitions of the boast.

"I was to pull through it I suppose, Mrs. Gradgrind. Whether I was to do it or not, ma'am, I did it, I pulled through it, though nobody threw me out a rope. Vagabond, errand-boy, vagabond, laborer, porter, clerk, chief manager, small partner, Josiah Bounderby of Coketown. Those are the antecedents, and the culmination. Josiah Bounderby of Coketown learnt his letters from the outsides of the shops, Mrs. Gradgrind, and was first able to tell the time upon a dial-plate, from studying the steeple clock of St. Giles's Church, London, under the direction of a drunken cripple, who was a convicted thief, and an incorrigible vagrant. Tell Josiah Bounderby of Coketown, of your district schools and your model schools, and your training schools, and your whole kettle-of-fish of schools; and Josiah Bounderby of Coketown, tells you plainly, all right, all correct—he hadn't such advantages—but let us have hard-headed, solid-fisted people—the education that made him won't do for everybody, he knows well—such and such his education was, however, and you may force him to swallow boiling fat, but you shall never force him to suppress the facts of his life."

Being heated when he arrived at this climax, Josiah

Bounderby of Coketown stopped. He stopped just as his eminently practical friend, still accompanied by the two young culprits, entered the room. His eminently practical friend, on seeing him, stopped also, and gave Louisa a reproachful look that plainly said, "Behold your Bounderby!"

"Well!" blustered Mr. Bounderby, "what's the matter? What is young Thomas in the dumps about?"

He spoke of young Thomas, but he looked at Louisa.

"We were peeping at the circus," muttered Louisa, haughtily, without lifting up her eyes, "and father caught us."

"And Mrs. Gradgrind," said her husband in a lofty manner, "I should as soon have expected to find my children reading poetry."

"Dear me," whimpered Mrs. Gradgrind. "How can you, Louisa and Thomas! I wonder at you. I declare you're enough to make one regret ever having had a family at all. I have a great mind to say I wish I hadn't. *Then* what would you have done, I should like to know."

Mr. Gradgrind did not seem favorably impressed by these cogent remarks. He frowned impatiently.

"As if, with my head in its present throbbing state, you couldn't go and look at the shells and minerals and things provided for you, instead of circuses!" said Mrs. Gradgrind. "You know, as well as I do, no young people have circus masters, or keep circuses in cabinets, or attend lectures about circuses. What can you possibly want to know of circuses then? I am sure you have enough to do, if that's what you want. With my head in its present state, I couldn't remember the mere names of half the facts you have got to attend to."

"That's the reason!" pouted Louisa.

"Don't tell me that's the reason, because it can be nothing of the sort," said Mrs. Gradgrind. "Go and be something ological directly." Mrs. Gradgrind was not a scientific character, and usually dismissed her children to their studies with this general injunction to choose their pursuit.

In truth, Mrs. Gradgrind's stock of facts in general was woefully defective; but Mr. Gradgrind in raising her to her high matrimonial position, had been influenced by two reasons. Firstly, she was most satisfactory as a question of figures ; and, secondly, she had "no nonsense" about her. By nonsense he meant fancy ; and truly it is probable she was as free from any alloy of that nature, as any human being not arrived at the perfection of an absolute idiot, ever was.

The simple circumstance of being left alone with her husband and Mr. Bounderby, was sufficient to stun this admirable lady again without collision between herself and any other fact. So, she once more died away, and nobody minded her.

"Bounderby," said Mr. Gradgrind, drawing a chair to the fireside, " you are always so interested in my young people—particularly in Louisa—that I make no apology for saying to you, I am very much vexed by this discovery. I have systematically devoted myself (as you know) to the education of the reason of my family. The reason is (as you know) the only faculty to which education should be addressed. And yet, Bounderby, it would appear from this unexpected circumstance of to-day, though in itself a trifling one, as if something had crept into Thomas's and Louisa's minds which is—or rather, which is not—I don't know that I can express myself better than by saying—which has never been intended to be developed, and in which their reason has no part."

"There certainly is no reason in looking with interest at a parcel of vagabonds," returned Bounderby. "When I was a vagabond myself, nobody looked with any interest at *me ;* I know that."

"Then comes the question," said the eminently practical father, with his eyes on the fire, "in what has this vulgar curiosity its rise?"

"I'll tell you in what. In idle imagination."

"I hope not," said the eminently practical; "I confess, however, that the misgiving *has* crossed me on my way home."

"In idle imagination, Gradgrind," repeated Bounderby. "A very bad thing for anybody, but a cursed bad thing for a girl like Louisa. I should ask Mrs. Gradgrind's pardon for strong expressions, but that she knows very well I am not a refined character. Whoever expects refinement in *me* will be disappointed. I hadn't a refined bringing up."

"Whether," said Mr. Gradgrind, pondering with his

hands in his pockets, and his cavernous eyes on the fire, " whether any instructor or servant can have suggested anything? Whether Louisa or Thomas can have been reading anything? Whether, in spite of all precautions, any idle storybook can have got into the house? Because, in minds that have been practically formed by rule and line, from the cradle upwards, this is so curious, so incomprehensible."

" Stop a bit!" cried Bounderby, who all this time had been standing, as before, on the hearth, bursting at the very furniture of the room with explosive humility. " You have one of those strollers' children in the school."

" Cecilia Jupe, by name," said Mr. Gradgrind, with something of a stricken look at his friend.

" Now, stop a bit!" cried Bounderby again. " How did she come there?"

" Why, the fact is, I saw the girl myself for the first time, only just now. She specially applied here at the house to be admitted, as not regularly belonging to our town, and—yes, you are right, Bounderby, you are right."

" Now, stop a bit!" cried Bounderby, once more. " Louisa saw her when she came?"

" Louisa certainly did see her, for she mentioned the application to me. But Louisa saw her, I have no doubt, in Mrs. Gradgrind's presence."

" Pray, Mrs. Gradgrind," said Bounderby, " what passed?"

" Oh, my poor health!" returned Mrs. Gradgrind. " The girl wanted to come to the school, and Mr. Gradgrind wanted girls to come to the school, and Louisa and Thomas both said that the girl wanted to come, and that Mr. Gradgrind wanted girls to come, and how was it possible to contradict them when such was the fact!"

" Now I tell you what, Gradgrind!" said Mr. Bounderby. " Turn this girl to the right about, and there's an end of it."

" I am much of your opinion."

" Do it at once," said Bounderby, " has always been my motto from a child. When I thought I would run away from my egg-box and my grandmother, I did it at once. Do you the same. Do this at once!"

" Are you walking?" asked his friend. " I have the

father's address.   Perhaps you would not mind walking
to town with me?"

"Not the least in the world," said Mr. Bounderby, "as
long as you do it at once!"

So Mr. Bounderby threw on his hat—he always threw
it on, as expressing a man who had been far too busily
employed in making himself, to acquire any fashion of
wearing his hat—and with his hands in his pockets,
sauntered out into the hall.   "I never wear gloves," it
was his custom to say.   "I didn't climb up the ladder in
them.   Shouldn't have been so high up, if I had."

Being left to saunter in the hall a minute or two while
Mr. Gradgrind went upstairs for the address, he opened
the door of the children's study and looked into that
serene floorclothed apartment, which, notwithstanding its
bookcases and its cabinets and its variety of learned and
philosophical appliances, had much of the genial aspect
of a room devoted to hair-cutting.   Louisa languidly
leaned upon the window looking out, without looking at
anything, while young Thomas stood sniffing revengefully
at the fire.   Adam Smith and Malthus, two younger
Gradgrinds, were out at lecture in custody ; and little
Jane, after manufacturing a great deal of moist pipe-clay
on her face with slate-pencil and tears, had fallen asleep
over vulgar fractions.

"It's all right now, Louisa: it's all right, young
Thomas," said Mr. Bounderby ; "you won't do so any
more.   I'll answer for it's being all over with father.
Well, Louisa, that's worth a kiss, isn't it?"

"You can take one, Mr. Bounderby," said Louisa, when
she had coldly paused, and slowly walked across the
room, and ungraciously raised her cheek towards him,
with her face turned away.

"Always my pet; ain't you, Louisa?" said Mr. Bounderby.   "Good bye, Louisa!"

He went his way, but she stood on the same spot, rubbing the cheek he had kissed, with her handkerchief, until
it was burning red.   She was still doing this, five minutes
afterwards.

"What are you about, Loo?" her brother sulkily remonstrated.   "You'll rub a hole in your face."

"You may cut the piece out with your penknife if you
like, Tom.   I wouldn't cry!"

CHAPTER V.

THE KEY-NOTE.

COKETOWN, to which Messrs. Bounderby and Gradgrind now walked, was a triumph of fact: it had no greater taint of fancy in it then Mrs. Gradgrind herself. Let us strike the key-note, Coketown, before pursuing our tune.

It was a town of red brick, or of brick that would have been red if the smoke and ashes had allowed it; but as matters stood it was a town of unnatural red and black like the painted face of a savage. It was a town of machinery and tall chimneys, out of which interminable serpents of smoke trailed themselves forever and ever, and never got uncoiled. It had a black canal in it, and a river that ran purple with ill-smelling dye, and vast piles of building full of windows where there was a rattling and a trembling all day long, and where the piston of the steam-engine worked monotonously up and down, like the head of an elephant in a state of melancholy madness. It contained several large streets all very like one another, and many small streets still more like one another, inhabited by people equally like one another, who all went in and out at the same hours, with the same sound upon the same pavements, to do the same work, and to whom every day was the same as yesterday and to-morrow, and every year the counterpart of the last and the next.

These attributes of Coketown were in the main inseparable from the work by which it was sustained; against them were to be set off, comforts of life which found their way all over the world, and elegances of life which made, we will not ask how much of the fine lady, who could scarcely bear to hear the place mentioned. The rest of its features were voluntary, and they were these.

You saw nothing in Coketown but what was severely workful. If the members of a religious persuasion built a chapel there—as the members of eighteen religious persuasions had done—they made it a pious warehouse of red brick, with sometimes (but this is only in highly ornamented examples) a bell in a bird-cage on the top of it. The solitary exception was the New Church; a stuccoed edifice with a square steeple over the door, terminating in four short pinnacles like florid wooden legs. All the public inscriptions in the town were painted alike, in severe characters of black and white. The jail might have been the infirmary, the infirmary might have been the jail, the town-hall might have been either, or both, or anything else, for anything that appeared to the contrary in the graces of their construction. Fact, fact, fact, everywhere in the material aspect of the town; fact, fact, fact, everywhere in the immaterial. The M'Choakumchild school was all fact, and the school of design was all fact, and the relations between master and man were all fact, and everything was fact between the lying-in hospital and the cemetery, and what you couldn't state in figures, or show to be purchasable in the cheapest market and salable in the dearest, was not, and never should be, world without end, Amen.

A town so sacred to fact, and so triumphant in its assertion, of course got on well? Why no, not quite well. No? Dear me!

No. Coketown did not come out of its own furnaces, in all respects like gold that had stood the fire. First the perplexing mystery of the place was, Who belonged to the eighteen denominations? Because, whoever did, the laboring people did not. It was very strange to walk through the streets on a Sunday morning, and note how few of *them* the barbarous jangling of bells that was driving the sick and nervous mad, called away from their own quarter, from their own close rooms, from the corners of their own streets, where they lounged listlessly, gazing at all the church and chapel going, as at a thing with which they had no manner of concern. Nor was it merely the stranger who noticed this, because there was a native organization in Coketown itself, whose members were to be heard of in the House of Commons every session, indignantly petitioning for acts of Parliament that should make these people religious by main force. Then came the Teetotal Society, who complained that these same people *would* get drunk, and showed in tabular statements that they did get drunk, and proved at tea parties that no inducement, human or Divine (except a medal), would induce them to forego their custom of getting drunk. Then came the chemist and druggist, with other tabular statements, showing that when they didn't get drunk, they took opium. Then came the experienced chaplain of the jail, with more tabular statements, outdoing all the previous tabular statements, and showing that the same people *would* resort to low haunts, hidden from the public eye, where they heard low singing and saw low dancing, and mayhap joined in it; and where A. B., aged twenty-four next birthday, and committed for eighteen months' solitary, had himself said (not that he had ever shown himself particularly worthy of belief) his ruin began, as he was perfectly sure and confident that otherwise he would have been a tip-top moral specimen. Then came Mr. Gradgrind and Mr. Bounderby, the two gentlemen at this present moment walking through Coketown, and both eminently practical, who could, on occasion, furnish more tabular statements derived from their own personal experience, and illustrated by cases they had known and seen, from which it clearly appeared —in short, it was the only clear thing in the case—that these same people were a bad lot altogether, gentlemen; that do what you would for them they were never thankful for it, gentlemen; that they were restless, gentlemen; that they never knew what they wanted; that they lived upon the best, and bought fresh butter; and insisted on Mocha coffee, and rejected all but prime parts of meat, and yet were eternally dissatisfied and unmanageable. In short it was the moral of the old nursery fable:

" There was an old woman, and what do you think ?
She lived upon nothing but victuals and drink ;
Victuals and drink were the whole of her diet.
And yet this old woman would NEVER be quiet."

Is it possible, I wonder, that there was any analogy between the case of the Coketown population and the case of the little Gradgrinds ? Surely, none of us in our sober senses and acquainted with figures, are to be told at this time of day, that one of the foremost elements in the existence of the Coketown working-people had been for scores of years, deliberately set at nought ? That there was any Fancy in them demanding to be brought into healthy existence instead of struggling on in convulsions? That exactly in the ratio as they worked long and monotonously, the craving grew within them for some physical relief—some relaxation, encouraging good humor and good spirits, and giving them a vent—some recognized holiday, though it were but for an honest dance to a stirring band of music—some occasional light pie in which even M'Choakumchild had no finger—which craving must and would be satisfied aright, or must and would inevitably go wrong, until the laws of the Creation were repealed?

"This man lives at Pod's End, and I don't quite know Pod's End," said Mr. Gradgrind. "Which is it, Bounderby?"

Mr. Bounderby knew it was somewhere down town, but knew no more respecting it. So they stopped for a moment, looking about.

Almost as they did so, they came running round the corner of the street at a quick pace and with a frightened look, a girl whom Mr. Gradgrind recognized. "Halloa!" said he. "Stop! Where are you going! Stop!" Girl number twenty stopped then, palpitating, and made him a curtsey.

"Why are you tearing about the streets," said Mr. Gradgrind, "in this improper manner?"

"I was—I was run after, sir," the girl, panted, "and I wanted to get away."

"Run after?" repeated Mr. Gradgrind. "Who would run after *you?*"

The question was unexpectedly and suddenly answered for her, by the colorless boy, Bitzer, who came round the corner with such blind speed and so little anticipating a stoppage on the pavement, that he brought himself up against Mr. Gradgrind's waistcoat and rebounded into the road.

"What do you mean, boy?" said Mr. Gradgrind. "What are you doing?" How dare you dash against—everybody—in this manner?"

Bitzer picked up his cap, which the concussion had knocked off; and backing, and knuckling his forehead, pleaded that it was an accident.

"Was this boy running after you, Jupe?" asked Mr. Gradgrind.

"Yes, sir," said the girl reluctantly.

"No, I wasn't, sir!" cried Bitzer. "Not till she run away from me. But the horse-riders never mind what they say, sir; they're famous for it. You know the horse-riders are famous for never minding what they say," addressing Sissy. "It's as well known in the town as—please, sir, as the multiplication table isn't known to the horse-riders." Bitzer tried Mr. Bounderby with this.

"He frightened me so," said the girl, "with his cruel faces!"

"Oh!" cried Bitzer. "Oh! An't you one of the rest! An't you a horse-rider! I never looked at her, sir. I asked her if she would know how to define a horse tomorrow, and offered to tell her again, and she ran away, and I ran after her, sir, that she might know how to answer when she was asked. You wouldn't have thought of saying such mischief if you hadn't been a horse-rider!"

"Her calling seems to be pretty well known among 'em," observed Mr. Bounderby. "You'd have had the whole school peeping in a row, in a week."

"Truly, I think so," returned his friend. "Bitzer, turn you about and take yourself home.   · · , stay here a moment. Let me hear of your runni _ m this manner any more, boy, and you will hear of me through the master of the school. You understand what I mean. Go along."

The boy stopped in his rapid blinking, knuckled his forehead again, glanced at Sissy, turned about, and retreated.

"Now, girl," said Mr. Gradgrind, "take this gentleman and me to your father's; we are going there. What have you got in that bottle you are carrying?"

"Gin," said Mr. Bounderby.

"Dear, no, sir! It's the nine oils."

"The what?" cried Mr. Bounderby.

"The nine oils, sir. To rub father with." Then, said Mr. Bounderby, with a loud short laugh, "What the devil do you rub your father with nine oils for?"

"It's what our people always use, sir, when they get any hurts in the ring," replied the girl, looking over her shoulder, to assure herself that her pursuer was gone. "They bruise themselves very bad sometimes."

"Serve 'em right," said Bounderby, "for being idle."

She glanced up at his face, with mingled astonishment and dread.

" By George ! " said Mr. Bounderby, " when I was four or five years younger than you, I had worse bruises upon me than ten oils, twenty oils, forty oils, would have rubbed off. I didn't get 'em by posture-making, but by being banged about. There was no rope-dancing for me ; I danced on the bare ground and was larruped with the rope."

Mr. Gradgrind, though hard enough, was by no means so rough a man as Mr. Bounderby. His character was not unkind, all things considered ; it might have been a very kind one indeed, if he had only made some round mistake in the arithmetic that balanced it, years ago. He said, in what he meant for a reassuring tone, as they turned down a narrow road, " And this is Pod's End ; is it, Jupe ! "

"This is it, sir, and—if you wouldn't mind, sir—this is the house."

She stopped, at twilight, at the door of a mean little public house, with dim red lights in it. As haggard and as shabby as if, for want of custom, it had itself taken to drinking, and had gone the way all drunkards go, and was very near the end of it.

It's only crossing the bar, sir, and up the stairs, if you wouldn't mind, and waiting there for a moment till I get a candle. If you should hear a dog, sir, it's only Merrylegs, and he only barks."

" Merrylegs and nine oils, eh ! " said Mr. Bounderby, entering last with his metallic laugh. " Pretty well this, for a self-made man ! "

CHAPTER VI.

SLEARY'S HORSEMANSHIP.

THE name of the public house was the Pegasus's Arms. The Pegasus's legs might have been more to the purpose ; but, underneath the winged horse upon the sign-board, the Pegasus's Arms was inscribed in Roman letters. Beneath that inscription again, in a flowing scroll, the painter had touched off the lines :

" Good malt makes good beer,
  Walk in, and they'll draw it here ;
  Good wine makes good brandy,
  Give us a call, and you'll find it handy."

Framed and glazed upon the wall behind the dingy little bar, was another Pegasus—a theatrical one—with real gauze let in for his wings, golden stars stuck on all over him, and his ethereal harness made of red silk.

As it had grown too dusky without, to see the sign, and as it had not grown light enough within to see the picture, Mr. Gradgrind and Mr. Bounderby received no offence from these idealities. They followed the girl up some steep corner-stairs without meeting any one, and stopped in the dark while she went on for a candle. They expected every moment to hear Merrylegs give tongue, but the highly trained performing dog had not barked when the girl and the candle appeared together.

"Father is not in our room, sir," she said, with a face of great surprise. "If you wouldn't mind walking in, I'll find him directly."

They walked in ; and Sissy, having set two chairs for them, sped away with a quick light step. It was a mean, shabbily furnished room, with a bed in it. The white night-cap, embellished with two peacock's feathers and a pigtail bolt upright, in which Signor Jupe had that very afternoon enlivened the varied performances with his chaste Shakesperean quips and retorts, hung upon a nail ; but no other portion of his wardrobe, or other token of himself or his pursuits, was to be seen anywhere. As to Merrylegs, that respectable ancestor of the highly trained animal who went aboard the ark, might have been accidentally shut out of it, for any sign of a dog that was manifest to eye or ear in the Pegasus's Arms.

They heard the doors of rooms above, opening and shutting as Sissy went from one to another in quest of her father ; and presently they heard voices expressing surprise. She came bounding down again in a great hurry, opened a battered and mangy old hair trunk, found it empty, and looked round with her hands clasped and her face full of terror.

"Father must have gone down to the Booth, sir. I don't know why he should go there, but he must be there ; I'll bring him in a minute!" She was gone directly, without her bonnet; with her long, dark, childish hair streaming behind her.

"What does she mean!" said Mr. Gradgrind. "Back in a minute? It's more than a mile off."

Before Mr. Bounderby could reply, a young man appeared at the door, and introducing himself with the words, "By your leaves, gentlemen!" walked in with his hands in his pockets. His face, close-shaven, thin, and sallow, was shaded by a great quantity of dark hair brushed into a roll all round his head, and parted up the centre. His legs were very robust, but shorter than legs of good proportions should have been. His chest and back were as much too broad, as his legs were too short. He was dressed in a Newmarket coat and tight-fitting trousers; wore a shawl round his neck; smelt of lamp-oil, straw, orange-peel, horses' provender, and sawdust; and looked a most remarkable sort of Centaur, compounded of the stable and the play-house. Where the one began, and the other ended, nobody could have told with any precision. This gentleman was mentioned in the bills of the day as Mr. E. W. B. Childers, so justly celebrated for his daring vaulting act as the Wild Huntsman of the North American Prairies; in which popular performance, a diminutive boy with an old face, who now accompanied him, assisted as his infant son: being carried upside down over his father's shoulder, by one foot, and held by the crown of his head, heels upwards, in the palm of his father's hand, according to the violent paternal manner in which wild huntsmen may be observed to fondle their offspring. Made up with curls, wreaths, wings, white bismuth, and carmine, this hopeful young person soared into so pleasing a Cupid as to constitute the chief delight of the maternal part of the spectators; but in private, where his characteristics were a precocious cutaway coat and an extremely gruff voice, he became of the Turf, turfy.

"By your leaves, gentlemen," said Mr. E. W. B. Childers, glancing round the room. "It was you, I believe, that were wishing to see Jupe!"

"It was," said Mr. Gradgrind. "His daughter has gone to fetch him, but I can't wait; therefore, if you please, I will leave a message for him with you."

"You see, my friend." Mr. Bounderby put in, "we are

the kind of people who know the value of time, and you are the kind of people who don't know the value of time."

"I have not," retorted Mr. Childers, after surveying him from head to foot, "the honor of knowing *you*,—but if you mean that you can make more money of your time than I can of mine, I should judge from your appearance, that you are about right."

"And when you have made it, you can keep it too, I should think," said Cupid.

"Kidderminster, stow that!" said Mr. Childers. (Master Kidderminster was Cupid's mortal name.)

"What does he come here cheeking us for, then?" cried Master Kidderminster, showing a very irascible temperament. "If you want to cheek us, pay your ochre at the doors, and take it out."

"Kidderminster," said Mr. Childers, raising his voice, "stow that!—Sir," to Mr. Gradgrind, "I was addressing myself to you. You may or you may not be aware (for perhaps you have not been much in the audience), that Jupe has missed his tip very often lately."

"Has—what has he missed?" asked Mr. Gradgrind, glancing at the potent Bounderby for assistance.

"Missed his tip."

"Offered at the Garters four times last night, and never done 'em once," said Master Kidderminster. "Missed his tip at the banners, too, and was loose in his ponging."

"Didn't do what he ought to do. Was short in his leaps and bad in his tumbling," Mr. Childers interpreted.

"Oh!" said Mr. Gradgrind, "that is tip, is it?"

"In a general way that's missing his tip," Mr. E. W. B. Childers answered.

"Nine oils, Merrylegs, missing tips, garters, banners, and Ponging, eh!" ejaculated Bounderby, with his laugh of laughs. "Queer sort of company, too, for a man who has raised himself."

"Lower yourself, then," retorted Cupid. "Oh Lord! if you've raised yourself so high as all that comes to, let yourself down a bit."

"This is a very obtrusive lad!" said Mr. Gradgrind, turning, and knitting his brows on him.

" We'd have had a young gentleman to meet you, if we had known you were coming," retorted Master Kidderminster, nothing abashed. "It's a pity you don't have a bespeak, being so particular. You're on the Tight-Jeff, ain't you?"

" What does this unmannerly boy mean," asked Mr. Gradgrind, eyeing him in a sort of desperation, " by Tight-Jeff?"

"There! Get out, get out!" said Mr. Childers, thrusting his young friend from the room, rather in the prairie manner. " Tight-Jeff or Slack-Jeff, it don't much signify: it's only tight-rope and slack-rope. You were going to give me a message for Jupe?"

" Yes, I was."

"Then," continued Mr. Childers, quickly, " my opinion is, he will never receive it. Do you know much of him?"

" I never saw the man in my life."

" I doubt if you ever *will* see him now. It's pretty plain to me, he's off."

" Do you mean that he has deserted his daughter?"

" Ay! I mean," said Mr. Childers, with a nod, " that he has cut. He was goosed last night, he was goosed the night before last, he was goosed to-day. He has lately got in the way of being always goosed, and he can't stand it."

" Why has he been—so very much—Goosed?" asked Mr. Gradgrind, forcing the word out of himself, with great solemnity and reluctance.

" His joints are turning stiff, and he is getting used up," said Childers. " He has his points as a Cackler still, but he can't get a living out of *them*."

" A Cackler!" Bounderby repeated. " Here we go again!"

" A speaker, if the gentleman likes it better," said Mr. E. W. B. Childers, superciliously throwing the interpretation over his shoulder, and accompanying it with a shake of his long hair—which all shook at once. " Now, it's a remarkable fact, sir, that it cut that man deeper, to know that his daughter knew of his being goosed, than to go through with it."

" Good!" interrupted Mr. Bounderby. " This is good, Gradgrind! A man so fond of his daughter, that he runs away from her! This is devilish good! Ha! ha! Now,

3

I'll tell you what, young man. I haven't always occupied my present station of life. I know what these things are. You may be astonished to hear it, but my mother ran away from *me.*"

E. W. B. Childers replied pointedly, that he was not at all astonished to hear it.

"Very well," said Bounderby. "I was born in a ditch, and my mother ran away from me. Do I excuse her for it? No. Have I ever excused her for it? Not I. What do I call her for it? I call her probably the very worst woman that ever lived in the world, except my drunken grandmother. There's no family pride about me, there's no imaginative, sentimental humbug about me. I call a spade a spade; and I call the mother of Josiah Bounderby, of Coketown, without any fear or any favor, what I should call her if she had been the mother of Dick Jones, of Wapping. So, with this man. He is a runaway rogue and a vagabond, that's what he is, in English."

"It's all the same to me what he is or what he is not, whether in English or whether in French," retorted Mr. E. W. B. Childers, facing about. "I am telling your friend what's the fact; if you don't like to hear it, you can avail yourself of the open air. You give it mouth enough, you do; but give it mouth in your own building, at least," remonstrated E. W. B. with stern irony. "Don't give it mouth in this building till you're called upon. You have got some building of your own, I dare say, now?"

"Perhaps so," replied Mr. Bounderby, rattling his money and laughing.

"Then give it mouth in your own building, will you, if you please?" said Childers. "Because this isn't a strong building, and too much of you might bring it down!"

Eyeing Mr. Bounderby from head to foot again, he turned from him, as from a man finally disposed of, to Mr. Gradgrind.

Jupe sent his daughter out on an errand not an hour ago, and then was seen to slip out himself, with his hat over his eyes, and a bundle tied up in a handkerchief under his arm. She will never believe it of him, but he has cut away and left her."

"Pray," said Mr. Gradgrind, "why will she never believe it of him?"

"Because those two were one. Because they were never asunder. Because, up to this time, he seemed to dote upon her," said Childers, taking a step or two to look into the empty trunk. Both Mr. Childers and Master Kidderminster walked in a curious manner; with their legs wider apart than the general run of men, and with a very knowing assumption of being stiff in the knees. This walk was common to all the male members of Sleary's company, and was understood to express that they were always on horseback.

"Poor Sissy! He had better have apprenticed her," said Childers, giving his hair another shake, as he looked up from the empty box. "Now, he leaves her without anything to take to."

"It is creditable to you, who have never been apprenticed, to express that opinion," returned Mr. Gradgrind, approvingly.

"*I* never apprenticed? I was apprenticed when I was seven years old."

"Oh! Indeed?" said Mr. Gradgrind, rather resentfully, as having been defrauded of his good opinion. "I was not aware of its being the custom to apprentice young persons to——"

"Idleness," Mr. Bounderby put in with a loud laugh. "No, by the Lord Harry! Nor I!"

"Her father always had it in his head," resumed Childers, feigning unconsciousness of Mr. Bounderby's existence, "that she was to be taught the deuce-and-all of education. How it got into his head, I can't say; I can only say that it never got out. He has been picking up a bit of reading for her, here—and a bit of writing for her, there—and a bit of ciphering for her, somewhere else—these seven years."

Mr. E. W. B. Childers took one of his hands out of his pocket, stroked his face and chin, and looked, with a good deal of doubt and a little hope, at Mr. Gradgrind. From the first he had sought to conciliate that gentleman, for the sake of the deserted girl.

"When Sissy got into the school here," he pursued, "her father was as pleased as Punch. I couldn't altogether make out why, myself, as we were not stationary here, being but comers and goers anywhere. I suppose, however, he had this move in his mind—he was always half-cracked—and then considered her provided for. If you should happen to have looked in to-night, for the purpose of telling him that you were going to do her any little service," said Mr. Childers, stroking his face again, and repeating his look, "it would be very fortunate and well-timed; *very* fortunate and well-timed."

"On the contrary," returned Mr. Gradgrind. "I came to tell him that her connections made her not an object for the school, and that she must not attend any more. Still, if her father really has left her, without any conni-vance on her part—Bounderby, let me have a word with you."

Upon this, Mr. Childers politely betook himself, with his equestrian walk, to the landing outside the door, and there stood stroking his face, and softly whistling. While thus engaged, he overheard such phrases in Mr. Bounderby's voice as "No. *I* say no. I advise you not. I say by no means." While, from Mr. Gradgrind, he heard in his much lower tone the words, "But even as an example to Louisa, of what this pursuit which has been the subject of a vulgar curiosity, leads to and ends in. Think of it, Bounderby, in that point of view."

Meanwhile, the various members of Sleary's company gradually gathered together from the upper regions, where they were quartered, and, from standing about, talking in low voices to one another and to Mr. Childers, gradually insinuated themselves and him into the room. There were two or three handsome young women among them, with their two or three husbands, and their two or three mothers, and their eight or nine little children, who did the fairy business when required. The father of one of the families was in the habit of balancing the father of another of the families on the top of a great pole; the father of a third family often made a pyramid of both those fathers, with Master Kidderminster for the apex, and himself for the base; all the fathers could dance upon rolling casks, stand upon bottles, catch knives and balls, twirl hand-basins, ride upon anything, jump over everything, and stick at nothing. All the mothers could (and did) dance, upon the slack wire and the tight rope, and perform rapid acts on bare-backed steeds; none of them were at all particular in respect of showing their legs; and one of them, alone in a Greek chariot, drove

six in hand into every town they came to. They all assumed to be mighty rakish and knowing, they were not
very tidy in their private dresses, they were not at all
orderly in their domestic arrangements, and the combined literature of the whole company would have produced but a poor letter on any subject. Yet there was a
remarkable gentleness and childishness about these
people, a special inaptitude for any kind of sharp practice,
and an untiring readiness to help and pity one another,
deserving often of as much respect, and always of as
much generous construction, as the every-day virtues of
any class of people in the world.

Last of all appeared Mr. Sleary : a stout man as already
mentioned, with one fixed eye, and one loose eye, a voice
(if it can be called so) like the efforts of a broken old pair
of bellows, a flabby surface, and a muddled head which
was never sober and never drunk.

"Thquire!" said Mr. Sleary, who was troubled with
asthma, and whose breath came far too thick and heavy
for the letter s, "Your thervant! Thith ith a bad piethe
of bithnith, thith ith. You've heard of my Clown and
hith dog being thuppothed to have morrithed?"

He addressed Mr. Gradgrind, who answered "Yes."

"Well, Thquire," he returned, taking off his hat, and
rubbing the lining with his pocket-handkerchief, which
he kept inside for the purpose. "Ith it your intenthion
to do anything for the poor girl, Thquire?"

"I shall have something to propose to her when she
comes back," said Mr. Gradgrind.

"Glad to hear it, Thquire. Not that I want to get rid
of the child, any more than I want to thtand in her way.
I'm willing to take her prentith, though at her age ith
late. My voithe ith a little huthky, Thquire, and not
eathy heard by them ath don't know me; but if
you'd been chilled and heated, heated and chilled, chilled
and heated in the ring when you wath young, ath often
ath I have been, *your* voithe wouldn't have lathted out,
Thquire, no more than mine."

"I dare say not," said Mr. Gradgrind.

"What thall it be, Thquire, while you wait? Thall it
be Therry? Give it a name, Thquire!" said Mr. Sleary,
with hospitable ease.

"Nothing for me, I thank you," said **Mr. Gradgrind.**

"Don't thay nothing, Thquire. What doth your friend thay? If you haven't took your feed yet, have a glath of bitterth."

Here his daughter Josephine—a pretty fair-haired girl of eighteen, who had been tied on a horse at two years old, and had made a will at twelve, which she always carried about with her, expressive of her dying desire to be drawn to the grave by the two piebald ponies—cried, "Father, hush! she has come back!" Then came Sissy Jupe, running into the room as she had run out of it. And when she saw them all assembled, and saw their looks, and saw no father there, she broke into a most deplorable cry, and took refuge on the bosom of the most accomplished tight-rope lady (herself in the family-way), who knelt down on the floor to nurse her, and to weep over her.

"Ith an infernal thame, upon my soul it ith," said Sleary.

"O my dear father, my good kind father, where are you gone? You are gone to try to do me some good, I know! You are gone away for my sake, I am sure! And how miserable and helpless you will be without me, poor, poor father, until you come back!" It was so pathetic to hear her saying many things of this kind, with her face turned upward, and her arms stretched out as if she were trying to stop his departing shadow and embrace it, that no one spoke a word until Mr. Bounderby (growing impatient) took the case in hand.

"Now, good people all," said he, "this is wanton waste of time. Let the girl understand the fact. Let her take it from me, if you like, who have been run away from, myself. Here, what's your name! Your father has absconded—deserted you—and you mustn't expect to see him again as long as you live."

They cared so little for plain Fact, these people, and were in that advanced state of degeneracy on the subject, that instead of being impressed by the speaker's strong common sense, they took it in extraordinary dudgeon. The men muttered "Shame!" and the women "Brute!" and Sleary, in some haste, communicated the following hint, apart to Mr. Bounderby.

"I tell you what, Thquire. To thpeak plain to you, my opinion ith that you had better cut it thort, and drop it.

They're a very good natur'd people, my people, but they're accuthtomed to be quick in their movementh; and if you don't act upon my advithe, I'm damned if I don't believe they'll pith you out o' winder."

Mr. Bounderby being restrained by this mild suggestion, Mr. Gradgrind found an opening for his eminently practical exposition of the subject.

" It is of no moment," said he, " whether this person is to be expected back at any time, or the contrary. He is gone away, and there is no present expectation of his re-ʊurn. That, I believe, is agreed on all hands."

" Thath agreed, Thquire. Thick to that! " From Sleary.

" Well then. I, who came here to inform the father of the poor girl, Jupe, that she could not be received at the school any more, in consequence of there being practical objections, into which I need not enter, to the reception there of the children of persons so employed, am prepared in these altered circumstances to make a proposal. I am willing to take charge of you, Jupe, and to educate you, and provide for you. The only condition (over and above your good behavior) I make is, that you decide now, at once, whether to accompany me or remain here. Also, that if you accompany me now, it is understood that you communicate no more with any of your friends who are here present. These observations comprise the whole of the case."

" At the thame time," said Sleary, " I mutht put in my word, Thquire, tho that both thides of the banner may be equally theen. If you like, Thethilia, to be prentitht, you know the natur of the work and you know your companionth. Emma Gordon, in whothe lap you're a lying at prethent, would be a mother to you, and Joth'phine would be a thithter to you. I don't pretend to be of the angel breed myself, and I don't thay but what, when you mith'd your tip, you'd find me cut up rough, and thwear an oath or two at you. But what I thay, Thquire, ith, that good tempered or bad tempered, I never did a horthe a injury yet, no more than thwearing at him went, and that I don't expect I thall begin otherwithe at my time of life, with a rider. I never wath much of a Cackler, Thquire, and I have thed my thay."

The latter part of this speech was addressed to Mr.

Gradgrind, who received it with a grave inclination of his head, and then remarked :

"The only observation I will make to you, Jupe, in the way of influencing your decision, is, that it is highly desirable to have a sound practical education, and that even your father himself (from what I understand) appears, on your behalf, to have known and felt that much."

The last words had a visible effect upon her. She stopped in her wild crying, a little detached herself from Emma Gordon, and turned her face full upon her patron. The whole company perceived the force of the change, and drew a long breath together, that plainly said, "she will go!"

"Be sure you know your own mind, Jupe," Mr. Gradgrind cautioned her; "I say no more. Be sure you know your own mind!"

"When father comes back," cried the girl, bursting into tears again after a minute's silence, "how will he ever find me if I go away!"

"You may be quite at ease," said Mr. Gradgrind, calmly; he worked out the whole matter like a sum; "you may be quite at ease, Jupe, on that score. In such a case, your father, I apprehend, must find out Mr. ——'

"Thleary. Thath my name, Thquire. Not athamed of it. Known all over England, and alwayth paythe ith way."

"Must find out Mr. Sleary, who would then let him know where you went. I should have no power of keeping you against his wish, and he would have no difficulty, at any time, in finding Mr. Thomas Gradgrind of Coketown. I am well known."

"Well known," assented Mr. Sleary, rolling his loose eye. "You're one of the thort, Thquire, that keepth a prethiouth thight of money out of the houthe. But never mind that at prethent."

There was another silence; and then she exclaimed, sobbing, with her hands before her face, "Oh give me my clothes, give me my clothes, and let me go away before I break my heart!"

The women sadly bestirred themselves to get the clothes together—it was soon done, for they were not many—and to pack them in a basket which had often travelled with them. Sissy sat all the time upon the ground, still sobbing, and covering her eyes. Mr. Gradgrind and his friend Bounderby stood near the door, ready to take her away. Mr. Sleary stood in the middle of the room, with the male members of the company about him, exactly as he would have stood in the centre of the ring during his daughter Josephine's performance. He wanted nothing but his whip.

The basket packed in silence, they brought her bonnet to her, and smoothed her disordered hair, and put it on. Then they pressed about her, and bent over her in very natural attitudes, kissing and embracing her: and brought the children to take leave of her; and were a tender-hearted, simple, foolish set of women altogether.

"Now, Jupe," said Mr. Gradgrind. "If you are quite determined, come!"

But she had to take her farewell of the male part of the company yet, and every one of them had to unfold his arms (for they all assumed the professional attitude when they found themselves near Sleary), and gave her a parting kiss—Master Kidderminster excepted, in whose young nature there was an original flavor of the misanthrope, who was also known to have harbored matrimonial views, and who moodily withdrew. Mr. Sleary was reserved until the last. Opening his arms wide he took her by both her hands, and would have sprung her up and down, after the riding-master manner of congratulating young ladies on their dismounting from a rapid act; but there was no rebound in Sissy, and she only stood before him crying.

"Good-bye, my dear!" said Sleary. "You'll make your fortun, I hope, and none of our poor folkth will ever trouble you, I'll pound it. I with your father hadn't taken hith dog with him; ith a ill-conwenienth to have the dog out of the billth. But on thecond thought, he wouldn't have performed without hith mathter, tho ith ath broad ath ith long!"

With that he regarded her attentively with his fixed, eye, surveyed his company with his loose one, kissed her, shook his head, and handed her to Mr. Gradgrind as to a horse.

"There the ith, Thquire," he said, sweeping her with

a professional glance as if she were being adjusted in her seat, " and the'll do you juthithe. Good-bye, Thethilia!"

" Good-bye, Cecilia!" " Good-bye, Sissy!" " God bless you, dear!" In a variety of voices from all the room.

But the riding-master's eye had observed the bottle of the nine oils in her bosom, and he now interposed with " Leave the bottle, my dear; ith large to carry; it will be of no uthe to you now. Give it to me!"

" No, no!" she said, in another burst of tears. " Oh, no! Pray let me keep it for father till he comes back! He will want it when he comes back. He had never thought of going away, when he sent me for it. I must keep it for him, if you please!"

" Tho be it, my dear. (You thee how it ith, Thquire!) Farewell, Thethilia! My lath wordth to you ith thith, Thtick to the termth of your engagement, be obedient to the Thquire, and forget uth. But if, when you're grown up and married and well off, you come upon any hortheriding ever, don't be hard upon it, don't be croth with it, give it a Bethpeak if you can, and think you might do wurth. People must be amused, Thquire, somehow," continued Sleary, rendered more pursy than ever, by so much talking; " they can't be alwayth a working, nor yet they can't be alwayth a learning. Make the betht of uth; not the wurtht. I've got my living out of the horthe riding all my life, I know ; but I conthider that I lay down the philothophy of the thubject when I thay to you, Thquire, make the betht of uth : not the wurtht!"

The Sleary philosophy was propounded as they went down stairs ; and the fixed eye of Philosophy—and its rolling eye, too—soon lost the three figures and the basket in the darkness of the street.

CHAPTER VII.

MRS. SPARSIT.

MR. BOUNDERBY being a bachelor, an elderly lady presided over his establishment, in consideration of a certain annual stipend. Mrs. Sparsit was this lady's name; and she was a prominent figure in attendance on Mr. Bounderby's car, as it rolled along in triumph with the Bully of humility inside.

For Mrs. Sparsit had not only seen different days, but was highly connected, She had a great aunt living in these very times called Lady Scadgers. Mr. Sparsit, deceased, of whom she was the relict, had been by the mothers side what Mrs. Sparsit still called " a Powler." Strangers of limited information and dull apprehension were sometimes observed not to know what a Powler was, and even to appear uncertain whether it might be a business or a political party, or a profession of faith. The better class of minds, however, did not need to be informed that the Powlers were an ancient stock, who could trace themselves so exceedingly far back that it was not surprising if they sometimes lost themselves—which they had rather frequently done, as respected horse-flesh, blind-hookey, Hebrew monetary transactions, and the Insolvent Debtors' Court.

The late Mr. Sparsit, being by the mother's side a Powler, married this lady, being by the father's side a Scadgers. Lady Scadgers (an immensely fat old woman, with an inordinate appetite for butcher's meat, and a mysterious leg which had now refused to get out of bed for fourteen years) contrived the marriage, at a period when Sparsit was just of age, and chiefly noticeable for a slender body, weakly supported on two long slim props, and surmounted by no head worth mentioning. He inherited a fair fortune from his uncle, but owed it all before he came into it, and spent it twice over immediately afterwards. Thus, when he died, at twenty-four (the scene of his decease, Calais, and the cause, brandy), he did not leave his widow, from whom he had been separated soon after the honeymoon, in affluent circumstances. That bereaved lady, fifteen years older than he, fell presently at deadly feud with her only relative, Lady Scadgers: and partly to spite her ladyship, and partly to maintain herself, went out at a salary. And here she was now, in her elderly days, with the Coriolanian style of nose and the dense black eyebrows which had captivated Sparsit, making Mr. Bounderby's tea as he took his breakfast.

If Bounderby had been a Conqueror, and Mrs. Sparsit a captive Princess whom he took about as a feature in his state-processions, he could not have made a greater flourish with her than he habitually did. Just as it belonged to his boastfulness to depreciate his own extraction, so it belonged to it to exalt Mrs. Sparsit's. In the measure that he would not allow his own youth to have been attended by a single favorable circumstance, he brightened Mrs. Sparsit's juvenile career with every possible advantage, and showered wagon-loads of early roses all over that lady's path. "And yet, sir," he would say, "how does it turn out after all? Why here she is at a hundred a year (I give her a hundred, which she is pleased to term handsome), keeping the house of Josiah Bounderby of Coketown!"

Nay, he made this foil of his so very widely known, that third parties took it up, and handled it on some occasions with considerable briskness. It was one of the most exasperating attributes of Bounderby, that he not only sang his own praises but stimulated other men to sing them. There was a moral infection of clap-trap in him. Strangers, modest enough elsewhere, started up at dinners in Coketown, and boasted, in quite a rampant way, of Bounderby. They made him out to be the Royal arms, the Union-Jack, Magna Charta, John Bull, Habeas Corpus, the Bill of Rights, An Englishman's house is his castle, Church and State, and God save the Queen, all put together. And as often (and it was very often) as an orator of this kind brought into his peroration,

> " Princes and lords may flourish or may fade,
> A breath can make them, as a breath has made,"

—it was, for certain, more or less understood among the company that he had heard of Mrs. Sparsit.

"Mr. Bounderby," said Mrs. Sparsit, "you are unusually slow, sir, with your breakfast this morning."

"Why, ma'am," he returned, "I am thinking about Tom Gradgrind's whim;" Tom Gradgrind, for a bluff independent manner of speaking—as if somebody were always endeavoring to bribe him with immense sums to say Thomas, and he wouldn't; "Tom Gradgrind's whim, ma'am, of bringing up the tumbling-girl."

"The girl is now waiting to know," said Mrs. Sparsit, "whether she is to go straight to the school, or up to the Lodge."

"She must wait, ma'am," answered Bounderby, "till I know myself. We shall have Tom Gradgrind down here

presently, I suppose. If he should wish her to remain
here a day or two longer, of course she can, ma'am."

"Of course she can if you wish it, Mr. Bounderby."

"I told him I would give her a shake-down here, last
night, in order that he might sleep on it before he decided
to let her have any association with Louisa."

"Indeed, Mr. Bounderby? Very thoughtful of you!"
Mrs. Sparsit's Coriolanian nose underwent a slight
expansion of the nostrils, and her black eyebrows contracted as she took a sip of tea.

"It's tolerably clear to *me*," said Bounderby, "that the
little puss can get small good out of such companionship."

"Are you speaking of young Miss Gradgrind, Mr.
Bounderby?"

"Yes, ma'am, I'm speaking of Louisa."

"Your observation being limited to 'little puss,'" said
Mrs. Sparsit, "and there being two little girls in question,
I did not know which might be indicated by that expres-
sion."

"Louisa," repeated Mr. Bounderby. "Louisa, Louisa."

"You are quite another father to Louisa, sir." Mrs.
Sparsit took a little more tea; and, as she bent her again
contracted eyebrows over her steaming cup, rather looked
as if her classical countenance were invoking the infernal
gods.

"If you had said I was another father to Tom—young
Tom, I mean, not my friend Tom Gradgrind—you might
have been nearer the mark. I am going to take young
Tom into my office. Going to have him under my wing,
ma'am."

"Indeed? Rather young for that, is he not, sir?" Mrs.
Sparsit's "sir," in addressing Mr. Bounderby, was a word
of ceremony, rather exacting consideration for herself in
the use, than honoring him.

"I'm not going to take him at once; he is to finish
his educational cramming before then," said Bounderby.
"By the Lord Harry, he'll have enough of it, first and
last! He'd open his eyes, that boy would, if he knew how
empty of learning *my* young maw was at his time of life."
Which, by the by, he probably did know, for he had heard
of it often enough. "But it's extraordinary the difficulty
I have on scores of such subjects, in speaking to any one
on equal terms. Here, for example, I have been speaking

to you this morning about tumblers. Why, what do *you* know about tumblers? At the time when, to have been a tumbler in the mud of the streets, would have been a godsend to me, a prize in the lottery to me, you were at the Italian Opera. You were coming out of the Italian Opera, ma'am, in white satin and jewels, a blaze of splendor, when I hadn't a penny to buy a link to light you."

"I certainly, sir," returned Mrs. Sparsit, with a dignity serenely mournful, "was familiar with the Italian Opera at a very early age."

"Egad, ma'am, so was I," said Bounderby, "—with the wrong side of it. A hard bed the pavement of its Arcade used to make, I assure you. People like you, ma'am, accustomed from infancy to lie on Down feathers, have no idea *how* hard a paving-stone is, without trying it. No, no, it's of no use my talking to *you* about tumblers. I should speak of foreign dancers, and the West End of London, and May Fair, and lords and ladies and honorables."

"I trust, sir," rejoined Mrs. Sparsit, with decent resignation, "it is not necessary that you should do anything of that kind. I hope I have learnt how to accommodate myself to the changes of life. If I have acquired an interest in hearing of your instructive experiences, and can scarcely hear enough of them, I claim no merit for that, since I believe it is a general sentiment."

"Well, ma'am," said her patron, "perhaps some people may be pleased to say that they do like to hear, in his own unpolished way, what Josiah Bounderby, of Coketown, has gone through. But you must confess that you were born in the lap of luxury, yourself. Come, ma'am, you know you were born in the lap of luxury."

"I do not, sir," returned Mrs. Sparsit with a shake of her head, "deny it."

Mr Bounderby was obliged to get up from the table and stand with his back to the fire, looking at her; she was such an enhancement of his position.

"And you were in crack society. Devilish high society," he said, warming his legs.

"It is true, sir," returned Mrs. Sparsit, with an affectation of humility the very opposite of his, and therefore in no danger of jostling it.

" You were in the tiptop fashion, and all the rest of it," said Mr. Bounderby.

" Yes, sir," returned Mrs. Sparsit, with a kind of social widowhood upon her. " It is unquestionably true."

Mr. Bounderby, bending himself at the knees, literally embraced his legs in his great satisfaction and laughed aloud. Mr. and Miss Gradgrind being then announced, he received the former with a shake of the hand, and the latter with a kiss.

" Can Jupe be sent here, Bounderby ? " asked Mr. Gradgrind.

Certainly. So Jupe was sent there. On coming in, she curtseyed to Mr. Bounderby, and to his friend Tom Gradgrind, and also to Louisa; but in her confusion unluckily omitted Mrs. Sparsit. Observing this, the blustrous Bounderby had the following remarks to make.

" Now I tell you what, my girl. The name of that lady by the teapot, is Mrs. Sparsit. That lady acts as mistress of this house, and she is a highly connected lady. Consequently, if ever you come again into any room in this house, you will make a short stay in it if you don't behave towards that lady in your most respectful manner. Now, I don't care a button what you do to *me*, because I don't affect to be anybody. So far from having high connections I have no connection at all, and I come of the scum of the earth. But towards that lady, I do care what you do; and you shall do what is deferential and respectful, or you shall not come here."

" I hope, Bounderby," said Mr. Gradgrind, in conciliatory voice," that this was merely an oversight."

" My friend Tom Gradgrind suggests, Mrs. Sparsit," said Bounderby, " that this was merely an oversight. Very likely. However, as you are aware, ma'am, I don't allow of even oversights towards you."

" You are very good indeed, sir," returned Mrs. Sparsit, shaking her head with her State humility. " It is not worth speaking of."

Sissy, who all this time had been faintly excusing herself with tears in her eyes, was now waved over by the master of the house to Mr. Gradgrind. She stood looking intently at him, and Louisa stood coldly by, with her eyes upon the ground, while he proceeded thus:

" Jupe, I have made up my mind to take you into my

house; and, when you are not in attendance at the school, to employ you about Mrs. Gradgrind, who is rather an invalid, I have explained to Miss Louisa—this is Miss Louisa—the miserable but natural end of your late career; and you are to expressly understand that the whole of that subject is past, and is not to be referred to any more. From this time you begin your history. You are, at present, ignorant, I know."

"Yes, sir, very," she answered, curtseying.

"I shall have the satisfaction of causing you to be strictly educated; and you will be a living proof to all who come in communication with you, of the advantages of the training you will receive. You will be reclaimed and formed. You have been in the habit now of reading to your father, and those people I found you among, I dare say?" said Mr. Gradgrind, beckoning her nearer to him before he said so, and dropping his voice.

"Only to father and Merrylegs, sir. At least I mean to father, when Merrylegs was always there."

"Never mind Merrylegs, Jupe," said Mr. Gradgrind, with a passing frown. "I don't ask about him. I understand you to have been in the habit of reading to your father?"

"O yes sir, thousands of times. They were the happiest—O, of all the happy times we had together, sir!"

It was only now when her sorrow broke out, that Louisa looked at her.

"And what," asked Mr. Gradgrind, in a still lower voice, "did you read to your father, Jupe?"

"About the Fairies, sir, and the Dwarf, and the Hunchback, and the Genies," she sobbed out; "and about—"

"Hush!" said Mr. Gradgrind, "that is enough. Never breathe a word of such destructive nonsense any more. Bounderby, this is a case for rigid training, and I shall observe it with interest."

"Well," returned Mr. Bounderby, "I have given you my opinion already, and I shouldn't do as you do. But, very well, very well. Since you are bent upon it, *very* well!"

So Mr. Gradgrind and his daughter took Cecilia Jupe off with them to Stone Lodge, and on the way Louisa never spoke one word, good or bad. And Mr. Bounderby went about his daily pursuits. And Mrs. Sparsit got behind her eyebrows and meditated in the gloom of that retreat, all the evening.

CHAPTER VIII.

NEVER WONDER.

LET us strike the key-note again, before pursuing the tune.

When she was half a dozen years younger, Louisa had been overheard to begin conversation with her brother one day, by saying "Tom, I wonder"—upon which Mr. Gradgrind, who was the person overhearing, stepped forth into the light and said, " Louisa, never wonder ! "

Herein lay the spring of the mechanical art and mystery of educating the reason without stooping to the cultivation of the sentiments and affections. Never wonder. By means of addition, subtraction, multiplication, and division, settle everything somehow, and never wonder. Bring to me, says M'Choakumchild, yonder baby just able to walk, and I will engage that it shall never wonder.

Now, besides very many babies just able to walk, there happened to be in Coketown a considerable population of babies who had been walking against time towards the infinite world, twenty, thirty, forty, fifty, years and more. These portentous infants being alarming creatures to stalk about in any human society, the eighteen denominations incessantly scratched one another's faces and pulled one another's hair by way of agreeing on the steps to be taken for their improvement—which they never did ; a surprising circumstance, when the happy adaptation of the means to the end is considered. Still, although they differed in every other particu'ar, conceivable and inconceivable (especially inconceivable), they were pretty well united on the point that these unlucky infants were never to wonder. Body number one, said they must take everything on trust. Body number two, said they must take everything on political economy. Body number three, wrote leaden little books for them, showing how the good grown-up baby invariably got to the Saving-bank, and the bad grown-up baby invariably

4

got transported. Body number four, under dreary pretence of being droll (when it was very melancholy indeed)
made the shallowest pretences of concealing pitfalls of
knowledge into which it was the duty of these babies to
be smuggled and inveigled. But, all the bodies agreed
that they were never to wonder.

There was a library in Coketown, to which general
access was easy. Mr. Gradgrind greatly tormented his
mind about what the people read in this library : a point
whereon little rivers of tabular statements periodically
flowed into the howling ocean of tabular statements,
which no diver ever got to any depth in and came up
sane. It was a disheartening circumstance, but a melancholy fact, that even these readers persisted in wondering. They wondered about human nature, human passions, human hopes and fears, the struggles, triumphs
and defeats, the cares and joys and sorrows, the lives and
deaths of common men and women! They sometimes,
after fifteen hours' work sat down to read mere fables
about men and women, more or less like themselves, and
about children, more or less like their own. They took
De Foe to their bosoms, instead of Euclid, and seemed to
be on the whole more comforted by Goldsmith than by
Cocker. Mr. Gradgrind was forever working, in print
and out of print, at this eccentric sum, and he never
could make out how it yielded this unaccountable pro-
duct.

"I am sick of my life, Loo. I hate it altogether, and
I hate everybody except you," said the unnatural young
Thomas Gradgrind in the hair-cutting chamber at twi-
light.

"You don't hate Sissy, Tom?"

"I hate to be obliged to call her Jupe. And she hates
me," said Tom, moodily.

"No, she does not, Tom, I am sure!"

"She must," said Tom. "She must just hate and
detest the whole set-out of us. They'll bother her head
off, I think, before they have done with her. Already
she's getting as pale as wax, and as heavy as—I am."

Young Thomas expressed these sentiments sitting
astride of a chair before the fire, with his arms on the
back, and his sulky face on his arms. His sister sat in
the darker corner by the fireside, now looking at him, now

looking at the bright sparks as they dropped upon the hearth.

"As to me," said Tom, tumbling his hair all manner of ways with his sulky hands, "I am a Donkey, that's what I am. I am as obstinate as one, I am more stupid than one, I get as much pleasure as one, and I should like to kick like one."

"Not me, I hope, Tom?"

"No, Loo; I wouldn't hurt *you*. I made an exception of you at first. I don't know what this—jolly old—Jaundiced Jail," Tom had paused to find a sufficiently complimentary and expressive name for the parental roof, and seemed to relieve his mind for a moment by the strong alliteration of this one, "would be without you."

"Indeed, Tom? Do you really and truly say so?"

"Why, of course I do. What's the use of talking about it!" returned Tom, chafing his face on his coatsleeve, as if to mortify his flesh, and have it in unison with his spirit.

"Because, Tom," said his sister, after silently watching the sparks awhile, "as I get older, and nearer growing up, I often sit wondering here, and think how unfortutate it is for me that I can't reconcile you to home better than I am able to do. I don't know what other girls know. I can't play to you, or sing to you. I can't talk to you so as to lighten your mind, for I never see any amusing sights or read any amusing books that it would be a pleasure or a relief to you to talk about, when you are tired."

"Well, no more do I. I am as bad as you in that respect; and I am a Mule too, which you're not. If father was determined to make me either a Pig or a Mule, and I am not a Pig, why, it stands to reason, I must be a Mule. And so I am," said Tom, desperately.

"It's a great pity" said Louisa, after another pause, and speaking thoughtfully out of her dark corner; "It's a great pity, Tom. It's very unfortunate for both of us."

"Oh! You," said Tom; "you are a girl, Loo, and a girl comes out of it better than a boy does. I don't miss anything in you. You are the only pleasure I have—you can brighten even this place—and you can always lead me as you like."

"You are a dear brother, Tom; and while you think I can do such things, I don't so much mind knowing better. Though I do know better, Tom, and am very sorry for it." She came and kissed him, and went back into her corner again.

"I wish I could collect all the Facts we hear so much about," said Tom, spitefully setting his teeth, "and all the Figures, and all the people who found them out: and I wish I could put a thousand barrels of gunpowder under them, and blow them all up together! However, when I go to live with old Bounderby, I'll have my revenge."

"Your revenge, Tom?"

"I mean I'll enjoy myself a little, and go about and see something, and hear something. I'll recompense myself for the way in which I have been brought up."

"But don't disappoint yourself beforehand, Tom. Mr. Bounderby thinks as father thinks, and is a great deal rougher, and not half so kind."

"Oh;" said Tom, laughing; "I don't mind that. I shall very well know how to manage and smooth old Bounderby!"

Their shadows were defined upon the wall, but those of the high presses in the room were all blended together on the wall and on the ceiling, as if the brother and sister were overhung by a dark cavern. Or, a fanciful imagination—if such treason could have been there—might have made it out to be the shadow of their subject, and of its lowering association with the future.

"What is your great mode of smoothing and managing, Tom? Is it a secret?"

"Oh!" said Tom, "if it is a secret, it's not far off. It's you. You are his little pet, you are his favorite; he'll do anything for you. When he says to me what I don't like, I shall say to him, 'My sister Loo will be hurt and disappointed, Mr. Bounderby. She always used to tell me she was sure you would be easier with me than this.' That'll bring him about, or nothing will."

After waiting for some answering remark, and getting none, Tom wearily relapsed into the present time, and twined himself yawning round and about the rails of his chair, and rumpled his head more and more, until he suddenly looked up, and asked:

"Have you gone to sleep, Loo?"

"No, Tom. I am looking at the fire."

"You seem to find more to look at in it than ever I could find," said Tom. "Another of the advantages, I suppose, of being a girl."

"Tom," inquired his sister, slowly, and in a curious tone, as if she were reading what she asked in the fire, and it were not quite plainly written there, "do you look forward with any satisfaction to this change to Mr. Bounderby's?"

"Why, there's one thing to be said of it," returned Tom, pushing his chair from him, and standing up; "it will be getting away from home."

"There is one thing to be said of it," Louisa repeated in her former curious tone; "it will be getting away from home. Yes."

"Not but what I shall be very unwilling, both to leave you, Loo, and to leave you here. But I must go, you know, whether I like it or not; and I had better go where I can take with me some advantage of your influence, than where I should lose it altogether. Don't you see?"

"Yes, Tom."

The answer was so long in coming, though there was no indecision in it that Tom went and leaned on the back of her chair, to contemplate the fire which so engrossed her, from her point of view, and see what he could make of it.

"Except that it is a fire," said Tom, "it looks to me as stupid and blank as everything else looks. What do you see in it? Not a circus?"

"I don't see anything in it, Tom, particularly. But since I have been looking at it, I have been wondering about you and me, grown up."

"Wondering again!" said Tom.

"I have such unmanageable thoughts," returned his sister, "that they *will* wonder."

"Then I beg of you, Louisa," said Mrs. Gradgrind, who had opened the door without being heard, "to do nothing of that description, for goodness' sake, you inconsiderate girl, or I shall never hear the last of it from your father. And Thomas, it is really shameful, with my poor head continually wearing me out, that a boy

brought up as you have been, and whose education
has cost what yours has, should be found encouraging
his sister to wonder, when he knows his father has expressly said that she is not to do it."

Louisa denied Tom's participation in the offence; but her
mother stopped her with the conclusive answer, "Louisa,
don't tell me, in my state of health; for unless you had
been encouraged, it is morally and physically impossible
that you could have done it."

"I was encouraged by nothing, mother, but by looking
at the red sparks dropping out of the fire, and whitening
and dying. It made me think, after all, how short my
life would be, and how little I could hope to do in it."

"Nonsense!" said Mrs. Gradgrind, rendered almost
energetic. "Nonsense! Don't stand there and tell me
such stuff, Louisa, to my face, when you know very well
that if it was ever to reach your father's ears I should
never hear the last of it. After all the trouble that has
been taken with you! After the lectures you have attended, and the experiments you have seen! After I have
heard you myself, when the whole of my right side has
been benumbed, going on with your master about combus-
tion, and calcination, and calorification, and I may say
every kind of ation that could drive a poor invalid distracted, to hear you talking in this absurd way about
sparks and ashes! I wish," whimpered Mrs. Gradgrind,
taking a chair, and discharging her strongest point before
succumbing under these mere shadows of facts, "yes, I
really *do* wish that I had never had a family, and then
you would have known what it was to do without me!"

CHAPTER IX.

SISSY'S PROGRESS.

SISSY JUPE had not an easy time of it, between Mr.
M'Choakumchild and Mrs. Gradgrind, and was not without strong impulses, in the first months of her probation,
to run away. It hailed facts all day long so very hard,
and life in general was opened to her as such a closely

ruled ciphering book, that assuredly she would have run away, but for only one restraint.

It is lamentable to think of; but this restraint was the result of no arithmetical process, was self-imposed in defiance of all calculation, and went dead against any table of probabilities that any Actuary would have drawn up from the premises. The girl believed that her father had not deserted her; she lived in hope that he would come back, and in the faith that he would be made the happier by her remaining where she was.

The wretched ignorance with which Jupe clung to this consolation, rejecting the superior comfort of knowing, on a sound arithmetical basis, that her father was an unnatural vagabond, filled Mr. Gradgrind with pity. Yet, what was to be done? M'Choakumchild reported that she had a very dense head for figures; that, once possessed with a general idea of the globe, she took the smallest conceivable interest in its exact measurements; that she was extremely slow in the acquisition of dates, unless some pitiful incident happened to be connected therewith; that she would burst into tears on being required (by the mental process) immediately to name the cost of two hundred and forty-seven muslin caps at fourteen-pence half-penny; that she was as low down, in the school, as low could be; that after eight weeks of induction into the elements of Political Economy, she had only yesterday been set right by a prattler three feet high, for returning to the question, "What is the first principle of this science?" the absurd answer, "To do unto other as I would that they should do unto me."

Mr. Gradgrind observed, shaking his head, that all this was very bad; that it showed the necessity of infinite grinding at the mill of knowledge, as per system, schedule, blue book, report, and tabular statements A to Z ; and that Jupe "must be kept to it." So Jupe was kept to it, and became low-spirited, but no wiser.

"It would be a fine thing to be you, Miss Louisa!" she said, one night, when Louisa had endeavored to make her perplexities for next day something clearer to her.

"Do you think so?"

"I should know so much, Miss Louisa. All that is difficult to me now, would be so easy then."

"You might not be the better for it, Sissy."

Sissy submitted, after a little hesitation. "I should not be the worse, Miss Louisa." To which Miss Louisa answered, "I don't know that."

There had been so little communication between these two—both because life at Stone Lodge went monotonously round like a piece of machinery which discouraged human interference, and because of the prohibition relative to Sissy's past career—that they were still almost strangers. Sissy, with her dark eyes wonderingly directed to Louisa's face, was uncertain whether to say more or to remain silent.

"You are more useful to my mother, and more pleasant with her than I can ever be," Louisa resumed. "You are pleasanter to yourself, than *I* am to *my* self."

"But, if you please, Miss Louisa," Sissy pleaded, "I am—O so stupid!"

Louisa, with a brighter laugh than usual, told her she would be wiser by and by.

"You don't know," said Sissy, half crying, "what a stupid girl I am. All through school hours I make mistakes. Mr. and Mrs. M'Choakumchild call me up, over and over again regularly to make mistakes. I can't help them. They seem to come natural to me."

"Mr. and Mrs. M'Choakumchild never make any mistakes themselves, I suppose, Sissy?"

"O no!" she eagerly returned. "They know everything."

"Tell me some of your mistakes."

"I am almost ashamed," said Sissy, with reluctance. "But to-day, for instance, Mr. M'Choakumchild was explaining to us about Natural Prosperity."

"National, I think it must have been," observed Louisa.

"Yes, it was.—But isn't it the same?" she timidly asked.

"You had better say, National, as he said so," returned Louisa, with her dry reserve.

"National Prosperity. And he said, Now, this school-room is a Nation. And in this nation, there are fifty millions of money. Isn't this a prosperous nation? Girl number twenty, isn't this a prosperous nation, and an't you in a thriving state?"

"What did you say?" asked Louisa.

"Miss Louisa, I said I didn't know. I thought I couldn't know whether it was a prosperous nation or not, and whether I was in a thriving state or not, unless I knew who had got the money, and whether any of it was mine. But that had nothing to do with it. It was not in the figures at all," said Sissy, wiping her eyes.

"That was a great mistake of yours," observed Louisa.

"Yes, Miss Louisa, I know it was, now. Then Mr. M'Choakumchild said he would try me again. And he said, This schoolroom is an immense town, and in it there are a million of inhabitants, and only five-and-twenty are starved to death in the streets, in the course of a year. What is your remark on that proportion? And my remark was—for I couldn't think of a better one—that I thought it must be just as hard upon those who were starved, whether the others were a million, or a million million. And that was wrong, too."

"Of course it was."

"Then Mr M'Choakumchild said he would try me once more. And he said, Here are the stutterings——"

"Statistics," said Louisa.

"Yes, Miss Louisa—they always remind me of stutterings, and that's another of my mistakes—of accidents upon the sea. And I find (Mr. M'Choakumchild said) that in a given time a hundred thousand persons went to sea on long voyages, and only five hundred of them were drowned or burnt to death. What is the percentage? And I said, Miss;" here Sissy fairly sobbed as confessing with extreme contrition to her greatest error; "I said it was nothing."

"Nothing, Sissy?"

"Nothing, Miss—to the relations and friends of the people who were killed. I shall never learn," said Sissy. "And the worst of all is, that although my poor father wished me so much to learn, and although I am so anxious to learn, because he wished me to, I am afraid I don't like it."

Louisa stood looking at the pretty modest head, as it drooped abashed before her, until it was raised again to glance at her face. Then she asked:

"Did your father know so much himself, that he wished you to be well taught too, Sissy?"

Sissy hesitated before replying, and so plainly showed her sense that they were entering on forbidden ground, that Louisa added, "No one hears us; and if any one did, I am sure no harm could be found in such an innocent question."

"No, Miss Louisa," answered Sissy, upon this encouragement, shaking her head; "father knows very little indeed. It's as much as he can do to write; and it's more than people in general can do to read his writing. Though it's plain to *me*."

"Your mother!"

"Father says she was quite a scholar. She died when I was born. She was;" Sissy made the terrible communication nervously; "she was a dancer."

"Did your father love her?" Louisa asked these questions with a strong, wild, wandering interest peculiar to her; an interest gone astray like a banished creature, and hiding in solitary places.

"O yes! As dearly as he loves me. Father loved me, first, for her sake. He carried me about with him when I was quite a baby. We have never been asunder from that time."

"Yet he leaves you now, Sissy?"

"Only for my good. Nobody understands him as I do; nobody knows him as I do. When he left me for my good—he never would have left me for his own—I know he was almost broken-hearted with the trial. He will not be happy for a single minute, till he comes back."

"Tell me more about him," said Louisa. "I will never ask you again. Where did you live?"

"We travelled about the country, and had no fixed place to live in. Father's a;" Sissy whispered the awful word, "a clown."

"To make the people laugh?" said Louisa, with a nod of intelligence.

"Yes. But they wouldn't laugh sometimes, and then father cried. Lately, they very often wouldn't laugh, and he used to come home despairing. Father's not like most. Those who didn't know him as well as I do, and didn't love him as dearly as I do, might believe he was not quite right. Sometimes they played tricks upon him; but they never knew how he felt them, and shrunk up, when he was alone with me. He was far, far timider than they thought!"

"And you were his comfort through everything?"

She nodded, with tears rolling down her face. "I hope so, and father said I was. It was because he grew so scared and trembling, and because he felt himself to be a poor, weak, ignorant, helpless man (those used to be his words), that he wanted me so much to know a great deal, and be different from him. I used to read to him to cheer his courage, and he was very fond of that. They were wrong books—I am never to speak of them here—but we didn't know there was any harm in them."

"And he liked them?" said Louisa, with a searching gaze on Sissy all this time.

"O very much! They kept him, many times, from what did him real harm. And often and often of a night, he used to forget all his troubles in wondering whether the Sultan would let the lady go on with the story, or would have her head cut off before it was finished."

"And your father was always kind? To the last?" asked Louisa; contravening the great principle, and wondering very much.

"Always, always!" returned Sissy, clasping her hands. "Kinder and kinder than I can tell. He was angry only one night, and that was not to me, but Merrylegs. Merrylegs;" she whispered the awful fact; "is his performing dog."

"Why was he angry with the dog?" Louisa demanded.

"Father, soon after they came home from performing, told Merrylegs to jump up on the backs of the two chairs and stand across them—which is one of his tricks. He looked at father, and didn't do it at once. Everything of father's had gone wrong that night, and he hadn't pleased the public at all. He cried out that the very dog knew he was failing, and had no compassion on him. Then he beat the dog, and I was frightened, and said, 'Father, father! Pray don't hurt the creature who is so fond of you! O Heaven forgive you, father, stop!' And he stopped, and the dog was bloody, and father lay down crying on the floor with the dog in his arms, and the dog licked his face."

Louisa saw that she was sobbing; and going to her, kissed her, took her hand, and sat down beside her.

"Finish by telling me how your father left you, Sissy. Now that I have asked you so much, tell me the end. The blame, if there is any blame, is mine, not yours."

"Dear Miss Louisa," said Sissy, covering her eyes, and sobbing yet; "I came home from the school that afternoon, and found poor father just come home too, from the booth. And he sat rocking himself over the fire, as if he was in pain. And I said, 'Have you hurt yourself, father?' (as he did sometimes, like they all did), and he said, 'A little, my darling. And when I came to stoop down and look up at his face, I saw that he was crying. The more I spoke to him, the more he hid his face; and at first he shook all over, and said nothing but 'My darling;' and 'My love!'"

Here Tom came lounging in, and stared at the two, with a coolness not particularly savoring of interest in anything but himself, and not much of that at present.

"I am asking Sissy a few questions, Tom," observed his sister. "You have no occasion to go away; but don't interrupt us for a moment, Tom dear."

"Oh! very well!" returned Tom. "Only father has brought old Bounderby home, and I want you to come into the drawing-room. Because if you come, there's a good chance of old Bounderby's asking me to dinner; and if you don't, there's none."

"I'll come directly."

"I'll wait for you," said Tom, "to make sure."

Sissy resumed in a lower voice. "At last poor father said that he had given no satisfaction again, and never did give any satisfaction now, and that he was a shame and disgrace, and I should have done better without him all along. I said all the affectionate things to him that came into my heart, and presently he was quiet and I sat down by him, and told him all about the school and everything that had been said and done there. When I had no more left to tell, he put his arms round my neck, and kissed me a great many times. Then he asked me to fetch some of the stuff he used, for the little hurt he had had, and to get it at the best place, which was at the other end of town from there; and then, after kissing me again, he let me go. When I had gone downstairs, I turned back that I might be a little bit more company to him yet, and looked in at the door, and said, 'Father dear, shall I take Merrylegs?' Father shook his head and said, 'No, Sissy, no; take nothing that's known to be mine, my darling;' and I left him sitting by the fire. Then the thought must have come upon him, poor, poor father! of going away to try something for my sake; for when I came back, he was gone."

"I say! Look sharp for old Bounderby, Loo!" Tom remonstrated.

"There's no more to tell, Miss Louisa. I keep the nine oils ready for him, and I know he will come back. Every letter that I see in Mr. Gradgrind's hand takes my breath away and blinds my eyes, for I think it comes from father, or from Mr. Sleary about father. Mr. Sleary promised to write as soon as ever father should be heard of, and I trust to him to keep his word."

"Do look sharp for old Bounderby, Loo!" said Tom, with an impatient whistle. "He'll be off if you don't look sharp!"

After this, whenever Sissy dropped a curtsey to Mr. Gradgrind in the presence of his family, and said in a faltering way, "I beg your pardon, sir, for being troublesome—but—have you had any letter yet about me?" Louisa would suspend the occupation of the moment, whatever it was, and look for the reply as earnestly as Sissy did. And when Mr. Gradgrind regularly answered, "No, Jupe, nothing of the sort," the trembling of Sissy's lip would be repeated in Louisa's face, and her eyes would follow Sissy with compassion to the door. Mr. Gradgrind usually improved these occasions by remarking, when she was gone, that if Jupe had been properly trained from an early age she would have remonstrated to herself on sound principles the baselessness of these fantastic hopes. Yet it did seem (though not to him, for he saw nothing of it) as if fantastic hope could take as strong a hold as Fact.

This observation must be limited exclusively to his daughter. As to Tom, he was becoming that not unprecedented triumph of calculation which is usually at work on number one. As to Mrs. Gradgrind, if she said anything on the subject, she would come a little way out of her wrappers, like a feminine dormouse, and say:

"Good gracious bless me, how my poor head is vexed and worried by that girl Jupe's so perseveringly asking over and over again, about her tiresome letters! Upon my word and honor I seem to be fated, and destined, and ordained, to live in the midst of things that I am never to hear the last of. It really is a most extraordinary circumstance that it appears as if I never was to hear the last of anything!"

At about this point, Mr. Gradgrind's eye would fall upon her; and under the influence of that wintry piece of fact, she would become torpid again.

CHAPTER X.

STEPHEN BLACKPOOL.

I ENTERTAIN a weak idea that the English people are as hardworked as any people upon whom the sun shines. I acknowledge to this ridiculous idiosyncrasy, as a reason why I would give them a little more play.

In the hardest working part of Coketown; in the innermost fortifications of that ugly citadel, where Nature was as strongly bricked out as killing airs and gases were bricked in; at the heart of the labyrinth of narrow courts upon courts, and close streets upon streets, which had come into existence piecemeal, every piece in a violent hurry for some one man's purpose, and the whole an unnatural family, shouldering, and trampling, and pressing one another to death; in the last close nook of this great exhausted receiver, where the chimneys, for want of air to make a draught, were built in an immense variety of stunted and crooked shapes, as though every house put out a sign of the kind of people who might be expected to be born in it; among the multitude of Coketown, generically called "the Hands,"—a race who would have found more favor with some people, if Providence had seen fit to make them only hands, or, like the lower creatures of the seashore, only hands and stomachs—lived a certain Stephen Blackpool, forty years of age.

Stephen looked older, but he had had a hard life. It is said that every life has its roses and thorns; there seemed, however, to have been a misadventure or mistake in Stephen's case, whereby somebody else had become possessed of his roses, and he had become possessed of the same somebody else's thorns in addition to his own. He had known, to use his words, a peck of trouble. He was usually called Old Stephen, in a kind of rough homage to the fact.

A rather stooping man, with a knitted brow, a pondering expression of face, and a hard-looking head sufficiently capacious, on which his iron-gray hair lay long and thin, Old Stephen might have passed for a particularly intelligent man in his condition. Yet he was not. He took no place among those remarkable "Hands," who, piecing together their broken intervals of leisure through many years, had mastered difficult sciences, and acquired a knowledge of most unlikely things. He held no station among the Hands who could make speeches and carry on debates. Thousands of his compeers could talk much better than he, at any time. He was a good power-loom weaver, and a man of perfect integrity. What more he was, or what else he had in him, if anything, let him show for himself.

The lights in the great factories, which looked, when they were illuminated, like Fairy palaces—or the travellers by express-train said so—were all extinguished; and the bells had rung for knocking off for the night, and had ceased again; and the Hands, men and women, boy and girl, were clattering home. Old Stephen was standing in the street, with the old sensation upon him which the stoppage of the machinery always produced—the sensation of its having worked and stopped in his own head.

"Yet I don't see Rachael, still!" said he.

It was a wet night, and many groups of young women passed him, with their shawls drawn over their bare heads and held close under their chins to keep the rain out. He knew Rachael well, for a glance at any one of these groups was sufficient to show him that she was not there. At last, there were no more to come; and then he turned away, saying in a tone of disappointment, "Why, then, I ha' missed her!"

But, he had not gone the length of three streets, when he saw another of the shawled figures in advance of him, at which he looked so keenly that perhaps its mere shadow indistinctly reflected on the wet pavement—if he could have seen it without the figure itself moving along from lamp to lamp, brightening and fading as it went—would have been enough to tell him who was there. Making his pace at once much quicker and much softer, he darted on until he was very near this figure, then fell into his former walk, and called " Rachael ! "

She turned, being then in the brightness of a lamp ; and raising her hood a little, showed a quiet oval face, dark and rather delicate, irradiated by a pair of very gentle eyes, and further set off by the perfect order of her shining black hair. It was not a face in its first bloom ; she was a woman five and thirty years of age.

" Ah, lad ! 'Tis thou ? " When she had said this, with a smile which would have been quite expressed, though nothing of her had been seen but her pleasant eyes, she replaced her hood again, and they went on together.

" I thought thou wast ahind me, Rachael ? "

" No."

" Early t' night, lass ? "

" 'Times I'm a little early, Stephen ! 'times a little late. I'm never to be counted on, going home."

" Nor going t' other way, neither, 't seems to me, Rachael ? "

" No, Stephen."

He looked at her with some disappointment in his face, but with a respectful and patient conviction that she must be right in whatever she did. The expression was not lost upon her ; she laid her hand lightly on his arm a moment as if to thank him for it.

" We are such true friends, lad, and such old friends, and getting to be such old folk, now."

" No, Rachael, thou'rt as young as ever thou wast."

" One of us would be puzzled how to get old, Stephen, without t' other getting so too, both being alive," she answered, laughing ; " but, any ways, we're such old friends, that t' hide a word of honest truth fro' one another would be a sin and a pity. 'Tis better not to walk too much together. 'Times, yes ! 'Twould be hard, indeed, if 'twas not to be at all," she said, with a cheerfulness she sought to communicate to him.

" 'Tis hard, anyways, Rachael."

" Try to think not ; and 'twill seem better."

" I've tried a long time, and 'ta'nt got better. But thou

'rt right; 'tmight mak fok talk, even of thee. Thou hast been that to me, Rachael, through so many year : thou hast done me so much good, and heartened of me in that cheering way, that thy word is a law to me. Ah, lass, and a bright good law! Better than some real ones."

" Never fret about them, Stephen," she answered quickly, and not without an anxious glance at his face. "Let the laws be."

" Yes," he said, with a slow nod or two. " Let 'em be. Let everything be. Let all sorts alone. 'Tis a muddle, and that's aw."

" Always a muddle ?" said Rachael, with another gentle touch upon his arm, as if to recall him out of the thoughtfulness, in which he was biting the long ends of his loose neckerchief as he walked along. The touch had its instantaneous effect. He let them fall, turned a smiling face upon her, and said, as he broke into a good-humored laugh, " Ay, Rachael, lass, awlus a muddle. That's where I stick. I come to the muddle many times and agen, and I never get beyond it."

They had walked some distance, and were near their own homes. The woman's was the first reached. It was in one of the many small streets for which the favorite undertaker (who turned a handsome sum out of the one poor ghastly pomp of the neighborhood) kept a black ladder, in order that those who had done their daily groping up and down the narrow stairs might slide out of this working world by the windows. She stopped at the corner, and putting her hand in his, wished him goodnight.

" Good-night, dear lass : good night! "

She went, with her neat figure and her sober womanly step, down the dark street, and he stood looking after her until she turned into one of the small houses. There was not a flutter of her coarse shawl, perhaps, but had its interest in this man's eyes; not a tone of her voice but had its echo in his innermost heart.

When she was lost to his view, he pursued his homeward way, glancing up sometimes at the sky, where the clouds were sailing fast and wildly. But, they were broken now, and the rain had ceased, and the moon shone,— looking down the high chimneys of Coketown on the deep furnaces below, and casting Titanic shadows of the steam

5

engines at rest, upon the walls where they were lodged. The man seemed to have brightened with the night, as he went on.

His home, in such another street as the first, saving that it was narrower, was over a little shop. How it came to pass that any people found it worth their while to sell or buy the wretched little toys, mixed up in its window with cheap newspapers and pork (there was a leg to be raffled for to-morrow night), matters not here. He took his end of candle from a shelf, lighted it at another end of candle on the counter, without disturbing the mistress of the shop who was asleep in her little room, and went upstairs into his lodging.

It was a room, not unacquainted with the black ladder under various tenants; but as neat, at present, as such a room could be. A few books and writings were on an old bureau in a corner, the furniture was decent and sufficient, and, though the atmosphere was tainted the room was clean.

Going to the hearth to set the the candle down upon a round three-legged table standing there, he stumbled against something. As he recoiled, looking down at it, it raised itself up into the form of a woman in a sitting attitude.

"Heaven's mercy, woman!" he cried, falling farther off from the figure. "Hast thou come back again!"

Such a woman! A disabled, drunken creature, barely able to preserve her sitting posture by steadying herself with one begrimed hand on the floor, while the other was so purposeless in trying to push away her tangled hair from her face, that it only blinded her the more with the dirt upon it. A creature so foul to look at, in her tatters, stains and splashes, but so much fouler than that in her moral infamy, that it was a shameful thing even to see her.

After an impatient oath or two, and some stupid clawing of herself with the hand not necessary to her support, she got her hair away from her eyes sufficiently to obtain a sight of him. Then she sat swaying her body to and fro, and making gestures with her unnerved arm, which seemed intended as the accompaniment to a fit of laughter, though her face was stolid and drowsy.

"Eigh lad? What yo'r there?" Some hoarse sounds,

meant for this, came mockingly out of her at last; and her head dropped forward on her breast.

"Back agen?" she screeched, after some minutes, as if he had that moment said it. "Yes! And back agen Back agen ever and ever so often. Back? Yes, back. Why not?"

Roused by the unmeaning violence with which she cried it out, she scrambled up, and stood supporting herself with her shoulders against the wall; dangling in one hand by the string, a dunghill-fragment of a bonnet, and trying to look scornfully at him.

"I'll sell thee off again, and I'll sell thee off again, and I'll sell thee off a score of times!" she cried, with something between a furious menace and an effort at a defiant dance. "Come awa' from th' bed!" He was sitting on the side of it, with his face hidden in his hands. "Come awa' from 't. 'Tis mine, and I 've a right to 't!"

As she staggered to it, he avoided her with a shudder, and passed—his face still hidden—to the opposite end of the room. She threw herself upon the bed heavily, and soon was snoring hard. He sunk into a chair, and moved but once all that night. It was to throw a covering over her; as if his hands were not enough to hide her, even in the darkness.

CHAPTER XI.

NO WAY OUT.

The Fairy palaces burst into illumination, before pale morning showed the monstrous serpents of smoke trailing themselves over Coketown. A clattering of clogs upon the pavement; a rapid ringing of bells; and all the melancholy mad elephants, polished and oiled up for the day's monotony, were at their heavy exercise again.

Stephen bent over his loom, quiet, watchful, and steady. A special contrast, as every man was in the forest of looms where Stephen worked, to the crashing, smashing, tearing piece of mechanism at which he labored. Never fear, good people of an anxious turn of mind, that Art, will consign Nature to oblivion. Set anywhere, side by side, the work of GOD and the work of man; and the former, even thought it be a troop of Hands of very small account, will gain in dignity from the comparison.

So many hundred Hands in this Mill; so many hundred horse Steam Power. It is known, to the force of a single pound weight, what the engine will do; but, not all the calculators of the National Debt can tell me the capacity for good or evil, for love or hatred, for patriotism or discontent, for the decomposition of virtue into vice, or the reverse, at any single moment in the soul of one of these its quiet servants, with the composed faces and the regulated actions. There is no mystery in it; there is an unfathomable mystery in the meanest of them, forever. —Supposing we were to reserve our arithmetic for material objects, and to govern these awful unknown quantities by other means!

The day grew strong, and showed itself outside, even against the flaming lights within. The lights were turned out, and the work went on. The rain fell, and the Smoke-serpent, submissive to the curse of all that tribe, trailed themselves upon the earth. In the wasteyard outside, the steam from the escape pipe, the litter of barrels and old iron, the shining heaps of coals, the ashes, everywhere, were shrouded in a veil of mist and rain.

The work went on, until the noon-bell rang. More clattering upon the pavements. The looms, and wheels, and Hands all out of gear for an hour.

Stephen came out of the hot mill into the damp wind and cold wet streets, haggard and worn. He turned from his own class and his own quarter, taking nothing but a little bread as he walked along, towards the hill on which his principal employer lived, in a red house with black outside shutters, green inside blinds, a black street door, up two white steps, BOUNDERBY (in letters very like himself) upon a brazen plate, and a round brazen door-handle underneath it, like a brazen full stop.

Mr. Bounderby was at his lunch. So Stephen had expected. Would his servant say that one of the Hands begged leave to speak to him? Message in return, requiring name of such hand. Stephen Blackpool. There was nothing troublesome against Stephen Blackpool; yes, he might come in.

Stephen Blackpool in the parlor. Mr. Bounderby (whom he just knew by sight), at lunch on chop and sherry. Mrs. Sparsit netting at the fireside, in a side-saddle attitude, with one foot in a cotton stirrup. It was a part, at once of Mrs. Sparsit's dignity and service, not to lunch. She supervised the meal officially, but implied that in her own stately person she considered lunch a weakness.

"Now, Stephen," said Mr. Bounderby, "what's the matter with *you?*"

Stephen made a bow. Not a servile one—these Hands will never do that! Lord bless you, sir, you'll never catch them at that, if they have been with you twenty years!—and, as a complimentary toilet for Mrs. Sparsit, tucked his neckerchief ends into his waistcoat.

"Now, you know," said Mr. Bounderby, taking some sherry, " we have never had any difficulty with you, and you have never been one of the unreasonable ones. You don't expect to be set up in a coach and six, and to be fed on turtle soup and venison, with a gold spoon, as a good many of 'em do! Mr. Bounderby always represented this to be the sole, immediate, and direct object of any Hand who was not entirely satisfied; ' and therefore I know already that you have not come here to make a complaint. Now, you know, I am certain of that beforehand."

" No, sir, sure I ha'not coom for nowt o' th' kind."

Mr. Bounderby seemed agreeably surprised, notwithstanding his previous strong conviction. " Very well," he returned. " You 're a steady Hand, and I was not mistaken. Now, let me hear what it's all about. As it's not that, let me hear what it is. What have you got to say? Out with it, lad!"

Stephen happened to glance towards Mrs. Sparsit. "I can go, Mr. Bounderby, if you wish it," said the self-sacrificing lady, making a feint of taking her foot out of the stirrup.

Mr. Bounderby stayed her, by holding a mouthful of chop in suspension before swallowing it, and putting out his left hand. Then, withdrawing his hand and swallowing his mouthful of chop, he said to Stephen :

" Now you know, this good lady is a born lady, a high lady. You are not to suppose because she keeps my house for me, that she hasn't been very high up the tree—ah, up at the top of the tree! Now, if you have got anything to say that can't be said before a born lady, this lady will leave the room. If what you have to say *can* be said before a born lady, this lady will stay where she is."

" Sir, I hope I never had nowt to say, not fitten for a born lady to year, sin' I were born mysen," was the reply, accompanied with a slight flush.

" Very well," said Mr. Bounderby, pushing away his plate, and leaning back. " Fire away!"

" I ha' coom," Stephen began, raising his eyes from the floor, after a moment's consideration, " to ask yo yor advice. I need 't overmuch. I were married on Eas'r Monday nineteen year sin, long and dree. She were a young lass—pretty enow—wi' good accounts of herseln. Well! She went bad—soon. Not along of me. Gon-nows I were not a unkind husband to her."

" I have heard all this before," said Mr. Bounderby. " She took to drinking, left off working, sold the furniture, pawned the clothes, and played old Gooseberry."

" I were patient wi' her."

(" The more fool you, I think," said Mr. Bounderby, in confidence to his wine-glass.)

" I were very patient wi' her. I tried to wean her fra't ower and ower agen. I tried this, I tried that, I tried t' other. I ha' gone home, many's the time, and found all vanished as I had in the world, and her without a sense left to bless herseln lying on bare ground. I ha' dun't not once, not twice—twenty time!"

Every line in his face deepened as he said it, and put in its affecting evidence of the suffering he had under-gone.

" From bad to worse, from worse to worsen. She left me. She disgraced herseln everyways, bitter and bad. She coom back, she coom back, she coom back. What could I do t' hinder her? I ha' walked the streets nights long, ere ever I'd go home. I ha' gone t' th brigg, minded to fling myseln ower, and ha' no more on't. I ha' bore that much, that I were owd when I were young."

Mrs. Sparsit, easily ambling along with her netting-needles, raised the Coriolanian eyebrows and shook her head, as much as to say, " The great know trouble as well as the small. Please to turn your humble eye in My direction."

"I ha' paid her to keep awa' fra' me. These five year I ha' paid her. I ha' gotten decent fewtrils about me agen. I ha' lived hard and sad, but not ashamed and fearfo' a' the minnits o' my life. Last night, I went 'home. There she lay upon my har-stone! There she is!"

In the strength of his misfortune, and the energy of his distress, he fired for the moment like a proud man. In another moment, he stood as he had stood all the time —his usual stoop upon him; his pondering face addressed to Mr. Bounderby, with a curious expression on it, half shrewd, half perplexed, as if his mind were set upon unravelling something very difficult; his hat held tight in his left hand, which rested on his hip; his right arm, with a rugged propriety and force of action, very earnestly emphasizing what he said : not least so when it always paused, a little bent, but not withdrawn, as he paused.

"I was acquainted with all this, you know," said Mr. Bounderby, "except the last clause, long ago. It's a bad job; that's what it is. You had better have been satisfied as you were, and not have got married. However, it's too late to say that."

"Was it an unequal marriage, sir, in point of years?" asked Mrs. Sparsit.

"You hear what this lady asks. Was it an unequal marriage in point of years, this unlucky job of yours?" said Mr. Bounderby.

"Not e'en so. I were one-and-twenty myseln; she were twenty nighbut."

"Indeed, sir?" said Mrs. Sparsit to her Chief, with great placidity. "I inferred, from its being so miserable a marriage, that it was probably an unequal one in point of years."

Mr. Bounderby looked very hard at the good lady in a sidelong way that had an odd sheepishness about it. He fortified himself with a little more sherry.

"Well? Why don't you go on?" he then asked, turning rather irritably on Stephen Blackpool.

"I ha' coom to ask yo, sir, how I am to be ridded o' this woman." Stephen infused a yet deeper gravity into the mixed expression of his attentive face. Mrs. Sparsit uttered a gentle ejaculation, as having received a moral shock.

"What do you mean?" said Bounderby, getting up to lean his back against the chimney-piece. "What are you talking about? You took her for better for worse."

"I mun' be ridden o' her. I cannot bear 't nommore. I ha' lived under 't so long, for that I ha' had'n the pity and comforting words o' th' best lass living or dead. Haply, but for her, I should ha' gone hottering mad."

"He wishes to be free, to marry the female of whom he speaks, I fear, sir," observed Mrs. Sparsit in an undertone, and much dejected by the immortality of the people.

"I do. The lady says what's right. I do. I were a coming to 't. I ha' read i' th' papers that great fok (fair faw 'em a'! I wishes 'em no hurt!) are not bonded together for better for worse so fast, but that they can be set free fro' *their* misfortnet marriages, and marry ower agen. When they dunnot agree, for that their tempers is ill-sorted, they has rooms o' one kind an another in their houses, above a bit, and they can live asunders. We fok ha' only one room, and we can't. When that won't do, they ha' gowd an' other cash, an' they can say 'This for yo' an' that for me,' an' they can go their separate ways. We can't. Spite o' all that, they can be set free for smaller wrongs than mine. So, I mun be ridden o' this woman, and I want 't know how?"

"No how," returned Mr. Bounderby.

"If I do her any hurt, sir, there's a law to punish me?"

"Of course there is."

"If I flee from her, there's a law to punish me?"

"Of course there is."

"If I marry t'oother dear lass, there's a law to punish ma?"

"Of course there is."

"If I was to live wi' her an' not marry her—saying such a thing could be, which it never could or would, an' her so good—there's a law to punish me, in every innocent child belonging to me?"

"Of course there is."

"No, 'a God's name," said Stephen Blackpool, "show me the law to help me!"

"Hem! There's a sanctity in this relation of life," said Mr. Bounderby, "and—and—it must be kept up."

"No no, dunnot say that, sir. 'Tan't kep' up that way. Not that way. 'Tis kep' down that way. I'm a weaver, I were in a fact'ry when a chilt, but I ha' gotten een to see wi' and eern to year wi'. I read in th' papers every 'Sizes, every Sessions—and you read too—I know it!—with dismay—how th' supposed unpossibility o' ever gettin' unchained from one another, at any price, on any terms, brings blood upon this land, and brings many common married fok to battle, murder, and sudden death. Let us ha' this right understood. Mine's a grievous case, an' I want—if yo' will be so good—t' know the law that helps me."

"Now, I tell you what!" said Mr. Bounderby, putting his hands in his pockets. "There *is* such a law."

Stephen, subsiding into his quiet manner, and never wandering in his attention, gave a nod.

"But it's not for you at all. It costs a mint of money."

"How much might that be?" Stephen kindly asked.

"Why you'd have to go to Doctors' Commons with a suit, and you'd have to go to a court of Common Law with a suit, and you'd have to go to the House of Lords with a suit, and you'd have to get an Act of Parliament to enable you to marry again, and it would cost you (if it was a case of very plain sailing), I suppose from a thousand to fifteen hundred pound," said Mr. Bounderby. "Perhaps twice the money."

"There's no other law?"

"Certainly not."

"Why then, sir," said Stephen, turning white, and motioning with that right hand of his, as if he gave everything to the four winds, "'*tis* a muddle. 'Tis just a muddle a' together, an the sooner I am dead, the better."

(Mrs. Sparsit again dejected by the impiety of the people.)

"Pooh, pooh! Don't you talk nonsense, my good fellow," said Mr. Bounderby, "about things you don't understand; and don't you call the institutions of your country a muddle, or you'll get yourself into a real muddle one of these fine mornings. The institutions of your country are not your piece-work, and the only thing you have got to do, is, to mind your piece-work. You didn't take your wife for fast and for loose; but for better for

worse. If she has turned out worse—why, all we have
got to say is, she might have turned out better."

"'Tis a muddle," said Stephen, shaking his head as he
moved to the door. "'Tis a' a muddle!"

"Now, I'll tell you what!" Mr. Bounderby resumed,
as a valedictory address. "With what I shall call your
unhallowed opinions, you have been quite shocking this
lady: who, as I have already told you, is a born lady,
and who, as I have not already told you, has had her own
marriage misfortunes to the tune of tens of thousands of
pounds—tens of Thousands of Pounds!" (he repeated it
with great relish). "Now, you have always been a
steady Hand hitherto; but my opinion is, and so I tell
you plainly, that you are turning into the wrong road.
You have been listening to some mischievous stranger or
other—they're always about—and the best thing you can
do is, to come out of that. Now you know;" here his
countenance expressed marvellous acuteness; "I can see
as far into a grindstone as another man; farther than a
good many, perhaps, because I had my nose well kept to
it when I was young. I see traces of the turtle soup, and
venison, and gold spoon in this. Yes I do!" cried Mr.
Bounderby, shaking his head with obstinate cunning.
"By the Lord Harry I do!"

With a very different shake of the head and deep sigh,
Stephen said, "Thank you, sir, I wish you good day." So
he left Mr. Bounderby swelling at his own portrait on the
wall, as if he were going to explode himself into it; and
Mrs. Sparsit still ambling on with her foot in her stirrup,
looking quite cast down by the popular vices.

CHAPTER XII.

THE OLD WOMAN.

OLD STEPHEN descended the two white steps, shutting
the black door with the brazen door-plate, by the aid of
the brazen full-stop, to which he gave a parting polish
with the sleeve of his coat, observing that his hot hand
clouded it. He crossed the street with his eyes bent
upon the ground, and thus was walking sorrowfully
away, when he felt a touch upon his arm.

It was not the touch he needed most at such a moment
—the touch that could calm the wild waters of his soul,
as the uplifted hand of the sublimest love and patience
could abate the raging of the sea—yet it was a woman's
hand too. It was an old woman, tall and shapely still,
though withered by time, on whom his eyes fell when he
stopped and turned. She was very cleanly and plainly
dressed, had country mud upon her shoes, and was newly
come from a journey. The flutter of her manner, in the
unwonted noise of the streets; the spare shawl, carried
unfolded on her arm; the heavy umbrella, and little
basket; the loose long-fingered gloves, to which her
hands were unused; all bespoke an old woman from the
country, in her plain holiday clothes come into Coketown
on an expedition of rare occurrence. Remarking this
at a glance, with the quick observation of his class,
Stephen Blackpool bent his attentive face—his face,
which, like the faces of many of his order, by dint of
long working with eyes and hands in the midst of a prodigious noise, had acquired the concentrated look with
which we are familiar in the countenances of the deaf—
the better to hear what she asked him.

"Pray, sir," said the old woman, "didn't I see you
come out of that gentleman's house?" pointing back to
Mr. Bounderby's. "I believe it was you, unless I have
had the bad luck to mistake the person in following?"

"Yes, missus," returned Stephen, "it were me."

"Have you—you'll excuse an old woman's curiosity—
have you seen the gentleman?"

"Yes, missus."

"And how did he look, sir? Was he portly, bold, out-
spoken, and hearty?" As she straightened her own
figure, and held up her head in adapting her action to
her words, the idea crossed Stephen that he had seen this
old woman before, and had not quite liked her.

"O yes," he returned, observing her more attentively,
"he were all that."

"And healthy," said the old woman, "as the fresh
wind?"

"Yes," returned Stephen. "He were ett'n and drinking—as large and as loud as a Hummobee."

"Thank you!" said the old woman, with infinite content. "Thank you!"

He certainly never had seen this old woman before. Yet there was a vague remembrance in his mind, as if he had more than once dreamed of some old woman like her.

She walked along at his side, and, gently accommodating himself to her humor, he said Coketown was a busy place, was it not? To which she answered "Eigh sure! Dreadful busy!" Then he said, she came from the country, he saw? To which she answered in the affirmative.

"By Parliamentary, this morning. I came forty mile by Parliamentary this morning, and I'm going back the same forty mile this afternoon. I walked nine mile to the station this morning, and if I find nobody on the road to give me a lift, I shall walk the nine mile back to-night. That's pretty well, sir, at my age!" said the chatty old woman, her eye brightening with exultation.

"'Deed 'tis. Don't do't too often, missus."

"No, no. Once a year," she answered, shaking her head. "I spend my savings so, once every year. I come regular, to tramp about the streets and see the gentlemen."

"Only to see 'em?" returned Stephen.

"That's enough for me," she replied, with great earnestness and interest of manner. "I ask no more! I have been standing about, on this side of the way, to see that gentleman," turning her head back towards Mr. Bounderby's again, "come out. But he's late this year and I have not seen him. You came out instead. Now, if I am obliged to go back without a glimpse of him—I only want a glimpse—well! I have seen you, and you have seen him, and I must make that do." Saying this, she looked at Stephen as if to fix his features in her mind, and her eye was not so bright as it had been.

With a large allowance for difference of tastes, and with all submission to the patricians of Coketown, this seemed so extraordinary a source of interest to take so much trouble about, that it perplexed him. But they were passing the church now, and as his eye caught the clock, he quickened his pace.

He was going to his work? the old woman said, quickening hers, too, quite easily. Yes, time was nearly out. On his telling her where he worked, the old woman became a more singular old woman than before.

" An't you happy?" she asked him.

" Why—there's awmost nobbody but has their troubles, missus." He answered evasively, because the old woman appeared to take it for granted that he would be very happy indeed, and he had not the heart to disappoint her. He knew that there was trouble enough in the world; and if the old woman had lived so long, and could count upon his having so little, why so much the better for her, and none the worse for him.

" Ay, ay! You have your troubles at home, you mean?" she said.

" Times. Just now and then," he answered, slightly.

" But, working under such a gentleman, they don't follow you to the Factory?"

No, no; they didn't follow him there, said Stephen. All correct there. Everything accordant there. (He did not go so far as to say, for her pleasure, that there was a sort of Divine Right there; but, I have heard claims almost as magnificent of late years.)

They were now in the black by-road near the place, and the Hands were crowding in. The bell was ringing, and the Serpent was a Serpent of many coils, and the Elephant was getting ready. The strange old woman was delighted with the very bell. It was the beautifullest bell she had ever heard, she said, and sounded grand!

She asked him, when he stopped goodnaturedly to shake hands with her before going in, how long he had worked there?

" A dozen year," he told her.

" I must kiss the hand," said she, " that has worked in this fine factory for a dozen year!" And she lifted it, though he would have prevented her, and put it to her lips. What harmony, besides her age and her simplicity, surrounded her, he did not know, but even in this fantastic action there was a something neither out of time nor place: a something which it seemed as if nobody else could have made as serious, or done with such a natural and touching air.

He had been at his loom full half an hour, thinking about this old woman, when, having occasion to move round the loom for its adjustment, he glanced through a window which was in his corner, and saw her still looking up at the pile of building, lost in admiration. Heedless of the smoke and mud and wet, and of her two long journeys, she was gazing at it, as if the heavy thrum that issued from its many stories were proud music to her.

She was gone by and by, and the day went after her, and the lights sprung up again, and the Express whirled in full sight of the Fairy Palace over the arches near: little felt amid the jarring of the machinery, and scarcely heard above its crash and rattle. Long before then his thoughts had gone back to the dreary room above the little shop, and to the shameful figure heavy on the bed, but heavier on his heart.

Machinery slackened; throbbing feebly like a fainting pulse; stopped. The bell again; the glare of light and heat dispelled; the factories, looming heavy in the black wet night—their tall chimneys rising up into the air like competing Towers of Babel.

He had spoken to Rachael only last night, it was true, and had walked with her a little way; but he had his new misfortune on him, in which no one else could give him a moment's relief, and, for the sake of it, and because he knew himself to want that softening of his anger which no voice but hers could effect, he felt he might so far disregard what she had said as to wait for her again. He waited, but she had eluded him. She was gone. On no other night in the year could he so ill have spared her patient face.

O! Better to have no home in which to lay his head, than to have a home and dread to go to it, through such a cause. He ate and drank, for he was exhausted—but he little knew or cared what; and he wandered about in the chill rain, thinking and thinking, and brooding and brooding.

No word of a new marriage had ever passed between them; but Rachael had taken great pity on him years ago, and to her alone he had opened his closed heart all this time, on the subject of his miseries; and he knew very well that if he were free to ask her, she would take him. He thought of the home he might at that moment have been seeking with pleasure and pride: of the different man he might have been that night; of the lightness then in his now heavy-laden breast; of the then restored honor, self-respect, and tranquillity all torn to pieces. He thought of the waste of the best part of his life, of the change it made in his character for the worse every day, of the dreadful nature of his existence, bound hand and foot, to a dead woman, and tormented by a demon in her shape. He thought of Rachael, how young when they were first brought together in these circumstances, how mature now, how soon to grow old. He thought of the number of girls and women she had seen marry, how many homes with children in them she had seen grow up around her, how she had contentedly pursued her own lone quiet path—for him—and how he had sometimes seen a shade of melancholy on her blessed face, that smote him with remorse and despair. He set the picture of her up, beside the infamous image of last night; and thought, Could it be, that the whole earthly course of one so gentle, good, and self-denying, was subjugate to such a wretch as that!

Filled with these thoughts—so filled that he had an unwholesome sense of growing larger, of being placed in some new and diseased relation towards the objects among which he passed, of seeing the iris round every misty light turn red—he went home for shelter.

CHAPTER XIII.

RACHAEL.

A CANDLE faintly burned in the window, to which the black ladder had often been raised for the sliding away of all that was most precious in this world to a striving wife and a brood of hungry babies; and Stephen added to his other thoughts the stern reflection, that of all the casualties of this existence upon earth, not one was dealt out with so unequal a hand as Death. The inequality of Birth was nothing to it. For, say that the child of a King and the child of a Weaver were born to-night in the same moment, what was that disparity, to the death of any human creature who was serviceable to, or beloved by, another, while this abandoned woman lived on!

From the outside of his home he gloomily passed to the inside, with suspended breath and with a slow footstep. He went up to his door, opened it, and so into the room.

Quiet and peace were there. Rachael was there, sitting by the bed.

She turned her head, and the light of her face shone in upon the midnight of his mind. She sat by the bed, watching and tending his wife. That is to say, he saw that some one lay there, and he knew too well it must be she; but Rachael's hands had put a curtain up, so that she was screened from his eyes. Her disgraceful garments were removed, and some of Rachael's were in the room. Everything was in its place and order as he had always kept it, the little fire was newly trimmed, and the hearth was freshly swept. It appeared to him that he saw all this in Rachael's face, and looked at nothing besides. While looking at it, it was shut out from his view by the softened tears that filled his eyes; but. not before he had seen how earnestly she looked at him, and how her own eyes were filled too.

She turned again towards the bed, and satisfying herself that all was quiet there, spoke in a low, calm, cheerful voice.

" I am glad you have come at last, Stephen. You are very late."

"I ha' been walking up an' down."

"I thought so. But 'tis too bad a night for that. The rain falls very heavy, and the wind has risen."

The wind? True. It was blowing hard. Hark to the thundering in the chimney, and the surging noise! To have been out in such wind, and not to have known it was blowing!

" I have been here once before, to-day, Stephen. Landlady came round for me at dinner-time. There was some one here that needed looking to, she said. And 'deed she was right. All wandering and lost, Stephen. Wounded too, and bruised."

He slowly moved to a chair and sat down, drooping his head before her.

" I came to do what little I could, Stephen; first, for that she worked with me when we were girls both, and for that you courted her and married her when I was her friend—"

He laid his furrowed forehead on his hand, with a low groan.

"And next, for that I know your heart, and am right sure and certain that 'tis far too merciful to let her die, or even so much as suffer, for want of aid. Thou knowest who said 'Let him who is without sin among you cast the first stone at her!' There have been plenty to do that. Thou art not the man to cast the last stone, Stephen, when she is brought so low."

"O Rachael, Rachael!"

"Thou hast been a cruel sufferer, Heaven reward thee!" she said, in compassionate accents. "I am thy poor friend, with all my heart and mind."

The wounds of which she had spoken, seemed to be about the neck of the self-made outcast. She dressed them now, still without showing her. She steeped a piece of linen in a basin, into which she poured some liquid from a bottle, and laid it with a gentle hand upon the sore. The three-legged table had been drawn close to the bedside, and on it there were two bottles. This was one.

It was not so far off, but that Stephen, following her hands with his eyes, could read what was printed on it in large letters. He turned of a deadly hue, and a sudden horror seemed to fall upon him.

"I will stay here, Stephen," said Rachael, quietly resuming her seat, "till the bells go Three. 'Tis to be done again at three, and then she may be left till morning."

"But thy rest agen to-morrow's work, my dear."

"I slept sound last night. I can wake many nights, when I am put to it. 'Tis thou who art in need of rest—so white and tired. Try to sleep in the chair there, while *I* watch. Thou hadst no sleep last night, I can well believe. To-morrow's work is far harder for thee than for me."

He heard the thundering and surging out of doors, and it seemed to him as if his late angry mood were going about trying to get at him. She had cast it out; she would keep it out; he trusted to her to defend him from himself.

"She don't know me, Stephen; she just drowsily mutters and stares. I have spoken to her times and again, but she don't notice! 'Tis as well so. When she comes to her right mind once more, I shall have done what I can, and she never the wiser."

6

"How long, Rachael, is't looked for, that she'll be so?"

"Doctor said she would haply come to her mind to-morrow."

His eyes fell again on the bottle, and a tremble passed over him, causing him to shiver in every limb. She thought he was chilled with the wet. "No," he said, "it was not that. He had had a fright."

"A fright?"

"Ay, ay! coming in. When I were walking. When I were thinking. When I—" It seized him again, and he stood up, holding by the mantel-shelf, as he pressed his dank cold hair down with a hand that shook as if it were palsied.

"Stephen!"

She was coming to him, but he stretched out his arm to stop her.

"No! Don't please; don't. Let me see thee setten by the bed. Let me see thee, a' so good, and so forgiving. Let me see thee as I see thee when I coom in. I can never see thee better than so. Never, never, never!"

He had a violent fit of trembling, and then sunk into his chair. After a time he controlled himself, and, rest—ing with an elbow on one knee, and his head upon that hand, could look towards Rachael. Seen across the dim candle with his moistened eyes, she looked as if she had a glory shining round her head. He could have believed she had. He did believe it, as the noise without shook the window, rattled at the door below, and went about the house clamoring and lamenting.

"When she gets better, Stephen, 'tis to be hoped she'll leave thee to thyself again, and do thee no more hurt. Anyways we will hope so now. And now I shall keep silence, for I want thee to sleep."

He closed his eyes, more to please her than to rest his weary head; but, by slow degrees as he listened to the great noise of the wind, he ceased to hear it, or it changed into the working of his loom, or even into the voices of the day (his own included) saying what had been really said. Even this imperfect consciousness faded away at last, and he dreamed a long, troubled dream.

He thought that he, and some one on whom his heart had long been set—but she was not Rachael, and that surprised him, even in the midst of his imaginary happi

ness—stood in the church being married. While the
ceremony was performing, and while he recognized among
the witnesses some whom he knew to be living, and many
whom he knew to be dead, darkness came on, succeeded
by the shining of a tremendous light. It broke from one
line in the table of commandments at the altar, and
illuminated the building with the words. They were
sounded through the church, too, as if there were voices
in the fiery letters. Upon this, the whole appearance
before him and around him changed, and nothing was
left as it had been, but himself and the clergyman. They
stood in the daylight before a crowd so vast, that if all
the people in the world could have been brought together
into one space, they could not have looked, he thought,
more numerous; and they all abhorred him, and there
was not one pitying or friendly eye among the millions
that were fastened on his face. He stood on a raised
stage, under his own loom; and, looking up at the shape
the loom took, and hearing the burial service distinctly
read, he knew that he was there to suffer death. In an
instant what he stood on fell below him, and he was
gone.

Out of what mystery he came back to his usual life,
and to places that he knew, he was unable to consider;
but he was back in those places by some means, and with
this condemnation upon him, that he was never, in this
world or the next, through all the unimaginable ages of
eternity, to look on Rachael's face or hear her voice.
Wandering to and fro, unceasingly, without hope, and in
search of he knew not what (he only knew that he was
doomed to seek it), he was the subject of a nameless, horrible dread, a mortal fear of one particular shape which
everything took. Whatsoever he looked at, grew into
that form sooner or later. The object of his miserable
existence was to prevent its recognition by any one among
the various people he encountered. Hopeless labor!
If he led them out of rooms where it was, if he shut up
drawers and closets where it stood, if he drew the curious
from places where he knew it to be secreted, and got
them out into the streets, the very chimneys of the mills
assumed that shape, and round them was the printed
word.

The wind was blowing again, the rain was beating on

the housetops, and the larger spaces through which he had strayed contracted to the four walls of his room. Saving that the fire had died out it was as his eyes had closed upon it. Rachael seemed to have fallen into a doze, in the chair by the bed. She sat wrapped in her shawl, perfectly still. The table stood in the same place, close by the bedside, and on it, in its real proportions and appearance, was the shape so often repeated.

He thought he saw the curtain move. He looked again, and he was sure it moved. He saw a hand come forth and grope about a little. Then the curtain moved more perceptibly, and the woman in the bed put it back, and sat up.

With her woful eyes, so haggard and wild, so heavy and large, she looked all round the room, and passed the corner where he slept in his chair. Her eyes returned to that corner, and she put her hand over them as a shade, while she looked into it. Again they went all round the room, scarcely heeding Rachael if at all, and returned to that corner. He thought, as she once more shaded them—not so much looking at him, as looking for him with a brutish instinct that he was there—that no single trace was left in those debauched features, or in the mind that went along with them, of the woman he had married eighteen years before. But that he had seen her come to this by inches, he never could have believed her to be the same.

All this time, as if a spell were on him, he was motionless and powerless, except to watch her.

Stupidly dozing, or communing with her incapable self about nothing, she sat for a little while with her hands at her ears, and her head resting on them. Presently, she resumed her staring round the room. And now, for the first time, her eyes stopped at the table with the bottles on it.

Straight way she turned her eyes back to his corner with the defiance of last night, and moving very cautiously and softly, stretched out her greedy hand. She drew a mug into the bed, and sat for a while considering which of the two bottles she should choose. Finally, she laid her insensate grasp upon the bottle that had swift and certain death in it, and, before his eyes, pulled out the cork with her teeth.

Dream or reality, he had no voice, nor had he power to stir. If this be real, and her allotted time be not yet come, wake, Rachael, wake!

She thought of that, too. She looked at Rachael, and very slowly, very cautiously, poured out the contents. The draught was at her lips.

A moment and she would be past all help, let the whole world wake and come about her with its utmost power. But in that moment Rachael started up with a suppressed cry. The creature struggled, and struck her, seized her by the hair ; but Rachael had the cup.

Stephen broke out of his chair. " Rachael, am I wakin' or dreamin' this dreadfo' night ? "

" 'Tis all well, Stephen. I have been asleep myself. " 'Tis near three. Hush ! I hear the bell."

The wind brought the sounds of the church clock to the window. They listened, and it struck three. Stephen looked at her, saw how pale she was, noted the disorder of her hair, and the red marks of fingers on her forehead, and felt assured that his senses of sight and hearing had been awake. She held the cup in her hand even now.

" I thought it must be near three," she said, calmly pouring from the cup into the basin, and steeping the linen as before. " I am thankful I stayed ! 'Tis done now, when I have put this on. There ! And now she's quiet again. The few drops in the basin I 'll pour away, for 'tis bad stuff to leave about, though ever so little of it," As she spoke, she drained the basin into the ashes of the fire, and broke the bottle on the hearth.

She had nothing to do, then, but to cover herself with her shawl before going out into the wind and rain.

" Thou'lt let me walk wi' thee at this hour, Rachael ? "

" No, Stephen. 'Tis but a minute, and I 'm home."

" Thou 'rt not fearfo' " he said it in a low voice as they went out at the door, " to leave me alone wi' her ! " As she looked at him, saying " Stephen ? " he went down on his knee before her, on the poor mean stairs, and put an end of her shawl to his lips.

" Thou art an angel. Bless thee, bless thee."

" I am, as I have told thee, Stephen, thy poor friend. Angels are not like me. Between them, and a working woman fu' of faults, there is a deep gulf set. My little sister is among them, but she is changed."

She raised her eyes for a moment as she said the words ; and then they fell again, in all their gentleness and mildness, on his face.

" Thou changest me from bad to good. Thou mak'st me humbly wishfo' to be more like thee, and fearfo' to lose thee when this life is ower, and a' the muddle cleared awa'. Thou'rt an Angel ; it may be, thou hast saved my soul alive ! "

She looked at him, on his knee at her feet, with her shawl still in his hand, and the reproof on her lips died away when she saw the working of his face.

" I coom home desp'rate. I coom home wi'out a hope, and mad wi' thinking that when I said a word o' complaint I was reckoned a onreasonable Hand. I told thee I had had a fright. It were the Poison-bottle on table. I never hurt a livin' creetur, but happenin' so suddenly upon 't, I thowt, ' How can *I* say what I might ha' done to myseln, or her, or both ! ' "

She put her two hands on his mouth, with a face of terror, to stop him from saying more. He caught them in his unoccupied hand, and holding them, and still clasping the border of her shawl, said hurriedly :

" But I see thee, Rachael, setten by the bed. I ha' seen thee, aw this night. In my troublous sleep I ha' known thee still to be there. Evermore I will see thee there. I nevermore will see her or think o' her, but thou shalt be beside her. I nevermore will see or think o' anything that angers me, but thou, so much better than me, shalt be by th' side on 't. And so I will try t' look 't th' time, and so I will try t' trust t' th' time, when thou and me at last shall walk together far awa', beyond the deep gulf, in th' country where thy little sister is."

He kissed the border of her shawl again, and let her go. She bade him good night in a broken voice, and went out into the street.

The wind blew from the quarter where the day would soon appear, and still blew strongly. It had cleared the sky before it, and the rain had spent itself or travelled elsewhere, and the stars were bright. He stood bareheaded in the road, watching her quick disappearance. As the shining stars were to the heavy candle in the window, so was Rachael, in the rugged fancy of this man, to the common experiences of his life.

CHAPTER XIV.

THE GREAT MANUFACTURER.

Time went on in Coketown like its own machinery: so much material wrought up, so much fuel consumed, so many powers worn out, so much money made. But, less inexorable than iron, steel, and brass, it brought its varying seasons even into that wilderness of smoke and brick, and made the only stand that ever *was* made in the place against its direful uniformity.

" Louisa is becoming," said Mr. Gradgrind, " almost a young woman."

Time, with his innumerable horse-power, worked away, not minding what anybody said, and presently turned out young Thomas a foot taller than when his father had last taken particular notice of him.

" Thomas is becoming," said Mr. Gradgrind, " almost a young man."

Time passed Thomas on in the mill, while his father was thinking about it, and there he stood in a long-tailed coat and a stiff shirt-collar.

" Really," said Mr. Gradgrind, " the period has arrived when Thomas ought to go to Bounderby."

Time, sticking to him, passed him on into Bounderby's Bank, made him an inmate of Bounderby's house, necessitated the purchase of his first razor, and exercised him diligently in his calculations relative to number one.

The same great manufacturer, always with an immense variety of work on hand, in every stage of development, passed Sissy onward in his mill, and worked her up into a very pretty article indeed.

" I fear, Jupe," said Mr. Gradgrind, " that your continuance at the school any longer would be useless."

" I am afraid it would, Sir," Sissy answered with a curtsey.

" I cannot disguise from you, Jupe," said Mr. Gradgrind, knitting his brow, " that the result of your probation there has disappointed me; has greatly disappointed me.

You have not acquired, under Mr. and Mrs. M'Choakum-child, anything like that amount of exact knowledge which I looked for. You are extremely deficient in your facts. Your acquaintance with figures is very limited. You are altogether backward, and below the mark."

"I am sorry, sir," she returned; "but I know it is quite true. Yet I have tried hard, sir."

"Yes," said Mr. Gradgrind, "yes, I believe you have tried hard; I have observed you, and I can find no fault in that respect."

"Thank you, sir. I have thought sometimes;" Sissy very timid here; "that perhaps I tried to learn too much, and that if I had asked to be allowed to try a little less, I might have——"

"No, Jupe, no," said Mr. Gradgrind, shaking his head in his profoundest and most eminently practical way. "No. The course you pursued, you pursued according to the system—the system—and there is no more to be said about it. I can only suppose that the circumstances of your early life were too unfavorable to the development of your reasoning powers, and that we began too late. Still, as I have said already, I am disappointed."

"I wish I could have made a better acknowledgment, sir, of your kindness to a poor forlorn girl who had no claim upon you, and of your protection of her.

"Don't shed tears," said Mr. Gradgrind. "Don't shed tears. I don't complain of you. You are an affectionate, earnest, good young woman—and—and we must make that do."

"Thank you, sir, very much," said Sissy, with a grateful curtsey.

"You are useful to Mrs. Gradgrind, and (in a generally pervading way) you are serviceable in the family also; so I understand from Miss Louisa, and, indeed, so I have observed myself. I therefore hope," said Mr. Gradgrind, "that you can make yourself happy in those relations."

"I should have nothing to wish, sir, if——"

"I understand you," said Mr. Gradgrind; "you still refer to your father. I have heard from Miss Louisa that you still preserve that bottle. Well! If your training in the science of arriving at exact results had been more successful, you would have been wiser on these points. I will say no more."

He really liked Sissy too well to have a contempt for her; otherwise he held her calculating powers in such very slight estimation that he must have fallen upon that conclusion. Somehow or other, he had become possessed by an idea that there was something in this girl which could hardly be set forth in a tabular form. Her capacity of definition might be easily stated at a very low figure, her mathematical knowledge at nothing; yet he was not sure that if he had been required, for example, to tick her off into columns in a parliamentary return, he would have quite known how to divide her.

In some stages of his manufacture of the human fabric, the processes of Time are very rapid. Young Thomas and Cissy being both at such a stage of their working up, these changes were effected in a year or two; while Mr. Gradgrind himself seemed stationary in his course, and underwent no alteration.

Except one, which was apart from his necessary progress through the mill. Time hustled him into a little noisy and rather dirty machinery, in a by-corner, and made him Member of Parliament for Coketown: one of the respected members for ounce weights and measures, one of the representatives of the multiplication table, one of the deaf honorable gentlemen, dumb honorable gentlemen, blind honorable gentlemen, lame honorable gentlemen, dead honorable gentlemen, to every other consideration. Else wherefore live we in a Christian land, eighteen hundred and odd years after our Master?

All this while, Louisa had been passing on, so quiet and reserved, and so much given to watching the bright ashes at twilight as they fell into the grate and became extinct, that from the period when her father had said she was almost a young woman—which seemed but yesterday— she had scarcely attracted his notice again, when he found her quite a young woman.

"Quite a young woman," said Mr. Gradgrind, musing. "Dear me!"

Soon after this discovery, he became more thoughtful than usual for several days, and seemed much engrossed by one subject. On a certain night, when he was going out, and Louisa came to bid him good-bye before his departure—as he was not to be home until late and she would not see him again until the morning—he held her in his arms, looking at her in his kindest manner, and said:

"My dear Louisa, you are a woman!"

She answered with the old, quick, searching look of the night when she was found at the Circus; then cast down her eyes. "Yes, father."

"My dear," said Mr. Gradgrind, "I must speak with you alone and seriously. Come to me in my room after breakfast to-morrow, will you?"

"Yes, father."

"Your hands are rather cold, Louisa. Are you not well?"

"Quite well, father."

"And cheerful?"

She looked at him again and smiled in her peculiar manner. "I am as cheerful, father, as I usually am, or usually have been."

"That's well," said Mr. Gradgrind. So, he kissed her and went away; and Louisa returned to the serene apartment of the hair-cutting character, and leaning her elbow on her hand, looked again at the short-lived sparks that so soon subsided into ashes.

"Are you there, Loo?" said her brother, looking in at the door. He was quite a young gentleman of pleasure now, and quite a prepossessing one.

"Dear Tom," she answered, rising and embracing him, "how long it is since you have been to see me!"

"Why, I have been otherwise engaged, Loo, in the evenings; and in the day-time old Bounderby has been keeping me at it rather. But I touch him up with you when he comes it too strong, and so we preserve an understanding. I say! Has father said anything particular to you to-day or yesterday, Loo?"

"No, Tom. But he told me to-night that he wished to do so in the morning."

"Ah! That's what I mean," said Tom. "Do you know where he is to-night?"—with a very deep expression.

"No."

"Then I'll tell you. He's with old Bounderby. They are having a regular confab together up at the Bank. Why at the Bank, do you think? Well. I'll tell you again. To keep Mrs. Sparsit's ears as far off as possible, I expect."

With her hand upon her brother's shoulder, Louisa still stood looking at the fire. Her brother glanced at her face with greater interest than usual, and, encircling her waist with his arm, drew her coaxingly to him.

"You are very fond of me, an't you, Loo?"

"Indeed I am, Tom, though you do let such long intervals go by without coming to see me."

"Well, sister of mine," said Tom, "when you say that, you are near my thoughts. We might be much oftener together—mightn't we? Always together, almost—mightn't we? It would do me a great deal of good if you were to make up your mind to I know what, Loo. It would be a splendid thing for me. It would be uncommonly jolly!"

Her thoughtfulness baffled his cunning scrutiny. He could make nothing of her face. He pressed her in his arm, and kissed her cheek. She returned the kiss, but still looked at the fire.

"I say, Loo! I thought I'd come, and just hint to you what was going on: though I supposed you'd most likely guess, even if you didn't know. I can't stay, because I'm engaged to some fellows to-night. You won't forget how fond you are of me?"

"No, dear Tom, I won't forget."

"That's a capital girl," said Tom. "Good-bye, Loo."

She gave him an affectionate good-night, and went out with him to the door, whence the fires of Coketown could be seen, making the distance lurid. She stood there, looking steadfastly towards them, and listened to his departing steps. They retreated quickly, as glad to get away from Stone Lodge; and she stood there yet, when he was gone and all was quiet. It seemed as if, first in her own fire within the house, and then in the fiery haze without she tried to discover what kind of woof Old Time, that greatest and longest-established Spinner of all, would weave from the threads he had already spun into a woman. But his factory is a secret place, his work is noiseless, and his Hands are mutes.

CHAPTER XV.

ALTHOUGH Mr. Gradgrind did not take after Blue Beard, his room was quite a blue chamber in its abundance of blue books. Whatever they could prove (which is usually anything you like), they proved there, in an army constantly strengthening by the arrival of new recruits. In that charmed apartment, the most complicated social questions were cast up, got into exact totals, and finally settled—if those concerned could only have been brought to know it. As if an astronomical observatory should be made without any windows, and the astronomer within should arrange the starry universe solely by pen, ink, and paper, so Mr. Gradgrind, in *his* Observatory (and there are many like it), had no need to cast an eye upon the teeming myriads of human beings around him, but could settle all their destinies on a slate, and wipe out all their tears with one dirty little bit of sponge.

To this Observatory, then : a stern room, with a deadly statistical clock in it, which measured every second with a beat like a rap upon a coffin-lid ; Louisa repaired on the appointed morning. A window looked towards Coketown and when she sat down near her father's table, she saw the high chimneys and the long tracts of smoke looming in the heavy distance gloomily.

"My dear Louisa," said her father, "I prepared you last night to give me your serious attention in the conversation we are now going to have together. You have been so well trained, and you do, I am happy to say, so much justice to the education you have received, that I have perfect confidence in your good sense. You are not impulsive, you are not romantic, you are accustomed to view everything from the strong dispassionate ground of reason and calculation. From that ground alone, I know you will view and consider what I am going to communicate."

He waited, as if he would have been glad that she said something. But she said never a word.

"Louisa, my dear, you are the subject of a proposal of marriage that has been made to me."

Again he waited, and again she answered not one word. This so far surprised him, as to induce him gently to repeat, "a proposal of marriage, my dear." To which she returned, without any visible emotion whatever:

"I hear you, father. I am attending, I assure you."

"Well!" said Mr. Gradgrind, breaking into a smile, after being for the moment at a loss, "you are even more dispassionate than I expected, Louisa. Or, perhaps, you are not unprepared for the announcement I have it in charge to make?"

"I cannot say that, father, until I hear it. Prepared or unprepared, I wish to hear it all from you. I wish to hear you state it to me, father."

Strange to relate, Mr. Gradgrind was not so collected at this moment as his daughter was. He took a paper-knife in his hand, turned it over, laid it down, took it up again, and even then had to look along the blade of it, considering how to go on.

"What you say, my dear Louisa, is perfectly reasonable. I have undertaken then to let you know that——in short, that Mr. Bounderby has informed me that he has long watched your progress with particular interest and pleasure, and has long hoped that the time might ultimately arrive when he should offer you his hand in marriage. That time, to which he has so long, and certainly with great constancy, looked forward, is now come. Mr. Bounderby has made his proposal of marriage to me, and has entreated me to make it known to you, and to express his hope that you will take it into your favorable consideration."

Silence between them. The deadly statistical clock very hollow. The distant smoke very black and heavy.

"Father," said Louisa, "do you think I love Mr. Bounderby?"

Mr. Gradgrind was extremely discomfited by this unexpected question. "Well, my child," he returned, "I—really—cannot take upon myself to say."

"Father," pursued Louisa in exactly the same voice as before, "do you ask me to love Mr. Bounderby?"

"My dear Louisa, no. No. I ask nothing."

"Father," she still pursued, " does Mr. Bounderby ask me to love him ? "

" Really, my dear," said Mr. Gradgrind, " it is difficult to answer your question—"

" Difficult to answer it, Yes or No, father ? "

" Certainly, my dear. Because ;" here was something to demonstrate, and it set him up again; " because the reply depends so materially, Louisa, on the sense in which we use the expression. Now, Mr. Bounderby does not do you the injustice, and does not do himself the injustice, of pretending to anything fanciful, fantastic, or (I am using synonymous terms) sentimental. Mr. Bounderby would have seen you grow up under his eyes, to very little purpose, if he could so far forget what is due to your good sense, not to say to his, as to address you from any such ground. Therefore, perhaps the expression itself—I merely suggest this to you, my dear—may be a little misplaced."

" What would you advise me to use in its stead, father ? "

" Why, my dear Louisa," said Mr. Gradgrind, completely recovered by this time, " I would advise you (since you ask me) to consider this question, as you have been accustomed to consider every other question, simply as one of tangible Fact. The ignorant and the giddy may embarrass such subjects with irrelevant fancies, and other absurdities that have no existence properly viewed —really no existence—but it is no compliment to you to say, that you know better. Now, what are the Facts of this case ? You are, we will say in round numbers, twenty years of age ; Mr. Bounderby is, we will say in round numbers, fifty. There is some disparity in your respective years, but in your means and positions there is none; on the contrary, there is a great suitability. Then the question arises, Is this one disparity sufficient to operate as a bar to such a marriage ? In considering this question, it is not unimportant to take into account the statistics of marriage, so far as they have yet been obtained, in England and Wales. I find, on reference to the figures, that a large proportion of these marriages are contracted between parties of very unequal ages, and that the elder of these contracting parties is, in rather more than three-fourths of these instances, the bridegroom.

It is remarkable as showing the wide prevalence of this law, that among the natives of the British possessions in India, also in a considerable part of China, and among the Calmucks of Tartary, the best means of computation yet furnished us by travellers, yield similar results. The disparity I have mentioned, therefore. almost ceases to be disparity, and (virtually) all but disappears."

"What do you recommend, father," asked Louisa, her reserved composure not in the least affected by these gratifying results, "that I should substitute for the term I used just now? For the misplaced expression?"

"Louisa," returned her father, "it appears to me that nothing can be plainer. Confining yourself rigidly to Fact, the question of Fact you state to yourself is: Does Mr. Bounderby ask me to marry him? Yes, he does. The sole remaining question then is: Shall I marry him? I think nothing can be plainer than that?"

"Shall I marry him?" repeated Louisa, with great deliberation.

"Precisely. And it is satisfactory to me, as your father, my dear Louisa, to know that you do not come to the consideration of that question with the previous habits of mind, and habits of life, that belong to many young women."

"No, father," she returned, "I do not."

"I now leave you to judge for yourself," said Mr. Gradgrind. "I have stated the case, as such cases are usually stated among practical minds; I have stated it, as the case of your mother and myself was stated in its time. The rest, my dear, Louisa, is for you to decide."

From the beginning, she had sat looking at him fixedly. As he now leaned back in his chair, and bent his deep-set eyes upon her in his turn, perhaps he might have seen one wavering moment in her, when she was impelled to throw herself upon his breast, and give him the pent-up confidences of her heart. But, to see it, he must have overleaped at a bound the artificial barriers he had for many years been erecting, between himself and all those subtle essences of humanity which will elude the utmost cunning of algebra until the last trumpet ever to be sounded shall blow even algebra to wreck. The barriers were too many and too high for such a leap. With his unbending, utilitarian, matter-of-fact face, he hardene?

her again; and the moment shot away into the plumbless depths of the past, to mingle with all the lost opportunities that are drowned there.

Removing her eyes from him, she sat so long looking silently towards the town, that he said, at length: "Are you consulting the chimneys of the Coketown works, Louisa?"

"There seems to be nothing there but languid and monotonous smoke. Yet when the night comes, Fire bursts out, father!" she answered, turning quickly.

"Of course I know that, Louisa. I do not see the application of the remark." To do him justice he did not, at all.

She passed it away with a slight motion of her hand, and concentrating her attention upon him again, said, "Father, I have often thought that life is very short."— This was so distinctly one of his subjects that he interposed.

"It is short, no doubt, my dear. Still, the average duration of human life is proved to have increased of late years. The calculations of various life assurance and annuity offices, among other figures which cannot go wrong, have established the fact."

"I speak of my own life, father."

"O indeed? Still," said Mr. Gradgrind, "I need not point out to you, Louisa, that it is governed by the laws which govern lives in the aggregate."

"While it lasts, I would wish to do the little I can, and the little I am fit for. What does it matter?"

Mr. Gradgrind seemed rather at a loss to understand the last four words; replying, "How, matter? What matter, my dear?"

"Mr. Bounderby," she went on in a steady, straight way, without regarding this, "asks me to marry him. The question I have to ask myself is, shall I marry him? That is so, father, is it not? You have told me so, father. Have you not?"

"Certainly, my dear."

"Let it be so. Since Mr. Bounderby likes to take me thus, I am satisfied to accept his proposal. Tell him, father, as soon as you please, that this was my answer. Repeat it, word for word, if you can, because I should wish him to know what I said."

" It is quite right, my dear," retorted her father approvingly, " to be exact. I will observe your very proper request. Have you any wish in reference to the period of your marriage, my child ? "

" None, father. What does it matter ! "

Mr. Gradgrind had drawn his chair a little nearer to her, and taken her hand. But her repetition of these words seemed to strike with some little discord on his ear. He paused to look at her, and, still holding her hand, said :

" Louisa, I have not considered it essential to ask you one question, because the possibility implied in it appeared to me to be too remote. But perhaps I ought to do so. You have never entertained in secret any other proposal ? "

" Father," she returned, almost scornfully, " what other proposal can have been made to *me?* Whom have I seen ? Where have I been ? What are my heart's experiences ? "

" My dear Louisa," returned Mr. Gradgrind, reassured and satisfied. " You correct me justly. I merely wished to discharge my duty."

What do *I* know, father," said Louisa, in her quiet manner, " of tastes and fancies ; of aspirations and affections ; of all that part of my nature in which such light things might have been nourished ? What escape have I had from problems that could be demonstrated, and realities that could be grasped ? " As she said it, she unconsciously closed her hand, as if upon a solid object, and slowly opened it as though she were releasing dust or ash.

" My dear," assented her eminently practical parent, " quite true, quite true."

" Why, father," she pursued, " what a strange question to ask *me !* The baby-preference that even I have heard of as common among children, has never had its innocent resting-place in my breast. You have been so careful of me, that I never had a child's heart. You have trained me so well, that I never dreamed a child's dream. You have dealt so wisely with me, father, from my cradle to this hour, that I never had a child's belief or a child's fear."

Mr. Gradgrind was quite moved by his success, and by

7

this testimony to it. " My dear Louisa," said he, " you abundantly repay my care. Kiss me, my dear girl."

So his daughter kissed him. Detaining her in his embrace, he said, " I may assure you now, my favorite child, that I am made happy by the sound decision at which you have arrived. Mr. Bounderby is a very remarkable man ; and what little disparity can be said to exist between you—if any—is more than counterbalanced by the tone your mind has acquired. It has always been my object so to educate you, as that you might, while still in your early youth, be (if I may so express myself) almost any age. Kiss me once more, Louisa. Now, let us go and find your mother.

Accordingly, they went down to the drawing-room, where the esteemed lady with no nonsense about her, was recumbent as usual, while Sissy worked beside her. She gave some feeble signs of returning animation when they entered, and presently the faint transparency was presented in a sitting attitude.

" Mrs. Gradgrind," said her husband, who had waited for the achievement of his feat with some impatience, " allow me to present to you Mrs. Bounderby."

" Oh ! " said Mrs. Gradgrind, " so you have settled it ! Well, I'm sure I hope your health may be good, Louisa ; for if your head begins to split as soon as you are married, which was the case with mine, I cannot consider that you are to be envied, though I have no doubt you think you are, as all girls do. However, I give you joy, my dear—and I hope you may now turn all your ological studies to good account, I am sure I do ! I must give you a kiss of congratulation, Louisa ; but don't touch my right shoulder, for there's something running down it all day long. And now you see," whimpered Mrs. Gradgrind, adjusting her shawls after the affectionate ceremony, " I shall be worrying myself, morning, noon, and night, to know what I am to call him ! "

" Mrs. Gradgrind," said her husband, solemnly, " what do you mean ? "

" Whatever I am to call him, Mr. Gradgrind, when he is married to Louisa ! I must call him something. It's impossible," said Mrs. Gradgrind, with a mingled sense of politeness and injury, " to be constantly addressing him and never giving him a name. I cannot call him Josiah, for the name is insupportable to me. You yourself wouldn't hear of Joe, you very well know. Am I to call my own son-in-law, Mister. Not, I believe, unless the time has arrived when, as an invalid, I am to be trampled upon by my relations. Then, what am I to call him!"

Nobody present having any suggestion to offer in this remarkable emergency, Mrs. Gradgrind departed this life for the time being after delivering the following codicil to her remarks already executed:

" As to the wedding, all I ask, Louisa, is,—and I ask it with a fluttering in my chest, which actually extends to the soles of my feet,—that it may take place soon. Otherwise, I know it is one of those subjects I shall never hear the last of."

When Mr. Gradgrind had presented Mrs. Bounderby, Sissy had suddenly turned her head, and looked, in wonder, in pity, in sorrow, in doubt, in a multitude of emotions, towards Louisa. Louisa had known it, and seen it, without looking at her. From that moment she was impassive, proud and cold—held Sissy at a distance—changed to her altogether.

CHAPTER XVI.

HUSBAND AND WIFE.

MR. BOUNDERBY'S first disquietude on hearing of his happiness, was occasioned by the necessity of imparting it to Mrs. Sparsit. He could not make up his mind how to do that, or what the consequences of the step might be. Whether she would instantly depart, bag and baggage, to Lady Scadgers, or would positively refuse to budge from the premises; whether she would be plaintive or abusive, tearful or tearing; whether she would break her heart, or break the looking-glass; Mr. Bounderby could not at all foresee. However, as it must be done, he had no choice but to do it; so, after attempting several letters, and failing in them all, he resolved to do it by word of mouth.

On his way home, on the evening he set aside for this momentous purpose, he took the precaution of stepping

into a chemist's shop and buying a bottle of the very
strongest smelling salts. "By George!" said Mr. Bounderby, "if she takes it in the fainting way, I'll have the
skin off her nose, at all events!" But, in spite of being
thus forearmed, he entered his own house with anything
but a courageous air; and appeared before the object of
his misgivings, like a dog who was conscious of coming
direct from the pantry.

"Good-evening, Mr. Bounderby!"

"Good-evening, ma'am, good-evening." He drew up
his chair, and Mrs. Sparsit drew back hers, as who should
say, "Your fireside, sir. I freely admit it. It is for you
to occupy it all, if you think proper."

"Don't go to the North Pole, ma'am!" said Mr. Bounderby.

"Thank you, sir." said Mrs. Sparsit, and returned
though short of her former position.

Mr. Bounderby sat looking at her, as, with the points
of a stiff, sharp pair of scissors, she picked out holes for
some inscrutable ornamental purpose, in a piece of cambric.
An operation which, taken in connection with the bushy
eyebrows and the Roman nose, suggested with some live-
liness the idea of a hawk engaged upon the eyes of a
tough little bird. She was so steadfastly occupied, that
many minutes elapsed before she looked up from her work;
when she did so Mr. Bounderby bespoke her attention
with a hitch of his head.

"Mrs. Sparsit, ma'am," said Mr. Bounderby, putting his
hands in his pockets, and assuring himself with his
right hand that the cork of the little bottle was ready for
use, "I have no occasion to say to you, that you are not
only a lady born and bred, but a devilish sensible woman."

"Sir," returned the lady, "this is indeed not the first
time that you have honored me with similar expressions
of your good opinion."

"Mrs. Sparsit, ma'am," said Mr. Bounderby, "I am
going to astonish you."

"Yes, sir?" returned Mrs. Sparsit, interrogatively,
and in the most tranquil manner possible. She generally
wore mittens, and she now laid down her work, and
smoothed those mittens. "I am going, ma'am," said
Bounderby, "to marry Tom Gradgrind's daughter."

"Yes, sir," returned Mrs. Sparsit. "I hope you may

be happy, Mr. Bounderby. Oh, indeed I hope you may be happy, sir!" And she said it with such great condescension as well as with such great compassion for him, that Bounderby,—far more disconcerted than if she had thrown her work-box at the mirror, or swooned on the hearth-rug,—corked up the smelling salts tight in his pocket, and thought, "Now confound this woman, who could ever have guessed that she would take it in this way!"

" I wish with all my heart, sir," said Mrs. Sparsit, in a highly superior manner; somehow she seemed in a moment, to have established a right to pity him ever afterwards ; " that you may be in all respects very happy."

" Well, ma'am," returned Bounderby, with some resentment in his tone : which was clearly lowered, though in spite of himself, " I am obliged to you. I hope I shall be."

" *Do* you sir!" said Mrs. Sparsit, with great affability. "But naturally you do ; of course you do."

A very awkward pause on Mr. Bounderby's part, succeeded. Mrs. Sparsit sedately resumed her work and occasionally gave a small cough, which sounded like the cough of conscious strength and forbearance.

" Well, ma'am," resumed Bounderby, "under these circumstances, I imagine it would not be agreeable to a character like yours to remain here, though you would be very welcome here."

" Oh, dear no, sir, I could on no account think of that !" Mrs. Sparsit shook her head, still in her highly superior manner, and a little changed the small cough—coughing now, as if the spirit of prophecy rose within her, but had better be coughed down.

" However, ma'am," said Bounderby, " there are apartments at the Bank, where a born and bred lady, as keeper of the place, would be rather a catch than otherwise ; and if the same terms——"

" I beg your pardon, sir. You were so good as to promise that you would always substitute the phrase, annual compliment."

" Well, ma'am, annual compliment. If the same annual compliment would be acceptable there, why, I see nothing to part us, unless you do."

" Sir," returned Mrs. Sparsit. " The proposal is like

yourself, and if the position I shall assume at the Bank is one that I could occupy without descending lower in the social scale——"

"Why of course it is," said Bounderby. "If it was not, ma'am, you don't suppose that I should offer it to a lady who has moved in the society you have moved in. Not that *I* care for such society, you know! But *you* do."

"Mr. Bounderby, you are very considerate."

"You'll have your own private apartments, and you'll have your coals and your candles, and all the rest of it, and you'll have your maid to attend upon you, and you'll have your light porter to protect you, and you'll be what I take the liberty of considering precious comfortable," said Bounderby.

"Sir," rejoined Mrs. Sparsit, "say no more. In yielding up my trust here, I shall not be freed from the necessity of eating the bread of dependence:" she might have said the sweet-bread, for that delicate article in a savory brown sauce was her favorite supper: "and I would rather receive it from your hand, than from any other. Therefore, sir, I accept your offer gratefully, and with many sincere acknowledgments for past favors. And I hope, sir," said Mrs. Sparsit, concluding in an impressively compassionate manner, "I fondly hope that Miss Gradgrind may be all you desire and deserve!"

Nothing moved Mrs. Sparsit from that position any more. It was in vain for Bounderby to bluster or to assert hinself in any of his explosive ways; Mrs. Sparsit was resolved to have compassion on him, as a Victim. She was polite, obliging, cheerful, hopeful; but, the more polite, the more obliging, the more cheerful, the more hopeful, the more exemplary altogether, she; the forlorner Sacrifice and Victim, he. She had that tenderness for his melancholy fate, that his great red countenance used to break out into cold perspirations when she looked at him.

Meanwhile the marriage was appointed to be solemnized in eight weeks' time, and Mr. Bounderby went every evening to Stone Lodge as an accepted wooer. Love was made on these occasions in the form of bracelets; and on all occasions during the period of betrothal, took a manufacturing aspect. Dresses were made, jewelery was made, cakes and gloves were made, settlements were made, and an extensive assortment of Facts did appropriate honor to the contract. The business was all Fact, from first to last. The Hours did not go through any of those rosy performances, which foolish poets have ascribed to them at such times ; neither did the clocks go any faster, or any slower, than at other seasons. The deadly statistical recorder in the Gradgrind observatory knocked every second on the head as it was born, and buried it with his accustomed regularity.

So the day came, as all other days come to people who will only stick to reason ; and when it came, they were married in the church of the florid wooden legs—that popular order of architecture—Josiah Bounderby Esquire of Coketown, to Louisa eldest daughter of Thomas Gradgrind Esquire of Stone Lodge, M.P. for that borough. And when they were united in holy matrimony, they went home to breakfast at Stone Lodge aforesaid.

There was an improving party assembled on the auspicious occasion, who knew what everything they had to eat and drink was made of, and how it was imported or exported, and in what quantities, and in what bottoms, whether native or foreign, and all about it. The bridesmaids, down to little Jane Gradgrind, were, in an intellectual point of view, fit helpmates for the calculating boy ; and there was no nonsense about any of the company.

After breakfast, the bridegroom addressed them in the following terms :

" Ladies and gentlemen, I am Josiah Bounderby of Coketown. Since you have done my wife and myself the honor of drinking our healths and happiness, I suppose I must acknowledge the same ; though, as you all know me and know what I am, and what my extraction was, you won't expect a speech from a man who, when he sees a Post, says ' that's a Post,' and when he sees a Pump, says ' that's a Pump,' and is not to be got to call a Post a Pump or a Pump a Post, or either of them a Toothpick. If you want a speech this morning, my friend and father-in-law, Tom Gradgrind, is a Member of Parliament, and you know where to get it. I am not your man. However, if I feel a little independent when I look around this table to-day, and reflect how little I thought of marrying Tom Gradgrind's daughter when I was a ragged street-boy, who never washed his face unless it was at a pump, and that not oftener than once a fortnight, I hope I may be excused. So, I hope you like my feeling independent; if you don't, I can't help it. I *do* feel independent. Now I have mentioned, and you have mentioned, that I am this day married to Tom Gradgrind's daughter. I am very glad to be so. It has long been my wish to be so. I have watched her bringing up, and I believe she is worthy of me. At the same time—not to deceive you—I believe I am worthy of her. So I thank you, on both our parts, for the good-will you have shown towards us ; and the best wish I can give the unmarried part of the present company, is this : I hope every bachelor may find as good a wife as I have found. And I hope every spinster may find as good a husband as my wife has found."

Shortly after which oration, as they were going on a nuptial trip to Lyons, in order that Mr. Bounderby might take the opportunity of seeing how the Hands got on in those parts, and whether they, too, required to be fed with gold spoons ; the happy pair departed for the railroad. The bride, in passing downstairs, dressed for her journey, found Tom waiting for her—flushed, either with his feelings or the vinous part of the breakfast.

"What a game girl you are to be such a first-rate sister, Loo ! " whispered Tom.

She clung to him as she should have clung to some far better nature that day, and was a little shaken in her reserved composure for the first time.

"Old Bounderby's quite ready," said Tom. "Time's up. Good bye ! I shall be on the lookout for you, when you come back. I say, my dear Loo ! An't it uncommonly jolly now ! "

END OF THE FIRST BOOK.

BOOK THE SECOND. REAPING.

CHAPTER I.

EFFECTS IN THE BANK.

A SUNNY midsummer day. There was such a thing
sometimes, even in Coketown.

Seen from a distance in such weather, Coketown lay
shrouded in a haze of its own, which appeared imper-
vious to the sun's rays. You only knew the town was
there, because you knew there could have been no such
sulky blotch upon the prospect without a town. A blur
of soot and smoke, now confusedly tending this way, now
that way, now aspiring to the vault of heaven, now murk-
ily creeping along the earth, as the wind rose and fell,
or changed its quarter: a dense formless jumble, with
sheets of cross light in it, that showed nothing but
masses of darkness:—Coketown in the distance was suggestive of itself, though not a brick of it could be seen.

The wonder was, it was there at all. It had been
ruined so often, that it was amazing how it had borne so
many shocks. Surely there never was such fragile china-
ware as that of which the millers of Coketown were made.
Handle them never so lightly, and they fell to pieces
with such ease, that you might suspect them of having
been flawed before. They were ruined, when they were
required to send laboring children to school; they were
ruined when inspectors were appointed to look into
their works; they were ruined, when such inspectors considered it doubtful whether they were quite justified in
chopping people up with their machinery; they were utterly undone, when it was hinted that perhaps they need
not always make quite so much smoke. Besides Mr.
Bounderby's gold spoon which was generally received in
Coketown, another prevalent fiction was very popular
105

there. It took the form of a threat. Whenever a Coke-towner felt he was ill-used—that is to say, whenever he was not left entirely alone, and it was proposed to hold him accountable for the consequences of any of his acts—he was sure to come out with the awful menace, that he would "sooner pitch his property into the Atlantic." This had terrified the Home Secretary within an inch of his life, on several occasions

However, the Coketowners were so patriotic after all, that they never had pitched their property into the At-antic yet, but, on the contrary, had been kind enough to take mighty good care of it. So there it was, in the haze yonder; and it increased and multiplied.

The streets were hot and dusty on the summer day, and the sun was so bright that it even shone through the heavy vapor drooping over Coketown, and could not be looked at steadily. Stokers emerged from low under-ground doorways into factory yards, and sat on steps, and posts, and palings, wiping their swarthy visages, and contemplating coals. The whole town seemed to be fry-ing in oil. There was a stifling smell of hot oil every-where. The steam-engines shone with it, the dresses of the Hands were soiled with it, the mills throughout their many stories oozed and trickled it. The atmosphere of those Fairy palaces was like the breath of the simoon: and their inhabitants, wasting with heat, toiled languidly in the desert. But no temperature made the melancholy mad elephants more mad or more sane. Their wearisome heads went up and down at the same rate, in hot weather and cold, wet weather and dry, fair weather and foul. The measured motion of their shadows on the walls, was the substitute Coketown had to show for the shadows of rustling woods; while, for the summer hum of insects, it could offer, all the year round, from the dawn of Monday to the night of Saturday, the whirr of shafts and wheels.

Drowsily they whirred all through this sunny day, making the passengers more sleepy and more hot as he passed the humming wall of the mills. Sunblinds, and sprinklings of water, a little cooled the main streets and the shops, but the mills, and the courts and alleys, baked at a fierce heat. Down upon the river that was black and thick with dye, some Coketown boys who were at large— a rare sight there—rowed a crazy boat, which made a spumous track upon the water as it jogged along, while every dip of an oar stirred up vile smells. But the sun itself, however beneficent, generally, was less kind to Coketown than hard frost, and rarely looked intently into any of its closer regions without engendering more death than life. So does the eye of Heaven itself become an evil eye, when incapable or sordid hands are interposed between it and the things it looks upon to bless.

Mrs. Sparsit sat in her afternoon apartment at the Bank, on the shadier side of the frying street. Office-hours were over: and at that period of the day, in warm weather, she usually embellished with her genteel presence, a managerial board-room over the public office. Her own private sitting-room was a story higher, at the window of which post of observation she was ready, every morning, to greet Mr. Bounderby, as he came across the road, with the sympathizing recognition appropriate to a victim. He had been married now a year; and Mrs. Sparsit had never released him from her determined pity a moment.

The Bank offered no violence to the wholesome monotony of the town. It was another red brick house, with black outside shutters, green inside blinds, a black street-door up two white steps, a brazen door-plate, and a brazen door-handle full stop. It was a size larger than Mr. Bounderby's house, as other houses were from a size to half-a-dozen sizes smaller; in all other particulars, it was strictly according to pattern.

Mrs. Sparsit was conscious that by coming in the evening tide among the desks and writing implements, she shed a feminine, not to say also aristocratic, grace upon the office. Seated with her needlework or netting apparatus, at the window, she had a self-laudatory sense of correcting, by her ladylike deportment, the rude business aspect of the place. With this impression of her interesting character upon her, Mrs. Sparsit considered herself, in some sort, the Bank Fairy. The townspeople who, in their passing and repassing, saw her there, regarded her as the Bank Dragon keeping watch over the treasures of the mine.

What those treasures were, Mrs. Sparsit knew as little as they did. Gold and silver coin, precious paper, secrets that if divulged would bring vague destruction upon vague persons (generally, however, people whom she disliked), were the chief items in her ideal catalogue thereof. For the rest, she knew that after office-hours, she reigned supreme over all the office furniture, and over a locked-up iron room with three locks against the door of which strong chamber the light porter laid his head every night, on a truckle bed, that disappeared at cockcrow. Further, she was lady paramount over certain vaults in the basement, sharply spiked off from communication with the predatory world; and over the relics of the current day's work, consisting of blots of ink, worn-out pens, fragments of wafers, and scraps of paper torn so small, that nothing interesting could ever be deciphered on them when Mrs. Sparsit tried. Lastly, she was guardian over a little armory of cutlasses and carbines, arrayed in vengeful order above one of the official chimneypieces; and over that respectable tradition never to be separated from a place of business claiming to be wealthy—a row of fire-buckets—vessels calculated to be of no physical utility on any occasion, but observed to exercise a fine moral influence almost equal to bullion, on most beholders.

A deaf serving-woman and the light porter completed Mrs. Sparsit's empire. The deaf serving-woman was rumored to be wealthy; and a saying had for years gone about among the lower orders of Coketown, that she would be murdered some night when the Bank was shut, for the sake of her money. It was generally considered, indeed, that she had been due some time, and ought to have fallen long ago; but she had kept her life, and her situation, with an ill-conditioned tenacity that occasioned much offence and disappointment.

Mrs. Sparsit's tea was just set for her on a pert little table, with its tripod of legs in an attitude, which she insinuated after office-hours, into the company of the stern leathern-topped, long-board-table that bestrode the middle of the room. The light porter placed the tea-tray on it, knuckling his forehead as a form of homage.

"Thank you, Bitzer," said Mrs. Sparsit.

"Thank *you*, ma'am," returned the light porter. He was a very light porter indeed; as light as in the days when he blinkingly defined a horse, for girl number twenty.

"All is shut up, Bitzer?" said Mrs. Sparsit.

"All is shut up, ma'am."

"And what," said Mrs. Sparsit, pouring out her tea, "is the news of the day? Anything?"

"Well, ma'am, I can't say that I have heard anything particular. Our people are a bad lot, ma'am; but that is no news unfortunately."

"What are the restless wretches doing now?" asked Mrs. Sparsit.

"Merely going on in the old way, ma'am. Uniting, and leaguing, and engaging to stand by one another."

"It is much to be regretted," said Mrs. Sparsit, making her nose more Roman and her eyebrows more Coriolanian in the strength of her severity, "that the united masters allow of any such class-combinations."

"Yes, ma'am," said Bitzer.

"Being united themselves, they ought one and all to set their faces against employing any man who is united with any other man," said Mrs. Sparsit.

"They have done that, ma'am," returned Bitzer; "but it rather fell through, ma'am."

"I do not pretend to understand these things," said Mrs. Sparsit, with dignity, "my lot having been signally cast in a widely different sphere; and Mr. Sparsit, as a Powler, being also quite out of the pale of any such dissensions. I only know that these people must be conquered, and that it's high time it was done, once for all."

"Yes, ma'am," returned Bitzer, with a demonstration of great respect for Mrs. Sparsit's oracular authority. "You couldn't put it clearer, I am sure, ma'am."

As this was his usual hour for having a little confidential chat with Mrs. Sparsit, and as he had already caught her eye and seen that she was going to ask him something, he made a pretence of arranging the rulers, inkstands, and so forth, while that lady went on with her tea, glancing through the open window, down into the street.

"Has it been a busy day, Bitzer? asked Mrs. Sparsit.

"Not a very busy day, my lady. About an average day." He now and then slided into my lady, instead of ma'am, as an involuntary acknowledgment of Mrs. Sparsit's personal dignity and claims to reverence.

"The clerks," said Mrs. Sparsit, carefully brushing an imperceptible crumb of bread and butter from her left hand mitten, "are trustworthy, punctual, and industrious of course?"

"Yes, ma'am, pretty fair, ma'am. With the usual exception."

He held the respectable office of general spy and informer in the establishment, for which volunteer service he received a present at Christmas, over and above his weekly wage. He had grown into an extremely clear-headed, cautious, prudent young man, who was safe to rise in the world. His mind was so exactly regulated, that he had no affections or passions. All his proceedings were the result of the nicest and coldest calculation; and it was not without cause that Mrs. Sparsit habitually observed of him, that he was a young man of the steadiest principle she had ever known. Having satisfied himself, on his father's death, that his mother had a right of settlement in Coketown, this excellent young economist had asserted that right for her with such a steadfast adherence to the principle of the case, that she had been shut up in the workhouse ever since. It must be admitted that he allowed her half a pound of tea a year, which was weak in him: first, because all gifts have an inevitable tendency to pauperize the recipient, and secondly, because his only reasonable transaction in that commodity would have been to buy it for as little as he could possibly give, and sell it for as much as he could possibly get; it having been clearly ascertained by philosophers that in this is comprised the whole duty of man—not a part of man's duty, but the whole.

"Pretty fair, ma'am. With the usual exception, ma'am," repeated Bitzer.

"Ah—h!" said Mrs. Sparsit, shaking her head over her teacup, and taking a long gulp.

"Mr. Thomas, ma'am, I doubt Mr. Thomas very much, ma'am, I don't like his ways at all."

"Bitzer," said Mrs. Sparsit, in a very impressive manner, "do you recollect my having said anything to you respecting names?"

"I beg your pardon, ma'am. It's quite true that you did object to names being used, and they're always best avoided."

"Please to remember that I have a charge here," said Mrs. Sparsit, with her air of state. "I hold a trust here,

Bitzer, under Mr. Bounderby. However improbable both Mr. Bounderby and myself might have deemed it years ago, that he would ever become my patron, making me an annual compliment, I cannot but regard him in that light. From Mr. Bounderby I have received every acknowledgment of my social station, and every recognition of my family descent, that I could possibly expect. More, far more. Therefore, to my patron I will be scrupulously true. And I do not consider, I will not consider, I cannot consider," said Mrs. Sparsit, with a most extensive stock on hand of honor and morality, " that I *should* be scrupulously true, if I allowed names to be mentioned under this roof, that are unfortunately—most unfortunately—no doubt of that—connected with his."

Bitzer knuckled his forehead again, and again begged pardon.

"No, Bitzer," continued Mrs. Sparsit, "say an individual, and I will hear you; say Mr. Thomas, and you must excuse me."

"With the usual exception, ma'am," said Bitzer, trying back, " of an individual."

"Ah—h!" Mrs. Sparsit repeated the ejaculation, the shake of the head over her tea-cup, and the long gulp, as taking up the conversation again at the point where it had been interrupted.

"An individual, ma'am," said Bitzer, " has never been what he ought to have been, since he first came into the place. He is a dissipated, extravagant idler. He is not worth his salt, ma'am. He wouldn't get it either, if he hadn't a friend and relation at court, ma'am!"

"Ah—h!" said Mrs. Sparsit, with another melancholy shake of her he d.

"I only ho ma'am," pursued Bitzer, " that his friend and relation may not supply him with the means of carrying on. Otherwise, ma'am, we know out of whose pocket *that* money comes."

"Ah—h!" sighed Mrs. Sparsit again, with another melancholy shake of her head. " He is to be pitied, m: m. The last party I have alluded to, is to be pitied, ma'an., ' said Bitzer.

"Yes, Bitzer," said Mrs. Sparsit. "I have always pitied the delusion, always."

"As to an individual, ma'am," said Bitzer, dropping his

voice and drawing nearer, " he is as improvident as any of the people in this town. And you know what *their* improvidence is, ma'am. No one could wish to know it better than a lady of your eminence does."

"They would do well," returned Mrs. Sparsit, "to take example by you, Bitzer."

"Thank you, ma'am. But, since you do refer to me, now look at me, ma'am. I have put by a little, ma'am, already. That gratuity which I receive at Christmas, ma'am : I never touch it. I don't even go the length of my wages, though they're not high, ma'am. Why can't they do as I have done, ma'am ? What one person can do, another can do."

This again, was among the fictions of Coketown. Any capitalist there, who had made sixty thousands pounds out of sixpence, always professed to wonder why the sixty thousand nearest Hands didn't each make sixty thousand pounds out of sixpence, and more or less reproached them every one for not accomplishing the little feat. What I did you can do. Why don't you go and do it ?

" As to their wanting recreations, ma'am," said Bitzer, it's stuff and nonsense. *I* don't want recreations. I never did, I never shall ; I don't like 'em. As to their combining together ; there are many of them, I have no doubt, that by watching and informing upon one another could earn a trifle now and then, whether in money or good will, and improve their livelihood. Then, why don't they improve it, ma'am ! It's the first consideration of a rational creature, and it's what they pretend to want."

"Pretend indeed ! " said Mrs. Sparsit.

" I am sure we are constantly hearing, ma'am, till it becomes quite nauseous, concerning their wives and families," said Bitzer. "Why look at me, ma'am ! *I* don't want a wife and family. Why should they ? "

" Because they are improvident," said Mrs. Sparsit.

"Yes, ma'am," returned Bitzer, "that's where it is. If they were more provident and less perverse, ma'am, what would they do? They would say, ' While my hat covers my family,' or, ' While my bonnet covers my family,'— as the case might be, ma'am—' I have only one to feed, and that's the person I most like to feed.' "

" To be sure," assented Mrs. Sparsit, eating muffin.

" Thank you, ma'am," said Bitzer, knuckling his forehead again, in return for the favor of Mrs. Sparsit's improving conversation. "Would you wish a little more hot water, ma'am, or is there anything else that I could fetch you?"

"Nothing just now, Bitzer."

"Thank you, ma'am. I shouldn't wish to disturb you at your meals, ma'am, particularly tea, knowing your partiality for it," said Bitzer, craning a little to look over into the street from where he stood; "but there's a gentleman been looking up here for a minute or so, ma'am, and he has come across as if he was going to knock. That *is* his knock, ma'am, no doubt."

He stepped to the window; and looking out, and drawing in his head again, confirmed himself with, "Yes, ma'am. Would you wish the gentleman to be shown in, ma'am?"

"I don't know who it can be," said Mrs. Sparsit, wiping her mouth and arranging her mittens.

"A stranger, ma'am, evidently."

"What a stranger can want at the Bank at this time of the evening, unless he comes upon some business for which he is too late, I don't know," said Mrs. Sparsit, "but I hold a charge in this establishment from Mr. Bounderby, and I will never shrink from it. If to see him is any part of the duty I have accepted, I will see him. Use your own discretion, Bitzer."

Here the visitor, all unconscious of Mrs. Sparsit's magnanimous words, repeated his knock, so loudly that the light porter hastened down to open the door; while Mrs. Sparsit took the precaution of concealing her little table, with all its appliances upon it, in a cupboard, and then decamped upstairs, that she might appear, if needful, with the greater dignity.

"If you please, ma'am, the gentleman would wish to see you," said Bitzer, with his light eye at Mrs. Sparsit's keyhole. So, Mrs. Sparsit, who had improved the interval by touching up her cap, took her classical features downstairs again, and entered the board-room in the manner of a Roman matron going outside the city walls to treat with an invading general.

The visitor having strolled to the window, and being then engaged in looking carelessly out, was as unmoved by this impressive entry as man could possibly be. He

8

stood whistling to himself with all imaginable coolness, with his hat still on, and a certain air of exhaustion upon him, in part arising from excessive summer, and in part from excessive gentility. For it was to be seen with half an eye that he was a thorough gentleman, made to the model of the time; weary of everything, and putting no more faith in anything than Lucifer.

"I believe, sir," quoth Mrs. Sparsit, "you wished to see me."

"I beg your pardon," he said, turning and removing his hat; "pray excuse me."

"Humph!" thought Mrs. Sparsit, as she made a stately bend. "Five and thirty, good-looking, good figure, good teeth, good voice, good breeding, well-dressed, dark hair, bold eyes." All which Mrs. Sparsit observed in her womanly way—like the Sultan who put his head in the pail of water—merely in dipping down and coming up again.

"Please to be seated, sir," said Mrs. Sparsit.

"Thank you. Allow me." He placed a chair for her, but remained himself carelessly lounging against the table. "I left my servant at the railway looking after the luggage —very heavy train and vast quantity of it in the van— and strolled on, looking about me. Exceedingly odd place. Will you allow me to ask you if it's *always* as black as this?"

"In general much blacker," returned Mrs. Sparsit, in her uncompromising way.

"Is it possible! Excuse me: you are not a native, I think?"

"No, sir," returned Mrs. Sparsit. "It was once my good or ill fortune, as it may be—before I became a widow—to move in a very different sphere. My husband was a Powler."

"Beg your pardon, really!" said the stranger. "Was ——?" Mrs. Sparsit repeated, "A Powler."

"Powler Family," said the stranger, after reflecting a few moments. Mrs. Sparsit signified assent. The stranger seemed a little more fatigued than before.

"You must be very much bored here?" was the inference he drew from the communication.

"I am the servant of circumstances, sir," said Mrs. Sparsit, "and I have long adapted myself to the governing power of my life."

"Very philosophical," returned the stranger, "and very exemplary and laudable, and—" It seemed to be scarcely worth his while to finish the sentence, so he played with his watch-chain wearily.

"May I be permitted to ask, sir," said Mrs. Sparsit, "to what I am indebted for the favor of——"

"Assuredly," said the stranger. "Much obliged to you for reminding me. I am the bearer of a letter of introduction to Mr. Bounderby the banker. Walking through this extraordinarily black town, while they were getting dinner ready at the hotel, I asked a fellow whom I met; one of the working people; who appeared to have been taking a shower-bath of something fluffy, which I assume to be the raw material—"

Mrs. Sparsit inclined her head.

"—Raw material—where Mr. Bounderby, the banker, might reside. Upon which, misled no doubt by the word Banker, he directed me to the Bank. Fact being, I presume, that Mr. Bounderby the Banker, does *not* reside in the edifice in which I have the honor of offering this explanation?"

"No, sir," returned Mrs. Sparsit, "he does not."

"Thank you. I had no intention of delivering my letter at the present moment, nor have I. But strolling on to the Bank to kill time, and having the good fortune to observe at the window," towards which he languidly waved his hand, then slightly bowed, "a lady of a very superior and agreeable appearance, I considered that I could not do better than take the liberty of asking that lady where Mr. Bounderby the Banker *does* live. Which I accordingly venture, with all suitable apologies, to do."

The inattention and indolence of his manner were sufficiently relieved, to Mrs. Sparsit's thinking, by a certain gallantry at ease, which offered her homage too. Here he was, for instance, at this moment, all but sitting on the table, and yet lazily bending over her, as if he acknowledged an attraction in her that made her charming —in her way.

"Banks, I know, are always suspicious, and officially must be," said the stranger, whose lightness and smoothness of speech were pleasant likewise; suggesting matter far more sensible and humorous than it ever contained— which was perhaps a shrewd device of the founder of this numerous sect, whosoever may have been that great man: "therefore I may observe that my letter—here it is—is from the member for this place—Gradgrind—whom I have had the pleasure of knowing in London."

Mrs. Sparsit recognized the hand, intimated that such confirmation was quite unnecessary, and gave Mr. Bounderby's address, with all needful clues and directions in aid.

"Thousand thanks," said the stranger. "Of course you know the Banker well?"

"Yes, sir," rejoined Mrs. Sparsit. "In my dependent relation towards him, I have known him ten years."

"Quite an eternity! I think he married Gradgrind's daughter?"

"Yes," said Mrs. Sparsit, suddenly compressing her mouth, "he had that—honor."

"The lady is quite a philosopher, I am told?"

"Indeed, sir," said Mrs. Sparsit. "*Is* she?"

"Excuse my impertinent curiosity," pursued the stranger, fluttering over Mrs. Sparsit's eyebrows, with a propitiatory air, "but you know the family, and know the world. I am about to know the family, and may have much to do with them. Is the lady so very alarming? Her father gives her such a portentously hardheaded reputation, that I have a burning desire to know. Is she absolutely unapproachable? Repellently and stunningly clever? I see, by your meaning smile, you think not. You have poured balm into my anxious soul. As to age, now. Forty! Five and thirty?"

Mrs. Sparsit laughed outright. "A chit," said she. "Not twenty when she was married."

"I give you my honor, Mrs. Powler," returned the stranger, detaching himself from the table, "that I never was so astonished in my life!"

It really did seem to impress him, to the utmost extent of his capacity of being impressed. He looked at his informant for full a quarter of a minute, and appeared to have the surprise in his mind all the time. "I assure you, Mrs. Powler," he then said, much exhausted, "that the father's manner prepared me for a grim and stony maturity. I am obliged to you, of all things, for correcting so absurd a mistake. Pray excuse my intrusion. Many thanks. Good-day!"

He bowed himself out; and Mrs. Sparsit, hiding in the window curtain, saw him languishing down the street on the shady side of the way, observed of all the town.

"What do you think of the gentleman, Bitzer?" she asked the light porter, when he came to take away.

"Spends a deal of money on his dress, ma'am."

"It must be admitted," said Mrs. Sparsit, "that it's very tasteful."

"Yes, ma'am," returned Bitzer, "if that's worth the money."

"Besides which, ma'am," resumed Bitzer, while he was polishing the table, "he looks to me as if he gamed."

"It's immoral to game," said Mrs. Sparsit.

"It's ridiculous, ma'am," said Bitzer, "because the chances are against the players."

Whether it was that the heat prevented Mrs. Sparsit from working, or whether it was that her hand was out, she did no work that night. She sat at the window, when the sun began to sink behind the smoke; she sat there, when the smoke was burning red, when the color faded from it, when darkness seemed to rise slowly out of the ground, and creep upward, upward, up to the house-tops, up the church steeple, up to the summits of the factory chimneys, up to the sky, Without a candle in the room, Mrs. Sparsit sat at the window, with her hands before her, not thinking much of the sounds of evening; the whooping of boys, the barking of dogs, the rumbling of wheels, the steps and voices of passengers, the shrill street cries, the clogs upon the pavement when it was their hour for going by, the shutting-up of shop-shutters. Not until the light porter announced that her nocturnal sweetbread was ready, did Mrs. Sparsit arouse herself from her reverie, and convey her dense black eyebrows—by that time creased with meditation, as if they needed ironing out —upstairs.

"O, you fool!" said Mrs. Sparsit, when she was alone at her supper. When she meant, she did not say; but she could scarcely have meant the sweetbread.

CHAPTER IL

MR. JAMES HARTHOUSE.

THE Gradgrind party wanted assistance in cutting the throats of the Graces. They went about recruiting; and where could they enlist recruits more hopefully, than among the fine gentlemen who having found out everything to be worth nothing, were equally ready for anything?

Moreover, the healthy spirits who had mounted to this sublime height were attractive to many of the Gradgrind school. They liked fine gentlemen; they pretended that they did not, but they did. They became exhausted in imitation of them; and they yaw-yawed in their speech like them; and they served out, with an enervated air, the little mouldy rations of political economy, on which they regaled their disciples. There never before was seen on earth such a wonderful hybrid race as was thus produced.

Among the fine gentlemen not regularly belonging to the Gradgrind school, there was one of a good family and a better appearance, with a happy turn of humor which had told immensely with the House of Commons on the occasion of his entertaining it with his (and the Board of Directors') view of a railway accident, in which the most careful officers ever known, employed by the most liberal managers ever heard of, assisted by the finest mechanical contrivances ever devised, the whole in action on the best line ever constructed, had killed five people and wounded thirty-two, by a casualty without which the excellence of the whole system would have been positively incomplete. Among the slain was a cow, and among the scattered articles unowned, a widow's cap. And the honorable member had so tickled the House (which has a delicate sense of humor) by putting the cap on the cow, that it became impatient of any serious reference to the Coroner's Inquest, and brought the railway off with Cheers and Laughter.

Now, this gentleman had a younger brother of still better appearance than himself, who had tried life as a

Cornet of Dragoons, and found it a bore ; and had afterwards tried it in the train of an English minister abroad, and found it a bore ; and had then strolled to Jerusalem, and got bored there; and had then gone yachting about the world, and got bored everywhere. To whom this honorable and jocular member fraternally said one day, " Jem, there's a good opening among the hard Fact fellows, and they want men. I wonder you don't go in for statistics." Jem, rather taken by the novelty of the idea, and very hard up for a change, was as ready to "go in " for statistics as for anything else. So, he went in. He coached himself up with a blue-book or two ; and his brother put it about among the hard Fact fellows, and said, " If you want to bring in, for any place, a handsome dog who can make you a devilish good speech, look after my brother Jem, for he's your man." After a few dashes in the public meeting way, Mr. Gradgrind and a council of political sages approved of Jem, and it was resolved to send him down to Coketown, to become known there and in the neighborhood. Hence the letter Jem had last night shown to Mrs. Sparsit, which Mr. Bounderby now held in his hand ; superscribed, " Josiah Bounderby, Esquire, Banker, Coketown. Specially to introduce James Harthouse, Esquire. Thomas Gradgrind."

Within an hour of the receipt of this despatch and Mr. James Harthouse's card Mr. Bounderby put on his hat and went down to the Hotel. There he found Mr. James Harthouse looking out of window, in a state of mind so disconsolate, that he was already half-disposed to " go in " for something else.

" My name, sir," said his visitor, " is Josiah Bounderby, of Coketown."

Mr. James Harthouse was very happy indeed (though he scarcely looked so), to have a pleasure he had long expected.

" Coketown, sir," said Bounderby, obstinately taking a chair, " is not the kind of place you have been accustomed to. Therefore, if you will allow me—or whether you will or not, for I am a plain man—I'll tell you something about it before we go any further."

Mr. Harthouse would be charmed.

" Don't be too sure of that," said Bounderby. " I don't promise it. First of all, you see our smoke. That's meat and drink to us. It's the healthiest thing in the world in all respects, and particularly for the lungs. If you are one of those who want us to consume it, I differ from you. We are not going to wear the bottoms of our boilers out any faster than we wear 'em out now, for all the humbugging sentiment in Great Britain and Ireland."

By way of "going in" to the fullest extent, Mr. Harthouse rejoined, "Mr. Bounderby, I assure you I am entirely and completely of your way of thinking. On conviction."

"I am glad to hear it," said Bounderby. "Now, you have heard a lot of talk about the work in our mills, no doubt. You have? Very good. I'll state the fact of it to you. It's the pleasantest work there is, and it's the lightest work there is, and it's the best paid work there is. More than that, we couldn't improve the mills themselves, unless we laid down Turkey carpets on the floors. Which we're not a-going to do."

"Mr. Bounderby, perfectly right."

"Lastly," said Bounderby, "as to our Hands. There's not a Hand in this town, sir, man, woman, or child, but has one ultimate object in life. That object is, to be fed on turtle soup and venison with a gold spoon. Now, they're not a-going—none of 'em—ever to be fed on turtle soup and venison with a gold spoon. And now you know the place."

Mr. Harthouse professed himself in the highest degree instructed and refreshed, by this condensed epitome of the whole Coketown question.

"Why, you see," replied Mr. Bounderby, "it suits my disposition to have a full understanding with a man, particularly with a public man, when I make his acquaintance. I have only one thing more to say to you, Mr. Harthouse, before assuring you of the pleasure with which I shall respond, to the utmost of my poor ability, to my friend Tom Gradgrind's letter of introduction. You are a man of family. Don't you deceive yourself by supposing for a moment that I am a man of family. I am a bit of dirty riff-raff, and a genuine scrap of tag, rag, and bobtail."

If anything could have exalted Jem's interest in Mr. Bounderby, it would have been this very circumstance. Or, so he told him.

"So now," said Bounderby, "we may shake hands on equal terms. I say, equal terms, because although I know what I am, and the exact depth of the gutter I have lifted myself out of, better than any man does, I am as proud as you are. I am just as proud as you are. Having now asserted my independence in a proper manner, I may come to how do you find yourself, and I hope you're pretty well."

The better, Mr. Harthouse gave him to understand as they shook hands, for the salubrious air of Coketown. Mr. Bounderby received the answer with favor.

"Perhaps you know," said he, "or perhaps you don't know, I married Tom Gradgrind's daughter. If you have nothing better to do than to walk up town with me, I shall be glad to introduce you to Tom Gradgrind's daughter."

"Mr. Bounderby," said Jem, "you anticipate my dearest wishes."

They went out without further discourse; and Mr. Bounderby piloted the new acquaintance who so strongly contrasted with him, to the private red-brick dwelling, with the black outside shutters, the green inside blinds, and the black street door up the two white steps. In the drawing-room of which mansion, there presently entered to them the most remarkable girl Mr. James Harthouse had ever seen. She was so constrained, and yet so careless; so reserved, and yet so watchful; so cold and proud, and yet so sensitively ashamed of her husband's braggart humility—from which she shrunk as if every example of it were a cut or a blow; that it was quite a new sensation to observe her. In face she was no less remarkable than in manner. Her features were handsome; but their natural play was so locked up, that it seemed impossible to guess at their genuine expression. Utterly indifferent, perfectly self-reliant, never at a loss, and yet never at her ease, with her figure in company with them there, and her mind apparently quite alone—it was of no use "going in" yet awhile to comprehend this girl, for she baffled all penetration.

From the mistress of the house, the visitor glanced to the house itself. There was no mute sign of a woman in the room. No graceful little adornment, no fanciful little device, however trivial, anywhere expressed her

influence. Cheerless and comfortless, boastfully and doggedly rich, there the room stared at its present occupants,
unsoftened and unrelieved by the least trace of any
womanly occupation. As Mr. Bounderby stood in the
midst of his household gods so those unrelenting divinities
occupied their places around Mr. Bounderby, and they
were worthy of one another, and well matched.

"This, sir," said Bounderby, "is my wife, Mrs. Bounderby : Tom Gradgrind's eldest daughter. Loo, Mr. James
Harthouse. Mr. Harthouse has joined your father's
muster-roll. If he is not Tom Gradgrind's colleague before long, I believe we shall at least hear of him in connection with one of our neighboring towns. You observe,
Mr. Harthouse, that my wife is my junior. I don't know
what she saw in me to marry me, but she saw something
in me, I suppose, or she wouldn't have married me. She
has lots of expensive knowledge, sir, political and otherwise. If you want to cram for anything, I should be
troubled to recommend you to a better adviser than Loo
Bounderby."

To a more agreeable adviser, or one from whom he
would be more likely to learn, Mr. Harthouse could never
be recommended.

"Come!" said his host. "If you're in the complimentary line, you'll get on here, for you'll meet with no com-
petition. I have never been in the way of learning compliments myself, and I don't profess to understand the
art of paying 'em. In fact, despise 'em. But, your bringing up was different from mine; mine was a real thing,
by George! You're a gentleman, and I don't pretend to
be one. I am Josiah Bounderby of Coketown, and that's
enough for me. However, though I am not influenced by
manners and station, Loo Bounderby may be. She hadn't
my advantages—disadvantages you would call 'em, but
I call 'em advantages—so you'll not waste your power, I
dare say."

"Mr. Bounderby," said Jem, turning with a smile to
Louisa, "is a noble animal in a comparatively natural state,
quite free from the harness in which a conventional hack
like myself works."

"You respect Mr. Bounderby very much," she quietly
returned. "It is natural that you should."

He was disgracefully thrown out, for a gentleman who

had seen so much of the world, and thought, "Now, how am I to take this?"

"You are going to devote yourself, as I gather from what Mr. Bounderby has said, to the service of your country. You have made up your mind," said Louisa, still standing before him where she had first stopped—in all the singular contrariety of her self-possession, and her being obviously very ill at ease—"to show the nation the way out of all its difficulties."

"Mrs. Bounderby," he returned, laughing, "upon my honor, no. I will make no such pretence to you. I have seen a little, here and there, up and down; I have found it all to be very worthless, as everybody has, and as some confess they have, and some do not; and I am going in for your respected father's opinions—really because I have no choice of opinions, and may as well back them as anything else."

"Have you none of your own?" asked Louisa.

"I have not so much as the slightest predilection left. I assure you I attach not the least importance to any opinions. The result of the varieties of boredom I have undergone, is a conviction (unless conviction is too industrious a word for the lazy sentiment I entertain on the subject), that any set of ideas will do just as much good as any other set, and just as much harm as any other set. There's an English family with a charming Italian motto —What will be, will be. It's the only truth going!"

This vicious assumption of honesty in dishonesty—a vice so dangerous, so deadly, and so common—seemed, he observed, a little to impress her in his favor. He followed up the advantage, by saying in his pleasantest manner: a manner to which she might attach as much or as little meaning as she pleased: "The side that can prove anything in a line of units, tens, hundreds, and thousands, Mrs. Bounderby, seems to me to afford the most fun, and to give a man the best chance. I am quite as much attached to it as if I believed it. I am quite ready to go in for it, to the same extent as if I believed it. And what more could I possibly do, if I did believe it!"

"You are a singular politician," said Louisa.

"Pardon me; I have not even that merit. We are the largest party in the state, I assure you, Mrs. Bounderby, if we all fell out of our adopted ranks and were reviewed together."

Mr. Bounderby, who had been in danger of bursting in silence, interposed here with a project for postponing the family dinner till half-past six, and taking Mr. James Harthouse in the meantime on a round of visits to the voting and interesting notabilities of Coketown and its vicinity. The round of visits was made; and Mr. James Harthouse, with a discreet use of his blue coaching, came off triumphantly, though with a considerable accession of boredom.

In the evening, he found the dinner-table laid for four, but they sat down only three. It was an appropriate occasion for Mr. Bounderby to discuss the flavor of the ha'p'orth of stewed eels he had purchased in the streets at eight years old; and also of the inferior water, especially used for laying the dust, with which he had washed down that repast. He likewise entertained his guest over the soup and fish, with the calculation that he (Bounderby) had eaten in his youth at least three horses under the guise of polonies and saveloys. These recitals, Jem, in a languid manner, received with "charming!" every now and then; and they probably would have decided him to "go in" for Jerusalem again to-morrow morning, had he been less curious respecting Louisa.

" Is there nothing," he thought, glancing at her as she sat at the head of the table, where her youthful figure, small and slight, but very graceful, looked as pretty as it looked misplaced; "is there nothing that will move that face?"

Yes! By Jupiter, there was something, and here it was, in an unexpected shape. Tom appeared. She changed as the door opened, and broke into a beaming smile.

A beautiful smile. Mr. James Harthouse might not have thought so much of it, but that he had wondered so long at her impassive face. She put out her hand—a pretty little soft hand; and her fingers closed upon her brother's, as if she would have carried them to her lips.

"Ay, ay?" thought the visitor. "This whelp is the only creature she cares for. So, so!"

The whelp was presented, and took his chair. The appellation was not flattering, but not unmerited.

" When I was your age, young Tom," said Bounderby, " I was punctual, or I got no dinner! "

" When you were my age," returned Tom, " you hadn't a wrong balance to get right, and hadn't to dress afterwards."

" Never mind, that now," said Bounderby.

" Well, then," grumbled Tom. " Don't begin with me."

" Mrs. Bounderby," said Harthouse, perfectly hearing this under-strain as it went on ; " your brother's face is quite familiar to me. Can I have seen him abroad ? Or at some public school, perhaps ? "

" No," she returned, quite interested, " he has never been abroad yet, and was educated here, at home. Tom, love, I am telling Mr. Harthouse that he never saw you abroad."

" No such luck, sir," said Tom.

There was little enough in him to brighten her face, for he was a sullen young fellow, and ungracious in his manner even to her. So much the greater must have been the solitude of her heart, and her need of some one on whom to bestow it. " So much the more is this whelp the only creature she has ever cared for," thought Mr. James Harthouse turning it over and over. " So much the more. So much the more."

Both in his sister's presence, and after she had left the room, the whelp took no pains to hide his contempt for Mr. Bounderby, whenever he could indulge it without the observation of that independent man, by making way faces, or shutting one eye. Without responding to these telegraphic communications, Mr. Harthouse encouraged him much in the course of the evening, and showed an unusual liking for him. At last, when he rose to return to his hotel, and was a little doubtful whether he knew the way by night, the whelp immediately proffered his services as guide, and turned out with him to escort him thither.

CHAPTER III.

THE WHELP.

It was very remarkable that a young gentleman who had been brought up under one continuous system of unnatural restraint, should be a hypocrite; but it was certainly the case with Tom. It was very strange that a young gentleman who had never been left to his own guidance for five consecutive minutes, should be incapable at last of governing himself; but so it was with Tom. It was altogether unaccountable that a young gentleman whose imagination had been strangled in his cradle, should be still inconvenienced by its ghost in the form of grovelling sensualities; but such a monster, beyond all doubt, was Tom.

"Do you smoke?" asked Mr. James Harthouse, when they came to the hotel.

"I believe you!" said Tom.

He could do no less than ask Tom up; and Tom could do no less than go up. What with a cooling drink adapted to the weather, but not so weak as cool; and what with a rarer tobacco than was to be bought in those parts; Tom was soon in a highly free and easy state at his end of the sofa, and more than ever disposed to admire his new friend at the other end. Tom blew his smoke aside, after he had been smoking a little while, and took an observation of his friend. "He don't seem to care about his dress," thought Tom, "and yet how capitally he does it. What an easy swell he is!"

Mr. James Harthouse, happening to catch Tom's eye, remarked that he drank nothing, and filled his glass with his own negligent hand.

"Thank'ee," said Tom. "Thank'ee. Well, Mr. Harthouse, I hope you have had about a dose of old Bounderby to-night." Tom said this with one eye shut up again, and looking over his glass knowingly at his entertainer.

"A very good fellow indeed!" returned Mr. James Harthouse.

"You think so, don't you?" said Tom. And shut up his eye again.

Mr. James Harthouse smiled ; and rising from his end of the sofa, and lounging with his back against the chimney-piece, so that he stood before the empty fire-grate as he smoked, in front of Tom and looking down at him observed :

" What a comical brother-in-law you are ! "

" What a comical brother-in-law old Bounderby is, I think you mean," said Tom.

" You are a piece of caustic, Tom," retorted Mr. James Harthouse.

There was something so very agreeable in being so intimate with such a waistcoat; in being called Tom, in such an intimate way, by such a voice; in being on such off-hand terms so soon, with such a pair of whiskers; that Tom was uncommonly pleased with himself.

" Oh ! I don't care for old Bounderby," said he, " if you mean that. I have always called old Bounderby by the same name when I have talked about him, and I have always thought of him in the same way. I am not going to begin to be polite now, about old Bounderby. It would be rather late in the day."

" Don't mind me," returned James; " but take care when his wife is by, you know."

" His wife ? " said Tom. " My sister Loo? O yes ! " And he laughed, and took a little more of the cooling drink.

James Harthouse continued to lounge in the same place and attitude, smoking his cigar in his own easy way, and looking pleasantly at the whelp, as if he knew himself to be a kind of agreeable demon who had only to hover over him, and he must give up his whole soul if required. It certainly did seem that the whelp yielded to this influence. He looked at his companion sneakingly, he looked at him admiringly, he looked at him boldly, and put up one leg on the sofa.

" My sister Loo ? " said Tom. " *She* never cared for old Bounderby."

" That's the past tense, Tom," returned Mr. James Harthouse, striking the ash from his cigar with his little finger. " We are in the present tense, now."

" Verb neuter, not to care. Indicative mood, present tense. First person singular, I do not care ; second person singular, thou dost not care ; third person singular, she does not care," returned Tom.

"Good! Very quaint!" said his friend. "Though you don't mean it."

"But I *do* mean it," cried Tom. "Upon my honor! Why, you won't tell me, Mr. Harthouse, that you really suppose my sister Loo does care for old Bounderby."

"My dear fellow," returned the other, "what am I bound to suppose, when I find two married people living in harmony and happiness?"

Tom had by this time got both his legs on the sofa. If his second leg had not been already there when he was called a dear fellow he would have put it up at that great stage of the conversation. Feeling it necessary to do something then, he stretched himself out at greater length, and, reclining with the back of his head on the end of the sofa, and smoking with an infinite assumption of negligence, turned his common face, and not too sober eyes, towards the face looking down upon him so carelessly yet so potently.

"You know our governor, Mr. Harthouse," said Tom, "and therefore, you needn't be surprised that Loo married old Bounderby. She never had a lover, and the governor proposed old Bounderby, and she took him."

"Very dutiful in your interesting sister," said Mr. James Harthouse.

"Yes, but she wouldn't have been as dutiful, and it would not have come off as easily," returned the whelp, "if it hadn't been for me."

The tempter merely lifted his eyebrows; but the whelp was obliged to go on.

"*I* persuaded her," he said, with an edifying air of superiority. "I was stuck into old Bounderby's bank (where I never wanted to be), and I knew I should get into scrapes there, if she put old Bounderby's pipe out; so I told her my wishes, and she came into them. She would do anything for me. It was very game of her, wasn't it?"

"It was charming, Tom!"

"Not that it was altogether so important to her as it was to me," continued Tom coolly, "because my liberty and comfort, and perhaps my getting on, depended on it; and she had no other lover, and staying at home was like staying in jail—especially when I was gone. It wasn't as if she gave up another lover for old Bounderby; but still it was a good thing in her."

"Perfectly delightful. And she gets on so placidly."

"Oh," returned Tom, with contemptuous patronage, "she's a regular girl. A girl can get on anywhere. She has settled down to the life, and *She* she don't mind. It does just as well as another. Besides, though Loo is a girl, she's not a common sort of girl. She can shut herself up within herself, and think—as I have often known her sit and watch the fire—for an hour at a stretch."

"Ay, ay? Has resources of her own," said Harthouse, smoking quietly.

"Not so much of that as you may suppose," returned Tom; "for our governor had her crammed with all sorts of dry bones and sawdust. It's his system."

"Formed his daughter on his own model?" suggested Harthouse.

"His daughter? Ah! and everybody else. Why he formed Me that way?" said Tom.

"Impossible!"

"He did, though," said Tom, shaking his head. "I mean to say, Mr. Harthouse, that when I first left home and went to old Bounderby's, I was as flat as a warming-pan, and knew no more about life, than any oyster does."

"Come, Tom! I can hardly believe that. A joke's a joke."

"Upon my soul!" said the whelp, "I am serious; I am indeed!" He smoked with great gravity and dignity for a little while, and then added, in a highly complacent tone, "Oh! I have picked up a little since. I don't deny that. But I have done it myself; no thanks to the governor."

"And your intelligent sister?"

"My intelligent sister is about where she was. She used to complain to me that she had nothing to fall back upon, that girls usually fall back upon; and I don't see how she is to have got over that since. But *she* don't mind," he sagaciously added, puffing at his cigar again. "Girls can always get on, somehow."

"Calling at the Bank yesterday evening, for Mr. Bounderby's address, I found an ancient lady, there, who seems to entertain great admiration for your sister," observed

9

Mr. James Harthouse, throwing away the last small remnant of cigar he had now smoked out.

"Mother Sparsit!" said Tom. "What! you have seen her already, have you?"

His friend nodded. Tom took his cigar out of his mouth, to shut up his eye (which had grown rather unmanageable) with the greater expression, and to tap his nose several times with his finger.

"Mother Sparsit's feeling for Loo is more than admiration, I should think," said Tom. "Say affection and devotion. Mother Sparsit never set her cap at Bounderby when he was a bachelor. Oh no!"

These were the last words spoken by the whelp, before a giddy drowsiness came upon him, followed by complete oblivion. He was roused from the latter state by an uneasy dream of being stirred up with a boot, and also of a voice saying: "Come, it's late. Be off!"

"Well!" he said, scrambling from the sofa. "I must take my leave of you though, I say. Yours is very good tobacco. But it's too mild."

"Yes, it's too mild," returned his entertainer.

"It's—it's ridiculously mild," said Tom. "Where's the door! Good-night!"

He had another odd dream of being taken by a waiter through a mist, which, after giving him some trouble and difficulty, resolved itself into the main street, in which he stood alone. He then walked home pretty easily, though not yet free from an impression of the presence and influence of his new friend—as if he were lounging somewhere in the air, in the same negligent attitude, regarding him with the same look.

The whelp went home, and went to bed. If he had had any sense of what he had done that night, and had been less of a whelp and more of a brother, he might have turned short on the road, might have gone down to the ill-smelling river that was dyed black, might have gone to bed in it for good and all, and have curtained his head forever with its filthy waters.

CHAPTER IV.

MEN AND BROTHERS.

"OH my friends, the down-trodden operatives of Coke-town! Oh my friends and fellow-countrymen, the slaves of an iron-handed and a grinding despotism! Oh my friends and fellow-sufferers, and fellow-workmen and fellow-men! I tell you that the hour is come, when we must rally round one another as One united power, and crumble into dust the oppressors that too long have battened upon the plunder of our families, upon the sweat of our brows, upon the labor of our hands, upon the strength of our sinews, upon the God-created glorious rights of Humanity, and upon the holy and eternal privileges of Brotherhood!"

"Good!" "Hear, hear, hear!" "Hurrah!" and other cries, arose in many voices from various parts of the densely crowded and suffocatingly close Hall, in which the orator, perched on a stage, delivered himself of this and what other froth and fume he had in him. He had declaimed himself into a violent heat, and was as hoarse as he was hot. By dint of roaring at the top of his voice under a flaring gas-light, clenching his fists, knitting his brows, setting his teeth, and pounding with his arms, he had taken so much out of himself by this time, that he was brought to a stop, and called for a glass of water.

As he stood there, trying to quench his fiery face with his drink of water, the comparison between the orator and the crowd of attentive faces turned towards him, was extremely to his disadvantage. Judging him by Nature's evidence, he was above the mass in very little but the stage on which he stood. In many great respects he was essentially below them. He was not so honest, he was not so manly, he was not so good-humored; he substituted cunning for their simplicity, and passion for their safe solid sense. An ill-made, high-shouldered man, with lowering brows, and his features crushed into an habitually sour expression, he contrasted most unfavorably, even in his mongrel dress, with the great body of his hearers in their plain working clothes. Strange as it always is to consider any assembly in the act of submissively resigning itself to the dreariness of some complacent person, lord or commoner, whom three-fourths of it could, by no human means, raise out of the slough of inanity to their own intellectual level, it was particularly strange, and it was even particularly affecting, to see this crowd of earnest faces, whose honesty in the main no competent observer free from bias could doubt, so agitated by such a leader.

Good! Hear, hear! Hurrah! The eagerness both of attention and intention, exhibited in all the countenances, made them a most impressive sight. There was no carelessness, no languor, no idle curiosity; none of the many shades of indifference to be seen in all other assemblies, visible for one moment there. That every man felt his condition to be, somehow or other, worse than it might be; that every man considered it incumbent on him to join the rest, towards the making of it better; that every man felt his only hope to be in his allying himself to the comrades by whom he was surrounded; and that in this belief, right or wrong (unhappily wrong then), the whole of that crowd were gravely, deeply, faithfully in earnest; must have been as plain to any one who chose to see what was there, as the bare beams of the roof and the whitened brick walls. Nor could any such spectator fail to know in his own breast, that these men, through their very delusions, showed great qualities, susceptible of being turned to the happiest and best account; and that to pretend (on the strength of sweeping axioms, howsoever cut and dried) that they went astray wholly without cause, and of their own irrational wills, was to pretend that there could be smoke without fire, death without birth, harvest without seed, anything or everything produced from nothing.

The orator having refreshed himself, wiped his corrugated forehead from left to right several times with his handkerchief folded into a pad, and concentrated all his revived forces, in a sneer of great disdain and bitterness.

"But, oh my friends and brothers! Oh men and Englishmen, the down-trodden operatives of Coketown! What shall we say of that man—that working-man, that I should find it necessary so to libel the glorious name— who, being practically and well acquainted with the grievances and wrongs of you, the injured pith and marrow of this land, and having heard you, with a noble and majestic unanimity that will make Tyrants tremble, resolve for to subscribe to the funds of the United Aggregate Tribunal, and to abide by the injunctions issued by that body for your benefit, whatever they may be—what, I ask you, will you say of that working-man, since such I must acknowledge him to be, who, at such a time, deserts his post, and sells his flag; who, at such a time, turns a traitor and a craven and a recreant; who, at such a time, is not ashamed to make to you the dastardly and humiliating avowal that he will hold himself aloof, and will *not* be one of those associated in the gallant stand for Freedom and for Right?"

The assembly was divided at this point. There were some groans and hisses, but the general sense of honor was much too strong for the condemnation of a man unheard. "Be sure you're right, Slackbridge!" "Put him up!" "Let's hear him!" Such things were said on many sides. Finally one strong voice called, "Is the man heer? If the man's heer, Slackbridge, let's hear the man himseln, 'stead o' yo." Which was received with a round of applause.

Slackbridge, the orator, looked about him with a withering smile; and holding out his right hand at arm's length (as the manner of all Slackbridges is), to still the thundering sea, waited until there was a profound silence.

"Oh my friends and fellow-men!" said Slackbridge then, shaking his head with violent scorn, "I do not wonder that you, the prostrate sons of labor, are incredulous of the existence of such a man. But he who sold his birthright for a mess of pottage existed, and Judas Iscariot existed, and Castlereagh existed, and this man exists!"

Here, a brief press and confusion near the stage, ended in the man himself standing at the orator's side before the concourse. He was pale and a little moved in the face—his lips especially showed it; but he stood quiet, with his left hand at his chin, waiting to be heard. There was a chairman to regulate the proceedings, and this functionary now took the case into his own hands.

"My friends," said he, "by virtue o' my office as your president, I askes o' our friend Slackbridge, who may be a little over hetter in this business, to take his seat, whiles this man Stephen Blackpool is heern. You all know this man Stephen Blackpool. You know him awlung o' his misfort'ns, and his good name."

With that, the chairman shook him frankly by the hand, and sat down again. Slackbridge likewise sat down, wiping his hot forehead—always from left to right, and never the reverse way.

"My friends," Stephen began, in the midst of a dead calm; "I ha' hed what's been spok'n o' me, and 'tis lickly that I shan't mend it. But I'd liefer you'd hearn the truth concernin' myseln, fro my lips than fro onny other man's though I never cud'n speak afore so monny, wi'out bein moydert and muddled."

Slackbridge shook his head as if he would shake it off, in his bitterness.

"I'm th' one single Hand in Bounderby's mill, o' a' the men theer, as don't coom in wi' th' proposed reg'lations. I canna' coom in wi' 'em. My friends, I doubt their doin' yo onny good. Licker they'll do you hurt."

Slackbridge laughed, folded his arms, and frowned sarcastically.

"But 't ant sommuch for that as I stands out. If that were aw, I'd coom in wi' th' rest. But I ha' my reasons—mine, yo see—for being hindered; not on'y now, but awlus—awlus—life long!"

Slackbridge jumped up and stood beside him, gnashing and tearing. "Oh my friends, what but this did I tell you? Oh my fellow-countrymen, what warning but this did I give you? And how shows this recreant conduct in a man on whom unequal laws are known to have fallen heavy? Oh you Englishmen, I ask you how does this subornation show in one of yourselves, who is thus consenting to his own undoing and to yours, and to your children's and your children's children's?"

There was some applause, and some crying of Shame upon the man; but the greater part of the audience were quiet. They looked at Stephen's worn face, rendered more pathetic by the homely emotions it evinced; and, in the kindness of their nature, they were more sorry than indignant.

"'Tis this Delegate's trade for t' speak," said Stephen, "an' he's paid for 't, and he knows his work. Let him keep to 't. Let him give no heed to what I ha had'n to bear. That's not for him. That's not for nobbody but me."

There was a propriety, not to say a dignity in these words, that made the hearers yet more quiet and attentive. The same strong voice called out, "Slackbridge, let the man be heern, and howd thee tongue?" Then the place was wonderfully still.

"My brothers," said Stephen, whose low voice was distinctly heard, "and my fellow-workmen—for that yo are to me, though not, as I knows on, to this delegate here— I ha but a word to sen, and I could sen nommore if I was to speak till Strike o' day. I know weel, aw what's afore me. I know weel that yo aw resolve to ha nommore ado wi' a man who is not wi' yo in this matter. I know weel that if I was a lyin' parist i' th' road, yo'd feel it right to pass me by, as a forrenner and stranger. What I ha getn, I mun mak th' best on."

"Stephen Blackpool," said the chairman, rising, "think on 't agen. Think on 't once agen, lad, afore thou'rt shunned by aw owd friends."

There was an universal murmur to the same effect, though no man articulated a word. Every eye was fixed on Stephen's face. To repent of his determination, would be to take a load from all their minds. He looked around him, and knew that it was so. Not a grain of anger with them was in his heart; he knew them, far below their surface weaknesses and misconceptions, as no one but their fellow-laborer could.

"I ha thowt on't, above a bit, sir. I simply canna coom in. I mun go th' way as lays afore me. I mun tak my leave o' aw heer."

He made a sort of reverence to them by holding up his arms, and stood for the moment in that attitude: not speaking until they slowly dropped at his sides.

"Monny's the pleasant word as soom heer has spok'n wi' me; monny's the face I see heer, as I first seen when I were yoong and lighter heart'n than now. I ha never had no fratch afore, sin ever I were born, wi' any o' my like; Gonnows I ha' none now that's o' my makin'. Yo'll ca' me traitor and that—yo I mean t' say," addressing Slackbridge, "but 'tis easier to ca' than mak' out. So let be."

He had moved away a pace or two to come down from the platform, when he remembered something he had not said, and returned again.

"Haply," he said, turning his furrowed face slowly about, that he might as it were individually address the whole audience, those both near and distant; "haply, when this question has been tak'n up and discoosed, there'll be a threat to turn out if I'm let to work among yo. I hope I shall die ere ever such a time cooms, and I shall work solitary among yo unless it cooms—truly, I mun do 't, my friends; not to brave yo, but to live. I ha nobbut work to live by; and wherever can I go, I who ha worked sin I were no heighth at aw, in Coketown heer? I mak' no complaints o' bein turned to the wa', o' being outcasten and overlooken fro this time forrard, but I hope I shall be let to work. If there is any right for me at aw, my friends, I think 'tis that."

Not a word was spoken. Not a sound was audible in the building, but the slight rustle of men moving a little apart, all along the centre of the room, to open a means of passing out, to the man with whom they had all bound themselves to renounce companionship. Looking at no one, and going his way with a lowly steadiness upon him that asserted nothing and sought nothing, Old Stephen, with all his troubles on his head, left the scene.

Then Slackbridge, who had kept his oratorical arm extended during the going out, as if he were repressing with infinite solicitude and by a wonderful moral power the vehement passions of the multitude, applied himself to raising their spirits. Had not the Roman Brutus, oh my British countrymen, condemned his son to death; and had not the Spartan mothers, oh my soon to be victorious friends, driven their flying children on the points of their enemies' swords? Then was it not the sacred duty of the men of Coketown, with forefathers before them, and an admiring world in company with them, and a posterity to come after them, to hurl out traitors from the tents they had pitched in a sacred and a God-like cause? The winds of heaven answered Yes; and bore Yes, east, west, north, and south. And consequently three cheers for the United Aggregate Tribunal!

Slackbridge acted as fugleman, and gave the time. The multitude of doubtful faces (a little conscience stricken) brightened at the sound, and took it up. Private feeling must yield to the common cause. Hurrah! The roof yet vibrated with the cheering, when the assembly dispersed.

Thus easily did Stephen Blackpool fall into the loneliest of lives, the life of solitude among a familiar crowd. The stranger in the land who looks into ten thousand faces for some answering look and never finds it, is in cheering society as compared with him who passes ten averted faces daily, that were once the countenances of friends. Such experience was to be Stephen's now, in every waking moment of his life; at his work, on his way to it and from it, at his door, at his window, everywhere. By general consent, they even avoided that side of the street on which he habitually walked; and left it, of all the working men, to him only.

He had been for many years, a quiet silent man, associating but little with other men, and used to companionship with his own thoughts. He had never known before the strength of the want in his heart for the frequent recognition of a nod, a look, a word; or the immense amount of relief that had been poured into it by drops through such small means. It was even harder than he could have believed possible, to separate in his own conscience his abandonment by all his fellows from a baseless sense of shame and disgrace.

The first four days of his endurance were days so long and heavy, that he began to be appalled by the prospect before him. Not only did he see no Rachael all the time, but he avoided every chance of seeing her; for, although he knew that the prohibition did not yet formally extend to the women working in the factories, he found that some of them with whom he was acquainted were changed to him, and he feared to try others, and dreaded that Rachael might be even singled out from the rest if she were seen in his company. So, he had been quite alone during the four days, and had spoken to no one, when, as he was leaving his work at night, a young man of a very light complexion accosted him in the street.

"Your name's Blackpool, ain't it?" said the young man.

Stephen colored to find himself with his hat in his hand, in his gratitude for being spoken to, or in the suddenness of it, or both. He made a feint of adjusting the lining, and said, "Yes."

"You are the Hand they have sent to Coventry, I mean?" said Bitzer, the very light young man in question.

Stephen answered " Yes," again.

" I supposed so, from their all appearing to keep away from you. Mr. Bounderby wants to speak to you. You know his house, don't you ? "

Stephen said " Yes," again.

Then go straight up there, will you ? " said Bitzer. " You're expected, and have only to tell the servant it's you. I belong to the Bank ; so, if you go straight up without me (I was sent to fetch you), you'll save me a walk."

Stephen, whose way had been in the contrary direction, turned about, and betook himself as in duty bound, to the red-brick castle of the giant Bounderby.

CHAPTER V.

MEN AND MASTERS.

" WELL Stephen," said Bounderby, in his windy manner, " what's this I hear ? What have these pests of the earth been doing to *you?* Come in, and speak up."

It was into the drawing-room that he was thus bidden. A tea-table was set out; and Mr. Bounderby's young wife, and her brother, and a great gentleman from London, were present. To whom Stephen made his obeisance, closing the door and standing near it, with his hat in his hand.

" This is the man I was telling you about, Harthouse," said Mr. Bounderby. The gentleman he addressed, who was talking to Mrs. Bounderby on the sofa, got up, saying in an indolent way, " Oh really ? " and dawdled to the hearthrug where Mr. Bounderby stood.

" Now," said Bounderby, " speak up ! "

After the four days he had passed, this address fell rudely and discordantly on Stephen's ear. Besides being a rough handling of his wounded mind, it seemed to assume that he really was the self-interested deserter he had been called.

" What were it, sir," said Stephen, " as yo were pleased to want wi' me ? "

" Why, I have told you," returned Bounderby. " Speak

up like a man, since you are a man, and tell us about yourself and this Combination."

" Wi' yor pardon, sir," said Stephen Blackpool, " I ha' nowt to sen about it.

Mr. Bounderby, who was always more or less like a Wind, finding something in his way here, began to blow at it directly.

" Now, look here, Harthouse," ssid he, " here's a specimen of 'em. When this man was here once before, I warned this man against the mischievous strangers who are always about—and who ought to be hanged wherever they are found—and I told this man that he was going in the wrong direction. Now, would you believe it, that although they have put this mark upon him, he is such a slave to them still, that he's afraid to open his lips about them ? "

" I sed as I had nowt to sen, sir; not as I was fearfo' o' openin' my lips."

" You said. Ah! *I* know what you said; more than that, I know what you mean, you see. Not always the same thing, by the Lord Harry ! Quite different things. You had better tell us at once, that that fellow Slackbridge is not in the town, stirring up the people to mutiny; and that he is not a regular qualified leader of the people: that is, a most confounded scoundrel. You had better tell us so at once; you can't deceive me. You want to tell us so. Why don't you?"

" I'm as sooary as yo, sir, when the people's leaders is bad," said Stephen shaking his head. " They take such as offers. Haply 'tis na the sma'est o' their misfortuns when they can get no better."

The wind began to get boisterous.

" Now, you'll think this pretty well, Harthouse," said Mr. Bounderby. " You'll think this tolerably strong. You'll say, upon my soul this is a tidy specimen of what my friends have to deal with; but this is nothing, sir ! You shall hear me ask this man a question. Pray, Mr. Blackpool "—wind springing up very fast—" may I take the liberty of asking you how it happens that you refused to be in this Combination ? "

" How't happens? "

" Ah ! " said Mr. Bounderby, with his thumbs in the arms of his coat, and jerking his head and shutting his eyes in confidence with the opposite wall: " how it happens."

" I'd leefer not coom to 't, sir ; but sin you put th' question—an not want'n t' be ill-maner'n—I'll answer. I ha passed a promess."

" Not to me, you know," said Bounderby. (Gusty weather with deceitful calms. One now prevailing.)

" O no, sir. Not to yo."

" As for me, any consideration for me has had just nothing at all to do with it," said Bounderby, still in confidence with the wall. " If only Josiah Bounderby of Coketown had been in question, you would have joined and made no bones about it?"

" Why, yes, sir. 'Tis true."

" Though he knows," said Mr. Bounderby, now blowing a gale, " that there are a set of rascals and rebels whom transportation is too good for! Now, Mr. Harthouse, you have been knocking about in the world some time. Did you ever meet with anything like that man out of this blessed country?" And Mr. Bounderby pointed him out for inspection, with an angry finger.

" Nay, ma'am," said Stephen Blackpool, staunchly protesting against the words that had been used, and instinctively addressing himself to Louisa, after glancing at her face. "Not rebels, nor yet rascals. Nowt o' th' kind, ma'am, nowt o the kind. They've not doon me a kindness, ma'am, as I know and feel. But there's not a dozen men amoong 'em, ma'am—a dozen? Not six—but what believes as he has done his duty by the rest and by himseln. God forbid as I, that ha' known, and had'n experience o' these men aw my life—I, that ha' ett'n an droonken wi' 'em, and seet'n wi' 'em and toil'n wi' 'em and lov'n em, should fail fur to stan by 'em wi' the truth, let 'em ha doon to me what they may !"

He spoke with the rugged earnestness of his place and character—deepened perhaps by a proud consciousness that he was faithful to his class under all their mistrust ; but he fully remembered where he was, and did not even raise his voice.

" No, ma'am, no. They're true to one another, faithfo' to one another, 'fectionate to one another, e'en to death. Be poor amoong 'em, be sick amoong 'em, grieve amoong 'em for onny o' th' monny causes that carries grief to the poor man's door, and they'll be tender wi' yo, gentle wi' yo, comfortable wi' yo, Chrisen wi' yo. Be sure o' that, ma'am. They'd be riven to bits, ere ever they'd be different."

"In short," said Mr. Bounderby, "it's because they are so full of virtues that they have turned you adrift. Go through with it while you are about it. Out with it."

"How 'tis, ma'am," resumed Stephen, appearing still to find his natural refuge in Louisa's face, "that what is in us fok, seems to turn us most to trouble an' misfort'n an' mistake, I dunno. But 'tis so. I know 'tis, as I know the heavens is over me ahint the smoke. We're patient too and wants in general to do right. An' I canna think the fawt is aw wi' us."

"Now, my friend," said Mr. Bounderby, whom he could not have exasperated more, quite unconscious of it though he was, than by seeming to appeal to any one else, "if you will favor me with your attention for half a minute, I should like to have a word or two with you. You said just now, that you had nothing to tell us about this business. You are quite sure of that before we go any further."

"Sir, I am sure on 't."

"Here's a gentleman from London present," Mr. Bounderby made a backhanded point at Mr. James Harthouse with his thumb, "a Parliament gentleman. I should like him to hear a short bit of dialogue between you and me, instead of taking the substance of it—for I know precious well, beforehand, what it will be ; nobody knows better than I do, take notice!—instead of receiving it on trust from my mouth."

Stephen bent his head to the gentleman from London, and showed a rather more troubled mind than usual. He turned his eyes involuntarily to his former refuge, but at a look from that quarter (expressive though instantaneous) he settled them on Mr. Bounderby's face.

"Now, what do you complain of?" asked Mr. Bounderby.

"I ha' not coom here, sir," Stephen reminded him, "to complain. I coom for that I were sent for."

"What," repeated Mr. Bounderby, folding his arms, "do you people, in a general way, complain of?"

Stephen looked at him with some lit le irresolution for a moment, and then seemed to make up his mind.

"Sir, I were never good at showin o't, though I ha had'n my share in feeling o't. 'Deed we are in a muddle, sir. Look round town—so rich as 'tis—and see the numbers o' people as has been broughten into bein heer, fur to weave, an to card, an to piece out a livin', aw the same one way, somehows, twixt their cradles and their graves. Look how we live, an wheer we live, an in what numbers, and by what chances, and wi' what sameness; and look how the mills is awlus a goin, and how they never works us no nigher to ony dis'ant object—ceptin awlus Death. Look how you considers of us; and writes of us, and talks of us, and goes up wi' yor deputation to Secretaries o' State 'bout us, and how yo are awlus right, and how we are awlus wrong, and never had'n no reason in us sin ever we were born. Look how this ha growen an growen, sir, bigger an bigger, broader an broader, harder an harder, fro year to year, fro generation unto generation. Who can look on 't, sir, and fairly tell a man 'tis not a muddle?"

"Of course," said Mr. Bounderby. "Now perhaps you'll let the gentleman know how you would set this muddle (as you're so fond of calling it) to rights."

"I donno, sir. I canna be expecten to 't. 'Tis not me as should be looken to for that, sir. 'Tis them as is put ower me, and ower aw the rest of us. What do they tak upon themseln, sir, if not to do 't?"

"I'll tell you something towards it, at any rate," returned Mr. Bounderby. "We will make an example of half a dozen Slackbridges. We'll indict the blackguards for felony, and get 'em shipped off to penal settlements."

Stephen gravely shook his head.

"Don't tell me we won't, man," said Mr. Bounderby, by this time blowing a hurricane, "because we will, I tell you!"

"Sir," returned Stephen, with the quiet confidence of absolute certainty, "if yo was t' tak a hundred Slackbridges—aw as there is, and aw the number ten times towd—an' was t' sew 'em up in separate sacks, an sink 'em in the deepest ocean as were made ere ever dry land coom to be, yo'd leave the muddle just wheer 'tis. Mischeevous strangers!" said Stephen, with an anxious smile; "when ha we not heern, I am sure, sin ever we can

call to mind, o' th' mischeevous strangers! 'Tis not by
them the trouble's made, sir. 'Tis nowt wi' *them* 't com-
mences. I ha no favor for 'em—I ha no reason to favor
'em—but 'tis hopeless and useless to dream o' taken them
fro their trade, 'stead o' taken their trade fro them! Aw
that's now about me in this room were heer afore I coom,
an will be heer when I am gone. Put that clock aboard
a ship an pack it off to Norfolk Island, an the time
will go on just the same. So 'tis wi' Slackbridge every
bit."

Reverting for a moment to his former refuge, he observed
a cautionary movement of her eyes towards the door.
Stepping back, he put his hand upon the lock. But he
had not spoken out of his own will and desire; and he
felt it in his heart a noble return for his late injurious
treatment to be faithful to the last to those who had re-
pudiated him. He stayed to finish what was in his mind.

"Sir, I canna, wi' my little learning an my common
way, tell the genelman what will better aw this—though
some working men o' this town could, above my powers
—but I can tell him what I know will never do 't. The
strong hand will never do 't. Vict'ry and triumph will
never do 't. Agreeing fur to mak one side unnat'rally
awlus and for ever right, and toother side unnat'rally
awlus and for ever wrong will never, never do 't. Nor
yet lettin alone will never do 't. Let thousands upon
thousands alone, aw leading the like lives and aw faw'en
into the like muddle and they will be as one, and yo will be
as anoother, wi' a black unpassable world betwixt yo, just
as long or short a time as sitch-like misery can last. Not
drawin nigh to fok, wi' kindness and patience an cheery
ways, that so draws nigh to one another in their monny
troubles, and so cherishes one another in their distresses
wi' what they need themseln—like, I humbly believe as no
people the genelman ha seen in aw his travels can beat
—will never do 't till th' Sun turns t' ice. Most o' aw,
rating 'em as so much Power, and reglatin 'em as if they
was figures in a soom, or machines: wi'out loves and
likens, wi'out memories and inclinations, wi'out souls to
weary and souls to hope—when aw goes quiet, draggin
on wi' 'em as if they'd nowt o' th' kind, and when aw
goes onquiet, reproachin 'em for their want o' sitch human-
ly feelins in their dealins wi' yo—this will never do 't sir,
till God's work is onmade.'

Stephen stood with the open door in his hand, waiting to know if anything more were expected of him.

"Just stop a moment," said Mr. Bounderby, excessively red in the face. "I told you, the last time you were here with a grievance, that you had better turn about and come out of that. And I also told you, if you remember, that I was up to the gold spoon look-out."

"I were not up to 't myseln, sir; I do assure yo."

"Now it's clear to me," said Mr. Bounderby, "that you are one of those chaps who have always got a grievance. And you go about, sowing it and raising crops. That's the business of *your* life, my friend."

Stephen shook his head, mutely protesting that indeed he had other business to do for his life.

"You are such a waspish, raspish, ill-conditioned chap, you see," said Mr. Bounderby, "that even your own Union, the men who know you best, will have nothing to do with you. I never thought those fellows could be right in anything; but I tell you what! I so far go along with them for a novelty, that I'll have nothing to do with you either."

Stephen raised his eyes quickly to his face.

"You can finish off what you're at," said Mr. Bounderby, with a meaning nod, "and then go elsewhere."

"Sir, yo know weel," said Stephen expressively, "that if I canna get work wi' yo, I canna get it elsewheer."

The reply was, "What I know, I know; and what you know, you know. I have no more to say about it."

Stephen glanced at Louisa again, but her eyes were raised to his no more; therefore, with a sigh, and saying, barely above his breath, "Heaven help us aw in this world!" he departed.

CHAPTER VI.

FADING AWAY.

It was falling dark when Stephen came out of Mr. Bounderby's house. The shadows of night had gathered so fast, that he did not look about him when he closed the door, but plodded straight along the street. Nothing was further from his thoughts than the curious old woman he had encountered on his previous visit to the same house, when he heard a step behind him that he knew, and turning, saw her in Rachael's company.

He saw Rachael first, as he had heard her only.

" Ah, Rachael, my dear ! Missus, thou wi' her ! "

" Well, and now you are surprised to be sure, and with reason I must say," the old woman returned. " Here I am again, you see."

" But how wi' Rachael ? " said Stephen, falling into their step, walking between them, and looking from one to the other.

" Why, I come to be with this good lass pretty much as I came to be with you," said the old woman, cheerfully, taking the reply upon herself. " My visiting time is later this year than usual, for I have been rather troubled with shortness of breath, and so put it off till the weather was fine and warm. For the same reason, I don't make all my journey in one day, but divide it into two days, and get a bed to-night at the Travellers' Coffee-House down by the rail-road (a nice clean house), and go back Parliamentary, at six in the morning. Well, but what has this to do with this good lass, says you? I'm going to tell you. I have heard of Mr. Bounderby being married. I read it in the paper, where it looked grand—oh, it looked fine ! " the old woman dwelt on it with strange enthusiasm : " and I want to see his wife. I have never seen her yet. Now, if you'll be-lieve me, she hasn't come out of that house since noon to-day. So not to give her up too easily, I was waiting about, a little last bit more, when I passed close to this good lass two or three times ; and her face being so friendly I spoke to her, and she spoke to me. There ! " said the old woman to Stephen, " you can make all the rest out for yourself now, a deal shorter than I can, I dare say ! "

Once again, Stephen had to conquer an instinctive pro-pensity to dislike this old women, though her manner was as honest and simple as a manner possibly could be. With a gentleness that was as natural to him as he knew it to be to Rachael, he pursued the subject that interested her in her old age.

" Well, missus," said he, " I ha seen the lady, and she were young and hansom. Wi' fine dark thinkin eyes, and a still way, Rachael, as I ha never seen the like on."

" Young and handsome. Yes ! " cried the old woman,

10

quite delighted. "As bonny as a rose! And what a happy wife!"

"Aye, missus, I suppose she be," said Stephen. But with a doubtful glance at Rachael.

"Suppose she be? She must be. She's your master's wife," returned the old woman.

Stephen nodded assent. "Though as to master," said he, glancing again at Rachael, "not master onny more. That's aw enden twixt him and me."

"Have you left his work, Stephen?" asked Rachael, anxiously and quickly.

"Why, Rachael," he replied, "whether I ha lef'n his work, or whether his work ha lef'n me, cooms t' th' same. His work and me are parted. 'Tis as weel so—better, I were thinkin when yo coom up wi' me. It would ha brought'n trouble upon trouble if I had stayed theer. Haply 'tis a kindness to monny that I go; haply 'tis a kindness to myseln; anyways it mun be done. I mun turn my face fro Coketown fur th' time, and seek a fort'n dear, by beginnin fresh."

"Where will you go, Stephen?"

"I dunno t' night," said he, lifting off his hat, and smoothing his thin hair with the flat of his hand. "But I'm not goin t' night, Rachael, not yet t' morrow. Tan't easy overmuch, t' know wheer t' turn, but a good heart will coom to me."

Herein, too, the sense of even thinking unselfishly aided him. Before he had so much as closed Mr. Bounderby's door, he had reflected that at least his being obliged to go away was good for her, as it would save her from the chance of being brought into question for not withdrawing from him. Though it would cost him a hard pang to leave her, and though he could think of no similar place in which his condemnation would not pursue him, perhaps it was almost a relief to be forced away from the endurance of the last four days, even to unknown difficulties and distresses.

So he said with truth, "I'm more leetsome, Rachael, under 't, than I couldn ha believed." It was not her part to make his burden heavier. She answered with her comforting smile, and the three walked on together.

Age, especially when it strives to be self-reliant and cheerful, finds much consideration among the poor. The old woman was so decent and contented, and made so light of her infirmities, though they had increased upon her since her former interview with Stephen, that they both took an interest in her. She was too sprightly to allow of their walking at a slow pace on her account, but she was very grateful to be talked to, and very willing to talk to any extent: so, when they came to their part of the town, she was more brisk and vivacious than ever.

"Coom to my poor place, missus," said Stephen, "and tak a coop o' tea. Rachael will coom then; and arter-wards I'll see thee safe t' thy Travellers' lodgin. 'T may be long, Rachael, ere ever I ha th' chance o' thy coompany agen."

They complied, and the three went on to the house where he lodged. When they turned into the narrow street, Stephen glanced at his window with a dread that always haunted his desolate home; but it was open, as he had left it, and no one was there. The evil spirit of his life had flitted away again, months ago, and he had heard no more of her since. The only evidence of her last return now, were the scantier movables in his room, and the grayer hair upon his head.

He lighted a candle, set out his little tea-board, got hot water from below, and brought in small portions of tea and sugar, a loaf, and some butter from the nearest shop. The bread was new and crusty, the butter fresh, and the sugar lump, of course—in fulfilment of the standard testimony of the Coketown magnates, that these people lived like princes, sir. Rachael made the tea (so large a party necessitated the borrowing of a cup), and the visitor enjoyed it mightily. It was the first glimpse of sociality the host had had for many days. He too, with the world a wide heath before them, enjoyed the meal—again in corroboration of the magnates, as exemplifying the utter want of calculation on the part of these people, sir.

"I ha never thowt yet, missus," said Stephen, "o' askin' thy name."

The old lady announced herself as "Mrs. Pegler."

"A widder, I think?" said Stephen.

"Oh, many long years?" Mrs. Pegler's husband (one of the best on record) was already dead, by Mrs. Pegler's calculation, when Stephen was born.

" 'Twere a bad job, too, to lose so good a one," said Stephen.

" Onny children ? "

Mrs. Pegler's cup rattling against her saucer as she held it, denoted some nervousness on her part. " No," she said. " Not now, not now."

" Dead, Stephen," Rachael softly hinted.

" I'm sooary I ha spok'n on't," said Stephen, " I ought t' hadn in my mind as I might touch a sore place. I—I blame myseln."

While he excused himself, the old lady's cup rattled more and more. " I had a son," she said, curiously distressed, and not by any of the usual appearances of sorrow ; " and he did well, wonderfully well. But he is not to be spoken of, if you please. He is—" Putting down her cup, she moved her hands as if she would have added, by her action, " dead ! " Then she said aloud, " I have lost him."

Stephen had not yet got the better of his having given the old lady pain, when his landlady came stumbling up the narrow stairs, and calling him to the door, whispered in his ear. Mrs. Pegler was by no means deaf, for she caught a word as it was uttered.

" Bounderby ! " she cried in a suppressed voice, starting up from the table. " Oh hide me ! Don't let me be seen for the world. Don't let him come up till I've got away. Pray, pray ! " She trembled, and was excessively agitated ; getting behind Rachael, when Rachael tried to reassure her ; and not seeming to know what she was about.

" But hearken, missus, hearken ; " said Stephen, astonished. " 'Tisn't Mr. Bounderby ; 'tis his wife. Yor not fearfo' o' her. Yo was hey-go-mad about her, but an hour sin."

" But are you sure it's the lady, and not the gentleman ? " she asked, still trembling.

" Certain sure ! "

" Well then, pray don't speak to me, nor yet take any notice of me," said the old woman. " Let me be quite to myself in this corner."

Stephen nodded ; looking to Rachael for an explanation, which she was quite unable to give him ; took the candle, went downstairs, and in a few moments returned, lighting Louisa into the room. She was followed by the whelp.

Rachael had risen, and stood apart with her shawl and bonnet in her hand, when Stephen, himself profoundly astonished by this visit, put the candle on the table. Then he too stood, with his doubled hand upon the table near it, waiting to be addressed.

For the first time in her life Louisa had come into one of the dwellings of the Coketown Hands; for the first time in her life she was face to face with anything like individuality in connection with them. She knew of their existence by hundreds and by thousands. She knew what results in work a given number of them would produce in a given space of time. She knew them in crowds passing to and from their nests, like ants or beetles. But she knew from her reading infinitely more of the ways of toiling insects than of these toiling men and women.

Something to be worked so much and paid so much, and there ended; something to be infallibly settled by laws of supply and demand; something that blundered against those laws, and floundered into difficulty; something that was a little pinched when wheat was dear, and over-ate itself when wheat was cheap; something that increased at such a rate of percentage, and yielded such another percentage of crime, and such another percentage of pauperism; something wholesale, of which vast fortunes were made; something that occasionally rose like a sea, and did some harm and waste (chiefly to itself), and fell again; this she knew the Coketown Hands to be. But, she had scarcely thought more of separating them into units, than of separating the sea itself into its component drops.

She stood for some moments looking round the room. From the few chairs, the few books, the common prints, and the bed, she glanced to the two women, and to Stephen.

"I have come to speak to you, in consequence of what passed just now. I should like to be serviceable to you, if you will let me. Is this your wife?"

Rachael raised her eyes, and they sufficiently answered no, and dropped again.

"I remember," said Louisa, reddening at her mistake; "I recollect, now, to have heard your domestic misfortunes spoken of, though I was not attending to the particulars at the time. It was not my meaning to ask a question that would give pain to any one here. If I should ask

any other question that may happen to have that result,
give me credit, if you please, for being in ignorance how
to speak to you as I ought."

As Stephen had but a little while ago instinctively
addressed himself to her, so she now instinctively addressed herself to Rachael. Her manner was short and
abrupt, yet faltering and timid.

" He has told you what has passed between himself and
my husband? You would be his first resource, I think."

"I have heard the end of it, young lady," said Rachael.

" Did I understand, that, being rejected by one employer, he would probably be rejected by all? I thought
he said as much?"

" The chances are very small, young lady—next to
nothing—for a man who gets a bad name among them."

" What shall I understand that you mean by a bad
name?"

" The name of being troublesome."

" Then, by the prejudices of his own class, and by the
prejudices of the other, he is sacrificed alike? Are the
two so deeply separated in this town, that there is no
place whatever, for an honest workman between them?"

Rachael shook her head in silence.

" He fell into suspicion," said Louisa, " with his fellow-
weavers, because he had made a promise not to be one of
them. I think it must have been to you that he made
that promise. Might I ask you why he made it?"

Rachael burst into tears. "I didn't seek it of him,
poor lad. I prayed him to avoid trouble for his own
good, little thinking he'd come to it through me. But I
know he'd die a hundred deaths, ere ever he'd break his
word. I know that of him well."

Stephen had remained quietly attentive, in his usual
thoughtful attitude, with his hand at his chin. He now
spoke in a voice rather less steady than usual.

" No one, excepting myseln, can ever know what honor,
an what love, an respect, I bear to Rachael, or wi' what
cause. When I passed that promess, I towd her true,
she were th' Angel o' my life. 'Twere a solemn promess.
'Tis gone fro' me, forever."

Louisa turned her head to him, and bent it with a deference that was new in her. She looked from him to
Rachael, and her features softened. "What will you

do?" she asked him. And her voice had softened too.

"Weel, ma'am," said Stephen, making the best of it, with a smile; "when I ha finished off, I mun quit this part, and try another. Fortnet or misfortnet, a man can but try; there's nowt to be done wi'out tryin'—'cept laying down and dying."

"How will you travel?"

"Afoot, my kind lady, afoot."

Louisa colored, and a purse appeared in her hand. The rustling of a bank-note was audible, as she unfolded one and laid it on the table.

"Rachael, will you tell him—for you know how, without offence—that this is freely his, to help him on his way? Will you entreat him to take it?"

"I canna do that, young lady," she answered, turning her head aside; "bless you for thinking o' the poor lad wi' such tenderness. But 'tis for him to know his heart, and what is right according to it."

Louisa looked, in part incredulous, in part frightened, in part overcome with quick sympathy, when this man of so much self-command, who had been so plain and steady through the late interview, lost his composure in a moment, and now stood with his hand before his face. She stretched out hers, as if she would have touched him; then checked herself, and remained still.

"Not e'en Rachael," said Stephen, when he stood again with his face uncovered, "could mak sitch a kind offerin, by onny words, kinder. T' show that I'm not a man wi'out reason and gratitude, I'll take two 'pound. I'll borrow 't for t' pay 't back. 'T will be the sweetest work as ever I had one, that puts it in my power to acknowledge once more my lastin thankfulness for this present action."

She was fain to take up the note again and to substitute the much smaller sum he had named. He was neither courtly, nor handsome, nor picturesque, in any respect; and yet his manner of accepting it, and of expressing his thanks without more words, had a grace in it that Lord Chesterfield could not have taught his son in a century.

Tom had sat upon the bed, swinging one leg and sucking his walking-stick with sufficient unconcern, until the

visit had attained this stage. Seeing his sister ready to
depart, he got up, rather hurriedly, and put in a word.

"Just wait a moment, Loo! Before we go, I should
like to speak to him a moment. Something comes into
my head. If you'll step out on the stairs, Blackpool, I'll
mention it. Never mind a light, man?" Tom was remarkably impatient of his moving towards the cupboard,
to get one. "It don't want a light."

Stephen followed him out, and Tom closed the room
door, and held the lock in his hand.

"I say!" he whispered. "I think I can do you a good
turn. Don't ask me what it is, because it may not come
to anything. But there's no harm in my trying."

His breath fell like a flame of fire on Stephen's ear, it
was so hot.

"That was our light porter at the Bank," said Tom,
"who brought you the message to-night. I call him our
light porter because I belong to the Bank too."

Stephen thought, "What a hurry he is in!" He spoke
so confusedly.

"Well!" said Tom. "Now look here! when are you
off?"

"T' day's Monday," replied Stephen, considering.
"Why, sir, Friday or Saturday, nigh 'bout."

"Friday or Saturday," said Tom. "Now, look here!
I am not sure that I can do you the good turn I want to
do you—that's my sister, you know, in your room—but I
may be able to, and if I should not be able to, there's no
harm done. So I tell you what. You'll know our light
porter again?"

"Yes sure," said Stephen.

"Very well," returned Tom. "When you leave work
of a night between this and your going away, just hang
about the Bank an hour or so, will you? Don't take on,
as if you meant anything, if he should see you hanging
about there ; because I shan't put him up to speak to
you, unless I find I can do you the service I want to do
you. In that case he'll have a note or a message for you,
but not else. Now look here! You are sure you understand."

He had wormed a finger, in the darkness, through a
buttonhole of Stephen's coat, and was screwing that
corner of the garment tight up round and round, in an
extraordinary manner.

"I understand, sir," said Stephen.

"Now look here!" repeated Tom. "Be sure you don't make any mistake then, and don't forget. I shall tell my sister as we go home, what I have in view, and she'll approve, I know. Now look here! You're all right, are you? You understand all about it? Very well then. Come along, Loo!"

He pushed the door open as he called to her, but did not return into the room or wait to be lighted down the narrow stairs. He was at the bottom when she began to descend, and was in the street before she could take his arm.

Mrs. Pegler remained in her corner until the brother and sister were gone, and until Stephen came back with the candle in his hand. She was in a state of inexpressible admiration of Mrs. Bounderby, and, like an unaccountable old woman, wept "because she was such a pretty dear." Yet Mrs. Pegler was so flurried lest the object of her admiration should return by chance, or anybody else should come, that her cheerfulness was ended for that night. It was late too, to people who rose early and worked hard; therefore the party broke up; and Stephen and Rachael escorted their mysterious acquaintance to the door of the Travellers' Coffee House, where they parted from her.

They walked back together to the corner of the street where Rachael lived, and as they drew nearer and nearer to it, silence crept upon them. When they came to the dark corner where their unfrequent meetings always ended, they stopped, still silent, as if both were afraid to speak.

"I shall strive t' see thee agen, Rachael, afore I go, but if not—"

"Thou wilt not, Stephen, I know. 'Tis better that we make up our minds to be open wi' one another."

"Thou'rt awlus right. 'Tis bolder and better. I ha been thinkin then, Rachael, that as 'tis but a day or two that remains, 'twere better for thee, my dear, not t' be seen wi' me. 'T might bring thee into trouble, fur no good."

"'Tis not for that, Stephen, that I mind. But thou know'st our old agreement. 'Tis for that."

"Well, well," said he. "'Tis better, onyways."

"Thou'lt write to me, and tell me all that happens, Stephen?"

"Yes. What can I say now, but Heaven be wi' thee, Heaven bless thee, Heaven thank thee and reward thee!'"

"May it bless thee, Stephen, too, in all thy wanderings, and send thee peace and rest at last!"

"I towd thee, my dear," said Stephen Blackpool—"that night—that I would never see or think o' onnything that angered me, but thou, so much better than me, should'st be beside it. Thou'rt beside it now. Thou mak'st me see it wi' a better eye. Bless thee. Good-night. Good-bye!"

It was but a hurried parting in a common street, yet it was a sacred remembrance to these two common people. Utilitarian economists, skeletons of schoolmasters, Commissioners of Fact, genteel and used-up infidels, gabblers of many little dog's-eared creeds, the poor you will have always with you. Cultivate in them, while there is yet time, the utmost graces of the fancies and affections, to adorn their lives so much in need of ornament; or, in the day of your triumph, when romance is utterly driven out of their souls, and they and a bare existence stand face to face, Reality will take a wolfish turn, and make an end of you.

Stephen worked the next day, and the next uncheered by a word from any one, and shunned in all his comings and goings as before. At the end of the second day, he saw land; at the end of the third, his loom stood empty.

He had overstayed his hour in the street outside the Bank, on each of the two first evenings; and nothing had happened there, good or bad. That he might not be remiss in his part of the engagement, he resolved to wait full two hours, on this third and last night.

There was the lady who had once kept Mr. Bounderby's house, sitting at the first floor window as he had seen her before; and there was the light porter, sometimes talking with her there, and sometimes looking over the blind below which had BANK upon it, and sometimes coming to the door and standing on the steps for a breath of air. When he first came out Stephen thought he might be looking for him, and passed near; but the light porter only cast his winking eyes upon him slightly, and said nothing.

Two hours were a long stretch of lounging about, after a long day's labor. Stephen sat upon the step of a door, leaned against a wall under an archway, strolled up and down, listened for the church clock, stopped and watched children playing in the street. Some purpose or other is so natural to every one, that a mere loiterer always looks and feels remarkable. When the first hour was out, Stephen even began to have an uncomfortable sensation upon him of being for the time a disreputable character.

Then came the lamplighter, and two lengthening lines of light all down the long perspective of the street, until they were blended and lost in the distance. Mrs. Sparsit closed the first floor window, drew down the blind. and went upstairs. Presently, a light went upstairs after her, passing first the fanlight of the door, and afterwards the two staircase windows, on its way up. By and by, one corner of the second floor blind was disturbed, as if Mrs. Sparsit's eye were there; also the other corner, as if the light porter's eye were on that side. Still, no communication was made to Stephen. Much relieved when the two hours were at last accomplished, he went away at a quick pace, as a recompense for so much loitering.

He had only to take leave of his landlady, and lie down on his temporary bed upon the floor; for his bundle was made up for to-morrow, and all was arranged for his departure. He meant to be clear of the town very early; before the Hands were in the streets.

It was barely daybreak, when, with a parting look round his room, mournfully wondering whether he should ever see it again, he went out. The town was as entirely deserted as if the inhabitants had abandoned it, rather than hold communication with him. Everything looked wan at that hour. Even the coming sun made but a pale waste in the sky, like a sad sea.

By the place where Rachael lived, though it was not in his way; by the red brick street; by the great silent factories, not trembling yet; by the railway, where the danger-lights were waning in the strengthening day; by the railway's crazy neighborhood, half pulled down and half built up; by scattered red brick villas, where the besmoked evergreens were sprinkled with a dirty powder, like untidy snuff-takers; by coal-dust paths and many varieties of ugliness; Stephen got to the top of the hill, and looked back.

Day was shining radiantly upon the town then, and the bells were going for the morning work. Domestic fires were not yet lighted, and the high chimneys had the sky to themselves. Puffing out their poisonous volumes, they would not be long in hiding it; but, for half an hour, some of the many windows were golden, which showed the Coketown people a sun eternally in eclipse, through a medium of smoked glass.

So strange to turn from the chimneys to the birds. So strange to have the road-dust on his feet instead of the coal-grit. So strange to have lived to his time of life, and yet to be beginning like a boy this summer morning! With these musings in his mind, and his bundle under his arm, Stephen took his attentive face along the high-road. And the trees arched over him, whispering that he left a true and loving heart behind.

CHAPTER VII.

GUNPOWDER.

Mr. James Harthouse, "going in" for his adopted party, soon began to score. With the aid of a little more coaching for the political sages, a little more genteel listlessness for the general society, and a tolerable management of the assumed honesty in dishonesty, most effective and most patronized of the polite deadly sins, he speedily came to be considered of much promise. The not being troubled with earnestness was a grand point in his favor, enabling him to take to the hard Fact fellows with as good a grace as if he had been born one of the tribe, and to throw all other tribes overboard, as conscious hypocrites.

"Whom none of us believe, my dear Mrs. Bounderby, and who do not believe themselves. The only difference between us and the professors of virtue or benevolence, or philanthropy—never mind the name—is, that we know it is all meaningless, and say so; while they know it equally and will never say so."

Why should she be shocked or warned by this reiteration? It was not so unlike her father's principles, and her early training, that it need startle her. Where was the great difference between the two schools, when each chained her down to material realities, and inspired her with no faith in anything else? What was there in her soul for James Harthouse to destroy, which Thomas Gradgrind had nurtured there in its state of innocence!

It was even the worse for her at this pass, that in her mind—implanted there before her eminently practical father began to form it—a struggling disposition to believe in a wider and nobler humanity than she had ever heard of, constantly strove with doubts and resentments. With doubts, because the aspirations had been so laid waste in her youth. With resentments, because of the wrong that had been done her, if it were indeed a whisper of the truth. Upon a nature long accustomed to self-suppression, thus torn and divided, the Harthouse philosophy came as a relief and justification. Everything being hollow and worthless, she had missed nothing and sacrificed nothing. What did it matter, she had said to her father, when he proposed her husband. What did it matter, she said still. With a scornful self-reliance, she asked herself, What did anything matter—and went on.

Towards what? Step by step, onward and downward, towards some end, yet so gradually, that she believed herself to remain motionless. As to Mr. Harthouse, whither *he* tended, he neither considered nor cared. He had no particular design or plan before him : no energetic wickedness ruffled his lassitude. He was as much amused and interested at present, as it became so fine a gentleman to be; perhaps even more than it would have been consistent with his reputation to confess. Soon after his arrival he languidly wrote to his brother, the honorable and jocular member, that the Bounderbys were "great fun;" and further, that the female Bounderby, instead of being the Gorgon he had expected, was young and remarkably pretty. After that, he wrote no more about them, and devoted his leisure chiefly to their house. He was very often in their house, in his flittings and visitings about the Coketown district; and was much encouraged by Mr. Bounderby. It was quite in Mr. Bounderby's gusty way to boast to all his world that *he* didn't care about your highly connected people, but that if his wife, Tom Gradgrind's daughter did, she was welcome to their company.

Mr. James Harthouse began to think it would be a

new sensation, if the face which changed so beautifully
for the whelp, would change for him.

He was quick enough to observe; he had a good memory,
and did not forget a word of the brother's revelations. He
interwove them with everything he saw of the sister, and
he began to understand her. To be sure, the better and
profounder part of her character was not within his scope
of perception : for in natures, as in seas, depth answers
unto depth ; but he soon began to read the rest with a
student's eye.

Mr. Bounderby had taken possession of a house and
grounds, about fifteen miles from the town, and accessible
within a mile or two, by a railway striding on many
arches over a wild country, undermined by deserted coal-
shafts, and spotted at night by fires and black shapes of
stationary engines at pits' mouths. This country gradually softening towards the neighborhood of Mr. Bounderby's retreat, there mellowed into a rustic landscape,
golden with heath, and snowy with hawthorn in the
spring of the year, and tremulous with leaves and their
shadows all the summer time. The bank had foreclosed
a mortgage effected on the property thus pleasantly
situated, by one of the Coketown magnates, who, in his
determination to make a shorter cut than usual to an
enormous fortune, overspeculated himself by about two
hundred thousand pounds. These accidents did sometimes happen in the best regulated families of Coketown, but the bankrupts had no connection whatever
with the improvident classes.

It afforded Mr Bounderby supreme satisfaction to install
himself in this snug little estate, and with demonstrative
humility to grow cabbages in the flower-garden. He
delighted to live, barrack-fashion, among the elegant
furniture, and he bullied the very pictures with his
origin. " Why, sir," he would say to a visitor, " I am
told that Nickets," the late owner, " gave seven hundred
pound for that Seabeach. Now, to be plain with you, if I
ever, in the whole course of my life, take seven looks at it,
at a hundred pound a look, it will be as much as I shall
do. No, by George! I don't forget that I am Josiah
Bounderby of Coketown. For years upon years, the only
pictures in my possession, or that I could have got into
my possession, by any means, unless I stole 'em, were the

engravings of a man shaving himself in a boot, on the blacking bottles that I was overjoyed to use in cleaning boots with, and that I sold when they were empty for a farthing a-piece, and glad to get it!"

Then he would address Mr. Harthouse in the same style.

"Harthouse, you have a couple of horses down here. Bring half a dozen more if you like, and we'll find room for 'em. There's stabling in this place for a dozen horses; and unless Nickits is belied, he kept the full number. A round dozen of 'em, sir. When that man was a boy, he went to Westminster School. Went to Westminster School as a King's Scholar, when I was principally living on garbage, and sleeping in market baskets. Why, if I wanted to keep a dozen horses—which I don't, for one's enough for me—I couldn' bear to see 'em in their stalls here, and think what my own lodging used to be. I couldn't look at 'em, sir, and not order 'em out. Yet so things come round. You see his place; you know what sort of a place it is; you are aware that there's not a completer place of its size in this kingdom or elsewhere—I don't care where— and here, got into the middle of it, like a maggot into a nut, is Josiah Bounderby. While Nickits (as a man came into my office, and told me yesterday), Nickits, who used to act in Latin, in the Westminster School plays, with the chief-justices and nobility of this country applauding him till they were black in the face, is drivelling at this minute drivelling, sir!—in a fifth floor up a narrow dark back street in Antwerp."

It was among the leafy shadows of this retirement, in the long sultry summer days, that Mr. Harthouse began to prove the face which had set him wondering when he first saw it, and to try if it would change for him.

"Mrs. Bounderby, I esteem it a most fortunate accident that I find you alone here. I have for some time had a particular wish to speak to you."

It was not by any wonderful accident that he found her, the time of day being that at which she was always alone, and the place being her favorite resort. It was an opening in a dark wood, where some felled trees lay, and where she would sit watching the fallen leaves of last year, as she had watched the falling ashes at home.

He sat down beside her, with a glance at her face.

"Your brother. My young friend Tom—"

Her color brightened and she turned to him with a look of interest. "I never in my life," he thought, "saw anything so remarkable and so captivating as the lighting of those features!" His face betrayed his thoughts—perhaps without betraying him, for it might have been according to its instructions so to do.

"Pardon me. The expression of your sisterly interest is so beautiful—Tom should be so proud of it—I know this is inexcusable, but I am so compelled to admire."

"Being so impulsive," she said composedly.

"Mrs. Bounderby, no: you know I make no pretence with you. You know I am a sordid piece of human nature, ready to sell myself at any time for any reasonable sum, and altogether incapable of any Arcadian proceeding whatever.

"I am waiting," she returned, "for your further reference to my brother."

"You are rigid with me, and I deserve it. I am as worthless a dog as you will find, except that I am not false—not false. But you surprised and started me from my subject, which was your brother. I have an interest in him."

"Have you an interest in anything, Mr. Harthouse?" she asked, half incredulously and half gratefully.

"If you had asked me when I first came here, I should have said no. I must say now—even at the hazard of appearing to make a pretence, and of justly awakening your incredulity—yes."

She made a slight movement, as if she were trying to speak, but could not find voice; at length she said, "Mr. Harthouse, I give you credit for being interested in my brother."

"Thank you. I claim to deserve it. You know how little I do claim, but I will go that length. You have done so much for him, you are so fond of him; your whole life, Mrs. Bounderby, expresses such charming self-forgetfulness on his account—pardon me again—I am running wide of the subject. I am interested in him for his own sake."

She had made the slightest action possible, as if she would have risen in a hurry and gone away. He had turned the course of what he said at that instant, and she remained.

"Mrs. Bounderby," he resumed, in a lighter manner, and yet with a show of effort in assuming it, which was even more expressive than the manner he dismissed; "it is no irrevocable offence in a young fellow of your brother's years, if he is heedless, inconsiderate, and expensive—a little dissipated, in the common phrase. Is he?"

"Yes?"

"Allow me to be frank. Do you think he games at all?"

"I think he makes bets." Mr. Harthouse waiting, as if that were not her whole answer, she added, "I know he does."

"Of course he loses?"

"Yes."

"Everybody does lose who bets. May I hint at the probability of your sometimes supplying him with money for these purposes?"

She sat, looking down; but, at this question, raised her eyes searchingly and a little resentfully.

"Acquit me of impertinent curiosity, my dear Mrs. Bounderby. I think Tom may be gradually falling into trouble, and I wish to stretch out a helping hand to him from the depths of my wicked experience.—Shall I say again, for his sake? Is that necessary?"

She seemed to try to answer, but nothing came of it.

"Candidly to confess everything that has occurred to me," said James Harthouse, again gliding with the same appearance of effort into his more airy manner; "I will confide to you my doubt whether he has had many advantages. Whether—forgive my plainness—whether any great amount of confidence is likely to have been established between himself and his most worthy father."

"I do not," said Louisa, flushing with her own great remembrance in that wise, "think it likely."

"Or, between himself, and—I may trust to your perfect understanding of my meaning, I am sure—and his highly esteemed brother-in-law."

She flushed deeper and deeper, and was burning red when she replied in a fainter voice, "I do not think that likely, either."

"Mrs. Bounderby," said Harthouse, after a short silence, "may there be a better confidence between yourself and me? Tom has borrowed a considerable sum of you?"

I I

"You will understand, Mr. Harthouse," she returned, after some indecision : she had been more or less uncertain, and troubled throughout the conversation, and yet had in the main preserved her self-contained manner ; "you will understand that if I tell you what you press to know, it is not by way of complaint or regret. I would never complain of anything, and what I have done I do not in the least regret."

"So spirited, too!" thought James Harthouse.

"When I married, I found that my brother was even at that time heavily in debt. Heavily for him, I mean. Heavily enough to oblige me to sell some trinkets. They were no sacrifice. I sold them very willingly. I attached no value to them. They were quite worthless to me."

Either she saw in his face that he knew, or she only feared in her conscience that he knew that she spoke of some of her husband's gifts. She stopped, and reddened again. If he had not known it before, he would have known it then, though he had been a much duller man than he was.

"Since then, I have given my brother, at various times, what money I could spare : in short, what money I have had. Confiding in you at all, on the faith of the interest you profess for him, I will not do so by halves. Since you have been in the habit of visiting here, he has wanted in one sum as much as a hundred pounds. I have not been able to give it to him. I have felt uneasy for the consequences of his being so involved, but I have kept these secrets until now, when I trust them to your honor. I have held no confidence with any one, because—you anticipated my reason just now." She abruptly broke off.

He was a ready man, and he saw and seized, an opportunity here of presenting her own image to her, slightly disguised as her brother.

"Mrs. Bounderby, though a graceless person, of the world worldly, I feel the utmost interest, I assure you, in what you tell me. I cannot possibly be hard upon your brother. I understand and share the wise consideration with which you regard his errors. With all possible respect both for Mr. Gradgrind and Mr. Bounderby, I think I perceive that he has not been fortunate in his training. Bred at a disadvantage towards the society in which he has his part to play, he rushes into these extremes for himself, from opposite extremes that have long been forced—with the very best intentions we have no doubt —upon him. Mr. Bounderby's fine bluff English independence, though a most charming characteristic, does not— as we have agreed—invite confidence. If I might venture to remark that it is the least in the world deficient in that delicacy to which a youth mistaken, a character misconceived, and abilities misdirected, would turn for relief and guidance, I should express what it presents to my own view."

As she sat looking straight before her, across the changing lights upon the grass into the darkness of the wood beyond, he saw in her face her application of his very distinctly uttered words.

"All allowance," he continued, "must be made.   I have one great fault to find with Tom, however, which I cannot forgive, and for which I take him heavily to account."

Louisa turned her eyes to his face, and asked him what fault was that?

"Perhaps," he returned, "I have said enough.   Perhaps it would have been better, on the whole, if no allusion to it had escaped me."

"You alarm me, Mr. Harthouse. Pray let me know it."

"To relieve you from needless apprehension—and as this confidence regarding your brother, which I prize I am sure above all possible things, has been established between us—I obey. I cannot forgive him for not being more sensible in every word, look, and act of his life of the affection of his best friend; of the devotion of his best friend; of her unselfishness; of her sacrifice. The return he makes her, within my observation, is a very poor one. What she has done for him demands his constant love and gratitude, not his ill-humor and caprice. Careless fellow as I am, I am not so indifferent, Mrs. Bounderby, as to be regardless of this vice in your brother, or inclined to consider it a venial offence."

The wood floated before her, for her eyes were suffused, with tears. They rose from a deep well, long concealed and her heart was filled with acute pain that found no relief in them.

"In a word, it is to correct your brother in this, Mrs.

Bounderby, that I must aspire. My better knowledge of his circumstances, and my direction and advice in extricating them—rather valuable, I hope, as coming from a scapegrace on a much larger scale—will give me some influence over him, and all I gain I shall certainly use towards this end. I have said enough, and more than enough. I seem to be protesting that I am a sort of good fellow, when upon my honor, I have not the least intention to make any protestation to that effect, and openly announce that I am nothing of the sort. Yonder, among the trees," he added, having lifted up his eyes and looked about; for he had watched her closely until now; "is your brother himself, no doubt, just come down. As he seems to be loitering in this direction, it may be as well, perhaps, to walk towards him, and throw ourselves in his way. He has been very silent and doleful of late Perhaps, his brotherly conscience is touched—if there are such things as consciences. Though, upon my honor, I hear of them much too often to believe in them."

He assisted her to rise, and she took his arm, and they advanced to meet the whelp. He was idly beating the branches as he lounged along: or he stooped viciously to rip the moss from the trees with his stick. He was startled when they came upon him while he was engaged in this latter pastime, and his color changed.

"Halloa!" he stammered; "I didn't know you were here."

"Whose name, Tom," said Mr. Harthouse, putting his hand upon his shoulder and turning him, so that they all three walked towards the house together, "have you been carving on the trees?"

"Whose name?" returned Tom. "Oh! You mean what girl's name?"

"You have a suspicious appearance of inscribing some fair creature's on the bark, Tom."

"Not much of that, Mr. Harthouse, unless some fair creature with a slashing fortune at her own disposal would take a fancy to me. Or she might be as ugly as she was rich, without any fear of losing me. I'd carve her name as often as she liked."

"I am afraid you are mercenary, Tom."

"Mercenary," repeated Tom. "Who is not mercenary? Ask my sister."

"Have you so proved it to be a failing of mine, Tom?" said Louisa, showing no other sense of his discontent and ill-nature.

"You know whether the cap fits you, Loo," returned her brother sulkily. "If it does, you can wear it."

"Tom is misanthropical to-day, as all bored people are now and then," said Mr. Harthouse. "Don't believe him, Mrs. Bounderby. He knows much better, I shall disclose some of his opinions of you, privately expressed to me, unless he relents a little."

"At all events, Mr. Harthouse," said Tom, softening in his admiration of his patron, but shaking his head sullenly too, "you can't tell her that I ever praised her for being mercenary. I may have praised her for being the contrary, and I should do it again if I had as good reason. However, never mind this now; it's not very interesting to you, and I am sick of the subject."

They walked on to the house, where Louisa quitted her visitor's arm and went in. He stood looking after her as she ascended the steps, and passed into the shadow of the door; then put his hand upon her brother's shoulder again, and invited him with a confidential nod to a walk in the garden.

"Tom, my fine fellow, I want to have a word with you."

They had stopped among a disorder of roses—it was part of Mr. Bounderby's humility to keep Nickits's roses on a reduced scale—and Tom sat down on a terrace-parapet, plucking buds and picking them to pieces; while his powerful Familiar stood over him, with a foot upon the parapet, and his figure easily resting on the arm supported by that knee. They were just visible from her window. Perhaps she saw them.

"Tom, what's the matter?"

"Oh! Mr. Harthouse," said Tom with a groan, "I am hard up, and bothered out of my life."

"My good fellow, so am I."

"You!" returned Tom. "You are the picture of independence. Mr. Harthouse, I am in a horrible mess. You have no idea what a state I have got myself into—what a state my sister might have got me out of, if she would only have done it."

He took to biting the rosebuds now, and tearing them away from his teeth with a hand that trembled like an

infirm old man's.   After one exceedingly observant look
at him, his companion relapsed into his lightest air.

"Tom, you are inconsiderate : you expect too much of
your sister. You have had money of her, you dog, you
know you have."

"Well, Mr. Harthouse, I know I have. How else was
I to get it? Here's old Bounderby always boasting that
at my age he lived upon twopence a month, or something
of that sort. Here's my father drawing what he calls a
line, and tying me down to it from a baby, neck and heels.
Here's my mother who never has anything of her own,
except her complaints. What *is* a fellow to do for money,
and where *am* I to look for it, if not to my sister?"

He was almost crying, and scattered the buds about by
dozens.   Mr. Harthouse took him persuasively by the
coat.

"But, my dear Tom, if your sister has not got it—"

"Not got it, Mr. Harthouse? I don't say she has got it.
I may have wanted more than she was likely to have got.
But then she ought to get it. She could get it. It's of
no use pretending to make a secret of matters now, after
what I have told you already ; you know she didn't marry
old Bounderby for her own sake, or for his sake, but for
my sake. Then why doesn't she get what I want, out of
him, for my sake? She is not obliged to say what she is
going to do with it ; she is sharp enough ; she could manage to coax it out of him, if she chose. Then why doesn't
she choose, when I tell her of what consequence it is? But
no. There she sits in his company like a stone, instead
of making herself agreeable and getting it easily. I don't
know what you may call this, but *I* call it unnatural
conduct."

There was a piece of ornamental water immediately
below the parapet, on the other side, into which Mr. James
Harthouse had a very strong inclination to pitch Mr.
Thomas Gradgrind Junior, as the injured men of Coketown threatened to pitch their property inio the Atlantic.
But he preserved his easy attitude ; and nothing more
solid went over the stone balustrades than the accumulated
rosebuds now floating about, a little surface-island.

"My dear Tom," said Harthouse, "let me try to be your
banker."

"For God's sake," replied Tom, suddenly, "don't talk

about bankers !" And very white he looked, in contrast with the roses. Very white.

Mr. Harthouse, as a thoroughly well bred man, accustomed to the best society, was not to be surprised—he could as soon have been affected—but he raised his eyelids a little more, as if they were lifted by a feeble touch of wonder. Albeit it was as much against the precepts of his school to wonder, as it was against the doctrines of the Gradgrind College.

"What is the present need, Tom? Three figures? Out with them. Say what they are."

"Mr. Harthouse," returned Tom, now actually crying; and his tears were better than his injuries, however pitiful a figure he made; "it's too late; the money is of no use to me at present. I should have had it before to be of use to me   But I am very much obliged to you; you're a true friend."

A true friend! "Whelp, whelp!" thought Mr. Harthouse, lazily; "what an Ass you are!"

And I take your offer as a great kindness," said Tom, grasping his hand. "As a great kindness, Mr. Harthouse."

"Well," returned the other, "it may be of more use by and by. And my good fellow, if you will open your bedevilments to me when they come thick upon you, I may show you better ways out of them than you can find for yourself."

"Thank you," said Tom, shaking his head dismally, and chewing rosebuds. "I wish I had known you sooner, Mr. Harthouse."

"Now, you see, Tom," said Mr. Harthouse in conclusion, himself tossing over a rose or two, as a contribution to the island, which was always drifting to the wall as if it wanted to become a part of the mainland : "every man is selfish in everything he does, and I am exactly like the rest of my fellow-creatures. I am desperately intent ; " the languor of his desperation being quite tropical ; "on your softening towards your sister—which you ought to do; and on your being a more loving and agreeable sort of brother—which you ought to be."

"I will be, Mr. Harthouse."

"No time like the present, Tom. Begin at once."

"Certainly I will. And my sister Loo shall say so."

"Having made which bargain, Tom," said Harthouse,

clapping him on the shoulder again, with an air which left him at liberty to infer—as he did, poor fool—that this condition was imposed upon him in mere careless good nature to lessen his sense of obligation, "we will tear ourselves asunder until dinner-time."

When Tom appeared before dinner, though his mind seemed heavy enough his body was on the alert; and he appeared before Mr. Bounderby came in. "I didn't mean to be cross, Loo," he said, giving her his hand, and kissing her. "I know you are fond of me, and you know I am fond of you."

After this, there was a smile upon Louisa's face that day, for some one else. Alas, for some one else!

"So much the less is the whelp the only creature that she cares for," thought James Harthouse, reversing the reflection of his first day's knowledge of her pretty face. "So much the less, so much the less."

CHAPTER VIII.

EXPLOSION.

The next morning was too bright a morning for sleep, and James Harthouse rose early, and sat in the pleasant bay window of his dressing-room, smoking the rare tobacco that had had so wholesome an influence on his young friend. Reposing in the sunlight, with the fragrance of his eastern pipe about him, and the dreamy smoke vanishing into the air, so rich and soft with summer odors, he reckoned up his advantages as an idle winner might count his gains. He was not at all bored for the time, and could give his mind to it.

He had established a confidence with her, from which her husband was excluded. He had established a confidence with her, that absolutely turned upon her indifference towards her husband, and the absence, now and at all times, of any congeniality between them. He had artfully, but plainly assured her, that he knew her heart in its last most delicate recesses; he had come so near to her through its tenderest sentiment; he had associated himself with that feeling; and the barrier behind which she lived, had melted away. All very odd, and very satisfactory!

And yet he had not, even now, any earnest wickedness of purpose in him. Publicly and privately, it were much better for the age in which he lived, that he and the legion of whom he was one were designedly bad, than indifferent and purposeless. It is the drifting icebergs setting with any current anywhere, that wreck the ships.

When the devil goeth about like a roaring lion, he goeth about in a shape by which few but savages and hunters are attracted. But, when he is trimmed, smoothed, and varnished, according to the mode; when he is aweary of vice, and aweary of virtue, used up as to brimstone, and used up as to bliss ; then, whether he take to the serving out of red tape, or to the kindling of red fire, he is the very Devil.

So, James Harthouse reclined in the window, indolently smoking, and reckoning up the steps he had taken on the road by which he happened to be travelling. The end to which it led was before him, pretty plainly ; but he troubled himself with no calculations about it. What will be, will be.

As he had rather a long ride to take that day—for there was a public occasion "to do" at some distance, which afforded a tolerable opportunity of going in for the Gradgrind men—he dressed early, and went down to breakfast. He was anxious to see if she had relapsed since the previous evening. No. He resumed where he had left off. There was a look of interest for him again.

He got through the day as much (or as little) to his own satisfaction, as was to be expected under the fatiguing circumstances; and came riding back at six o'clock. There was a sweep of some half mile between the lodge and the house, and he was riding along at a foot pace over the smooth gravel, once Nickits's, when Mr. Bounderby burst out of the shrubbery, with such violence as to make his horse shy across the road.

"Harthouse! " cried Mr. Bounderby. "Have you heard ? "

"Heard what?" said Harthouse, soothing his horse, and inwardly favoring Mr. Bounderby with no good wishes.

"Then you *haven't* heard ! "

"I have heard you and so has this brute. I have heard nothing else."

Mr. Bounderby, red and hot, planted himself in the centre of the path before the horse's head, to explode his bombshell with more effect.

" The Bank's robbed ! "

" You don't mean it ! "

" Robbed last night, sir. Robbed in an extraordinary manner. Robbed with a false key."

" Of much ? "

Mr. Bounderby, in his desire to make the most of it, really seemed mortified by being obliged to reply, " Why, no; not of very much. But it might have been."

" Of how much ? "

" Oh ! as a sum—if you stick to a sum—of not more than a hundred and fifty pound," said Bounderby, with impatience. " But it's not the sum; it's the fact. It's the fact of the Bank being robbed, that's the important circumstance. I am surprised you don't see it."

" My dear Bounderby," said James, dismounting, and giving his bridle to his servant, " I *do* see it; and am as overcome as you can possibly desire me to be, by the spectacle afforded to my mental view. Nevertheless, I may be allowed, I hope, to congratulate you—which I do with all my soul, I assure you—on your not having sustained a greater loss."

" Thank 'ee," replied Bounderby, in a short, ungracious manner. " But I tell you what. It might have been twenty thousand pound."

" I suppose it might."

" Suppose it might ! By the Lord, you *may* suppose so. By George ! " said Mr. Bounderby, with sundry menacing nods and shakes of his head. " It might have been twice twenty. There's no knowing what it would have been, or wouldn't have been, as it was, but for the fellows being disturbed."

Louisa had come up now, and Mrs. Sparsit, and Bitzer.

" Here's Tom Gradgrind's daughter knows pretty well what it might have been, if you don't," blustered Bounderby. " Dropped, sir, as if she was shot when I told her ! Never knew her do such a thing before. Does her credit, under the circumstances, in my opinion ! "

She still looked faint and pale. James Harthouse begged her to take his arm; and as they moved on very slowly, asked her how the robbery had been committed.

"Why, I am going to tell you," said Bounderby, irritably giving his arm to Mrs. Sparsit. "If you hadn't been so mighty particular about the sum, I should have begun to tell you before. You know this lady (for she *is* a lady), Mrs. Sparsit?"

"I have already had the honor"—

"Very well. And this young man, Bitzer, you saw him too on the same occasion?" Mr. Harthouse inclined his head in assent, and Bitzer knuckled his forehead.

"Very well. They live at the Bank. You know they live at the Bank, perhaps? Very well. Yesterday afternoon, at the close of business hours, everything was put away as usual. In the iron room that this young fellow sleeps outside of, there was never mind how much. In the little safe in young Tom's closet, the safe used for petty purposes, there was a hundred and fifty odd pound."

"A hundred and fifty-four, seven, one," said Bitzer.

"Come!" retorted Bounderby, stopping to wheel round upon him, "let's have none of *your* interruptions. It's enough to be robbed while you're snoring because you're too comfortable, without being put right with *your* four seven ones. I didn't snore myself, when I was your age, let me tell you. I hadn't victuals enough to snore. And I didn't four seven one. Not if I knew it."

Bitzer knuckled his forehead again, in a sneaking manner, and seemed at once particularly impressed and depressed by the instance last given of Mr. Bounderby's moral abstinence.

"A hundred and fifty odd pound," resumed Mr. Bounderby. "That sum of money, young Tom locked in his safe, not a very strong safe, but that's no matter now. Everything was left, all right. Some time in the night, while this young fellow snored—Mrs. Sparsit, ma'am, you say you have heard him snore?"

"Sir," returned Mrs. Sparsit, "I cannot say that I have heard him precisely snore, and therefore must not make that statement. But on winter evenings, when he has fallen asleep at his table, I have heard him, what I should prefer to describe as partially choke. I have heard him on such occasions produce sounds of a nature similar to what may be sometimes heard in Dutch clocks. Not," said Mrs. Sparsit, with a lofty sense of giving strict evidence, " that I would convey any imputation on his moral character. Far from it. I have always considered Bitzer a young man of the most upright principle; and to that I beg to bear my testimony."

" Well! " said the exasperated Bounderby, " while he was snoring, *or* choking, *or* Dutch-clocking *or* something or other—being asleep—some fellows, somehow, whether previously concealed in the house or not remains to be seen, got to young Tom's safe, forced it, and abstracted the contents. Being then disturbed, they made off; letting themselves out at the main door, and double-locking it again (it was double-locked, and the key under Mrs. Sparsit's pillow) with a false key, which was picked up in the street near the Bank, about twelve o'clock to-day. No alarm takes place, till this chap, Bitzer, turns out this morning, and begins to open and prepare the offices for business. Then, looking at Tom's safe, he sees the door ajar, and finds the lock forced, and the money gone."

" Where is Tom, by the by ? " asked Harthouse, glancing round.

" He has been helping the police," said Bounderby, " and stays behind at the Bank. I wish these fellows had tried to rob me when I was at his time of life. They would have been out of pocket if they had invested eighteenpence in the job; I can tell 'em that."

" Is anybody suspected ? "

" Suspected ? I should think there was somebody suspected. Egod ! " said Bounderby, relinquishing Mrs. Sparsit's arm to wipe his heated head. " Josiah Bounderby of Coketown is not to be plundered and nobody suspected. No, thank you! "

Might Mr. Harthouse inquire Who was suspected ?

" Well," said Bounderby, stopping and facing about to confront them all, " I'll tell you. It's not to be mentioned everywhere; it's not to be mentioned anywhere : in order that the scoundrels concerned (there's a gang of 'em) may be thrown off their guard. So take this in confidence. Now wait a bit." Mr. Bounderby wiped his head again. " What should you say to; " here he violently exploded ; " to a Hand being in it ? "

" I hope," said Harthouse, lazily, " not our friend Blackpot ? "

"Say Pool instead of pot, sir," returned Bounderby, "and that's the man."

Louisa faintly uttered some word of incredulity and surprise.

"O yes! I know!" said Bounderby, immediately catching at the sound. "I know! I am used to that. I know all about it. They are the finest people in the world, these fellows are. They have got the gift of the gab, they have. They only want to have their rights explained to them, they do. But I tell you what. Show me a dissatisfied Hand, and I'll show you a man that's fit for anything bad, I don't care what it is." Another of the popular fictions of Coketown, which some pains had been taken to disseminate—and which some people really believed.

"But I am acquainted with these chaps," said Bounderby. "I can read 'em off, like books. Mrs. Sparsit, ma'am, I appeal to you. What warning did I give that fellow, the first time he set foot in the house, when the express object of his visit was to know how he could knock Religion over, and floor the Established Church! Mrs. Sparsit, in point of high connections, you are on a level with the aristocracy,—did I say, or did I not say, to that fellow, 'you can't hide the truth from me: you are not the kind of fellow I like; you'll come to no good'?"

"Assuredly, sir," returned Mrs. Sparsit, "you did, in a highly impressive manner, give him such an admonition."

"When he shocked you, ma'am," said Bounderby; "when he shocked your feelings?"

"Yes, sir," returned Mrs. Sparsit, with a meek shake of her head, "he certainly did so. Though I do not mean to say but that my feelings may be weaker on such points—more foolish if the term is preferred—than they might have been, if I had always occupied my present position."

Mr. Bounderby stared with a bursting pride at Mr. Harthouse, as much as to say, "I am the proprietor of this female, and she's worth your attention, I think." Then, resumed his discourse.

"You can recall for yourself, Harthouse, what I said to him when you saw him. I didn't mince the matter with him. I am never mealy with 'em. I KNOW 'em. Very well, sir. Three days after that he bolted. Went off, nobody knows where : as my mother did in my infancy—only with this difference, that he is a worse subject than my mother, if possible. What did he do before he went? What do you say;" Mr. Bounderby, with his hat in his hand, gave a beat upon the crown at every little division of his sentences, as if it were a tambourine; "to his being seen —night after night—watching the Bank?—to his lurking about there—after dark?—to its striking Mrs. Sparsit—that he could be lurking for no good—To her calling Bitzer's attention to him, and their both taking notice of him—And to its appearing on inquiry to-day—that he was also noticed by the neighbors?" Having come to the climax, Mr. Bounderby, like an oriental dancer, put his tambourine on his head.

"Suspicious," said James Harthouse, "certainly."

"I think so, sir," said Bounderby, with a defiant nod. "I think so. But there are more of 'em in it. There's an old woman. One never hears of these things till the mischief's done; all sorts of defects are found out in the stable door after the horse is stolen; there's an old woman turns up now. An old woman who seems to have been flying into town on a broomstick, every now and then. *She* watches the place a whole day before this fellow begins, and on the night when you saw him, she steals away with him, and holds a council with him—I suppose, to make her report on going off duty, and be damned to her."

There was such a person in the room that night, and she shrunk from observation, thought Louisa.

"This is not all of 'em, even as we already know 'em." said Bounderby, with many nods of hidden meaning. "But I have said enough for the present. You'll have the goodness to keep it quiet, and mention it to no one. It may take time, but we shall have 'em. It's policy to give 'em line enough, and there's no objection to that."

"Of course, they will be punished with the utmost rigor of the law, as noticeboards observe," replied James Harthouse, "and serve them right. Fellows who go in for Banks must take the consequences. If there were no consequences, we should all go in for Banks." He had gently taken Louisa's parasol from her hand, and had put it up for her; and she walked under its shade, though the sun did not shine there.

"For the present, Loo Bounderby," said her husband, "here's Mrs. Sparsit to look after. Mrs. Sparsit's nerves have been acted upon by this business, and she'll stay here a day or two. So, make her comfortable."

"Thank you very much, sir," that discreet lady observed, "but pray do not let my comfort be a consideration. Anything will do for Me."

It soon appeared that if Mrs. Sparsit had a failing in her association with that domestic establishment, it was that she was so excessively regardless of herself and regardful of others, as to be a nuisance. On being shown her chamber, she was so dreadfully sensible of its comforts as to suggest the inference that she would have preferred to pass the night on the mangle in the laundry. True, the Powlers and the Scadgerses were accustomed to splendor, "but it is my duty to remember," Mrs. Sparsit was fond of observing with a lofty grace: particularly when any of the domestics were present, " that what I was, I am no longer. Indeed " said she, "if I could altogether cancel the remembrance that Mr. Sparsit was a Powler, or that I myself am related to the Scadgers family; or if I could even revoke the fact, and make myself a person of common descent and ordinary connections; I would gladly do so. I should think it, under existing circumstances, right to do so." The same Hermitical state of mind led to her renunciation of made-dishes and wines at dinner, until fairly commanded by Mr. Bounderby to take them; when she said. "Indeed you are very good, sir; " and departed from a resolution of which she had made rather formal and public announcement, to "wait for the simple mutton." She was likewise deeply apologetic for wanting the salt; and, feeling amiably bound to bear out Mr. Bounderby to the fullest extent in the testimony he had borne to her nerves, occasionally sat back in her chair and silently wept; at which periods a tear of large dimensions, like a crystal ear-ring, might be observed (or rather, must be, for it insisted on public notice) sliding down her Roman nose.

But Mrs. Sparsit's greatest point, first and last, was her determination to pity Mr. Bounderby. There were occasions when in looking at him she was involuntarily moved to shake her head, as who would say, " Alas poor Yorick ! " After allowing herself to be betrayed into these evidences of emotion, she would force a lambent brightness, and would be fitfully cheerful, and would say," You have still good spirits, sir, I am thankful to find ; " and would appear to hail it as a blessed dispensation that Mr. Bounderby bore up as he did. One idiosyncrasy for which she often apologized, she found it excessively difficult to conquer. She had a curious propensity to call Mrs. Bounderby " Miss Gradgrind," and yielded to it some three or four score times in the course of the evening. Her repetition of this mistake covered Mrs. Sparsit with modest confusion ; but indeed, she said, it seemed so natural to say Miss Gradgrind : whereas, to persuade herself that the young lady whom she had had the happiness of knowing from a child could be really and truly Mrs. Bounderby, she found almost impossible. It was a further singularity of this remarkable case, that the more she thought about it, the more impossible it appeared ; " the differences," she observed, " being such."

In the drawing-room after dinner, Mr. Bounderby tried the case of the robbery, examined the witnesses, made notes of the evidence, found the suspected persons guilty, and sentenced them to the extreme punishment of the law. That done, Bitzer was dismissed to town with instructions to recommend Tom to come home by the mail-train.

When candles were brought, Mrs. Sparsit murmured, " Don't be low, sir. Pray let me see you cheerful, sir, as I used to do." Mr. Bounderby, upon whom these consolations had begun to produce the effect of making him, in a bull-headed blundering way, sentimental, sighed like some large sea-animal. " I cannot bear to see you so, sir," said Mrs. Sparsit. " Try a hand at backgammon, sir, as you used to do when I had the honor of living under your roof." " I haven't played backgammon, ma'am," said Mr. Bounderby, " since that time." " No, sir," said Mrs. Sparsit, soothingly, " I am aware that you have not. I remember that Miss Gradgrind takes no interest in the game. But I shall be happy, sir, if you will condescend."

They played near a window, opening on the garden. It was a fine night : not moonlight, but sultry and fragrant. Louisa and Mr. Harthouse strolled out into the garden, where their voices could be heard in the stillness, though not what they said. Mrs. Sparsit, from her place at the backgammon board, was constantly straining her eyes to pierce the shadows without. "What's the matter, ma'am?" said Mr. Bounderby; "you don't see a Fire, do you?" "Oh dear no, sir," returned Mrs. Sparsit, "I was thinking of the dew." "What have you got to do with the dew, ma'am?" said Mr. Bounderby. "It's not myself, sir," returned Mrs. Sparsit, "I am fearful of Miss Gradgrind's taking cold." "She never takes cold," said Mr. Bounderby. "Really, sir?" said Mrs. Sparsit. And was affected with a cough in her throat.

When the time drew near for retiring, Mr. Bounderby took a glass of water. "Oh, sir?" said Mrs. Sparsit. "Not your sherry warm, with lemon-peel and nutmeg?" "Why I have got out of the habit of taking it now, ma'am," said Mr. Bounderby. "The more's the pity, sir," returned Mrs. Sparsit; "you are losing all your good old habits. Cheer up, sir! If Miss Gradgrind will permit me, I will offer to make it for you, as I have often done."

Miss Gradgrind readily permitting Mrs. Sparsit to do anything she pleased, that considerate lady made the beverage, and handed it to Mr. Bounderby. "It will do you good, sir. It will warm your heart. It is the sort of thing you want, and ought to take, sir." And when Mr. Bounderby said, "Your health, ma'am!" she answered with great feeling, "Thank you, sir. The same to you, and happiness also." Finally, she wished him good-night, with great pathos; and Mr. Bounderby went to bed, with a maudlin persuasion that he had been crossed in something tender, though he could not, for his life, have mentioned what it was.

Long after Louisa had undressed and lain down, she watched and waited for her brother's coming home. That could hardly be, she knew, until an hour past midnight; but in the country silence, which did anything but calm the trouble of her thoughts, time lagged wearily. At last, when the darkness and stillness had seemed for hours to thicken one another, she heard the bell at the gate. She felt as though she would have been glad that it rang on until daylight; but it ceased, and the circles of its last sound spread out fainter and wider in the air, and all was dead again.

She waited yet some quarter of an hour, as she judged. Then she arose, put on a loose robe, and went out of her room in the dark, and up the staircase to her brother's

12

room.   His door being shut, she softly opened it and spoke to him, approaching his bed with a noiseless step.

She kneeled down beside it, passed her arm over his neck, and drew his face to hers.   She knew that he only feigned to be asleep, but she said nothing to him.

He started by and by as if he were just then awakened, and asked who that was, and what was the matter?

"Tom, have you anything to tell me?   If ever you loved me in your life, and have anything concealed from every one besides, tell it to me."

"I don't know what you mean, Loo.   You have been dreaming."

"My dear brother:" she laid her head down on his pillow, and her hair flowed over him as if she would hide him from every one but herself: "is there nothing that you have to tell me?   Is there nothing you can tell me if you will?   You can tell me nothing that will change me. O Tom, tell me the truth!"

"I don't know what you mean, Loo!"

"As you lie here alone, my dear, in the melancholy night, so you must lie somewhere one night when even I, if I am living then, shall have left you.   As I am here beside you, barefoot, unclothed, undistinguishable in darkness, so must I lie through all the night of my decay until I am dust.   In the name of that time, Tom, tell me the truth now!"

"What is it you want to know?"

"You may be certain;" in the energy of her love she took him to her bosom as if he were a child; "that I will not reproach you.   You may be certain that I will be compassionate and true to you.   You may be certain that I will save you at whatever cost.   O Tom, have you nothing to tell me?   Whisper very softly.   Say only 'yes' and I shall understand you!"

She turned her ear to his lips, but he remained doggedly silent.

"Not a word, Tom?"

"How can I say Yes, or how can I say No, when I don't know what you mean?   Loo, you are a brave, kind girl, worthy I begin to think of a better brother than I am. But I have nothing more to say.   Go to bed, go to bed."

"You are tired," she whispered presently, more in her usual way.

"Yes, I am quite tired out."

"You have been so hurried and disturbed to-day. Have any fresh discoveries been made?"

"Only those you have heard of, from—him."

"Tom, have you said to any one that we made a visit to those people, and that we saw those three together?"

"No. Didn't you yourself particularly ask me to keep it quiet when you asked me to go there with you?"

"Yes. But I did not know then what was going to happen."

"Nor I neither. How could I?"

He was very quick upon her with this retort.

"Ought I to say, after what has happened," said his sister, standing by the bed—she had gradually withdrawn herself and risen, "that I made that visit? Should I say so? Must I say so?"

"Good Heavens, Loo," returned her brother, "you are not in the habit of asking my advice. Say what you like. If you keep it to yourself, I shall keep it to *my*self. If you disclose it, there's an end of it."

It was too dark for either to see the other's face; but each seemed very attentive, and to consider before speaking.

"Tom, do you believe the man I gave the money to, is really implicated in this crime?"

"I don't know. I don't see why he shouldn't be."

"He seemed to me an honest man."

"Another person may seem to you dishonest, and yet not be so."

There was a pause, for he had hesitated and stopped.

"In short," resumed Tom, as if he had made up his mind, "if you come to that, perhaps I was so far from being altogether in his favor, that I took him outside the door to tell him quietly, that I thought he might consider himself very well off to get such a windfall as he had got from my sister, and that I hoped he would make good use of it. You remember whether I took him out or not. I say nothing against the man: he may be a very good fellow, for anything I know; I hope he is."

"Was he offended by what you said?"

"No, he took it pretty well; he was civil enough. Where are you, Loo?" He sat up in bed and kissed her. "Good-night, my dear, good-night!"

" You have nothing more to tell me ? "

" No.   What should I have ?   You wouldn't have me tell you a lie ? "

" I wouldn't have you do that to-night, Tom, of all the nights in your life ; many and much happier as I hope they will be."

" Thank you, my dear Loo.   I am so tired, that I am sure I wonder I don't say anything to get to sleep.   Go to bed, go to bed."

Kissing her again, he turned round, drew the coverlet over his head, and lay as still as if that time had come by which she had adjured him.   She stood for some time at the bedside before she slowly moved away.   She stopped at the door, looked back when she had opened it, and asked him if he had called her ?   But he lay still, and she softly closed the door and returned to her room.

Then the wretched boy looked cautiously up and found her gone, crept out of bed, fastened his door, and threw himself upon his pillow again : tearing his hair, morosely crying, grudgingly loving her, hatefully but impenitently spurning himself, and no less hatefully and unprofitably spurning all the good in the world.

CHAPTER IX.

HEARING THE LAST OF IT.

Mrs. Sparsit, lying by to recover the tone of her nerves in Mr. Bounderby's retreat, kept such a sharp look-out, night and day, under her Coriolanian eyebrows, that her eyes, like a couple of lighthouses on an iron-bound coast, might have warned all prudent mariners from that bold rock her Roman nose and the dark and craggy region in its neighborhood, but for the placidity of her manner. Although it was hard to believe that her retiring for the night could be anything but a form, so severely wide awake were those classical eyes of hers, and so impossible did it seem that her rigid nose could yield to any relaxing influence, yet her manner of sitting, smoothing her uncomfortable, not to say, gritty mittens (they were constructed of a cool fabric like a meat-safe), or of ambling to unknown places of destination with her foot in her cotton stirrup, was so perfectly serene, that most observers would have been constrained to suppose her a dove, embodied by some freak of nature, in the earthly tabernacle of a bird of the hook-beaked order.

She was a most wonderful woman for prowling about the house. How she got from story to story was a mystery beyond solution. A lady so decorous in herself, and so highly connected, was not to be suspected of dropping over the bannisters or sliding down them, yet her extraordinary facility of locomotion suggested the wild idea. Another noticeable circumstance in Mrs. Sparsit was, that she was never hurried. She would shoot with consummate velocity from the roof to the hall, yet would be in full possession of her breath and dignity on the moment of her arrival there. Neither was she ever seen by human vision to go at a great pace.

She took very kindly to Mr. Harthouse, and had some pleasant conversation with him soon after her arrival. She made him her stately curtsey in the garden, one morning before breakfast.

"It appears but yesterday, sir," said Mrs. Sparsit, "that I had the honor of receiving you at the Bank, when you were so good as to wish to be made acquainted with Mr. Bounderby's address."

"An occasion, I am sure, not to be forgotten by myself in the course of Ages," said Mr. Harthouse, inclining his head to Mrs. Sparsit with the most indolent of all possible airs.

"We live in a singular world, sir," said Mrs. Sparsit.

"I have had the honor, by a coincidence of which I am proud, to have made a remark, similar in effect, though not so epigrammatically expressed."

"A singular world, I would say, sir," pursued Mrs. Sparsit; after acknowledging the compliment with a drooping of her dark eyebrows, not altogether so mild in its expression as her voice was in its dulcet tones; "as regards the intimacies we form at one time, with individuals we were quite ignorant of, at another. I recall, sir, that on that occasion you went so far as to say you were actually apprehensive of Miss Gradgrind."

"Your memory does me more honor than my insignificance deserves. I availed myself of your obliging hints to correct my timidity, and it is unnecessary to add that they were perfectly accurate. Mrs. Sparsit's talent for —in fact for anything requiring accuracy—with a combination of strength of mind—and Family—is too habitually developed to admit of any question." He was almost falling asleep over this compliment; it took him so long to get through, and his mind wandered so much in the course of its execution.

"You found Miss Gradgrind—I really cannot call her Mrs. Bounderby; it's very absurd of me—as youthful as I described her?" asked Mrs. Sparsit, sweetly.

"You drew her portrait perfectly," said Mr. Harthouse. "Presented her dead image."

"Very engaging, sir," said Mrs. Sparsit, causing her mittens slowly to revolve over one another.

"Highly so."

"It used to be considered," said Mrs. Sparsit, "that Miss Gradgrind was wanting in animation, but I confess she appears to me considerably and strikingly improved in that respect. Ay, and indeed here *is* Mr. Bounderby!" cried Mrs. Sparsit, nodding her head a great many times, as if she had been talking and thinking of no one else. "How do you find yourself this morning, sir? Pray let us see you cheerful, sir."

Now, these persistent assuagements of his misery, and lightenings of his load, had by this time begun to have the effect of making Mr. Bounderby softer than usual towards Mrs. Sparsit, and harder than usual to most other people from his wife downward. So, when Mrs. Sparsit said with forced lightness of heart, "You want your breakfast, sir, but I dare say Miss Gradgrind will soon be here to preside at the table," Mr. Bounderby replied, "If I waited to be taken care of by my wife, ma'am, I believe you know pretty well I should wait till Doomsday, so I'll trouble *you* to take charge of the teapot." Mrs. Sparsit complied, and assumed her old position at table.

This again made the excellent woman vastly sentimental. She was so humble withal, that when Louisa appeared, she rose, protesting she never could think of sitting in that place under existing circumstances, often as she had had the honor of making Mr. Bounderby's breakfast, before Mrs. Gradgrind—she begged pardon, she meant to say Miss Bounderby—she hoped to be excused, but she really could not get it right yet, though she trusted to become familiar with it by and by—had assumed her present position. It was only (she observed) because Miss Gradgrind happened to be a little late, and Mr. Bounderby's time was so very precious, and she knew it of old to be so essential that he should breakfast to the moment, that she had taken the liberty of complying with his request; long as his will had been a law to her.

"There! Stop where you are, ma'am," said Mr. Bounderby, "stop where you are! Mrs. Bounderby will be very glad to be relieved of the trouble, I believe."

"Don't say that, sir," returned Mrs. Sparsit, almost with severity, "because that is very unkind to Mrs. Bounderby. And to be unkind is not to be you, sir."

"You may set your mind at rest, ma'am.—You can take it very quietly, can't you, Loo?" said Mr. Bounderby, in a blustering way to his wife.

"Of course. It is of no moment. Why should it be of any importance to me?"

"Why should it be of any importance to any one, Mrs. Sparsit, ma'am;" said Mr. Bounderby, swelling with a sense of slight. "You attach too much importance to these things, ma'am. By George, you'll be corrupted in some of your notions here. You are old-fashioned, ma'am. You are behind Tom Gradgrind's children's time."

"What is the matter with you?" asked Louisa, coldly surprised. "What has given you offence?"

"Offence!" repeated Bounderby. "Do you suppose if there was any offence given me, I shouldn't name it, and request to have it corrected? I am a straightforward man, I believe. I don't go beating about for side-winds."

"I suppose no one ever had occasion to think you too diffident, or too delicate," Louisa answered him composedly: "I have never made that objection to you, either as a child or as a woman. I don't understand what you would have."

"Have?" returned Mr. Bounderby. "Nothing. Otherwise, don't you, Loo Bounderby, know thoroughly well that I, Josiah Bounderby of Coketown, would have it?"

She looked at him, as he struck the table and made the teacups ring, with a proud color in her face that was a new change, Mr. Harthouse thought. "You are incomprehensible this morning," said Louisa. "Pray take no

further trouble to explain yourself. I am not curious to
know your meaning. What does it matter?"

Nothing more was said on this theme, and Mr. Harthouse was soon idly gay on indifferent subjects. But
from this day, the Sparsit action upon Mr. Bounderby
threw Louisa and James Harthouse more together, and
strengthened the dangerous alienation from her husband
and confidence against him with another, into which she
had fallen by degrees so fine that she could not retrace
them if she tried. But whether she ever tried or no, lay
hidden in her own closed heart.

Mrs. Sparsit was so much affected on this particular
occasion, that, assisting Mr. Bounderby to his hat after
breakfast, and being then alone with him in the hall, she
imprinted a chaste kiss upon his hand, murmured " My
benefactor !" and retired, overwhelmed with grief. Yet
it is an indubitable fact, within the cognizance of this
history, that five minutes after he had left the house in
the self-same hat, the same descendant of the Scadgerses
and connection by matrimony of the Powlers, shook her
right-hand mitten at his portrait, made a contemptuous
grimace at that work of art, and said " Serve you right,
you Noodle, and I am glad of it."

Mr. Bounderby had not been long gone, when Bitzer
appeared. Bitzer had come down by train, shrieking
and rattling over the long line of arches that bestrode
the wild country of past and present coalpits, with an
express from Stone Lodge. It was a hasty note to inform
Louisa, that Mrs. Gradgrind lay very ill. She had never
been well within her daughter's knowledge ; but, she
had declined within the last few days, had continued
sinking all through the night, and was now as nearly
dead, as her limited capacity of being in any state that
implied the ghost of an intention to get out of it, allowed.

Accompanied by the lightest of porters, fit colorless
servitor at Death's door when Mrs. Gradgrind knocked,
Louisa rumbled to Coketown, over the coalpits past and
present, and was whirled into its smoky jaws. She dismissed the messenger to his own devices, and rode away
to her old home.

She had seldom been there since her marriage. Her
father was usually sifting and sifting at his parliamentary
cinder-heap in London (without being observed to turn

up many precious articles among the rubbish), and was still hard at it in the national dust-yard. Her mother had taken it rather as a disturbance than otherwise, to be visited, as she reclined upon her sofa ; young people, Louisa felt herself all unfit for ; Sissy she had never softened to again, since the night when the stroller's child had raised her eyes to look at Mr. Bounderby's intended wife. She had no inducements to go back, and had rarely gone.

Neither, as she approached her old home now, did any of the best influences of old home descend upon her. The dreams of childhood—its airy fables ; its graceful, beautiful, humane, impossible adornments of the world beyond : so good to be believed in once, so good to be remembered when outgrown, for then the least among them rises to the stature of a great Charity in the heart, suffering little children to come into the midst of it, and to keep with their pure hands a garden in the stony ways of this world, wherein it were better for all the children of Adam that they should oftener sun themselves, simple and trustful, and not worldly-wise—what had she to do with these ? Remembrances of how she had journeyed to the little that she knew, by the enchanted roads of what she and millions of innocent creatures had hoped and imagined ; of how, first coming upon Reason through the tender light of Fancy, she had seen it a beneficent god, deferring to gods as great as itself : not a grim Idol cruel and cold, with its victims bound hand to foot, and its big dumb shape set up with a sightless stare, never to be moved by anything but so many calculated tons of leverage—what had she to do with these ? Her remembrances of home and childhood were remembrances of the drying up of every spring and fountain in her young heart as it gushed out. The golden waters were not there. They were flowing for the fertilization of the land where grapes are gathered from thorns, and figs from thistles.

She went, with a heavy, hardened kind of sorrow upon her, into the house and into her mother's room. Since the time of her leaving home, Sissy had lived with the rest of the family on equal terms. Sissy was at her mother's side ; and Jane, her sister, now ten or twelve years old, was in the room.

There was great trouble before it could be made known to Mrs. Gradgrind that her eldest child was there. She reclined, propped up, from mere habit, on a couch : as nearly in her old usual attitude, as anything so helpless could be kept in. She had positively refused to take to her bed ; on the ground that if she did, she would never hear the last of it.

Her feeble voice sounded so far away in her bundle of shawls, and the sound of another voice addressing her seemed to take such a long time in getting down to her ears, that she might have been lying at the bottom of a well. The poor lady was nearer Truth than she ever had been : which had much to do with it.

On being told that Mrs. Bounderby was there, she replied at cross-purposes, that she had never called him by that name since he married Louisa ; that pending her choice of an objectionable name, she had called him J ; and that she could not at present depart from that regulation not being yet provided with a permanent substitute. Louisa had sat by her for some minutes, and had spoken to her often, before she arrived at a clear understanding who it was. She then seemed to come to it all at once.

"Well, my dear," said Mrs. Gradgrind, "and I hope you are going on satisfactorily to yourself. It was all your father's doing. He set his heart upon it. And he ought to know."

"I want to hear of you, mother ; not of myself."

"You want to hear of me, my dear ? That's something new, I am sure, when anybody wants to hear of me. Not at all well, Louisa. Very faint and giddy."

"Are you in pain, dear mother ?"

"I think there's a pain somewhere in the room," said Mrs. Gradgrind, "but I couldn't positively say that I have got it."

After this strange speech, she lay silent for some time. Louisa, holding her hand, could feel no pulse ; but kissing it, could see a slight thin thread of life in fluttering motion.

"You very seldom see your sister," said Mrs. Gradgrind. "She grows like you. I wish you would look at her. Sissy, bring her here."

She was brought, and stood with her hand in her

sister's. Louisa had observed her with her arm round Sissy's neck, and she felt the difference of this approach.

" Do you see the likeness, Louisa?"

" Yes, mother. I should think her like me. But——"

" Eh ! Yes, I always say so," Mrs. Gradgrind cried, with unexpected quickness. " Aud that reminds me. I—I want to speak to you, my dear. Sissy, my good girl, leave us alone a minute."

Louisa had relinquished the hand : had thought that her sister's was a better and brighter face than hers had ever been : had seen in it, not without a rising feeling of resentment, even in that place and at that time, something of the gentleness of the other face in the room ; the sweet face with the trusting eyes, made paler than watching and sympathy made it, by the rich dark hair.

Left alone with her mother, Louisa saw her lying with an awful lull upon her face, like one who was floating away upon some great water, all resistance over, content to be carried down the stream. She put the shadow of a hand to her lips again, and recalled her.

" You were going to speak to me, mother."

" Eh? Yes, to be sure, my dear. You know your father is almost always away now, and therefore I must write to him about it."

" About what, mother? Don't be troubled. About what ? "

" You must remember, my dear, that whenever I have said anything, on any subject, I have never heard the last of it : and consequently, that I have long left off saying anything."

" I can hear you, mother." But, it was only by dint of bending down to her ear, and at the same time attentively watching the lips as they moved, that she could link such faint and broken sounds into any chain of connection.

" You learnt a great deal, Louisa, and so did your brother. Ologies of all kinds from morning to night. If there is any Ology left, of any description, that has not been worn to rags in this house, all I can say is, I hope I shall never hear its name."

" I can hear you, mother, when you have strength to go on." This, to keep her from floating away.

But there is something—not an Ology at all—that your father has missed, or forgotten, Louisa. I don't know what it is. I have often sat with Sissy near me, and thought about it. I shall never get its name now. But your father may. It makes me restless. I want to write to him, to find out for God's sake, what it is. Give me a pen, give me a pen."

Even the power of restlessness was gone, except from the poor head, which could just turn from side to side.

She fancied, however, that her request had been complied with, and that the pen she could not have held was in her hand. It matters little what figures of wonderful no-meaning she began to trace upon her wrappers. The hand soon stopped in the midst of them; the light that had always been feeble and dim behind the weak transparency, went out; and even Mrs. Gradgrind, emerged from the shadow in which man walketh and disquieteth himself in vain, took upon her the dread solemnity of the sages and patriarchs.

CHAPTER X.

MRS. SPARSIT'S STAIRCASE.

Mrs. Sparsit's nerves being slow to recover their tone, the worthy woman made a stay of some weeks in duration at Mr. Bounderby's retreat, where, notwithstanding her anchorite turn of mind based upon her becoming consciousness of her altered station, she resigned herself with noble fortitude to lodging, as one may say, in clover, and feeding on the fat of the land. During the whole term of this recess from the guardianship of the Bank, Mrs. Sparsit was a pattern of consistency; continuing to take such pity on Mr. Bounderby to his face as is rarely taken on man, and to call his portrait a Noodle to *its* face, with the greatest acrimony and contempt.

Mr. Bounderby, having got it into his explosive composition that Mrs. Sparsit was a highly superior woman to perceive that he had that general cross upon him in his deserts (for he had not yet settled what it was), and further that Louisa would have objected to her as a frequent visitor if it had comported with his greatness that she should object to anything he chose to do, resolved not to lose sight of Mrs. Sparsit easily. So when her nerves were strung up to the pitch of again consuming sweet-breads in solitude, he said to her at the dinner-table, on the day before her departure, I tell you what, ma'am; you shall come down here of a Saturday, while the fine weather lasts, and stay till Monday." To which Mrs. Sparsit returned, in effect, though not of the Mahomedan persuasion: "To hear is to obey." Now, Mrs. Sparsit was not a poetical woman; but she took an idea in the nature of an allegorical fancy, into her head. Much watching of Louisa, and much consequent observation of her impenetrable demeanor, which keenly whetted and sharpened Mrs. Sparsit's edge, must have given her as it were a lift, in the way of inspiration. She erected in her mind a mighty Staircase, with a dark pit of shame and ruin at the bottom; and down those stairs from day to day and hour to hour she saw Louisa coming.

It became the business of Mrs. Sparsit's life to look up at her staircase, and to watch Louisa coming down. Sometimes slowly, sometimes quickly, sometimes several steps at one bout, sometimes stopping, never turning back. If she had once turned back, it might have been the death of Mrs. Sparsit in spleen and grief.

She had been descending steadily, to the day, and on the day, when Mr. Bounderby issued the weekly invitation recorded above. Mrs. Sparsit was in good spirits, and inclined to be conversational.

"And pray, sir," said she, "if I may venture to ask a question appertaining to any subject on which you show reserve—which is indeed hardy in me, for I well know you have a reason for everything you do—have you received intelligence respecting the robbery?"

"Why, ma'am, no; not yet. Under the circumstances, I didn't expect it yet. Rome wasn't built in a day, ma'am"

"Very true, sir," said Mrs. Sparsit, shaking her head.

"Nor yet in a week, ma'am."

"No, indeed, sir," returned Mrs. Sparsit, with a gentle melancholy upon her.

"In a similar manner, ma'am," said Bounderby, "I can wait, you know. If Romulus and Remus could wait, Josiah Bounderby can wait. They were better off in their

youth than I was, however. They had a she-wolf for a
nurse; *I* had only a she-wolf for a grandmother. She
didn't give any milk, ma'am; she gave bruises. She was a
regular Alderney at that."

"Ah!" Mrs Sparsit sighed and shuddered.

"No, ma'am," continued Bounderby, "I have not heard
anything more about it. It's in hand, though; and young
Tom who rather sticks to business at present—something
new for him; he hadn't the schooling *I* had—is helping.
My injunction is, Keep it quiet, and let it seem to blow
over. Do what you like under the rose, but don't give a
sign of what you're about; or half a hundred of 'em will
combine together and get this fellow who has bolted,
out of reach for good. Keep it quiet, and the thieves
will grow in confidence by little and little, and we, hall
have 'em."

"Very sagacious indeed, sir," said Mrs. Sparsit. "Very
interesting. The old woman you mentioned, sir——"

"The old woman I mentioned, ma'am," said Bounderby
cutting the matter short, as it was nothing to boast about,
"is not laid hold of; but she may take her oath she will be
if that is any satisfaction to her villainous old mind. In
the mean time, ma'am, I am of opinion, if you ask me my
opinion, that the less she is talked about the better."

That same evening, Mrs. Sparsit, in her chamber window, resting from her packing operations, looked towards
her great staircase and saw Louisa still descending.

She sat by Mr. Harthouse, in an alcove in the garden,
talking very low, he stood leaning over her, as they whispered together, and his face almost touched her hair. "If
not quite!" said Mrs. Sparsit, straining her hawk's eyes to
the utmost. Mrs. Sparsit was too distant to hear a word
of their discourse, or even to know that they were speaking softly, otherwise than from the expression of their
figures; but what they said was this:

"You recollect the man, Mr. Harthouse?"

"Oh, perfectly!"

"His face and his manner, and what he said?"

"Perfectly. And an infinitely dreary person he appeared to me to be. Lengthy and prosy in the extreme. It
was knowing to hold forth, in the humble-virtue school of
eloquence; but, I assure you I thought at the time, 'My
good fellow, you are over-doing this!'"

"It has been very difficult to me to think ill of that man."

"My dear Louisa—as Tom says." Which he never did say. "You know no good of the fellow?"

"No, certainly."

"Nor of any other such person?"

"How can I," she returned, with more of her first manner on her then he had lately seen, "when I know nothing of them, men or women?"

"My dear Louisa, then consent to receive the submissive representation of your devoted friend, who knows something of several varieties of his excellent fellow-creatures—for excellent they are, I am quite ready to believe, in spite of such little foibles as always helping themselves to what they can get hold of. This fellow talks. Well; every fellow talks. He professes morality. Well; all sorts of humbugs profess morality. From the House of Commons to the House of Correction, there is a general profession of morality, except among our people; it really is that exception which makes our people quite reviving. You saw and heard the case. Here was one of the fluffy classes pulled up extremely short by my esteemed friend Mr. Bounderby—who, as we know, is not possessed of that delicacy which would soften so tight a hand. The member of the fluffy classes was injured, exasperated, left the house grumbling, met somebody who proposed to him to go in for some share in this Bank business, went in, put something in his pocket which had nothing in it before, and relieved his mind extremely. Really he would have been an uncommon, instead of a common, fellow, if he had not availed himself of such an opportunity. Or he may have orignated it altogether if he had the cleverness."

"I almost feel as though it must be bad in me," returned Louisa, after sitting thoughtful awhile, "to be so ready to agree with you, and to be so lightened in my heart by what you say."

"I only say what is reasonable; nothing worse. I have talked it over with my friend Tom more than once—of course I remain on terms of perfect confidence with Tom—and he is quite of my opinion, and I am quite of his. Will you walk?" They strolled away, among the lanes beginning to be indistinct in the twilight—she leaning on his arm—and she little thought how she was going down, down, down, Mrs. Sparsit's staircase.

Night and day, Mrs. Sparsit kept it standing. When Louisa had arrived at the bottom and disapeared in the gulf, it might fall in upon her if it would; but, until then, there it was to be, a Building, before Mrs. Sparsit's eyes. And there Louisa always was upon it. And always gliding down, down, down!

Mrs. Sparsit saw James Harthouse come and go; she heard of him here and there; she saw the changes of the face he had studied; she too remarked to a nicety how and when it clouded, how and when it cleared; she kept her black eyes wide open, with no touch of pity, with no touch of compunction, all absorbed in interest. In thei nterest of seeing her, ever drawing with no hand to stay her, nearer and nearer to the bottom of this new Giant's Staircase.

With all her deference for Mr. Bounderby as contradistinguished from his portrait, Mrs. Sparsit had not the smallest intention of interrupting the descent. Eager to see it accomplished, and yet patient, she waited for the last fall, as for the ripeness and fulness of the harvest of her hopes. Hushed in expectancy, she kept her wary gaze upon the stairs; and seldom so much as darkly shook her right mitten (with her fist in it), at the figure coming down.

CHAPTER XI.

LOWER AND LOWER.

THE figure descended the great stairs, steadily, steadily; always verging, like a weight in deep water, to the black gulf at the bottom.

Mr. Gradgrind, apprised of his wife's decease, made an expedition from London, and buried her in a business-like manner. He then returned with promptitude to the national cinder-heap, and resumed his sifting for the odds and ends he wanted, and his throwing of the dust about into the eyes of other people who wanted other odds and ends—in fact resumed his parliamentary duties.

In the meantime, Mrs. Sparsit kept unwinking watch and ward. Separated from her staircase, all the week, by the length of iron road dividing Coketown from the country-house, she yet maintained her cat-like observation of Louisa, through her husband through her brother, through James Harthouse, through the outsides of letters and packets, through everything animate and inanimate that at any time went near the stairs. " Your foot on the last step, my lady," said Mrs. Sparsit, apostrophizing the descending figure with the aid of her threatening mitten, "and all your art shall never blind me."

Art or nature though, the original stock of Louisa's character or the graft of circumstances upon it,—her curious reserve did baffle, while it stimulated, one as sagacious as Mrs. Sparsit. There were times when Mr. James Harthouse was not sure of her. There were times when he could not read the face he had studied so long; and when this lonely girl was a greater mystery to him then any woman of the world with a ring of satellites to help her.

So the time went on ; until it happened that Mr. Bounderby was called away from home by business which required his presence elsewhere, for three or four days. It was on a Friday that he intimated this to Mrs. Sparsit at the Bank, adding : " But you'll go down to morrow, ma'am, all the same. You'll go down just as if I was there. It will make no difference to you."

" Pray, sir," returned Mrs. Sparsit, reproachfully, " let me beg you not to say that. Your absence will make a vast difference to me, sir, as I think you very well know."

" Well, ma'am, then you must get on in my absence as well as you can," said Bounderby, not displeased.

" Mr. Bounderby," retorted Mrs. Sparsit, " your will is to me a law, sir ; otherwise, it might be my inclination to dispute your kind commands, not feeling sure that it will be quite so agreeable to Miss Gradgrind to receive me, as it ever is to your own munificent hospitality. But you shall say no more, sir. I will go upon your invitation."

" Why, when I invite you to my house, ma' am," said Bounderby, opening his eyes, " I should hope you want no other invitation."

" No, indeed, sir," returned Mrs. Sparsit, " I should hope not. Say no more, sir. I would, sir, I could see you gay again."

" What do you mean, ma'am ?" blustered Bounderby.

13

"Sir," rejoined Mrs. Sparsit, "there was wor.t to be an elasticity in you which I sadly miss. Be buoyant, sir!"

Mr. Bounderby, under the influence of this difficult adjuration, backed up by her compassionate eye, could only scratch his head in a feeble and ridiculous manner, and afterwards assert himself at a distance, by being heard to bully the small fry of business all the morning.

"Bitzer," said Mrs. Sparsit that afternoon, when her patron was gone on his journey, and the Bank was closing, "present my compliments to young Mr. Thomas, and ask him if he would step up and partake of a lamb chop and walnut ketchup, with a glass of India ale?" Young Mr. Thomas being usually ready for anything in that way returned a gracious answer, and followed on its heels.

"Mr. Thomas," said Mrs. Sparsit, "these plain viands being on table, I thought you might be tempted."

"Thank'ee, Mrs. Sparsit," said the whelp. And gloomily fell to.

"How is Mr. Harthouse, Mr. Tom?" asked Mrs. Sparsit.

"Oh, he's all right," said Tom.

"Where may he be at present?" Mrs. Sparsit asked in a light conversational manner, after mentally devoting the whelp to the Furies for being so uncommunicative.

"He is shooting in Yorkshire," said Tom. "Sent Loo a basket half as big as a church, yesterday."

"The kind of gentleman, now," said Mrs. Sparsit, sweetly, "whom one might wager to be a good shot!"

"Crack," said Tom.

He had long been a down-looking young fellow, but this characteristic had so increased of late, that he never raised his eyes to any face for three seconds together. Mrs. Sparsit consequently had ample means of watching his looks, if she were so inclined.

"Mr. Harthouse is a great favorite of mine," said Mrs. Sparsit, "as indeed he is of most people. May we expect to see him again shortly, Mr. Tom?"

"Why, I expect to see him to-morrow," returned the whelp.

"Good news!" cried Mrs. Sparsit, blandly.

"I have got an appointment with him to meet him in the evening at the station here," said Tom, "and I am going to dine with him afterwards, I believe. He is not

coming down to the country house for a week or so,
being due somewhere else. At least, he says so; but I
shouldn't wonder if he was to stop here over Sunday,
and stray that way."

" Which reminds me!" said Mrs. Sparsit. " Would
you remember a message to your sister, Mr. Tom, if I
was to charge you with one?"

" Well? I'll try," returned the reluctant whelp, " if it
isn't a long un."

" It is merely my respectful compliments," said Mrs.
Sparsit, " and I fear I may not trouble her with my
society this week; being still a little nervous, and better
perhaps by my poor self."

" Oh! If that's all," observed Tom, " it wouldn't
much matter, even if I was to forget it, for Loo's not
likely to think of you unless she sees you."

Having paid for his entertainment with this agreeable
compliment, he relapsed into a hangdog silence until there
was no more India ale left, when he said, " Well, Mrs.
Sparsit, I must be off!" and went off.

Next day, Saturday, Mrs. Sparsit sat at her window
all day long looking at the customers coming in and out,
watching the postmen, keeping an eye on the general
traffic of the street, revolving many things in her mind,
but, above all, keeping her attention on her staircase.
The evening come, she put on her bonnet and shawl, and
went quietly out: having her reasons for hovering in a
furtive way about the station by which a passenger would
arrive from Yorkshire, and for preferring to peep into it
round pillars and corners, and out of ladies' waiting-
room windows, to appearing in its precincts openly.

Tom was in attendance, and loitered about until the
expected train came in. It brought no Mr. Harthouse.
Tom waited until the crowd had dispersed, and the bustle
was over; and then referred to a posted list of trains, and
took counsel with porters. That done, he strolled away
idly, stopping in the street and looking up it and down
it, and lifting his hat off and putting it on again, and
yawning and stretching himself, and exhibiting all the
symptoms of mortal weariness to be expected in one who
had still to wait until the next train should come in, an
hour and forty minutes hence.

" This is a device to keep him out of the way," said

Mrs. Sparsit, starting from the dull office window whence she had watched him last. "Harthouse is with his sister now!"

It was the conception of an inspired moment, and she shot off with her utmost swiftness to work it out. The station for the country house was at the opposite end of the town, the time was short, the road not easy; but she was so quick in pouncing on a disengaged coach, so quick in darting out of it, producing her money, seizing her ticket, and diving into the train, that she was borne along the arches spanning the land of coal-pits past and present, as if she had been caught up in a cloud and whirled away.

All the journey, immovable in the air though never left behind; plain to the dark eyes of her mind, as the electric wires which ruled a colossal strip of music-paper out of the evening sky, were plain to the dark eyes of her body; Mrs. Sparsit saw her staircase, with the figure coming down. Very near the bottom now. Upon the brink of the abyss.

An overcast September evening, just at nightfall, saw beneath its drooping eyelid Mrs. Sparsit glide out of her carriage, pass down the wooden steps of the little station into a stony road, cross it into a green lane, and become hidden in a summer-growth of leaves and branches. One or two late birds sleepily chirping in their nests, and a bat heavily crossing and recrossing her, and the reek of her own tread in the thick dust that felt like velvet, were all Mrs. Sparsit heard or saw until she very softly closed a gate.

She went up to the house, keeping within the shrubbery, and went round it, peeping between the leaves at the lower windows. Most of them were open, as they usually were in such warm weather, but there were no lights yet, and all was silent. She tried the garden with no better effect. She thought of the wood, and stole towards it, heedless of long grass and briers: of worms, snails, and slugs, and all the creeping things that be. With her dark eyes and her hook nose warily in advance of her, Mrs. Sparsit softly crushed her way through the thick undergrowth, so intent upon her object that she probably would have done no less, if the wood had been a wood of adders.

Hark!

The smaller birds might have tumbled out of their nests, fascinated by the glittering of Mrs. Sparsit's eyes in the gloom, as she stopped and listened.

Low voices close at hand. His voice and hers. The appointment *was* a device to keep the brother away! There they were yonder, by the felled tree.

Bending low among the dewy grass, Mrs. Sparsit advanced closer to them. She drew herself up, and stood behind a tree, like Robinson Crusoe in his ambuscade against the savages; so near to them that at a spring, and that no great one, she could have touched them both. He was there secretly, and had not shown himself at the house. He had come on horseback, and must have passed through the neighboring fields; for his horse was tied to the meadow side of the fence, within a few paces.

"My dearest love," said he, "What could I do? Knowing you were alone, was it possible that I could stay away?"

"You may hang your head, to make yourself the more attractive; *I* don't know what they see in you when you hold it up," thought Mrs. Sparsit; "but you little think, my dearest love, whose eyes are on you!"

That she hung her head, was certain. She urged him to go away, she commanded him to go away; but she neither turned her face to him nor raised it. Yet it was remarkable that she sat as still as ever the amiable woman in her ambuscade had seen her sit, at any period in her life. Her hands rested in one another, like the hands of a statue; and even her manner of speaking was not hurried.

"My dear child," said Harthouse; Mrs. Sparsit saw with delight that his arm embraced her; "will you not bear with my society for a little while?"

"Not here."

"Where, Louisa?"

"Not here."

"But we have so little time to make so much of, and I have come so far, and am altogether so devoted, and distracted. There never was a slave at once so devoted and illused by his mistress. To look for your sunny welcome that has warmed me into life, and to be received in your frozen manner, is heartrending."

"Am I to say again, that I must be left to myself here?"

"But we must meet, my dear Louisa. Where shall we meet?"

They both started. The listener started, guiltily, too; for she thought there was another listener among the trees. It was only rain, beginning to fall fast, in heavy drops.

"Shall I ride up to the house a few minutes hence, innocently supposing that its master is at home and will be charmed to receive me?"

"No!"

"Your cruel commands are implicitly to be obeyed; though I am the most unfortunate fellow in the world, I believe, to have been insensible to all other women, and to have fallen prostrate at last under the foot of the most beautiful, and the most engaging, and the most imperious. My dearest Louisa, I cannot go myself, or let you go, in this hard abuse of your power."

Mrs. Sparsit saw him detain her with his encircling arm, and heard him then and there, within her (Mrs. Sparsit's) greedy hearing, tell her how he loved her, and how she was the stake for which he ardently desired to play away all that he had in life. The objects he had lately pursued, turned worthless beside her; such success as was almost in his grasp, he flung away from him like the dirt it was, compared with her. Its pursuit, nevertheless, if it kept him near her, or its renunciation if it took him from her, or flight if she shared it, or secrecy if she commanded it, or any fate, or every fate all was alike to him, so that she was true to him,—the man who had seen how cast away she was, whom she had inspired at their first meeting with an admiration, an interest, of which he had thought himself incapable, whom she had received into her confidence, who was devoted to her and adored her. All this, and more, in his hurry, and in hers, the whirl of her own gratified malice, in the dread of being discovered, in the rapidly increasing noise of heavy rain among the leaves, and a thunderstorm rolling up—Mrs. Sparsit received into her mind, set off with such an unavoidable halo of confusion and indistinctness, that when at length he climbed the fence and led his horse away, she was not sure where they were to meet, or when, except that they had said it was to be that night.

But one of them yet remained in the darkness before her; and while she tracked that one she must be right.

"Oh, my dearest love," thought Mrs. Sparsit, "you little think how well attended you are!"

Mrs. Sparsit saw her out of the wood, and saw her enter the house. What to do next? Ir rained now, in a sheet of water. Mrs. Sparsit's white stockings were of many colors, green predominating; prickly things were in her shoes; caterpillars slung themselves, in hammocks of their own making, from various parts of her dress; rills ran from her bonnet, and her Roman nose. In such condition, Mrs. Sparsit stood hidden in the density of the shrubbery, considering what next?

Lo, Louisa coming out of the house! Hastily cloaked and muffled, and stealing away. She elopes! She falls from the lowermost stair, and is swallowed up in the gulf.

Indifferent to the rain, and moving with a quick determined step, she struck into a side-path parallel with the ride. Mrs. Sparsit followed in the shadow of the trees, at but a short distance; for it was not easy to keep a figure in view going quickly through the umbrageous darkness.

When she stopped to close the side-gate without noise, Mrs. Sparsit stopped. When she went on, Mrs. Sparsit went on. She went by the way Mrs. Sparsit had come, emerged from the green lane, crossed the stony road, and ascended the wooden steps to the railroad. A train for Coketown would come through presently, Mrs. Sparsit knew; so she understood Coketown to be her first place of destination.

In Mrs. Sparsit's limp and streaming state, no extensive precautions were necessary to change her usual appearance; but, she stopped under the lee of the station wall, tumbled her shawl into a new shape, and put it on over her bonnet. So disguised she had no fear of being recognized when she followed up the railroad steps, and paid her money in the small office. Louisa sat waiting in a corner. Mrs. Sparsit sat waiting in another corner. Both listened to the thunder, which was loud, and to the rain, as it washed off the roof, and pattered on the parapets of the arches. Two or three lamps were rained out and blown out; so both saw the lightning to advantage as it quivered and zigzagged on the iron tracks.

The seizure of the station with a fit of trembling, gradually deepening to a complaint of the heart, announced the train. Fire and steam, and smoke, and red light: a hiss, a crash, a bell, and a shriek; Louisa put into one carriage, Mrs. Sparsit put into another: the little station a desert speck in the thunder-storm.

Though her teeth chattered in her head from wet and cold, Mrs. Sparsit exulted hugely. The figure had plunged down the precipice, and she felt herself, as it were, attending on the body. Could she, who had been so active in the getting up of the funeral triumph, do less than exult? "She will be at Coketown long before him," thought Mrs. Sparsit, "though his horse is never so good. Where will she wait for him? And where will they go together? Patience. We shall see."

The tremendous rain occasioned infinite confusion, when the train stopped at its destination. Gutters and pipes had burst, drains had overflowed, and streets were under water. In the first instant of alighting, Mrs. Sparsit turned her distracted eyes towards the waiting coaches, which were in great request. "She will get into one," she considered, "and will be away before I can follow in another. At all risks of being run over, I must see the number, and hear the order given to the coachman."

But Mrs. Sparsit was wrong in her calculation. Louisa got into no coach, and was already gone. The black eyes kept upon the railroad-carriage in which she had travelled, settled upon it a moment too late. The door not being opened after several minutes, Mrs. Sparsit passed it and repassed it, saw nothing, looked in, and found it empty. Wet through and through: with her feet squelching and squashing in her shoes whenever she moved; with a rash of rain upon her classical visage; with a bonnet like an over-ripe fig; with all her clothes spoiled; with damp impressions of every button, string, and hook-and-eye she wore, printed off upon her highly connected back; with a stagnant verdure on her general exterior, such as accumulates on an old park fence in a mouldy lane; Mrs. Sparsit had no resource but to burst into tears of bitterness and say, "I have lost her!"

CHAPTER XII.

DOWN.

THE national dustmen, after entertaining one another with a great many noisy little fights among themselves, had dispersed for the present, and Mr. Gradgrind was at home for the vacation.

He sat writing in the room with the deadly statistical clock, proving, something no doubt—probably, in the main, that the Good Samaritan was a Bad Economist. The noise of the rain did not disturb him much; but it attracted his attention sufficiently to make him raise his head sometimes, as if he were rather remonstrating with the elements. When it thundered very loudly, he glanced towards Coketown, having it in his mind that some of the tall chimneys might be struck by lightning.

The thunder was rolling into distance, and the rain was pouring down like a deluge, when the door of his room opened. He looked round the lamp upon his table, and saw, with amazement, his eldest daughter.

" Louisa ! "

" Father, I want to speak to you."

" What is the matter? How strange you look! And good Heaven," said Mr. Gradgrind, wondering more and more, " have you come here exposed to this storm ? "

She put her hands to her dress, as if she hardly knew. " Yes." Then she uncovered her head, and letting her cloak and hood fall where they might, stood looking at him : so colorless, so dishevelled, so defiant and de-spairing, that he was afraid of her.

" What is it ? I conjure you, Louisa, tell me what is the matter."

She dropped into a chair before him, and put her cold hand on his arm.

" Father, you have trained me from my cradle ? "

" Yes, Louisa."

" I curse the hour in which I was born to such a destiny."

He looked at her in doubt and dread, vacantly repeating: "Curse the hour? Curse the hour?"

"How could you give me life, and take from me all the inappreciable things that raise it from the state of conscious death? Where are the graces of my soul? Where are the sentiments of my heart? What have you done, O father, what have you done, with the garden that should have bloomed once, in this great wilderness here!"

She struck herself with both her hands upon her bosom.

"If it had ever been here, its ashes alone would save me from the void in which my whole life sinks. I did not mean to say this; but, father, you remember the last time we conversed in this room?"

He had been so wholly unprepared for what he heard now, that it was with difficulty he answered, "Yes, Louisa."

"What has risen to my lips now, would have risen to my lips then, if you had given me a moment's help. I don't reproach you, father. What you have never nurtured in me, you have never nurtured in yourself; but O! if you had only done so, long ago, or if you had only neglected me, what a much better and much happier creature I should have been this day!"

On hearing this, after all his care, he bowed his head upon his hand and groaned aloud.

"Father, if you had known, when we were last together here, what even I feared while I strove against it—as it has been my task from infancy to strive against every natural prompting that has arisen in my heart; if you had known that there lingered in my breast, sensibilities, affections, weaknesses capable of being cherished into strength, defying all the calculations ever made by man, and no more known to his arithmetic than his Creator is, —would you have given me to the husband whom I am now sure that I hate?"

He said, "No. No, my poor child."

"Would you have doomed me, at any time, to the frost and blight that have hardened and spoiled me? Would you have robbed me—for no one's enrichment—only for the greater desolation of this world—of the immaterial part of my life, the spring and summer of my belief, my refuge from what is sordid and bad in the real things

around me, my school in which I should have learned to
be more humble and more trusting with them, and to
hope in my little sphere to make them better?"

"O no, no. No, Louisa."

"Yet, father if I had been stone blind; if I had groped
my way by my sense of touch, and had been free, while
I knew the shapes and surfaces of things, to exercise my
fancy somewhat, in regard to them; I should have been
a million times wiser. happier, more loving, more contented, more innocent and human in all good respects,
than I am with the eyes I have. Now, hear what I have
come to say."

He moved, to support her with his arm. She rising as
he did so, they stood close together: she, with a hand
upon his shoulder, looking fixedly in his face.

"With a hunger and thirst upon me, father, which have
never been for a moment appeased; with an ardent impulse towards some region where rules, and figures, and
definitions were not quite absolute; I have grown up,
battling every inch of my way."

"I never knew you were unhappy, my child."

"Father, I always knew it. In this strife I have almost
repulsed and crushed my better angel into a demon.
What I have learned has left me doubting, misbelieving,
despising, regretting, what I have not learned; and my
dismal resource has been to think that life would soon go
by, and that nothing in it could be worth the pain and
trouble of a contest."

"And you so young, Louisa!" he said with pity.

"And I so young. In this condition, father—for I show
you now, without fear or favor, the ordinary deadened
state of my mind as I know it—you proposed my husband
to me. I took him. I never made a pretence to him or
you that I loved him. I knew, and, father, you knew,
and he knew, that I never did. I was not wholly indifferent, for I had a hope of being pleasant and useful to
Tom. I made that wild escape into something visionary,
and have slowly found out how wild it was. But Tom
had been the subject of all the little tenderness of my
life; perhaps he became so because I knew so well how to
pity him. It matters little now, except as it may dispose
you to think more leniently of his errors."

As her father held her in his arms, she put her other

hand upon his other shoulder, and still looking fixedly in his face, went on.

" When I was irrevocably married, there rose up into rebellion against the tie, the old strife, made fiercer by all those causes of disparity which arise out of our two individual natures, and which no general laws shall ever rule or state for me, father, until they shall be able to direct the anatomist where to strike his knife into the secrets of my soul."

" Louisa! " he said, and said imploringly; for he well remembered what had passed between them in their former interview.

" I do not reproach you, father, I make no complaint. I am here with another object."

" What can I do, child? Ask me what you will."

"I am coming to it. Father, chance then threw into my way a new acquaintance; a man such as I had had no experience of; used to the world; light, polished, easy; making no pretences; avowing the low estimate of everything, that I was half afraid to form in secret; conveying to me almost immediately, though I don't know how or by what degrees, that he understood me, and read my thoughts. I could not find that he was worse than I. There seemed to be a near affinity between us. I only wondered it should be worth his while, who cared for nothing else, to care so much for me."

" For you, Louisa! "

Her father might instinctively have loosened his hold, but that he felt her strength departing from her, and saw a wild dilating fire in the eyes steadfastly regarding him.

" I say nothing of his plea for claiming my confidence. It matters very little how he gained it. Father, he did gain it. What you know of the story of my marriage, he soon knew, just as well."

Her father's face was ashy white, and he held her in both his arms.

" I have done no worse, I have not disgraced you. But if you ask me whether I have loved him, or do love him, I tell you plainly, father, that it may be so. I don't know."

She took her hands suddenly from his shoulders, and pressed them both upon her side; while in her face, not like itself—and in her figure, drawn up, resolute to finish by a last effort what she had to say—the feelings long suppressed broke loose.

"This night, my husband being away, he has been with me, declaring himself my lover. This minute he expects me, for I could release myself of his presence by no other means. I do not know that, I am sorry I do not know that I am ashamed, I do not know that I am degraded in my own esteem. All that I know is, your philosophy and your teaching will not save me. Now, father, you have brought me to this. Save me by some other means!"

He tightened his hold in time to prevent her sinking on the floor, but she cried out in a terrible voice, "I shall die if you hold me! Let me fall upon the ground!" And he laid her down, there, and saw the pride of his heart and the triumph of his system, lying, an insensible heap, at his feet.

END OF THE SECOND BOOK.

BOOK THE THIRD. GARNERING.

CHAPTER 1.

ANOTHER THING NEEDFUL.

LOUISA awoke from a torpor, and her eyes languidly opened on her old bed at home, and her old room. It seemed, at first, as if all that happened since the days when these objects were familiar to her were the shadows of a dream; but gradually, as the objects became more real to her sight, the events became more real to her mind.

She could scarcely move her head for pain and heaviness, her eyes were strained and sore, and she was very weak. A curious passive inattention had such possession of her, that the presence of her little sister in the room did not attract her notice for some time. Even when their eyes had met, and her sister approached the bed, Louisa lay for minutes looking at her in silence, and suffering her timidly to hold her passive hand, before she asked:

"When was I brought to this room?"

"Last night, Louisa?"

"Who brought me here?"

"Sissy, I believe."

"Why do you believe so?"

"Because I found her here this morning. She didn't come to my bedside to wake me, as she always does; and I went to look for her. She was not in her own room either; and I went looking for her all over the house until I found her here taking care of you and cooling your head. Will you see father? Sissy said I was to tell him when you woke."

"What a beaming face you have, Jane!" said Louisa, as her young sister—timidly still—bent down to kiss her.

"Have I? I am very glad you think so. I am sure it must be Sissy's doing."

The arm Louisa had begun to twine about her neck, unbent itself. "You can tell father if you will." Then, staying her a moment, she said, "It was you who made my room so cheerful, and gave it this look of welcome?"

"Oh no, Louisa, it was done before I came. It was ——" Louisa turned upon her pillow, and heard no more. When her sister had withdrawn, she turned her head back again, and lay with her face towards the door, until it opened and her father entered.

He had a jaded anxious look upon him, and his hand, usually steady, trembled in hers. He sat down at the side of the bed, tenderly asking how she was, and dwelling on the necessity of her keeping very quiet after her agitation and exposure to the weather last night. He spoke in a subdued and troubled voice, very different from his usual dictatorial manner; and was often at a loss for words.

"My dear Louisa. My poor daughter." He was so much at a loss at that place, that he stopped altogether. He tried again.

"My unfortunate child." The place was so difficult to get over, that he tried again.

"It would be hopeless for me, Louisa, to endeavor to tell you how overwhelmed I have been, and still am, by what broke upon me last night. The ground on which I stand has ceased to be solid under my feet. The only support on which I leaned, and the strength of which it seemed and still does seem, impossible to question, has given way in an instant. I am stunned by these discoveries. I have no selfish meaning in what I say; but I find the shock of what broke upon me last night, to be very heavy indeed."

She could give him no comfort herein. She had suffered the wreck of her whole life upon the rock.

"I will not say, Louisa, that if you had by any happy chance undeceived me some time ago, it would have been better for us both; better for your peace, and better for mine. For I am sensible that it may not have been a

part of my system to invite any confidence of that kind.
I had proved my—my system to myself, and I have rigidly administered it; and I must bear the responsibility
of its failures. I only entreat you to believe, my favorite child, that I have meant to do right."

He said it earnestly, and to do him justice he had. In
gauging fathomless deeps with his little mean excise-rod,
and in staggering over the universe with his rusty stiff-
legged compasses, he had meant to do great things.
Within the limits of his short tether he had tumbled
about, annihilating the flowers of existence with greater
singleness of purpose than many of the blatant personages
whose company he kept.

"I am well assured of what you say, father, I know
I have been your favorite child. I know you have intended to make me happy. I have never blamed you, and
never shall."

He took her outstretched hand, and retained it in his.

"My dear, I have remained all night at my table, pondering again and again on what has so painfully passed
between us. When I consider your character; when I
consider that what has been known to me for hours, has
been concealed by you for years; when I consider under
what immediate pressure it has been forced from you at
last; I come to the conclusion that I cannot but mistrust
myself."

He might have added more than all, when he saw the
face now looking at him. He did add it in effect, perhaps,
as he softly moved her scattered hair from her forehead
with his hand. Such little actions, slight in another
man, were very noticeable in him; and his daughter
received them as if they had been words of contrition.

"But," said Mr. Gradgrind, slowly, and with hesitation
as well as with a wretched sense of helplessness, "If I
see reason to mistrust myself for the past, Louisa, I should
also mistrust myself for the present and the future. To
speak unreservedly to you, I do. I am far from feeling
convinced now, however differently I might have felt only
this time yesterday, that I am fit for the trust you repose
in me; that I know how to respond to the appeal you
have come home to make to me; that I have the right
instinct—supposing it for the moment to be some quality

of that nature—how to help you, and to set you right, my child."

She had turned upon her pillow, and lay with her face upon her arm, so that he could not see it. All her wildness and passion had subsided; but, though softened, she was not in tears. Her father was changed in nothing so much as in the respect that he would have been glad to see her in tears.

"Some persons hold," he pursued, still hesitating, "that there is a wisdom of the Head, and that there is a wisdom of the Heart. I have not supposed so; but as I have said, I mistrust myself now. I have supposed the Head to be all-sufficient. It may not be all-sufficient; how can I venture this morning to say it is! If that other kind of wisdom should be what I have neglected, and should be the instinct that is wanted, Louisa——"

He suggested it very doubtfully, as if he were half unwilling to admit it even now. She made him no answer, lying before him on her bed, still half-dressed, much as he had seen her lying on the floor of his room last night.

"Louisa," and his hand rested on her hair again, "I have been absent from here, my dear, a good deal of late; and though your sister's training has been pursued accordingly to—the system," he appeared to come to that word with great reluctance always, "it has necessarily been modified by daily associations begun, in her case, at an early age. I ask you—ignorantly and humbly, my daughter—for the better, do you think?"

"Father," she replied, without stirring, "if any harmony has been awakened in her young breast that was mute in mine until it turned to discord, let her thank Heaven for it, and go upon her happier way, taking it as her greatest blessing that she has avoided my way."

"O my child, my child!" he said, in a forlorn manner, "I am an unhappy man to see you thus! What avails it to me that you do not reproach me, if I so bitterly reproach myself!" He bent his head and spoke low to her. "Louisa, I have a misgiving that some change may have been slowly working about me in this house, by mere love and gratitude: that what the Head had left undone and could not do, the Heart may have been doing silently. Can it be so?"

19

She made him no reply.

" I am not too proud to believe it, Louisa.　How could I be arrogant, and you before me !　Can it be so ?　Is it so, my dear ? "

He looked upon her once more, lying cast away there ; and without another word went out of the room.　He had not been long gone, when she heard a light tread near the door, and knew that some one stood beside her.

She did not raise her head.　A dull anger that she should be seen in her distress, and that the involuntary look she had so resented should come to this fulfilment, smouldered within her like an unwholesome fire.　All closely imprisoned forces rend and destroy.　The air that would be healthful to the earth, the water that would enrich it, the heat that would ripen it, tear it when caged up.　So in her bosom even now ; the strongest qualities she possessed, long turned upon themselves, became a heap of obduracy, that rose against a friend.

It was well that soft touch came upon her neck, and that she understood herself to be supposed to have fallen asleep.　The sympathetic hand did not claim her resentment.　Let it lie there, let it lie.

It lay there, warming into life a crowd of gentler thoughts ; and she rested.　As she softened with the quiet, and the consciousness of being so watched, some tears made their way into her eyes.　The face touched hers, and she knew that there were tears upon it too, and she the cause of them.

As Louisa feigned to rouse herself, and sat up, Sissy retired, so that she stood placidly near the bedside.

" I hope I have not disturbed you.　I have come to ask if you would let me stay with you ? "

" Why should you stay with me ?　My sister will miss you.　You are everything to her."

" Am I ? " returned Sissy, shaking her head.　" I would be something to you if I might."

" What ? " said Louisa, almost sternly.

" Whatever you want most, if I could be that.　At all events, I would like to try to be as near it as I can.　And however far off that may be, I will never tire of trying.　Will you let me ? "

" My father sent you to ask me."

" No indeed," replied Sissy.　" He told me that I might

come in now, but he sent me away from the room this morning—or at least—" She hesitated and stopped.

"At least, what?" said Louisa, with her searching eyes upon her.

"I thought it best myself that I should be sent away, for I felt very uncertain whether you would like to find me here."

"Have I always hated you so much?"

"I hope not, for I have always loved you and have always wished that you should know it. But you changed to me a little, shortly before you left home. Not that I wondered at it. You knew so much, and I knew so little, and it was so natural in many ways, going as you were among other friends, that I had nothing to complain of, and was not at all hurt."

Her color rose as she said it modestly and hurriedly. Louisa understood the loving pretence, and her heart smote her.

"May I try?" said Sissy, emboldened to raise her hand to the neck that was insensibly drooping towards her.

Louisa, taking down the hand that would have embraced her in another moment, held it in one of hers, and answered:

"First, Sissy, do you know what I am? I am so proud and so hardened, so confused and troubled, so resentful and unjust to every one and to myself, that everything is stormy, dark, and wicked to me. Does not that repel you?"

"No!"

"I am so unhappy, and all that should have made me otherwise is so laid waste, that if I had been bereft of sense to this hour, and instead of being as learned as you think me, had to begin to acquire the simplest truths, I could not want a guide to peace, contentment, honor, all the good of which I am quite devoid, more abjectly than I do. Does not that repel you?"

"No!"

In the innocence of her brave affection, and the brimming up of her old devoted spirit, the once deserted girl shone like a beautiful light upon the darkness of the other.

Louisa raised the hand that it might clasp her neck and join its fellow there. She fell upon her knees, and clinging to this stroller's child looked up at her almost with veneration.

" Forgive me, pity me, help me ! Have compassion on my great need, and let me lay this head of mine upon a loving heart ? "

" O lay it here ! " cried Sissy. "Lay it here, my dear."

CHAPTER II.

VERY RIDICULOUS.

Mr. James Harthouse passed a whole night and a day in a state of so much hurry, that the World, with its best glass in its eye, would scarcely have recognized him during that insane interval, as the brother Jem of the honorable and jocular member. He was positively agitated. He several times spoke with an emphasis, similar to the vulgar manner. He went in and went out in an unaccountable way, like a man without an object. He rode like a highwayman. In a word, he was so horribly bored by existing circumstances, that he forgot to go in for boredom in the manner prescribed by the authorities.

Afer putting his horse at Coketown through the storm, as if it were a leap, he waited up all night : from time to time ringing his bell with the greatest fury, charging the porter who kept watch with delinquency in withholding letters or messages that could not fail to have been entrusted to him, and demanding restitution on the spot. The dawn coming, the morning coming, and the day coming, and neither message nor letter coming with either, he went down to the country-house. There, the report was, Mr. Bounderby away, and Mrs. Bounderby in town. Left for town suddenly last evening. Not even known to be gone until receipt of message, importing that her return was not to be expected for the present.

In these circumstances he had nothing for it but to follow her to town. He went to the house in town. Mrs. Bounderby not there. He looked in at the Bank. Mr. Bounderby away, and Mrs. Sparsit away. Mrs. Sparsit away ? Who could have been reduced to sudden extremity for the company of that griffin !

"Well! I don't know," said Tom, who had his own reasons for being uneasy about it. "She was off somewhere at daybreak this morning. She's always full of mystery; I hate her. So I do that white chap; he's always got his blinking eyes upon a fellow."

"Where were you last night, Tom?"

"Where was I last night!" said Tom. "Come! I like that. I was waiting for you, Mr. Harthouse, till it came down as *I* never saw it come down before. Where was I too! Where were you, you mean."

"I was prevented from coming—detained."

"Detained!" murmured Tom. "Two of us were detained. I was detained looking for you, till I lost every train but the mail. It would have been a pleasant job to go down by that on such a night, and have to walk home through a pond. I was obliged to sleep in town after all."

"Where?"

"Where? Why in my own bed at Bounderby's."

"Did you see your sister?"

"How the deuce," returned Tom, staring, "could I see my sister when she was fifteen miles off?"

Cursing these quick retorts of the young gentleman to whom he was so true a friend, Mr. Harthouse disembarrassed himself of that interview with the smallest conceivable amount of ceremony, and debated for the hundredth time what all this could mean? He made only one thing clear. It was, that whether she was in town or out of town, whether he had been premature with her who was so hard to comprehend, or she had lost courage, or they were discovered, or some mischance or mistake, at present incomprehensible, had occurred, he must remain to confront his fortune, whatever it was. The hotel where he was known to live when condemned to that region of blackness, was the stake to which he was tied. As to all the rest—What will be, will be.

"So, whether I am waiting for a hostile message, or an assignation, or a penitent remonstrance, or an impromptu wrestle with my friend Bounderby in the Lancashire manner—which would seem as likely as anything else in the present state of affairs—I'll dine," said Mr. James Harthouse. Bounderby has the advantage in point of weight; and if anything of a British nature is to come off between us, it may be as well to be in training."

Therefore he rang the bell, and tossing himself negligently on a sofa, ordered " Some dinner at six—with a beefsteak in it," and got through the intervening time as well as he could. That was not particularly well; for he remained in the greatest perplexity, and, as the hours went on, and no kind of explanation offered itself, his perplexity augmented at compound interest.

However, he took affairs as coolly as it was in human nature to do, and entertained himself with the facetious idea of the training more than once. " It wouldn't be bad," he yawned at one time, "to give the waiter five shillings, and throw him." At another time it occurred to him " Or a fellow of about thirteen or fourteen stone might be hired by the hour." But these jests did not tell materially on the afternoon, or his suspense; and, sooth to say, they both lagged fearfully.

It was impossible, even before dinner, to avoid often walking about in the pattern of the carpet, looking out of the window, listening at the door for footsteps, and occasionally becoming rather hot when any steps approached that room. But, after dinner, when the day turned to twilight, and the twilight turned to night, and still no communication was made to him, it began to be as he expressed it, " like the Holy Office and slow torture." However, still true to his conviction that indifference was the genuine high-breeding (the only conviction he had), he seized this crisis as the opportunity for ordering candles and a newspaper.

He had been trying in vain, for half an hour, to read this newspaper, when the waiter appeared and said, at once mysteriously and apologetically :

" Beg your pardon, sir. You are wanted, sir, if you please."

A general recollection that this was the kind of thing the Police said to the swell mob, caused Mr. Harthouse to ask the waiter in return, with bristling indignation, what the Devil he meant by " wanted ? "

" Beg your pardon, sir. Young lady outside, sir, wishes to see you."

" Outside ? Where ? "

" Outside this door, sir."

Giving the waiter to the personage before mentioned, as a blockhead duly qualified for that consignment, Mr.

Harthouse hurried into the gallery. A young woman whom he had never seen stood there. Plainly dressed, very quiet, very pretty. As he conducted her into the room and placed a chair for her, he observed, by the light of the candles, that she was even prettier than he had at first believed. Her face was innocent and youthful, and its expression remarkably pleasant. She was not afraid of him, or in any way disconcerted; she seemed to have her mind preoccupied with the occasion of her visit, and to have substituted that consideration for herself.

"I speak to Mr. Harthouse?" she said, when they were alone.

"To Mr. Harthouse." He added in his mind, "And you speak to him with the most confiding eyes I ever saw, and the most earnest voice (though so quiet) I ever heard."

"If I do not understand—and I do not, sir"—said Sissy, "what your honor as a gentleman binds you to, in other matters:" the blood really rose in his face as she began in these words: "I am sure I may rely upon it to keep my visit secret, and to keep secret what I am going to say. I will rely upon it, if you will tell me I may so far trust——"

"You may, I assure you."

"I am young, as you see; I am alone, as you see. In coming to you, sir, I have no advice or encouragement beyond my own hope."

He thought "But that is very strong," as he followed the momentary upward glance of her eyes. He thought besides, "This is a very odd beginning. I don't see where we are going."

"I think," said Sissy, "you have already guessed whom I left just now!"

"I have been in the greatest concern and uneasiness during the last four-and-twenty hours (which have appeared as many years)," he returned, "on a lady's account. The hopes I have been encouraged to form that you come from that lady, do not deceive me, I trust."

"I left her within an hour."

"At——?"

"At her father's."

Mr. Harthouse's face lengthened in spite of his coolness, and his perplexity increased. "Then I certainly," he thought, "do *not* see where we are going."

"She hurried there last night. She arrived there in great agitation, and was insensible all through the night. I live at her father's, and was with her. You may be sure sir, you will never see her again as long as you live."

Mr. Harthouse drew a long breath; and, if ever man found himself in the position of not knowing what to say, made the discovery beyond all question that he was so circumstanced. The child-like ingenuousness with which his visitor spoke, her modest fearlessness, her truthfulness which put all artifice aside, her entire forgetfulness of herself in her earnest quiet holding to the object with which she had come; all this, together with her reliance on his easily given promise—which in itself shamed him—presented something in which he was so inexperienced, and against which he knew any of his usual weapons would fall so powerless; that not a word could he rally to his relief.

At last he said:

"So startling an announcement, so confidently made, and by such lips, is really disconcerting in the last degree. May I be permitted to inquire, if you are charged to convey that information to me in those hopeless words, by the lady of whom we speak?"

"I have no charge from her."

"The drowning man catches at the straw. With no disrespect for your judgment, and with no doubt of your sincerity, excuse my saying that I cling to the belief that there is yet hope that I am not condemned to perpetual exile from that lady's presence."

"There is not the least hope. The first object of my coming here, sir, is to assure you that you must believe that there is no more hope of your ever speaking with her again, than there would be if she had died when she came home last night."

"Must believe? But if I can't—or if I should, by infirmity of nature, be obstinate—and won't——"

"It is still true. There is no hope."

James Harthouse looked at her with an incredulous smile upon his lips; but her mind looked over and beyond him, and the smile was quite thrown away.

He bit his lip, and took a little time for consideration.

"Well! If it should unhappily appear," he said, "after due pains and duty on my part, that I am brought to a position so desolate as this banishment, I shall not become the lady's persecutor. But you said you had no commission from her?"

"I have only the commission of my love for her, and her love for me. I have no other trust, than that I have been with her since she came home, and that she has given me her confidence. I have no further trust, than that I know something of her character and her marriage. O Mr. Harthouse, I think you had that trust too!"

He was touched in the cavity where his heart should have been—in that nest of addled eggs, where the birds of heaven would have lived if they had not been whistled away—by the fervor of this reproach.

"I am not a moral sort of fellow," he said, "and I never make any pretensions to the character of a moral sort of fellow. I am as immoral as need be. At the same time, in bringing any distress upon the lady who is the subject of the present conversation, or in unfortunately compromising her in any way, or in committing myself by any expression of sentiments towards her, not perfectly reconcilable with—in fact with—the domestic hearth; or in taking any advantage of her father's being a machine, or of her brother's being a whelp, or of her husband's being a bear; I beg to be allowed to assure you that I have had no particularly evil intentions, but have glided on from one step to another with a smoothness so perfectly diabolical, that I had not the slightest idea the catalogue was half so long until I began to turn it over. Whereas I find," said Mr. James Harthouse, in conclusion, "that it is really in several volumes."

Though he said all this in his frivolous way, the way seemed, for that once, a conscious polishing of but an ugly surface. He was silent for a moment; and then proceeded with a more self-possessed air, though with traces of vexation and disappointment that would not be polished out.

"After what has been just now represented to me, in a manner I find it impossible to doubt—I know of hardly any other source from which I could have accepted it so readily—I feel bound to say to you, in whom the confidence you have mentioned has been reposed, that I cannot refuse to contemplate the possibility (however unexpected) of my seeing the lady no more. I am solely to blame for the thing having come to this—and—and, I cannot say," he added, rather hard up for a general peroration, that I have any sanquine expectation of ever becoming a moral sort of fellow, or that I have any belief in any moral sort of fellow whatever."

Sissy's face sufficiently showed that her appeal to him was not finished.

"You spoke," he resumed, as she raised her eyes to him again, "of your first object. I may assume that there is a second to be mentioned?"

"Yes."

"Will you oblige me by confiding it?"

"Mr. Harthouse," returned Sissy, with a blending of gentleness and steadiness that quite defeated him, and with a simple confidence in his being bound to do what she required, that held him at a singular disadvantage, "the only reparation that remains with you, is to leave here immediately and finally. I am quite sure that you can mitigate in no other way the wrong and harm you have done. I am quite sure that it is the only compensation you have left it in your power to make. I do not say that it is much, or that it is enough; but it is something, and it is necessary. Therefore, though without any other authority than I have given you, and even without the knowledge of any other person than yourself and myself, I ask you to depart from this place to-night, under an obligation never to return to it."

If she had asserted any influence over him beyond her plain faith in the truth and right of what she said; if she had concealed the least doubt or irresolution, or had harbored for the best purpose any reserve or pretence; if she had shown, or felt, the lightest trace of any sensitiveness to his ridicule or his astonishment, or any remonstrance he might offer; he would have carried it against her at this point. But he could as easily have changed a clear sky by looking at it in surprise, as affect her.

"But do you know," he asked, quite at a loss, "the extent of what you ask? You probably are not aware that

I am here on a public kind of business, preposterous enough in itself, but which I have gone in for, and sworn by, and am supposed to be devoted to in quite a desperate manner? You probably are not aware of that, but I assure you it's the fact."

It had no effect on Sissy, fact or no fact.

"Besides which," said Mr. Harthouse, taking a turn or two across the room, dubiously, " it's so alarmingly absurd. It would make a man so ridiculous, after going in for these fellows, to back out in such an incomprehensible way."

" I am quite sure," repeated Sissy, "that it is the only reparation in your power, sir. I am quite sure, or I would not have come here."

He glanced at her face, and walked about again. " Upon my soul, I don't know what to say. So immensely absurd!"

It fell to his lot, now, to stipulate for secrecy.

" If I were to do such a very ridiculous thing," he said, stopping again presently, and leaning against the chimney-piece, " it could only be in the most inviolable confidence."

" I will trust to you, sir," returned Sissy, "and you will trust to me."

His leaning against the chimney-piece reminded him of the night with the whelp. It was the self-same chimney-piece, and somehow he felt as if *he* were the whelp to-night. He could make no way at all.

"I suppose a man never was placed in a more ridiculous position," he said, after looking down, and looking up, and laughing, and frowning, and walking off, and walking back again. " But I see no way out of it. What will be, will be. *This* will be, I suppose. I must take off myself, I imagine—in short, I engage to do it."

Sissy rose. She was not surprised by the result, but she was happy in it, and her face beamed brightly.

"You will permit me to say," continued Mr. James Harthouse, "that I doubt if any other ambassador, or ambassadress, could have addressed me with the same success. I must not only regard myself as being in a very ridiculous position, but as being vanquished at all points. Will you allow me the privilege of remembering my enemy's name?"

" *My* name?" said the ambassadress.

"The only name I could possibly care to know, to-night."

"Sissy Jupe."

" Pardon my curiosity at parting. Related to the family ? "

" I am only a poor girl," returned Sissy. " I was separated from my father—he was only a stroller—and taken pity on by Mr. Gradgrind. I have lived in the house ever since."

She was gone.

" It wanted this to complete the defeat," said Mr. James Harthouse, sinking, with a resigned air, on the sofa, after standing transfixed a little while. " The defeat may now be considered perfectly accomplished. Only a poor girl—only a stroller—only James Harthouse made nothing of—only James Harthouse a Great Pyramid of failure."

The Great Pyramid put it into his head to go up the Nile. He took a pen upon the instant, and wrote the following note (in appropriate hieroglyphics) to his brother:

" Dear Jack,—All up at Coketown. Bored out of the place, and going in for camels. Affectionately, JEM."

He rang the bell.

" Send my fellow here."

"Gone to bed, sir."

"Tell him to get up, and pack up."

He wrote two more notes. One, to Mr. Bounderby, announcing his retirement from that part of the country, and showing where he would be found for the next fortnight. The other, similar in effect, to Mr. Gradgrind. Almost as soon as the ink was dry upon their superscriptions, he had left the tall chimneys of Coketown behind, and was in a railway carriage, tearing and glaring over the dark landscape.

The moral sort of fellows might suppose that Mr. James Harthouse derived some comfortable reflections afterwards from this prompt retreat, as one of his few actions that made any amends for anything, and as a token to himself that he had escaped the climax of a very bad business. But it was not so, at all. A secret sense of having failed and been ridiculous—a dread of what other fellows who went in for similar sorts of things, would say at his expense if they knew it—so oppressed him, that what was about the very best passage in his life was the one of all others he would not have owned to on any account, and the only one that made him ashamed of himself.

CHAPTER III.

VERY DECIDED.

THE indefatigable Mrs. Sparsit, with a violent cold upon her, her voice reduced to a whisper, and her stately frame so racked by continual sneezes that it seemed in danger of dismemberment, gave chase to her patron until she found him in the metropolis; and there, majestically sweeping in upon him at his hotel in St. James's Street, exploded the combustibles with which she was charged, and blew up. Having executed her mission with infinite relish, this high-minded woman then fainted away on Mr. Bounderby's coat-collar.

Mr. Bounderby's first procedure was to shake Mrs. Sparsit off, and leave her to progress as she might through various stages of suffering on the floor. He next had recourse to the administration of potent restoratives, such as screwing the patient's thumbs, smiting her hands, abundantly watering her face, and inserting salt in her mouth. When these attentions had recovered her (which they speedily did), he hustled her into a fast train without offering any other refreshment, and carried her back to Coketown more dead than alive.

Regarded as a classical ruin, Mrs. Sparsit was an interesting spectacle on her arrival at her journey's end; but considered in any other light, the amount of damage she had by that time sustained was excessive, and impaired her claims to admiration. Utterly heedless of the wear and tear of her clothes and constitution, and adamant to her pathetic sneezes, Mr. Bounderby immediately crammed her into a coach, and bore her off to Stone Lodge.

"Now, Tom Gradgrind," said Bounderby, bursting into his father-in-law's room late at night; "here's a lady here—Mrs. Sparsit—you know Mrs. Sparsit—who has something to say to you that will strike you dumb."

"You have missed my letter!" exclaimed Mr. Gradgrind, surprised by the apparition.

"Missed your letter, sir!" bawled Bounderby. "The present time is no time for letters. No man shall talk to Josiah Bounderby of Coketown about letters, with his mind in the state it's in now."

"Bounderby," said Mr. Gradgrind, in a tone of temperate remonstrance, "I speak of a very special letter I have written to you, in reference to Louisa."

"Tom Gradgrind," replied Bounderby, knocking the flat of his hand several times with great vehemence on the table, "I speak of a very special messenger who has come to me, in reference to Louisa. Mrs. Sparsit, ma'am, stand forward!"

That unfortunate lady hereupon essaying to offer testimony, without any voice and with painful gestures expressive of an inflamed throat, became so aggravating and underwent so many facial contortions, that Mr. Bounderby, unable to bear it, seized her by the arm and shook her.

"If you can't get it out, ma'am," said Bounderby, "leave *me* to get it out. This is not a time for a lady, however highly connected, to be totally inaudible, and seemingly swallowing marbles. Tom Gradgrind, Mrs. Sparsit latterly found herself, by accident, in a situation to overhear a conversation out of doors between your daughter and your precious gentleman friend, Mr. James Harthouse."

"Indeed!" said Mr. Gradgrind.

"Ah! Indeed!" cried Bounderby. "And in that conversation——"

"It is not necessary to repeat its tenor, Bounderby. I know what passed."

"You do? Perhaps," said Bounderby, staring with all his might at his so quiet and assuasive father-in-law, "you know where your daughter is at the present time!"

"Undoubtedly. She is here."

"Here?"

" My dear Bounderby, let me beg you to restrain these loud outbreaks, on all accounts. Louisa is here. The moment she could detach herself from that interview with the person of whom you speak, and whom I deeply regret to have been the means of introducing to you, Louisa hurried here, for protection. I myself had not been at home many hours, when I received her—here in this room. She hurried by the train to town, she ran from town to this house through a raging storm, and presented herself before me in a state of distraction. Of course, she has remained here ever since. Let me entreat you, for your own sake and for hers, to be more quiet."

Mr. Bounderby silently gazed about him for some moments, in every direction except Mrs. Sparsit's direction ; and then, abruptly turning upon the niece of Lady Scadgers, said to that wretched woman :

" Now, ma'am ! We shall be happy to hear any little apology you may think proper to offer, for going about the country at express pace, with no other luggage than a Cock-and-a-Bull, ma'am ! "

" Sir," whispered Mrs. Sparsit, " my nerves are at present too much shaken, and my health is at present too much impaired, in your service, to admit of my doing more than taking refuge in tears."

(Which she did.)

" Well, ma'am," said Bounderby, " without making any observation to you that may not be made with propriety to a woman of good family, what I have got to add to that, is that there is something else in which it appears to me you may take refuge, namely, a coach. And the coach in which we came here, being at the door, you'll allow me to hand you down to it, and pack you home to the Bank : where the best course for you to pursue, will be to put your feet into the hottest water you can bear, and take a glass of scalding rum and butter after you get into bed." With these words, Mr. Bounderby extended his right hand to the weeping lady, and escorted her to the conveyance in question, shedding many plaintive sneezes by the way. He soon returned alone.

" Now, as you showed me in your face, Tom Gradgrind, that you wanted to speak to me," he resumed, " here I am. But, I am not in a very agreeable state, I tell you plainly : not relishing this business, even as it is, and not

considering that I am at any time as dutifully and submissively treated by your daughter, as Josiah Bounderby
of Coketown ought to be treated by his wife. You have
your opinion, I daresay; and I have mine, I know. If
you mean to say anything to me to-night, that goes
against this candid remark, you had better let it alone."

Mr. Gradgrind, it will be observed, being much softened, Mr. Bounderby took particular pains to harden
himself at all points. It was his amiable nature.

"My dear Bounderby," Mr. Gradgrind began in reply.

"Now, you'll excuse me," said Bounderby, "but I don't
want to be too dear. That, to start with. When I begin to be dear to a man, I generally find that his intention is to come over me. I am not speaking to you politely; but, as you are aware, I am *not* polite. If you like
politeness, you know where to get it. You have your
gentleman-friends you know, and they'll serve you with
as much of the article as you want. I don't keep it myself."

"Bounderby," urged Mr. Gradgrind, "we are all liable
to mistakes——"

"I thought **you** couldn't make 'em," interrupted
Bounderby.

"Perhaps I thought so. But, I say we are all liable to
mistakes; and I should feel sensible of your delicacy,
and grateful for it, if you would spare me these references
to Harthouse. I shall not associate him in our conversation with your intimacy and encouragement; pray do
not persist in connecting him with mine."

"I never mentioned his name!" said Bounderby.

"Well, well!" returned Mr. Gradgrind, with a patient,
even a submissive air. And he sat for a little while pondering. "Bounderby, I see reason to doubt whether we
have ever quite understood Louisa."

"Who do you mean by We?"

"Let me say I, then," he returned, in answer to the
coarsely blurted question; "I doubt whether I have understood Louisa. I doubt whether I have been quite right
in the manner of her education."

"There you hit it," returned Bounderby. "There I
agree with you. You have found it out at last have you?
Education! I'll tell you what education is—To be tumbled out of doors, neck and crop, and put upon the shortest

allowance of everything except blows. That's what *I* call education."

"I think your good sense will perceive," Mr. Gradgrind remonstrated in all humility, "that whatever the merits of such a system may be, it would be difficult of general application to girls."

"I don't see it at all, sir," returned the obstinate Bounderby.

"Well," sighed Mr. Gradgrind, "we will not enter into the question. I assure you I have no desire to be controversial. I seek to repair what is amiss, if I possibly can; and I hope you will assist me in a good spirit, Bounderby, for I have been very much distressed."

"I don't understand you, yet," said Bounderby, with determined obstinacy, "and therefore I won't make any promises."

"In the course of a few hours, my dear Bounderby," Mr. Gradgrind proceeded, in the same depressed and propitiatory manner, "I appear to myself to have become better informed as to Louisa's character, than in previous years. The enlightenment has been painfully forced upon me, and the discovery is not mine. I think there are— Bounderby, you will be surprised to hear me say this— I think there are qualities in Louisa, which—which have been harshly neglected, and—and a little perverted. And —and I would suggest to you, that—that if you would kindly meet me in a timely endeavor to leave her to her better nature for a while—and to encourage it to develop itself by tenderness and consideration—it—it would be the better for the happiness of all of us. Louisa," said Mr. Gradgrind, shading his face with his hand, "has always been my favorite child."

The blustrous Bounderby crimsoned and swelled to such an extent on hearing these words, that he seemed to be, and probably was, on the brink of a fit. With his very ears a bright purple shot with crimson, he pent up his indignation, however, and said:

"You'd like to keep her here for a time?"

"I—I had intended to recommend, my dear Bounderby, that you should allow Louisa to remain here on a visit, and be attended by Sissy (I mean of course Cecilia Jupe), who understands her, and in whom she trusts."

15

" I gather from all this, Tom Gradgrind," said Bound-erby, standing up with his hands in his pockets, " that you are of opinion that there's what people call some in-compatibility between Loo Bounderby and myself."

" I fear there is at present a general incompatibility between Louisa, and—and—and almost all the relations in which I have placed her," was her father's sorrowful reply.

" Now, look you here, Tom Gradgrind," said Bounderby the flushed, confronting him with his legs wide apart, his hands deeper in his pockets, and his hair like a hayfield wherein his windy anger was boisterous. " You have said your say ; I am going to say mine. I am a Coketown man. I am Josiah Bounderby of Coketown. I know the bricks of this town, and I know the works of this town, and I know the chimneys of this town, and I know the smoke of this town, and I know the Hands of this town. I know 'em all pretty well. They're real. When a man tells me anything about imaginative qualities, I always tell that man, whoever he is, that I know what he means. He means turtle-soup and venison, with a gold spoon, and that he wants to be set up with a coach and six. That's what your daughter wants. Since you are of opinion that she ought to have what she wants, I recom-mend you to provide it for her. Because, Tom Gradgrind, she will never have it from me."

" Bounderby," said Mr. Gradgrind, " I hoped, after my entreaty, you would have taken a different tone."

" Just wait a bit," retorted Bounderby, " you have said your say, I believe. I heard you out ; hear me out, if you please. Don't make yourself a spectacle of unfairness as well as inconsistency, because, although I am sorry to see Tom Gradgrind reduced to his present position, I should be doubly sorry to see him brought so low as that. Now, there's an incompatibility of some sort or another, I am given to understand by you, between your daughter and me. I'll give *you* to understand, in reply to that, that there unquestionably is an incompatibility of the first magnitude—to be summed up in this—that your daughter don't properly know her husband's merits, and is not impressed with such a sense as would become her, by George! of the honor of his alliance. That's plain speaking, I hope."

"Bounderby," urged Mr. Gradgrind, "that is unreasonable."

"Is it?" said Bounderby. "I am glad to hear you say so. Because when Tom Gradgrind with his new lights, tells me that what I say is unreasonable, I am convinced at once it must be devilish sensible. With your permission I am going on. You know my origin; and you know that for a good many years of my life I didn't want a shoeing-horn, in consequence of not having a shoe. Yet you may believe or not, as you think proper, that there are ladies—born ladies—belonging to families—Families! —who next to worship the ground I walk on."

He discharged this like a Rocket, at his father-in-law's head.

"Whereas your daughter," proceeded Bounderby, "is far from being a born lady. That you know, yourself. Not that I care a pinch of candle-snuff about such things, for you are very well aware I don't; but that such is the fact, and you, Tom Gradgrind, can't change it. Why do I say this?"

"Not, I fear," observed Mr. Gradgrind, in a low voice, "to spare me."

"Hear me out," said Bounderby, "and refrain from cutting in till your turn comes round. I say this, because highly connected females have been astonished to see the way in which your daughter has conducted herself, and to witness her insensibility. They have wondered how I have suffered it. And I wonder myself now, and I won't suffer it."

"Bounderby," returned Mr. Gradgrind, rising, "the less we say to-night the better, I think."

"On the contrary, Tom Gradgrind, the more we say to-night, the better, I think. That is," the consideration checked him, "till I have said all I mean to say, and then I don't care how soon we stop. I come to a question that may shorten the business. What do you mean by the proposal you made just now?"

"What do I mean, Bounderby?"

"By your visiting proposition," said Bounderby, with an inflexible jerk of the hayfield.

"I mean that I hope you may be induced to arrange in a friendly manner, for allowing Louisa a period of repose and reflection here, which may tend to a gradual alteration for the better in many respects."

"To a softening down of your ideas of the incompatibility?" said Bounderby.

"If you put it in those terms."

"What made you think of this?" said Bounderby.

"I have already said, I fear Louisa has not been understood. Is it asking too much, Bounderby, that you, so
far her elder, should aid in trying to set her right? You
have accepted a great charge of her; for better, for worse,
for——"

Mr. Bounderby may have been annoyed by the repetition of his own words to Stephen Blackpool, but he cut
the quotation short with an angry start.

"Come!" said he, "I don't want to be told about that.
I know what I took her for, as well as you do. Never
you mind what I took her for; that's my lookout."

"I was merely going on to remark, Bounderby, that we
may all be more or less in the wrong, not even excepting
you; and that some yielding on your part, remembering
the trust you have accepted, may not only be an act of
true kindness, but perhaps a debt incurred towards
Louisa."

"I think differently," blustered Bounderby. "I am
going to finish this business according to my own opinions.
Now, I don't want to make a quarrel of it with you, Tom
Gradgrind. To tell you the truth, I don't think it would
be worthy of my reputation to quarrel on such a subject.
As to your gentleman-friend, he may take himself off,
wherever he likes best. If he falls in my way, I shall
tell him my mind; if he don't fall in my way, I shan't,
for it won't be worth my while to do it. As to your
daughter, whom I made Loo Bounderby, and might have
done better by leaving Loo Gradgrind, if she don't come
home to-morrow, by twelve o'clock at noon, I shall understand that she prefers to stay away, and I shall send her
wearing apparel and so forth over here, and you'll take
charge of her for the future. What I shall say to people
in general, of the incompatibility that led to my so laying
down the law, will be this. I am Josiah Bounderby, and
I had my bringing-up; she's the daughter of Tom Gradgrind, and she had her bringing-up; and the two horses
wouldn't pull together. I am pretty well known to be
rather an uncommon man, I believe; and most people
will understand fast enough that it must be a woman

rather out of the common, also, who, in the long run, would come up to my mark."

"Let me seriously entreat you to reconsider this, Bounderby," urged Mr. Gradgrind, "before you commit yourself to such a decision."

"I always come to a decision," said Bounderby, tossing his hat on : "and whatever I do, I do at once. I should be surprised at Tom Gradgrind's addressing such a remark to Josiah Bounderby of Coketown, knowing what he knows of him, if I could be surprised by anything Tom Gradgrind did, after his making himself a party to sentimental humbug. I have given you my decision, and I have got no more to say. Good-night !"

So Mr. Bounderby went home to his town house to bed. At five minutes past twelve o'clock next day, he directed Mrs. Bounderby's property to be carefully packed up and sent to Tom Gradgrind's; advertised his country retreat for sale by private contract; and resumed a bachelor life.

CHAPTER IV.

LOST.

The robbery at the Bank had not languished before, and did not cease to occupy a front place in the attention of the principal of that establishment now. In boastful proof of his promptitude and activity, as a remarkable man, and a self-made man, and a commercial wonder more admirable than Venus, who had risen out of the mud instead of the sea, he liked to show how little his domestic affairs abated his business ardor. Consequently, in the first few weeks of his resumed bachelorhood, he even advanced upon his usual display of bustle, and every day made such a rout in renewing his investigations into the robbery, that the officers who had it in hand almost wished it had never been committed.

They were at fault too, and off the scent. Although they had been so quiet since the first outbreak of the matter, that most people really did suppose it to have been abandoned as hopeless, nothing new occurred. No implicated man or woman took untimely courage, or made a self-betraying step. More remarkable yet, Stephen Black-pool could not be heard of, and the mysterious old woman remained a mystery.

Things having come to this pass, and showing no latent signs of stirring beyond it, the upshot of Mr. Bounderby's investigations was, that he resolved to hazard a bold burst. He drew up a placard, offering Twenty Pounds reward for the apprehension of Stephen Blackpool, suspected of complicity in the robbery of the Coketown Bank on such a night; he described the said Stephen Blackpool by dress, complexion, estimated height, and manner, as minutely as he could; he recited how he had left the town; and in what direction he had been last seen going; he had the whole printed in great black letters on a staring broadsheet; and he caused the walls to be posted with it in the dead of night, so that it should strike upon the sight of the whole population at one blow.

The factory-bells had need to ring their loudest that morning to disperse the groups of workers who stood in the tardy daybreak, collected round the placards, devouring them with eager eyes. Not the least eager of the eyes assembled, were the eyes of those who could not read. These people, as they listened to the friendly voice that read aloud—there was always some such ready to help them—stared at the characters which meant so much with a vague awe and respect that would have been half ludicrous, if any aspect of public ignorance could ever be otherwise than threatening and full of evil. Many ears and eyes were busy with a vision of the matter of these placards, among turning spindles, rattling looms, and whirring wheels, for hours afterwards; and when the Hands cleared out again into the streets, there were still as many readers as before.

Slackbridge, the delegate, had to address his audience too that night; and Slackbridge had obtained a clean bill from the printer, and had brought it in his pocket. O my friends and fellow-countrymen, the down-trodden operatives of Coketown, oh my fellow-brothers and fellow workmen and fellow-citizens and fellow-men, what a to-do was there, when Slackbridge unfolded what he called "that damning document," and held it up to the gaze, and for the execration of the working-man community! "Oh my fellow-men, behold of what a traitor in the camp

of those great spirits who are enrolled upon the holy
scroll of Justice and of Union, is appropriately capable!
Oh my prostrate friends, with the galling yoke of tyrants
on your necks and the iron foot of despotism treading
down your fallen forms into the dust of the earth, upon
which right glad would your oppressors be to see you
creeping on your bellies all the days of your lives, like
the serpent in the garden—oh my brothers, and shall I
as a man not add, my sisters too, what do you say, *now*,
of Stephen Blackpool, with a slight stoop in his shoulders
and about five foot seven in height, as set forth in this
degrading and disgusting document, this blighting bill,
this pernicious placard, this abominable advertisement;
and with what majesty of denouncement will you crush
the viper, who would bring this stain and shame upon the
God-like race that happily has cast him out forever! Yes,
my compatriots, happily cast him out and sent him forth!
For you remember how he stood here before you on this
platform; you remember how, face to face and foot to
foot, I pursued him through all his intricate windings;
you remember how he sneaked and slunk, and sidled, and
splitted of straws, until, with not an inch of ground to which
to cling, I hurled him out from amongst us; an object for
the undying finger of scorn to point at, and for the aveng-
ing fire of every free and thinking mind to scorch and
sear! And now my friends—my laboring friends, for I
rejoice and triumph in that stigma—my friends whose
hard but honest beds are made in toil, and whose scanty
but independent pots are boiled in hardship; and, now I
say, my friends, what appellation has that dastard craven
taken to himself, when, with the mask torn from his
features, he stands before us in all his native deformity,
a What? A thief! A plunderer! A proscribed fugitive,
with a price upon his head; a fester and a wound upon
the noble character of the Coketown operative! Therefore, my band of brothers in a sacred bond, to which
your children and your children's children yet unborn
have set their infant hands and seals, I propose to you on
the part of the United Aggregate Tribunal, ever watchful for your welfare, ever zealous for your benefit, that
this meeting does Resolve: That Stephen Blackpool,
weaver, referred to in this placard, having been already
solemnly disowned by the community of Coketown Hands,

the same are free from the shame of his misdeeds, and cannot as a class be reproached with his dishonest actions!"

Thus Slackbridge; gnashing and perspiring after a prodigious sort. A few stern voices called out "No!" and a score or two hailed, with assenting cries of "Hear, hear!" the caution from one man, "Slackbridge, y' or over hetter int; y' or a goen too fast!" But these were pigmies against an army; the general assemblage subscribed to the gospel according to Slackbridge, and gave three cheers for him, as he sat demonstratively panting at them.

These men and women were yet in the streets, passing quietly to their homes, when Sissy, who had been called away from Louisa some minutes before, returned.

"Who is it?" asked Louisa.

"It is Mr. Bounderby," said Sissy, timid of the name, "and your brother Mr. Tom, and a young woman who says her name is Rachael, and that you know her."

"What do they want, Sissy dear?"

"They want to see you. Rachael has been crying, and seems angry."

"Father," said Louisa, for he was present, "I cannot refuse to see them, for a reason that will explain itself. Shall they come in here?"

As he answered in the affirmative, Sissy went away to bring them. She reappeared with them directly. Tom was last; and remained standing in the obscurest part of the room, near the door.

"Mrs. Bounderby," said her husband, entering with a cool nod, "I don't disturb you, I hope. This is an unseasonable hour, but here is a young woman who has been making statements which render my visit necessary. Tom Gradgrind, as your son, young Tom, refuses for some obstinate reason or other to say anything at all about those statements, good or bad, I am obliged to confront her with your daughter."

"You have seen me once before, young lady," said Rachael, standing in front of Louisa.

Tom coughed.

"You have seen me, young lady," repeated Rachael, as she did not answer, "once before."

Tom coughed again.

"I have."

Rachael cast her eyes proudly towards Mr. Bounderby, and said, " Will you make it known, young lady, where, and who was there?"

" I went to the house where Stephen Blackpool lodged, on the night of his discharge from his work, and I saw you there. He was there too; and an old woman who did not speak, and whom I could scarcely see, stood in a dark corner. My brother was with me."

"Why couldn't you say so, young Tom?" demanded Bounderby.

"I promised my sister I wouldn't." Which Louisa hastily confirmed. "And besides," said the whelp bitterly, " she tells her own story so precious well—and so full—that what business had I to take it out of her mouth ! "

" Say, young lady, if you please," pursued Rachael, " why in an evil hour, you ever came to Stephen's that night."

"I felt compassion for him," said Louisa, her color deepening, " and I wished to know what he was going to do, and wished to offer him assistance."

"Thank you, ma'am," said Bounderby. " Much flattered and obliged."

"Did you offer him," asked Rachael, " a bank-note?"

"Yes; but he refused it, and would only take two pounds in gold."

Rachael cast her eyes towards Mr. Bounderby again.

"Oh certainly!" said Bounderby. "If you put the question whether your ridiculous and improbable account was true or not, I am bound to say it's confirmed."

" Young lady," said Rachael, " Stephen Blackpool is now named as a thief in public print all over this town, and where else! There have been a meeting to-night where he have been spoken of in the same shameful way. Stephen! The honestest lad, the truest lad, the best!" Her indignation failed her, and she broke off sobbing.

"I am very, very sorry," said Louisa.

"O young lady, young lady," returned Rachael, "I hope you may be, but I don't know! I can't say what you may ha' done! The like of you don't know us, don't care for us, don't belong to us. I am not sure why you may ha' come that night. I can't tell but what you may ha' come wi' some aim of your own, not mindin' to what trouble you brought such as the poor lad. I said then, Bless you for coming; and I said it of my heart, you seemed to take so pitifully to him; but I don't know now, I don't know!"

Louisa could not reproach her for her unjust suspicions; she was so faithful to her idea of the man, and so afflicted.

"And when I think," said Rachael through her sobs, "that the poor lad was so grateful, thinkin' you so good to him—when I mind that he put his hand over his hard-worken face to hide the tears that you brought up there—O, I hope you may be sorry, and ha' no bad cause to be it; but I don't know, I don't know!"

"You're a pretty article," growled the whelp, moving uneasily in his dark corner, "to come here with these precious imputations! You ought to be bundled out for not knowing how to behave yourself, and you would be by rights."

She said nothing in reply; and her low weeping was the only sound that was heard, until Mr. Bounderby spoke.

"Come!" said he, "you know what you have engaged to do. You had better give your mind to that; not this."

"'Deed, I am loath," returned Rachael, drying her eyes, "that any here should see me like this; but I won't be seen so again. Young lady, when I had read what's put in print of Stephen—and what has just as much truth in it as if it had been put into print of you—I went straight to the Bank to say I knew where Stephen was, and to give a sure and certain promise that he should be here in two days. I couldn't meet wi' Mr. Bounderby then, and your brother sent me away, and I tried to find you, but you was not to be found, and I went back to work. Soon as I come out of the Mill to-night, I hastened to hear what was said of Stephen—for I know wi' pride he will come back to shame it!—and then I went again to seek Mr. Bounderby, and I found him, and I told him every word I knew; and he believed no word I said, and brought me here."

"So far, that's true enough," assented Mr. Bounderby, with his hands in his pockets and his hat on. "But I have known you people before to-day, you'll observe, and I know you never die for want of talking. Now, I recommend you not so much to mind talking just now, as doing. You have undertaken to do something; all I remark upon that at present is, do it!"

"I have written to Stephen by the post that went out this afternoon, as I have written to him once before sin' he went away," said Rachael: "and he will be here, at furthest, in two days."

"Then I'll tell you something. You are not aware perhaps," retorted Mr. Bounderby, "that you yourself have been looked after now and then, not being considered quite free from suspicion in this business, on account of most people being judged according to the company they keep. The post-office hasn't been forgotten either. What I'll tell you is, that no letter to Stephen Blackpool has ever got into it. Therefore, what has become of yours, I leave you to guess. Perhaps you're mistaken, and never wrote any."

"He hadn't been gone from here, young lady," said Rachael, turning appealingly to Louisa, "as much as a week, when he sent me the only letter I have had from him, saying that he was forced to seek work in another name."

"Oh, by George!" cried Bounderby, shaking his head, with a whistle, "he changes his name, does he! That's rather unlucky, too, for such an immaculate chap. It's considered a little suspicious in Courts of Justice, I believe, when an Innocent happens to have many names."

"What," said Rachael, with the tears in her eyes again, "what, young lady, in the name of Mercy, was left the poor lad to do! The masters against him on one hand, the men against him on the other, he only wantin to work hard in peace, and do what he felt right. Can a man have no soul of his own, no mind of his own? Must he go wrong all through wi' this side, or must he go wrong all through wi' that, or else be hunted like a hare?"

"Indeed, indeed, I pity him from my heart," returned Louisa; "and I hope that he will clear himself."

"You need have no fear of that, young lady. He is sure!"

"All the surer, I suppose," said Mr. Bounderby, "for your refusing to tell where he is? Eh?"

"He shall not, through any act of mine, come back wi' the unmerited reproach of being brought back. He shall

come back of his own accord to clear himself, and put all
those that have injured his good character, and he not
here for its defence, to shame. I have told him what has
been done against him," said Rachael, throwing off all
distrust as a rock throws off the sea, "and he will be here
at furthest, in two days."

"Notwithstanding which," added Mr. Bounderby, "if
he can be laid hold of any sooner, he shall have an earlier
opportunity of clearing himself. As to you, I have nothing against you; what you came and told me turns out
to be true, and I have given you the means of proving it
to be true, and there's an end of it. I wish you good-
night all! I must be off to look a little further into
this."

Tom came out of his corner when Mr. Bounderby moved,
moved with him, kept close to him, and went away with
him. The only parting salutation of which he delivered
himself was a sulky "Good-night, father!" With a brief
speech, and a scowl at his sister, he left the house.

Since his sheet-anchor had come home, Mr. Gradgrind
had been sparing of speech. He still sat silent, when
Louisa mildly said:

"Rachael, you will not distrust me one day, when you
know me better."

"It goes against me," Rachael answered, in a gentler
manner, "to mistrust any one; but when I am so mistrusted—when we all are—I cannot keep such things
quite out of my mind. I ask your pardon for having
done you an injury. I don't think what I said now. Yet
I might come to think it again, wi' the poor lad so
wronged."

"Did you tell him in your letter," inquired Sissy, "that
suspicion seemed to have fallen upon him, because he
had been seen about the Bank at night? He would then
know what he would have to explain on coming back,
and would be ready."

"Yes, dear," she returned; "but I can't guess what
can have ever taken him there. He never used to go
there. It was never in his way. His way was the same
as mine, and not near it."

Sissy had already been at her side asking her where
she lived, and whether she might come to-morrow night,
to inquire if there were news of him.

"I doubt," said Rachael, "if he can be here till next day."

"Then, I will come next night too," said Sissy

When Rachael, assenting to this, was gone, Mr. Gradgrind lifted up his head, and said to his daughter:

"Louisa, my dear, I have never, that I know of, seen this man. Do you believe him to be implicated?"

"I think I have believed it, father, though with great difficulty. I do not believe it now."

"That is to say, you once persuaded yourself to believe it, from knowing him to be suspected. His appearance and manner; are they so honest?"

"Very honest."

"And her confidence not to be shaken! I ask myself," said Mr. Gradgrind, musing, "does the real culprit know of these accusations? Where is he? Who is he?"

His hair had latterly begun to change its color. As he leaned upon his hand again, looking gray and old, Louisa, with a face of fear and pity, hurriedly went over to him, and sat close at his side. Her eyes by accident met Sissy's, at the moment. Sissy flushed and started, and Louisa put her finger on her lip.

Next night, when Sissy returned home and told Louisa that Stephen was not come, she told it in a whisper. Next night again, when she came home with the same account, and added that he had not been heard of, she spoke in the same low frightened tone. From the moment of that interchange of looks, they never uttered his name, or any reference to him, aloud; nor ever pursued the subject of the robbery, when Mr. Gradgrind spoke of it.

The two appointed days ran out, three days and nights ran out, and Stephen Blackpool was not come, and remained unheard of. On the fourth day, Rachael, with unabated confidence, but considering her dispatch to have miscarried, went up to the Bank, and showed her letter from him with his address at a working colony, one of many, not upon the main road, sixty miles away. Messengers were sent to that place, and the whole town looked for Stephen to be brought in next day.

During this whole time the whelp moved about with Mr. Bounderby like his shadow, assisting in all the proceedings. He was greatly excited, horribly fevered, bit his nails down to the quick, spoke in a hard rattling voice, and with lips that were black and burnt up. At the hour when the suspected man was looked for, the whelp was at the station; offering to wager that he had made off before the arrival of those who were sent in quest of him, and that he would not appear.

The whelp was right. The messengers returned alone. Rachael's letter had gone, Rachael's letter had been delivered, Stephen Blackpool had decamped in that same hour; and no soul knew more of him. The only doubt in Coketown was, whether Rachael had written in good faith, believing that he really would come back, or warning him to fly. On this point opinion was divided.

Six days, seven days, far on into another week. The wretched whelp plucked up a ghastly courage, and began to grow defiant. " *Was* the suspected fellow the thief ? A pretty question! If not, where was the man, and why did he not come back ?"

Where was the man, and why did he not come back? In the dead of night the echoes of his own words, which had rolled Heaven knows how far away in the daytime, came back instead, and abided by him until morning.

CHAPTER V.

FOUND.

DAY and night again, day and night again. No Stephen Blackpool. Where was the man, and why did he not come back?

Every night, Sissy went to Rachael's lodging, and sat with her in her small neat room. All day, Rachael toiled as such people must toil, whatever their anxieties. The smoke-serpents were indifferent who were lost or found, who turned out bad or good; the melancholy mad elephants, like the Hard Fact men, abated nothing of their set routine, whatever happened. Day and night again, day and night again. The monotony was unbroken. Even Stephen Blackpool's disappearance was falling into the general way, and becoming as monotonous a wonder as any piece of machinery in Coketown.

"I misdoubt," said Rachael, "if there is as many as twenty left in all this place, who have any trust in the poor dear lad now."

She said it to Sissy, as they sat in her lodging, lighted only by the lamp at the street corner. Sissy had come there when it was already dark, to await her return from work; and they had since sat at the window where Rachael had found her, wanting no brighter light to shine on their sorrowful talk.

"If it hadn't been mercifully brought about, that I was to have you to speak to," pursued Rachael, "times are, when I think my mind would not have kept right. But I get hope and strength through you; and you believe that though appearances may rise against him, he will be proved clear?"

"I do believe so," returned Sissy, "with my whole heart. I feel so certain, Rachael, that the confidence you hold in yours against all discouragement, is not like to be wrong, that I have no more doubt of him than if I had known him through as many years of trial as you have."

"And I, my dear," said Rachael, with a tremble in her voice, "have known him through them all, to be, according to his quiet ways, so faithful to everything honest and good, that if he was never to be heard of more, and I was to live to be a hundred years old, I could say with my last breath, God knows my heart, I have never once left trusting Stephen Blackpool!"

"We all believe, up at the Lodge, Rachael, that he will be freed from suspicion, sooner or later."

"The better I know it to be so believed there, my dear," said Rachael, "and the kinder I feel it that you come away from there, purposely to comfort me, and keep me company, and be seen wi' me when I am not yet free from all suspicion myself, the more grieved I am that I should ever have spoken those mistrusting words to the young lady. And yet——"

"You don't mistrust her now, Rachael?"

"Now that you have brought us more together, no. But I can't at all times keep out of my mind——"

Her voice so sunk into a low and slow communing with herself, that Sissy, sitting by her side, was obliged to listen with attention.

"I can't at all times keep out of my mind, mistrustings

of some one. I can't think who 'tis, I can't think how or why it may be done, but I mistrust that some one has put Stephen out of the way. I mistrust that by his coming back of his own accord, and showing himself innocent before them all, some one would be confounded, who—to prevent that—has stopped him, and put him out of the way."

"That is a dreadful thought," said Sissy, turning pale.

"It *is* a dreadful thought to think that he may be murdered.

Sissy shuddered, and turned paler yet.

"When it makes its way into my mind, dear," said Rachael, "and it will come sometimes, though I do all I can to keep it out, wi' counting on to high numbers as I work, and saying over and over again pieces that I knew when I were a child—I fall into such a wild, hot hurry, that, however tired I am, I want to walk fast, miles and miles. I must get the better of this before bed-time. I'll walk home wi' you."

"He might fall ill upon the journey back," said Sissy, faintly offering a worn-out scrap of hope; "and in such a case, there are many places on the road where he might stop."

"But he is in none of them. He has been sought for in all, and he is not there."

"True," was Sissy's reluctant admission.

"He'd walked the journey in two days. If he was foot-sore and couldn't walk, I sent him, in the letter he got, the money to ride, lest he should have none of his own to spare."

"Let us hope that to-morrow will bring something better, Rachael. Come into the air!"

Her gentle hand adjusted Rachael's shawl upon her shining black hair in the usual manner of her wearing it, and they went out. The night being fine, little knots of Hands were here and there lingering at street corners; but it was supper-time with the greater part of them, and there were but few people in the streets.

"You're not so hurried now, Rachael, and your hand is cooler."

"I get better, dear, if I can only walk, and breathe a little fresh. 'Times when I can't, I turn weak and confused."

" But you must not begin to fail, Rachael, for you may be wanted at any time to stand by Stephen. To-morrow is Saturday. If no news comes to-morrow, let us walk in the country on Sunday morning, and strengthen you for another week. Will you go?"

" Yes, dear."

They were by this time in the street where Mr. Bounderby's house stood. The way to Sissy's destination led them past the door, and they were going straight towards it. Some train had newly arrived in Coketown, which had put a number of vehicles in motion, and scattered a considerable bustle about the town. Several coaches were rattling before them and behind them as they approached Mr. Bounderby's, and one of the latter drew up with such briskness as they were in the act of passing the house, that they looked round involuntarily. The bright gaslight over Mr. Bounderby's steps showed them Mrs. Sparsit in the coach, in an ecstasy of excitement, struggling to open the door; Mrs. Sparsit seeing them at the same moment, called to them to stop.

" It's a coincidence," exclaimed Mrs. Sparsit, as she was released by the coachman. " It's a Providence! Come out, ma'am!" then said Mrs. Sparsit, to some one inside, " come out, or we'll have you dragged out!"

Hereupon, no other than the mysterious old woman descended. Whom Mrs. Sparsit incontinently collared.

" Leave her alone, everybody!" cried Mrs. Sparsit, with great energy. "Let nobody touch her. She belongs to me. Come in, ma'am!" then said Mrs. Sparsit, reversing her former word of command. "Come in, ma'am, or we'll have you dragged in!"

The spectacle of a matron of classical deportment, seizing an ancient woman by the throat, and haling her into a dwelling-house, would have been under any circumstances, sufficient temptation to all true English stragglers so blest as to witness it, to force a way into that dwelling-house and see the matter out. But when the phenomenon was enhanced by the notoriety and mystery by this time associated all over the town, with the Bank robbery, it would have lured the stragglers in, with an irresistible attraction, though the roof had been expected to fall upon their heads. Accordingly, the chance witnesses on the ground, consisting of the busiest of the

16

neighbors to the number of some five-and-twenty, closed in after Sissy and Rachael, as they closed in after Mrs. Sparsit and her prize; and the whole body made a disorderly irruption into Mr. Bounderby's dining-room, where the people behind lost not a moment's time in mounting on the chairs, to get the better of the people in front.

"Fetch Mr. Bounderby down!" cried Mrs. Sparsit. "Rachael, young woman; you know who this is?"

"It's Mrs. Pegler," said Rachael.

"I should think it is!" cried Mrs. Sparsit, exulting. "Fetch Mr. Bounderby. Stand away, everybody!" Here old Mrs. Pegler, muffling herself up, and shrinking from observation, whispered a word of entreaty. "Don't tell me," said Mrs. Sparsit, aloud, "I have told you twenty times, coming along, that I will *not* leave you till I have handed you over to him myself."

Mr. Bounderby now appeared, accompanied by Mr. Gradgrind and the whelp, with whom he had been holding conference upstairs. Mr. Bounderby looked more astonished than hospitable, at sight of this uninvited party in his dining-room.

"Why, what's the matter now!" said he. "Mrs. Sparsit, ma'am?"

"Sir," explained that worthy woman, "I trust it is my good fortune to produce a person you have much desired to find. Stimulated by my wish to relieve your mind, sir, and connecting together such imperfect clues to the part of the country in which that person might be supposed to reside, as have been afforded by the young woman, Rachael, fortunately now present to identify, I have had the happiness to succeed, and to bring that person with me—I need not say most unwillingly on her part. It has not been, sir, without some trouble that I have effected this: but trouble in your service is to me a pleasure, and hunger, thirst, and cold a real gratification."

Here Mrs. Sparsit ceased; for Mr. Bounderby's visage exhibited an extraordinary combination of all possible colors and expressions of discomfiture, as old Mrs. Pegler was disclosed to his view.

"Why, what do you mean by this?" was his highly unexpected demand, in great warmth. "I ask you, what do you mean by this, Mrs. Sparsit, ma'am?"

"Sir?" exclaimed Mrs. Sparsit, faintly.

"Why don't you mind your own business, ma'am?" roared Bounderby. "How dare you go and poke your officious nose into my family affairs?"

This allusion to her favorite feature overpowered Mrs. Sparsit. She sat down stiffly in a chair, as if she were frozen; and with a fixed stare at Mr. Bounderby, slowly grated her mittens against one another, as if they were frozen too.

"My dear Josiah!" cried Mrs. Pegler, trembling. "My darling boy! I am not to blame. It's not my fault, Josiah. I told this lady over and over again, that I knew she was doing what would not be agreeable to you, but she would do it."

"What did you let her bring you for? Couldn't you knock her cap off, or her tooth out, or scratch her, or do something or other to her?" asked Bounderby.

"My own boy! She threatened me that if I resisted her, I should be brought by constables, and it was better to come quietly than make that stir in such a—" Mrs. Pegler glanced timidly but proudly round the walls— "such a fine house as this. Indeed, indeed, it is not my fault! My dear, noble, stately boy! I have always lived quiet and secret, Josiah, my dear. I have never broken the condition once. I have never said I was your mother. I have admired you at a distance: and if I have come to town sometimes, with long times between, to take a proud peep at you, I have done it unbeknown, my love, and gone away again."

Mr. Bounderby with his hands in his pockets, walked in impatient mortification up and down at the side of the long dining-table, while the spectators greedily took in every syllable of Mrs. Pegler's appeal, and at each succeeding syllable became more and more round-eyed. Mr. Bounderby still walking up and down when Mrs. Pegler had done, Mr. Gradgrind addressed that maligned old lady:

"I am surprised, madam," he observed with severity, "that in your old age you have the face to claim Mr. Bounderby for your son, after your unnatural and in-human treatment of him."

"*Me* unnatural!" cried poor old Mrs. Pegler. "*Me* inhuman! To my dear boy?"

"Dear!" repeated Mr. Gradgrind. "Yes; dear in his

self-made prosperity, madam, I dare say. Not very dear,
however, when you deserted him in his infancy, and left
him to the brutality of a drunken grandmother."

"*I* deserted my Josiah!" cried Mrs. Pegler, clasping
her hands, "Now, Lord forgive you, sir, for your wicked
imaginations, and for your scandal against the memory
of my poor mother, who died in my arms before Josiah
was born. May you repent of it, sir, and live to know
better!"

She was so very earnest and injured, that Mr. Gradgrind, shocked by the possibility which dawned upon him,
said in a gentler tone:

"Do you deny, then, madam, that you left your son to
—to be brought up in the gutter?"

"Josiah in the gutter!" exclaimed Mrs. Pegler. "No
such a thing, sir. Never! For shame on you! My dear
boy knows, and will give *you* to know, that though he
come of humble parents, he come of parents that loved
him as dear as the best could, and never thought it hardship on themselves to pinch a bit that he might write
and cipher beautiful, and I've his books at home to show
it! Aye, have I!" said Mrs. Pegler, with indignant
pride. "And my dear boy knows, and will give *you* to
know, sir, that after his beloved father died when he was
eight years old, his mother, too, could pinch a bit, as it
was her duty and her pleasure and her pride to do it, to
help him out in life, and put him 'prentice. And a steady
lad he was, and a kind master he had to lend him a hand,
and well he worked his own way forward to be rich and
thriving. And *I*'ll give you to know, sir—for this my
dear boy won't—that though his mother kept but a little
village shop, he never forgot her, but pensioned me on
thirty pound a year—more than I want, for I put by out
of it—only making the condition that I was to keep down
in my own part, and make no boasts about him, and not
trouble him. And I never have, except with looking at
him once a year, when he has never knowed it. And it's
right," said poor old Mrs. Pegler, in affectionate cham-
pionship, "that I *should* keep down in my own part, and
I have no doubts that if I was here I should do a many
unbefitting things, and I am well contented, and I can
keep my pride in my Josiah to myself, and I can love for
love's own sake! And I am ashamed of you, sir," said

Mrs. Pegler, lastly, "for your slanders and suspicions. And for I never stood here before, nor never wanted to stand here when my dear son said no. And I shouldn't be here now, if it hadn't been for being brought here. And for shame upon you, O for shame, to accuse me of being a bad mother to my son, with my son standing here to tell you so different!"

The bystanders, on and off the dining-room chairs, raised a murmur of sympathy with Mrs. Pegler, and Mr. Gradgrind felt himself innocently placed in a very distressing predicament, when Mr. Bounderby, who had never ceased walking up and down, and had every moment swelled larger and larger, and grown redder and redder, stopped short.

"I don't exactly know," said Mr. Bounderby, "how I come to be favored with the attendance of the present company, but I don't inquire. When they're quite satisfied perhaps they'll be so good as to disperse; whether they're satisfied or not, perhaps they'll be so good as to disperse. I'm not bound to deliver a lecture on my family affairs, I have not undertaken to do it and I'm not a going to do it. Therefore those who expect any explanation whatever upon that branch of the subject, will be disappointed—particularly Tom Gradgrind, and he can't know it too soon. In reference to the Bank robbery, there has been a mistake made, concerning my mother. If there hadn't been over-officiousness it wouldn't have been made, and I hate over-officiousness at all times, whether or no. Good evening!"

Although Mr. Bounderby carried it off in these terms, holding the door open for the company to depart, there was a blustering sheepishness upon him, at once extremely crestfallen and superlatively absurd. Detected as the Bully of humility, who had built his windy reputation upon lies, and in his boastfulness had put the honest truth as far away from him as if he had advanced the mean claim (there is no meaner) to tack himself on to a pedigree, he cut a most ridiculous figure. With the people filing off at the door he held, who he knew would carry what had passed to the whole town, to be given to the four winds, he could not have looked a Bully more shorn and forlorn, if he had had his ears cropped. Even that unlucky female, Mrs. Sparsit, fallen from her pinnacle of exultation into the Slough of Despond, was not in so bad a plight as that remarkable man and self-made Humbug, Josiah Bounderby of Coketown.

Rachael and Sissy, leaving Mrs. Pegler to occupy a bed at her son's for that night, walked together to the gate of Stone Lodge and there parted. Mr. Gradgrind joined them before they had gone very far, and spoke with much interest of Stephen Blackpool ; for whom he thought this signal failure of the suspicions against Mrs. Pegler was likely to work well.

As to the whelp ; throughout this scene as on all other late occasions, he had stuck close to Bounderby. He seemed to feel that as long as Bounderby could make no discovery without his knowledge, he was so far safe. He never visited his sister, and had only seen her once since she went home : that is to say on the night when he still stuck close to Bounderby, as already related.

There was one dim unformed fear lingering about his sister's mind, to which she never gave utterance, which surrounded the graceless and ungrateful boy with a dreadful mystery. The same dark possibility had presented itself in the same shapeless guise, this very day, to Sissy, when Rachael spoke of some one who would be confounded by Stephen's return, having put him out of the way. Louisa had never spoken of harboring any suspicion of her brother in connection with the robbery, she and Sissy had held no confidence on the subject, save in that one interchange of looks when the unconscious father rested his gray head on his hand ; but it was understood between them, and they both knew it. This other fear was so awful, that it hovered about each of them like a ghostly shadow; neither daring to think of its being near herself, far less of its being near the other.

And still the forced spirit which the whelp had plucked up, throve with him. If Stephen Blackpool was not the thief, let him show himself. Why didn't he ?

Another night. Another day and night. No Stephen Blackpool. Where was the man, and why did he not come back ?

CHAPTER VI.

THE STARLIGHT.

THE Sunday was a bright Sunday in autumn, clear and cool, when early in the morning Sissy and Rachael met, to walk in the country.

As Coketown cast ashes not only on its own head but on the neighborhood's too—after the manner of those pious persons who do penance for their own sins by putting other people into sackcloth—it was customary for those who now and then thirsted for a draught of pure air, which is not absolutely the most wicked among the vanities of life, to get a few miles away by the railroad, and then begin their walk, or their lounge in the fields. Sissy and Rachael helped themselves out of the smoke by the usual means, and were put down at a station about midway between the town and Mr. Bounderby's retreat.

Though the green landscape was blotted here and there with heaps of coal, it was green elsewhere, and there were trees to see, and there were larks singing (though it was Sunday), and there were pleasant scents in the air, and all was over-arched by a bright blue sky. In the distance one way, Coketown showed as a black mist; in another distance hills began to rise; in a third, there was a faint change in the light of the horizon where it shone upon the far-off sea. Under their feet, the grass was fresh; beautiful shadows of branches flickered upon it, and speckled it; hedgerows were luxuriant; everything was at peace. Engines at pits' mouths and lean old horses that had worn the circle of their daily labor into the ground, were alike quiet; wheels had ceased for a short space to turn; and the great wheel on earth seemed to revolve without the shocks and noises of another time.

They walked on across the fields and down the shady lanes, sometimes getting over a fragment of a fence so rotten that it dropped at a touch of the foot, sometimes passing near a wreck of bricks and beams overgrown with grass, marking the site of deserted works. They followed paths and tracks, however slight. Mounds where the grass was rank and high, and where brambles, dock-weed, and such-like vegetation, were confusedly heaped together, they always avoided; for dismal stories were told in that country, of the old pits hidden beneath such indications.

The sun was high when they sat down to rest. They had seen no one, near or distant, for a long time; and the solitude remained unbroken. "It is so still here, Rachael, and the way is so untrodden, that I think we must be the first who have been here all the summer."

As Sissy said it, her eyes were attracted by another of those rotten fragments of fence upon the ground. She got up to look at it. "And yet I don't know. This has not been broken very long. The wood is quite fresh where it gave way. Here are footsteps too.—O Rachael!"

She ran back, and caught her round the neck. Rachael had already started up.

"What is the matter?"

"I don't know. There is a hat lying in the grass."

They went forward together. Rachael took it up, shaking from head to foot. She broke into a passion of tears and lamentations: Stephen Blackpool was written in his own hand on the inside.

"O the poor lad, the poor lad! He has been made away with. He is lying murdered here!"

"Is there—has the hat any blood upon it?" Sissy faltered.

They were afraid to look; but they did examine it, and found no mark of violence, inside or out. It had been lying there some days, for rain and dew had stained it, and the mark of its shape was on the grass where it had fallen. They looked fearfully about them, without moving, but could see nothing more. "Rachael," Sissy whispered, "I will go on a little by myself."

She had unclasped her hand, and was in the act of stepping forward, when Rachael caught her in both arms with a scream that resounded over the wide landscape. Before them, at their very feet, was the brink of a black ragged chasm hidden by the thick grass. They sprang back, and fell upon their knees, each hiding her face upon the other's neck.

"O, my good Lord! He's down there! Down there!" At first this and her terrific screams, were all that could be got from Rachael, by any tears, by any prayers, by any representations, by any means. It was impossible to hush her; and it was deadly necessary to hold her, or she would have flung herself down the shaft.

"Rachael, dear Rachael, good Rachael, for the love of Heaven, not these dreadful cries! Think of Stephen, think of Stephen, think of Stephen!"

By an earnest repetition of this entreaty, poured out in all the agony of such a moment, Sissy at last brought her to be silent, and to look at her with a tearless face of stone.

"Rachael, Stephen may be living. You wouldn't leave him lying maimed at the bottom of this dreadful place, a moment, if you could bring help to him?"

"No, no, no!"

"Don't stir from here, for his sake! Let me go and listen."

She shuddered to approach the pit; but she crept towards it on her hands and knees, and called to him as loud as she could call. She listened, but no sound replied. She called again and listened; still no answering sound. She did this, twenty, thirty times. She took a little clod of earth from the broken ground where he had stumbled, and threw it in. She could not hear it fall.

The wide prospect, so beautiful in its stillness but a few minutes ago, almost carried despair to her brave heart, as she rose and looked all round her, seeing no help. "Rachael, we must lose not a moment. We must go in different directions, seeking aid. You shall go by the way we have come, and I will go forward by the path. Tell any one you see, and every one what has happened. Think of Stephen, think of Stephen!"

She knew by Rachael's face that she might trust her now. And after standing for a moment to see her running, wringing her hands as she ran, she turned and went upon her own search; she stopped at the hedge to tie her shawl there as a guide to the place, then threw her bonnet aside, and ran as she had never run before.

Run, Sissy, run, in Heaven's name! Don't stop for breath. Run, run! Quickening herself by carrying such entreaties in her thoughts, she ran from field to field,

and lane to lane, and place to place, as she had never run
before; until she came to a shed by an engine-house,
where two men lay in the shade, asleep on straw.

First to wake them, and next to tell them, all so wild
and breathless as she was, what had brought her there,
were difficulties; but they no sooner understood her
than their spirits were on fire like hers. One of the men
was in a drunken slumber, but on his comrade's shouting
to him that a man had fallen down the Old Hell Shaft,
he started out to a pool of dirty water, put his head in it,
and came back sober.

With these two men she ran to another half-a-mile
further, and with that one to another, while they ran
elsewhere. Then a horse was found; and she got another man to ride for life or death to the railroad, and
send a message to Louisa, which she wrote and gave
him. By this time a whole village was up; and wind-
lasses, ropes, poles, lanterns, all things necessary, were fast
collecting and being brought into one place, to be carried
to the Old Hell Shaft.

It seemed now hours and hours since she had left the
lost man lying in the grave where he had been buried
alive. She could not bear to remain away from it any
longer—it was like deserting him—and she hurried swiftly
back, accompanied by half-a-dozen laborers, including the
drunken man whom the news had sobered, and who was
the best man of all. When they came to the Old Hell
Shaft, they found it as lonely as she had left it. The
men called and listened as she had done, and examined
the edge of the chasm, and settled how it had happened,
and then sat down to wait until the implements they
wanted should come up.

Every sound of insects in the air, every stirring of the
leaves, every whisper among these men, made Sissy
tremble, for she thought it was a cry at the bottom of
the pit. But the wind blew idly over it, and no sound
arose to the surface, and they sat upon the grass, waiting
and waiting. After they had waited some time, straggling people who had heard of the accident began to
come up; then the real help of implements began to arrive. In the midst of this, Rachael returned; and with
her party there was a surgeon, who brought some wine
and medicines. But, the expectation among the people

tLat the man would be found alive, was very slight indeed.

There being now people enough present to impede the work, the sobered man put himself at the head of the rest, or was put there by the general consent, and made a large ring round the Old Hell Shaft, and appointed men to keep it. Besides such volunteers as were accepted to work, only Sissy and Rachael were at first permitted within this ring; but, later in the day, when the message brought an express from Coketown, Mr. Gradgrind and Louisa, and Mrs. Bounderby, and the whelp, were also there.

The sun was four hours lower than when Sissy and Rachael had first sat down upon the grass, before a means of enabling two men to descend securely was rigged with poles and ropes. Difficulties had arisen in the construction of this machine, simple as it was; requisites had been found wanting and messages had had to go and return. It was five o'clock in the afternoon of the bright autumnal Sunday before a candle was sent down to try the air, while three or four rough faces stood crowded close together, attentively watching it: the men at the windlass lowering as they were told. The candle was brought up again, feebly burning, and then some water was cast in. Then the bucket was hooked on; and the sobered man and another got in with lights, giving the word " Lower away ! "

As the rope went out, tight and strained, and the windlass creaked, there was not a breath among the one or two hundred men and women looking on, that came as it was wont to come. The signal was given and the windlass stopped, with abundant rope to spare. Apparently so long an interval ensued with the men at the windlass standing idle, that some women shrieked that another accident had happened ! But the surgeon who held the watch, declared five minutes not to have elapsed yet, and sternly admonished them to keep silence. He had not well done speaking, when the windlass was reversed and worked again. Practised eyes knew that it did not go as heavily as it would if both workmen had been coming up, and that only one was returning.

The rope came in tight and strained ; and ring after ring was coiled upon the barrel of the windlass, and all eyes were fastened on the pit. The sobered man was brought up, and leaped out briskly on the grass. There was an universal cry of " Alive or dead? " and then a deep, profound hush.

When he said " Alive! " a great shout arose and many eyes had tears in them.

" But he's hurt very bad," he added, as soon as he could make himself heard again. " Where's doctor? He's hurt so very bad, sir, that we donno how to get him up."

They all consulted together, and looked anxiously at the surgeon, as he asked some questions, and shook his head on receiving the replies. The sun was setting now; and the red light in the evening sky touched every face there, and caused it to be distinctly seen in all its rapt suspense.

The consultation ended in the men returning to the windlass, and the pitman going down again, carrying the wine and some other small matters with him. Then the other man came up. In the meantime, under the surgeon's directions, some men brought a hurdle, on which others made a thick bed of spare clothes covered with loose straw, while he himself contrived some bandages and slings from shawls and handkerchiefs. As these were made, they were hung upon an arm of the pitman who had last come up, with instructions how to use them: and as he stood, shown by the light he carried, leaning his powerful loose hand upon one of the poles, and sometimes glancing down the pit, and sometimes glancing round upon the people, he was not the least conspicuous figure in the scene. It was dark now, and torches were kindled.

It appeared from the little this man said to those about him, which was quickly repeated all over the circle, that the lost man had fallen upon a mass of crumbled rubbish with which the pit was half choked up, and that his fall had been further broken by some jagged earth at the side. He lay upon his back with one arm doubled under him, and according to his own belief had hardly stirred since he fell, except that he had moved his free hand to a side pocket, in which he remembered to have some bread and meat (of which he had swallowed crumbs, and had likewise scooped up a little water in it now and then. He had come straight away from his work, on being written to, and had walked the whole journey; and was on his way to Mr. Bounderby's country-house after dark, when he fell. He was crossing that dangerous country at such a dangerous time, because he was innocent of what was laid to his charge, and couldn't rest from coming the nearest way to deliver himself up. The Old Hell Shaft, the pitman said, with a curse upon it, was worthy of its bad name to the last; for though Stephen could speak now, he believed it would soon be found to have mangled the life out of him.

When all was ready, this man, still taking his last hurried charges from his comrades and the surgeon after the windlass had begun to lower him, disappeared into the pit. The rope went out as before, the signal was made as before, and the windlass stopped. No man removed his hand from it now. Every one waited with his grasp set, and his body bent down to the work, ready to reverse and wind in. At length the signal was given, and all the ring leaned forward.

For, now, the rope came in, tightened and strained to its utmost as it appeared, and the men turned heavily, and the windlass complained. It was scarcely endurable to look at the rope, and think of its giving way. But ring after ring was coiled upon the barrel of the windlass safely, and the connecting chains appeared, and finally the bucket with the two men holding on at the sides—a sight to make the head swim, and oppress the heart—and tenderly supporting between them, slung and tied within, the figure of a poor, crushed, human creature.

A low murmur of pity went round the throng, and the women wept aloud, as this form, almost without form, was moved very slowly from its iron deliverance, and laid upon the bed of straw. At first, none but the surgeon went close to it. He did what he could in its adjustment on the couch, but the best that he could do was to cover it. That gently done, he called to him Rachael and Sissy. And at that time the pale, worn, patient face was seen looking up at the sky, with the broken right hand lying bare on the outside of the covering garments, as if waiting to be taken by another hand.

They gave him drink, moistened his face with water, and adminstered some drops of cordial and wine. Though he lay quite motionless looking up at the sky, he smiled and said, " Rachael."

She stooped down on the grass at his side, and bent over him until her eyes were between his and the sky, for he could not so much as turn them to look at her.

" Rachael, my dear."

She took his hand. He smiled again and said, " Don't let 't go."

" Thou 'rt in great pain, my own dear Stephen ? "

" I ha' been, but not now. I ha' been—dreadful, and dree, and long, my dear—but 'tis ower now. Ah, Rachael, aw a muddle ! Fro' first to last, a muddle ! "

The spectre of his old look seemed to pass as he said the word.

" I ha' fell into th' pit, my dear, as have cost wi'in the knowledge o' old fok now livin, hundreds and hundreds o' men's lives—fathers, sons, brothers, dear to thousands an thousands, an keeping 'em fro' want and hunger. I ha' fell into a pit that ha' been wi' Fire-damp crueller than battle. I ha' read on 't in the public petition, as onny one may read, fro' the men that works in pits, in which they ha' pray'n and pray'n the lawmakers for Christ's sake not to let their work be murder to 'em, but to spare 'em for th' wives and children that they loves as well as gentlefok loves theirs. When it were in work, it killed wi'out need; when 'tis let alone, it kills wi'out need. See how we die an no need, one way an another—in a muddle—every day ! "

He faintly said it, without any anger against any one. Merely as the truth.

" Thy little sister, Rachael, thou hast not forgot her. Thou 'rt not like to forget her now, and me so nigh her. Thou know'st—poor, patient, suff'rin dear—how thou didst work for her, seet'n all day long in her little chair at thy winder, and how she died, young and misshapen, awlung o' sickly air as had'n no need to be, an awlung o' working people's miserable homes. A muddle ! Aw a muddle ! "

Louisa approached him, but he could not see her, lying with his face turned up to the night sky.

" If aw th' things that touches us, my dear, was not so muddled, I should'n ha' had'n need to coom heer. If we was not in a muddle among ourseln, I should'n ha' been by my own fellow weavers and workin' brothers, so mistook. If Mr. Bounderby had ever know'd me right—if he'd ever know'd me at aw—he would'n ha' took'n offence wi' me. He would'n ha' suspect'n me. But look up yonder, Rachael! Look aboove!"

Following his eyes, she saw that he was gazing at a star.

"It ha' shined upon me," he said reverently, "in my pain and trouble down below. It ha' shined into my mind. I ha' look'n at 't and thowt o' thee, Rachael, till the muddle in my mind have cleared awa, above a bit, I hope. If soom ha' been wantin' in unnerstan'in me better, I, too, ha' been wantin' in unnerstan'in them better. When I got thy letter, I easily believe that what the young ledy sen and done to me, and what her brother sen and done to me, was one, and that there were a wicked plot betwixt 'em. When I fell, I were in anger wi' her, and hurryin' on t' be as onjust t' her as oothers was t' me. But in our judgments, like as in our doins, we mun bear and forbear. In my pain an trouble, lookin up yonder,—wi' it shinin' on me—I ha' seen more clear, and ha' made it my dying prayer that aw th' world may on'y coom toogether more, an get a better unnerstan'in o' one another, than when I were in 't my own weak seln."

Louisa hearing what he said, bent over him on the opposite side to Rachael, so that he could see her.

"You ha' heard?" he said, after a few moments' silence. "I ha' not forgot you, ledy."

"Yes, Stephen, I have heard you. And your prayer is mine."

"You ha' a father. Will yo tak' a message to him?"

"He is here," said Louisa, with dread. "Shall I bring him to you?"

"If yo please."

Louisa returned with her father. Standing hand-innand, they both looked down upon the solemn countenance.

"Sir, yo will clear me an mak my name good wi' aw men. This I leave to yo."

Mr. Gradgrind was troubled and asked how?

"Sir," was the reply: "yor son will tell yo how. Ask him. I mak no charges: I leave none ahint me; not a single word. I ha' seen and spok'n wi' yor son, one night.

I ask no more o' yo than that yo clear me—an I trust to yo to do 't."

The bearers now being ready to carry him away, and the surgeon being anxious for his removal, those who had torches or lanterns, prepared to go in front of the litter. Before it was raised, and while they were arranging how to go, he said to Rachael, looking upward at the star:

"Often as I coom to myseln, and found it shinin on me down there in my trouble, I thowt it were the star as guided to Our Saviour's home. I awmust think it be the very star!"

They lifted him up, and he was overjoyed to find that they were about to take him in the direction whither the star seemed to him to lead.

"Rachael, beloved lass! Don't let go my hand. We may walk toogether t'night, my dear!"

"I will hold thy hand, and keep beside thee, Stephen, all the way."

"Bless thee! Will soombody be pleased to coover my face!"

They carried him very gently along the fields, and down the lanes, and over the wide landscape; Rachael always holding the hand in hers. Very few whispers broke the mournful silence. It was soon a funeral procession. The star had shown him where to find the God of the poor; and through humility, and sorrow, and forgiveness, he had gone to his Redeemer's rest.

CHAPTER VII.

WHELP-HUNTING.

BEFORE the ring formed round the Old Hell Shaft was broken, one figure had disappeared from within it. Mr. Bounderby and his shadow had not stood near Louisa, who held her father's arm, but in a retired place by themselves. When Mr. Gradgrind was summoned to the couch, Sissy, attentive to all that happened, slipped behind that wicked shadow—a sight in the horror of his face, if there had been eyes there for any sight but one—and whispered in his ear. Without turning his head, he conferred with her a few moments, and vanished. Thus the whelp had gone out of the circle before the people moved.

When the father reached home, he sent a message to Mr. Bounderby's, desiring his son to come to him directly. The reply was, that Mr. Bounderby having missed him in the crowd, and seeing nothing of him since, had supposed him to be at Stone Lodge.

"I believe, father," said Louisa, "he will not come back to town to-night." Mr. Gradgrind turned away, and said no more.

In the morning, he went down to the Bank himself as soon as it was opened, and seeing his son's place empty (he had not the courage to look in at first) went back along the street to meet Mr. Bounderby on his way there. To whom he said that, for reasons he would soon explain, but entreated not then to be asked for, he had found it necessary to employ his son at a distance for a little while. Also, that he was charged with the duty of vindicating Stephen Blackpool's memory, and declaring the thief. Mr. Bounderby, quite confounded, stood stock-still in the street after his father-in-law had left him, swelling like an immense soap-bubble, without its beauty.

Mr. Gradgrind went home, locked himself in his room, and kept it all that day. When Sissy and Louisa tapped at his door, he said, without opening it, "Not now, my dears; in the evening." On their return in the evening, he said, "I am not able yet—to-morrow." He ate nothing all day, and had no candle after dark; and they heard him walking to and fro late at night.

But, in the morning he appeared at breakfast at the usual hour, and took his usual place at the table. Aged and bent he looked, and quite bowed down; and yet he looked a wiser man, and a better man, than in the days when in this life he wanted nothing but Facts. Before he left the room, he appointed a time for them to come to him; and so, with his gray head drooping, went away.

"Dear father," said Louisa, when they kept their appointment, "you have three young children left. They will be different, *I* will be different yet, with Heaven's help."

She gave her hand to Sissy, as if she meant with her help too.

17

"Your wretched brother," said Mr. Gradgrind "Do you think he had planned this robbery, when he went with you to the lodging?"

"I fear so, father. I know he had wanted money very much, and had spent a great deal."

"The poor man being about to leave the town, it came into his evil brain to cast suspicion on him?"

"I think it must have flashed upon him while he sat there, father. For, I asked him to go there with me. The visit did not originate with him."

"He had some conversation with the poor man. Did he take him aside?"

"He took him out of the room. I asked him afterwards, why he had done so, and he made a plausible excuse; but since last night, father, and when I remember the circumstances by its light, I am afraid I can imagine too truly what passed between them."

"Let me know," said her father, "if your thoughts present your guilty brother in the same dark view as mine."

"I fear father," hesitated Louisa, "that he must have made some representation to Stephen Blackpool—perhaps in my name, perhaps in his own—which induced him to do in good faith and honesty, what he had never done before, and to wait about the Bank those two or three nights before he left the town."

"Too plain!" returned the father. "Too plain!"

He shaded his face, and remained silent for some moments. Recovering himself, he said:

"And now, how is he to be found? How is he to be saved from justice? In the few hours that I can possibly allow to elapse before I publish the truth, how is he to be found by us, and only by us? Ten thousand pounds could not effect it."

"Sissy has effected it, father."

He raised his eyes to where she stood, like a good fairy in his house, and said in a tone of softened gratitude and grateful kindness, "It is always you, my child!"

"We had our fears," Sissy explained, glancing at Louisa, "before yesterday; and when I saw you brought to the side of the litter last night, and heard what passed (being close to Rachael all the time), I went to him when no one saw, and said to him, 'Don't look at me. See

where your father is. Escape at once, for his sake and
your own!' He was in a tremble before I whispered to
him, and he started and trembled more then, and said,
'Where can I go? I have very little money, and I don't
know who will hide me!' I thought of father's old circus.
I have not forgotten where Mr. Sleary goes at this time
of year, and I read of him in a paper only the other day.
I told him to hurry there, and tell his name, and ask Mr.
Sleary to hide him till I came. 'I'll get to him before the
morning,' he said. And I saw him shrink away among
the people."

"Thank Heaven!" exclaimed his father. "He may be
got abroad yet."

It was the more hopeful as the town to which Sissy
had directed him was within three hours' journey of
Liverpool, whence he could be swiftly despatched to any
part of the world. But, caution being necessary in communicating with him—for there was a greater danger
every moment of his being suspected now, and nobody
could be sure at heart but that Mr. Bounderby himself,
in a bullying vein of public zeal, might play a Roman
part—it was consented that Sissy and Louisa should repair to the place in question, by a circuitous course, alone;
and that the unhappy father, setting forth in an opposite
direction, should get round to the same bourne by another and wider route. It was further agreed that he
should not present himself to Mr. Sleary, lest his intentions should be mistrusted, or the intelligence of his arrival should cause his son to take flight anew; but that
the communication should be left to Sissy and Louisa to
open; and that they should inform the cause of so
much misery and disgrace, of his father's being at hand
and of the purpose for which they had come. When
these arrangements had been well considered and were
fully understood by all three, it was time to begin to
carry them into execution. Early in the afternoon, Mr.
Gradgrind walked direct from his own house into the
country, to be taken up on the line by which he was to
travel; and at night the remaining two set forth upon
their different course, encouraged by not seeing any face
they knew.

The two travelled all night, except when they were left,
for odd numbers of minutes, at branch-places, up illimit-

able flights of steps, or down wells—which was the only
variety of those branches—and, early in the morning,
were turned out on a swamp, a mile or two from the
town they sought. From this dismal spot they were res-
cued by a savage old postilion, who happened to be up
early, kicking a horse in a fly; and so were smuggled
into the town by all the back lanes where the pigs lived;
which, although not a magnificent or even savory approach, was, as is usual in such cases, the legitimate
highway.

The first thing they saw on entering the town was the
skeleton of Sleary's Circus. The company had departed for
another town more than twenty miles off, and had opened
there last night. The connection between the two places
was by a hilly turnpike-road, and the travelling on that
road was very slow. Though they took but a hasty
breakfast, and no rest (which it would have been in vain
to seek under such anxious circumstances), it was noon
before they began to find the bills of Sleary's Horse-riding
on barns and walls, and one o'clock when they stopped
in the market-place.

A Grand Morning Performance by the Riders, commencing at that very hour, but in course of announcement by
the bellman as they set their feet upon the stones of the
street. Sissy recommended that, to avoid making inquiries and attracting attention in the town, they should
present themselves to pay at the door. If Mr. Sleary
were taking the money, he would be sure to know her,
and would proceed with discretion. If he were not he
would be sure to see them inside; and, knowing what he
had done with the fugitive, would proceed with discretion
still.

Therefore, they repaired, with fluttering hearts, to the
well-remembered booth. The flag with the inscription
Sleary's Horse-riding was there; and the Gothic niche
was there; but Mr. Sleary was not there. Master Kid-
derminister, grown too maturely turfy to be received by
the wildest credulity as Cupid any more, had yielded to
the invincible force of circumstances (and his beard), and,
in the capacity of a man who made himself generally
useful, presided on this occasion over the exchequer—
having also a drum in reserve, on which to expend his
leisure moments and superfluous forces. In the extreme

sharpness of his lookout for base coin, Mr. Kidderminster, as at present situated, never saw anything but money; so Sissy passed him unrecognized, and they went in.

The Emperor of Japan, on a steady old white horse stencilled with black spots, was twirling five wash-hand basins at once, as it is the favorite recreation of that monarch to do. Sissy, though well acquainted with his Royal line, had no personal knowledge of the present Emperor, and his reign was peaceful. Miss Josephine Sleary, in her celebrated graceful Equestrian Tyrolean Flower-Act, was then announced by a new clown (who humorously said Cauliflower Act) and Mr. Sleary appeared, leading her in.

Mr. Sleary had only made one cut at the Clown with his long whip-lash, and the Clown had only said, "If you do it again, I'll throw the horse at you!" when Sissy was recognized both by father and daughter. But they got through the Act with great self-possession; and Mr. Sleary, saving for the first instant, conveyed no more expression into his locomotive eye than into his fixed one. The performance seemed a little long to Sissy and Louisa, particularly when it stopped to afford the Clown an opportunity of telling Mr. Sleary (who said "Indeed, sir!" to all his observations in the calmest way and with his eye on the house), about two legs sitting on three legs looking at one leg, when in came four legs, and laid hold of one leg, and up got two legs, caught hold of three legs, and threw 'em at four legs, who ran away with one leg. For, although an ingenious Allegory relating to a butcher, a three-legged stool, a dog, and a leg of mutton, this narrative consumed time; and they were in great suspense. At last, however, little fair-haired Josephine made her curtsey amid great applause; and the Clown, left alone in the ring, had just warmed himself, and said, "Now I'll have a turn!" when Sissy was touched on the shoulder, and beckoned out.

She took Louisa with her; and they were received by Mr. Sleary in a very little private apartment, with canvas sides, a grass floor, and a wooden ceiling all aslant, on which the box company stamped their approbation, as if they were coming through. "Thethilia," said Mr. Sleary, who had brandy and water at hand, "it doth me good to thee you. You wath alwayth a favorite with uth, and

you've done uth credith thinth the old timeth I'm thure.
You mutht thee our people, my dear, afore we thpeak of
bithnith, or they'll break their hearth—ethpethially the
women. Here 'th Jothphine hath been and got married
to E. W. B. Childerth, and thee hath got a boy, and though
he 'th only three yearth old, he thtickth on to any pony
you can bring againtht him. He'th named The Little
Wonder of Thcolathtic Equitation; and if you don't hear
of that boy at Athley'th, you'll hear of him at Parith.
And you recollect Kidderminthter, that wath thought to
be rather thweet upon yourthelf? Well. He'th married
too. Married a widder. Old enough to be hith mother.
Thee wath Tightrope, thee wath, and now thee'th nothing
—on accounth of fat. They've got two children, tho we're
thtrong in the Fairy bithnith and the Nurthery dodge.
If you wath to thee our Children in the Wood, with their
father and mother both a dyin' on a horthe—their uncle
a rethieving of 'em ath hith wardth, upon a horthe—them-
thelvth both a goin' a blackberryin' on a horthe—and
the Robinth a coming in to cover 'em with leavth, upon
a horthe—you'd thay it wath the completetht thing ath
ever you thet your eyeth on! And you remember Emma
Gordon, my dear, ath wath a'motht a mother to you? Of
courthe you do; I needn't athk. Well! Emma, thee
lotht her huthband. He wath throw'd a heavy back-fall
off a Elephant in a thort of a Pagoda thing ath the
Thultan of the Indieth, and he never got the better
of it; and thee married a thecond time—married a Cheeth-
monger ath fell in love with her from the front—and
he'th a Overtheer and makin' a fortun."

These various changes, Mr. Sleary, very short of breath
now, related with great heartiness, and with a wonderful
kind of innocence, considering what a bleary and brandy-
and-watery-old veteran he was. Afterwards he brought in
Josephine, and E. W. B. Childers (rather deeply-lined in
the jaws by daylight) and the Little Wonder of Scholastic
Equitation, and in a word all the company. Amazing
creatures they were in Louisa's eyes, so white and pink
of complexion, so scant of dress, and so demonstrative of
legs; but it was very agreeable to see them crowding
about Sissy, and very natural in Sissy to be unable to refrain from tears.

"There! Now Thethilia hath kithd all the children,

and hugged all the women, and thaken handth all round with all the men, clear, every one of you, and ring in the band for the second part!"

As soon as they were gone, he continued in a low tone, "Now, Thethilia, I don't athk to know any thecreth, but I thuppothe I may consthider thith to be Mithe Thquire."

"This is his sister. Yes."

"And t' other on'th daughter. That 'th what I mean. Hope I thee you well, mith. And I hope the Thquire 'th well?"

"My father will be here soon," said Louisa, anxious to bring him to the point. "Is my brother safe?"

"Thafe and thound!" he replied. "I want you jutht to take a peep at the Ring, mith, through here. Thethilia, you know the dodgeth; find a thpy-hole for yourthelf."

They each looked through the chinks in the boards.

"That 'th Jack the Giant Killer—piethe of comic infant bithnith," said Sleary. "There 'th a property-houthe, you thee, for Jack to hide in; there'th my Clown with a thauthepan-lid and a thpit, for Jack 'th thervant; there'th little Jack himthelf in a thplendid thoot of armor; there 'th two comic black thervanth twithe ath big ath the houthe, to thtand by it and to bring it in and clear it; and the Giant (a very ecthpenthive bathket one), he an't on yet. Now, do you thee 'em all?"

"Yes," they both said.

"Look at 'em again," said Sleary, "look at 'em well. You thee 'em all? Very good. Now, mith;" he put a form for them to sit on; "I have my opinionth, and the Thquire your father hath hith. I don't want to know what your brother 'th been up to; ith better for me not to know. All I thay ith, the Thquire hath thtood by Thethilia, and I'll thand by the Thquire. Your brother ith one o' them black thervanth."

Louisa uttered an exclamation, partly of distress, partly of satisfaction.

"Ith a fact," said Sleary, "and even knowin' it, you couldn't put your finger on him. Let the Thquire come. I thall keep your brother here after the performanth. I thant undreth him, nor yet wath hith paint off. Let the Thquire come here after the performanth, or come here yourthelf after the performanth, and you thall find your brother and have the whole plathe to talk to him in.

Never mind the lookth of him, ath long ath he 'th well hid."

Louisa, with many thanks and with a lightened load, detained Mr. Sleary no longer then. She left her love for her brother, with her eyes full of tears; and she and Sissy went away until later in the afternoon.

Mr. Gradgrind arrived within an hour afterwards. He too had encountered no one whom he knew; and was now sanguine with Sleary's assistance, of getting his disgraced son to Liverpool in the night. As neither of the three could be his companion without almost identifying him under any disguise, he prepared a letter to a correspondent whom he could trust, beseeching him to ship the bearer off at any cost, to North or South America, or any distant part of the world to which he could be the most speedily and privately dispatched.

This done, they walked about, waiting for the Circus to be quite vacated; not only by the audience, but by the company and by the horses. After watching it a long time, they saw Mr. Sleary bring out a chair and sit down by the side-door, smoking; as if that were his signal that they might approach.

" Your thervant, Thquire," was his cautious salutation as they passed in. "If you want me you'll find me here. You muthn't mind your thon having a comic livery on."

They all three went in; and Mr. Gradgrind sat down forlorn, on the Clown's performing chair in the middle of the ring. On one of the back benches, remote in the subdued light and the strangeness of the place, sat the villanous whelp, sulky to the last, whom he had the misery to call his son.

In a preposterous coat, like a beadle's, with cuffs and flaps exaggerated to an unspeakable extent; in an immense waistcoat, knee-breeches, buckled shoes, and a mad cocked hat; with nothing fitting him, and everything of coarse material, moth-eaten and full of holes; with seams in his black face, where fear and heat had started through the greasy composition daubed all over it; anything so grimly, detestably, ridiculously shameful as the whelp in his comic livery, Mr. Gradgrind never could by any other means have believed in, weighable and measurable fact though it was. And one of his model children had come to this!

At first the whelp would not draw any nearer, but persisted in remaining up there by himself. Yielding at length, if any concession so suddenly made can be called yielding, to the entreaties of Sissy—for Louisa he disowned altogether—he came down, bench by bench, until he stood in the sawdust, on the verge of the circle, as far as possible, within its limits from where his father sat.

" How was this done ? " asked the father.

" How was what done ? " moodily answered the son.

" This robbery," said the father, raising his voice upon the word.

" I forced the safe myself over night, and shut it up ajar before I went away. I had had the key that was found, made long before. I dropped it that morning, that it might be supposed to have been used. I didn't take the money all at once. I pretended to put my balance away every night, but I didn't. Now you know all about it."

" If a thunderbolt had fallen on me," said the father, " it would have shocked me less than this ! "

" I don't see why," grumbled the son. " So many people are employed in situations of trust; so many people, out of so many, will be dishonest. I have heard you talk, a hundred times, of its being a law. How can *I* help laws ? You have comforted others with such things, father. Comfort yourself ! "

The father buried his face in his hands, and the son stood in his disgraceful grotesqueness, biting straw : his hands, with the black partly worn away inside, looking like the hands of a monkey. The evening was fast closing in ; and from time to time, he turned the whites of his eyes restlessly and impatiently towards his father. They were the only parts of his face that showed any life or expression, the pigment upon it was so thick.

" You must be got to Liverpool, and sent abroad."

" I suppose I must. I can't be more miserable anywhere," whimpered the whelp, " than I have been here, ever since I can remember. That's one thing."

Mr. Gradgrind went to the door, and returned with Sleary, to whom he submitted the question, How to get this deplorable object away ?

" Why, I've been thinking of it, Thquire. There'th not muth time to lothe, tho you muth thay yeth or no. Ith over twenty mileth to the rail. There'th a coath in half an hour, that goeth *to* the rail, 'purpothe to catch the mail train. That train will take him right to Liverpool."

"But look at him," groaned Mr. Gradgrind. "Will any coach——"

"I don't mean that he thould go in the comic livery," said Sleary. "Thay the word, and I'll make a Jothkin of him, out of the wardrobe, in five minutes."

"I don't understand," said Mr. Gradgrind.

"A Jothkin—a Carter. Make up your mind quick, Thquire. There'll be beer to feth. I've never met with nothing but beer ath'll ever clean a comic blackamoor."

Mr. Gradgrind rapidly assented; Mr. Sleary rapidly turned out from a box, a smock frock, a felt hat, and other essentials; the whelp rapidly changed clothes behind a screen of baize: Mr. Sleary rapidly brought beer, and washed him white again.

"Now," said Sleary, "Come along to the coath, and jump up behind; I'll go with you there, and they'll thuppoth you one of my people. Thay farewell to your family, and tharp'th the word." With which he delicately retired.

"Here is your letter," said Mr. Gradgrind. "All necessary means will be provided for you. Atone, by repentance and better conduct, for the shocking action you have committed, and the dreadful consequence to which it has led. Give me your hand, my poor boy, and may God forgive you as I do!"

The culprit was moved to a few abject tears by these words and their pathetic tone. But, when Louisa opened her arms, he repulsed her afresh.

"Not you. I don't want to have anything to say to you!"

"O Tom, Tom, do we end so, after all my love!"

"After all your love!" he returned obdurately. "Pretty love! Leaving old Bounderby to himself, and packing my best friend Mr. Harthouse off, and going home just when I was in the greatest danger. Pretty love that! Coming out with every word about our having gone to that place, when you saw the net was gathering round me. Pretty love that! You have regularly given me up. You never cared for me."

"Tharp 'th the word!" said Sleary, at the door.

They all confusedly went out: Louisa crying to him that she forgave him, and loved him still, and that he would one day be sorry to have left her so, and glad to think of these her last words, far away : when some one ran against them. Mr. Gradgrind and Sissy, who were both before him while his sister yet clung to his shoulder, stopped and recoiled.

For, there was Bitzer, out of breath, his thin lips parted, his thin nostrils distended, his white eyelashes quivering, his colorless face more colorless than ever, as if he ran himself into a white heat, when other people ran themselves into a glow. There he stood panting and heaving, as if he had never stopped since the night, now long ago, when he had run them down before.

"I'm sorry to interfere with your plans," said Bitzer, shaking his head, "but I can't allow myself to be done by horse-riders. I must have young Mr. Tom; he mustn't be got away by horse-riders; here he is in a smock frock, and I must have him!"

By the collar, too, it seemed. For so he took possession of him.

CHAPTER VIII.

PHILOSOPHICAL.

They went back into the booth, Sleary shutting the door to keep intruders out. Bitzer, still holding the paralyzed culprit by the collar, stood in the Ring, blinking at his old patron through the darkness of the twilight.

"Bitzer," said Mr. Gradgrind, broken down and miserably submissive to him, "have you a heart?"

"The circulation, sir," returned Bitzer, smiling at the oddity of the question, "couldn't be carried on without one. No man, sir, acquainted with the facts established by Harvey relating to the circulation of the blood, can doubt that I have a heart."

"Is it accessible," cried Mr. Gradgrind, "to any compassionate influence?"

"It is accessible to Reason, sir," returned the excellent young man. "And to nothing else."

They stood looking at each other; Mr. Gradgrind's face as white as the pursuer's.

"What motive—even what motive in reason—can you have for preventing the escape of this wretched youth," said Mr. Gradgrind, "and crushing his miserable father? See his sister here. Pity us!"

"Sir," returned Bitzer, in a very business-like and logical manner, "since you ask me what motive I have in reason, for taking young Mr. Tom back to Coketown, it is only reasonable to let you know. I have suspected young Mr. Tom of this bank-robbery from the first. I had had my eye upon him before that time, for I knew his ways. I have kept my observations to myself, but I have made them; and I have got ample proofs against him now, besides his running away, and besides his own confession, which I was just in time to overhear. I had the pleasure of watching your house yesterday morning, and following you here. I am going to take young Mr. Tom back to Coketown, in order to deliver him over to Mr. Bounderby. Sir, I have no doubt whatever that Mr. Bounderby will then promote me to young Mr. Tom's situation. And I wish to have his situation, sir, for it will be a rise to me, and will do me good."

"If this is solely a question of self-interest with you——" Mr. Gradgrind began.

"I beg your pardon for interrupting you, sir," returned Bitzer; "but I am sure you know that the whole social system is a question of self-interest. What you must always appeal to, is a person's self-interest. It's your only hold. We are so constituted. I was brought up in that catechism when I was very young, sir, as you are aware."

"What sum of money," said Mr. Gradgrind, "will you set against your expected promotion?"

"Thank you, sir," returned Bitzer, "for hinting at the proposal; but I will not set any sum against it. Knowing that your clear head would propose that alternative, I have gone over the calculations in my mind; and I find that to compound a felony, even on very high terms indeed, would not be as safe and good for me as my improved prospects in the Bank."

"Bitzer," said Mr. Gradgrind, stretching out his hands as though he would have said, See how miserable I am! "Bitzer, I have but one chance left to soften you. You were many years at my school. If, in remembrance of the pains bestowed upon you there, you can persuade yourself in any degree to disregard your present interest and release my son, I entreat and pray you to give him the benefit of that remembrance."

" I really wonder, sir," rejoined the old pupil in an argumentative manner, " to find you taking a position so untenable. My schooling was paid for; it was a bargain; and when I came away, the bargain ended."

It was a fundamental principle of the Gradgrind philosophy that everything was to be paid for. Nobody was ever on any account to give anybody anything, or render anybody help without purchase. Gratitude was to be abolished, and the virtues springing from it were not to be. Every inch of the existence of mankind, from birth to death, was to be a bargain across a counter. And if we didn't get to Heaven that way, it was not a politico-economical place, and we had no business there.

" I don't deny," added Bitzer, " that my schooling was cheap. But that comes right, sir. I was made in the cheapest market, and have to dispose of myself in the dearest."

He was a little troubled here, by Louisa and Sissy crying.

" Pray don't do that," said he, " it's of no use doing that: it only worries. You seem to think that I have some animosity against young Mr. Tom; whereas I have none at all. I am only going, on the reasonable grounds I have mentioned, to take him back to Coketown. If he was to resist, I should set up the cry of Stop Thief! But, he won't resist, you may depend upon it."

Mr. Sleary, who, with his mouth open and his rolling eye as immovably jammed in his head as his fixed one, had listened to these doctrines with profound attention, here stepped forward.

" Thquire, you know perfectly well, and your daughter knowth perfectiy well (better than you, becauthe I thed it to her), that I didn't know what your thon had done, and that I didn't want to know—I thed it wath better not, though I only thought, then, it wath thome thky-larking. However, thith young man having made it known to be a robbery of a bank, why, that 'th a theriouth thing; muth too theriouth a thing for me to compound, ath thith young man hath very properly called it.

Conthequently, Thquire, you muthn't quarrel with me if I take thith young man'th thide, and thay he 'th right and there 'th no help for it. But I tell you what I'll do, Thquire; I'll drive your thon and thith young man over to the rail, and prevent expothure here. I can't conthent to do more, but I'll do that."

Fresh lamentations from Louisa, and deeper affliction on Mr. Gradgrind's part, followed this desertion of them by their last friend. But, Sissy glanced at him with great attention; nor did she in her own breast misunderstand him. As they were all going out again, he favored her with one slight roll of his movable eye, desiring her to linger behind. As he locked the door, he said excitedly:

"The Thquire thtood by you, Thethilia, and I'll thtand by the Thquire. More than that: thith ith a prethiouth rathcal, and belongth to that bluthtering Cove that my people nearly pitht out o' winder. It'll be a dark night; I've got a horthe that'll do anything but thpeak; I've got a pony that'll go fifteen mile an hour with Childerth driving of him; I've got a dog that'll keep a man to one plathe four-and-twenty hourth. Get a word with the young Thquire. Tell him, when he theeth our horthe begin to danthe, not to be afraid of being thpilt, but to look out for a pony-gig coming up. Tell him, when he theeth that gig clothe by, to jump down, and it'll take him off at a rattling pathe. If my dog leth thith young man thtir a peg on foot, I give him leave to go. And if my horthe ever thtirth from that thpot where he beginth a danthing, till the morning—I don't know him!—Tharp 'th the word!"

The word was so sharp, that in ten minutes Mr. Childers, sauntering about the market-place in a pair of slippers, had his cue, and Mr. Sleary's equipage was ready. It was a fine sight, to behold the learned dog barking round it, and Mr. Sleary instructing him, with his one practicable eye, that Bitzer was the object of his particular attentions. Soon after dark they all three got in and started; the learned dog (a formidable creature) already pinning Bitzer with his eye, and sticking close to the wheel on his side, that he might be ready for him in the event of his showing the slightest disposition to alight.

The other three sat up at the inn all night in great suspense. At eight o'clock in the morning Mr. Sleary and the dog reappeared: both in high spirits.

"All right, Thquire!" said Mr. Sleary, "Your thon may be aboard-a-thip by thith time. Childerth took him off, an hour and a half after we left here latht night. The horthe danthed the polka till he wath dead beat (he would have walthed if he hadn't been in harneth), and then I gave him the word and he went to thleep comfortable. When that prethiouth young Rathcal thed he'd go for'ard· afoot, the dog hung on to hith neck-handkercher with all four legth in the air and pulled him down and rolled him over. Tho he come back into the drag, and there he that, till I turned the horthe'th head, at halfpatht thixth thith morning."

Mr. Gradgrind overwhelmed him with thanks, of course; and hinted as delicately as he could, at a handsome remuneration in money.

"I don't want money mythelf, Thquire; but Childerth ith a family man, and if you wath to like to offer him a five-pound note, it mightn't be unactheptable. Likewithe if you wath to thtand a collar for the dog, or a thet of bellth for the horthe, I thould be very glad to take 'em. Brandy and water I alwayth take." He had already called for a glass, and now called for another. "If you wouldn't think it going too far, Thquire, to make a little thpread for the company at about three and thixth a head, not reckoning Luth, it would make 'em happy."

All these little tokens of his gratitude, Mr. Gradgrind very willingly undertook to render. Though he thought them far too slight, he said, for such a service.

"Very well, Thquire; then if you'll only give a Hortheriding, a bethpeak, whenever you can, you'll more than balanthe the account. Now, Thquire, if your daughter will ethcuthe me, I should like one parting word with you."

Louisa and Sissy withdrew into an adjoining room; Mr. Sleary, stirring and drinking his brandy and water as he stood, went on:

"Thquire, you don't need to be told that dogth ith wonderful animalth."

"Their instinct," said Mr. Gradgrind, "is surprising."

" Whatever you call it—and I'm bletht if I know what to call it "—said Sleary, "it ith athtonithing. The way in with a dog 'll find you—the dithtanthe he 'll come ! "

"His scent," said Mr. Gradgrind, "being so fine."

" I'm bletht if I know what to call it," repeated Sleary, shaking his head, " but I have had dogth find me, Thquire, in a way that made me think whether that dog hadn't gone to another dog, and thed, 'You don't happen to know a perthon of the name of Thleary, do you? Perthon of the name of Thleary, in the Horthe-riding way— thtout man—game eye ?' And whether that dog mightn't have thed,' Well, I can't thay I know him myself, but I know a dog that I think would be likely to be acquainted with him.' And whether that dog mightn't have thought it over, and thed, ' Thleary, Thleary ! O yeth, to be sure ! A friend of mine mentioned him to me at one time. I can get you hith addreth directly.' In conthequenth of my being afore the public, and going about tho muth, you thee, there mutht be a number of dogth acquainted with me, Thquire, that *I* don't know ! "

Mr. Gradgrind seemed to be quite confounded by this speculation.

"Any way," said Sleary, after putting his lips to his brandy and water, "ith fourteen months ago, Thquire, thinthe we wath at Chethter. We wath getting up our Children in the Wood one morning, when there cometh into our Ring, by the thtage door, a dog. He had travelled a long way, he wath in very bad condithon, he wath lame, and pretty well blind. He went round to our children, one after another, as if he wath a theeking for a child he know'd ; and then he come to me, and throwd hithelf up behind, and thtood on hith two forelegth, weak ath he wath, and then he wagged hith tail, and died. Thquire, that dog wath Merrylegth."

" Sissy's father's dog ! "

"Thethilia'th father'th old dog. Now, Thquire, I can take my oath, from my knowledge of that dog, that that man wath dead—and buried—afore that dog came back to me. Joth'phine and Childerth and me talked it over a long time, whether I thould write or not. But we agreed, 'No. There'th nothing comfortable to tell ; why unthettle her mind, and make her unhappy ?' Tho, whether her father bathely detherted her ; or whether he broke hith own heart alone, rather than pull her down along with him, never will be known, now, Thquire, till —no, not till we know how the dogth findth uth out!"

"She keeps the bottle that he sent her for, to this hour; and she will believe in his affection to the last moment of her life," said Mr. Gradgrind.

"It theemth to prethent two thingth to a perthon, don't it, Thquire?" said Mr. Sleary, musing as he looked down into the depths of his brandy and water: "one, that there ith a love in the world, not all Thelf-interetht after all, but thomething very different; t'other, that it hath a way of ith own of calculating or not calculating, whith thomehow or another ith at leatht ath hard to give a name to, ath the wayth of the dogth ith!"

Mr. Gradgrind looked out of window, and made no reply. Mr. Sleary emptied his glass and recalled the ladies.

"Thethilia my dear, kith me and good-bye! Mith Thquire, to thee you treating of her like a thither that you trutht and honor with all your heart and more, ith a very pretty thight to me. I hope your brother may live to be better dethervin of you, and a greater comfort to yoo. Thquire, thake handth, firtht and latht! Don't be croth with uth poor vagabondth. People mutht be amuthed. They can't be alwayth a learning, nor yet they can't be alwayth a working, they an't made for it. You *mutht* have uth, Thquire. Do the withe thing and the kind thing too, and make the betht of uth; not the wurtht!"

"And I never thought before," said Mr. Sleary, putting his head in at the door again to say it, "that I wath tho muth of a Cackler!"

CHAPTER IX.

FINAL.

It is a dangerous thing to see anything in the sphere of a vain blusterer, before the vain blusterer sees it himself. Mr. Bounderby felt that Mrs. Sparsit had audaciously anticipated him, and presumed to be wiser than he. Unappeasably indignant with her for her triumphant discovery of Mrs. Pegler, he turned this presumption, on the part of a woman in her dependent position, over and over in his mind, until it accumulated with turning like a great snowball. At last he made the discovery that to discharge this highly connected female—to have it in his power to say, " She was a woman of family, and wanted to stick to me, but I wouldn't have it, and got rid of her " —would be to get the utmost possible amount of crowning glory out of the connection, and at the same time to punish Mrs. Sparsit according to her deserts.

Filled fuller than ever, with this great idea, Mr. Bounderby came in to lunch, and sat himself down in the dining-room of former days, where his portrait was. Mrs. Sparsit sat by the fire, with her foot in her cotton stirrup, little thinking whither she was posting.

Since the Pegler affair, this gentlewoman had covered her pity for Mr. Bounderby with a veil of quiet melancholy and contrition. In virtue thereof, it had become her habit to assume a woful look, which woful look she now bestowed upon her patron.

" What's the matter now, ma'am ? " said Mr. Bounderby, in a very short rough way.

" Pray, sir," returned Mrs. Sparsit, " do not bite my nose off."

" Bite your nose off, ma'am ? " repeated Mr. Bounderby. " *Your* nose ! " meaning, as Mrs. Sparsit conceived, that it was too developed a nose for the purpose. After which offensive implication, he cut himself a crust of bread, and threw the knife down with a noise.

Mrs. Sparsit took her foot out of her stirrup, and said, " Mr. Bounderby, sir ! "

" Well, ma'am ? " retorted Mr. Bounderby. " What are you staring at ? "

" May I ask, sir," said Mrs. Sparsit, " have you been ruffled this morning ? "

" Yes, ma'am."

" May I inquire, sir," pursued the injured woman, " whether *I* am the unfortunate cause of your having lost your temper ? "

" Now, I'll tell you what, ma'am," said Bounderby, " I am not come here to be bullied. A female may be highly connected, but she can't be permitted to bother and badger a man in my position, and I am not going to put up with it." (Mr. Bounderby felt it necessary to get on, foreseeing that if he allowed of details, he would be beaten.)

Mrs. Sparsit first elevated, then knitted, her Coriolanian eyebrows; gathered up her work into its proper basket; and rose.

" Sir," said she majestically. " It is apparent to me that I am in your way at present. I will retire to my own apartment."

" Allow me to open the door, ma'am."

"Thank you, sir; I can do it for myself."

" You had better allow me, ma'am," said Bounderby, passing her, and getting his hand upon the lock; " because I can take the opportunity of saying a word to you, before you go. Mrs. Sparsit, ma'am, I rather think you are cramped here, do you know? It appears to me, that, under my humble roof, there's hardly opening enough for a lady of your genius in other people's affairs."

Mrs. Sparsit gave him a look of the darkest scorn, and said with great politeness, " Really, sir?"

" I have been thinking it over, you see, since the late affairs have happened, ma'am," said Bounderby; "and it appears to my poor judgment——"

" Oh! Pray sir," Mrs. Sparsit interposed, with sprightly cheerfulness, "don't disparage your judgment. Everybody knows how unerring Mr. Bounderby's judgment is. Everybody has had proofs of it. It must be the theme of general conversation. Disparage anything in yourself but your judgment, sir," said Mrs. Sparsit, laughing.

Mr. Bounderby, very red and uncomfortable, resumed:

" It appears to me, ma'am, I say, that a different sort of establishment altogether would bring out a lady of *your* powers. Such an establishment as your relation, Lady Scadgers's, now. Don't you think you might find some affairs there, ma'am, to interfere with?"

" It never occurred to me before, sir," returned Mrs. Sparsit; " but now you mention it, I should think it highly probable."

" Then suppose you try, ma'am," said Bounderby, laying an envelope with a cheque in it in her little basket. " You can take your own time for going, ma'am; but perhaps in the meanwhile, it will be more agreeable to a lady of your powers of mind, to eat her meals by herself, and not to be intruded upon. I really ought to apologize to you—being only Josiah Bounderby of Coketown—for having stood in your light so long."

"Pray don't name it, sir," returned Mrs. Sparsit. "If that portrait could speak, sir—but it has the advantage over the original of not possessing the power of committing itself and disgusting others,—it would testify, that a long period has elapsed since I first habitually addressed it as the picture of a Noodle. Nothing that a Noodle does, can awaken surprise or indignation; the proceedings of a Noodle can only inspire contempt."

Thus saying, Mrs. Sparsit, with her Roman features like a medal struck to commemorate her scorn of Mr. Bounderby, surveyed him fixedly from head to foot, swept disdainfully past him, and ascended the staircase. Mr. Bounderby closed the door, and stood before the fire; projecting himself after his old explosive manner into his portrait—and into futurity.

Into how much of futurity? He saw Mrs. Sparsit fighting out a daily fight at the points of all the weapons in the female armory, with the grudging, smarting, peevish, tormenting Lady Scadgers, still laid up in bed with her mysterious leg, and gobbling her insufficient income down by about the middle of every quarter, in a mean little airless lodging, a mere closet for one, a mere crib for two; but did he see more? Did he catch any glimpse of himself making a show of Bitzer to strangers, as the rising young man, so devoted to his master's great merits, who had won young Tom's place, and had almost captured young Tom himself, in the times when by various rascals he was spirited away? Did he see any faint reflection of his own image making a vain-glorious will, whereby five-and-twenty Humbugs, past five and fifty years of age, each taking upon himself the name, Josiah Bounderby of Coketown, should forever dine in Bounderby Hall, forever lodge in Bounderby Buildings, forever attend a Bounderby chapel, forever go to sleep under a Bounderby chaplain, forever be supported out of a Bounderby estate, and forever nauseate all healthy stomachs, with a vast amount of Bounderby balderdash and bluster? Had he any prescience of the day, five years to come, when Josiah Bounderby of Coketown was to die of a fit in the Coketown street, and this same precious will was to begin its long career of quibble, plunder, false pretences, vile example, little service and much law? Probably not. Yet the portrait was to see it all out.

Here was Mr. Gradgrind on the same day, and in the same hour, sitting thoughtful in his own room. How much of futurity did *he* see? Did he see himself, a white-haired, decrepit man, bending his hitherto inflexible theories to appointed circumstances; making his facts and figures subservient to Faith, Hope, and Charity; and no longer trying to grind that Heavenly trio in his dusty little mills? Did he catch sight of himself, therefore, much despised by his late political associates? Did he see them, in the era of its being quite settled that the national dustmen have only to do with one another, and owe no duty to an abstraction called a People, "taunting the honorable gentleman" with this and with that and with what not, five nights a week, until the small hours of the morning? Probably he had that much fore-knowledge knowing his men.

Here was Louisa on the night of the same day, watching the fire as in days of yore, though with a gentler and humbler face. How much of the future might arise before *her* vision? Broadsides in the street, signed with her father's name, exonerating the late Stephen Blackpool, weaver, from misplaced suspicion, and publishing the guilt of his own son, with such extenuation as his years and temptation (he could not bring himself to add, his education) might beseech; were of the Present. So, Stephen Blackpool's tombstone, with her father's record of his death, was almost of the Present, for she knew it was to be. These things she could plainly see. But, how much of the Future?

A working woman, christened Rachael, after a long illness once again appearing at the ringing of the Factory bell, and passing to and fro at the set hours, among the Coketown hands; a woman of pensive beauty, always dressed in black, but sweet-tempered and serene and even cheerful; who, of all the people in the place, alone appeared to have compassion on a degraded, drunken wretch of her own sex, who was sometimes seen in the town secretly begging of her, and crying to her; a woman working, ever working, but content to do it, and preferring to do it as her natural lot, until she should be too old to labor any more? Did Louisa see this? Such a thing was to be.

A lonely brother, many thousand of miles away, writing, on paper blotted with tears, that her words had too soon come true, and that all the treasures in the world would be cheaply bartered for a sight of her dear face? At length this brother coming nearer home, with hope of seeing her, and being delayed by illness; and then a letter, in a strange hand, saying "he died in hospital, of fever, such a day, and died in penitence and love for you: his last word being your name?" Did Louisa see these things? Such things were to be.

Herself again a wife—a mother—lovingly watchful of her children, ever careful that they should have a childhood of the mind no less than a childhood of the body, as knowing it to be even a more beautiful thing, and a possession, any hoarded scrap of which, is a blessing and happiness to the wisest? Did Louisa see this? Such a thing was never to be.

But happy Sissy's happy children loving her; all children loving her; she, grown learned in childish lore; thinking no innocent and pretty fancy ever to be despised; trying hard to know her humbler fellow-creatures, and to beautify their lives of machinery and reality with those imaginative graces and delights, without which the heart of infancy will wither up, the sturdiest physical manhood will be morally stark death, and the plainest national prosperity figures can show, will be the Writing on the Wall,—she holding this course as part of no fantastic vow, or bond or brotherhood, or sisterhood, or pledge, or covenant, or fancy dress, or fancy fair; but simply as a duty to be done—did Louisa see these things of herself? These things were to be.

Dear reader! It rests with you and me, whether in our two fields of action, similar things shall be or not. Let them be! We shall sit with lighter bosoms on the hearth, to see the ashes of our fires turn gray and cold.

THE END.